MARY A. LARKIN OMNIBUS

For Better, For Worse
Playing With Fire

MARY A. LARKIN OMNIBUS

For Better, For Worse
Playing With Fire

MARY A. LARKIN

timewarner
paperbacks

A *Time Warner* Paperback

This omnibus edition first published in Great Britain by
Time Warner Paperbacks in 2003
Mary A. Larking Omnibus Copyright © Mary A. Larking 2003

Previously published separately:
For Better, For Worse first published in Great Britain in 1996 by
Judy Piatkus (Publishers) Ltd
Published by Warner Books in 1967
Copyright © Mary A. Larking 1996

Playing With Fire first published in Great Britain in 2001 by
Little, Brown and Company
Reprinted by Time Warner Paperbacks in 2002
Copyright © Mary A. Larking 2001

The moral right of the author has been asserted.

A CIP catalogue record for this book is available from the British Library.

ISBN 0 7515 3514 1

Printed and bound in Great Britain by
Mackays of Chatham plc, Chatham, Kent

Time Warner Paperbacks
An imprint of
Time Warner Books UK
Brettenham House
Lancaster Place
London WC2E 7EN

www.TimeWarnerBooks.co.uk

For Better, For Worse

For my husband Con

I would like to thank Alison Quigley, Chief Registrar at Gretna Green, and the staff of the Belfast Reference Library for all their kind assistance during the writing of this book.

And special thanks go to my son Con for his patience and understanding when I came unstuck with my new computer!

Chapter One

Belfast 1946

Johnny Cleary stood against the rubble stone wall that hid from view Beechmount Hospital, home for old people. He faced the bright lights illuminating the Broadway Picture House and scant shadow was offered by the large beech trees that lined the road. His tall figure in the good quality sports jacket and pale grey, flannel trousers drew many curious and admiring glances from passersby.

The wall ran for about a quarter of a mile along the Falls Road and the picture house opposite the lower end of it was his target. He stood head back, peering down his long straight nose, eyes trained on the entrance to the cinema. The bright coloured lights around the more brilliant name above the entrance gave him great pleasure. He remembered how, this time a year ago, even a single light would have been unheard of because of the blackout during the bleak days of the war. He was glad the war was over. Surely soon the rationing must end?

It had taken him a year to save enough clothing coupons to purchase his sports jacket. His hand unconsciously caressed the sleeve. He was very proud of it and had only managed to obtain enough clothing coupons by exchanging his own sweet coupons with the woman next door who had young children. He was also aware that it showed off the breadth of his shoulders and hinted at the slimness of his waist. Before the war he had been

1

quite podgy, but four years in the army had changed all that. Now a keep fit fanatic, he was determined to keep his body trim and in good shape.

It was also great to be free of the arrogant Yanks thronging the dance halls, promising much-coveted nylon stockings to girls who would go out on dates with them. On his few precious leaves home he had been disgusted at the way the local girls were throwing themselves at the Yanks. The Plaza Ballroom in Chichester Street had been thronged nightly with American service men, and the girls had shown their preference for them by refusing to dance with the local lads. Stupid fools! Had they thought the war would last forever? There must be a lot of unhappy girls in Belfast today . . . yes, a lot! A few who had been foolish were known to him personally and they had been very silly making no effort to hide their wantonness, shamelessly allowing themselves to be seen in the company of American servicemen, causing gossip and speculation. Now they must pay the price! What decent man would want to take on secondhand goods? Not that all the girls were playing around, but quite a few who frequented the Plaza were out for a good time and some had paid the penalty. If a girl wanted to keep her reputation above reproach she would give the Plaza a wide berth. At the age of twenty-six, with his stint in the army behind him, he would like to settle down and raise a family, but he wanted a pure girl as the mother of his children. No secondhand goods for him! True, the Americans' choosing Northern Ireland from which to launch their attack against Hitler's armies had brought prosperity to the city, but the girls didn't have to treat them like gods!

Who would have thought that Belfast would play such an important part in the war? Geographically placed as it was, and with its industrial capacity, the city had played a vital role. The blitz had been terrible, and Belfast, like most large cities, had had its share of the bombing, but it had thrown Catholics and Protestants together and reduced the animosity they bore each other. Johnny remembered how Catholic and Protestant alike had stood proud, shoulder to shoulder, when General Eisenhower saluted them from the steps of the City Hall. Now, as ships, planes and buildings ruined during the war were being rebuilt, there was plenty of work and harmony prevailed between the religions.

Tonight he had been to a reunion of the soldiers from his regiment. Not being a drinking man Johnny had left early, before the men had become too maudlin as they relived the war. It was best forgotten, if that was possible. He was one of the lucky few who had been welcomed back into his former employment. After three months back in Short and Harland's he was now settled in, and his natural drawing talents were attracting comments from his employers. The manager had just that day hinted that Johnny would soon be offered promotion. He had also implied that married men advanced quicker and wanted to know if Johnny had any plans in that direction? Sadly, he'd had to admit that a wedding wasn't planned for the immediate future.

The opening of the doors of the cinema brought him to attention, to move forward to the edge of the footpath where he would get a better view. The crowds spilled out on to the pavement and he scanned faces. As the crowd thinned out he grew anxious. Was his mother not here tonight? Had she left by a side or back door? Unrest assailed him as he was struck by a thought. Perhaps she was ill! Only if she was ill would she miss her Friday night out at the Broadway. She suffered from high blood pressure, giving cause for concern lately as she became prone to fainting spells. She had been all right when he'd left the house that morning but perhaps she had felt unwell during the day. He should have gone home; checked that she was well before meeting the lads. With a slight shake of the head he ridiculed himself. He was being silly! She wasn't expecting him to be waiting for her. It was only as he'd approached the Broadway earlier that he'd recalled it was her night out and decided to wait outside the cinema. He was devoted to his mother who had always been so understanding when he and his father had been at loggerheads. His father's temper had been quick and often cruel, and when Johnny was a young lad his mother had taken many a blow that was meant for him.

At last he caught sight of her large figure in a bright blue coat, her henna-dyed hair a red halo around her head. Sometimes he wished his mother would grow old gracefully; let her hair stay grey. Go without the rouge and lipstick that only called attention to her wrinkles. Still, she was a warm gentle person and he loved her dearly. With a sigh of relief he crossed the road to join her. As he reached his mother's side his attention was caught by a girl – a beautiful girl! As she left the shelter of the foyer of the cinema her deep auburn hair lifted in the slight breeze and Johnny felt a lump rise in his throat at the beauty of her. All else faded as he gazed at her small pale oval face, high cheekbones and a wide sensuous mouth. His mother followed his gaze and smiled fondly, making him aware that he was gaping. A blush warmed his face, but to his relief he noted that the girl was completely unaware of his presence and his obvious embarrassment.

However, Eileen Ross's companion was very much aware of him. Kate Rafferty had had a crush on Johnny Cleary for many a long day before the war took him away. It should have been out of sight, out of mind, but thoughts of him had lingered, and since his return the old feelings were rekindled. She'd dreamt of one day bumping into him and his being bowled over by her. Now it dismayed her to see him gaping in admiration at her best friend. Catching his eye, she gave him a slight nod of acknowledgement and was rewarded by a wide grin, before moving ahead of him and his mother.

Johnny was jubilant. What a bit of luck! This girl was a friend of Kate Rafferty's. He knew Kate slightly, her brother Kevin had been in the same class as him at St Malachy's College. He had done his homework many a time in Kevin's home. Now he would have to cultivate Kate's friendship. Get introduced to this beautiful girl.

The two girls walked slowly up the road in front of him and his mother. They walked with arms linked, giggling and whispering. Every now and again one would nudge the other with an elbow or hip and laughter would fill the air.

Even her laughter was musical, he thought. Who was she? Where did she live? How come he'd never noticed her before? Of course she was young, perhaps that was why she had escaped his notice. She was younger than Kate, and Kate was about twenty; six years younger than Kevin and him. The redhead would probably still have been at school when he joined the army.

When they reached the corner of St James's Park, in spite of his mother's silent mirth, Johnny slowed down and watched the girls walk down the street, thinking, My, but she moves like poetry in motion! He loved the way the green skirt hugged her hips and then flowed gently to below her calves, displaying slim ankles. The motion of her long hair rippling down her back delighted him. He just had to meet this girl! Did she go to the Broadway every Friday night? He'd soon find out. If that failed he would just have to call on Kevin Rafferty on some pretext or other; renew his acquaintance.

'Well, now . . . she certainly bowled you over, didn't she, son?' Madge Cleary teased, as she gently urged her son away from the top of St James's Park and across the Falls Road towards Rockmore Road where they lived.

Johnny laughed ruefully. 'You can say that again, Ma!' As Madge playfully proceeded to do so: 'She certainly . . .'

Johnny laughed and nudged her arm. 'Come off it, Ma. Do you know her?' he asked excitedly.

Madge chuckled and admitted, 'Just to see. She's one of Sarah Ross's daughters. She's not very old, mind.'

'I realize that . . . but I would still like to meet her.'

Madge Cleary sighed. 'Knowing you, son, no doubt you will!'

Unaware of the interest being bestowed upon her, Eileen Ross bade Kate Rafferty good night and entered the driveway to her home. She walked through the garden and down the side of the house, round the back to the kitchen door. Here she paused to inhale the fragrance from the stock and wallflowers being wafted on the light breeze. Her father was a keen gardener and even at this late hour the garden was a riot of colour. Approaching the small plot of herbs which was her father's pride and joy, she rubbed her fingers gently on the rosemary and thyme leaves, releasing their perfume, sniffing blissfully at her fingers before entering the kitchen. Passing through to the hall she paused, head tilted in surprise, eyebrows high at the sound of raised voices and laughter coming from the living room.

Who on earth's visiting this late? she wondered. Hanging her coat on the rack at the foot of the stairs, she opened the living-room door and put her head around it. A swift glance left her more surprised still; the room was crowded. Even her grandparents were there and although they only lived across the street, they never stayed out late. What was going on? It was Kate's mother Kathleen Rafferty, a close friend of the family, who greeted her.

'Come on, Eileen! What kept you? We've been waitin' for you.' She turned to Eileen's father. 'Well, Mick, she's here. You can pour the champagne now.'

Eileen's mother beckoned her forward. 'Come and see Beth's ring. She has agreed to marry Tommy.'

As she admired her sister's solitaire diamond ring,

Eileen could not help thinking. Agreed? She's been nudging Tommy towards marriage since the day she met him! Still, he was a good catch . . . and nice as well.

She smiled at them. 'Congratulations, you two!'

Tommy was grinning. 'Thanks, Eileen.' He closed his eyes and shook his head. 'I can't believe it. I must be the happiest man on the Falls Road.'

Beth's eyes teased her. She knew Eileen's opinion of her, but she was unrepentant. Tommy was very precious to her. She loved him very much.

To Eileen's chagrin it was a glass of orange juice she was offered, to toast the happy couple.

'I thought you were waiting for me before opening the champagne?'

'You're too young for champagne,' her father reprimanded her. 'We were waiting for you for the toast. Anyway we've only one bottle! And that's thanks to Barney. Thank goodness he's still got friends working on the boats.'

'Ah, Dad . . . I'm eighteen! It's a big bottle, so it is! Can't I have a little drink? Eh? I've never tasted champagne, so I haven't. Or anything alcoholic, for that matter,' she finished wistfully.

Mick Ross was not to be persuaded. 'If we give you intoxicating drink, they'll want some,' he informed her, nodding in the direction of the two youngest members of the family, fifteen-year-old Claire and nine-year-old Emma. 'I have to draw the line somewhere.'

Knowing from experience that her father never backed down once he had taken a stand, Eileen accepted the orange juice with bad grace and went to sit beside her grandmother.

As usual, her moment of temper did not last long and she smiled warmly at her grannie. 'How are you, Gran?'

Maggie Grahame bestowed a fond look on her granddaughter. Although she tried hard not to show favouritism for any of her grandchildren, in her heart she knew

7

that Eileen was special to her. Perhaps it was because this young girl was the spit of her, that she seemed closer than the others. Now she answered with a smile, 'Not too bad, love. Just the odd ache and pain.'

'Why's Bernard not with you?'

Seeing a pained expression flit across her grandmother's face, Eileen was sorry she had asked after her young uncle. Born late in life to his parents, Bernard was her mother's half-brother, thus uncle to her and her sisters. He was younger than Beth and her but older than Claire and Emma. At the moment his behaviour was causing concern and it was her grandfather who answered her question with one of his own.

'You didn't notice him at the corner of the Whiterock Road, then?'

Well aware that the Whiterock corner, where all the young lads gathered, had been empty tonight, Eileen lied to spare their feelings. 'No, Granda, I was talking to Kate Rafferty and never noticed.'

She didn't want to cause any trouble for Bernard. If she said the corner was empty and Bernard arrived home and stated he had been standing there talking to friends, he would be in trouble. She could understand how he felt. He was sixteen and rebelling against his parents' strict views, whereas they were afraid of his getting in with the wrong company.

They were all brought to attention by Mick raising his glass for the toast. 'To the happy couple.' And after they had all sipped from their glasses, he added, 'Roll on September 'till I get one daughter off my hands.' These words caused everyone to laugh and after they all had added their congratulations, Mick turned to Eileen. 'Hope you wait a couple of years and give me chance to save up for your wedding reception.'

'Oh, you needn't worry about that, Dad,' she assured him. 'I don't intend getting married before I'm twenty-five.'

8

'Good! Good! I'm glad to hear that. That gives me plenty of time.'

'What about me, Dad? I might get married before Eileen,' Claire teased him.

Mick turned a look of reproach on his wife. 'Why didn't you give me a couple of sons, eh? It would have been much cheaper.'

He laughed as he teased her, but although Sarah smiled in return, her heart was sad. Did Mick regret having all daughters? He said not . . . but was there some deep longing for a son? The name Ross would die out as far as they were concerned. Mick had been an orphan reared in Milltown Boys' Home, so there was no one left to carry on the family name.

As if sensing her unease, he raised his glass again. 'Another toast . . . to my four lovely daughters! I wouldn't change one of them for a prince.'

There was more laughter when Sarah retorted, 'Just let someone offer me a prince for one of them!'

'Which one of us would you exchange for him?' Claire was quick to ask. Sarah gazed at Mick. Only he was aware why Claire held a special place in her heart. He returned her look, eyes full of love. In the fourth year of their marriage, trouble had brewed. For some months Sarah had been besotted with a young student, Gerry Docherty, who at that time had lived across the street in the house next door to her mother. Mick had been sure he'd lost her. In his misery he had turned to another woman, Maisie O'Hara, an attractive young widow. Then Maggie had almost lost her life giving birth to young Bernard and somehow things had fallen into perspective and Claire was the result of their reunion.

There was a pause as Sarah pretended to ponder. It was no secret that Claire was her favourite daughter. However she was not to be drawn. 'I don't think I could part with any of you. So, one of you will have to *marry* a prince.'

* * *

9

After an hour of talk and banter, Barney and Maggie at last crossed the street to their home to find it still in darkness.

As Barney was opening the door Maggie recognized her son's approaching footsteps and, gripping her husband's arm, whispered 'Please, love . . . please.'

Entering the driveway, Bernard came to an abrupt halt with a start of surprise and gaped at his parents. 'You're out late! Where were you?'

'Looking for you!' Barney exclaimed testily. 'Where else?' His temper was smouldering on a short fuse these days where his son was concerned and only Maggie's pleas on his behalf kept it from erupting. He wanted to give him an ultimatum – Toe the line or get out – but knew it would break his wife's heart should their son leave home.

For a moment Bernard believed him. It was just like something his father would do. He treated him like a child. Where were you? Who were you with? What were you doing? was what passed for conversation in their house. His mates were never questioned about their whereabouts. Their parents were broad-minded.

Once inside the house father and son faced each other.

Barney was the first to break the silence. 'Well . . . where were you?'

'Ah, Dad, give it a rest! Listening to you's like listening to a record with . . .'

Maggie screamed when she saw her husband's fist rise in the air. Bernard was so surprised he stood and took the full force of the blow. Anger lent extra weight to Barney's fist and his son was lifted off his feet. As he staggered back, saved from falling by clutching hold of the sideboard, blood gushed from his nose. Seeing bright red stains spatter and spread across his shirt front, Bernard pushed himself away from the sideboard and, with a howl of rage, lurched at his father. It was

Maggie hanging on to his arm that brought him to his senses. For some seconds father and son glared at each other, then shrugging off his mother's restraining hand, Bernard angrily turned on his heel and left the room.

When the door closed on him, Barney's shoulders slumped in despair. Going to the fireside, he sank down in the armchair. Maggie stared at the door for some seconds, ears strained. What would Bernard do? Would he leave the house? She heard him thump up the stairs and along the landing. The door to his room slammed, then silence. She relaxed. At least he wasn't packing! It was too quiet for that. With a sigh, she turned towards her husband.

He met her accusing gaze and cried defensively, 'I can't put up with this any longer, Maggie. If he can't treat us with respect, he'll have to go.'

'Barney, he's young and impressionable . . . give him time. He'll change, I know he will. After all, he hasn't done anything wrong. Now has he?'

'How can you say that? He ignores me at every turn. Thwarts my wishes . . . and he's not studying enough! At this rate he'll never pass his exams. Never!'

Going to him, Maggie sat on the arm of the chair. She put her arm across his shoulders, ruffling his hair with her cheek. Hair that was still thick and blond, not like hers that was liberally threaded with silver. But then, he was ten years younger than she and looked even younger than his forty-seven years.

'I remember when I first met you . . . you told me how your grandparents had great plans for their only grandson, but you talked them into letting you go to sea. Remember? And I'm glad they did! Otherwise we might never have met. That doesn't bear thinking about, does it?'

He moved restlessly in her embrace. 'No . . . no. But I was in a different position. Both my parents were dead. If my father had lived, I would probably have listened to him.'

11

'Now, now,' she chided. 'That's easy to say. But Bernard's you all over again. Stubborn.' She kissed his cheek to take the sting from her words. 'I often regret talking him out of joining the navy. The sea's in his blood, just like it was in yours.'

'Ah, Maggie, don't! I've often regretted that too. But it's a hard life at sea and he's so brainy. If he studies hard, he'll go far.'

Out of sight Maggie crossed her fingers. 'I've been thinking. Perhaps if we suggest he joins the Royal Navy . . . you know what I mean. If he gets good grades he could become a Radio Engineer or something like that. Would you object to that?'

'Tut, Maggie. It would be such a waste. He's lucky to be studying at St Malachy's College. They bring out the very best in their students. He's so brainy. Why, he could go on to Queen's University. Enter the law or medicine, or some other profession. He's better at home. The sea can be treacherous. Besides, I don't want to back down now.'

The last words were muttered low. Maggie sighed with relief; she was winning him over. Everything would pan out, as her old friend Mollie used to say, so long as Barney didn't have to lose face.

The following Friday night saw Johnny Cleary at the Broadway Picture House, but although he walked up and down the aisles, he could not see Kate Rafferty and the other girl. Near the end of the film he left his seat and took up a stand from where he could see the people coming down the stairs from the balcony, but alas, there was no sign of the two girls. Undaunted, the following day he made his way down St James's Park and presented himself at the Raffertys' door. It was Kevin's father Jim who opened the door and he immediately thrust his hand towards Johnny in welcome.

'This is a surprise,' he bellowed as he pumped Johnny's hand up and down. 'Long time, no see. Come in, son.

Come on in. Here . . . let me take your coat.' As he hung the coat in the hall he called upstairs, 'Kevin, guess who's here? It's Johnny Cleary.'

From the living room Kate heard all this commotion, and when her father and Johnny entered the room, she warned her heart to behave. Hadn't she a good idea why Johnny was here?

As Kate listened to her father question Johnny about his time in the army, she was amused at her brother's barely concealed surprise.

Johnny was also aware of Kevin's perplexity, and for the first time felt embarrassed at his own actions. Imagine, after all these years when he hadn't even seen Kevin, years before the war, now having the cheek to land on the Raffertys' doorstep!

When a lull in the conversation presented itself he rose quickly to his feet. He had forgotten just how talkative Jim Rafferty could be.

'I'll have to be going now.'

'Come again, son. Don't wait so long next time. You'll always be welcome here. You know . . .'

In desperation Johnny interrupted Jim in mid-sentence. 'I will come back, Mr Rafferty. It was lovely seeing you all again.'

A slight tilt of the head indicated he would like to speak to Kevin alone. Coming to his rescue, Kevin led the way through the hall and outside. Relieved, Johnny nodded a farewell to Kate and, grabbing his coat from the clothes rack, followed closely behind.

Kate's heart was heavy as she watched him go. She had never stood much chance with Johnny before, but now it looked as if he fancied Eileen Ross, otherwise he would never have made such a fool of himself, coming here like this. Why, it must be six years since he'd last set foot inside this house. At least she had one thing to be thankful for: she had never said to anyone how much she fancied Johnny. Nobody would have cause to pity her.

13

On the pavement outside the garden gate Johnny smiled ruefully at Kevin. 'You must be wondering what brings me to your home?'

Kevin nodded, but remained silent. Johnny continued. 'I want a word in with your Kate's friend. I think her name's Ross. Can you help me?'

'Young Eileen? She's just a kid! Why do you want a word in with her?'

Eileen! Even her name sounded lovely. Johnny stood bemused for a few seconds. 'Is she not as old as Kate, then?' he asked.

'No, she's not! She's only eighteen.' Kevin could not understand how a mature man like Johnny Cleary, who could pick and choose his girls, wanted a word in with young Eileen Ross. Why, she looked even younger than her eighteen years.

In spite of feeling a fool, Johnny insisted, 'I would still like to meet her.'

With a shrug, Kevin turned towards the house again, saying over his shoulder, 'It's our Kate you need to speak to. Hey, Kate ... Johnny would like a word with you. Maybe I'll see more of you now, Johnny?' he added slyly.

Johnny had the grace to blush. 'Probably ... yes, more than likely.'

Kate's heart leapt when she heard Kevin calling out her name and she quite literally flew out of the house to join them. Had she misjudged the situation? Could Johnny possibly want a date with her? However, when Kevin explained the reason for Johnny's unexpected visit her heart felt like lead. He must really be smitten by Eileen to go to such lengths.

Johnny shuffled his feet in embarrassment. What had possessed him? Any other girl and he would have just left it to chance, confident that, given the opportunity, he would be able to date her. But since he had set eyes on Eileen Ross, she had filled his every waking thought. He was besotted with her.

Seeing how embarrassed he was, Kate took pity on him, and forced a smile to her lips. 'So, you want to meet Eileen Ross?'

He smiled wryly in return. 'Yes. I feel such a fool now but I wanted to do things right . . . you know what I mean? I didn't want just to try to pick her up. I don't think she's that kind of girl . . .' His voice trailed off and sadly Kate agreed with him.

'You're right. She's not that kind of girl. Tell you what! Go to the nine o'clock in St John's tomorrow and I'll introduce you to her after Mass.'

'Thanks, Kate, I'm indebted to you.'

With a slight bow of acknowledgement, Johnny once more bade her farewell and strode up the street, content. Tomorrow he would meet Eileen Ross.

That evening, when Kate told Eileen that Johnny Cleary wanted a word in with her, she gasped in surprise. 'Who on earth's Johnny Cleary.'

'Oh, he's very nice. Went to St Malachy's College with our Kevin. He's one of the old school. Likes to do things properly, ye know . . . hence the introduction.'

'Well, I don't want to meet him, so there!'

'He's nice. Good-looking. A bit older than you . . .'

'How old?' Eileen interrupted her.

'Twenty-six.'

'Twenty-six?' If Kate had said one hundred, Eileen could not have been more astounded. 'Twenty-six? He's an old man as far as I'm concerned.'

Kate laughed outright; she was aware that anyone over twenty was regarded as past it by Eileen. 'Well, I've promised to introduce you to him outside St John's in the morning. So you can make up your mind then.'

'You're joking! I'll go to a later Mass tomorrow, or else go down to St Paul's, so I will!' Eileen cried.

'Please, Eileen. He'll be so embarrassed if you're not with me. Just pass yourself. It's not a commitment, you know. You're just meeting him, for heaven's sake! If you don't like him, you needn't go out with him.'

To her relief, Eileen begrudgingly agreed to meet Johnny. 'Mind you ... I won't go out with him,' she vowed. 'Twenty-six? Huh!'

Kate smiled her thanks. She felt as if she was signing her own death warrant. But who knows? Perhaps when Johnny met Eileen he would realize how immature she was and maybe, just maybe, then he would see Kate's potential ...

The next morning, having covertly watched Eileen all during Mass, Johnny waited outside St John's. Passing throught the small churchyard, he stood beyond the gates on the pavement, a little way back from the crowds. He didn't want to stand shaking Eileen's hand and making small conversation under the interested gaze of his mother who was also there.

Eileen was embarrassed as Kate gripped her firmly by the arm and led her towards him.

'Johnny, this is my friend Eileen Ross. Eileen ... Johnny Cleary.'

They eyed each other. Johnny thought Eileen was even more beautiful than before and Eileen thought him handsome, but old. And she didn't like red-haired men.

However, as he walked with them to the top of St James's Park he soon set her at ease and when he politely asked her if she would accompany him to the Broadway the following night, she found herself nodding in agreement; almost laughing aloud when he said he would pick her up at her house at six-thirty.

She thought it quaint that he was calling to her home for her. Men only did that when they had come to know a girl well and their intentions were serious. Never on a first date! On a first date you either met at the corner or outside the cinema. If the boy happened to be a Protestant, you met well away from your home

16

ground, in the town centre. Her parents were in for a big surprise!

The following night she was still amused as she awaited his arrival. She had informed her parents that she was being picked up by a man and her mother was like a cat on hot bricks, hovering behind the net curtains, watching for him to put in an appearance at the gate.

A minute to the half hour Johnny was there, knocking on the door, looking quite nervous.

Rising to her feet, Eileen went to open the door, asking teasingly, 'Do you want to be introduced to him?'

'Of course we want to be introduced. Bring him in!' her mother ordered, and with a smile Eileen obeyed. She didn't feel as if she was going on a date. More like going out with a distant cousin, and you didn't date your cousin!

Johnny was immaculate in a dark grey suit and snow white shirt. His usually tousled bright red hair had been subdued with Brylcreem and Eileen had to admit that he looked very handsome. Not the kind of man that she would be attracted to – she liked dark-haired men – but still, he was handsome and she could see that her parents were impressed. He got on well with her father, she noted. But then . . . they were almost on the same wavelength. Finally she had to remind him that if they didn't leave soon they would miss the start of the big picture.

They had to queue outside the Broadway for a short time and Johnny was thrilled to have Eileen by his side; to note the admiring glances directed at her. Glances that he could see she was completely unaware of. He made up his mind that one day she would be his wife. And, as his mother had a habit of saying, he usually got what he wanted.

By a trick of fate, Eileen found herself dating two men at the same time. The Saturday night after her first date

17

with Johnny, she met Billy Greer at a dance in the Orpheus Ballroom. He asked her out and she agreed, even though he was a Protestant, and she knew she would be wiser not to see him. However, she enjoyed his company and against the advice of Kate, agreed to go to the pictures with him. In no time at all she was seeing him regularly and tried to stop her Monday night outings to the Broadway with Johnny, but in vain. He was determined to win Eileen over and, unaware that she was dating someone else, pressured her to continue seeing him. Under the disapproving eye of Kate, Eileen saw Johnny every Monday night, and Saturdays and Tuesdays she dated Billy Greer. Then Victor Sylvester's band came to town and to her great delight, Billy treated her and Kate to tickets for this great ball. The dance was to be held in the Floral Hall out at Bellevue, on the outskirts of Belfast. Full of excitement, Eileen showed Kate the tickets, expecting her to be as excited as she was.

Seeing her tight lips, and the determined thrust of Kate's chin, Eileen's heart sank. She just had to persuade her friend to go to the dance with her! Just had to! It was the chance of a lifetime.

They were in Kate's bedroom. Sitting cross-legged on the bed, Eileen leant forward and pleaded, 'Please say you'll come to the dance, Kate. If you don't go, Dad won't let me go.'

'No!' Kate's tone was adamant, her face mutinous.

'Look, he won't hear tell of me going on me own. Please come, Kate. You know he won't ... please, Kate?'

'Tut ... go and play gooseberry? Sitting like a wallflower all night while you dance with Billy Greer? At a big dance like that all the men will have their own partners with them. No, thanks! I'd rather go to the pictures on me own, so I would.'

Eileen almost fell off the bed in her excitement. 'But you won't be alone.' She thumped her brow with the heel of her hand in mock dismay. 'Billy's bringing a friend. Imagine me forgetting to say. He says you'll like Bobby Price. Oh, please, Kate . . . please . . . please! The Floral Hall is supposed to be beautiful. Say you'll come with me?' She thrust her face closer to Kate's. 'When have we ever been anywhere exceptional? Eh? It'll be a new experience, so it will. Why, it would be a sin to miss the chance. It's not every day I get two tickets to a big dance. You must admit it's very good of Billy to treat us. Think of it, Kate. Victor Sylvester! We'll be the envy of all the girls in work, so we will.'

Kate heard her out and looking at her friend's flushed face, alight with eager excitement, said quietly, 'You like Billy Greer a lot, don't you?'

Eileen sighed resignedly and sank back on the bed. She knew she was about to receive a lecture.

Sure enough, Kate wailed, 'I warned you not to go out with him in the first place, didn't I? What good can come of it? Your dad would go mad if he knew you were dating a Protestant.'

'He won't find out. Just another few dates, that's all I ask. Please, Kate, do this for me. The last three months have been the happiest of my life. Billy respects me. Do you know something . . .' once more she thrust her face towards Kate to emphasize her point, '. . . he has never ever touched me.' She lifted a finger in the air. 'Not once! Just a quick good night kiss that no priest could find fault with. Not like some good Catholic boys who can't keep their hands to themselves! Ninepence into the pictures and they think they own you. No, Billy's not like that! We've been out in the country, miles from anywhere on his motor bike, and he has never made a wrong move. Not once!' Another wag of her raised finger. 'All I want is a few more dates with him.'

By the end of this tirade, Kate was gazing at her friend open-mouthed. 'You're in love with him!' she accused.

Eileen's eyes widened and she stared at Kate in silence.

19

Then, her voice full of wonder, she whispered, 'Yes . . . yes, I believe I am.'

'There you are then! You shouldn't see him again. Ah, Eileen, I can't go with you. Can't you see? I can't be a party to your downfall. You mustn't see him again.'

Kate was frantic with worry. Two years older than Eileen, she felt she should be looking after her. Keeping her on the straight and narrow as it were. If big Mick Ross ever found out his daughter was dating a Protestant from the Shankill Road, there would be wigs on the green. And furthermore, he would want to know why Kate had not tried to put a stop to it, or failing that . . . told him, so that he could nip it in the bud.

Rising from the bed Eileen approached her friend. 'Look, Kate, if you come to the Floral Hall with me, I promise I'll just see him a few more times.' She crossed her heart. 'Cross my heart and hope to die. Please, Kate! I'd do it for you, so I would,' she accused plaintively.

'Tut!' Kate swung away and gazed blankly out of the window for a few seconds. She was at sixes and sevens. It was a fact that Eileen would go out of her way to please her. This was what swayed Kate. She swung towards Eileen again. 'Oh, all right then!' She gave in ungraciously. 'You've worn me down, but remember your promise.'

It was her turn to wag a finger in front of Eileen's face, and catching hold of it, Eileen cried gratefully, 'I'll remember. Thanks, Kate. You're a smashing friend.' She sank back on the bed, eyes sparkling with excitement. This would be her first late dance and she felt grown-up. Kate was a real pal. A true friend, indeed.

Eileen spent all day Saturday preparing for her date with Billy. Her long auburn hair was set in huge rollers to give it lift when brushed out. She caused dissension with her sisters, she spent so much time in the bathroom. At last she was ready. When she descended the stairs her father

20

was in the hall. He gazed at her in wonder and she knew her efforts had not been in vain.

'You look lovely,' he muttered. 'The spitting image of your grannie. Sarah, come and see our Eileen!'

Coming slowly from the kitchen, Sarah's eyes widened in wonder when she saw her daughter. In a primrose-coloured dress, one that Eileen had spent long hours cutting out and sewing, she was the image of her grannie. All her clothing coupons had been spent on the soft silky material and she was indebted to Maggie for supplying the coupons for her new black patent court shoes. With Beth's wedding so near, Sarah had thought the coupons could have been put to better use. Now her eyes misted over at the beauty of her young daughter. She was taken aback; she had been aware Eileen resembled her grannie, but tonight she was her double. The yellow dress threw colour into her daughter's pale grey eyes, which glowed tawny like a tiger's, bringing to Sarah's mind vivid pictures of her mother's beauty as a young woman. Bright auburn hair sprang in curls around Eileen's face and tumbled down her back in a soft cloud. Excitement coloured her high cheekbones.

'Here . . . let's have a look at your dress.'

Slowly Eileen turned full circle and Sarah gave a tug here, a pull there, and gently flattened the sash that spanned her daughter's slim waist. 'It's a bit low,' she lamented, trying to pull the neckline higher.

'Ah, Mam . . . it's not low! You can't see any cleavage.' Eileen wriggled the dress down again, and chuckled as she added, 'I should be so lucky. I'm as flat as a pancake!'

Sarah smiled in return. 'You'll be the belle of the ball,' she whispered huskily. 'Watch no one doctors your drink,' she warned anxiously.

'I'll be careful,' Eileen promised. A loud blast from a car's horn brought a smile to her face and, after kissing her parents farewell, she rushed outside to answer its summons. Kate had persuaded her father to take them to the dance and return at one o'clock to collect them, so they were to travel in style.

The journey down the Falls, across town and along the Antrim Road, did not take long and soon they arrived at the Cave Hill, where some years earlier the Floral Hall had been built. Excitement kept Eileen on the edge of her seat as the car wound its way in and out, up the side of the hill. Up past the zoo and the elephant house. On the other side of the high wire fence Eileen could see some of the animals prowling and her ears picked up the unmistakable roar of a lion, mixed with the excited chattering of monkeys on the still air.

At last the Floral Hall came into view and her gasp of surprise was echoed by Kate. It was breathtaking! Big and imposing, its curved white facade was lit up like a Christmas tree. Coloured lights also threaded the trees that surrounded it, and swayed in the gentle breeze, giving it a fairy tale appearance.

They left the car, and stood in awe of the scene before them, only half-hearing Jim Rafferty's warning to be careful, as they took in all the splendour. Inside the foyer where they were to meet Billy Greer and his mate, they stood gazing around at the soft subdued lighting and the wonderful murals, Eileen with suppressed excitement, Kate with apprehension.

'Isn't it lovely, Kate?' Eileen whispered in her friend's ear. 'Oh, I feel all grown-up! Aren't you glad you came?'

Kate's nod was non-committal. It wasn't easy being a friend of Eileen's. Men gravitated to her like moths to a flame. Even now she was being eyed speculatively. As Kate watched the few young men who were unattached move closer, still eyeing Eileen, she sighed. Well, at least tonight Billy Greer was bringing a friend along with him. Her evening would depend on that friend. He would probably turn out to be a drip, and she would be stuck with him for five long hours, but that would be better than being a wallflower. Not for the first time she envied her friend's glowing beauty.

Butterflies fluttered in Eileen's stomach. All week she had been haunted by Kate's words: 'You're in love with him.' Now, for the first time, she was nervous of meeting Billy. Nervous and excited. The emotions that tied her stomach in knots were new to her and she hoped she was not in love. It would present so many problems. At last she saw him making his way through the crowd towards her. Tall, dark and handsome, just like the heroes she read about in books. His blue eyes, dark with love and admiration, awakened an answering spark within her. Her heart gave a leap and joy flooded through her as she acknowledged to herself that, problems or not, she did indeed love him.

'You look lovely,' he whispered, pressing her hands to his chest.

Oblivious to everyone else, his eyes roamed over her face as if seeing her for the first time. Never had she looked lovelier: her hair a bright cloud framing a face that was pale but for pink tinges of excitement. Big tawny eyes, like pools of mystery. He could see the love shining in their yellow depths and, heart thumping against his breast, bent to kiss her. A discreet cough from his companion brought him to attention with a laugh.

'Pardon me!' Bill quickly made the introductions. 'Eileen, Kate, this is Bobby Price. Bobby, these two beauties are our dates for the night.'

Looking at the tall dark-haired lad whose smile was infectious, Kate relaxed. He looked all right. Nice, and handsome as well. When he raised his brows and said, 'Dance?' she nodded her approval at Eileen before allowing herself to be led away to the ballroom.

'Didn't I tell you she'd like him?' Billy pulled Eileen closer and she nodded happily. She felt so full of joy she thought she would burst. It was going to be a wonderful evening.

'We're wasting time, my love. Let's dance.'

Well aware that he was the recipient of many envious glances, Billy kept his arm possessively around Eileen's shoulders and led her into the ballroom. It was huge. Tables adorned with lamps and floral arrangements circled the walls and the edge of the dance floor. Eileen felt she had entered Wonderland as they glided across the floor. The lights on the tables and walls were soft and muted, but a spotlight directed on the big multi-faceted silver ball revolving slowly in the centre of the ceiling sent probing fingers of light into the teeming mass of dancers, picking out the brightness of the ladies' dresses, and emphasizing the whiteness of the mens' shirts. At the top of the ballroom, on a raised dais, the orchestra played softly.

Eileen was right: it was a wonderful evening. Billy's sister Ruth and her husband George were present, and he introduced Eileen to them. Ruth was pleasant and friendly, George a bit of a clown. They spent about an hour with them, and Eileen enjoyed their company immensely.

Before they parted company, Ruth, giving Billy a meaningful look, said, 'Why don't you bring Eileen home to meet Mother and Father?' And when he smilingly nodded his agreement, Eileen's cup was full.

The band was rated the best in the land, and Billy was a marvellous dancer. Their bodies moved as one. Closer than was decent really, due to the vast crowd. Eileen was light-headed with happiness.

Every now and then they met up with Kate and Bobby at the bar for a drink. The girls were drinking fruit juice, but the two young men were drinking beer. Tired and footsore, Eileen at last cried, 'That's enough, Billy! I must sit out a dance. My feet are killing me.' Ruefully, she looked down at her shoes. She should have known better than to wear new ones to a dance. They felt a size too small – especially after attempting that new crazy dance, the Jitterbug, which was all the rage in the dance halls since the American servicemen had introduced it during the war.

'Have you ever seen the lough by moonlight?' Billy asked, and when Eileen shook her head, took her by the elbow and led her to a side door and out into the grounds.

It was dark outside, the moon obscured by slow-moving grey clouds, and in the gloom all Eileen could see was the Cave Hill rearing up in front of her, dark and menacing. She shivered. With a protective arm around her shoulders, Billy guided her round the side of the hall, past the duck pond, to the other side; pleased when she gasped in amazement at the scene before her eyes.

'Isn't it a sight to behold?' he asked softly.

Enraptured, she nodded, at a loss for words to tell how she felt. She had never seen anything so beautiful, so magnificent, and it left her speechless.

It was a warm night. Slowly they made their way down the grassy slope, away from the bright lights of the ballroom. Billy removed his jacket and spread it on the grass for them to sit on. Entwined in each other's arms, they sat contented and happy, gazing out over the lough. It stretched for miles, the lights from the distant County Down coast reflected on the water. The overall effect was of a huge diamond necklace shimmering and moving with the motion of the water.

'It's beautiful,' Eileen whispered in awe.

His cheek against hers, Billy nodded in agreement and pointed to the right of the lough. 'See over there, love? To the right . . . see the outline of the cranes? That's Harland and Wolff shipyard.' His finger moved slowly to the left, along the lights. 'And those lights directly across from here are from Sydenham, Helen's Bay, Hollywood, and that's Bangor along to the left . . .'

'Sydenham?' she interrupted him. 'I've been there!'

She had not liked Sydenham. But then, the two

occasions she had been there were sad times. The first she had been very young; her great-grandfather had died suddenly from a heart attack. All she remembered was the crowds of people weeping when the coffin was carried from the house. The second time she was there was for another funeral, this time her great-grandmother's.

Eileen could still recall the fear she had felt when someone had lifted her up to kiss her great-grannie goodbye. The sight of the still figure in its brown shroud had brought a wail of protest from her lips. Her mother had dragged her from the man's arms, crying indignantly, 'She's too young for that! For heaven's sake . . . she's only seven!'

Oh, yes, she could do without Sydenham! Billy was still talking and she brought her attention back to him.

'Do you see these lights down here to the left, love?'

He was pointing to the near side of the lough and she nodded when she saw where he meant.

'Well . . . that's Glengormley. It would be a good place to rear children. It's a lovely village. My gran lives there. If possible, that's where I'd like us to live when we get married.'

Eileen's breath caught in her throat. Had she heard him right? Had he said 'when *we* get married', or 'when *I* get married'? She remained motionless, not knowing how to react. Not daring to take anything for granted. This was the first time Billy had indicated that his intentions were serious.

Shaking her gently, he said, 'I'm asking you to marry me, Eileen. Will you?'

Oh, this wonderful thing could not be happening to her. She must be dreaming. Could it possibly be true? Billy was speaking again. She had heard him right.

'Eileen? Answer me! Will you marry me?' He sounded nervous and she turned eagerly in his arms, anxious to reassure him.

'Could we? Could we possibly get married? What about

26

our parents? Would your father let you marry in a Catholic Church? I couldn't marry anywhere else, mind.'

'It doesn't matter what our parents think. That is . . .' His hands cupped her face and his eyes adored her. 'If you love me. Do you, Eileen? Do you?'

Again she was fervent in her reply. 'So much! So very much.'

'That's all that matters then.' He sighed contentedly. 'We love each other. If our parents agree, fair enough. If not, then we'll go over to England. Or even America! I'll have no trouble getting a job over there now that I've served my time.'

Full of joy she snuggled close to him. From the ballroom the strains of 'My Foolish Heart' drifted out on the still air, and Eileen thought, Oh, everything is so perfect! I'll always love this song. I just hope I'm not dreaming. She gave her arm a pinch and was delighted to feel the pain. She was awake all right!

'Ah, Eileen, Eileen, my love.'

In the dim light her eyes glowed with love and trust. Her lips trembled when he touched them with his. She was so beautiful, and she had promised to marry him.

Eileen tasted the beer on his breath and her nose wrinkled with distaste, but she did not draw away. Not even when he urged her back flat on the grass and his mouth became more urgent. Savagely crushing her lips against her teeth, trying to force them apart; hurting her. Only when his hands roughly caressed her body did she feel uneasy. Didn't the priests warn them from the pulpit not to go into dark lonely places with boys? Ah, but Billy loved her. He wouldn't harm her. Would he? Would he? Panic rose in her throat as doubt set in. He was going too far! She must stop him!

What was he doing? Oh, dear God, what was he doing? Oh, no. No! He mustn't! He mustn't! When he rolled on top of her, crushing her against the hard lumpy ground, she tried to speak, to pull away, to reason with him. But

27

the pressure of his mouth was choking her, making her gag.

She struggled frantically, pushing at his chest with all her might, but it was like trying to move a brick wall. Caught up in a frenzy of passion, aware of nothing but his own urgent need, Billy was unaware of her distress. His hands were cruel, fingers biting into the soft flesh of her upper arms. His thrusts at her body were brutal and her dream became a nightmare as she struggled and pushed to be free of him. When at last he rolled off her and lay back on the grass, she curled up in a ball and wept. Deep silent sobs of despair that racked her slight frame.

At last her distress penetrated Billy's stupor and the enormity of what he had done sobered him. He tried to draw her into his arms, wanting to comfort her, to tell her how sorry he was. She cowered away from him like a wounded animal, and shame and guilt consumed him.

When at last the sobs that racked her body subsided, she sat up and with hands that trembled, smoothed her dress and petticoats.

His voice urgent, he pleaded, 'Eileen, I'm sorry. I didn't mean for this to happen. Honestly, love. It must've been the drink. I don't usually drink so much. Can you ever forgive me?'

She wiped her eyes with the handkerchief he thrust at her and, declining to answer, started to rise from the grass. Gently he helped her. This time she did not draw away, though inwardly marvelling that this was the same man who minutes ago, had hurt and humiliated her.

Her thoughts were racing ahead. How could she face Kate? She was sure to guess. Oh, how she wished she was home! She wished she had never heard tell of the Floral Hall.

'I must go to the cloakroom,' she whispered shakily.

Aghast at her pallor, at the tears he could see threatening to fall anew, Billy nodded to show he understood.

'Come on, I'll show you a door near the cloakrooms, love.'

He led her around the building to a door adjacent to the cloakrooms and she hurried into the Ladies, glad to find it was empty. Examining herself in the mirror, she was appalled at her appearance. She looked demented: huge, staring, tearful eyes and hair standing on end. Locking herself into one of the cubicles, she combed her hair and powdered her face. Next she examined her dress. Except for a few small grass stains near the hem, and some wrinkles, it looked all right. She did not dare look beneath the dress to where she ached. She felt as if she had been torn in two. Oh, the shame, that this should happen to her!

As tears filled her eyes, she urged herself not to cry again. Later . . . she could cry later. Not now! Now she must face Kate, put on a show, pretend she was happy. It would not be easy, but she had only herself to blame. Heaven knows the priests had warned often enough from the pulpit about this very danger. Boys were weak! It was up to the girl to keep them in their place. Did Billy think her easy? A loose woman? Was that why he had done this awful thing to her? Would he not respect her any more?

Tremors coursed through her body and she squeezed her eyes shut and clenched her fists to try and gain control of her emotions. She must hurry; get outside where it was dark and wait for Kate. She could not afford to meet her under the bright lights. Her friend was no fool, she would be sure to guess something was wrong and would question Eileen.

In the corridor near the door of the ladies' room, Billy leant against the wall staring in blind misery at the floor, unaware of the milling crowds. How could he have done *that* to Eileen? Why, he worshipped her! She was so young and innocent and lovely. Now he had spoilt her, had taken away her virginity. He cringed when he recalled the episode outside. To have taken her like that! Why, an animal would have been kinder, more tender. He deserved to be horse-whipped. Would she ever forgive him? Oh, Lord, she must. He could not live without her. Her face was in his thoughts all day long. She was so lovely and she had confessed that she loved him. And he had treated her like that! What must she be thinking of him? She must forgive him! He could not imagine life without her.

He would take her home to meet his parents, he silently vowed. Thoughts of his parents brought a worried frown to his brow. It was all right for his sister to urge him to bring Eileen home, but his father would not be easy to win over. Would he be expelled from the Orange Order if his son married a Catholic? If so, it would kill him, he was such a staunch member. What if he was given the choice to stay in the Order by putting the traitor out of the house? Would his father obey and put Billy out? Well then, as he had said to Eileen, he would go over to England, and once he was settled, he would send for her. It would be a big upheaval. His poor mother would break her heart . . . but he loved Eileen, and she must come first. If only she was a Protestant everything would be all right. But she wasn't and still he wanted her for his wife.

He moved restlessly from one foot to the other. What was keeping her? She had been in there such a long time. Suddenly he straightened up in alarm. Was there another door out of the cloakroom? Had she slipped out to avoid him? Fear gripped him. What if he never saw her again? He didn't even know where she lived! Imagine, he didn't know where she lived. On the Falls Road, yes, but the Falls Road stretched for miles and was a warren of streets. Not meaning for the relationship to become serious, he had never inquired into her personal life; never shown any interest in where she lived. Now, he regretted this. He loved her, must have her for his wife.

Hearing a crowd enter the cloakroom, Eileen guessed the dance was over and left the cubicle with face averted, not wanting to talk to anyone. She must wait outside in the shadows for her friend. She must wait outside, otherwise Kate would be bound to guess that something was wrong.

When Billy saw her leave the cloakroom, he breathed a sigh of relief and hurried anxiously towards her.

'Are you all right, love?'

She nodded, but kept her eyes downcast and headed for the exit.

'Eileen, I'm sorry. Can you ever forgive me?' he whispered, hurrying after her.

She could not bear to meet his eyes, such was her shame. To have let him do that to her!

'Eileen, look at me. Do you forgive me?' His voice was urgent. She must forgive him.

She nodded, but still refused to meet his eyes.

'Listen, love, tomorrow night I'm taking you home to meet my parents.' He had to make her understand. Had to reassure her, before they parted company.

At last her eyes flew to his face and he was dismayed at the misery reflected there. Did he mean it? Eileen wondered. Was there still hope for them?

Seeing her sadness replaced by hope, Billy rushed on, 'I intend to make you my wife, come what may. Trust me, love.' He gripped her hand tightly. 'Please trust me. As far as I'm concerned you're already my wife. Everything is going to be all right and I don't want you to worry. Do you understand me? Everything's going to be all right, I promise.'

She managed a trembling smile, then catching sight of Kate, ran to meet her beside Jim Rafferty's car.

'Eileen?' Anxiously Billy shouted after her: 'Tomorrow night? Usual time and place?'

He was rewarded by another wobbly smile before she climbed into the car.

*   *   *

Johnny Cleary arrive late at the Floral Hall. When Eileen had proudly informed him that she and Kate would be at the Victor Sylvester Ball, he had moved heaven and earth to obtain tickets for himself. He had paid double the price for the tickets, but counted himself fortunate to get them at such short notice. He had also been lucky enough to persuade Angie Carson to accompany him. Unfortunately Angie worked as a receptionist at one of the hotels in town. She had been working the late shift and so it was after eleven when they finally stepped from a taxi and entered the Floral Hall.

Angie gazed about her in delight. 'Oh, this is lovely! Don't you agree?'

Johnny was also impressed. 'It is rather . . . very nice indeed.'

Angie was aware of his reason for being at the dance and now she challenged him. 'Well . . . let's go find this girl who's managed to dent your heart.'

'Thanks, Angie, for coming with me.'

They had been friends since school days. Angie grinned at him. 'I just hope she appreciates your worth.' With these words she led the way into the ballroom, only to stop in dismay.

The dance floor was one huge mass of moving bodies. How could he hope to find anyone in this crowd? It would be like looking for a needle in a haystack.

It was almost midnight when Johnny at last spotted Kate Rafferty. Keeping her in sight, he danced Angie around until at last Kate and her partner made their way off the floor, but though he watched for some time, there was no sign of Eileen.

'I would love a drink, Johnny.'

'Angie . . . I'm sorry. I'm neglecting you.'

'Oh, it's all right, Johnny. After all I know why we're here. Listen, while you get the drinks I'll go and powder my nose and meet you back here, OK?'

It was while he was waiting his turn at the bar,

watching the dancers do the Jitterbug, that he caught sight of Eileen. He examined her partner. Tall, rugged and swarthy . . . and young. About twenty-one, he would guess. And obviously Eileen was fond of him. Even as Johnny watched, she stopped at the edge of the dance floor, and laughing, pointed down at her feet. Johnny's heart ached when he saw the lad lead her towards the open door and out into the moonlit grounds.

He sighed. If only he could make Eileen see him as a possible suitor. The past few months had been the happiest of his life. He was aware that she only went to the pictures with him out of kindness, but since she appeared to have no interest in anyone else, he had been hopeful. He had to admit that he had pressured her to continue going out with him. He was also aware that it was obvious to all that he doted on her. When he had sought Kevin Rafferty out and asked to be introduced to Eileen, Kevin had been amused, had silently implied that he was cradle snatching, but nothing had deterred Johnny. Now every Monday night, without fail, Eileen and he frequented the Broadway Picture House together. Afraid of what he might hear, he had not questioned her about other boyfriends. It had come as a shock to him when she had casually mentioned she had tickets for the Floral Hall; tickets bought for her by a man. A boy, really, if her dance partner was the benefactor.

That was the only glimpse he was to have of Eileen, and although Angie was willing to offer him solace when they arrived at her flat, Johnny respectfully declined. He wanted only Eileen. Angie was a good friend but a bit too willing where men were concerned. He had set his sights on Eileen and didn't want any complications from the likes of Angie.

On the journey home Eileen was glad that Kate was full of the dance. She talked non-stop. When they arrived at Eileen's door, Jim Rafferty turned in his seat with a rueful smile for her. Under his scrutiny, she was glad of the shadows.

'What about you, Eileen? Did you enjoy the dance?' he asked kindly. 'This daughter of mine didn't let you get a word in edgeways.'

'It was great. Mr Rafferty. Just great,' she enthused in a bright voice. 'Thanks awfully for the lift there and back. Good night. See you tomorrow, Kate.'

'Hey! Wait a minute, Eileen. Are you going to eleven o'clock Mass?'

'No! An early one,' she shouted over her shoulder.

'An early one?' Kate gasped. 'It's almost two already.'

But Eileen was through the gate and unlocking the door. Annoyed, Kate shouted, 'Well ... I'll see you sometime.'

With relief, Eileen let herself into the silent house. Hoping everyone would be asleep, she closed the outer door gently. To her dismay the living-room door opened and her father entered the hall.

'Here you are at last. Did you enjoy yourself?'

Aware that the light from the living room shone full on her, Eileen quailed and waited for his wrath to explode. Surely he would guess? She must look different. But no, he was smiling kindly at her.

'You look tired, love. I'll put the teapot on and you can tell me all about the dance.'

'No, Dad! No tea for me, thanks. The dance was smashing, but I'm dead beat. I just want to take a quick bath and go to bed. My feet are aching in these new shoes.' She eased them from her feet. 'Ah ... look at the blisters. A soak in the tub will do me good.' The look she directed at her father was reproachful. 'Really, Dad ... you shouldn't have waited up for me.'

'This is the latest any of you has ever been out, and you expected me to go to bed?' He was amazed at her naivety. I wouldn't have slept. But you go on up, love. You can tell us all about the dance tomorrow.'

'Good night, Dad.'

'Good night, Eileen.'

Wearily, she climbed the stairs. Going into the bathroom, she set the taps running. She ached all over. Perhaps a bath would soothe her. Tears flowed freely when she removed her torn underwear. How was she going to explain those to her mother? She would have to try and repair them before her mother saw them.

Lying in water just bearably hot, she scrubbed and scrubbed, but still felt dirty. Dirty and wicked, and so ashamed. How could she have been so stupid? Tears rained down her face and despair engulfed her once more.

'Are you all right, Eileen?'

Her father's voice, full of concern, startled her. In a daze, she realized she had been in the bath a long time, the water was almost cold.

'Yes, Dad. I must have dozed off.'

'That's dangerous, love. Get t'bed.'

'All right, Dad.'

As she dried her body, she was dismayed to see bruises already appearing on her thighs and arms. She would have to keep her arms covered, otherwise her father would want to know how she had acquired the marks. As she creamed her face, tears mingled with the cream and she admonished herself: Stop it! For heaven's sake, stop crying or tomorrow you'll look awful. And you know what that'll mean. Questions from Mam, questions from Dad, and questions from the girls. Questions! Questions! She wouldn't be able to bear it!

Her mind alive with the events of the dance, she tossed and turned all night, afraid of sleeping in for eight o'clock Mass. If she went as usual to eleven o'clock Mass, at least one of her family would be there and they would notice if she didn't receive Holy Communion. Johnny Cleary would also be there and would wait outside to walk her to the top of the street. Such was her shame, she thought all eyes would be on her. That everyone would be aware that she had committed a grave sin. She had never had reason to miss receiving Holy Communion before and now she felt damned. At Communion time, she bowed her head and asked God's forgiveness for the terrible sin she had committed. When Mass was over she hurried out, not wanting to talk to any of the congregation.

At the corner of the street she met Claire and Emma on their way to nine o'clock Mass.

'You look awful!' Claire greeted her.

'You're no oil painting yourself,' Eileen retorted.

'Huh! You're in bad humour. Sorry I spoke.'

At another time Eileen would have apologized for her outburst, but she was so miserable she just grunted and continued on her way, leaving Claire staring after her, a surprised look on her face.

Her father was finishing his breakfast when Eileen entered the kitchen. One look at her face caused him to bawl, 'No more late dances for you, me girl! If that's how you look after a late night out, you'll be an old hag in no time at all.'

Sarah examined her daughter's face anxiously. So pale, dark purple shadows under her eyes. 'Do you think you're sickening for something?' she asked anxiously, her mind on Beth's wedding two weeks away.

Pushing her plate of bacon and eggs away from her, Eileen replied, 'No, Mam. I'm just tired. I guess I danced too much last night. I'll go back to bed for a while.'

When she left the room, Beth threw her mother a worried glance. 'She looks ill. Do you think she's sickening for something? The 'flu is rife at the moment. It would be awful if we all caught it, with the wedding so near.'

'I think she's probably run down. A bit bloodless, you know? I'll buy a jar of malt tomorrow, and make her take it,' vowed Sarah.

Extract of malt was Sarah's cure for all ails and she was sure it would solve this problem.

Lying on top of the bedclothes, Eileen tried to sleep, but her mind kept going over the events of the night before, filling her with misery and shame, and sleep eluded her.

At dinnertime she picked at her food, causing more comments and worried frowns from the family. At last it was time to get ready and she was glad to escape to her room to prepare to meet Billy. She did so with great care: using more make-up than usual to hide the tell-tale marks of her sleepless night and bouts of weeping. She wanted to make a good impression on Billy's parents. Wanted them to like her. Suppose they refused to meet her? Or supposing they met her and then her parents refused to meet Billy? Her father was quite capable of showing him the door if she brought him home. Usually an easy-going person, he was very strict about Catholics dating Protestants, often warning his daughters to bear in mind that in the long run it was better to stick to your own kind. Enough of that! One thing at a time. First she must meet Billy's parents. She let herself out of the house quietly and walked quickly down the street, glad she did not see any of her family in case they asked more questions.

When she had met Billy at a dance one night and started dating him, she had not meant to deceive everybody. If anyone had asked where she was going or who she was going with, she would have told them. However, as time passed and she saw more of him, realizing they thought she was either with Kate or Johnny Cleary, she just did not enlighten them. After all ... Billy was a Protestant, nothing could come of it. She wasn't doing anything wrong, so surely a few dates wouldn't matter? Now this awful thing had happened. But she had not meant to deceive them, not really!

1

So lost in thought was she, standing at the bottom of the Donegall Road where she usually met Billy, it came as a shock to her when it became obvious he was not going to show up. Her back ached, and even with plasters on her heels, her feet were sore in the new shoes, so she caught a tram up the Donegall Road, a luxury she did not often indulge in.

Not wanting to go home so early and face a barrage of questions, she called at Kate's house, hoping to find her at home. It was Kate herself who opened the door and motioned her inside, a surprised look on her face.

Leading the way into the sitting room, she asked, 'Where's Billy tonight? I thought you saw him on a Sunday night as well now?' Then, with a laugh, she answered her own question. 'I suppose he has a hangover. By, but him and that Bobby fella supped a lot of beer last night!'

With a start of surprise, Eileen realized this could indeed be the reason Billy had not turned up. Why had she not thought of it? And why had she not realized that he was drunk last night? Then she would have known better than to go outside with him. How different she would be feeling today. Instead, she was convinced that he would finish with her, now that he had got what he wanted. Ah, did she really think that? He loved her! Oh, surely he loved her? Hadn't he told her so?

Kate was bewildered at her silence. 'Is anything wrong?'

'Billy didn't turn up tonight.'

'Well, maybe he has a hangover,' Kate repeated.

'He was to take me to meet his parents tonight. Last night he asked me to marry him.'

Kate's legs gave beneath her and she sank slowly down on to a chair, and cried in dismay, 'Ah, Eileen, stick to your own kind! It's easier in the long run.'

Eileen's mouth twisted as if in pain. 'Maybe I'll have to,' she wailed. 'Perhaps his parents have forbidden him to see me again.'

'That's the best thing that could happen,' Kate stated

firmly. She was riddled with guilt: she should have talked Eileen out of dating Billy Greer at the beginning, before she grew too fond of him. At first she had hoped that dating him would put a stop to Eileen's seeing Johnny Cleary, and then maybe he would have turned his attentions to her. That was wishful thinking! Eileen still went to the pictures with Johnny every Monday night. It wasn't fair the way she kept him on a string while she dated Billy Greer. But then, it was kindness that motivated her. She thought Johnny was too old to take seriously. She enjoyed his company but didn't love him. Never dreamt that Kate carried a torch for him, so why not date him? Really ... she should be encouraging Eileen to meet Billy's parents; urging her to marry the man she loved. Then perhaps she would catch Johnny on the rebound. If only Billy was a Catholic everything would be all right.

'Don't say that, Kate. Other Catholics have married Protestants. And you know yourself, all the new estates that are being built have mixed denominations. The war made a great difference, you know. It's not like the old days when mixed marriages were a scandal. People are more lenient these days. At least, that's what I think.'

It was on the tip of Kate's tongue to say. Try telling your dad that! Seeing the misery in her friend's eyes, she said instead, 'Oh, don't worry about it. Billy will probably be there as usual on Tuesday night, full of apologies. Just wait, you'll see. And if you are both serious ... well it will be your choice. Here, give me your coat and we'll listen to the radio.'

Billy did not turn up on Tuesday night, nor did he come the following Saturday. With every day that passed Eileen's heart broke a little more, as hope grew fainter and fainter. She tried to put him from her mind, tried to forget about him, telling herself that Kate was right and that it was for the best, but in vain. He was in her thoughts every waking moment.

* * *

Sarah worried about Eileen and shovelled spoonfuls of malt into her every morning, wanting her to be well for Beth's wedding, but with so much on her mind she neglected to question her.

The malt turned Eileen's stomach, and every morning in work she retched and retched into the wash basin in the ladies' cloakroom, feeling miserable.

Kate eyed her worriedly, afraid to voice her thoughts. It was unthinkable that Eileen could be . . . no, not Eileen Ross! Anybody but Eileen. At last she could bear it no longer and cried, 'Eileen, you couldn't be . . .' her voice trailed off. 'Oh, never mind.'

Eileen's pale, woebegone face turned towards her. 'Couldn't be what?'

'Well . . . ah, I know it sounds crazy . . . and you'll hate me for suggesting it, but . . .' Again she hesitated. Eileen would be angry, but what if she was right? She had to ask her. Bravely she took the plunge. 'Well, you couldn't be pregnant, could you?'

It seemed impossible that Eileen could go any whiter, but she did! Sagging against the wash-stand in dismay; gripping the cold basin to keep a hold on her senses. She realized that Kate was right. That's what was wrong with her. She was expecting a baby. It was not the malt that was making her sick every morning. And her period . . . it should have arrived . . . Oh, dear God, no! Please don't let it be that. Oh, God, please don't let it be that. Unable to face the enormity of it, her mind sank towards oblivion, but Kate's cry of horror held her back.

'Oh, my God! Say I'm wrong, Eileen!' Kate cried in dismay, but she knew by her friend's horrified eyes that she had hit the nail on the head.

'What will I do? Oh, Kate, what will I do?' Eileen wailed. 'Dear God, what will I do?' She couldn't think straight. The enormity of it! Her, expecting a baby!

'Hush, Eileen, hush now. Look, I'll get our coats, and

ask Mr Mooney if I can take you home. I'll tell him you're not well.'

Kate turned to leave the cloakroom, but Eileen grabbed her arm and clung to her. 'No! I can't go home like this. Mam will guess.'

Kate snorted. 'Well, she'll have to know sometime, you'll not be able to hide this for long.'

'Perhaps I'm wrong. Eh, Kate? What if I'm wrong? It won't be the first time my period was late. It might still come.' Eileen was babbling. 'If it doesn't come, I'll tell me mam after the wedding. I can't spoil Beth's wedding. Ah, God, no. I can't spoil our Beth's big day.'

Reluctantly, Kate nodded in agreement; no good upsetting everyone before the wedding. 'Are you well enough to work?' she asked solicitously, and receiving a nod in reply, she promised, 'I'll cover for you all I can.' And she did, but it was to be one of the longest days of Eileen's young life.

'Can I come to your house for tea, Kate? I can't face the family.'

'Of course you can. Mam will be glad to see you.'

After a long miserable day, they walked up the Donegall Road on their way home from work.

'I can't face Dad.' Eileen's face was drawn and haggard and her friend's heart went out to her. 'Ah, Kate, what am I going to do?'

Kate, who had been racking her brains all day, trying to find a solution, could find no words of consolation and glumly shook her head.

Entering St James's Park, and seeing Emma playing in the garden, Eileen called her over.

'Tell Mam I'm having tea at Kate's house tonight, Emma, will you, love?'

'Why?'

'Because I want to. Go on,' Eileen gave her a gentle push, 'tell her.'

41

With a shrug, Emma ran across the road and entered the house. Mournfully Eileen turned to her friend. 'Your mam won't mind, will she, Kate?'

'Mam's always glad to have company. She misses the brood, you know.'

Of Kathleen's seven children just Kevin and Kate still lived at home, and she missed the hustle and bustle of a crowded house. She fussed over Eileen. 'Tut, tut. So you're not feeling well, love?'

Eileen smiled wanly and Kathleen said, 'I know what. I'll make you a nice omelette. You should be able to hold that down.'

Much to her surprise, Eileen enjoyed the omelette, having eaten nothing all day. However, her despair returned later when Kate and she were alone.

'What can I do, Kate? How will I tell my dad? He'll kill me.'

'No, he won't! But I've been thinking . . . what you're going to do is this. You're going to see Billy Greer and tell him about the baby. For heaven's sake, Eileen, he'll have to stand by you. Anyway, once he gets over the shock, he'll probably be all right. After all . . . he did ask you to marry him, didn't he?' When Eileen nodded, Kate said, 'There's your answer then. Go see him and tell him the truth.'

'I can't.'

'Look, Eileen, I understand how you feel, but this is no time for false pride. You must tell him.' Kate was amazed at her friend's refusal.

'You don't understand, Kate. I really can't tell him. I don't know where he lives.'

'You don't know where he lives?' Kate was scandalized. 'You've been going out with him for three months or more, and you've been . . . intimate . . . and you don't know where he lives? Bah! I don't believe you.'

She turned away in disgust. If Eileen didn't trust her, that was that.

Gripping Kate's arm, Eileen pulled her round to face her. 'Honestly, Kate, I don't know. I'm speaking the truth.' She was bobbing her head up and down in an effort to convince her friend that she was indeed telling the truth. 'I only know that he lives somewhere on the Shankill Road, but how many streets are there on the Shankill?'

'Hundreds,' whispered Kate. Then a thought struck her and she cried excitedly, 'You must know where he works.'

Sadly, Eileen shook her head. 'I know he's a plumber, but I don't know where he works. You see, Kate we didn't discuss things like that, we had so many other interests.'

'Obviously!' Kate grunted.

'You're wrong, Kate.' Eileen turned away shamefaced. 'That only happened once.'

'Once? And you're pregnant?'

'Once!' Eileen repeated, but she could see that Kate didn't believe her.

'Was it as wonderful as Big Aggie says it is?' Kate's voice was low. She felt ashamed asking such a question, but she longed to know what it was like, and she knew Eileen would tell her the truth. Big Aggie, who worked with them, was forever saying that they didn't know what they were missing. She was always boasting of her conquests.

To Kate's dismay, Eileen, head in hands, burrowed into the arms of the settee, and her slight frame shook with great silent sobs.

'Ah, Eileen, don't cry. I'm sorry I asked.' Distracted, Kate went down on her knees beside her friend. Putting her arms around her, she consoled her. 'Something will turn up. You'll see.' She continued murmuring words of comfort, until at last, with a long shuddering sigh, Eileen wiped her eyes dry and sat upright.

'It was awful, Kate. Horrible!' She shuddered at the

memory. 'Don't you believe a word Big Aggie says. It was awful!' Her voice was bleak, when she asked, 'I don't suppose Bobby Price mentioned where Billy works?'

Regretfully, Kate shook her head. It seemed to her that Billy Greer had won Eileen's love and trust, and had successfully pulled the wool over her eyes. She doubted very much that Eileen would ever hear from him again.

The bastard! The dirty mean bastard!

Many girls had been foolish during the war, when handsome American servicemen had turned their heads with promises of marriage and a new life in the United States. It was a well-known fact that a woman down the Donegall Road got rid of unwanted pregnancies when unfortunate victims were left in the the lurch. The thought of an illegal abortion had been niggling at Kate's mind for a couple of hours now. In normal circumstances she would not dream of condoning abortion, but in the face of Eileen's distress she was tempted. Should she mention it to her? No! No, Eileen would never hear tell of it! Besides, if she chanced an abortion and anything went wrong, how would Kate live with herself? Even so, Eileen would never hear tell of it. Back street abortions had been rife for a while after the war, but to imagine that a girl like Eileen Ross would sink so low was unthinkable. Why, it was a sin for Kate even to think along those lines! There was only one solution to her friend's problem. Somehow, they must track down Billy Greer and make him take responsibility for his actions. It was the only answer. They must find Billy Greer, somehow!

Chapter Two

With each day that passed Eileen became more and more frightened. The longed for period did not materialize and her mind baulked when she thought that a child was growing inside her. Her, Eileen Ross! Who had looked in disdain and disgust at the girls in work who admitted to doing *just that*. She clung to Kate for comfort, talking about Billy, thinking up reasons why he had not been in contact with her. Refusing to believe that he had abandoned her.

Guessing that he probably did not know which street she lived in, Eileen haunted the bottom of the Donegall Road, hoping against hope that one night he would be there, and somehow everything would be all right. At last Kate, unable to bear it any longer, put her arms around Eileen, and weeping with frustration, told her she had better face up to the fact that Billy was not going to put in an appearance. His parents must have objected to his marrying a Catholic and he had not been strong enough to stand up to them. She advised Eileen to tell her parents; explain her predicament to them. Eileen promised she would ... but not just yet. She could not spoil the preparations for Beth's wedding. Could not cause a scandal before the big day.

Luckily, at home everyone was too preoccupied with the approaching wedding to pay much attention to Eileen and she was able to hide her pain and distress. The house revolved around the wedding. Morning, noon and night it was the subject of discussion. Sarah and Mick were delighted with their eldest daughter's choice of a husband. A motor mechanic! And a good one at that! He was also very shrewd. He'd have his own business one day. He had already purchased a small house and he and Beth spent all their spare time renovating it. Tommy Rogan was an easy-going young man and it was obvious to them he adored Beth. They were confident she would be safe in his hands.

Still aware of Eileen's pallor, Sarah made sure she took a large spoonful of malt every morning, but otherwise paid little attention to her, her mind being full of last-minute preparations. As mother of the bride, everything fell on her shoulders. More so than usual as Tommy's mother was a widow, and an invalid. Not that Sarah minded. Quite the contrary! She revelled in all the excitement leading up to the big day.

It came as a surprise to her when one morning Mick took her to one side. 'Our Eileen isn't a bit well-looking. Have you any idea what's worrying her?'

'You think she's worrying about something?' she asked in dismay.

'Aye, I do. She looks as if the weight of the world's on her shoulders. An' surely you've noticed she eats hardly anything?'

'No. No, I hadn't.' Sarah sighed. 'I've had so much on my mind this past couple of weeks. We're having a dress-fitting this evening, I'll have a word with her afterwards.'

That evening when she saw how the bridesmaid's dress, which a few weeks earlier had fitted perfectly, now hung on Eileen, she was appalled. Pinning the dress at the waist where she would have to take it in, she scolded, 'If you don't start eating properly, girl, you'll end up in a sanatorium. That's what'll happen to you. You'll end up in Purdysburn, so ye will! After the wedding we'll go down and see young Dr Hughes and get you a tonic.'

Dr Hughes wasn't all that young, but was so called to

distinguish him from his father who had retired years ago. His surgery was on the Springfield Road, where her mother had worked for many years as receptionist to the older doctor. Sarah had great confidence in his son and both her mother and she had refused to transfer to another doctor when they had moved from Waterford Street to St James's Park further up the Falls Road. A knock on the door interrupted Sarah's tirade and brought them to attention. They listened in silence. Heard the living-room door open and footsteps in the hall. The murmur of voices, too low to distinguish, reached them. Then, after tapping on the sitting-room door and being bidden to enter, Mick's head appeared around it.

'Johnny Cleary's here with a present for Beth. I'll talk to him in the living room 'till you're finished in here.'

'Now, isn't that nice of him Beth?' Sarah addressed her eldest daughter but she eyed Eileen as she spoke. Was Eileen serious about Johnny? She didn't seem to be; said he was too old! That Johnny cared for her was obvious but only time would tell if he would win Eileen round. She was young; had plenty of time to make up her mind.

Unaware of her mother's scrutiny, Eileen sighed. Johnny was another problem. She would have to tell him the truth soon, because it was obvious that he would be regarded as the father of her child. Why couldn't she have fallen in love with him? He was kind and courteous. Treated her like a queen . . . but he was old. She couldn't imagine herself married to him.

Once the dress-fitting was over the girls joined Mick and Johnny in the sitting room while Sarah made a pot of tea. Beth was delighted at the beautiful china tea set Johnny had bought. Eileen was daft if she let him slip through her fingers. Why, he could have any girl he wanted! He was handsome and kind and didn't appear to be short of money. And eight years was nothing between husband and wife. She'd have a talk

47

with Eileen. Advise her to make up her mind before it was too late.

Because of the unexpected visit, Sarah once again neglected to question Eileen, and Mick, knowing how preoccupied she was, didn't press her. He decided to tackle his daughter himself. Claire and Eileen had to be in by half-past ten each night. That night he waylaid Eileen at the door, and ushered her into the sitting room.

There was fear in her eyes as she gazed at him and he cried in exasperation, 'For heaven's sake, Eileen, don't look at me like that! Anyone would think I beat you regularly.' He could see that she was still ill at ease and to help her relax, added jokingly, 'Instead of once a month.'

Mick had never lifted his hand to any of his children, finding when they were young, that brandishing his slipper in front of their faces was enough to make them toe the line. These words brought a faint smile to her face.

'What's wrong, love?' he asked, voice full of compassion.

For a moment she was tempted to tell him. To pour all her troubles on to his broad shoulders. To weep against his chest and risk his wrath. With a great effort of will, she resisted the temptation.

'Nothing.'

'Ah, come on, Eileen. A blind man could see you're worried.'

She shook her head vehemently. 'Nothing's wrong, Dad. I guess I'm just run down.' How could she confide in her dad whom she adored? It would break his heart and spoil Beth's wedding. She realized she would have to tell him soon. But not until after the wedding, because she now knew without a doubt that she was pregnant. There had been no reprieve.

Disappointed, Mick turned aside. He had made the

effort. He had done his best. 'Well, I'm here if you should change your mind, remember that,' he said sadly, and Eileen watched his shoulders slump as he turned and left the room. If only she could tell him . . .

The next few days were spent putting the finishing touches to the small kitchen house in Clondara Street, where Beth and Tommy were going to start married life together. Although just a short distance away from St James's Park, Clondara Street in contrast was a narrow street of old terraced houses. They had worked hard the past few months renovating the house, and now had it looking like a small palace. Downstairs was a kitchen, a tiny narrow scullery, with a small room off, and upstairs were two bedrooms. Tommy was planning to extend it. To build a bathroom at the back. He did not intend to let Beth use an outside toilet for long. Not when she was used to a bathroom. It was just a first home. Later, when they came to sell the house, Tommy was confident that they would make money on it, enabling them to buy a bigger house, perhaps up the Glen Road or Andersonstown. He would work his fingers to the bone, and one day he would have his own garage. He adored Beth and often wondered what she saw in him, but vowed she would never regret marrying him.

Breathtaking in her white satin dress which had used up everybody's quota of clothing coupons, Beth took her father's arm and smiled up at him. For some seconds Mick paused, breath catching in his throat at the beauty of her. Then, with a glance behind to make sure Eileen and Claire were ready and that Emma had the long train lifted clear of the ground, he nodded to Jim Rafferty who was one of the ushers. Jim, from his position inside the church, in turn nodded up at the organist, and as the strains of 'Here Comes the Bride' filled the air, Mick proudly led his eldest daughter up the aisle.

Tommy never once took his eyes off Beth. When

she finally joined him at the altar rails, he cleared his throat and smiled nervously. Watching the way Tommy worshipped her sister with his eyes, and hearing the reverence in his voice as he took his vows, Eileen felt like weeping. Never for her a white wedding. Indeed her chances of marriage were ruined, and all because she had trusted Billy Greer.

As communion time drew near Eileen's stomach churned with nerves. How could she receive Holy Communion and her in mortal sin? She had been afraid to go to confession. Never having committed a sin of such magnitude before, she did not know what the priest's reaction would be. What if he insisted on her telling her parents about the baby? No ... she couldn't risk that. Time enough after Beth's wedding.

Now she felt faint with worry. Should she pretend to be ill? In fact she did feel ill, but it would spoil Beth's big day. Begging God's forgiveness, Eileen received the Eucharist. She expected to be struck dead, but God is good and nothing happened, and she spent the remainder of the service thanking Him for His mercy. Soon the register was signed and they passed out into the churchyard. Here, her grannie's brother, Great Uncle William, was waiting to take the wedding photographs. This was a great honour! William was now famous in England. In fact, on quite a few occasions he had been commissioned to photograph members of the Royal Family. He had arrived early that morning and was returning to England the same night.

William had them posing here and there, this way and that, until everyone became quite restless. Sarah watched her uncle and remembered her own wedding day. She remembered her Aunt Emma had had a crush on William. Seeing him now, Emma must be relieved that he had married Elsie, leaving her free to marry kind, humorous Uncle Tim. Even as she thought of her, Sarah caught sight of Emma, still slim and attractive, dressed in a pale green coat. A Dior model. He had gone against the restrictions still imposed after the war. Realizing women were tired of square-shouldered skimpy dresses, his new line had sloping shoulders and fitted waists and skirts that flared to below the calf. Emma had no children and could well afford the clothing coupons, easily obtainable on the black market. Working as a buyer for a small select dress shop, she was always exquisitely turned out in the latest fashions from London and Paris. Sarah chuckled quietly to herself when she saw her aunt move closer to Tim and gaze in bemused wonder at William, possibly wondering what on earth she had ever seen in him.

Elsie had been unable to accompany William to the wedding, but she had kept in touch with Maggie and Sarah over the years with the odd letter or card. This was the first time they had seen William since before the war. Sarah knew her mother was disappointed that her only brother was not staying. Even a few days would have pleased Maggie, but William was a very busy man and was returning to England that night. Sarah had to admit that if she had met her uncle in the street, she would have passed him by, he had changed so much. He was grossly overweight and his once bright fair hair was now non-existent. Only his eyes were the same clear green, like her own. Catching her appraising gaze, William winked, bringing a guilty flush to her cheeks. What on earth was she blushing for? He could not possibly know what she was thinking.

'Won't be long now, Sarah, I'm almost finished,' he called out. 'One shot of all the guests together and that's it!'

Laughing, she replied, 'Take all the time you want, Uncle William. We're honoured to have you.' And she meant it. The wedding album was to be William's wedding present to Beth and Tommy, and Sarah knew it would be unique. Crossing the churchyard, she joined the tall, silver-haired priest, standing talking to her mother and Barney.

'I'm glad you could come, Uncle Brendan,' she greeted him.

'So am I. I'm just sorry I couldn't perform the Nuptial Mass, but at least I'm here, and so happy to see you all.' Head tilted back, he looked down his nose at her, a comical expression on his face. 'Your mother and I have just been remarking how changed William is.'

With a grin, she agreed with him. 'He has indeed.' Then, knowing how disappointed he had been not to have obtained permission to say Nuptial Mass, she added, 'Perhaps in a couple of years time, you'll be able to say Nuptial Mass for Eileen.'

'Perhaps. Who knows what can happen in a couple of years. Things change so quickly these days and I'm not getting any younger.' He nodded across at a tall handsome lad and turned to Maggie. 'I also see a great change in young Bernard. My, but he has grown. He's quite the young man now! It must be four years since I last saw you all.'

'Yes, it's his height that makes him look so mature,' Maggie agreed fondly. 'That and the collar and tie. Barney's so proud of him. He does look well, doesn't he?' she asked proudly. Her eyes ran over her son's well turned out frame, dressed in the best of everything. 'He's a good lad.'

Brendan agreed that Bernard did look well, but he saw the grimace on Sarah's face as she turned away and surmised that her half-brother was not one of his niece's favourites.

With a sigh of relief, Maggie said, 'At last! William's finished. Will you come in the same car as Barney and me, Brendan?'

'I have my own car, Maggie.' He turned to Sarah. 'I'll be able to take some guests to the reception for you, if you like?'

He laughed outright at her surprised expression. 'Priests in country parishes need cars, Sarah. Not that it's anything grand, mind you. But it gets me around, and at my age what more could I want?'

The reception was held in the Imperial Hotel, on Donegall Place, and after the wedding breakfast was finished – a breakfast that Eileen could not eat – the floor was cleared for dancing.

This was the moment Johnny had been waiting for, dreaming about. The chance to hold Eileen in his arms. To his surprise, he felt quite nervous. Matthew Rogan, Tommy's brother, who had been his best man, claimed the first dance with her, and Johnny watched jealously as he swung Eileen around the floor to the strains of 'We'll Gather Lilacs in the Spring Again'. Next her father waltzed off with her and again Johnny was left watching. Preparing to ask her for the third dance, he was pleased when the 'Moonlight Saunter' was requested. The 'Moonlight Saunter' was one of those dances where everyone had to dance in sequence and Johnny knew he was very good at it. At the dances, girls loved to partner him.

At first Eileen demurred, saying that she could not do the 'Moonlight Saunter', but when he assured her that he would guide her round the floor, she silently entered his arms. A thrill coursed through him at her nearness. She felt like a feather in his arms and he guided her into the dance routine expertly.

Thoughts of the Floral Hall haunted Eileen's mind as she glided around the floor. The sweetness and the shame of it. And when they played 'My Foolish Heart' her heightened emotions brought her close to tears. The fact that Billy Greer had abandoned her without a word tore at her heartstrings and she hated the child that was growing inside her. Hated it with such intensity, she was surprised it didn't leave her body. She wondered where Billy was today. Why, oh why, was he doing this to her? He had seemed so kind, and she had trusted him utterly.

His parents must have forbidden him to see her again, but he should have been man enough to tell her to her face. She despised him for being so cowardly. That was the only reason she could think of to cause him to abandon her. Unless he had been planning this all along? But she could not believe that of him. He had never attempted to touch her before. She had believed him when he had said that if their parents didn't agree to their marrying, they would go over to England. Well, obviously his parents had not given their consent and they were more important to him than she was. He had been leading her on. The sooner she faced the fact that she would never see him again, the better. Tomorrow she must tell her parents about the baby. Her face blanched at the very idea.

When the dance ended, Johnny noticed her pallor and asked anxiously, 'Are you all right, Eileen?'

Forcing a smile to her lips, she nodded. When he asked her for the next dance, to his delight she remained by his side and as the music started up again, listlessly entered his arms. Johnny held her as if she was made of fine china. He thought she had never looked lovelier than now, in a pale blue dress that showed off the whiteness of her skin, the soft contours of her body, and flowed gently around her ankles. She looked so fragile, like a delicate tropical flower. The awareness of her body, with its small pointed breasts, so close to his, gave him great pleasure. He felt exalted to be holding her, to have that soft beautiful hair brushing his cheek. Her perfume filled his nostrils and he longed to draw her closer, to feel her body actually touch his, but refrained, afraid of incurring her displeasure.

'Beth looks lovely. And so happy,' he said, when the bride and groom danced past gazing raptly at each other.

'Yes, she's beautiful,' Eileen agreed, and hoped the envy she felt did not come across in her voice.

'So are you, Eileen.'

At these words a faint smile touched her lips. If only she *was* beautiful! Maybe then Billy Greer would have faced up to his parents and married her. To her surprise Johnny dared to draw her closer. He was not usually forward. The film was nearly over every Monday night before he took her hand and held it clasped in his, a fact she was grateful for. Why did she still see him? He was too old for her. Now that she was pregnant she would have to stop seeing him. He would get a right shock when he heard about her condition.

Mouth close to her ear, Johnny whispered daringly, 'I wish this was our wedding day, Eileen.'

Her heart missed a beat and she stumbled. 'I'm sorry,' she apologized.

'My fault.' Gallantly, he took the blame.

She felt winded. Could this be the answer to her prayers? Was she meant to marry Johnny? Good God, no! She didn't love him! It was Billy Greer she loved. Billy, with his dark intense good looks; his young muscular body. She couldn't possibly marry Johnny Cleary. He had no effect on her whatsoever. She just could not marry a man eight years older than herself. Why not? her mind shouted. What had she to look forward to otherwise? Spinsterhood, with an illegitimate child. If she married Johnny, at least her child would have a name. Oh, Billy, Billy, where are you? Where are you? her heart cried.

'So do I, Johnny,' she heard herself whisper in reply.

So great was his amazement, it was Johnny's turn to stumble. Recovering his step, he gently pushed her from him and eyed her intently. Was he hearing things? Could she possibly care?

'Do you mean that, Eileen?'

She looked into his eyes. Kind eyes that reminded her of her father's. That was the way she thought of him: a father figure. It would be wrong to marry him. It wouldn't be fair! He deserved better. In spite of all these objections that her mind conjured up, she found herself nodding her agreement.

'When, Eileen?' He sounded winded, could not believe his luck.

Anxiously, she cried, 'I don't want all the fuss and bother our Beth went through, mind.' She knew full well that all the beautiful trimmings were denied her. 'Just a quiet wedding is all I want, you know. Is that all right with you?'

'Whatever you like, Eileen. I'll agree to anything you say. Soon, Eileen? Can we be married soon?'

Johnny was sure he was dreaming and would soon wake up to reality. Never had he imagined that Eileen cared for him in that way. Liked him, yes, but not really cared.

'Whenever you like, Johnny.'

If she did not sound overjoyed, he was too happy to notice. She cared! Oh, he hoped he wasn't dreaming.

'Let's tell everyone,' he cried eagerly. He wanted her to commit herself before she had a chance to change her mind; wanted everyone to know that she had agreed to marry him.

'No, Johnny!' Frantically Eileen pulled him back as he headed for the top of the room. 'This is our Beth's big day. Besides, I must tell my parents first, and you must tell your mother.'

'You're right as usual, Eileen.' He pulled her possessively close, content to wait now that he knew she cared.

Closing her eyes to hide her distaste, Eileen felt panic grip her. Was she doing the right thing? Oh, Billy Greer, I hate you. I hate you! Her heart cried as all her hopes died.

The day after Beth's wedding Eileen tried to force herself into the living room where her mother and father sat, unwinding after the hectic previous day. She should be glad that she had a solution to her problem; that Johnny wanted to marry her. However, she still trembled at the thought of what her parents' reaction might be. Expecially her mother! She was such a prude, expected so much from her four daughters. Would worry about what the neighbours might think.

Not that Eileen blamed her. Normally she would not have dreamed of playing about before marriage. Good girls didn't! It was just the way things had happened. Billy had been so strong, she hadn't stood a chance. Still ... she should not have been out there alone in the dark with him in the first place. She should have known better. At last, in despair, she decided to ask her grandmother's advice. Her grannie was kind. Yes, she would talk to her first; ask her advice.

Eileen felt relieved when she'd made this decision and, leaving the house, slowly crossed the street to her grannie's. Going around to the back, she waved to her granda who was digging at the bottom of the garden and let herself into the kitchen. Maggie was at the stove and greeted her warmly.

'Hello, love. How are you?' she said kindly, but her eyes showed surprise.

'Hello, Grannie. Can I have a word with you?'

Noting her granddaughter's pale face and dark-ringed eyes, Maggie felt apprehensive. She lowered the gas under the pot, and turned to lead the way into the sitting room.

'In here, love. We won't be disturbed. Bernard is out and Barney is weeding out the back garden.'

A smile tugged at her lips when Eileen replied forlornly, 'I know ... I saw him.' But noting that Eileen was in no mood for smiling at the idea that she could have possibly missed her granda's tall figure, Maggie motioned to a large comfortable armchair.

'I can see that the wedding has taken its toll on you, love. Sit down and put your feet up. Would you like a nice wee cup of tea?'

Eileen sat down but refused the tea. She sat silent so long, Maggie prompted her. 'You wanted to ask me something, love?'

To her amazement, Eileen rose from the chair. Throwing herself at Maggie's feet, she buried her head in her lap. 'Ah, Grannie, I don't know how to tell me mam. I don't know what's going to happen to me,' she wailed.

Concerned, Maggie gathered her close. 'Hush, love . . . hush. Nothing can be that bad.'

Gulping back great sobs, Eileen assured her, 'Oh, it can. It can!' She lifted a face drowned in tears and gasped, 'I'm expecting a baby. Oh, dear God . . . what am I going to do? What am I going to do, Grannie?'

Shock kept Maggie frozen for some moments. This frail young body was carrying a child? 'Ah, Eileen . . . Eileen.'

At the sorrow in her grannie's voice, Eileen hastened to assure her. 'I know, I know it's awful! But Johnny Cleary wants to marry me. It'll be all right . . . won't it, Grannie?'

Resentment against Johnny Cleary filled Maggie with bitterness. That a mature man like him should bring a young innocent girl like her granddaughter down, made her very angry.

'Does anyone else know?' she asked.

Once again the head was buried in Maggie's lap but muffled words reached her. 'Just Kate Rafferty. I don't know how to tell me mam and dad. Me mam will be mad. They'll kill me, so they will! They'll be so mad!'

'No, they won't. Would you like me to be there, Eileen, when you break the news to them?'

Eileen's head rose and big grey eyes, so like Maggie's own, beseeched her. 'Would you, Grannie? Would you, please?'

'Shall we tell them now?' Maggie's mind was running ahead. If her granddaughter was getting married, well . . . the sooner the better.

At Eileen's grateful nod, Maggie pulled off her slippers, stepped into a pair of shoes and reached for her coat. 'Come on. Let's get it over with then.'

They found Sarah and Mick relaxing in the living room, Sarah curled up on the settee and Mick stretched out in an armchair, reading a Zane Grey western. When Maggie entered the room, Sarah sat up and swung her legs to the floor.

'Well, now ... this is a surprise,' she exclaimed. 'I thought you'd be taking it easy, Mam, after all the excitement yesterday.'

Maggie motioned her granddaughter forward. 'Eileen has something to tell you two,' she said gruffly.

One look at her daughter's face and Sarah guessed the news was bad, but her heart sank when Eileen whispered, 'Johnny and I want to get married as soon as possible, Dad, Mam.' Her glance flickered from one to the other and seeing alarm register on their faces, she hurried on. 'We don't want a big reception. Just a quiet wedding with the families present.'

Mick was on his feet at once, towering over her. 'You can't be serious! Why the big rush? You'll wait and get married decent like Beth did!'

Meeting her mother's eyes, Eileen whispered, 'Mam, I have to get married.'

Disbelief registered on Sarah's face. Her eyes swung towards her husband and they gaped in dismay at each other.

Maggie stood silent, her eyes watchful. She wanted to see Sarah's reaction to Eileen's news. Her daughter was such a pillar of the church now. Very commendable, but it made her forgetful of her own past failings.

Now Sarah met Maggie's eye and unspoken thoughts passed between them. With a sigh she turned back to her husband and nodded towards the door. Looking stunned, he placed the book he held face down on the chair and, like a blind man, groped his way from the room.

Sarah patted the place beside her. 'Come and sit down, love.'

With one look her mother had jogged her memory and she recalled making the very same announcement to her, more than twenty years ago. Sarah could still recall the look of horror on Maggie's face and remembered shouting, 'I'm not the first and I won't be the last.' Her mother had slapped her face and fled from the house. Now history was repeating itself.

When, after a grateful glance at Maggie, Eileen sat down beside her mother, Maggie quietly left the room. Sarah would be kind to Eileen now that her own memory had been jogged.

Sarah was alarmed at how thin her daughter was. She hadn't realized Eileen was losing so much weight. Why, she felt like a bag of bones! She could feel tremors coursing through the frail body close to hers, and said kindly, 'Don't worry, love. You're not the first, and you won't be the last.' Smiling ironically at her choice of words. The words that she had shouted at her mother all those years ago. The words that had caused Maggie to slap her face.

She was surprised that Johnny Cleary had seduced her daughter. Couldn't comprehend it. He seemed such a gentleman. Why hadn't he done things decent? However . . . she herself knew from experience that men could get carried away, expecially if the girl was willing. She had to be honest with herself and admit that she had trapped Mick in the same way. These things happened and were often greatly regretted. But once a child was involved, regrets were not enough. Still, Eileen hadn't seemed serious about Johnny, she had kept insisting that he was too old. Had she changed her mind?

To be truthful, both she and Mick had hoped that eventually the couple would marry. But not like this! Not in disgrace. Eileen was so immature for her age. Somehow, they had thought that she was safe with

Johnny. They had made him welcome in their home; made him a friend. How could he betray their kindness like this? There was no doubt that there would be gossip and everybody would point the finger of shame at Eileen.

For one horrible moment, the thought of abortion entered Sarah's mind, only to be discarded. What on earth was she coming to? How could she even entertain such a thought? God forgive her! Tentatively, she continued, 'Are you sure you want to marry Johnny? Your dad and I'll help you all we can, so why not wait an' see how you feel after the baby's born? Don't worry about the neighbours . . .' Unconsciously she sighed at the idea of the neighbours' reaction to this juicy piece of scandal, and Eileen felt like weeping at the shame she was bringing to her parents' door. '. . . they'll talk anyhow, but it'll be a nine-day wonder.' Sarah was remembering her own first pregnancy; how she had miscarried. If they could get Eileen to wait . . .

Eileen digested her mother's words. Dare she wait? Then she realized she could not afford to. If she did and Johnny became aware of her condition, he would soon make it known that he was not responsible, because it was obvious that he would be blamed.

What would she do then? Tell her parents that she was carrying a Protestant's bastard? Her mind shied away from that word. She had never used it before, not even in her thoughts, but it was the truth. No! Her parents must never know a Protestant from the Shankill Road had used her then discarded her. She was too ashamed to tell them that. It would kill her dad. Was Billy Greer leading some other girl on now? Did he make a habit of it?

'I want my baby to have a name. I want to marry Johnny,' she said forlornly.

Sarah sensed something was amiss, but what could it be? Eileen must have some feelings for Johnny, or surely she would not be in this position in the first place? The

61

more Sarah thought of it, the less she could see Johnny in the role of villain. She could not imagine his taking advantage of her daughter, so Eileen must have been willing. Johnny always treated Eileen with respect. Bought her flowers, chocolates and small gifts; had indicated that his intentions were honourable.

'All right,' Sarah agreed. 'Tomorrow night we'll go round and see Father McGouran. Since you both have lived in the parish all your lives and have never been away for any length of time, except when Johnny was in the army, he should be able to marry you soon. That is, if you're sure you still want to go through with it? Do you, love?'

There it was again. The chance to opt out. Sarah looked at Eileen, brows raised inquiringly. Regretfully, she nodded her head. This way her baby would have a name; she really did not have any other choice. She was relieved at how understanding her mother was being and tried to thank her. Sarah waved her thanks away. 'It's what we're here for. Your dad and I'll do all we can to help, though it's been a terrible shock to us, ye know,' she said, and as she hugged her daughter close, her heart was heavy and tears stung her eyes.

Johnny was surprised at his mother's reaction to his news. For years she had been on at him to get married and give her grandchildren, but when he told her he had asked Eileen Ross to marry him and that she had agreed, Madge stared at him in surprise. She couldn't believe it!

'She's too young to marry!' she cried, aghast.

'Oh . . . and what age were you when you married Dad, eh, Mam?'

'It was different in those days. If you were lucky enough to get a man to propose to you . . . ye grabbed him. Especially if you were a plain Jane like me. And some of us lived to regret it.'

Johnny did not have to ask her what she meant.

He knew his mother had come to hate her late husband.

'Surely you know I'll not ill-treat Eileen? I don't take after me dad. I'm a big softie ... like you,' he teased her.

However, Madge was not to be appeased. 'Is she pregnant?' She immediately regretted the words. Johnny threw her a look of contempt and turned on his heel. Her voice stopped him in his tracks. 'Son, please bear with me.' A frown puckered her brow and as he turned towards her she queried, 'Tell me, if she's not pregnant, why the big rush then?'

Johnny relaxed. There was an excuse for his mother. She had been taken unawares. Why, he himself was still unable to believe that Eileen was to be his wife. 'Eileen doesn't want any fuss, Mam,' he explained.

Still Madge questioned him. She had been at Mass on Saturday morning and had waited outside the church to see the bridal party leave. Now she snorted with surprise. 'Huh! Her sister seemed to enjoy all the fuss last Saturday, so she did! A lovely bride she was. An' yon dress must have cost a bob or two, not to mention the clothing coupons.'

'That's exactly why Eileen wants a quiet wedding,' Johnny assured her. 'She's had enough fuss already. Besides her parents couldn't afford another big wedding so soon after Beth's. And they won't hear tell of me paying for it.'

'Why not wait, then? Eh, son? Give the girl a big day.'

'Mam ... I know Eileen is the girl for me. I don't want to wait. She's willing, I'm willing, so why waste any more time?'

'You're afraid of her changing her mind, that's what's wrong with you!' she accused him.

He acknowledged this with a slight nod.

'Son ... if you and her are meant for each other ... another year won't make any difference.'

'Mam, I'm doing the right thing. I'm sure of this. I love Eileen.'

Unconvinced, Madge said, 'When am I going to meet her?'

'Tomorrow night, Mam. If that's all right with you?'

She nodded, but he could see that she was far from pleased. Disbelief creased her brow as, with an exaggerated sigh, she sank back in the armchair. The old adage entered her mind: Marry in haste, repent at leisure. But try telling Johnny that!

The following night Johnny was nervous when he answered Eileen's knock on the door and ushered her into his home. Close up, Madge discovered the girl was even lovelier than she had thought. And so young! So very young!

When the introductions were over and conversation lagged, Madge turned to her son. 'Johnny . . . fetch the photo album down.'

It was obvious to him that his mother wanted to speak to Eileen on her own. 'Tut, Ma, Eileen doesn't want to look at old photos.'

'Ah, now, I'm sure Eileen would be interested to see what you looked like when you were young.' She raised her eyebrows. 'Wouldn't you, love?'

At her nod of approval, Johnny rose reluctantly to his feet and left the room. While they waited Eileen tried to keep her eyes from wandering around the room. She had never seen so much furniture in one place before, all old and battered. Why, her mother would have thrown out most of it a long time ago!

Madge's voice broke in on her thoughts. 'What age are you, girl?'

'Eighteen, Mrs Cleary,' she cried, startled out of her musing.

'You know Johnny's twenty-six, don't you?'

'Yes, he told me.'

'He's a bit old for you, isn't he?'

Eileen remained silent. After all, she agreed with Madge, so what could she say?

'Mind you, Johnny's ready for marriage . . . but I think you're too young for him. You're biting off more than you can chew. He's ready to settle down. But you, love, you should be out enjoying yourself for another year or two, before even thinking of marriage. Unless of course there's a reason for all this haste?'

'No! No . . . we just want to get married.'

A bright flush suffused Eileen's face. The arrival of Johnny with the photo album brought the difficult conversation to an end.

With a deep sigh, Madge rose to her feet. 'You two look at the photos. I'll make a cup of tea. Do you take sugar, Eileen?'

When she left the room, ignoring the album, Johnny turned eagerly to Eileen. 'Have you seen the priest yet?'

Relieved to be getting a breather from Madge's overpowering presence, Eileen nodded.

'What did he have to say? How soon can we be married?'

'He says we can be married in three weeks' time.' Eileen clamped her lips tightly together. To her horror, she had almost added, 'On account of my condition.'

She hoped Father McGouran would not mention her condition to Johnny when he went to see him. He had assumed that Johnny knew all about the baby, thought the child was his, and she had not disillusioned him. She intended telling Johnny about the baby, sure of his understanding and sympathy. But not just yet. When they were married, on their honeymoon, that was when she would tell him.

Three weeks later, on a Wednesday morning, they were married in St John's Church at eight o'clock Mass. It was indeed a quiet wedding, just Maggie, Barney and Bernard, Sarah, Mick, Beth, Tommy, Claire and Emma, from the bride's side. On the groom's were Madge and Johnny's brother Phillip, who had arrived from England the previous day to be his brother's best man, and a distraught Kate Rafferty who was bridesmaid.

Eileen felt guilty when she heard the reverence in Johnny's voice and saw the love in his eyes as he vowed to take her, for better, for worse, in sickness and in health, till death do us part. She felt everybody must be aware that her replies were automatic as she whispered her vows, and silently promised God that she would do all in her power to be a good wife to Johnny.

An amateur photography student friend of Bernard's had kindly offered to take the wedding photographs. A far cry from Uncle William, but beggars couldn't be choosers. To her surprise, Eileen found Phillip Cleary kind and attentive. Not a bit like the rogue Johnny had made him out to be. Could he possibly be jealous of his brother's dark good looks?

Mick seethed with rage as he watched Johnny Cleary, saw the possessive way he stayed by Eileen's side during the small reception, held at home in St James's Park. He looked so bloody proud! Cocky even. What had he to be proud about? He should be ashamed of himself! He had brought Eileen down. Rushed her into marriage; done her out of all the trimmings that she deserved. And he was proud? Then, remembering that he had been married in similar circumstances, Mick hung his head in shame. Who was he to judge? But, he reminded himself, although Sarah had been only seventeen when they were married, she had been very mature for her age. Eileen seemed even younger than her eighteen years. That was the difference.

Sarah moved closer to her husband. She knew he was torturing himself with regrets and wanted to ease his pain. 'Don't be so upset, love. It's not the end of the world. She must really want him.'

Mick's eyes widened with amazement and he muttered in despair, 'Does she look as if she's in love? Good God, Sarah, you only have to look into her eyes to see she's unhappy, the poor wee soul.'

Seeing Eileen approach them, Sarah whispered, 'Hush, love. Don't make it worse for her.'

'Thanks, Mam, Dad, for being so good.'

Eileen's eyes begged forgiveness. She could see her father was upset and it hurt; how it hurt. She wished it was time to leave on her honeymoon. How she longed to escape from all this false gaiety. A smile pasted itself across Mick's face as he reached for her and held her close. A smile? A terrible failure of a smile. Eileen's eyes met her mother's and Sarah felt a lump rise in her throat when she saw the sorrow there. Dear God, so much misery on what should be the happiest day of her life.

Pushing Eileen gently away from him, Mick gazed down at her. 'Now you be happy! Do ye hear me? You be happy!' he warned.

Eileen defied the tears to fall as she gazed up at him. 'I will, Dad. I will,' she promised.

'It's time we were leaving, Eileen.'

When Johnny put his arm possessively around her, Mick reared back and Sarah gripped his arm warningly. 'Yes,' she agreed with Johnny. 'It's time you two were away.' Then, taking Eileen in her arms, she hugged her tight.

Johnny had noticed Mick's action and Sarah's warning look, and his lips tightened. He could not understand Mick's attitude. Before Eileen had agreed to marry him, her father had always been friendly towards him. He and Johnny had a lot of interests in common and Johnny had been sure that an engagement would be met with approval. However, from the minute the wedding plans got under way, things had changed. Mick was distant and unfriendly, and Johnny could only suppose he was upset at losing another daughter so quickly. Was it because they were getting married in a rush? Determined not to let anyone spoil the day for him, he smiled brightly and reached for Eileen's coat. The sooner they were alone, the better he would like it.

Sarah was disappointed that Eileen was going away in the suit she had been married in. It was a two-piece with matching overcoat. Johnny held the coat for her to slip her arms into. Made of soft pale blue wool, it was a lovely outfit, and without Madge's generous help they would not have managed the clothing coupons for it so soon after Beth's wedding. Even so, Sarah lamented the fact that Eileen had not been married in a long dress. Not white, but some pale colour – cream or ivory. Johnny Cleary had spoiled her daughter's wedding day, had done her out of all the glory that this day implied, and Sarah could never forgive him for that.

'Say your goodbyes, love. The taxi's at the door,' Sarah said, and gently pushed Eileen in the direction of her guests. She was afraid Mick would lose control and break down; they could cry later.

Eileen smiled wryly as she hugged her friend in farewell. When she had told Kate Rafferty that she was marrying Johnny, she had been unprepared for her wrath.

'Are you mad?' she had cried. 'You can't marry him! You don't love him. He's too old for you.' Gripping her by the shoulders, Kate had shaken her roughly. 'For heaven's sake, Eileen, you're only eighteen. You've your whole life ahead of you. There's plenty of time to look around and meet someone else. You're not the first girl to have a baby. And it's not fair saddling Johnny with another man's child. He deserves better.'

Angrily pulling free from her hold, Eileen's cry had been derisive. 'Do you really think some *nice* boy will take me on with a child? Do you? Honestly now, Kate, do you really believe that? Huh! They'll all think I'm an easy lay.' Her lips tightened. 'This way, at least my baby will have a name. I'll do all in my power to make Johnny happy. I'll be a good wife to him.'

Kate was silent for a minute. She knew how cruel people could be. Eileen was right. A child born out of wedlock was a terrible burden. 'Does Johnny know about the baby?' she asked.

'No! I'll tell him on our honeymoon.'

Kate was scandalized and it showed. 'Huh! You're taking a hell of a chance, aren't you? What if he doesn't want to rear another man's child? Eh? Have you thought about that? Remember he's one of the old school! He'd have grounds for an annulment. Think of the scandal *that* would cause.'

'You don't know Johnny. He can be so kind. He's always been good to me. He'll understand, so he will.'

Kate's heart was heavy. Johnny was very good-living. Would he accept the baby? She doubted it. She very much doubted it!

'I'm sorry, Eileen. I hope you're right. But I think you should tell him before it's too late. Do your parents know the baby isn't Johnny's?'

'No!' Eileen's face quivered as she fought back the tears. 'And they aren't going to know.'

Seeing a ray of hope, Kate urged her. 'Tell them, Eileen! Tell them, and be guided by them. Please, Eileen. Please?'

'No, Kate! My mind's made up and if you ever tell anyone, I'll never forgive you. Do you hear me? This is my business . . . and I'll sort it out as I see fit!'

With those words, she had sealed Kate's lips, and valuing Eileen's friendship, Kate held her tongue and prayed that things would work out for her friend and Johnny.

Now, she gripped Eileen close. 'I wish you all the happiness in the world, Eileen. I really do. All the happiness.'

Damn Billy Greer! she fumed inwardly. Damn him! Hell will never be full until he's in it.

On the long train journey down to Galway where they were to honeymoon, Johnny treated Eileen like a queen; anticipating her every need. Making sure she was comfortable, had a magazine to read; some sweets close at hand. He excitedly confided in her that his mother had managed to get the key to a house in Rockmore Road. An old house, in need of a lot of repair, but he assured her that he had saved most of his money while in the army and had a small nest egg. He had already set wheels in motion to renovate the house.

He was glad to note that this news brightened Eileen's demeanour. She had seemed so depressed and it had worried him. Now he guessed the reason for her gloom. She must have dreaded living at home with her parents. Then why hadn't she agreed to live with his mother? Still, she was young, immature. A thrill coursed through him at the thought that she was his to awaken. A virgin! He considered himself very fortunate.

At Dublin they had to change trains and on the second leg of the journey across country to the west coast, Johnny sat admiring his wife as she dozed in the seat opposite him. She was beautiful and she was his! Rich auburn hair framed a face that was a pure cameo. Thick lashes cast shadows on high cheekbones, full sensuous lips were parted slightly, and he longed to kiss her. Kiss her properly; not the pecks he had made do with during their short courtship. She had removed her overcoat and jacket and the slight curve of her breasts as they rose and fell beneath the fine lawn of her blouse pleased his eye. He liked slim women. A shiver of anticipation ran down his spine. Soon she would be his!

It was late when they arrived at the Majestic Hotel where Johnny had booked a room for the week. A whole week!

Why, some couples thought themselves lucky if they got away for a few days to Bangor or Newcastle. While Johnny signed the register, Eileen stood in the foyer and looked around at all the grandeur. The red and gold flocked wallpaper, the ornate gold trimmings, and the great, big old-fashioned paintings that hung on the walls. From where she stood she could see into the lounge and immediately fell in love with the big open hearth on which turf burned brightly. She was very impressed. It would cost a lot of money to stay at this hotel. Well . . . hadn't Johnny told her he wasn't short of a bob or two? Eileen's feet sank in the thick carpets as they followed the bellboy to the lift and she revelled in the luxury of it. Now that was a feeling she would love to get used to!

Once in their bedroom, since the restaurant was closed for the night, Johnny ordered tea and sandwiches to be brought to their room.

Going to the curtains, he pulled them back and displayed a french window that opened on to a small balcony. With an exclamation of pleasure he beckoned her forward, out on to the balcony. 'Come and look at the view, Eileen.'

From the circle of his arm she stood looking out over Galway Bay. It was a calm night and the water caressed the beach, dark and mysterious, then rolled back to sea. A moon low in the sky turned the sands to silver. It looked so tranquil. If only she could be at peace. Calm the churning in her stomach that was making her feel ill. The scene brought to mind the last time she had admired a view from the circle of a man's arm. Then it had been Belfast Lough. Look where she had ended up that night! Soon she must confess her terrible secret to Johnny. Was she a fool to believe that he would understand? Only time would tell. Soon she would know. She shivered at the very thought of it.

At once he was all solicitude, drawing her back into the room and closing the window. His voice, close to her ear, broke into her muddled thoughts. 'I'm sorry, love, keeping you out there in the night air.' His lips trailed her cheek, her throat, and her lips. She trembled in his arms.

'Johnny, please . . . I . . .'

'Don't worry, love I won't rush you.

To her relief, a knock on the door heralded the arrival of the night porter with their supper, and Johnny released his hold on her. She was in a turmoil. His mounting excitement was apparent and she dreaded what lay ahead of her. She must tell him the truth before he found out for himself. She remembered whispered conversations in work. A man could tell if a girl wasn't a virgin. Isn't that what they had said? Even if he didn't guess she would still have to tell him. Johnny was far from stupid. Once she started to show he would know the child wasn't his.

The meal over, Eileen unpacked her suitcase; taking longer than was necessary. At last she could delay no longer and turned to him with a pleading look. The words of confession so carefully rehearsed in her mind while they ate refused to leave her mouth, and she gazed at him in mute appeal.

Mistaking the reason for the look, Johnny responded at once. 'I'll go down to the bar and have a drink. I'll be about fifteen minutes.' He was touched that she was shy of undressing in front of him. He would give her plenty of time to get to know him. Play it by ear; teach her to want him.

Reprieved, Eileen thanked him for his thoughtfulness and when he left the room, undressed with shaking hands. Putting on the sheer nightdress that Beth had given her, she examined herself in the full-length mirror and was horrified at how thin she was. She turned sideways. No sign of a bump and the sickness had stopped . . . could she have made a mistake? Would her period eventually appear? Oh, if only it would come and Johnny didn't have to know of her shame. Should she refrain from telling him? Hope he didn't realize she was not a virgin? If he didn't guess and her period came, she would become a model wife. Devote her life to Johnny. Oh, please God, don't let him find out! she prayed.

Johnny felt self-conscious as he sat at the bar. He imagined that everyone knew just why he was sitting there on his own. Nevertheless, he lingered half an hour over his drink before returning to their room. Eileen was already in bed and when he started to undress she turned her head away. She had never seen a naked man before and was in no mood to look at one now. All her thoughts were on her dilemma. Should she tell him the truth?

Johnny slipped into bed beside her and, raising himself on an elbow, gazed down at her. 'Eileen . . . if you want me to stop, just say so and I will. That's a promise!'

She gazed into his eyes, dark and intense with passion, and gulped deep in her throat as she recalled her previous experience with Billy Greer. She wished it was all over. Then, to her very great surprise, under the touch of his hands, the tension slowly left her body. His lips would leave hers, only to return again and again, each kiss more consuming, more arousing, than the last. Eileen found herself anticipating his moves and met them with caresses of her own. Pulling herself back from the well of passion he was awakening, she whispered, 'Johnny, I have something to tell you.'

'Later, love. We can talk later. Just relax.'

'I think I should . . .'

'Later, love. Just relax.'

With a sigh of relief she obeyed him and, closing her eyes, gave herself up to the magic of his touch. As she was caught more and more in a well of passion, a laughing face with dark blue eyes hovered against her eyelids. As she shuddered beneath Johnny, it was Billy Greer who held her thoughts.

They clung together in the aftermath of the wonderful storm they had created. Eileen was sated, but bewildered.

It greatly surprised her that she had enjoyed Johnny's lovemaking. It was far removed from her encounter with Billy Greer. Perhaps it wouldn't be so bad being married to Johnny after all. He had been so tender, leading her all the way; making her aware of the sensuous side of her nature. And . . . he hadn't realized that she wasn't a virgin. Her prayers had been answered. That was a blessing. She'd wait and see if her period came. If it didn't then she would have to confess about the baby. If he accepted the child she would be all right married to him. A feeling of well-being filled her. Yes . . . she would be all right married to Johnny.

The well-being was short lived. As realization dawned on Johnny he pushed her from him. Gazing down at her in horror, he croaked, 'You're not a virgin!' His look begged her to deny this awful accusation but as hot colour flooded her face and she writhed in shame, he knew he was right.

She recoiled at the contempt in his eyes. 'That's what I was trying to tell you,' she whimpered.

Rising swiftly from the bed, he pulled on his pyjama trousers. He left the room and stood on the balcony, gazing blindly out over the bay. His mind was in a turmoil. Was Eileen one of those very girls he abhorred? Had she knocked about with servicemen during the war? Unable to bear the thought of it, he rounded on her and shouted, 'Did you go to the Plaza? Did you dance with Yanks?'

Deciding to be truthful, she had deceived him enough, Eileen nodded her head. She opened her mouth to explain that she had only been to the Plaza on one occasion and had not enjoyed it at all. It had been too crowded. Too many men had wanted to dance with her. But with an exclamation of disgust, Johnny reached for his clothes and started to dress.

Forgetful of her nudity, Eileen left the bed to stand gazing at him. 'Where are you going?' she asked anxiously.

Averting his eyes from the beauty before him, Johnny grunted, 'I'm going for a walk. I need time to think! Decide what to do.'

When the door closed on him Eileen crept back into bed. Kate Rafferty's words haunted her. She had said Johnny could seek an annulment. But that could only happen if the marriage wasn't consummated. It was too late for that now, wasn't it? What would Johnny do? Would he leave her after less than one day of marriage?

When Sarah opened the door and saw Madge Cleary on the step, she hid her surprise with difficulty and invited her in. She led the way to the sitting room which she always kept tidy for unexpected callers.

'Sit down, Mrs Cleary, and I'll make us a cup of tea.'

With a wave of her hand Madge replied, 'I'll be more at home in the kitchen.' Seeing Sarah's surprise, she added lamely, 'That's if you don't mind?'

'Not at all. No, I don't mind. Just as you like.' Sarah answered, wondering why she felt so uncomfortable in this woman's company.

While Sarah made the tea Madge looked around the kitchen in admiration, noting the stainless steel sink and the white enamelled stove. It would be a pleasure to work here. It was easy to see that Sarah was married to a man who cared about his family and home. She turned her attention to Sarah. Still a fine-looking woman, with a slim figure, and thick chestnut hair without a trace of grey, Madge figured that Sarah must be about thirty-eight or nine, but she still looked young enough to pass as sister to her daughters. Turning from the stove, Sarah caught Madge's appraising look and blushed. Seeing she had embarrassed her, Madge rushed into conversation. 'I thought I'd let you know that I managed to get the key to a house at the top of our street,' she announced proudly.

'Oh, that's wonderful! Wonderful! How on earth did you manage it?'

Smiling at her pleasure, Madge replied airily, 'Oh, I know some people in the right places. Mind you, it's in an awful state. An old man has lived in it alone for fifteen years, so you can guess what it's like.'

'Soap and water comes cheap,' Sarah declared, and added in wonder, 'Those houses have bathrooms, don't they?'

'Aye, they do, and they'll need a new bathroom suite, but Johnny will soon get that.'

'How much was the key, Mrs Cleary?'

'Call me Madge, please. Oh, Johnny has paid for it! The reason I'm here is ... well, I thought you and I could clean the house out for them returning from Galway ... move their wedding presents in and things like that. Johnny has arranged to get some estimates for repairs, but meanwhile it needs a good cleaning out. It's filthy, so it is. I didn't like just to go ahead on me own ... ye know ... with Eileen being your daughter.'

Sarah was relieved about the house, knowing that Mick had dreaded the idea of Johnny's living with them. He couldn't forgive Johnny for leading Eileen into a shotgun wedding, and Eileen had refused point-blank to live with her mother-in-law.

Madge watched Sarah covertly to see how she would react to this suggestion. She was ready to back down if Sarah showed any repugnance at the idea. She would not intrude where she was not wanted.

Her worries were unnecessary. Sarah said at once, 'No, I'm glad you came for me Madge. That's a good idea, and I'll rope in the rest of the family to help. The more the merrier.'

'I'll get Phillip to help an' all,' Madge agreed, happily.

The two women smiled at each other, and although

they were never to be close friends, they respected each other.

Sarah discovered that the house was indeed in a terrible state. Dirty cracked linoleum curled from the floors and paper hung loosely on the walls, even coming away in places. As they passed down the narrow hall her nose twitched in distaste at the stench of stale tobacco smoke trapped in damp airless rooms. Madge had not been joking when she said it was in an awful state. The kitchen was a mess, with grease everywhere and the sink badly discoloured. Upstairs was no better. The rooms would all need to be stripped of paper and paint, and everything started from scratch again. As for the bathroom . . . there was no way they would be able to use the bath. That would have to be replaced as soon as possible and the toilet pot was filthy and cracked.

There was no way that Johnny and Eileen could move straight into this hovel. They would have to live with Sarah for a time, until at least some of the rooms were made habitable.

A sigh escaped her, and catching her eye, Madge nodded. 'I know how you feel, pet, but mind you, these houses are beautiful when decorated and cared for.' She added consolingly, 'They'll be all right! We'll get stuck in tomorrow an' at least it'll be clean for them coming home.'

Sadly, Sarah nodded her agreement. Yes, they could at least clean the place up and make it a bit more respectable for them.

The following week, while the couple were on honeymoon, both families worked hard, scrubbing and cleaning, but all agreed it would be a long time before the house looked half-decent. Still, it was a rented house, and not to be sneezed at, and after all, Johnny and Eileen had the rest of their lives to make a home of it.

* * *

It was with relief that Eileen packed her suitcase and left, for the last time, the room where she had spent six long miserable nights. After the first night she had slept alone in the huge bed while Johnny slept on the uncomfortable chair. At first she had not been unduly worried, sure that somehow things would work out. She was now aware of the extent of his feelings for her. Why, his protestations of love and passion had scared her a little. No one should care that much. Still, the knowledge had given her hope. Johnny loved her! She was his wife! Surely if she tried she could make him understand?

However, as time passed and he continued to give her the cold shoulder, she grew resentful. How could she put things right if Johnny refused to talk to her, except when it was absolutely necessary? The days passed amicably enough as her husband seemed determined to put on an act for the benefit of the staff and other hotel guests, but at night he kept her at a distance. They retired late and each morning when she awoke he had already gone for his daily walk along the beach. Lonely, she had tentatively suggested that she join him on his walks, but this suggestion was answered by an abrupt shake of the head. So by the end of their so-called honeymoon she was glad to dust the last of the Majestic Hotel off her feet and step into the taxi that was to take them to the railway station. It would be great to get home, to return to work and some kind of normality.

The journey home was not as pleasant as the trip down. Johnny left her more or less to fend for herself and when the train drew in to Great Victoria Street station Eileen felt weary in mind and body. It came as a terrible blow to find out on top of all this, that they would have to live with her parents for a short while after all. It was going to be awkward. Johnny never touched her; hardly spoke to her. Such a change from his attitude before they were married. What would everyone think? She had dreaded the idea of seeing her father and Johnny together. Now it would be even worse. That her father was disappointed in her, she knew, try though he did to hide it. And it hurt. She idolized her father, and the bond between them had been very strong, but now he could not hide his disappointment. And worse still . . . he blamed Johnny!

She was ashamed at the difference her condition made between Johnny and her father. They had got on so well together and the knowledge that she was to blame for the present discord filled her with guilt. She quailed inside when she tried to picture Johnny's reaction when he found out she was pregnant. After the horrified reception to his accusation that she was not a virgin, Eileen had been afraid to tell him about the baby. Should she pretend it was his? Hope to go over her time and pretend it was premature? Oh, what a web of deceit she would be weaving but it would be folly to admit the truth at this time. She was very much afraid of the anger she knew her husband was keeping on a tight rein.

So she was glad about the house; couldn't wait to move in. However, when she saw the state it was in, she could have wept. But at least a start had been made and she would be able to escape to it each evening when she came home from work. The idea of putting a bright face on every evening for the benefit of the family, had filled her with dread. She knew that her family was talking about her, wondering what was wrong, but in the face of her aloofness, no one dared question her. At work Kate tried to gain her confidence and was hurt when Eileen rebuffed her. Eileen was too ashamed to confide in Kate. Hadn't her friend warned her that Johnny might object to rearing another man's child? And it looked like she might be right. Eileen further offended Kate by refusing her offer to help get the house shipshape, but it would be too much of a strain to be under her watchful eye.

With her morose husband, Eileen escaped to the house on Rockmore Road in the evenings and at weekends.

They needed no excuse to go; there was plenty of work to be done.

Slowly but surely, under Johnny's skilful hands the house took on a new look. Night after night when they had finished their evening meal they silently made their way up to Rockmore Road where they were joined by Phillip. Johnny had gently but firmly refused offers of help from her family and for this Eileen was grateful. At least she didn't have to put on a brave front for Phillip; she didn't care what he thought. Soon a new bathroom suite replaced the old, and a new sink and stove were fitted in the kitchen. They worked side by side, stripping paper from the walls, Johnny's face a tight controlled mask. As Eileen watched the changes taking place under his capable hands, she could have wept for the hurt she knew festered in her husband's heart.

That Phillip was puzzled was very apparent. He couldn't understand what was wrong. Johnny had been so besotted with his young bride that Phillip had been disgusted at him. In his opinion no man should be so dependent on a woman for his happiness. Now his brother hardly acknowledged his wife. What on earth had happened to cause such discord? Was Eileen frigid? Had the honeymoon been a disaster? This was the only reason Phillip could think of for the disharmony between them. Sure of his ability to win a woman's confidence, he set out to charm Eileen; find out what was wrong.

Great bitterness welled up in Johnny's breast as he covertly observed Eileen's depression lift under Phillip's flirting. Johnny knew he should be trying to put things right between himself and his young wife, but for the life of him he just couldn't. He had returned to the hotel on the first morning of their honeymoon determined to talk things over, but at the sight of Eileen, looking so innocent and pure, words had failed him. How could he ever trust her again? She looked as if butter wouldn't melt in her mouth and yet she must have been with at least one other man. He was afraid to ask how many! After all, he had not asked her about other men. He had assumed that he would be her first lover. He argued with himself. Why was it so important to him that Eileen should be a virgin? He was far from being a saint himself, so why expect her to be unsullied?

When a laugh escaped Eileen's lips at some absurdity of Phillip's, the urge to hit his brother became over-powering. It was the first time she had laughed since their wedding night and it angered Johnny that his brother should be the instigator of her happiness. To resist the urge to lash out at Phillip, he grabbed his coat and left the house, slamming the door behind him. When it had settled on its hinges, Eileen gazed at it with tear-filled eyes. Slowly, Phillip reached for her hand and clasped it to his breast.

'What on earth's wrong between you two, Eileen?'

Snatching her hand away, she answered curtly, 'Nothing.' She was wary of Phillip. His constant attention and kind-ness made her want to trust him; make an ally of him; to confide in him. However, she knew she must never give in to this desire. No one must ever know of her dark secret. It would be bad enough when she had to tell Johnny. Perhaps he wouldn't forgive her. Would make known to all and sundry why she had been in such a hurry to get married, but until then it must remain her secret.

'Come off it! Everybody's talking about you two, won-dering what happened on your honeymoon . . .'

'Everybody? Everybody?' she squealed. 'But why? It's nobody's business but mine and Johnny's.'

'We're worried about you, that's why! We want to help.' His voice was kind, compassionate, and when he reached once more for her hand, Eileen responded to his kindness by moving closer.

His arm encircled her waist and drew her close. 'A trouble shared is a trouble halved, Eileen,' he said softly. 'Are you sure that you don't want to talk about it?'

'No ... thank you for caring, Phillip, but no, I don't want to discuss my private business.'

At the corner of the street Johnny stopped in his tracks. Was he daft, leaving his own house like that? It was up to him to tell Phillip to get out and not come back. Tell him that they didn't need his assistance any further. On this thought he turned on his heel and strode back up the street.

Phillip heard the key turn in the lock and bent his head lower as if to catch Eileen's whispered reply. He wanted Johnny to think the worst. Wanted to see what his reaction would be. Eileen was completely unaware of her husband's return until Phillip was swung away from her and Johnny's fist smashed into his face. The sight of his brother so close to Eileen had made Johnny's temper explode and weeks of restrained anger were behind his punch. The blow drew blood. 'Get out! Do you hear me? Get out and don't ever come back.'

Mopping at his nose with a handkerchief, Phillip cried, 'I'm only trying to give the girl a bit of comfort. Any fool can see you're making her miserable ...'

Once more Johnny's fist rose in the air but Phillip was ready this time. Parrying the blow with his forearm, he caught Johnny with an uppercut, sending him flying across the room to crash heavily against the stepladder, bringing it crashing to the bare floor boards.

'Stop it! For heaven's sake, stop it!' As Johnny rose groggily to his feet, Eileen hovered shakily between him and his brother. 'Get out, Phillip. Go on ... get out!'

'Only because you ask me, Eileen. That's the only reason I'm going. I've never walked away from a fight in my life, but for you ... I'll go. And, Eileen, if you ever need anything, you know where to come.' The look he shot Johnny was disdainful. 'I'm not afraid of him, and don't you let him bully you. If he gives you any bother, you let me know.'

With a howl of rage Johnny lunged at his brother. 'Get out! Get out, or so help me I'll swing for you!'

When the door closed on him, Johnny swung back to his wife. 'You slut . . . you dirty wee slut! The minute I turned my back you were ready to fall into his arms, weren't you? Just how far would you have gone if I hadn't come back so soon? Eh? Go on . . . tell me! How far were you prepared to go?'

Pride kept tears at bay as Eileen faced him. 'He was only being kind. He meant no harm.'

'Our Phillip is only kind when he's after something and you'd better make sure you steer clear of him.'

Stung at his tone of voice, Eileen taunted him: 'Why? What difference would it make? You don't want me! You won't even speak to me. So what if I do want some company? Someone to talk to?'

She was unprepared for the effect her words had on him.

With a howl of rage, he grabbed her. At first he made as if to throw her from him in disgust, but as her perfume wafted around him, he gripped her close with a smothered exclamation. 'You're my wife! That's the difference it makes! You're mine! So you want to talk? Well, I'll talk to you, so I will. The only kind of talk you know.'

Eileen clung to him, hope in her heart. He wanted her! However, it was soon obvious that it wasn't love that drove him and she fought against him with all her might, pleading with him to stop. Her distress was obvious to him but still he forced his attentions on her until at last her piteous cries broke through the rage that blinded him. Pushing her away from him, he turned his back on her, fighting for control. Eileen stood hugging herself for comfort. At least when Billy Greer had attacked her there had been an excuse. He had been drunk. This time there was no excuse. Johnny wasn't drunk. Johnny was her husband. He was supposed to love and cherish her, not treat her like an animal.

Shaking with rage and hurt, she growled at him, 'If you ever touch me again, I'll leave you, so help me. Do you hear me? You lay one finger on me again and I'll go. That's a promise.' The way he was behaving towards her he would probably be glad to see the back of her, but she was hurt and it was the only threat she could think of before blundering from the house.

Tears blinded her as she staggered down the street. She couldn't go to her parents in this state. Her father would be only too glad of an excuse to have a go at Johnny, and much as she hated her husband at this moment, she couldn't face another fight.

What could she do? It was only seven o'clock. She'd take a walk. Tears still falling, she turned up the Whiterock Road towards the quietness of the countryside. Soon the houses were left behind and the peace of the fields and hedges bathed in the warm amber and brown of early-autumn soothed her tortured soul as she walked. When she reached the mountain loney she was much calmer. Here, she bathed her face at the small waterfall, glad to be alone. After a short rest she felt composed enough to retrace her steps. She had made up her mind. She would tell Johnny about the baby; force him to make a decision. She could not live in a constant state of fear and deceit, wondering what was going to happen next. It would be better to make a clean breast of everything; hope her parents would stand by her when they learnt the truth. If not ... well, there was always her grannie. She could always depend on her grannie.

It was dark when at last she arrived at St James's Park, and making her way down the street, she went around the back of the house. With a bit of luck she would be able to escape to the room she shared with Johnny without anyone seeing her. Voices and laughter came from the living room as she tip-toed past the door. She was in luck and managed to climb the stairs unobserved. She was glad to find the bedroom in darkness. It was too late to have a confrontation tonight, so determined to be asleep when Johnny came home – *if* he came home – she undressed quickly in the dark and slipped into bed. He was there before her. She cringed away from him in dismay. How had she not realized he was already in bed? She had been too preoccupied with the events of the previous few hours.

Johnny reached for her and in spite of the fact that her family were awake downstairs, with an exclamation of disgust she hit out at him, leaping from the bed, and switching on the light.

The glare she turned on him was full of hatred and her words came out in a low hiss. 'I warned you never to touch me again. I won't be treated like an animal. No matter how bad a woman may be, she's too good for the likes of you, so she is. I don't want to live with you any more. I'm not going back to Rockmore Road. We're finished!'

He was out of bed and reaching for her. The hurt vulnerable look on her face as she cowered away from him brought a lump to his throat.

'Eileen . . . don't look like that . . . please. I'm sorry, I don't know what possessed me. Can you ever forgive me?'

Her brows drew together and she looked bewildered. Did all men think they could treat you like dirt and if they said they were sorry, everything would be all right?

'Please, forgive me. I'm sorry . . . truly sorry.' His voice was low and pleading.

'I can't!' She ran her hands through her hair in her anguish. 'I can't! Do you think I'm not wise or something? How can you expect me to put up with the likes of that? Eh? I don't know where I stand with you anymore. I just want to be left alone. Just leave me alone, and get the hell out of here!'

He hovered near her, afraid to touch her. The state she was in, she was very likely to scream blue murder and that would be enough to bring big Mick racing up the stairs followed by the rest of the family. He knew Mick would be glad of the chance to interfere. He was watching them like a hawk, wondering what was wrong. The whole bloody family was watching them; grandparents and all! It was like living in a goldfish bowl. If only their own house was habitable, perhaps they could sort things out.

'Eileen . . . I swear I'll never treat you like that again. I swear it!'

Once more he reached for her, but still, with raised hand, she fended him off and her voice rose. 'No! Don't touch me. I mean what I say! I'm not going back to that house of misery. I'll rear the child on me own, so I will.'

Shock held them both silent as her words echoed between them. The silence was deafening as Eileen groped about in her mind to find words to explain her bombshell. Johnny moved closer, a look of awe on his face.

'You're pregnant? How did you know so soon?' But then women knew these things, didn't they? And they had been married five weeks so if she had conceived on their wedding night, then she would know.

'Yes . . . but . . .' Her words trailed off.

'Why didn't you tell me?'

'I tried, but you wouldn't listen. I wanted you to know but, Johnny, I didn't mean . . .'

'Ah, Eileen . . . that's wonderful news.'

Slowly, the realization dawned on her that Johnny thought he was the father. And here she was thinking that she had just made the great confession. How could he be so naive?

'Eileen, this changes everything. Did .you think I wouldn't want a child? I know I haven't been much of a husband lately but all that will change. Why, this is wonderful news.'

Once more he reached for her but again she warded him off. She must tell him the truth; get it off her chest. 'It's no good, Johnny . . .'

'Look, Eileen, please give me a chance to prove how much I care. Come back to bed.' When her head swung from side to side and her mouth opened to protest, he forestalled her. 'I won't touch you. Not until I've won your respect again. Just share the bed with me. This is between us, Eileen. Let's keep it that way.'

She agreed with him on that score! She didn't want all her dirty linen washed in public. Now she allowed him to draw her to the bed.

Her heart was thumping and she was sure the whole house must hear it.

'Eileen . . . I can't explain why I've been acting so strange since our wedding night. But let me try. I've always hated easy women. Willing to give their all at the sight of a uniform. Remember, I was in uniform in foreign countries. It was no different out there! I know what I'm talking about. When I came home on leave during the war I used to watch the local girls make spectacles of themselves down in the dance halls and I vowed I'd never marry one of them. Then I met you and I fell in love. Not for one minute did I doubt you were a virgin . . . so you can guess how shocked I was on our honeymoon.'

'Johnny, listen, you've got it all wrong. I only went to the Plaza once and I hated it. That's the truth. Just the once! Kate and I sneaked down one night. Our parents would have killed us had they known. But we wanted to see what all the fuss was about. We didn't let anyone see us home and we didn't date any servicemen. But really, most of the girls just danced with them. Because, you see, they really knew how to make a girl feel attractive. But that didn't mean that the girls were having it off with them. I

87

know a lot of girls who brought them home to meet their families because they were homesick. They only wanted to talk about their folks back home. Wanted to enjoy a home cooked meal. Maybe the odd girl was easy, but you can't tar us all with the same brush.'

'I know! In my heart I know that. Can you ever forgive me, love?'

'Well . . . I was to blame too. But I wasn't easy. It only happened the once. And that's the truth, so it is.'

Gently he drew her close and when she squirmed, was quick to reassure her: 'I just want to hold you. Go to sleep, love. From now on things will be different, you'll see.'

The following morning Eileen realized that she should have told Johnny the truth when she had the chance. Cleared the air once and for all. She mulled things over in her mind. He had promised to be more affable; more understanding. Win her love and respect. She couldn't bear to spoil the chance of a normal life, especially while she was living with her parents. She was fed up with being watched and whispered about. She decided to take a chance. Maybe the child would have her colouring and somehow or other she would be able to hoodwink Johnny into believing that he was the natural father and everything would be all right. She knew she was grasping at straws but she didn't want to risk upsetting the applecart until she had to. Better to have his love and respect for the next lot of months than not at all. She would leave it to fate to decide for her. Take each day at a time.

Two weeks later they moved into their own home in Rockmore Road. That evening Eileen sat in the living room and for the first time since her wedding day, she felt relaxed. It was great to be in their own home at last.

As if on cue, Johnny echoed her thoughts. 'It's great to be alone, isn't it, Eileen?'

'Yes ... yes, I agree with you there! You must be fed up with me hissing at you.'

A smile twisted Johnny's mouth at this understatement. 'It will be a relief to talk naturally,' he agreed. 'We might even become more than just friends ... eh, Eileen?' Tentatively his hand pressed her shoulder.

A warm rosy glow brightened her face. She felt shy. She had grown very fond of Johnny over the past few weeks; had become used to being cosseted by him. While living with her parents she had kept him at arm's length, but now they were alone, how should she react to him? Should she forgive him and start anew? Yes, that's what she'd do. Start afresh. To give their marriage a chance, she must forgive and forget. She covered his hand with her own and returned the pressure.

Johnny leant down and looked into her eyes. 'Eileen, don't let me make any stupid mistakes. Do you mean ... does this mean ...'

She came to his rescue. 'Yes, Johnny, it means what you think.'

Slowly, he sank to his knees and gathering her close, sank his face in her hair. 'Ah, Eileen,' he whispered hoarsely, 'you'll never regret it.' And when he sought her lips, she willingly surrendered to him.

Once settled in, Christmas seemed to come in a rush. Madge invited Johnny and Eileen to her house for their Christmas dinner. Johnny was keen to go and Eileen didn't blame him. Her cooking was coming on, but very slowly. However, she would only agree to go if he consented to go to her parents for tea later in the day. Still smarting from Mick's attitude towards him, Johnny reluctantly agreed, much to Eileen's relief. To have accepted Madge's invitation and refused her mother's would have been a terrible insult to her parents. Besides, due to Johnny's generosity she had bought everyone presents and wanted to hand them out personally. Show off a bit.

Cathy Monaghan, Phillip's latest girlfriend, was also at Madge's for Christmas dinner, and Eileen thought she was lovely. It was obvious that she doted on Phillip, and that Madge was disappointed that an engagement ring had not been produced and an announcement made. She hinted about an Easter wedding, to Cathy's great embarrassment, but the hints fell on deaf ears. Phillip was not to be drawn. Eileen agreed with Madge that he should get married, and the sooner the better. He had started to call at her house when he knew Johnny would not be at home and it made her uneasy. He was always the perfect gentleman, so she could not fault him ... still, he made her feel uneasy. What would Johnny think if he ever found out?

Madge was thinking along similar lines to Eileen. She was aware that Phillip was making a play for his brother's wife. Whether he was really attracted to Eileen or just wanted to put one over on Johnny, she didn't know. Phillip had always envied whatever Johnny achieved; always had to try to go one better than him. There was fear in Madge's heart as she watched. What if Johnny twigged on? Or, was that what Phillip was hoping for?

The afternoon passed pleasantly, with Phillip and Johnny apparently burying the hatchet, and it was with reluctance that Eileen rose to go. She hoped the evening would be as pleasant as the afternoon. If only her father could call a truce with Johnny, everything would be all right. As she stood at the hall mirror wrapping a scarf around her throat, Phillip caught her around the waist and deftly turned her to face him.

'Got you!' He laughingly pointed at the mistletoe above the mirror and, to Eileen's dismay, bent to kiss her. Glad that Johnny was upstairs, she stood tense in Phillip's arms and twisted her head away from him, endeavouring to escape his lips. Phillip was very conscious of his mother's warning glance but he could no more have passed by this chance than fly to the moon. Eileen strained back in his arms but he refused to release her. Deciding that she may as well get it over with, she relaxed against him. After all it was only a kiss. With a bit of luck it would be over before Johnny came downstairs.

'Ah, there you are, Johnny. I thought you couldn't find the coats.' It was Madge's voice that caused the entwined figures to part and there was consternation in the look she threw Phillip.

'Sorry . . . I was in the loo. I didn't realize there was any need to hurry.' Johnny looked perplexed.

Taking Eileen's coat from him, Phillip held it open and she slipped her arms into the sleeves, keeping her gaze averted. Dear God, please make him get married or return to England! I've enough to worry about. I just want to be left alone, she thought.

It was with relief that she escaped out into the brisk frosty air, glad that Johnny had not noticed her agitation.

When they arrived at St James's Park, Beth and Tommy were already there. Fifteen minutes later their grandparents arrived, and ignoring Mick's quietness, Johnny sat with Maggie and Barney. At least in their company he felt welcome, not tolerated. Watching the easy camaraderie between her grandparents and husband Eileen relaxed, breathed a sigh of relief, and determined to enjoy herself.

Happy and smiling, she stacked her parcels under the Christmas tree, well aware that all eyes were on her. And why not? She was looking her best! Her long auburn hair was plaited and wound around her head, then caught in at the back again. The loose white sweater she wore over a full skirt to hide her small bump made her eyes gleam like diamonds, and pregnancy added a bloom to her clear creamy skin.

Beth watched her enviously. How she wished she was pregnant. Married before Eileen and here she was as flat as a pancake. Although nothing had ever been said, she suspected that Eileen was pregnant before she was married. Why else the mad rush? Well, she would change places with her any time. Surely something must be wrong with her or Tommy, or she would be with child by now?

Tommy Rogan saw the envious looks his wife cast at her sister and frowned. He knew Beth was blaming him for their childlessness. She would never admit to fearing being barren. To him children were a bonus. He would love a family, but if it was not to be, it was God's will, and so long as he had Beth it would be bearable. Beth now, that was another matter. She would brood, but he supposed any woman would be the same. He gave himself a little shake. Catch yourself on, man. You've only been married a few months, he derided himself.

Mick was also watching Eileen. He had seen very little of her since they had moved to Rockmore Road. A short duty visit twice a week on her way home from work was all they got and for this he blamed Johnny. This was the happiest he had seen his daughter since before her marriage. Today her expression was soft, her features relaxed. It had broken his heart to watch her when she had lived with them. Once again his heart cried: Why? Why had she ruined her life? He remembered how she had looked the night she had gone to the Floral Hall; so radiant. Why, she could have taken the Falls by storm. Instead she had let Johnny Cleary seduce her.

Leaning over the back of Mick's chair, Sarah put an arm around him and gave him a hug. 'Cheer up. It's Christmas.'

He saw the concern in her eyes and smiled. 'Sorry, love. I was wool gathering.'

92

'It's nice to have all the girls here, isn't it?'

He nodded in agreement. 'We don't see enough of Eileen.'

'Oh, I suppose once they have the house decorated and all, we'll be invited up,' she assured him with more confidence than she felt.

'Don't count on it. I've a feeling that Johnny will never make us welcome,' he replied, with a sarcastic twist to his lips.

'Now don't be like that. Let's give him the benefit of the doubt.'

'What on earth are you two whispering about? Or shouldn't I ask?' Beth laughed as she teased them but her gaiety was a bit forced. However, no one seemed to notice, except Tommy.

'I was just saying what a lovely family we have,' Sarah replied with a smile. 'How about a game of charades?'

After tea, one game led to another and it was past midnight when Maggie and Barney decided to call it a day and made their farewells. When the door closed on them, Eileen asked the question that had hovered on her lips but been forced back during the events of the evening. She had been loath to spoil the happiness that prevailed.

'Where's Bernard tonight?'

It was her mother who answered her. 'He's got himself a girlfriend.'

'You didn't invite her for tea?'

'Oh . . . she's from the Malone Road.' With a wry twist of her lips Sarah continued, 'Actually her grannie and your grannie went to school together.'

'Grannie's pleased then?'

'No. She doesn't think the girl's parents will accept Bernard, but he was invited over there to tea tonight. so time'll tell.'

Tired and contented, Eileen linked Johnny's arm as they

dandered home. It had been a wonderful day. If only it could be like this always.

'Did you enjoy yourself?' she asked.

With a slight shrug, he answered, 'It was all right.' After a short silence, he added, 'I can't understand why your father has turned against me.'

'What on earth gives you that idea?'

'Ah, Eileen, you know what I mean. And for the life of me I don't know why. I mean . . . you could have done worse, couldn't you? And he seemed to like me at the beginning, you know, before we were married.'

Knowing only too well what had turned her father against him, Eileen replied, 'Give him time, Johnny. Give him time.'

Dismissing her words with a shrug, he smiled down at her. 'It doesn't really matter. You enjoyed yourself, didn't you?' He hugged her arm close to his side. 'So long as you're happy, nothing else matters. I love to see you happy. I love you, Eileen.'

He waited expectantly, hoping she would say the words he longed to hear. With a contented sigh Eileen moved closer to him but she didn't speak and Johnny had to be content with the thought that at least she was his wife. Their first Christmas together had been pleasant enough. Perhaps 1947 would be a good year for them. He would do all in his power to make it so.

Chapter Three

Sarah rose to her feet, a questioning look in her eyes when Barney Grahame entered the room. Ever since her mother had broken her leg some weeks ago, Barney rarely left her side in the evenings, so Sarah was somewhat surprised to see him. When the shop that he and Jim Rafferty ran on the corner of Rockmore Road closed each day, Barney rushed straight home and fussed around Maggie like a protective hen. The following day's meals would be prepared the night before and all the dirty dishes washed and put neatly away. It irritated Sarah that her step-father was so independent. Anyone else would have been more than glad of any assistance, but not Barney Grahame. Still, at least he was capable and clearly doted on Maggie.

Now Sarah greeted him, an anxious frown on her brow. 'Hello, Barney. Is anything wrong?'

'No.' He smiled slightly at her expression. 'Don't look so worried. Your mother just wants to have a wee word with you. If you've got the time, that is?'

A glance towards the mantelpiece clock confirmed that it was almost ten o'clock. Whatever her mother wanted to see her about at this late hour must be very important, otherwise surely it could wait until morning? Sarah visited her mother every morning to see if she could be of any help, but in vain. The house was always spick and span; that would be Barney's long years at sea coming in useful. Still, her mother was always glad of her company for an hour or so each day. When Sarah

95

had donned her coat she looked askance at Barney. He answered her unspoken question. 'I'll stay here and chat with Mick for a while. She wants to see you alone.'

Mick smiled when the frown on his wife's brow deepened. 'Away ye go,' he chided her, 'the sooner you see Maggie, the sooner the mystery will be solved.'

Leaving the house, Sarah crossed the road and made her way round to the back of her mother's house, entering the kitchen.

Maggie's voice reached her. 'Sarah ... is that you? There's a bottle of sherry in here. Bring two glasses in with you. They're in the cupboard to the left of the cooker.'

When Sarah was settled in the armchair facing her, a glass of sherry in her hand, Maggie smiled and raised her glass, 'To the future.'

Still looking mystified, Sarah leant forward and clinked her glass against her mother's. 'Good health, Mam.'

At these words Maggie grimaced. 'Don't remind me! The specialist at the hospital today wasn't too happy with my leg. He thinks it may have to be reset.'

'Ah, Mam ... that's awful! Why didn't you send for me sooner? I thought that it was just your usual routine visit. You know, Barney should let me accompany you to the hospital, there is really no need for him to go with you. I'd be only too glad to do it. Is it your leg you wanted to talk about?'

'Huh! Have a bit of sense, Sarah. That's not important. It could have waited until morning. I sent for you because I want to know how Eileen is. She has been on my mind all day long and I couldn't wait until tomorrow.'

'Eileen?'

'Yes, Eileen. You know, Johnny's wife! Don't tell me you haven't been up to see her? Isn't the baby almost due?'

Sarah felt her face flush at the sarcasm in her mother's voice. 'I saw her last week just after she left work,' she cried defensively. 'And you know they're not too keen on visitors calling on them until the house has been properly furnished. To tell you the truth, we feel uneasy in Johnny's company. Anyhow, we saw Eileen twice a week when she was working. You can't criticize us if he chose not to accompany her.'

'Do you class yourself a visitor? You're her mother, for heaven's sake! Did you ever ask Eileen to invite Johnny along with her?' Maggie asked quietly.

'No. But, good God, you don't stand on ceremony with your own family! He knew he was welcome to come any time. Tommy Rogan doesn't wait for an invitation,' Sarah finished triumphantly. 'He's never out of our house!'

'That's because he's treated as one of the family. The way Mick treats Johnny you'd think he was a leper or something! Honestly, Sarah, Mick's the last person who should point the finger. Many a man gets a girl into trouble . . . but they don't all rush into marriage. Nor do they make up for it the way Johnny has. Why, Eileen should be very happy. Instead, she's obviously worried about something! Surely you've noticed?'

'No . . . no, Mam, I haven't. She seems all right to me.'

'Huh!'

'Look, Mam, just what are you getting at? Are you implying that we neglect our Eileen?'

Maggie sighed, and the look she threw Sarah was sad. 'Yes, I am. Furthermore, you don't even realize you're doing it.' Seeing that Sarah was about to refute her accusation, she raised a hand to silence her. 'Just let me finish. The last time I saw Eileen, I could see she had something on her mind. I tried to wheedle it out of her, find out what was worrying her, but it was like trying to get blood out of a stone. She remained tight-lipped. Has she said anything to you?'

'No . . . no, she hasn't. She'd be more likely to confide in you, than me. She's probably worrying about the birth. I remember I was terrified just before Beth was born.'

'No, there's more to it than that. I'm sure it's something else.'

'Well . . . Eileen's changed since she got married, that's for sure! She never tells me anything now. Remember when they came home from their honeymoon, how strange they both acted? Not one of us dared question Eileen.' Sarah sat silent for a moment, then voiced her thoughts. 'You know, our Eileen is the last person I would have thought to let anyone touch her outside of marriage . . . yet she did. And she's not exactly head over heels in love with Johnny, so why did she do it?'

'I don't know. But this much I do know. Johnny loves her dearly,' Maggie said firmly.

'I had my doubts about that for a while . . . just after the honeymoon, when he seemed to enjoy making her miserable. Do you think she loves him?'

'To be truthful, I don't. Fond of him, yes. But love . . . ?' Maggie finished with a sad shake of the head.

'Then why did Eileen marry him?'

'You forget, a child was involved.'

'Huh! Don't remind me! I just can't understand how it all came about. Our Eileen was so good-living. I did try to get her to put the wedding off until after the baby was born, but she wouldn't hear tell of it.'

'Well, we all make mistakes. I trusted you, remember? I never dreamt that you . . .'

Sarah paled at these words. Imagine her mother throwing that up in her face after all these years! Her one fall from grace. 'That was different. Mick was a good man . . .'

'Ah, but I didn't know that at the time, did I? To me he was just someone you had been seeing for a few short months. So don't you be so quick to judge others, Johnny's a good man too.'

Silence reigned for some seconds. Sarah's hump was

up at her mother's interference, and Maggie was deep in thought. She agreed with her daughter. Eileen was not the type to mess about just for the fun of it. She was too good-living. So how had she landed herself in a pickle that led to the altar rails? It wasn't love that prompted her. She did not love Johnny. This Maggie was certain of. As far as she could see, her granddaughter had all her wants now, yet still she looked haunted.

'Anyhow, ... Mick's water under the bridge now. I'm worried about Eileen. If it wasn't for this,' Maggie gestured towards her plastered leg, 'I wouldn't see you in my way. I'd go and see for myself how she is getting on. But the child will probably be born before I'm mobile again. Won't you go?'

'Ah, Mam, of course I will. You're right. I should be keeping an eye on her. Do you know something? I don't even know when my first grandchild is due. I'll call over tomorrow and have a wee chat with her. How's that?'

'Fine by me. By the way, when is Beth's baby due?'

At the mention of her eldest daughter's name, a happy smile spread across Sarah's face. 'The twenty-ninth of November ...' Her voice trailed off at the look of contempt Maggie threw her. 'Well, Beth told me the date. I didn't have to ask!' she cried defensively, obviously distressed. 'Look, Mam, you've made your point. From now on things will be different. That's a promise.'

'Good! I'm glad to hear that. Now, pour us another sherry and we'll change the subject.'

Glasses replenished, Sarah asked, 'What exactly did the specialist have to say about your leg?'

'He thinks the bone isn't knitting properly and it may need a pin in it.'

'Ah, Mam, that's awful, so it is.'

'He's not sure, so perhaps it will be all right.'

'I hope so ... I really hope so. You're fed up, aren't you?'

'I am . . . but whatever will be, will be. I'll just have to grin and bear it.'

Without thinking Sarah inquired after Bernard. 'How's Bernard these days? Have you seen his flat yet?'

The pain that crossed her mother's face at the mention of her son caused Sarah to regret her words. However, the hurt that had been inflicted on her regarding Eileen still rankled and she hardened her heart. Although nothing had been said about Bernard's departure from home other than, 'He's got a flat over near St Malachy's College,' and whenever anyone inquired after him, they were told he was doing well, Sarah guessed that Barney had washed his hands of his son and Maggie must be torn between the two of them. Let her mother try and justify not going to visit Bernard! Sarah hadn't been in the least surprised when her half-brother had left home. He had been spoilt rotten. Her mother and Barney could see no wrong in him. They thought the sun shone out of his backside!

A sad little smile played on Maggie's lips and she raised her glass. 'Touché.'

Sarah had the grace to look ashamed. 'Ah, Mam, I'm sorry. I didn't really mean to be catty. But you've got to admit that he is spoilt.'

'No more than you, Sarah, at that age. You tend to forget just how things were with you then. Did you ever heed my advice? Oh, no, you went your own sweet way, and it's only by good fortune that you're still married . . . and happily . . . to Mick.'

'All right! All right! I give in. Bernard's just going through a phase. There's hope for him yet. I'm sorry I opened my mouth.'

'It's all right, Sarah. Bernard is a sore point in this house at present. As you well know, Barney can't bear to hear his name mentioned.'

Silence fell. Sarah was about to break it when Maggie continued, 'Nevertheless, in spite of Barney I did go and visit my son.' At Sarah's start of surprise, she smiled. 'Now, that surprises you, doesn't it? But . . . how could I have done otherwise? Still, I hope Barney never finds out. He'd be very angry.'

Her gaze was intent, and Sarah hastened to assure her, 'I won't say a word, Mam. But . . . how did you manage to get away over to the other side of town on your own?' She gestured towards Maggie's leg.

'Oh, I went just before this happened. I got a taxi there and back. Bernard's *flat* . . . for want of a better name . . . is one room. It's in one of those big houses on the Antrim Road near Duncairn Gardens.' Maggie ran a hand wearily across her face. 'Ah, Sarah, it was awful. Squalid and dirty. My hands just itched to give it a good scrubbing out. But . . . Emily Gordon was there.'

Sarah's lips formed a silent 'Oh' and curiosity brought her to the edge of her chair in anticipation. She couldn't believe what she was hearing. The wonderful Bernard living in sin? She wouldn't have thought he had the guts to live with a girl. Emily Gordon must be the domineering type. Now she asked, 'Are Bernard and Emily living together?'

'Well . . . when Emily left the room for a few minutes, I asked him that. He denied it of course, but then, he would, wouldn't he?'

'They might get married in a Register Office. Do you think they would, Mam?' Sarah ventured to say.

Sadly Maggie nodded in agreement.

'Mam, you can stop them? Bernard's not eighteen yet. He's underage. You could even have him made a ward of court.'

'What good would it do, Sarah? They'd just live together, and if a child was born it would be a bastard. We'll have to avoid that at all costs.'

'Is there anything I can do? Will me and Mick go over and see him, and try to talk some sense into him?'

'Oh, no! Barney wouldn't hear tell of that. And, Sarah,

for the time being, please don't mention it to anyone else. Not even to Mick ... promise?'

Sarah sighed. 'All right, Mam. My lips are sealed.'

In spite of her promise to visit Eileen, the following evening Sarah was loath to do so. She and Mick had yet to be invited over to Eileen's house and the one time they had gone uninvited had been a disaster, with Johnny hardly saying a word to them. On the way home that night Mick had vowed he would never return unless Johnny himself invited them. Now Sarah dithered about, urging herself to go. Anyone would think it was a stranger she was about to visit, instead of her own daughter.

With an exasperated sigh, Mick marked the place in the book he was reading and, putting it to one side, turned to his wife. 'OK, come on, out with it. What's wrong? You're like a cat on a hot griddle.'

'Mmm ...'

'Sarah ... Sarah! Yo ho! Come on, I can't read with you prowling about. What's the matter with you? What's going on?'

With a start Sarah came back to reality and a faint smile touched her lips when she noted his concern. He was so tuned in to her moods.

'I'm sorry, love. It's just that I'm worried,' she confessed.

'Eh? What about? What are you worried about?'

Still smarting from her mother's sarcasm over their alleged neglect of Eileen, Sarah had not acquainted Mick of the true reason for the summons the night before, making the news of the possible resetting of her mother's leg an excuse for the late visit. Now she was telling the truth, albeit a bit late. 'It's our Eileen ... I haven't seen her for over a week and the baby must be almost due.'

'Well then, what's your problem? Away up and see her.'

'I am going . . . but to tell you the truth, I feel guilty. I feel I've neglected her. She might show me the door.'

'Have a titter of wit, Sarah! Eileen would never offend you. If she thinks we're neglectful, she has only Johnny to blame. Way up and see her, love. Do you want me to come with you?' He made as if to rise and Sarah hurriedly forestalled him.

'You're right, Mick. I'll nip up, but I'd better go alone. I wouldn't like to be the instigator of you breaking your word . . . if you know what I mean?'

'What word?'

'The vow you made, never to visit them again unless invited by Johnny himself. Remember?'

A grin spread across Mick's face. 'For you, my love, I'd even break my word.'

'No . . . no, I'd better go on me own.'

Before he could object, she went into the hall and returned, pushing her arms into the sleeves of her coat. 'I won't be long.' Going to him, she put her arms around him and planted a kiss on his cheek. 'I love you,' she whispered.

Grabbing hold of her, Mick tried, without success, to hide his pleasure at her action. 'Hey! what brought this on?'

Sarah laughed and freed herself from his arms. 'I'd better go now, or I won't get out at all,' she teased. As he pretended to lunge at her she ran from the room.

All laughter left her on the way up the street as she remonstrated with herself. Why on earth didn't I go up today when Johnny was at work? But why should I? Anyone would think I was afraid of him. He was the one at fault! He'd a cheek, taking umbrage just because we hadn't welcomed him with open arms, after the way he'd acted, bringing Eileen down!

A sigh of relief escaped her lips as she waited to cross over the Falls Road. There was Johnny walking briskly down the far side, a holdall slung over his shoulder.

She had been reprieved. She was glad she wasn't any earlier or she'd have bumped into him. Come to think of it . . . it was Friday. If she remembered rightly, Johnny went down to a gymnasium at the bottom of Divis Street every Friday night. Watching his tall figure striding along, Sarah had to admit to herself that he looked fit, and he wasn't bad-looking either.

Eileen was unable to hide her shock when she opened the door to her mother's knock. 'This is a surprise,' she gasped, mouth agape.

'Well . . . are you going to ask me in?'

'Oh, sorry, Mam.' Eileen laughed and moved to one side. 'I'm just so surprised at seeing you.'

Sarah strode down the hall, her eyes taking in the pale wallpaper and bright white paint; such a change from the dingy dark wallpaper and dull paint that had previously been on the walls and doors. Why, the hall seemed twice as wide as before. A new hallstand graced one wall and a small table was home to a shiny black telephone. She gaped. Imagine . . . they had a phone! 'When did you get that?' she asked with a nod towards the phone.

'Last weekend. Johnny insisted we get it in case I need help in a hurry. I told him I'd get plenty of warning before the baby finally arrives, but he wouldn't listen to me.'

'It's handy having a phone, so it is. Have you finished all the decorating then?'

'Not quite. We've the two big bedrooms and the living room to do yet. And we've to put the finishing touches to most of the other rooms, but we're getting there!'

'And you didn't think to invite us over to see what you've done?'

'Why should I? Although you wouldn't think it, I'm your daughter. I wanted you to come of your own accord. I wanted you to show you cared for me . . . no matter how you felt about Johnny. Madge doesn't wait for an invitation, but then, Johnny's precious to her.' Eileen's voice broke slightly. 'Do you wait for an invitation from Beth? Eh, do you?'

Eileen was grim-faced as she led the way into the parlour. She softened slightly at her mother's small gasp of appreciation when she entered the room.

'Oh, this is lovely!' Sarah exclaimed, her eyes instinctively going to her feet as they sank into the thick pile of the carpet square. Pale silvery green in colour, it covered most of the floor and complemented the curtains which were a deeper shade of green. The high ceiling and frieze were brilliant white and the wallpaper was pale grey with small sprigs of flowers in a scattered pattern. Just the perfect background for the dark grey suite. Sarah could see that they must have got it specially made. This wasn't one of the utility designs manufactured during the war. The suite was dark embossed velvet and contrasted with the two-tone pale grey tiles of the kitchenette grate. The grate itself was well blackleaded and set with paper spills and coal ready to light, and above it the ornate mantelpiece gleamed white. Johnny must have connections on the black market to have obtained so many luxuries. The goods were available all right but you had to be in the know and be prepared to pay through the nose to get them. They looked expensive. Where would Johnny get that kind of money?

The look Sarah turned on Eileen was worried. 'This room must have cost a small fortune. Did you get it all on tick?'

'No, Mam. Strange though it may seem to you, Johnny is a very responsible person. He wouldn't dream of getting into debt. He is very careful with his money and he has some savings. Just wait till you see the nursery!'

With these words she led the way down the hall. A warm glow enveloped her as she climbed the stairs. She was aware that her mother was very impressed; saw the way she touched the banister that Johnny had sanded down and varnished; saw her let her fingers trail the new wallpaper.

Sarah was indeed impressed. Paint and paper certainly made a big difference! It was hard to believe that this was the same house that she had first seen just a few short months ago. The landing seemed wider and each door had a motif on it indicating which room it was. Johnny was rising a couple of notches in her opinion. Only a devoted man would have achieved so much in such a short time. Bemused, she followed Eileen through the door marked with a baby motif, to stand in awe in the nursery.

It was the smallest bedroom. Painted in soft pastel shades of blue, pink and lemon, it was suitable for either boy or girl. A large white cot stood beneath the window and a sheepskin rug lay alongside it, while little nursery pictures decorated the walls.

'I'm not buying curtains for in here until I see what I get.'

'What would you prefer?'

'Oh, I'm not fussy,' Eileen confessed, and inwardly lamented: Just so long as it has red hair. She was two weeks overdue! What would happen if the child was dark like its father? God only knew. She begged Him daily to let her go a month over her time, then perhaps she would be able to pull the wool over Johnny's eyes. She was happy with him. To have to leave this beautiful house now would break her heart, after all the hard work she had put into it. She felt so secure and safe here. What would happen to her and the baby if she had to rear the child alone? The shame of everybody knowing the truth! Would she be brave enough to face it, or would she feel compelled to move to where nobody knew her? The worry of it was driving her around the bend.

'You can't have much longer to go now.' Sarah's voice brought her out of her daydream.

It was a statement but Eileen knew her mother was fishing. 'No,' she agreed, and changed the subject, 'How's Beth?'

'Not too bad. The morning sickness has stopped and she is starting to show. Very proud of her bump, she is.'

'You see her regularly, don't you?' The bitter note was back in Eileen's voice.

Sarah's lips tightened. Obviously Eileen wanted her pound of flesh. 'Look, Eileen . . . the last time we visited you, Johnny was very distant. We didn't feel welcome, so we didn't come back. It's as simple as that.'

'Now you know how Johnny felt when he had to live under your roof. He wasn't made to feel at home either. He was barely tolerated! Not like Tommy Rogan . . . he's treated like one of the family. No wonder he's never out of your house!'

To Sarah's dismay, she detected tears in Eileen's eyes. Guilt swamped all other emotions and she hastened to make amends.

'Look, Eileen, we never meant to hurt you . . . or Johnny, for that matter! We were just so disappointed. Your father made a friend of Johnny and when he forced you into a shotgun wedding, well . . . Mick couldn't forgive him.'

'You're blaming it all on Johnny and it wasn't his fault!' Sarah's brows rose in surprise at these words and knowing her mother was about to inquire sarcastically who was to blame then, Eileen hurried on. 'Johnny didn't seduce me, you know. It takes two to play that game.' She felt ashamed that Johnny's character was being blackened and he not being in a position to defend himself. If only she had not gone to the Floral Hall with Billy that night, everything would have been so different now. But . . . would she have still married Johnny? No, she would have been looking for a dark handsome hero to sweep her off her feet.

'Look, are we going to stand here all night arguing? Let's go downstairs. And how's about making me a cup of tea, eh? Or am I not going to be offered a cup?'

'Ah, Mam, I'm sorry. Of course I'll make a cup of tea.'

When they were seated in the partially decorated kitchen, with a wave around, Sarah said, 'You're very lucky, you know.'

'I realize that. Johnny's a good man. I want for nothing.'

This was the opening that Sarah was waiting for. 'Then why do you always seem weighed down with worry?'

'What do you mean?'

Not for the world was Sarah going to admit that she hadn't noticed that her daughter always looked worried. 'I noticed you weren't yourself lately . . . and so did your grannie.'

'Have you all been talking about me again, eh? Discussing me behind my back?'

'Ach, Eileen, knock that chip off your shoulder and tell me what's wrong, please.'

'Mam, there's nothing wrong! I'm just nervous about the birth.' She was pleased with her answer. She had told the truth. She *was* worried about the birth, but not the way her mother imagined.

Sarah smiled. 'That's what I told your grannie. It's only natural that you'd be worried, with it being your first child, but you'll be all right. How's about you and me going down town tomorrow? Eh? We'll have a dander round the shops and buy something nice for the baby. I've a few clothing coupons left over this month.'

'I'd love to get out for a while, Mam. Break the monotony. But you don't need to buy anything for the baby. You've bought enough already.' This was one way Eileen could not fault her mother. Whatever Sarah bought for Beth, Eileen got likewise and vice versa.

'Well then, I'll buy you something for yourself. How are you off for nightdresses?'

'Ah, Mam . . . you don't have to.'

'I want to, so I do. Meet me at the bus stop tomorrow

morning at nine and we'll go down and paint the town red. Eh, love?'

Eileen nodded in agreement. 'That would be nice.' And they smiled at each other. Silently, Sarah vowed to buy her mother a box of chocolates while in town the next day. She was glad that Maggie had shown her how foolish she was. From now on everything would be different.

Saturday morning was dry but frosty and a pale sun high above the rooftops promised better things to come. From her stand at the bus stop Sarah watched Eileen waddle towards her. She was huge! What if she had twins? She remembered that twins ran in the family. Her father's brother and sister were twins: Aunt Jean and Uncle Liam. With a smile she greeted her daughter. 'You look lovely this morning.'

In fact, in spite of her bulk, Eileen looked beautiful. Her auburn hair was a soft cloud and the dark green of the loose coat she wore, made her eyes green luminous pools. She took after her grannie in the respect that her eyes reflected any deep colour she wore.

'I feel great, Mam. I'm looking forward to our outing, so I am.'

Once they were seated on the trolleybus, Sarah cast an eye over her daughter's huge bump. 'I hope you aren't expecting twins.'

To tease her worry, Eileen confessed, 'I'm two weeks overdue.'

'What? And you only left work a week ago? Were you not afraid of dropping it in the match factory?'

'Ah, now Mam . . . you know you get plenty of warning, especially with the first baby.'

'Still . . . I'm surprised Johnny let you work on so long.'

'Johnny's not my keeper. I do as I please.' How could Eileen confess, that although Johnny thought

109

she had another month to go, he had wanted her to leave work much sooner? She had pretended she was leaving six weeks before the birth. Most expectant mothers worked as close to the approximate date of the birth as was prudent. They weren't all as fortunate as her.

'Oh, sorry I spoke . . .'

Sadly, Eileen interrupted her mother. 'Ah, Mam. Let's not argue.' For a moment she was tempted to tell Sarah the truth; share the great burden of guilt that was weighing her down, but shame held her silent. If the child had red hair no one need ever know.

The bus arriving at the bottom of Castle Street came as a welcome relief. With a smile, Eileen thanked her mother as she gripped her arm to assist her to her feet. The bus stop was right outside the doors of the London Mantle Warehouse and Eileen paused for some minutes to admire a style that she would soon be able to wear. Once she was rid of this great big bump, Johnny had promised to buy her a new outfit. Again she prayed inwardly. Please God let everything work out for me.

For the next three hours they dandered up and down Royal Avenue, along High Street and down Ann Street, in and out of shops until Sarah called for a halt. Stopping outside a small cafe she cried, 'Right, that's it! I must have a cup of tea or I'll pass out.'

The tearoom was crowded but Eileen managed to find an empty table along the wall, while Sarah queued for tea and crumpets.

Closing her eyes, Eileen relaxed as the tension eased from her body, and sat back contentedly. It was funny how a bit of sun and family harmony gave rise to hope. Today she was confident that everything would work out all right. A somehow familiar voice shattered this confidence.

'Is it all right if we share your table, missus?'

110

Looking up, Eileen found herself gazing into the bright blue eyes of Ruth Greer.

'Why . . . it's you, Eileen, isn't it?'

'Hello, Ruth.' Eileen felt winded, Ruth's eyes, so like Billy's, had thrown her into confusion. 'Yes, of course you can sit here.'

Setting the tray down, Ruth motioned the woman with her into the seat facing Eileen. Sitting down beside her, she unloaded the tray. Her face showed little trace of friendliness.

Eileen felt her own face redden. She had seen the contempt in Ruth's eyes when she had noted her obvious pregnancy. When Sarah arrived at the table she could see that her daughter was distressed and wondered what on earth was wrong.

'Are you all right?' she inquired, peering anxiously at Eileen before emptying the tray.

'Yes, I'm fine, Mam. This is a friend of mine. Ruth . . . ?' Eileen looked inquiringly at Ruth. 'I'm afraid I don't know your married name.

'Smyth . . . my married name is Smyth. I'm pleased to meet you.' Ruth exchanged nods with Sarah and then turned to her companion. 'Mam, this is Eileen Ross and her mother.'

'Eileen Ross?' The woman was suddenly alert and her eyes questioned her daughter. When Ruth nodded, her mother's eyes swung to Eileen, avidly examining her; making her squirm uncomfortably.

'I'm very pleased to meet you, Eileen,' she said softly. 'And your mother.' She smiled and nodded at Sarah, who nodded in return.

Silence reigned for some minutes and Eileen could feel Mrs Greer examining her covertly. At last she could bear it no longer, and decided that she had nothing to be ashamed of – after all they could not expect all Billy's girlfriends to remain single – she asked, 'How is Billy? Any word of him getting married?'

Eileen watched in wonder as Ruth's mouth dropped open and her eyes widened in amazement. At last she gasped, 'You don't know! You really don't know!'

'Don't know what?' A shiver of apprehension coursed through Eileen's body. She sensed that she was about to hear something terrible.

Placing a comforting hand over her mother's, Ruth said flatly, 'Billy's dead.'

'Dead?' Eileen's voice came out in a squeak, causing Sarah to turn and gape at her in astonishment. 'What happened? When did he die?'

'The night after that dance in the Floral Hall. He was on his way to meet you. A young lad ran out in front of his motorbike. He swerved to avoid him, right into the path of a tram. He died instantly.'

There wasn't enough room for Eileen to fall when she fainted, but she slumped down in the seat beside her bewildered mother.

Who were these women? Sarah, not knowing just what was wrong, nevertheless placed the blame on the strangers. She glared balefully at them before bending anxiously over Eileen.

'Oh, dear God, how am I going to get her home?' she cried as she feverishly rubbed her daughter's hands in an effort to revive her.

'Open her coat,' Ruth ordered. 'Look, she's coming round. Please let me help. I'll take you home. My car's parked round in Rosemary Street.'

Seeing Sarah was about to refuse, she pleaded. 'Please? I thought she knew. It was splashed across the front of the *Telegraph*.'

'We don't get the *Telegraph*, so we don't. We get the *Irish News*!' Sarah answered curtly.

'I'll fetch my car. Give me five minutes, then come to the door. You stay here with them, Mother.' Before Sarah could object, Ruth hurried away, tea forgotten.

While they waited outside the tearoom, Eileen suddenly doubled over in pain. Sarah guessed the baby had decided to come.

'Take deep breaths, love.' Putting an arm around her daughter she whispered in her ear, 'That's right, love. Big deep breaths. We'll soon have you home.'

After what seemed ages, but was in reality only a few minutes, Ruth arrived. Sarah helped her daughter into the back seat of the car and clambered in beside her, muttering words of thanks. When Mrs Greer was at last settled in the front seat beside her daughter, Ruth asked, 'Well, where to?'

'St James's Park! It's up . . .'

'I know where it is.' Ruth carefully manoeuvred the car into the stream of traffic and they were off. On the journey up the Falls Road she glanced worriedly over her shoulder at Eileen.

'She's in shock as well as labour, so she is.'

'How do you know that?' Worry made Sarah's voice strident.

'I'm a nurse, that's how I know.'

Mick was taking advantage of the fine weather to tidy the front garden. He straightened to attention when a small dark blue saloon car stopped outside the house and Sarah scrambled out of it. When a stranger hurried from the far side of the car and helped her assist Eileen from the back seat, Mick was out on the pavement in a flash, questions tumbling from his lips.

Shooting him a worried glance, Sarah cried, 'Go fetch Nurse Lancaster, love. And hurry! Eileen's in labour. And you'd better let Johnny know that she's over here.'

Without another word, Mick turned on his heel and hurried up the street, coatless, his old work boots clattering on the pavement. Between them Sarah and Ruth managed to get Eileen upstairs and undressed. When she was settled in bed, Sarah turned to Ruth and thanked her, making it plain that she wanted her to leave. Downstairs, Ruth turned appealingly to her.

'Can I call back tomorrow to see how she is?'

'Well . . . I don't know. If she holds on she'll probably be over in her own house. I'm a stupid fool, so I am. I should have got you to take us to Eileen's house. I don't know what I was thinking of. Johnny won't be too pleased.'

Ruth was not to be put off. 'Well, can I call here just in case?'

'I . . . well . . .' Sarah was dubious. She didn't know if Eileen would want to see this woman again. Who was she anyway? How come Eileen knew her?

'Please. I don't think Eileen will mind.'

Reluctantly Sarah nodded. 'OK, then.'

Relieved, Ruth slipped her arm through her mother's and with a final farewell, they left the house.

Ruth was glad Sarah had not opposed her request to return to see Eileen because she was determined to see her again, by fair means or foul. On the journey up the Falls road with Eileen, her thoughts had been racing. Her brother was dead just over nine months. Eileen was huge; she could easily be over her time. Was the baby Billy's? Tomorrow she intended to find out.

All through the fifteen long hours of labour, Eileen clung to the thought that Billy had loved her. He hadn't abandoned her after all. He had been coming to take her home to meet his parents. Somehow, it made a difference to her. It didn't change her predicament, but the knowledge of his love warmed her heart and seemed to ease the terrible pains that were racking her.

At last she managed to push the baby free from her exhausted body. When Dr Hughes had finished stitching her up, he congratulated her on producing a fine healthy son and hurried off on another call, muttering, 'Babies are like bananas. They seem to come

114

in bunches – and usually in the early hours of the morning.'

Nurse Lancaster held the child for Eileen to see. Eileen gazed on her son for the first time, and her heart contracted with fear when she saw the thatch of dark hair. She had no chance of pulling the wool over Johnny's eyes. He was bound to guess. Could two red-haired people produce a dark-haired child? She had no idea. Would Johnny be any the wiser? Tentatively, she reached out and touched the baby's head. Poor wee mite; he didn't ask to be born. No matter what happened, she would devote her life to looking after this child. With or without Johnny. But the thought of life without Johnny filled her with despair. It would be difficult to rear a baby on her own, under the disapproving eyes of the neighbours. Especially after the loving care Johnny had lavished on her.

The baby started to cry, and Nurse Lancaster said, 'I'll give him a wash, Eileen, and then we'll try him at your breast. That's a hungry cry, if ever I heard one.'

Once the child was lying in the crook of Eileen's arm, Sarah smiled benignly down at him. 'I'll go down and tell Johnny that he can come up now. He's worried sick about you.'

To her amazement Eileen gripped her arm and pulled her down so that she could whisper in her ear, 'Mam . . . will you explain to Johnny that premature babies need extra care for a while?'

'What?' Sarah frowned at Eileen. What on earth did she mean? Why, hadn't Eileen herself confessed that she was two weeks over her time? Then comprehension dawned. The child wasn't Johnny's! Dear God . . . then who was the father?

Eileen frantically shook her mother's arm. 'Mam, do this for me, please.'

Sarah glanced towards Nurse Lancaster but that good lady was apparently unaware of the situation.

'Mam?'

'All right! All right, I'll tell him, but he'll never believe me!' The baby was big; eight pounds, two ounces. Johnny would never believe her, but she would try. She was apprehensive when she stood at the top of the stairs and summoned her son-in-law up to see his son.

Johnny took the stairs two at a time and fell on his knees beside the bed. 'Are you all right, Eileen?'

'Of course I am. Just tired.'

Johnny turned his attention to the baby in his wife's arms. Eileen watched closely for any sign of doubt. 'He's very dark, isn't he?'

'Yes, he is,' Eileen agreed. 'I think perhaps he'll take after my father in colouring.'

Sarah felt her mouth drop open at these words. Why, the audacity of Eileen! Who would have thought that she could be so brazen? But then, she had a lot to lose. When her daughter continued in a light teasing voice, Sarah thought she would faint.

'But look at his nose ... that's yours all over again, Johnny!'

When Johnny leant closer to examine the baby, above his head Eileen nodded slightly at her mother.

Sarah wasn't very happy at the deception she was being asked to condone. She was remembering how the family had treated Johnny; how they had blamed him for Eileen's condition – and all the time he had been innocent. Apparently, he hadn't even known Eileen was pregnant when they got married. Her daughter had duped him! Someone else was the culprit. How on earth had she managed this deception? Still ... it was true what they said! There was none so blind as those who didn't want to see, and Johnny was besotted with Eileen. No wonder he couldn't stand the sight of them! After the way they'd behaved he must feel very bitter towards them. And with just cause! Why, he must think they were nutcases.

'He'll have to be watched carefully for the first few weeks on account of being premature, Johnny.' Sarah's voice sounded false to her ears but he seemed unaware of it. She was glad that he had his back to Nurse Lancaster and did not see the nurse's start of surprise. Sarah wasn't worried about Nurse Lancaster. No, midwives were like doctors in that they knew when to keep their mouths shut.

'I was thinking he was a bit early . . . about a month, isn't it?'

So he had been counting the months. 'Mmm . . . but he looks healthy enough.' It was Eileen who answered him.

'Still, we had better keep an eye on him, just in case.'

'To tell you the truth, Eileen, I'm glad he didn't inherit my red hair,' Johnny confessed, and touched the dark down on the baby's head. 'It's a curse when the kids nickname you Carrot Top or Ginger. I would like him to have inherited your colouring though.'

Johnny's fingers trailed lightly over her hair and down her cheek, and when Sarah saw the way her daughter turned her face so that her lips touched his fingers, fear smote her and she prayed silently: Please God forgive Eileen and let her get away with this. For it was obvious to her that, whether Eileen realized it or not, she loved Johnny Cleary.

'I've been thinking, Johnny, how's about Eileen staying here for a few days?'

Both Eileen and Johnny turned surprised looks on Sarah.

'I just thought it would give her a chance to get her strength back and get used to motherhood. That way you would have more time to get everything ready for them coming home, Johnny.'

'What do you think, Eileen? It would give me a chance to finish our bedroom.'

'It's up to you. I'll do whatever you like.'

'All right, Sarah. If you're sure you don't mind the

117

extra work, we'll be glad to take you up on your kind offer.' He glanced at his watch. 'It's four o'clock, I'd better go home and snatch a few hours sleep or I'll be fit for nothing tomorrow. If you're staying here for a . . .' He turned to Sarah. 'Is it all right if she stays until next Friday?' When she answered him with a quick nod, he continued, 'Then I'll just go into work next week, Eileen, and take the following week off. You'll need me at home more then. Is that OK with you, love?'

'Yes, Johnny, that's a good idea,' Eileen agreed. 'See you later, love.'

'Good night, nurse. Thanks for all your help.'

'I'm only doing my job, son. Good night.'

When Nurse Lancaster at last bade them good night and departed, Sarah stood at the side of the bed and bestowed on Eileen a stern look. 'Now, explain yourself, girl. Who's the father of this young man?'

'Mam . . . I don't want to talk about it. Thanks for helping me out, I'm obliged. But, least said, soonest mended.'

'Ah, now, you listen to me, girl. I'll have to tell your father that we've been blaming . . .'

'Mam! That's the worst possible thing you could do. Good God, me dad wouldn't be able to put on an act. We might as well tell Johnny the truth as tell me dad. You know that's right don't you, Mam?'

Sarah stood in thought for some seconds. Eileen was right! Mick would feel so guilty about the way he'd treated Johnny that he'd be extra nice to him, and Johnny would surely twig on. 'Well, you can at least tell me who the father is? I can't remember you ever going out with any other boy.'

'Mam, it's no one you know . . .'

Suddenly an idea dawned on Sarah and she interrupted Eileen excitedly. 'I know who it is. It's that young lad who was killed on the motorbike, isn't it? No wonder you went into labour when you learnt of his death! But how on earth . . . where did you . . . I don't understand!' Sarah finished lamely, slumping down on the bed, completely at a loss.

'Mam, you don't have to understand. Just forget all about it. As far as everybody is concerned, this is Johnny's son. Now I know me dad is waiting to come up to see his grandson, so go down and send him up. Then maybe we'll all get some sleep.'

Stopping her car outside Sarah's drive the following day, Ruth Smyth sat for a moment to compose herself. As she stubbed out her cigarette in the ashtray, her hand shook. Convinced that the child was Billy's, she was determined to make Eileen admit that her brother was indeed the child's father. But would she? She had to! She just had to! It would mean so much to Ruth's parents to know that part of Billy lived on; that they had a grandchild. Since discovering some years ago that she was barren, Ruth felt that she had let her parents down. After years of tests, hopes raised only to be dashed, she and George were reconciled to being childless. He had wanted a son to carry on the small shop he ran in Upper North Street, but alas, it was not to be. Ruth and George had a wonderful relationship and could live without children but her parents had been saddened at the prospect. Ruth had been depending on Billy to provide grandchildren for their parents. Then he had died so suddenly. But if this baby was Billy's . . . it was almost too exciting to think about. A grandchild for her parents?

Throwing open the car door, Ruth almost knocked against a tall red-haired man and apologized profusely. He acknowledged her apology with a nod and a wide grin, and entering the driveway of Sarah's house, walked down the side and around the back.

As she waited for an answer to her knock on the front door, Ruth idly wondered who he was. With that colouring he could be Eileen's brother. Or perhaps he was her husband?

'Ah, hello, Ruth. Come on in.' Sarah's welcome was cordial and Ruth was relieved. She had been afraid that Eileen might refuse to see her.

'How is Eileen today?' she asked.

'She's fine and I have a lovely wee grandson. Weighed in at eight pounds two ounces, so he did.'

'Oh, that's wonderful.'

'Come on up and see her.'

Sarah led the way upstairs. Tapping on the door of the bedroom which Eileen was occupying, she entered.

'You've a visitor,' she said, and ushered Ruth in.

Eileen's eyes were wary but she greeted the visitor civilly enough. 'Hello, Ruth. It's good of you to come.'

With a glance and a smile at Eileen, Ruth's gaze then fastened on the baby in her arms. 'He's lovely! Oh, so beautiful. You must be very proud of him.'

'We certainly are.' Sarah pulled a chair over beside the bed. 'Here, sit down, Ruth. While you two have a natter, I'll put the tea pot on.'

When Sarah left the room, Ruth gently touched the baby's head. 'He's very dark. Is your husband dark?'

Unaware that Johnny was downstairs and might come up at any minute, Eileen nodded.

'Have you picked a name for him yet?'

'Yes, we've decided on Paul. After my first grandfather. Grannie will be pleased.'

'Paul?' Ruth repeated, but she was abstracted. She was wondering if the baby really looked like her brother or if it was just wishful thinking on her part.

With a tap on the door, Johnny entered the room. 'Sorry to disturb you ladies but I just popped in to see my son. I still can't believe I'm a father.'

With a smile at Ruth, he bent to kiss Eileen and gently touched the baby's face.

'Hold him, Johnny. Go on ... he won't bite you,' Eileen teased.

Gingerly, Johnny gathered the little bundle up in his arms and as he gazed down on its features Ruth examined him. Noting the bright red hair, she was more than ever convinced that Billy was the father of this dark-haired baby. Why else would Eileen lie about her husband's colouring?

The baby opened its eyes and gazed at Johnny with big unfocused orbs. He stifled the doubts that rose in him; doubts that had assailed him during the night. Of course this was his child. Who else could be the father? He must never let Eileen know that he had ever for one moment thought otherwise. Why, it would ruin their marriage.

With a final kiss on the baby's brow, Johnny gently placed him back into his wife's arms. 'My mam will be over later this afternoon, if that's all right with you, Eileen?'

'Of course it's all right! She can come any time. Tell her not to stand on ceremony ... come as often as she likes.'

'I'll be off then, I'm finishing the kitchen today. See you later.' He turned to Ruth. 'This young fellow took us all by surprise, you know, arriving early,' he confided with a smile.

Hoping Johnny didn't hear Ruth's indrawn breath at the news that the baby was premature, Eileen made the introductions.

'Let me introduce you to a friend of mine, Johnny. This is Ruth Smyth, Ruth this is my husband, Johnny.'

'It's always nice to meet a friend of Eileen's.' Johnny offered Ruth his hand. 'Maybe you'll visit us some time? You'd be more than welcome. Wouldn't she, Eileen?'

'I'd enjoy that.' Ruth knew by the look on Eileen's face that she would never be a welcome visitor.

When Johnny left the room the silence stretched, both

women being loth to break it. At last Ruth blurted out, 'He's Billy's child, isn't he?'

'No! He is not!' Eileen was tight-lipped and adamant. 'What gives you the right to say an awful thing like that?'

'Ah, Eileen, I know he's Billy's. He's the picture of him, so he is.'

'He's the spit of my dad! And I won't have you putting doubts into people's minds with your wicked accusations.'

Eileen's voice had risen shrilly and Sarah, entering the room, gave Ruth a resentful look. Placing the tray she carried on the small table, she took the baby from Eileen's arms and cuddled him close. It was wonderful to hold a baby again. 'I'll take him downstairs and change his nappy. Will you pour the tea, Ruth?'

At the door she hesitated, her eyes anxious. 'Are you all right, Eileen?'

Eileen forced a smile and nodded. With a warning look at Ruth, Sarah left the room.

Ruth poured the tea and the conversation was general. Ruth was full of admiration for the house and garden.

'It is a lovely house,' Eileen agreed. 'We used to live in Waterford Street but Mam always wanted to live up here. You see, my grandfather ... the one I'm naming Paul after ... died young and Grannie married again. She and her second husband, Granda Barney, bought a house up here. They still live in it, across the street from here. So once Mam saw Grannie's bathroom and the gardens she wanted a house like it. She tortured Dad until he agreed to move.'

'How long have you lived here?'

'Since 1938. The threat of war had the shipyard working round the clock. Me dad was earning great money and he gave into Mam's pleas and bought this house. If you think this is nice ... you should see me grannie's. Her house still has the old-fashioned slate mantels and cast iron grates. They're gorgeous. And most of me grannie's furniture is antique. Furniture that she and an old friend that she used to live with in Waterford Street restored themselves. It was during the 1920 troubles when they used to be confined to the house during curfew. I think it's lovely, but me mam likes the latest fashions, so when we moved here, as soon as she could afford to, she changed the mantelpieces and bought modern furniture. Still ... everyone to their own taste.'

'You're right there! It wouldn't do if we all had the same taste. I'm like your mam, I prefer to have the latest fashions.'

'I'm like my grannie, I love old things.'

'You seem very fond of your grannie.'

'Oh, I am.' Eileen's love for Maggie came through in her softly spoken words. 'She's a marvellous person, so she is. You know ... she's originally from the Malone Road. Quite upper-class. Her parents disowned her when she married my grandfather. Can you imagine, giving up a beautiful big home and the chance of inheriting some money, to live in two rooms in Waterford Street?'

Personally, Ruth thought Eileen's grannie must have been a fool but keeping her opinions to herself, she replied, 'She must have been very much in love.'

'Yes. My grandfather must have been a remarkable man. She has a photograph of him. One of the old sepia kind. He was very handsome. You know ... dark and intense and passionate-looking. Perhaps that's who Paul takes after. A throwback, you know?' Eileen was glad of the chance to add this piece of information, and paused to let it sink in but Ruth did not take her up on it. 'Unfortunately, my granda was only twenty-five when he died. He was struck down with TB and only lasted a few months. Grannie was expecting her second child at the time. The shock sent her into premature labour and the baby, a boy whom they also named Paul, died.'

'How sad.'

Eileen was on her hobby horse now! She loved talking about Maggie. Besides, it kept the conversation away from Paul. 'Grannie had a hard time rearing my mam on her own. During the the troubles in the 1920s she was regarded with suspicion, a Protestant living in the heart of the Falls. Mam says the neighbours were jealous of her. They thought she was too posh! Said she talked as if she had a marble in her mouth! She still speaks lovely. You'd think that living surrounded all these years by us lot, she'd have lapsed into our way of talking, but no, she still rounds all her words off. I never tire of listening to her. I'm supposed to be her double.'

'She must have been very beautiful.' Ruth's gaze was admiring and Eileen blushed at the implied compliment.

'Thank you. You're very kind.' She was overcome with shyness for some seconds, then continued. 'My grannie was thirty-seven when she met Granda Barney. 'He's ten years younger than her. They got married two years later and moved up here. This was one of the posh districts then. There was no Whiterock or St James's estates. All up the Whiterock was fields ... right up to the Black Mountain. It must have been beautiful.' She paused to dwell on how lovely it must have been, especially in the summertime. She pictured green fields colourful with wild flowers, hedges laden with hawthorn blossom, right up to the mountain where the waterfall tumbled down the hill side. With a sigh of regret at the loss of all this beauty, she continued, 'They thought that they were doomed to be childless, but when my grannie was forty-two she became pregnant. She almost died in childbirth, but thank God she pulled through and so did her son, my Uncle Bernard.'

Eileen knew that she was babbling but couldn't stop. She wished her mother would return. She wanted this woman to leave and never come back.

'What a tragic life your grannie had. Why, you could write a book about it!'

Eileen smiled at the very idea of this. 'All tears and snatters? Doom and gloom? Who would want to read it? I only hope I haven't inherited my grannie's tendency to tragedy, as well as her looks.'

'Still, it obviously had its happier side.' The tension had eased as Eileen rambled on and Ruth smiled happily at her, displaying a set of even white teeth, just like Billy's. Ruth resembled Billy a lot and Eileen felt tears gather as she pondered on his tragic death.

Conversation lagged again and it was Ruth who broke the silence. 'Our Billy was besotted with you. He never stopped talking to me about how beautiful you were.'

'Did he? Did he, really?' In spite of herself, Eileen sounded eager. She wanted to find out all she could about Billy without appearing too interested.

'Yes, he did. My parents could see that he was serious about you . . . that's why they consented to meet you.' Ruth fell silent and they both sat deep in thought for some seconds. 'If only he had left the house earlier that night! Or taken a different route! My dad says it wouldn't have made any difference. He believes that when your time's up, you go. No matter where you are.'

'My dad believes if you die young it's because something better is in store for you. But . . . how can one know?'

'That's just it! We can't! Nobody ever comes back to tell what it's like.'

Sadness settled like a cloak on Eileen as she pondered how different life might have been had Billy lived. She remained silent.

Ruth continued, 'When Billy was killed we didn't know how to contact you. We thought you would be sure to see it in the *Telegraph* . . . it was the headlines . . . and we waited for you to come. When you failed to put in an appearance, we thought your parents had forbidden you to.'

'I didn't know! You see, we only get the *Irish News*. If it was in the other paper I would have missed it, so I knew nothing about his death.'

Ruth reached over and clasped Eileen's hand between hers. 'It must have been awful for you, not knowing . . . wondering why Billy didn't show up that night.'

Unconsciously, Eileen nodded her head in agreement. However, when Ruth whispered softly, 'Did you know then that you were pregnant?' she reacted furiously.

Snatching her hand away, she hissed, 'I was not pregnant! Do you hear me? I was not pregnant! Why do you keep on like this?'

Wringing her hands in anguish, Ruth leant closer to the bed. Her mother's happiness was at stake here. 'Please, Eileen, tell me the truth. You don't know how much it would mean to my parents to know that they had a grandchild. You see . . . I can't have children.'

Eileen felt the blood drain from her face as the implication of these words sank in. She pictured Ruth's parents coming to see their grandson. Oh, dear God, the scandal it would cause! She could imagine the effect it would have on Johnny. Could visualize his anger.

Dear God, help me, she prayed silently. Her face crumpled in self-pity, then anger took over. This was her son's future she was fighting for here. Afraid of being overheard, she kept her voice low.

The words came out in a hiss. 'How dare you! How dare you come here with these wild accusations? Do you realize that if my husband heard you it could ruin our marriage?'

Ruth slumped back in her chair in defeat. Eileen's words had made her aware of the other side of the story. She had just been considering her own family. Now she was aware that Eileen could never confess that Billy was the father of her child. Especially as her husband seemed to believe that the baby was his. It would be unreasonable to expect her to admit anything. Ruth was only thankful that she had not confided her suspicions to anyone else; had not raised her parents' hopes.

'It's all right, Eileen! It's all right! Don't upset yourself. I just wasn't thinking straight.' She rose to her feet and whilst she smoothed on her gloves, tried to find words to reassure Eileen.

'I promise I'll never mention my suspicions to anyone else.'

When Eileen did not speak, Ruth stressed, 'I mean that! But . . .' she rummaged in her handbag and produced a pen and a scrap of paper. Scribbling on the paper, she handed it to Eileen. 'Just in case. If you ever need any help, please contact me. Now, remember, any time at all. No matter how much time has elapsed, don't be afraid to get in touch with me.' Hearing Sarah on the stairs she fell silent.

Entering the room, Sarah was at once conscious of the tension. 'Oh, are you going already, Ruth?' she asked when she saw that Ruth had her gloves on and her bag tucked under her arm.

'Ruth has an appointment, Mam,' Eileen said hurriedly, and Sarah knew she was being warned not to urge this woman to stay.

'Can I hold the baby a minute before I go?'

'Of course you can.' Sarah handed the child over and was amazed to see tears on Ruth's cheeks. With a hasty kiss on the child's head, Ruth thrust him back into Sarah's arms and hurried to the door, muttering, 'I'll see myself out. Thanks for the tea.'

'What on earth was all that about?' Sarah asked suspiciously. 'Does she know her brother is Paul's father?'

Eileen had no intention of admitting anything. 'Ah, Mam, don't you start. Ruth is just emotional because she can't have children of her own. I told you, Johnny is Paul's father. Remember that!' she warned. Scanning

127

the piece of paper on which Ruth had written her address, she then tore it up into small pieces. 'Mam, will you throw these into the waste bin for me, please?'

Reaching for her son, she cuddled him close. When she bared her breast to him, he suckled contentedly. Kissing the crown of his head, Eileen silently vowed, No one will ever harm you, if I can prevent it.

The week passed quickly, with Claire and Emma vying with their parents to spoil Paul, watched by a proud Eileen. Even Maggie, in spite of being housebound, was guilty of spoiling her great-grandchild. She demanded that the baby be brought over to her house daily so that she could see how he was faring. Once Eileen was on her feet she herself brought Paul over to visit her grannie. She knew that seeing Paul helped to salve the pain inflicted on Maggie by Bernard.

'Grannie, you'll have to visit us often when you're feeling better.'

'I was very relieved to discover that I didn't need to get my leg reset. Another week or so and I should get this plaster off. You might regret that invitation. You'll soon get fed up looking at my old face.'

'Ah, Grannie, we could never see enough of you. Why, you spoil me rotten.'

'Couldn't spoil a better person,' Maggie assured her, with a fond smile.

Embarrassed, Eileen said haltingly, 'Grannie ... I'm not the good person you think I am. If you knew what I've done ...'

With an abrupt movement of her hand Maggie stopped her. 'I don't want to know your secrets! Save that for the confessional. I know that at heart you're a good person and that's all that matters to me. However ... there's one thing, Eileen, that I want to say. If I'm being too forthright, please stop me. Johnny loves you very much.' Maggie didn't look at her granddaughter as she spoke.

'You are very fond of him . . . but do you love him? If you married him on the rebound, I want you to remember one thing. Few marriages are made in heaven and all have to be worked at. Never be tempted to unburden yourself to Johnny. He would not understand. It's up to you, Eileen, to make your marriage work. Do you know what I mean?'

Eileen sat dumbfounded. She couldn't believe her ears. Her grannie knew Paul wasn't Johnny's son. No! She guessed the truth.

No one could possibly know, with the exception of Kate Rafferty and Sarah. But if her grannie had guessed, how many more were speculating about her son's parenthood?

'Eileen, don't look so worried. I don't think anyone else guesses.'

'Did me mam tell you?'

'No! Oh, no! I wasn't even aware that Sarah knew. Ah, Eileen, I'm sorry. I didn't mean to upset you. I should have kept my big mouth shut!'

'It's all right, Grannie. It's just . . . well, I thought no one guessed. I realize that you're right. I *have* been tempted to tell Johnny. You know what I mean . . . get rid of the guilt . . . I feel so deceitful, he is so good to me.'

'I don't think that would be a good idea, Eileen. He idolizes you.'

'Mmmm . . . I think you're right. I'll concentrate on making a good life for Johnny and Paul.'

'Good! And remember, if you ever need a shoulder to cry on, you're old grannie is always here. Come to me, won't you, love?'

'Ah, Grannie, you're not old.'

'You're as old as you feel and at the moment I feel about eighty. But remember, I'm here if you ever need me.'

'I will, Grannie. I sure will.'

Imagine her grannie worrying about her, and her with troubles of her own. Silently, Eileen vowed to stay close to her. That Maggie grieved for Bernard there was no doubt. To make it worse Granda Barney refused to speak about him; couldn't bear to hear his son's name mentioned. It was almost as if Bernard had died. So in a sense Maggie suffered her son's betrayal alone. Paul had been born at the right time. He had captured Maggie's heart and Eileen would make sure that she saw him as often as possible.

Chapter Four

Young Paul brought a whole new meaning to Eileen's life. She idolized him so much, Johnny secretly begrudged the child the attention Eileen lavished on him, although his own devotion to Paul was unquestionable. He was however relieved that Eileen seemed content with her lot. He was aware that her feelings for him were not as deep as he would wish them to be and was glad that Paul fully occupied her time.

During the fine summer days, walks in the Falls Park became a regular occurrence for Eileen. With Paul in his pram, she would load up with all the necessary requirements for the baby and herself and head up the Falls Road. Her young sister Emma never missed an opportunity to accompany her and was as proud as Punch whenever Eileen let her push the pram. Eileen's favourite spot was the part of the park up near the bus depot. They would dander through the length of the park and then, there by the stream, Eileen would sit for hours watching the water tumble along over age-worn stones. Seeing older children paddling happily in its clear shallow depths was her delight and she dreamed about the day when Paul would paddle there too. She felt restful here, proud and contented, sunbathing while Emma rocked the pram, lulling Paul to sleep. She was a lucky girl! Johnny was good to her and she had no money worries. Life wasn't so bad after all.

The park was a haven of tranquillity, especially in the summer and autumn months. Now, flower beds were in full bloom and the smell of new mown grass filled the air. In the surrounding trees song thrushes sang in contention with blackbirds and Eileen could happily have sat all day long drinking in this beauty that surrounded her, and making desultory conversation with other young mothers. However time passed all too quickly on these idyllic afternoons, and it seemed only minutes had elapsed when Paul, awakening with a cry, would warn her that not only did he need feeding, but that it was time to go home and make her husband's tea.

They had a very quiet social life. Whenever a good film came to the Broadway or Windsor Picture Houses, Eileen would ask Claire to babysit and she and Johnny would go out together. However, most evenings were spent quietly at home. They settled into a routine, with Johnny spending one night a week at the gymnasium and Eileen keeping herself busy around the house. All their spare money was used to make their home more comfortable. If at times Johnny examined his son with suspicion Eileen was unaware of it. She had confessed her sins in the confessional, and the priest had lectured her on her morals. Then he had told her to forget the past and concentrate on keeping her husband and child happy.

It was in the autumn, when the days shortened and the trees flaunted their beautiful changing mantle of yellow, bronze and gold, preparing to shed their leaves for another season, that Eileen, confined to the house in the evenings, began to fret for lost chances. When Claire visited her she was full of talk of the dances she frequented in the Club Orchid and Orpheus Ballrooms, and the boys who partnered her. Eileen longed to be free. That she loved her son there was no doubt but he tied her down. How she longed to dress up in the latest style and go out dancing! Tentatively, she asked Johnny to take her to the Orpheus Ballroom on a Saturday night

132

but he refused. Aware of his wife's restlessness, Johnny was afraid to take her to public places where he knew men would show how attractive they found her. Eileen was so young. What if she was attracted to some man in return? It was far too risky! So he made all sorts of excuses whenever she asked him to take her dancing.

Maggie watched her granddaughter with apprehension. She remembered how Sarah, tied down with two children before she was twenty-one, had chafed at the ties that bound her to Mick. She remembered how horrified she had been when she realized that Sarah was infatuated with Gerry Docherty, who at that time was Maggie's next-door neighbour. It had been a traumatic time and had led to so much conflict that Sarah had asked Mick to leave the house. In despair of ever winning his young wife back, he had turned to another woman for solace, a young widow called Maisie Simpson. Not wanting history to repeat itself, Maggie considered ways to occupy Eileen. At last she came up with a bright idea and the first chance she got she outlined her plan to her granddaughter.

True to the vow she had made when Paul was born, Eileen visited Maggie regularly and the bond between them had grown and strengthened. However, she reacted with surprise when her grannie voiced the plan she had come up with regarding her granddaughter's future.

'Go out to work?' Eileen was puzzled and showed it. 'Ah, Grannie, Johnny would never hear tell of it! You know that! He won't even take me out to the odd dance.'

'No ... I don't mean for you to go out to work ... I mean for you to work from home.' When Eileen still looked perplexed, Maggie explained, 'Barney was saying how he needed someone to look after his books. You know, keep him right with the tax man? That's what you did at Maguire's factory, wasn't it?'

'Yes, it was, and I was very good at my job,' Eileen assured her. 'Mr Mooney was very sorry to lose me. He suggested I might like to return to work after the baby was born, but I knew Johnny would object, so I didn't bother to ask him.'

'And would you not fancy working from home? Surely Johnny couldn't object to that?'

Eileen sat for some moments in thought, then she nodded as she came to a decision. 'I think you're right, Grannie! So . . . whether Johnny likes it or not, I'll give it a try. I'm bored stiff stuck at home all day long. I'll soon not know how to conduct a sensible conversation any more unless it's in baby talk. I'll need to talk Johnny into buying me a typewriter, but that shouldn't be a problem.'

'No, Eileen. Be independent! I'll lend you the money to get started. You can pay me back when you get established.'

'*If* I get established.'

'Ah, Eileen . . . be positive! *When* you get established,' Maggie chided her, 'Barney will spread the word and he is sure that a few business friends of his will also be glad to employ you, so it could work out all right for you.'

'Do you know something, Grannie? You've just made my day! The more I think about it, the better I like the idea. I was feeling so frustrated. Now I will have something to occupy me.' Eileen raised an eyebrow at Maggie. 'Are you by any chance making work for idle hands, eh? Making sure I keep out of mischief?'

Maggie laughed, but Eileen noted that her cheeks were quite rosy. Reaching over, she squeezed her hand. 'Thanks, Grannie. I'm indebted to you. I'll make a go of it, even if it kills me.'

'I know you will put every effort into it. I have faith in you, so I'll lift some money from the bank and you can buy a typewriter, and all the odds and ends that you will need to go with it. How much do you think you'll need?'

They sat for some time discussing just what Eileen would need to get started and how much it would all cost. It was with a light heart that Eileen left to go home and talk it over with Johnny.

To her surprise, Johnny raised no objections to her working from home. The only fault he found was her intention to borrow money from Maggie, saying he would be more than willing to buy her a typewriter. Eileen refused his offer, knowing that she would have more incentive to work hard if her success depended on her alone. The typewriter was purchased and Eileen set to work with a will. An advertisement was placed in her granda's shop window but most of her contacts came by word of mouth as her grandfather and Jim Rafferty spread the news. Slowly but surely her little business took off and as more work came her way, she discovered that she was pregnant again. She decided to ask Claire to assist her; suggesting that her sister worked two hours, Monday and Wednesday evenings. Claire was now a typist in an office in Bedford Street and was only too glad to comply. Besides giving her the opportunity to earn some extra money, it was also good experience for her. It helped her increase her typing speed, and since she had her sights set on becoming a secretary this was a bonus for her.

Paul was fifteen months old when Louise was born. Red-haired and blue-eyed, she captured Johnny's heart in a way his son never had but still Johnny pulled his weight about the house and cared for the children when Eileen had to work late or on Saturdays.

At last the day arrived when Eileen was in a position to clear her debt with Maggie. Armed with a huge box of chocolates, she set off down the street, feeling very happy within herself. She had tried to repay the debt earlier, but Maggie assured her that there was no hurry and told her to wait until her business was well off the ground. Now at last she was well established. She was also four months pregnant.

After a protracted wait, it was Maggie who opened the door to her knock, and to Eileen's dismay she noticed that her grannie's eyes were red-rimmed and puffy, showing signs of recent tears. Concerned, Eileen closed the door and put the chocolates to one side. Taking Maggie in her arms, she held her close.

'What's wrong, Grannie? Are you not feeling well?'

Since Bernard's departure from the house Maggie's health had caused concern all round. The weight slowly disappearing from her formerly buxom figure had left her gaunt and frail-looking.

Maggie let her granddaughter render comfort to her for some moments. Then she gently released herself from Eileen's embrace and led the way into the living room.

'I had some bad news earlier today. Bernard got married in a Register Office yesterday. Imagine . . . he didn't even invite us to the wedding, or even let us know that he was getting married. Where did I go wrong, Eileen?'

'Ah, Grannie, I'm so sorry. And listen, you didn't do anything wrong, so don't you go blaming yourself! Why, you have always been a good mother.'

'Perhaps I should have made a greater effort to persuade him to come home. I thought that, given time, it would all blow over. I was so sure that he would tire of Emily Gordon. But I was wrong.'

'How's Granda Barney taking it?'

'Awful . . . he's locking it all inside himself. Won't even talk to me about it. He's so disappointed, so he is. He's down in Rafferty's at the moment.'

'Is there anything I can do to help?'

'Well . . . I was wondering how to break the news to the rest of the family . . . will you tell them, Eileen? I don't want everybody coming here offering their condolences as if Bernard was dead. Explain to them that Barney and I don't want to talk about it. At least, not for the moment. Perhaps later, when it doesn't hurt so much.'

'I'll make sure nobody intrudes on your privacy, Grannie. Can I do anything else?'

'Yes, love. Talk to me! Take my mind off it. Tell me, what brings you here at this time of night?'

'Well . . . I thought I'd nip down and repay my debt. It's also an excuse to have a wee chat with you.'

'Are you sure you can afford to pay me now? I told you there was no hurry, didn't I?'

'Yes, I know you did, but I can afford the money now, Grannie. Thanks to Granda and Jim Rafferty, my wee business is flourishing.'

Eileen counted several five pound notes into Maggie's hand, but when she would have added an extra five pounds for interest, Maggie would not hear tell of it.

'I don't want to make any money from you. What's family for if they can't help each other?'

There were tears in Eileen's eyes when she hugged Maggie close. Her grannie was so good to her. 'I've brought you a big box of chocolates. They're your favourites! You won't refuse them, I hope?'

'Now you're appealing to my weakness. You know I would never refuse chocolates.'

The sound of the back door opening, caused Maggie to put a finger to her lips. 'Mum's the word,' she whispered, and when Barney entered the room, they were discussing Eileen's welfare.

Five months later Eileen gave birth to another baby girl, Marie. This child favoured Eileen with dark auburn hair and grey eyes. As he gazed on her, Johnny once again experienced emotions he had never felt towards his son. Perhaps that was how it worked; men loved their daughters and women doted on their sons. His heart swelled with pride and when, directly after her birth, his tiny daughter gripped his proffered finger and appeared to smile at him, he thought his heart would burst.

Fearful of another pregnancy too soon, Eileen eventually plucked up the courage to voice her concern to Johnny. To her dismay he disagreed with her, saying that they had lived up to their religion so far and were doing very well, so why spoil things? He reminded her that the family came first, and if her job was proving too much for her she would have to give it up. She assured him that her work was not the problem but that she did not want a house full of children. She also assured him that she did not intend using artifical contraception but tentatively suggested that they try the rhythm method which was permitted by the church and which Dr Hughes had mentioned to her on one of her visits to his surgery. Johnny would not hear of this, so each month Eileen breathed a sigh of relief when her period arrived. However her frequent headaches put a strain on their marriage. Determined not to become pregnant, she kept Johnny at arm's length whenever possible. She was trying to use the rhythm method without her husband's knowledge and so far it was working fine.

Giving a deep chuckle, Eileen laughed across the table at her husband. She was reading a letter which had just arrived in the morning post. Johnny's heart gave a lurch as he gazed at her. Lately her smiles were few and far between and he sensed that she was yearning for something beyond his scope. He loved her so very much. However, he was aware that he cared more than she did. To outsiders they appeared a happily married couple, but Johnny knew there were parts of Eileen he could never fathom. Physically she was his, although their unions were now few and far between, but mentally, well . . . there was something . . . a barrier that he had never been able to break through.

'What do you think?' she asked, with a light laugh. 'Kate Rafferty's getting married.'

'Ah, now that is good news!'

'Yes, I'm delighted for her. She's a good person. Really genuine!' Eileen agreed with him, 'I'm glad she's met someone at last. She wants me to be matron of honour.'

Johnny continued buttering a slice of toast. He knew what that would mean. A big function where men would ogle his wife and want to dance with her. That he could do without!

'Oh, won't it be great, Johnny? Just think! A day out.'

Johnny sighed. How could he refuse, especially after all Kate had done for them? Hadn't she brought them together? Against his better judgement, he asked, 'Would you like to be matron of honour?' He wanted to see her smile again, longed to please her.

Eileen inclined her head and waited, breathless. She had every intention of being matron of honour, but marriage to Johnny had taught her that it was better if he thought he was in control of every situation, and she was learning how to manoeuvre things so that he thought he was boss.

'All right then,' he said, and his reward was another wide smile.

At a knock on the door Eileen addressed her son, 'That'll be your grannie, Paul. Go and let her in, please.'

Paul, who had just celebrated his fifth birthday the week before, ran to obey her, followed as usual by his shadow, Louise.

Sarah entered the room, a teasing question on her lips. 'Have the children been good this morning?'

'Well now, let me think,' Eileen teased, but seeing a worried frown crease her son's brow, she relented. 'Yes, Paul and Louise have been as good as gold, but Marie is still asleep.'

'Here you are then, Paul.' A small bag of dolly mixtures was placed in his hand, and eyes aglow he beamed his thanks at his grannie. Next Louise received her gift, and after receiving a thank you kiss from her granddaughter, Sarah inquired after the baby of the family, 'Is Marie poorly, then?'

'Yes, Mam,' Eileen grimaced. 'We had a bad night with her. I wish those back teeth would hurry up and come through.'

'Poor wee mite.' Sarah was all sympathy. Then she turned her gaze on her son-in-law. 'And how are you this morning, Johnny?'

'I'm fine, Mrs Ross, and I don't have to ask how you are, you look full of beans. How's Mr Ross?'

'Working hard as usual.'

'Sorry I'm so like him.' Johnny sighed, and rising from the table, lifted his coat and slipped his arms into it. 'I'd better be off now, or I'll be late for work. See you soon, Mrs Ross.'

'Goodbye, Johnny.'

Johnny kissed Eileen on the cheek and hugged his two children before hurrying off. When the back door closed on him, Eileen turned to her mother. 'I had a letter from Kate this morning, Mam, and what do you think? She's getting married . . . to a schoolteacher no less!'

'Well now, isn't that nice? Kathleen'll be tickled pink.'

'I'm going to be matron of honour,' Eileen announced, with a happy smile.

'Oh! And what had His Nibs to say about that?' Sarah's voice was dry. It annoyed her the way Johnny still kept Eileen on a short rein and rarely took her out anywhere special. The kids had more freedom! Why Eileen put up with it, she would never know.

'Actually, he was quite agreeable.'

'Huh! That's a change for him. When's the wedding?'

'In July! The twelfth fortnight. I suppose she's having it then because everybody will be off for the summer break. It's on a Friday and . . . wait for it!' She held up her hand dramatically, 'She's bringing her fiancé home

140

this weekend to meet the family, and deliver his letters of freedom to Father McKenna.'

Sarah's eyebrows climbed. 'Posh, eh? No ordinary boyfriend for Kate. Well, she deserves the best, she's a good girl.'

Noting the sad droop to Eileen's mouth, she hurried on, 'I've some good news too. Claire brought her boyfriend home last night. He's a lovely lad. It looks serious between them.'

'Yes, I've met him.'

'You never said!'

'Well, when I say I've met him, I'm exaggerating a bit. He's picked Claire up from here a few times, after she finished work. But . . . from the way Claire talks, I don't think that she's serious about him.'

'That's a pity. He seems a nice lad. He's from the Glen Road. Him and your da got on well.'

'Hmm.'

Sarah was sorry she had mentioned that. Even though he'd tried to befriend Johnny, Mick found it hard to be sincere with him, and her daughter was aware of it. Of course Mick didn't know how Eileen had deceived Johnny, so blamed him for ruining his daughter's life. Not that her life was ruined! As Sarah frequently pointed out to her husband, hadn't she all her wants? Still, Mick thought that she had married too young; lamented that Johnny had wasted Eileen's youth.

Sarah continued. 'I've another bit of good news. Sister Carmel sent for me yesterday. She wants us to let Emma go to St Dominic's School of Further Education. What do you think of that?'

'Oh, Mam. Now that is good news. It's a wonderful opportunity for her, but will she go?'

Sarah nodded. 'Aye, she surprised us. She's thrilled to bits at the idea. Your dad's ever so proud, and your grannie's delighted. She's even offered to buy her school uniform for her.'

'Can you afford to keep her on at school?'

'Just about, it'll be worth a few sacrifices. Beth was pleased when she heard the news. She was worrying about how she'd get Mary to school when Emma left. Now she doesn't have to worry. If Emma goes to St Dominic's she'll still be able to take Mary down to St Vincent's every morning. Save Beth the journey.'

'She should have sent her to St John's School. But, oh no ... that's not good enough for Tommy Rogan's kids! At least they wouldn't have to troop up and down that road when the weather's bad. I think if kids have any brains at all they'll learn, no matter what school they go to.' Eileen broke off and sighed. 'Listen to the rants of me. It's none of my business which school Beth sends her kids to. That's her and Tommy's decision. Anyhow, how is Beth?'

Sarah didn't agree with Eileen. Where education was concerned the Sisters of Charity in St Vincent's School in Dunlewey Street had a reputation for getting good results. Professional people sent their children from as far away as Fort William on the other side of town to receive their primary education there.

However, Sarah had no intention of arguing with her daughter. 'She's fed up to the teeth, so she is. And she takes it all out on Tommy. I went round to see her last night and she was in a tizzy. Poor Tommy will be glad when this pregnancy comes to an end, he gets the backlash of all her frustration.' Sarah sighed deeply. 'To tell you the truth, I think that she has her dates mixed up or else it's a boy. Boy's are lazy, you know.'

'Beth will be delighted if she does get a boy.'

'At the moment she doesn't care what she gets, so long as the child is all right. All she wants is to get it over and done with.' Sarah laughed softly and confided, 'I know this much ... Tommy Rogan will be glad when it's all over. To think that Beth thought she was going to be childless because she didn't conceive right away.

And then to have three children inside five years! That should keep her quiet. I suppose she will be like you and want a break after this one.'

'Our Beth is spoilt, so she is! She wears the trousers in that house. You can bet that there will be no more children, if she says so! She doesn't know she's living. Why, she can fly her kite, do whatever she likes, and Tommy will just smile benignly . . .' Eileen paused for breath but seeing that her mother was about to dispute this statement, she hurried on, 'Oh, I know! I know that she doesn't do anything out of the ordinary, but . . . she could if she wanted to! That's the difference between Beth and me. She's in control!'

Eileen started to clear the table and Sarah watched her closely. Less than six years of marriage and three children had changed her daughter. Gone was the flat-chested teenager and in her place was a beautiful young woman with a high rounded bust and slim hips. Sarah marvelled how anyone could come through all that Eileen had and still look so beautiful. However, the big grey eyes always seemed to be shadowed, giving Eileen a haunted look. And no wonder! Eileen should tell Johnny the truth about Paul. The child favoured no one on their side of the family; he was probably the picture of his real father, and although the jokes of 'What colour hair has the coalman?' were now few and far between, Johnny must look at Paul sometimes with suspicion. Not that he showed it! He obviously loved the boy. Eileen should tell him the truth and then perhaps the shadow would leave her eyes.

Eileen paused in her task and eyed her mother. 'Why are you looking at me like that, Mam?' she inquired, a puzzled frown creasing her brow.

'I'm just thinking how young you still look,' Sarah replied. 'Look . . . don't you bother coming out this morning. I'll take Paul over to school for you if you like?'

'Oh, Mam, would you? That would be great! I have

some invoices to get off today and I'm behind with my audits.' Impulsively, Eileen hugged Sarah. 'Thanks for everything, Mam. I don't know how I'd manage without you.'

Embarrassed but pleased, Sarah cried, 'Oh, get away. You'd manage all right. You're a fighter, so you are. Come on, son.' She lifted Paul's blazer. 'Here, put this on and let's get you over to school, son.'

Madge Cleary was standing on a chair cleaning her parlour window. When they drew near she climbed down and leant on the garden gate to greet them.

'You're out a early this mornin', Sarah.'

After many years they were at last on easy terms with each other.

'Well, you know what they say, Madge. The early bird catches the worm,' Sarah jested. 'But to be truthful . . . all I ever catch is the cold.'

Madge chuckled, and reaching over the gate she chucked Paul under the chin. 'How're you, Paul? Is your grannie taking you to school?'

Paul grinned and nodded; both his grannies spoilt him.

Madge dug into her apron pocket and produced a penny. 'Here, son, buy yourself a couple of gobstoppers.' Her look at Sarah was inquiring. 'Is Eileen not well?'

'Oh, she's fine. Just very busy. She's a wee bit behind with her work so I offered to take Paul over to school,' Sarah assured her.

Madge's attention returned to her grandson. 'Amp't I goin' to get a big kiss for that penny then?' she cried reproachfully.

Dutifully Paul raised his face and Madge kissed him.

'I'll have to run on now,' Sarah cried, and grabbed the hand that Paul was using to wipe Madge's kiss from his lips. 'See you later, Madge. Say goodbye to your Grannie Cleary, Paul.'

'Bye-bye, Grannie.'

'Goodbye, son, goodbye, Sarah.'

With a final wave Sarah continued down the street, wishing Madge had not mentioned gobstoppers. Those big sweets were a curse. Why, a child could choke on one of them. But her worries were allayed, Paul was content to settle for some wine gums. After she had left him at St John's School, she turned down into Clondara Street. She had decided to call and take young Margaret, Beth's second child, home with her, and give her daughter a bit of a break.

It was Tommy who opened the door to his mother-in-law's knock and she could see that he was in a right state.

'Thanks be to God you're here, Sarah. I've just been down to your house. Beth's started! Will you stay with her while I go for Nurse Lancaster?'

Sarah had already removed her coat and was on the stairs. 'Away you go, son. Is wee Margaret upstairs?'

'Aye, I didn't know what else to do with her.'

'Mam? Is that you, Mam? Oh, thank God!' Beth's voice, ending in a wail of pain, reached Sarah and she continued in haste up the stairs. 'Yes, love, I'm here. Everything is going to be all right.'

Her eldest daughter lay on top of the bedclothes, her face the colour of death, and three-year-old Margaret stood wide-eyed by the side of the bed.

'Come here, pet. Come on, love.' Taking the child by the hand, Sarah led her from the room and down the stairs. Making sure that the fireguard was securely in place and her granddaughter could come to no harm, she said, 'Will you stay here, love, and play with your toys, while I help your mammy?'

Without waiting for an answer, Sarah rushed back up the stairs again in answer to Beth's renewed cries of pain. 'Mam, it's different this time. Something's wrong, I know it is. Ahhh, I know something's wrong.'

Sarah looked down at her daughter and wished she knew more about delivering babies. Kathleen Rafferty now, she'd know what to do. Everybody sent for Kathleen. Well, Kathleen wasn't here, so it was up to her. With this thought, Sarah rolled up her sleeves and said with more confidence than she felt, 'You're going to be all right, love. Let's get that dressing gown off and get you under the bedclothes in case of accidents. We don't want any unnecessary washing, do we?'

When Tommy returned he was distraught. 'Nurse Lancaster's out on another call. What are we going to do, Sarah?' he cried, and she could see panic reflected in his eyes.

Eyeing the basin, towels, and baby gowns spread out ready for use, she said, 'Put plenty of water on to boil. Then go and fetch Kathleen Rafferty. If Kathleen's not at home, fetch me mam.' Maggie could be relied on in times of trouble; she could probably deliver the baby if called upon, for that matter.

With another worried look at his wife moaning and writhing about on the bed, Tommy flew down the stairs.

'Ah, Mam! It's coming, it's coming! Ohhh . . . where's that nurse? She should be here, so she should! It's coming. Ahhh!' Beth yelled aloud.

'Well then, love, let it come. Don't fight it. Come on now. Hang on to me and push.'

Beth clung on to Sarah's hand and strained hard.

'That's right, love,' Sarah encouraged her. 'Now take a breather. Just pant . . . pant, love. Good . . . now when another pain comes, use it. Push for all you're worth.'

They had not long to wait for another pain and Sarah panicked a bit as she realized that the baby could be born any minute now. Was she capable of delivering it? She could only do her best! She was all Beth had to help her at the moment. When Sarah saw the head start to emerge she realized that the time for the nurse was past. There wasn't even time to send for the doctor. It was up to her to deliver this baby; her and Beth. Then all rational thoughts fled as maternal instinct took over and she was caught up in the most memorable moment of her life.

'Right, Beth. Push! Come on now, push! Good girl. Now rest a minute. Hold on, just pant ... take deep breaths ... that's my girl, use your pains. The baby's almost here, love.' But in spite of all Beth's pushing and straining the baby stayed firmly wedged. Perspiration gathered on Sarah's brow, as she cajoled and pleaded with her daughter. 'Come on now, Beth, come on, push! That's right, love ... come on now, one good big push. Good! That's right, love.' Once the head was free Sarah sighed with relief. 'One more big push will do it, love.' Beth obliged her. The shoulders came through and the baby slithered out. 'It's a girl,' Sarah yelled. 'My hasn't she got a good pair of lungs?'

A flushed, triumphant Sarah turned to greet Kathleen Rafferty when she hurried into the room, closely followed by an anxious Maggie. 'What do ye think of that, Kathleen? I've just delivered my first baby. Isn't that great?'

Beth was up on an elbow. 'Is she all right? For heaven's sake, let me see her, Mam.'

'Sorry, love. Sorry ...' As she turned, Sarah realized that the cord was still attached. 'Kathleen, will you do the needful with that?'

A loud knock on the door caught the women's attention. They heard Nurse Lancaster's voice in the hall and Tommy ushered her up the stairs and into the room.

Sarah gladly relinquished her place at the bedside. 'You've another wee daughter, Tommy,' she informed her son-in-law. 'My first delivery.'

Downstairs, she sat on the settee beside her granddaughter. 'You've a new wee sister, Margaret,' she said, hugging her close. 'A beautiful wee baby sister.'

147

'Baby . . . baby . . . Grannie?'

'Yes, love. A wee sister.'

Reaction was now setting in, and much to her surprise Sarah began to shake like a leaf. This was her first experience of delivering a baby and she hoped it was her last. For a while there she had been panic-stricken, picturing the baby dying through her inexperience. Poor Beth, with not having had time to send for the doctor she had torn herself; she would probably need a few stitches. The baby was big, much bigger than Mary or Margaret. Ah, well, the worst was over. Beth would soon be up and about and in the excitement of looking after the new baby all her pain would be forgotten. After all, it was part of married life.

'Has Beth any whiskey or brandy in the house, Sarah? You could do with a drop, so you could, to settle your nerves.'

Sarah turned gratefully to Maggie. 'I don't know, Mam. Look in that cupboard over there.'

A bottle of Bushmills was uncovered and when the drinks were passed round, Maggie raised her glass. 'To the baby's good health.'

Sarah raised her glass, and clinking it against Maggie's and then Kathleen's, repeated, 'To the baby.' When they had all drunk the baby's health Sarah gestured towards Kathleen. 'And a toast to your Kate. May she have a long and happy marriage.'

Kathleen gaped at her with surprise. 'How did you know? I was just about to tell you the good news myself.'

'Our Eileen got a letter this morning. Kate wants her to be matron of honour.'

'I know she does. And do you know something else? That's all my prayers answered. Our Kate's almost twenty-six. I thought she was going to be left on the shelf. Mind you . . . that'll still leave Kevin at home, although I don't think he'll ever get married.'

'Why not? He's a good-looking lad . . . of course

he will. Some girl will soon snap him up,' Maggie assured her.

A sad look settled on Kathleen's face. 'I think he's in love with a married woman,' she confessed.

Sarah's eyes widened; she had heard rumours, but to hear it put into words by Kathleen, took her breath away. 'Who? Who is she?'

'Oh, never mind. Perhaps I'm wrong. Least said, soonest mended . . . that's what I say.' Unhappy with the interest she had aroused, Kathleen pleaded, 'Please forget I ever mentioned it. I'm probably wrong anyway.'

And try though Sarah did, Kathleen was not to be drawn.

Eileen hugged Kate close and cried, 'Oh, it's good to see you again, Kate.'

Her friend drew back, and still holding Eileen, looked at her questioningly. 'You will be matron of honour, won't you, Eileen?'

Eileen nodded happily and with a sigh of relief Kate turned to the man behind her and drew him forward. 'Eileen, this is Peter Madden.'

Eileen could see at once why Kate had called him her fiancé, and not just her boyfriend. This was no boy. He was a mature man. Not much taller than her friend, he was of muscular build and gave off an air of assurance. Dark hair tumbled boyishly over a high forehead, and from behind horn rimmed spectacles brown eyes twinkled.

'Am I glad to meet you at last!' he greeted her. 'Kate never stops talking about you.'

Eileen loved his soft Southern brogue and as he clasped her hand warmly in his, she instinctively trusted him. 'All good, I hope?' Glancing at Kate she gave a small nod of approval before continuing. 'Well, you won't have a very good opinion of me, keeping you standing here in the draughty hall. Come on in and meet my husband.'

149

Johnny rose to his feet to greet them. His arms opened wide to embrace Kate and she closed her eyes as he hugged her close. It was a wonderful sensation to be in his arms for the first time. When he released her and turned to welcome Peter, Kate went to the settee and sat down. She needed a few moments to gather her wits about her. Her feelings for Johnny had been the main reason why she had sought work in the South. The very idea of Eileen and Johnny being married and living together had been the cause of an unbearable ache in her and she had to get away. But that was long ago! She loved Peter Madden, so why did Johnny still affect her so much! Why, she was trembling like a young teenager in love for the first time. Did one's first love always have the power to thrill? Eileen could see that Kate was distinctly ruffled and wondered why. Later, when Kate followed her out to the kitchen as she retired to make the tea, Eileen questioned her, 'Are you all right? You seemed a bit ill at ease at first.'

Alarmed that Eileen had noticed her reaction to Johnny, Kate said teasingly, 'I'm fine. I see your imagination still works overtime.'

Sitting beside the comforting presence of Peter had put things back in perspective again for Kate and now she had her emotions under control. It was her turn to question Eileen.' 'How are you enjoying married life?'

'Hummmm, not bad . . . not bad at all.'

'Are you happy, Eileen?' Kate asked softly, her eyes alert.

Not realizing the sadness that lurked deep in her eyes, Eileen smiled. 'Yes. Johnny and I get along fine.' Her smile broadened. 'And I have the children. Would you like to see them before we make the tea?'

'Oh, yes. Indeed I would.' There was a deep ache within Kate. For years she had envied her friend. In spite of the way Eileen and Johnny had got married, Kate could not imagine her friend being anything but happy married to a man like Johnny Cleary, but there was something amiss. An outsider would not be aware of it but Kate knew Eileen too well to be taken in. As for Johnny, well, he was the perfect host and it was apparent that he still adored Eileen, so why didn't Eileen count her blessings? Kate realized that her friend had missed out on a lot by marrying so young. Did she now regret her marriage to Johnny? Kate managed to hide her concern, and running her eyes over Eileen's figure she looked down at her own ample curves, and sighed. 'How do you manage to stay so slim, Eileen?'

'I'm far from thin! Why, I've put on a stone since the kids were born.'

'I didn't say thin, I said slim! There's a difference, you know. You could afford to put on weight. Remember how you used to lament about not having a cleavage?' When Eileen laughed outright at the memory, Kate added, 'Now you're curved in all the right places.' She followed Eileen out of the kitchen and up the stairs.

Quietly, they entered the back room and Kate gazed in wonder at Louise and Marie. 'They're beautiful,' she whispered, lifting a lock of Louise's hair and gently twisting it around her finger. 'Her hair's like silk. Oh, they are both just gorgeous.' As she turned away, with a grin and a widening of the eyes, she patted her stomach. 'Perhaps next year!'

'Quite probably!' Eileen agreed, and took her into the small box room where Paul slept. Looking down at his chubby face flushed with deep sleep, long dark eyelashes fanned out on pink cheeks, Kate thought of all the heartbreak he had unwittingly caused. She looked Eileen in the eye.

'Does Johnny know?'

'No!' Eileen's answer was abrupt and accompanied by a quick glance over her shoulder towards the bedroom door.

151

'It's all right! He can't possibly hear. Did Billy Greer ever make any effort to contact you?'

Eileen hesitated, debating whether or not to tell Kate the truth. At the time she had been too upset. Then shortly after Paul's birth, much to Eileen's surprise, Kate had gone down South to work and the opportunity had never presented itself again. Should she let sleeping dogs lie? No! Kate had a right to know.

'Billy's dead.'

Slowly Kate straightened up from her position by Paul's bed and mouthed one word, 'No!' her face full of anguish.

'Yes.' Eileen nodded. 'He crashed his motorbike on his way to meet me that night. Remember he was to take me home to meet his parents? Isn't it awful to think about? Me standing there waiting, and him lying under a tram, dead.'

'Would it have made any difference, Eileen? I mean, if you had known Billy was dead? Would you still have married Johnny?'

'I don't know.' Eileen shrugged and pondered for a moment. 'How do I know how I'd have reacted?'

'How did you find out about Billy?'

'It's a long story, Kate. I'll tell you about it some day, but not just now. Come on, let's go back down and make the tea.'

Eileen did not want to stir up emotions that were best forgotten and she led the way down the stairs, followed by a bemused Kate.

Primrose yellow was the colour Eileen and Kate had chosen for her to wear as matron of honour. The dress was made of taffeta with a silk overdress, and it suited Eileen to perfection, emphasizing the rich auburn sheen of her hair and adding a deep glow to her eyes. As she gazed at herself in the mirror, Eileen recalled the last time she had worn this colour: the night of the dance in the Floral Hall. Sadness settled like a mantle on her as memories were awakened. How different her life might have been had she not gone to that dance. She might in due course have met someone she could truly love, someone dark and handsome, and Johnny would surely have met another girl who would have lived up to his high standards.

Enough of that! she chastised herself. No regrets. Had she not a lot to be thankful for? Three lovely children and a beautiful home. Indeed, she had a lot to be thankful for! She could be a lot worse off. Johnny was jealous and possessive, there was no doubt about that, he watched her closely, but if she behaved herself she had nothing to fear, and she had no intention of misbehaving. After all, what you never had, you never missed.

As she left the bedroom Phillip's voice greeted her from the hall. 'You look stunning, Eileen.'

She had been greatly relieved when, shortly before Paul's birth, Phillip had gone over to work in England. His Friday night visits had been a terrible strain on her and his presence had proved overpowering. He was so dark and handsome, and his eyes had constantly tried to seduce her. He still came home every July for the twelfth holiday fortnight but most times she managed to stay out of his way. Today he must have come to collect the children. Madge was having them overnight, and they were all excited at the prospect, knowing that their grannie would pander to their every whim.

As she descended the stairs, Eileen saw Phillip's eyes rove over her body and felt naked. He always had the knack of making her feel vulnerable. His dark good looks reminded her of Billy Greer and she was wary of the emotions he managed to arouse in her. Hot colour stained her cheeks. He was ogling her lewdly. When she reached the hall she saw the flare of renewed interest darken his eyes and was glad Johnny was still in the bedroom. She had better keep out of Phillip's way, because if Johnny ever suspected his brother was making a pass at her, there would be hell to pay.

'Welcome home, Phillip. Are you enjoying your holiday?'

'Holiday? Ma has about fifty wee jobs all lined up for me to do, and you know what her wee jobs are like. It would take tradesmen a month to do them, but she expects me to do them in two weeks.' Phillip's voice was light, he had seen the warning in Eileen's eyes and brought himself under control. His guard had slipped just for a minute; he had forgotten how beautiful she was.

'Don't let Ma shove it on to you,' Johnny said, as he left the bedroom and came down the stairs behind Eileen. There was a scowl on his face. He dreaded this wedding, knowing full well all the young men would flock around his wife. How could they help it? She looked so lovely. If only he felt sure of her, things could be so different. If he could just be convinced that she loved him, he could cope. But he wasn't! She had never once said she loved him. Not once in six years of marriage. That must be a record of some sort, surely? Still, she must care. Surely she cared? She had married him, hadn't she? What further proof did he need? Still, he felt uneasy when he saw how other men were attracted to her. He preferred to keep her away from social gatherings. He only felt safe when she was with him or confined within these four walls. Now he regretted giving his permission for her to be Kate's matron of honour. It was going to be a long day for him.

'I'll do as many of the jobs as I can, Johnny. Then perhaps you'll do the rest,' Phillip answered slyly.

'I look after Ma all year round. It won't be out of turn for you to pull your weight. Have you come for the kids?'

'Aye!' Phillip lifted Marie up in his arms and glanced down at Louise and Paul. 'Say goodbye to your mam and dad, and we'll go down to the shop for some sweets.'

To Eileen's relief they obeyed him, and giving her the thumbs up sign he ushered them out of the house, just as the car arrived to take her and Johnny to the church.

The wedding ceremony brought a lump to Eileen's throat and when Kate and Peter made their vows she shed a few tears. Everything went smoothly and soon they were piling into the hired cars to go across town to Belfast Castle where the wedding luncheon was booked. Once the delicious luncheon was over Eileen left the bridal table and joined Johnny at the table he shared with her grandparents. She intended staying close to him, then he would have no cause for complaint. Really, they should go out more often, make new friends. If only she could persuade him to take her out dancing. Even as the thought entered her mind she discarded it. Johnny didn't want to make new friends. All he wanted was her and the kids. He was a stick in the mud. Well, Madge had tried to warn her, hadn't she? Still she really hadn't had any other choice at the time.

Once the dancing got under way, Eileen was besieged with partners. Peter's friends up from Dublin for the wedding all asked for a dance. Johnny could not complain without appearing surly because she danced every other dance with him. He tried to take his mind off her by giving duty dances to Beth and Maggie, Sarah and young Claire. He even managed to dance with the bride. However, try though he did to hold resentment at bay, jealousy still plagued him.

Glad that Johnny seemed to be enjoying himself, Eileen closed her eyes and succumbed to the rhythm of the music as her feet glided over the floor. Breathless and happy, she entreated Johnny to consider going to a dance once a week.

'It would break the monotony!' she cried. 'Give us something to look forward to.'

'Monotonous? Is that how you see our marriage?'

'No, of course not! I love the kids. Wouldn't be without them . . . but it would be nice to have a night out once a week. It's not as if we can't afford it.'

Johnny pondered on her words. She loved the kids. No mention of her feelings for him. He gazed at his wife: cheeks flushed with happiness, eyes aglow. So lovely! No wonder the men were queuing up to dance with her. His tone, when he answered her was non-committal. 'Perhaps. Perhaps we could go out, now and again.'

With this half-hearted promise Eileen had to be content.

Maggie observed Johnny's unrest as he watched Eileen twirl around the floor in the arms of different men and whenever possible engaged him in conversation, but his replies were abstracted. He was locked in his own tortured world of possessiveness. His eyes followed every move Eileen made, and Maggie's heart went out to him. He was a prisoner of his own jealousy, and only he could conquer it.

In the midst of all this gaiety and laughter, Eileen felt totally relaxed. Unused to alcohol, the Babychams she was drinking went to her head and she was really enjoying herself. The beer Johnny was consuming was having the opposite effect on him. He was sinking deeper and deeper into resentment against his wife. Why didn't she sit with him instead of dancing with every Tom, Dick and Harry? he asked himself. Seeing Kevin Rafferty heading their way, he silently answered his own question. Because he wasn't dark and handsome like Kevin Rafferty.

Eileen saw Kevin approach and quickly turned to her husband. 'Will you dance this one with me, Johnny?' she coaxed. 'It's your favourite, the "Moonlight Saunter".'

Aware that he was behaving like a child, Johnny declined and when Kevin asked her to dance with him, Eileen excused herself and entered his arms.

Johnny watched their every move. Kevin was a good

dancer and as he effortlessly led Eileen in and out of the steps of the 'Moonlight Saunter', he engaged her in light conversation. Eileen laughed up at something he said and Johnny felt rage build up inside him. They looked so well together. Kevin's dark curly hair a perfect foil for Eileen's auburn locks. They were so at ease with each other. Like everyone else, Johnny was aware of the rumours that circulated about Kevin chasing a married woman. Could it possibly be Eileen? Did everybody know but him? Were they all laughing at him behind his back? These thoughts brought him abruptly to his feet and unsteadily he made his way down the side of the dance floor and out of the door on to the curved stone stairway that led down into the castle gardens.

The cool air on his face soothed him. Lighting a cigarette, he descended the steps and dandered across the neat lawn and down a sloping bank. Dragging the smoke deep into his lungs, he released it in rings that hung on the still air. He would stay out here for a while and get control of himself. Otherwise he would not be responsible for his actions.

From the dance floor, Eileen watched her husband leave the room. When the dance was over she absent-mindedly nodded when Kevin asked her if she would like a drink, before making her way out on to the stone stairway and descending into the grounds. There was no sign of Johnny and there were so many paths that he could have taken that she realized it would be foolish to try and follow him. She was about to retrace her steps when Kevin arrived with drinks for them both.

'Oh, this is very kind of you, but you shouldn't have bothered.'

Kevin laughed softly. 'I asked you if you wanted a drink and you said yes,' he reminded her.

'Did I? Did I really?'

'Yes, you did!' Kevin assured her.

Eileen also laughed and sipped at the Babycham. 'I'm

a bit tipsy, you know. I don't usually drink alcohol,' she confided. 'In fact . . . I don't do anything much. Just work and look after the house and kids,' she added sadly.

At a loss how to take these confidences, he said, 'At least you have a home and kids. I have very little to look forward to.'

Eileen's sympathy was aroused. Like everyone else, she had heard the rumours. Now she questioned him, 'It's true then . . . these rumours I've heard.'

'Now what rumours would they be, Eileen?'

'Ah, come on now, Kevin. You must know people are talking. They say you're having an affair with a married woman.'

'Oh, are they now?'

'Yes. Is there any truth in it?'

'Will this information be for your ears only, Eileen?'

'For my ears only,' she eagerly agreed.

He moved away from the stone stairway and across the lawn towards a bench shaded by a large yew tree. Slowly she followed him. He waited until she was seated then sat down beside her.

'Who are they saying it is, then?' he asked with a wry smile.

'No one knows. In spite of all the snooping and prying.' Eileen's eyes teased him. 'You must be very careful.'

'I have to be. I love her very much and wouldn't do anything that might cause her pain. You see, she loves her husband and any hint of a scandal would result in her sending me packing.'

'Then you're not having an affair?'

'Oh, yes . . . I am, but on her terms.'

Eileen thought that this woman, whoever she was, must be very selfish, or else she would not keep a man like Kevin dangling on a string. Why, she was ruining his life. 'Aren't you being foolish?' she countered. 'I mean, a handsome man like you could pick and choose.'

'You don't understand, we love each other.'

'But you just said . . .'

'I know. I'm afraid I didn't make myself very clear. We are very much in love but her husband was injured in the war and he can't . . . you know.' He gestured with his hands and quirked a brow at her. A blush stained her cheeks but she nodded to show that she understood. Amused at her embarrassment, Kevin continued, 'He actually gives us his blessing but if she left him he would be devastated. He's a fine guy. I wouldn't do anything that would make him unhappy.'

'Ah, Kevin. How sad.' Eileen moved closer and placed her hand over his in a comforting gesture. 'You're a good person. You deserve a wife and children. I'm so sorry for you.'

Taking her hand between his, he sighed, 'It's a relief to talk to someone about it. You won't tell anyone . . . sure you won't? Just let them keep on guessing.'

'Of course I won't.' Leaning closer still, Eileen kissed him on the cheek and asked tentatively, 'Is it anyone I know?'

His eyes teased her. 'Still for your ears only?' When she nodded excitedly, he leant closer, his lips touching her ear, and whispered, 'No.'

She laughed. 'Perhaps you're right not to tell me. There are so many people near dead to find out who she is, I mightn't be able to keep my big mouth shut.'

'Oh, I think if you once gave your word my secret would be safe with you. But, honestly, it's no one you know.'

'Still . . . it's not fair! You deserve better, Kevin.'

As she moved away from him a movement amongst the trees to her left caught her attention. She turned in time to see Johnny take off across the lawn and dismay filled her. What had her husband seen? What construction had he put on her actions? What would he be thinking? The worst, that was for sure!

The room had been booked until nine o'clock and when the last waltz of the evening was announced Johnny still had not put in an appearance. To Eileen's surprise, her granda asked her to dance the last waltz with him.

'Why, Granda, this is an honour! But a surprise,' she teased. 'I thought you were supposed to have two left feet and only dared to dance with Grannie?'

'If I trample on you, you can blame her. I'm here on Maggie's orders. We noticed that Johnny seems to have left early?'

Eileen sighed. 'It would appear so. He went without saying a word to me.'

'Well then you must share our taxi home. All right?'

'That would be great, Granda. Thanks very much.'

Eileen was relieved; Kevin also aware of her plight, had offered to let her share his taxi. However, she had not thought that a good idea. Johnny was already incensed; to arrive home in the same car as Kevin would be adding fuel to the flames. Her grandparents had taken her off the hook.

The journey home was a quiet affair. Maggie and Barney, having for a few short hours managed to forget their disappointment over Bernard, had really enjoyed themselves. They were tired and happy and ordered the taxi driver to drop Eileen off first.

'Would you like us to come in for a minute, Eileen?' Maggie asked tentatively.

'No, Grannie, I'll be all right. I'll see you tomorrow, and thanks for the lift home. Good night . . . good night, Granda.'

The front of the house was in darkness and Eileen sent a little prayer heavenwards that Johnny would be in bed. If so she would spend the night on the settee. She was quickly disillusioned; when she entered the hall Johnny opened the living-room door. Ignoring his tight-lipped disapproval, she said lightly, 'Oh, are you still up? Would you like a cup of tea?' He did not deign to answer, so with a slight shrug, she said, 'Well then, I'm off the bed.'

She had enjoyed herself today; time enough tomorrow for recriminations. She headed for the stairs but was not to escape so lightly. Johnny was beside her in an instant and his fingers dug cruelly into her arm.

'You're hurting me.'

Still hanging on to her,. he growled, 'Tell me, Eileen. How come you and Kevin Rafferty are so pally? Have you two been carrying on behind my back? I've heard rumours about him and some married woman. Is it you? Is it?'

Amazed at his line of thinking, her hand rose in the air to slap his face, but he caught hold of it. She pulled away from him and when he abruptly released his hold on her she was taken unawares. Unable to keep her balance she fell heavily, catching her head on the sharp corner of the hallstand. For some seconds she lay stunned, trying to clear her blurred vision. Aghast, Johnny fell to his knees beside her.

'Ah, love . . .'

'Don't touch me, you brute! You sicken me, do you hear? You sicken me.' She staggered when she was at last upright, but when he once again moved to assist her, she cringed away from him. 'Leave me alone! You couldn't bear to see me enjoying myself, could you? For six years I've done everything your way, bowed to your every whim, but you couldn't bear to see me happy for a few short hours. And just tell me this: when would I have had the time to have an affair? Eh? You know every move I make! This beautiful house is like a prison to me. I may as well be in Armagh Jail for all the freedom I have here. Well, no more, do you hear me? No more! I've had enough.'

Again Johnny reached for her, a pleading look on his face, but this time she actually flailed wildly at him with clenched fists, her blows making contact with his face. Afraid of the great anger that seethed within him, he grabbed his jacket and quickly left the house. As the door

161

slammed behind him, Eileen's legs buckled beneath her as she fainted.

It was dark when she came to and for some seconds she was completely disorientated. She was stiff and cold and her head throbbed. Memory returned slowly, bringing with it a great well of bitterness and frustration. Sinking down on to the settee, she wept long and hard. Her life was all work and no play. Women twice her age had more fun. At last she wiped her eyes and, realizing that it was dark, rose stiffly on legs that tingled with pins and needles as circulation returned. Painfully she made her way across the room, clinging to the mantelpiece, and peering at the clock. Half-past ten! She had been unconscious for about an hour. Where was Johnny? God alone knew, but she had to get out before he returned.

She couldn't bear to face him now. She must get out of the house; get time to think.

Where could she go? To her grannie, where she brought all her troubles? No! It was late and her grannie was not a young woman. Anyhow, her grandparents would have retired by now. She couldn't knock them up. It wouldn't be fair. Her parents? No, she would hate to admit to her father that she had failed. She knew that over the years she had fooled most people, but she had never been able to pull the wool over his eyes. Her father knew that lately she was very restless, but she wouldn't bring her sorrows to his door. The first thing he was likely to do was seek Johnny out and give him a good hiding. This would be the excuse that her father had been waiting for ever since the day she had married Johnny. No, that would never do. So St James's Park was out of the question. Where then? Madge? Yes, she would go down to Madge's. She could trust her mother-in-law to keep her mouth shut.

Pulling on a coat to cover her dress, she quickly left the house. Men were straggling up from the pub. Some eyed her curiously as she hurried down the street. She kept her head bent, hoping no one would recognize her and stop to speak. She was struggling to lift the stiff latch of the garden gate when Phillip came up the street. Dismayed, she paused undecided as he joined her on the path. What would she do now? She had forgotten that he would be home too.

'Hello . . . this is a surprise. I suppose you've come to look in on the kids before you go to bed?'

Grasping at this pretence of normality, Eileen agreed with him. 'I wouldn't have believed I could miss them so much.'

'Hell!' Phillip was rummaging in his pockets. 'I've forgotten my key. I hope me ma hears us. She'll be in the kitchen preparing the vegetables for tomorrow's soup.'

He knocked on the door, very much aware of Eileen's closeness as the smell of her perfume filled his nostrils. Receiving no answer he knocked again, louder this time.

'I'm comin', I'm comin'. For heaven's sake, hang on. I can't move any faster!' Madge shouted indignantly, as she shuffled down the hall. Opening the door, she stepped back in surprise. 'Eileen . . . what brings you here at this time of night?'

'She just wants to see the kids. Well, can we come in, Ma?' Phillip sounded indignant. He couldn't understand why his mother was staring in dismay at Eileen, but with the light from the hall full on her face, Madge had seen what Phillip hadn't. The side of Eileen's face that was hidden from her son's gaze was discoloured, and blood had crusted on a wound on her temple. There were also telltale signs that she had been crying.

Eileen had forgotten about bumping her head. In her anxiety to escape before Johnny's return she hadn't bothered to look in the mirror. Now her hand went instinctively to her temple.

'Ma . . . will ye let us in, for heaven's sake?' Phillip cried in exasperation.

Madge turned and walked down the hall and they followed her. In the kitchen she faced Eileen.

'What happened?'

Only then did Phillip become aware that all was not well. His eyes scanned Eileen's face, noting the swelling at her temple, the dried blood. 'Who did that? Did our Johnny do that?' he roared.

'No! No, he didn't, I fell.' Eileen could see that they didn't believe her and repeated, 'Honestly . . . I did fall. He never touched me.'

'Here, love, sit down. I'll bathe that wound.' Madge pushed her gently towards the armchair, then turned to her son. 'Phillip, heat some water, and while you're at it, make us a pot of tea.'

He left the room, and Madge moved closer to Eileen. 'What happened?'

'Johnny was jealous of me dancing with other men,' she whispered. If she had remembered that Phillip was at home she would never have come here, but the damage was done so she must make the best of it. 'He left the reception early.'

Gently, Madge touched the bump on Eileen's head, causing her to wince. 'Did he do this?'

'No . . . he didn't. Ah, Madge, you know he's not violent! We had a bit of a scuffle and I fell, I hit my head against the hallstand, that's the truth Madge.'

'I thought maybe he'd found out about the boy. That would be enough to make any man violent.'

Eileen drew back in dismay and her mother-in-law laughed softly, 'Ah, daughter, did ye think you'd fooled me? Do you think I don't know a full-term baby when I see one?'

'What boy? What are you talking about?'

They were not aware that Phillip had entered the room.

164

'Never mind.' Madge's voice was curt.

Bewildered, he looked from one to the other and repeated, 'What boy? Who are you talking about?'

Madge said reluctantly, 'Paul isn't Johnny's child.' She immediately regretted the words. Why hadn't she kept her big mouth shut? When Paul was first born, Madge had assumed that Johnny, although he had denied it, in an endeavour to be sure of Eileen, had made her pregnant. However, as time passed, Madge was only too aware that Johnny was not the father of this dark-haired infant. There was no likeness to any of their family in him. She had been surprised that Johnny seemed to think that he was the father. Now she had let the cat out of the bag, and to Phillip of all the people! This was dangerous knowledge for him to have. Madge could see that her son was dumbfounded. He had always thought Eileen the epitome of innocence itself.

Speechless, Phillip stared at Eileen, waiting for her to deny this terrible accusation, but to his horror he could see it was the truth. Guilt and shame was written all over her face. He could not believe it! A good girl like Eileen Ross with an illegitimate child? Who was the child's father? How had Eileen managed to hoodwink Johnny? Johnny of all people. Didn't she realise that his brother idolized her? Why, if Johnny ever found out, he would kill her. Shaking his head in bewilderment, Phillip left the room.

After she had bathed the caked blood from the wound at Eileen's temple, and cleansed it with disinfectant, Madge fetched a nightdress and persuaded her daughter-in-law to sleep in her bed tonight. When she had taken a cup of hot sweet tea up to her, Madge then poured Phillip a cup and carried it into the parlour where he sat.

The look he gave her was full of anguish. 'Don't son. Don't blame her,' she entreated. 'Remember she was only a child herself when it happened, and she chose what she thought was the only way out. And mind you . . . they were getting on all right, so they were. It was jealousy that triggered this off. Something must have happened at the wedding today.'

'They were getting on all right?' The look Phillip threw his mother was derisive. 'Ah, Ma, catch yourself on ... how could she be happy? Why, she may as well be in Armagh Jail for all the freedom she has with him. Who is this other man and why didn't he marry her?'

'I've no idea, and I doubt if we'll ever know.' Madge sadly shook her head. 'Perhaps he was already married. Just remember, son, it's none of our business. And they were getting on all right, in spite of what you think. She has all her wants! Not many marriages are all love and kisses, ye know. There's many a girl would gladly exchange places with Eileen.'

Abruptly, Phillip rose to his feet and left the room. He couldn't bear to listen any more. Madge followed him into the hall and saw that he intended going out.

'Now, don't you do anything foolish,' she warned. 'Remember, it was her choice to marry Johnny. He's the one who was deceived, and she'll go back to him. Nothing's surer. For the kids' sake, she'll go back to him. So watch your step.'

'I need time to think. I'm going out for a walk.'

Outside the gate Phillip stopped, undecided, and gazed up the street. Then resolutely he strode up towards his brother's house. He had to find out if Eileen was telling the truth when she said that Johnny had not hit her. Finding the back door unbarred he stormed in, causing Johnny to rear up from his seat at the table in surprise.

Recognizing his brother, he sank down again in relief. 'You gave me a hell of a start there, barging in like that. What do you want at this time of night?'

Phillip could see that his brother was rightly; not drunk; but rightly, and this was very unusual. Had Johnny hit Eileen because of the drink?

'I came to find out how Eileen got the bump on her head.'

'What bump? And what the hell has it got to do with you, anyhow?'

'Did you hit Eileen? I want the truth, mind.'

'For your information, she fell.'

'And you just left her lying there? Eh? Eh? Why, you cowardly bastard! She told us she was unconscious for over an hour.'

'Unconscious?'

'Oh, don't act soft! You left her lying there . . .'

'I didn't!' Johnny interrupted him. 'She was standing in the living room when I left. As a matter of fact, she quite literally threw me out of the house.'

'Is that the truth?'

Johnny had had enough of this interference. Rising to his feet, he faced his brother. 'Tell me this! What friggin' business is it of yours how I treat my wife?'

'You ever touch her . . . and you'll soon find out! I'll make it my business, that's a promise. Lay one finger on her and you're for it, do you hear me?'

'Huh! What's been going on here then . . . right under my nose?'

Uttering an oath, Phillip teetered in front of Johnny. 'Nothing has been going on. Do you hear me . . . nothing! Your jealousy's making you imagine things. Eileen's too good-living to do any flirting about. How the hell she stays in this house with you I'll never know. She's got no freedom whatsoever, and it's easy to see she doesn't love you.'

'Did she say she doesn't love me? Did she? She married me of her own free will, you know! I didn't hold a gun to her head to make her do it. So what makes you think she doesn't love me? Eh?'

There was a great aching hurt in Johnny's breast. Was everyone aware that Eileen didn't love him?

It was on the tip of Phillip's tongue to say: Because she

was bearing another man's child, that's why! Somehow he swallowed the words, turning on his heels and leaving the house. When the door closed on him, Johnny locked and barred it. Obviously Eileen would not be home tonight and he did not want any more unexpected visitors.

Madge had given her some aspirins, but still Eileen could not sleep. The throbbing pain in her head had, for a while, subsided to a dull ache and she yearned for sleep, but in vain. She knew she would need all her strength next day if she was to convince Johnny that her actions with Kevin Rafferty were innocent. To be fair, it must have looked bad, her holding Kevin's hand and kissing him on the cheek and him whispering in her ear. Johnny probably thought that Kevin was kissing her. She couldn't really blame her husband if he thought the worst. However, one thing she was sure of . . . there was no way she was going to leave the house. She had put too much hard work into the last six years just to walk away from it. So somehow or other she had to convince Johnny that she wasn't in the least bit interested in Kevin. She wept long and sore for all she had missed out on. Tears are a waste of time, she warned herself, but somehow she felt better for them and at last sleep claimed her.

On the other side of the wall, Phillip could hear her muffled sobs and lay clenching his fists in frustration. He was surprised at the great storm of emotions that had been awakened when he saw Eileen in need. He longed to go to her, to hold and console her, but he knew she would not want him to witness her humiliation. When he thought he could bear the anguish no longer, the sobs trailed off and he knew she was asleep. However sleep still eluded him. He was debating whether or not he should give up his job in England and stay here, to be nearby in case she needed his protection. But would that be wise? It would be difficult to obtain his kind of work in Belfast at the moment and to leave a good job in England to go on the dole would be foolish. The best thing to do would be to persuade Eileen to leave Johnny and return to England with him.

These thoughts astounded him. Phillip Cleary wanting to run off with a married woman who had three children? And his sister-in-law to boot? The scandal it would cause! His mother, and Eileen's family, would all be up in arms against them and the church would excommunicate them. Still he would be willing to face anything to have Eileen for his own. He was amazed at the strength of his feelings for her. This deep passion was new to him. If she was willing he didn't see any reason to worry about her husband or family. He knew it was wrong, yet here he was contemplating asking her to leave Johnny and set up home with him. He tossed and turned, until at last, still undecided, he fell into a troubled sleep.

Johnny was not at home next morning when Madge called at the house to collect clean clothes for Eileen. She was glad that she didn't have to face him. After all, he was her son and he had been deceived. What if Eileen was lying and Johnny had hit her? Madge would find it difficult to condemn him. She was heart-broken for him, as well as Eileen. He was a good husband and father and that he loved Eileen, there could be no doubt. A possessive misguided love, but a love he had carried for many a long year. Eileen should never have married him. If she loved him there would be no problem, for he would get her the sun if he could, but he must be aware that there was no deep affection in Eileen for him, and that was the root of the trouble. He was afraid of losing her and his desire to keep her was pushing her further away.

When Eileen was dressed and ready to go home, she descended the stairs and the children clambered up to greet her.

'Did you sleep in Grannie's bed last night, Mammy?' asked Paul, his eyes bright and inquisitive.

'Yes, love, I did.'

Marie held her arms up to be lifted and when Eileen obliged, she tentatively touched her mother's face. 'Did you fall down, Mammy?'

'Yes, I fell down, love.'

Louise, whilst endeavouring to give her mother a kiss, accidentally bumped heads with her, and Eileen winced.

Paul cried in sympathy. 'Is it very sore, Mammy? How did you hurt it?'

'I bumped it when I fell, love.'

'Did you hurt your eye too, Mammy?' Louise queried.

Eileen and Madge looked at each other, and Madge said, 'Oh, for the innocence of children!'

Wrapping a scarf around her head, Eileen covered as much as possible of the bruises left by her accident. To her dismay, when she rose to leave, Phillip was waiting in the hall. He insisted on carrying Marie up the street. At the door she thanked him, making it obvious that she did not want him to come in.

Reluctantly, he set Marie down and slowly turned away, but not without a last word. 'Remember, I'm just down the street if you need me.' He left her standing surrounded by her children, and his heart was heavy.

Ushering the children into the parlour, Eileen warned Paul to keep his sisters there until she called them. Johnny was at the stove when she entered the kitchen. He was stirring something in a pot and did not look up, not even when she approached and stood close to him.

'Johnny . . . it wasn't what you think.'

At these words he swung round to face her. 'Oh! And how do you know what I think? Eh? Eh? I saw you yesterday!' he accused.

'I know you did, Johnny, but I was only comforting him.'

'Hah! I wish you'd comfort me sometime.'

'Comfort you?' Eileen was bewildered. 'I don't understand.'

'No, of course you don't! I'm just the mug that tries to make things run smoothly for you. The one who would die to please you ... and what do I get in return? Headaches and more headaches. And you like it, Eileen. You enjoy lovemaking. So there must be another man! And from what I saw yesterday, it looks like that man's Kevin Rafferty.'

Eileen couldn't believe what she was hearing. She cried indignantly, 'You're wrong, Johnny. Honestly! I know I've been using headaches as an excuse lately, but it was because I was afraid.'

'Afraid?'

'I was afraid of becoming pregnant again. I want a break from childbirth, Johnny! I don't want to spend the best years of my life up to my eyes in nappies. You wouldn't agree to trying the rhythm method, so what could I do? Eh? I was trying to use the safe period without your help. So there! That's why I kept fobbing you off, and if I gave you the wrong impression I'm sorry.'

She could see that he was taken aback. He examined her face through narrowed eyelids and she met his gaze unblinkingly. As she watched the desire to believe her fight doubt, she whispered entreatingly, 'Please believe me, Johnny.'

The silence stretched. He was battling within himself. He was aware that he was putty in Eileen's hands. He so desperately wanted to believe her. At last he shrugged and gestured helplessly towards her and she moved closer still. Slowly his hands lifted and cupped her poor bruised face.

'Eileen ... believe me, I didn't know you had hurt yourself. There's no way I would have left you lying there had I known.'

'I know that, Johnny.'

'When Phillip came here last night he acted as if I was some kind of a monster.'

'Phillip came here last night?' Eileen was indignant

and the breath caught in her throat with fear. Madge had had no right to tell Phillip about Paul; had he said anything to Johnny? She relaxed when she realized that Phillip could not have mentioned anything about Paul. If he had, her husband would not be holding her so tenderly.

Johnny answered her question with a nod. 'Mmm . . .' Gently he kissed her temple and eye. 'You look like a battered wife.'

'I'll have to stay indoors until these marks fade or the neighbours will start talking about us.'

Her lips were inviting and he kissed them. As the kiss deepened she pushed him away. A frown gathered on his brow and his lips tightened angrily.

'Oh, for heaven's sake, another headache?' he asked sarcastically.

She laughed softly and her fingers covered his mouth to still any more angry comments. 'No . . . not a headache! But there are three children in the parlour waiting for me to call them in.'

He relaxed. 'Tonight?'

'Tonight,' she vowed.

It was his turn to laugh. 'I hear the lads in work joke about being on a promise. Now I know what they mean.' He kissed her again, and as passion mounted between them he laughed softly in triumph. Gently turning her about, he pushed her towards the door. 'You'd better get the kids in.'

He gestured ruefully towards the pot on the stove. 'So much for my scrambled eggs. I'll dump this lot. Everybody for scrambled eggs?'

Relieved that things had sorted themselves out, Eileen nodded her head and went to fetch the children.

Phillip waited for a chance to see Eileen alone before returning to England. To his knowledge, she had not been outside the door since he had left her home a

172

week ago. It was Friday night and he was travelling to England the next day. He watched from behind the net curtains, and regular as clockwork Johnny passed down the street, holdall over his shoulder, on his way to the gymnasium. Once his brother was out of sight Phillip left the house and made his way up the street. It was obvious when Eileen opened the door that she was not pleased to see him. However, standing to one side, she motioned him in with a wave of her hand.

'I never did thank you for your help and kindness. I don't know what I would have done without you and your mother last weekend.'

'Bah! I don't want any thanks. Do you know what you should have done? You should have gone down to your da. That's the best thing that could have happened, 'cause he'd have taken you in. He'd have made you leave Johnny.' As she stood mutely shaking her head in disagreement, Phillip moved closer. 'Leave him, Eileen,' he urged. 'A blind man on a galloping horse could see how miserable you are with him.'

'I'm not miserable with him! You've got it all wrong,' she cried, aghast. Did she look the picture of misery?.

'I'd take you away to England with me, so I would, Eileen.'

Eyes wide with surprise, she faced him speechlessly. Bemused, she reached out and touched his cheek. This was a surprise. She had not dreamt that he really cared for her. Lusted after her, yes, but she had never dreamt that he really cared. 'Thanks, Phillip. Thanks for being concerned, but you're mistaken. I'm quite content with my life here. Please don't waste your time on me.'

The feel of her fingers on his cheek sent a thrill coursing through his body, right to the core of his being, and before she could move his arms circled her waist. She tried to draw away from him but he hung on, pressing her close; his desire making him rough.

'No, Phillip, no, please!' she begged. He was strong

and she was remembering another time when she had struggled in vain against a man's passion.

'Eileen . . . Eileen, I love you so much. I didn't realize it until last weekend. Now I know why I can't get interested in another woman.'

'Stop it! Do you hear me, Phillip? Stop it at once, or I'll scream.' She meant what she said; no man was going to take advantage of her again.

'Eileen . . . you're attracted to me, I know you are. So don't act all innocent!'

'I'm warning you, Phillip, stop it or I'll shout. I was raped once before and if I can help it, I won't ever be raped again. I will scream blue murder, mind!'

He relaxed his hold on her and she quickly put some distance between them. 'You were raped?' he cried, astounded.

'Ah, he was drunk, and I should have known better than to go out into the dark with him. But I'm in my own home here and I won't stand for any nonsense. I admit I find you attractive. You're a handsome man, lots of women must find you attractive. But I would never risk ruining my marriage. It is very important to me.'

'I thought you hated Johnny? I never could understand why you married him until I learnt about Paul. I thought you would be glad to leave him.'

'Well, you're wrong. Johnny may not be your idea of a perfect husband, but I love him!'

Eileen hoped that Phillip was not aware that she was as surprised as he at this declaration. They gazed at each other. Slowly, Phillip turned towards the door then stopped. Abruptly he swung around and the look he threw her was puzzled. Eileen didn't blame him. Wasn't she bewildered herself?

'If you're putting on an act for my benefit . . .'

'I'm not!' she hastily interrupted.

Still his gaze was wary. 'Well, there's nothing more to

be said then. But if ever you should change your mind, will you send for me?'

'Ever is a long time, Phillip. Forget about me! Find yourself a nice girl and settle down. You should have married Cathy Monaghan. She loved you!'

Cathy was now married and the mother of a baby boy but Eileen knew that given the chance she would have married Phillip.

'And made her unhappy? How can I get married now that I know I love you?'

'Ah, Phillip . . . don't let me ruin things for you. I've no intention of changing my way of life. Go back to England and find yourself a nice girl.'

'Will you promise to send for me, if ever you need me?'

'All right, I promise.'

He opened the door but her voice stayed him. 'Phillip . . . it's not as bad as it may have sounded. Paul's father had asked me to marry him.'

'Then why didn't you marry him? Did you not love him?'

'I was young and foolish. I thought I loved him. But . . . he died in a motorbike accident. He didn't live long enough to know about Paul.'

His gaze was compassionate. 'It must have been awful for you.'

'It was . . . terrible. But I've survived. Please promise that you will never tell Johnny about Paul?'

'I promise. But really, Eileen, you shouldn't take chances! You should tell him yourself. It will be bad enough coming from you . . . but if he was to find out some other way, he'd go mad.'

'I know.' Her voice was forlorn. 'But I'm afraid of the consequences. What if he left me?'

'Does he really mean so much to you, Eileen?'

She nodded her head but could see that he still doubted her. 'He does,' she assured him.

'Well, then, there's nothing more to say. I wish you every happiness, Eileen. Goodbye, love.'

'Goodbye, Phillip.'

Long after the door closed she stood staring blankly at it. Did she really love Johnny? Oh, he was a terrific lover . . . hadn't she missed him like hell? But did she love him?

She was brought back to reality by a scream from Louise. As she rushed out into the yard to see what had caused such a cry, all thoughts of Johnny faded. She would investigate her feelings for him another time. After all they were married, so did it matter just how deep her feelings were?

Chapter Five

Claire Ross sat on the ledge of the shop window and admired her handiwork. She had just finished rearranging the window display and knew she had done a good job. She was now in charge of the typing pool in the solicitor's office where she worked, and loved the responsibility attached to it. On Saturdays, however, she helped out in her grandfather's shop and here she was in her glory, especially when setting out the window displays. Until a few years ago the shop had been run solely as a greengrocery concern. Then Jim Rafferty had been forced to retire from the shoe repair business he ran at the corner of Alma Street, because of the crippling rheumatism in his hands. The shop, facing the Falls Baths, had been acquired in the 1920s during the troubles in the city, after Jim had been fire bombed out of the premises he rented in Donegall Street. He had now left this business in the capable hands of his elder son, and turned his full attention to the greengrocer's he shared with Barney Grahame. At his suggestion the two friends had decided to expand the business. A double-fronted shop, they had decided to keep one side for greengroceries and the other for newspapers and confectionery.

Since the end of the war it had become a thriving concern and Claire enjoyed working here on a Saturday. She was kept up to date on all the local gossip and occasionally made new friends. Becoming aware that she was being watched now, she slowly lifted her head and met a pair of dark blue eyes full of admiration. The young man standing outside on the pavement was tall, over six feet, she guessed, if he was to straighten up. His hair shone like pale gold in the afternoon sun. He grinned at her, displaying even white teeth, a bright flash set in a tanned handsome face. She found herself smiling in return before dismissing him with an abrupt nod and disappearing from view.

Michael O'Hara hurriedly straightened and with quick steps entered the shop, only to stop in dismay. The girl was nowhere to be seen. Buying a newspaper from the tall grey-haired man behind the counter, he turned and left. For some minutes he stood outside at the window, hoping to catch sight of the vision again. However, she did not reappear, and somewhat crestfallen, he headed down the Falls Road. But he would be back! He was determined to meet this girl. She was beautiful and she had smiled at him. He had also noted the absence of any rings on her left hand.

It must have been fate that had brought him up the Falls Road today. He never travelled in this direction except when going to the Falls Park or to visit his father's grave in Milltown Cemetery, and then he always took a trolleybus. He would be forever grateful to Irene Parks for neglecting to post the firm's invoices to Mrs Cleary. He smiled shamefacedly, remembering his reaction when, about to leave the workshop, he was approached by his boss and asked if he would deliver the documents to the house in Rockmore Road today, as a great favour. He had been so ungracious, but now he thanked his lucky stars that Irene had forgotten to post them, otherwise he might have waited years before meeting this girl. That he would have eventually met her he didn't doubt for one minute. She was the one for him. He was convinced that he had just seen his future wife. That was how sure he was that this girl was meant for him. He had dated plenty of girls but had always felt sure that when he met the right one he would know immediately. And she was the one. It was definitely providence that had guided him to this shop today!

Unaware of the profound effect she'd had upon the stranger, Claire spent some time in the back of the shop. Her actions were automatic, her thoughts far away, as she unpacked and sorted boxes of chocolates and sweets. She had a lot on her mind. Brian Muldoon was becoming a problem to her. When she had first started work as a typist in the solicitor's office in Bedford Street, she had kept him at arm's length, knowing full well that it would be prudent to keep her private life separate from her working life. However, after much coaxing she had finally allowed herself to be talked into going out on a date with him. Now it had become a habit and she felt trapped. He was becoming serious . . . but how did she feel? Was she expecting too much from life? Her friends all assured her that she could wait in vain for the earth to move at a glance from a man.

However, one day when she and Eileen had been helping their grannie spring clean, Maggie had reminisced about the past. She told them that she had been swept off her feet by a single glance from each of her husbands. Her first, a bricklayer, had been working on a building site in Shaftesbury Square when she had passed by. Their eyes had met and it was love at first sight. And in spite of coming from entirely different backgrounds and different religions they had eventually married. It had been the same years later, Grannie had assured them. She had been a widow when Granda Barney had come on the scene. She had answered the door to his knock and fallen in love at first sight. At least, that was what Grannie had said. Was it all hindsight? Was she just an old romantic at heart? Was she seeing things as she would have wished them to be, rather than as they actually were? Quite likely! It all sounded so romantic and Claire imagined it would be lovely for two people to be committed to each other just like that. But was it possible?

Would she not be wise to hang on to Brian? Wasn't he a great catch? Didn't he have his own house and car, and wasn't it well known that he had a bit of money in the bank? She smiled wryly to herself . . . didn't she sound mercenary? And . . . sometimes Brian made her feel ill at ease, uncomfortable. She could not put her finger on the reason why, but was this a sign that they were not compatible? Surely she should be completely at ease with him if marriage was in question? Claire laughed softly to herself. Hark at her! Perhaps Brian had no intention of asking her to marry him. The best thing to do would be to stop dating him for a time and see if they missed each other. Would he agree to that? She thought not. He would talk and talk, and persuade her to see him at least once a week. He could be very persuasive. Besides, it would be awkward to break it off, with them working in the same office. Not that she saw much of him at work; he was upstairs and she was on the ground floor. However everyone knew they dated. There would be gossip. In a small firm everybody knew each other's business and it was not considered nosy to ask prying questions. But it wasn't as if they were engaged. You didn't automatically get married because you dated someone.

Hearing her sister's voice, she returned to the front of the shop. 'Hi, Eileen. You're late today.'

Eileen smiled. 'Not my fault. George Flynn's invoices arrived late. It seems Irene Parks forgot to post them yesterday, so they were delivered by hand. By a handsome young man, no less! But then, Irene's in love . . . she just got engaged last week, so we must excuse her. George is in a hurry for this particular one.' She raised the envelope she held. 'I didn't like to ask the young lad to wait for it. I'll nip out and put it in the post box, then George will get it first thing on Monday morning. Won't be a minute.'

As the door closed on her, Barney Grahame came from the back of the shop and gazed thoughtfully after her, then turned to Claire. 'You're grannie and I were just saying how different Eileen has been this past month.'

'Different? What do you mean?'

'Happy . . . we've never seen her so free and easy. So contented.'

Claire pondered for a moment. 'To be truthful, I never really noticed, but thinking back, you're probably right. She has been acting different of late.'

Barney called across the shop to where Jim Rafferty had just finished serving a customer. 'What do you think, Jim?'

'What do I think about what, Barney?'

'Our Eileen . . . doesn't she look unusually happy lately?'

'Now, it's funny you should say that. Kathleen said the very same thing the other night. So there must be a difference if she noticed.' He didn't add that Kathleen had hinted that Eileen looked like a woman in love. Her return put an end to the conversation and after Eileen had passed the time of day with their grandfather and Jim Rafferty, Claire led the way into the little room at the rear, where every Saturday Eileen made up the shop's books.

'Grandfather was just saying how different you are lately. For the better, mind you! And I must admit, I agree with him. Have you won the pools or something, and never let on?'

'Me, different? You're imagining things. But . . .' Eileen smiled wryly. 'I've got to confess, I do feel a lot happier these days. More contented with my lot.' Not for the world would she admit it, but Eileen knew that they were right. She was acting differently! The discovery of how deep her feelings for Johnny were had opened up a whole new world for her. She hugged the knowledge of her love for him close to herself. She had never expected to fall in

181

love with her husband and found herself secretly eyeing him when he wasn't looking. She must have been blind not to see just how attractive he was. His hair, though a might bright, was thick and curly. His face was strong, with a firm cleft chin and sensitive lips. His eyes, framed in golden lashes, were deep blue and usually warm and smiling. Since he had agreed to give the rhythm method a try, they were getting on so well together. Their love life had added awareness to it. It was like continually planning naughty weekends together, and added spice to their relationship. So, yes, she'd be the first to admit that she was different, but she would never say why!

Claire's voice broke in on her musing.

'Eileen . . . what do you think of Brian Muldoon?'

'Mmmm? Oh, nice . . . quiet . . . respectable . . . handsome . . . good job. Need I go any further? Why do you ask?'

'Well, it's just . . . I think he's getting a wee bit too serious about me and I don't know how I feel about him.'

'Why are you dating him, then? You seemed happy enough when you brought him to meet Johnny and me last week.'

'Oh, I started to go out with him because . . . well . . . he kept pestering me for a date, and now it's become a weekly routine.'

'But you must fancy him?' Eileen reasoned. She remembered how she and Johnny had started off and felt somewhat apprehensive. 'Why, you've been seeing him for about four months now.'

'I feel sorry for him.' At her sister's look of surprise, Claire cried, 'I know. I know! He's not the kind of person to feel sorry for. He's worked his way up from office boy to junior partner. Has a car. Earns good money. Girls throw themselves at him. But still . . .' her voice trailed off. 'I don't know why, but I find myself pitying him.'

She drew back, startled, when Eileen leant forward and gripped her arm.

'Drop him! Pity isn't enough. At first I thought you weren't serious about him, but then, when you visited us last Wednesday, you seemed to be enjoying his company so I thought I had misjudged things. But obviously you don't really care for him . . . so drop him.'

'It's not that easy. With us working in the same office it would be awkward to break it off. I realize that I should never have gone out with him in the first place. I feel so trapped now. Another thing . . . Mam will be disappointed. She thinks a lot of him.'

'Huh! That's only because he's a solicitor. Never mind what Mam thinks. Or anyone else for that matter! You're the one who'll have to live with him, and it won't be easy. Please, Claire, stop seeing him. I know what I'm talking about. Without love, well, life is just . . . mediocre.'

Seeing the surprise in her sister's eyes, and sensing questions hovering on her lips, Eileen released her hold on Claire and turned away. 'I'd better start work or I'll be here all night,' she stated firmly, forestalling Claire's questions. Crossing the room, she sat down at the desk, her back to her sister. She had no intention of admitting how she had felt towards Johnny at the beginning of their marriage. How her stupidity could easily have wrecked their relationship. Anyhow, didn't it just go to show that you could grow to love someone? Claire might grow to love Brian.

For some moments Claire gazed at her. The auburn hair, thick and silky, was now cut close to her head. Everyone had been scandalized when some months earlier Eileen had had her long tresses cut off. However, the new look suited her; showed off her high cheekbones and long, frail-looking neck. Long necks always looked vulnerable to Claire, and now the sight of her sister's long elegant neck made her feel sad. But without cause. Eileen may well look delicate, but she was far from frail!

She had worked hard to get established. Hadn't she herself helped Eileen burn the midnight oil on many occasions? Eileen was respected and looked up to. Her home was beautiful and her children, under Johnny's guidance, were well-behaved. Claire agreed that Eileen was right. Pity was not a good foundation for a lasting relationship. Tonight she would break it off with Brian. Yes, tonight she would take the plunge and tell him that she did not want to see him again.

That night when Brian's car drew up in front of the house, Claire was waiting, ready to leave. She was surprised at how nervous she felt. Good heavens, she chastized herself, he's only a man after all. That he had a sharp tongue when displeased, she knew, having been on the receiving end of it one day when one of the new typists had made a few spelling errors. But then, that was his privilege. It was her job to see that everything ran smoothly in the typing pool. Still, it had been her first week in charge so he could have been more lenient. She hadn't been dating him at the time and the following day he had apologized to her. In fact he had been very sweet and that was one of the reasons she had consented to go out with him. No ... he wouldn't bite her. But even with this assurance she still felt nervous as she slipped into the passenger seat beside him.

'You're looking very nice.' His voice was light but his eyes were wary.

Why had she not waited until he came to the door for her? He always had a chat with her father when he picked her up. Big Mick Ross was offhand with him; didn't go out of his way to make him welcome, the way her mother did. So Brian was working on him; he wanted to be liked. After all, he hoped to marry Mick's daughter. He sensed Claire's unrest and watched her covertly.

'Thank you.'

'Well . . . let's go.' With these words he eased the car away from the kerb. 'The Club Orchid as usual?'

'Of course! Where else?'

'You seem strange tonight. I thought perhaps . . .'

'I'm all right. I want to go to the dance.'

Brian grew more worried as they travelled down the Falls Road to King Street. Claire was usually very talkative but tonight she sat in silence.

'You're very quiet. Is anything wrong?'

'No . . . no! I've told you, there's nothing wrong. I'm just a bit tired, that's all.'

'We don't have to go to the dance. We could go for a drive out to Carrickfergus or Bangor and have a bite to eat, if you like?'

The thought of being alone in his company for any length of time did not appeal to Claire. 'I just want to go to the dance,' she assured him. 'I love the Club Orchid on a Saturday night.'

As usual the dance hall was packed. Claire left Brian and joined the queue along the stairs leading up to the ladies' cloakroom. After handing in her coat and receiving her ticket, she powdered her nose and combed her hair before making her way down to the ballroom. It was as she descended the stairs to join Brian that she noticed a familiar face. The young man nodded to her and she nodded back, at a loss to put a name to the face. The stranger was joined by a petite blonde and as he turned to enter the ballroom, still eyeing her over his shoulder, Claire realized who he was. This was the man who that afternoon had watched her through the window of the shop. Funny, she had never noticed him before . . . now she supposed she would fall over him every turn she made. Life was strange that way.

Located above a public house on the corner of Divis Street and King Street, the Club Orchid Ballroom had limited space. The small dance floor was crowded, and as the night wore on Claire began to wish she was elsewhere.

That the stranger seemed to be on their heels every time they took to the floor was a bit unnerving to her, and as the night progressed the heat in the ballroom became oppressive.

Brian was taking advantage of the packed dance floor this night to clasp her close, and Claire felt uneasy. It wasn't right to move together like this. She tried to hold him off but he ignored her efforts and pressed against her. This was immoral; an occasion of sin. She should stop him acting like this. Well, why didn't she? She didn't have to put up with this kind of behaviour from anyone. Pushing him roughly away, she broke free of his hold and hurried from the dance floor.

He followed her to a corner of the room and watched through narrowed eyes as she sat down. 'Is anything wrong, Claire?'

A combination of embarrassment and stifling heat had made her cheeks bright red. She glared angrily at him. He knew fine well what was wrong! He had been indecent! She had never been so close to a man before and had felt vulnerable. In a crowded room, he had taken advantage of her and she objected strongly to his actions.

Not wanting to cause a scene in public, she said, 'I'm too hot.'

Her voice was curt and he frowned. Anyone would think he had done something wrong. Surely she had danced close with other men? Good heavens, she was twenty-two years old! Not some wee schoolgirl.

'Would you like a cold drink?'

'Yes, please.'

'Orange?'

At her nod of agreement he left her side, and pushing his way through the crowd, went downstairs to the bar.

Michael O'Hara breathed a sigh of relief when he saw Claire push her companion away and hurry from the dance floor. Resentment was burning deep inside him at the way this man was treating the girl he longed to meet. Why, the dirty bastard acted as if he owned her! A terrible thought assailed him. What if the couple were engaged? You didn't need to wear a ring to be planning to get married. Some girls thought the money better spent on material things. Oh, he hoped she wasn't engaged. It would put paid to his plans.

'What on earth's the matter with you, Michael?'

With a start of surprise, he swung his partner round on the dance floor. Involuntarily, his feet had been leading them to where Claire sat.

'I'm sorry, Eve. I don't know what's the matter with me tonight.' He shook his head. 'I'm not with it.'

'Who is she?'

Dismayed, he cried, 'What . . . what do you mean?'

'Oh, come off it! Do you think I'm daft? Do you know that girl you've been ogling all night?'

'What girl? Hey . . .'

Eve had had enough. Leaving him standing on the dance floor, she turned on her heel and with a determined step left the ballroom, heading for the stairs and cloakroom. She was going home. Michael strode after her, very much aware that he had been in the wrong, and that *that* girl had been sitting watching their antics.

He caught up with Eve on the stairs. 'I'm sorry. Let me make amends.' When she remained stiff and unrelenting, he pleaded, 'Please?' Seeing she was softening, he added, 'Look . . . how's about us going round to Johnny Long's for a fish supper? Eh? Anyway, it's too hot in here tonight. Let's go now,' he coaxed.

Eve dithered and then relented. He was right; the heat was becoming unbearable. 'All right. I'll get my coat.'

As he waited at the foot of the stairs, Michael pondered on fate. Twice in one day he had seen *that* girl. He had not been to the Club Orchid for a couple of years, preferring the Orpheus Ballroom above the Co-op in York Street, which was big and spacious. It was Eve who frequented the Orchid. He had been dating her just a few short weeks and had already made up his mind to end it, even before he had seen Claire. Eve was nice, but she was not for him. He would tell her so tonight.

Making his way back to where Claire sat, Brian warned himself to be cautious. He mustn't make an issue of Claire's prudery. Because that was what it all boiled down to; she was a prude! He had danced very close with girls that he didn't even know and they hadn't objected. On a crowded dance floor most men chanced their arm.

'Here you are, Claire. Orange juice for the lady.'

Eyeing the other drink he held, she said dryly, 'You should be drinking fruit juice as well. You're driving . . . remember?'

His lips tightened but he managed to keep his voice light. 'One beer won't do any harm.'

'Oh, no?' Her voice was cynical.

'It will be sweated out of me by the end of the night,' he assured her. 'The heat in here is overpowering.'

'I don't want to stay until the end of the dance.' Claire's voice was fretful. The idea of going back on to the floor with him did not appeal to her. 'I would like to go home as soon as we finish our drinks. You're right, it's too hot for dancing.'

'Fair enough! We'll take a drive down the coast to Carrickfergus.'

'No, I don't want to go to Carrickfergus. I'd prefer to go home.'

'The night's still young, Claire. Look . . . what about going round to Johnny Long's for something to eat? If we leave now we'll beat the crowds.'

Relieved that he wasn't pressing her to go for a drive, and glad to escape the closeness that dancing with him entailed, Claire agreed to go to Johnny Long's fish and chip shop. Situated in an out of the way back street near the town centre, Johnny's was nevertheless always packed because of its reputation for delicious fish suppers. It had been a happy haunt of Claire and her friends when they had attended learner dancing classes in the Kingsway Ballroom. Every Tuesday night after the dance had seen them in Johnny Long's, where high-heeled shoes had been eased off to let their aching feet cool off on the cold tiled floor while they ate their fish and chips. If the weather was dry they usually carried their shoes on the long trek up the Grosvenor Road towards home. The dance classes always ended too late to catch the last bus home unless you were willing to miss the last waltz. That was unheard of as far as they were concerned! As for taxis, they were taboo. Why waste money that would take them to another dance? So, providing the weather was dry, they endured the journey home on bare feet, but certainly not in silence! The air was always alive with laughter as they compared notes of their experiences on the dance floor with different partners. There were also occasional yelps of pain when one of them would stub a toe on a raised flagstone. This brought howls of laughter from the others as the unfortunate girl hobbled about on one leg and grabbed at a friend for support. Claire wished that this was one of those happy nights and she was with her mates instead of Brian.

Fifteen minutes later found Brian and Claire outside the Club Orchid. It was a beautiful evening and to Claire's relief Brian agreed that it would be a good idea to collect the car later. Leaving it parked in Castle Street, they made their way along King Street and cut through narrow side streets to the small fish and chip shop. Early though they were, it was already full but after a short wait they got a table. The demonstration on the dance floor had made Claire more determined than ever to break off her relationship with Brian. On the way here she had been going over in her mind just what she would say to him. As they waited for their order, she broached the subject of their friendship.

'Brian, I . . . I don't know how to put this . . . but I'm

189

not ready for a serious relationship just yet.' She paused, hoping he would help her out. He just raised his brows enquiringly and she continued, 'You know what I mean, don't you?'

'Oh, so you don't want to be serious? I wasn't aware I had indicated that I wanted you to be?' he said dryly.

At his tone of voice colour blazed across her face. My, but he could be cutting! She felt about two feet tall. To her relief, she managed a quick retort. 'Well then, that's fine. I just didn't want to be misleading you.' Grabbing a chance to get her own back, she continued, 'The way you were dancing with me, I thought you were staking a claim. Or do you dance like that with all your partners?'

'Of course I don't,' he lied.

Aware that he lied, she taunted. 'Oh, so it's only me you don't respect?'

'You've got it all wrong! I do respect you, Claire,' he argued. 'I respect you very much.'

'Huh! You could have fooled me!' Her cheeks grew hotter at the remembered embrace.

Brian leant across the table and gripped her hand. 'Listen, Claire, I didn't mean any offence. Everybody dances like that now, and . . .'

'No, they don't!' she interrupted him angrily. 'No one has ever attempted to dance with me like that.'

'It won't happen again, I promise. I have to confess that I'm very fond of you. However, whatever you say goes. I enjoy your company very much and I thought you liked me?'

'I do like you, but I'm too young to be tied down. I want to enjoy myself before I'm married and saddled with children.'

'I understand. But surely we can still be friends? You will come out with me from time to time, won't you?'

His voice was soft, wheedling, the anger he felt well concealed. He was aware that many girls found him attractive. Why, he could pick and choose! The cheek of her treating him like this! Just who the hell did she think she was? However, he had better tread lightly as it was Claire that he had set his sights on. Her family were respected; looked up to. Not like his!

His father, a jailbird, had walked out on his wife when Brian was nine years old. His mother had sought comfort in the bottle. Brian bore a great deal of resentment towards his parents. An only child, he should have had all his wants, but instead he'd had to wear other children's cast-off clothes, brought to his home by the Sisters of Charity. He had lived in dread of seeing that nun, her big butterfly wimple attracting the neighbours' attention, standing there on the doorstep with her brown paper parcel. Everybody knew just why she was there; what the parcel contained. How he had hated it! He had detested the pity directed at him every time his mother was admitted to hospital after one of her binges. It came as a relief to him when she eventually passed away. With hindsight he realized that she must have been unhappy and lonely, but how was a child supposed to cope with that?

Matthew Ryan had been his salvation. Matthew had taken him in and treated him as one of his own family. At fourteen, when he left school, Matthew had got him employed in a solicitor's office as messenger boy. Now, at twenty-seven, he was one of the junior partners with great prospects ahead of him. He was proud of his achievements. Having studied hard at evening classes at the College of Technology, he had passed all his exams with merit. The only snag was that Matthew hoped he would become his son-in-law. Brian knew that Theresa Ryan would be more than willing to become his wife. At one time he had actually thought it an ideal plan. Then he had set eyes on Claire Ross.

He remembered the day he had first became aware of her. One of the typists had made a mess of a letter he had dictated. Claire was in charge of the typing pool

191

and he'd sought her out to complain. Watching the colour come and go in her face as he ticked her off, Brian realized how lovely she was. He loved the way the thick chestnut hair swept back from her face; the way her smooth, fine-textured skin coloured so easily. Her face had lingered in his mind all day and he had even dreamt about her that night. He must have been blind not to have noticed her before. A few discreet inquiries gave him the information that she was unattached and apparently heart free. The next day he had apologized for losing his temper and asked her out.

She had graciously declined, but undeterred he had pursued her and a few weeks later she had at last agreed to accompany him to the cinema. That was four months ago and they had dated ever since. He had thought he was making headway; was sure that Claire liked him. He had felt confident enough to take a chance while dancing. Had thought that she might even enjoy the contact as much as he did. Well, obviously he had been mistaken! Here she was saying that she didn't want to be serious. Why the sudden change? Was it just because of the incident on the dance floor or – had she met someone else? Now there was a thought! That was more likely to be the reason. She was just using his dancing as an excuse. He'd make it his business to find out if he had a rival.

Meanwhile it was vital that he keep in touch outside office hours. 'You will come out with me from time to time, won't you, Claire?' he coaxed.

Glad to find him so affable, she nodded her head. She was relieved when the arrival of the waitress with their meal meant that he had to relinquish his hold on her hand. It was there again, that uneasy feeling. She would only go out with him now and again, until he got fed up and found someone more gullible than her. She didn't know how to take him! With a word he could cut you to the quick and the next minute, like now, he practically whined when he wanted something.

Claire watched him turn on the charm for the benefit of the waitress. Saw the colour come and go in the young girl's face as he teased her. She had to admit that he was very attractive, and when he chose, could be charming. A little on the short side perhaps, he was nevertheless of muscular build and handled himself well. Dark-haired and brown-eyed, he was the recipient of many an admiring glance from the opposite sex. The single girls in the office envied her. Why he had singled her out she would never know. He was very attentive; bought her flowers and chocolates, and until tonight had never put a foot wrong. So why did she sometimes feel ill at ease in his company? There was no apparent reason. His actions on the dance floor had come as a surprise to her. So far his good night kisses had been brief, no cause for complaint there! Always the perfect gentleman. Still, after his antics earlier on in the Club Orchid, she sensed that he was serious about her. The cheek of him, thinking she liked the sort of thing he had attempted on the dance floor! She expected respect from her partners and was glad to have got her point across in no uncertain manner. Romantically he had no effect on her whatsoever. She may as well be sitting here with her father for all the emotion Brian aroused in her. It would be better to break off with him altogether, but gently, she must do it gently. Not cause any conflict that might spill over into the office.

After they had finished their meal and were leaving the premises she once again made eye contact with the stranger. He was sitting near the door. Tight-lipped, she avoided his avid stare and hurried outside. She was beginning to think he was haunting her.

During the journey up the Falls Road, Claire went over the evening's events and felt depressed. If only she could get away for a while. Suddenly a thought struck her. Why not? Last Thursday Maureen Dillon had arrived at work in a dither. Her mother had been taken into hospital

193

suddenly. The holiday Maureen had booked for ten days in the Isle of Man with two other girls from the office to start next Friday would have to be cancelled. She had asked around for someone to buy her ticket and hotel deposit for half price but at such short notice had received no offers. Now Claire decided to take her up on her offer. She had done her boss a favour by working a week of the twelfth fortnight when she should have been off work and was certain that he would not object to her taking time off now, even if it was at such short notice. Money would be a bit tight but she could borrow some from her grandfather or Eileen. Why, it would be a blessing in disguise! Get her away from Brian for a while. Perhaps by the time she returned he would be seeing someone else and that would solve her dilemma.

When they arrived at her driveway, Claire quickly jumped out of the car and before Brian could join her on the pavement, said, 'You won't mind if I don't ask you in for tea tonight, will you? I'm tired and I want to go straight to bed.'

Face like thunder, her stared at her. His mouth opened and closed, but no words came out. Claire smiled grimly. Imagine, Brian Muldoon speechless! Wonders would never cease. Taking advantage of the stunned silence, Claire said, 'See you on Monday, Brian. Thanks for everything.' And closing the car door firmly, quite literally flew up the garden path.

Brian sat for some time grim-faced, hands gripping the steering wheel so tight his knuckles showed white. Just who the hell did she think she was? He'd soon show her! But first he must win her over. It would not be easy but he loved a challenge. One day she would marry him.

Having made up her mind, Claire quickly set the wheels in motion. First she phoned Maureen and made sure that the holiday was still available. Then the next day she approached her grandfather for a loan. Once assured of the money, on Monday she asked and received permission from her boss to take a fortnight off. She was not working for Eileen on Monday night as her sister and brother-in-law were going to the Broadway Picture House. An avid Humphrey Bogart fan, Johnny wanted to see his Oscar-winning role in *The African Queen*. She could tell Eileen on Tuesday night when she visited her. The three elder sisters had started to meet every Tuesday night for a drink and a natter, either in Beth's or Eileen's house, and this Tuesday it was Eileen's turn to be hostess. If Eileen was shorthanded while Claire was away, Emma, who was progressing very well at St Dominic's School, might be able to give her a hand.

From her seat on the bedsettee that Eileen had bought for the parlour, Claire watched her sister pour the wine. She had been surprised when a month earlier Eileen had started using this lovely room as an office. Eileen had pointed out that the room wasn't used much and the furniture would soon grow old-fashioned so she might as well get some enjoyment out of it. She had moved the three-piece suite into the living room, to make room for her desk and typewriter, and bought the bedsettee to take its place, and was now using the parlour as her office. She explained that the settee was for when she worked late. Johnny retired early most nights and this way she didn't have to disturb him.

When Beth arrived and the sisters were settled down with drinks in their hands, Claire addressed Eileen. 'Can you manage without me for a while, Eileen?'

'Why? Where are you going?'

'To the Isle of Man!' Smiling at their amazed expressions, Claire explained about Maureen Dillon's mother being taken into hospital and how she had got the holiday at a cut price.

'Can you do without me, Eileen?'

'I'll manage. Good luck to you! I wish I was going with you. Besides,' she added knowingly, 'you need to get away and have some time alone to decide on your future.'

Beth was looking from one to the other in bewilderment. 'Have I missed something? I feel as if I've come in near the end of a film.'

'Sorry, Beth,' Claire apologized. 'I forgot you didn't know. Brian Muldoon is getting too serious for my liking and I need to get away for a while.'

'You could do a lot worse than Brian, mind. He'd be coming home clean every night. Not covered in oil and grease, like someone I know.'

Eileen and Claire exchanged a glance. It was intercepted by Beth and she reacted angrily. 'All right! All right! So I'm an old fusspot. But it is very annoying washing dirty overalls every other day.'

'Are you all right, Beth?' Eileen reached over and touched her sister's hand. 'A bit of dirt never annoyed you before. You've been different ever since the baby was born.'

Beth sighed and admitted, 'I don't feel one bit well. I'm healthy enough but I'm always down in the dumps. Tommy deserves a medal for putting up with me and my moods.'

Eileen and Claire exchanged a smile. They had often voiced that opinion where Tommy was concerned. Beth wasn't looking at them and they remained silent, sensing that more was to come.

They were right. 'I don't want any more children. I'm determined about that! I've my eye on one of those new houses they're building on the open ground between Broadway and the Christian Brothers' home.'

'Oh, how lovely!' Eileen had herself been thinking about those houses. Now that she was well established she didn't want to move too far from Rockmore Road. The new houses being built above the Broadway Picture House would be ideal for her, and Johnny had agreed with her that they could now afford to buy a house.

According to reports in the local newspapers the houses were to be semi-detached, big and roomy. However, if Beth intended purchasing one that would hit her idea on the head. Johnny would not want to live so close to any of his in-laws. If only Eileen had voiced her intentions sooner.

'Yes, they should be lovely,' Beth agreed. 'And closer to St Vincent's School as well.'

'What's the problem then? Surely you can afford it now that Tommy's got that big yard at the bottom of Spinner Street? Why, he must be coining it, with two mechanics working for him. Or, doesn't Tommy fancy moving to a new house?'

'Oh, yes! Yes, he does. He's all for it. But you see . . . I don't want any more children.'

Seeing that Eileen was as mystified as she was, Claire said tentatively, 'I don't understand. What have children to do with it?'

'Well, as you know, I really had an awful pregnancy with young Elizabeth. Right from the beginning I was sick or in pain. And then I had all those stitches. You know how bad I was.'

They both nodded in agreement. Beth did have a bad time with Elizabeth, but then, Eileen had had a bad time with Marie. No two pregnancies were alike. The next birth could be easier.

Beth was continuing, 'I'm so afraid of getting caught again, I won't even take a chance with the rhythm method.'

'Well . . . it's early days. Give yourself a chance,' Claire consoled her.

Beth threw her a wrathful look. 'What do you know about it? Eh? I shouldn't even be talking like this in front of you. I'll be putting you right off marriage.'

'Oh, I wouldn't worry about that,' Claire assured her. 'I'm not exactly partial to marriage at the moment.'

'Then what's your problem with Brian? If in doubt . . .'

kick it out! That's always been my motto and so far it hasn't failed me.'

Eileen eyed Beth and tentatively voiced her thoughts. 'Tommy has always struck me as being very considerate. If he's willing to try the rhythm method, you should go along with him. It's not every man that's willing, you know. A lot demand their so-called conjugal rights!'

'Huh! I'd like to see Tommy try to railroad me into doing something I didn't want. And what if it doesn't work, eh? That will be me saddled with another child. It would drive me round the bend, so it would!'

'Would it matter so much if you didn't do ... you know what I mean?' Claire sounded puzzled. Could it possibly mean so much after years of marriage? Didn't the novelty wear off? Her voice trailed away at the expression on Beth's face.

'Of course it matters! You don't understand. Wait until you fall in love. It's awful not being able to express your love for one another.'

Claire sat silent. It was obvious to her that Brian would never affect her in this way. Still, did it matter? Surely there was more to marriage than sex?

'Would you not talk it over with the priest? Ask his advice?' Eileen ventured to ask. But she did not really think that the priest would be very helpful in that department.

She was right! Beth was shaking her head. Putting on a pompous voice, her sister retorted, 'One must remember that one married for procreation. Any pleasure derived from the sex act is a bonus.' She grimaced. 'He didn't actually use those words but that's what he meant. It's all right for them! They don't have to rear families.' Her look grew puzzled as she fixed her gaze on Eileen. 'Are you not afraid of another pregnancy?'

She decided to be truthful. 'Yes ...' She nodded towards the bedsettee. 'Hence this. We're using the rhythm method and . . .' She raised a hand, fingers crossed. 'So far, so good.'

'But you have the room to do this,' Beth argued, and it was her turn to nod towards the settee. 'With just having the two bedrooms, Tommy and I have to share a bed.'

'No, you don't!' Eileen disagreed with her. 'Tommy could sleep downstairs on the sofa during the danger periods. Where there's a will, there's a way.'

Beth was still apprehensive. 'Do you really think it would work?'

Eileen shrugged, 'One can only hope. It's better than nothing. But don't you go blaming me if it doesn't work, mind,' she warned. 'Remember, I'm no marriage guidance counsellor, or doctor for that matter! So long as you can get your dates sorted out there shouldn't be any problem.'

Seeing that she had given her sister food for thought, Eileen adroitly changed the subject.

The holiday on the Isle of Man passed all too quickly. The weather had been marvellous and Claire returned home tanned and relaxed. Mick and Sarah were genuine in their praise of how well she looked, although Mick admonished her for wearing shorts, saying they were indecent.

'Don't listen to him, Claire. They let people see how lovely your legs are,' Sarah assured her, and sighed. 'How I wish I was young again! You young ones have so much freedom these days.' She added slyly, 'I'm sure Brian will be glad to see you back again.' There was something amiss between her daughter and Brian and Sarah was determined to find out just what was wrong.

At the mention of Brian, Claire's lips tightened. A frown gathered on Sarah's brow. If Claire wasn't careful she'd lose him. What on earth was wrong with this daughter of hers? Brian had everything a girl could want.

'Will you be seeing him tonight?' she probed.

'No! Look, Mam, I told you, Brian and I are just good friends. There are no strings attached. I'll see him at work on Monday.' Claire dreaded seeing him. She had managed to avoid him the week before going away and had only worked half day on Friday, the day he always came to make sure they were going out together on the Saturday night. He wouldn't be too happy about missing her. Well . . . she didn't owe him anything! Hadn't she told him that she didn't want to be tied down to any one man? Still, it would have been good manners to let him know that she was going on holiday. Her mother was still lamenting and Claire irritably brought her attention back to her.

'You listen to me, Claire Ross! You know I don't believe in poking my nose in where it's not wanted, but . . .'

'Oh, no?' Claire interrupted her mother. 'Hah! That's a laugh.'

Sarah was scandalized. 'Tell me, when have I ever tried to advise you on anything? Eh? Though many a time I've been tempted, mind you,' she admitted. 'You think you know it all, girl! But I really do think you're making a terrible mistake where Brian Muldoon is concerned. Many a girl would be glad of his attentions.'

'Well then . . . let him get someone else. I couldn't care less.'

'You may well live to regret it, you know,' Sarah warned her.

'I'll risk it! Now can we please change the subject?'

Michael O'Hara entered the shop in a determined state of mind. He had every intention of finding out just what had happened to the girl with the lovely chestnut hair. She had been absent from the shop for the past two Saturdays and he was beginning to think she had been a mirage. Today he intended to find out her name and address. To his great delight, when he entered the shop there she stood behind the counter. He was also pleased to recognize the woman she was conversing with. It was Mrs Cleary.

'This is a surprise,' he greeted Eileen, but it was Claire who held his attention.

Noting his interest in her sister, Eileen raised an eyebrow, 'Yes . . . isn't it strange that I should be shopping in my grandfather's shop at the corner of the road I live on? What are you doing here?'

'Your grandfather's shop? I didn't know. I just happened to be passing and I came in for some chocolates for my mother.'

At these words Eileen winked at Claire and teased him. 'Just passing? Don't you live over Beechmount?'

Hot colour flooded Michael's face and neck. Seeing his embarrassment, Claire threw her sister a reproachful look and came to his rescue.

'Take no notice of her. Can I help you?'

Michael threw her a grateful glance and turned towards the display of chocolates. 'I'll just pick one of these boxes. And I also want a *Daily Mirror.*'

While his back was turned Claire motioned to her sister, indicating that she wanted to be introduced to him.

As Claire was wrapping the chocolates, Eileen said, 'By the way, this is my sister, Claire, Claire Ross.'

'Your sister?'

'Yes, my sister.' Eileen was grinning from ear to ear as she turned to Claire. 'Claire . . . meet Michael O'Hara. This past few weeks he has delivered documents to me from his firm. I wondered about that. Why they had stopped posting them out. Now I can guess!'

Michael gripped Claire's hand and Eileen, seeing she was fast becoming invisible to these two, gathered up her shopping bags and headed for the door. 'I'll leave you to get acquainted.'

At the door she turned to say farewell but neither of them was looking in her direction. With an envious sigh, she left the shop.

Although Michael had relinquished his hold on Claire's hand, he still stood gazing sheepishly at her. 'You must think me a bit of an idiot, but I thought I had lost my chance to get to know you. Where have you been lately?'

He asked the question as if he had the right to know and Claire smiled slightly as she answered him. 'I've been on holiday,' she informed him, and added cheekily, 'that is, if it's any business of yours.'

'I'm sorry. I didn't mean to be forward.'

'It's all right. I was only teasing you.'

'I should have guessed, with you having a tan like that. Have you been abroad?'

'No such luck! I went to the Isle of Man and the weather was glorious.'

'You look great.'

'Thank you.'

Claire handed him his parcel and change. Michael dithered, not knowing what to say next. A customer entered the shop and he glanced round in exasperation. He had no excuse to linger any longer. Was he to lose this chance to ask this beautiful girl for a date? Dare he ask her?

Claire made no effort to serve the newcomer and Jim Rafferty came from the back of the shop to attend to the woman. Realizing that Claire was deliberately giving him a chance to talk to her, Michael leant across the counter and whispered, 'Will you come out with me some time?'

Eyes alight with laughter, Claire whispered back, 'How's about tonight?'

He gaped in amazement at her. 'Really?'

'Yes, really. I live in St James's Park. Meet me at the corner at half-six. Does that suit you?'

'Any time . . . any time at all.' He was backing towards the door as he spoke, unable to take his eyes off her. At last, with a grin and a wave of the hand, he left the shop.

On his way down the Falls Road, Michael smiled at all who passed him. He was so happy he wanted to shout for joy. Her name was Claire Ross and tonight he was taking her out on a date. Where could they go? Would she want to go to the Club Orchid? He hoped not. Half-six was a bit early for the dance so perhaps she had somewhere else in mind. He wanted to be alone with her; find out all about her. Many people turned to look after the tall young man with the broad smile. Some fondly; some enviously. Michael was completely unaware of them. Tonight he was going out with the loveliest girl in Belfast and he was over the moon at the thought of it.

As Claire walked up St James's Park that evening she could see Michael's tall lanky figure waiting at the corner. For the life of her she could not understand just why she had agreed to go out with him. In fact, she had positively jumped at the chance. What on earth had possessed her?

Michael smiled and gazed admiringly at her. 'You look lovely.'

Aware that she did look her best, Claire smiled at the compliment. She was wearing a pale green cotton dress; sleeveless and with a brief bodice that emphasized her high bust and long neck. The skirt was full and swirled about long tanned legs, and around her shoulders was draped a white cardigan. White flat-heeled sandals encased her feet and a small clutch purse was tucked under her arm. The white and green of the outfit emphasized her newly acquired tan and her hair was a soft chestnut cloud shot with golden highlights. Michael stood entranced at the beauty of her, admiring the dusting of gold freckles across the bridge of a small straight nose, and the soft pink lipstick that called attention to wide sensuous lips.

To cover her embarrassment at this close scrutiny, Claire teased him.

'Did you just ask me out to stand at the corner gaping at me?'

Flustered, Michael blushed bright red. 'Sorry! Where would you like to go?'

'Have you anywhere in mind?'

'No, I am yours to command,' he assured her.

'Well, since it is such a lovely evening, it seems a shame to spend it indoors. Would you fancy going for a walk?'

His grin widened. Here was a girl after his own heart. 'I'd love to walk with you. Have you any particular direction in mind?'

'Yes, let's go up the mountain loney. It's lovely up there at this time of the year.'

They crossed the Falls Road, and as they climbed the Whiterock Road conversation flowed easily between them. There were no awkward pauses, no searching for something to say. They were in complete harmony. Soon the built up area was left behind and fields stretched to left and right of them, as far as the eye could see. Snapping a twig off the hawthorn hedge, Claire sniffed at it then handed it to Michael.

'Doesn't it smell lovely? Oh, how I'd love to own a house with a view of the countryside.'

Michael smelt the blossom and agreed with her that it would be nice to awaken to a view of hills and fields each morning. The heat was becoming too much for him and, loosening his tie, he removed it and placed it in the pocket of his sports coat. Then shrugging out of the jacket, he slung it over one shoulder. 'Ah, that's better! I can breathe now.'

Although Claire was five foot seven, she barely came up to his shoulder. She smiled up at him. 'Hi, you up there. How tall are you?'

'Six two! Big and bad, my dad used to say.'

'Used to?'

'He died three years ago.'

'I'm sorry to hear that. You must miss him.' At his silent nod she continued, 'Have you any brothers or sisters?'

'I have a stepbrother, four years older than me. My mother was widowed twice. I have two younger sisters, Patsy and Bridget.'

'What age are you?'

'Twenty-two.' At her start of surprise, he laughed. 'Yes, I know I look older, but I'd a hard paper round,' he jested. 'And this . . .' a finger tapped the side of his nose, obviously broken at some time, '. . . doesn't help any.'

'How did you break it?'

'I was climbing a tree in the Falls Park. It was a very tall tree and when I reached the top a branch broke and I came tumbling down. I also broke my leg. I was fourteen at the time and should have known better. My dad was furious. I had just left school and Dad had managed to get me an apprenticeship at carpentry.' He raised a finger in the air. 'Not, mind you, to be confused with joinery, which is much easier. For six weeks I travelled to work with a plaster cast on my leg. But I did learn one lesson, I haven't climbed a tree since! Tell me about yourself. First now, how old are you?'

'I'm also twenty-two, but the only tree I've ever climbed is the apple tree at the bottom of my grannie's garden. I took many a tumble from it but didn't break any bones. When I was fourteen, I started work in a solicitor's office. I was called a trainee typist, but for the first year I was the gofer. You know . . . go for this or go for that. However I did finally become a typist and now I'm in charge of the typing pool.'

'Congratulations! That's a great achievement.'

They had come to the foot of the Black Mountain and, taking the path to the left, started to wend their way upwards. Claire was amazed at herself. Imagine coming up here with a stranger! True, on a beautiful evening like this there were plenty of people about, but even so,

205

she would never have trusted Brian Muldoon enough to come up here alone with him. Yet here she was with a complete stranger, thinking nothing of it. As they walked along she became aware that they were in Lover's Lane and smiled slightly at the idea. Couples were walking, arms entwined or holding hands. Michael reached for her hand and when she did not demur, he drew it through his arm, drawing her close to his side. They walked for a long time, delighted to find that they shared so many common interests. At last they came to an open clearing. Spreading his jacket on the ground, Michael invited her to sit down. Claire sat and stared at the scene before her, surprised that they had climbed so high. The view was wonderful. Fields tumbled down one after the other in every imaginable shade of green, separated by unruly hedges. It was like a great big patchwork quilt spread out in front of them. Small streams meandered in and out, flashing silver in the sunlight. It made Claire imagine a giant darning needle sewing the fields together, the hedges being the big dark stitches. In the far distance the city slumbered in a heat haze and a skylark filled the air with music as it soared high above them. Everything was so peaceful here.

Claire sat, arms around knees, and drank in the beauty of her surroundings. Michael could not take his eyes off her. At last she turned an amused gaze on him. 'Well, do I meet with your approval?'

'You sure do! You're even lovelier than I thought at first. Tell me, why did you agree to come out with me?'

Claire stretched out on the grass and examined the bright blue of the sky. Everything was so still; even the fluffy white clouds were motionless. They hung about the sky like cotton wool buds, and the lark was a mere speck against the blue.

When Michael was about to repeat the question, she shook her head and confessed, 'I really don't know.'

'Have you any serious men friends?' He held his breath

as he awaited an answer to his question. Surely a girl as lovely as Claire was spoken for? He relaxed when once again she shook her head, and prompted her: 'What about the guy you were with at the Club Orchid?'

Hot colour swept across her face as she shook her head vehemently. 'No! Definitely not. What about the blonde you were with?' she countered, brows raised enquiringly. 'Is she anyone special?'

'No! No, I wouldn't do that, ask you out while I was seeing someone else. Eve and I went out together for a short time but it wasn't anything serious.'

'Did she think it was serious?'

Remembering Eve's reaction when he explained to her that he had met someone else, he became flustered. 'Well . . .'

Claire touched his arm gently. 'Forget I asked. It's really none of my business,' she assured him.

'Oh, but that's where you're wrong! I broke off with Eve after I saw you in the shop.'

Embarrassed but flattered, she laughed. 'Really?'

'Really! I made up my mind that day that I was going to marry you.'

'Hey! Aren't you jumping the gun a bit?' she teased. 'For heaven's sake, we've only known each other a few short hours.'

He leant on his elbow, his face inches from hers. 'That doesn't make any difference. I knew I would know the girl for me the minute I set eyes on her, and you're that girl. And you also know that there is something special between us, don't you?'

His eyes slowly scanned her face and it was like a caress. He inched towards her and she waited breathlessly. His lips were gentle on hers and when they trailed her face and the warm contours of her throat, shivers of anticipation passed through her body. Amazed at herself, Claire actually longed for more and her face moved restlessly, lips seeking his. The kiss was long and soul-consuming, leaving her breathless and wide-eyed with wonder. So this was what it was like when you really fancied someone. Wonderful!

'Do you believe me now, that we are meant for each other?' he whispered softly. Bemused, Claire found herself nodding in agreement with him and offered him her lips yet again.

This kiss was deeper still and she wriggled towards him, wanting more contact with him. As passion flared between them, he put her firmly from him and rose to his feet. Grasping her hands, he pulled her up to face him. Cupping her face in his hands, he said softly, 'It will be dark soon. We'd better be heading back.'

They were silent on the way down the mountain path, content to dander along, arms around each other's waist, glad just to be close together. When they eventually arrived at her home he followed her down the side of the house and into the kitchen as if he had been doing it all his life. Sarah jumped to her feet in surprise when her daughter ushered the tall stranger into the living room.

'Mam, Dad, I want you to meet Michael O'Hara.'

Sarah blinked, taken aback by the pride in her daughter's voice. Who was this young man? And what about Brian Muldoon?

Bewildered, she nevertheless took the stranger's hand and bade him welcome. Once Mick had greeted him, Sarah invited Michael to sit down.

'Would you like a cup of tea ... or coffee?' she asked.

'Tea, please.' He accepted the offer gratefully and conversed easily with Mick when Sarah and Claire left the room.

As soon as the kitchen door closed on them, Sarah rounded on her daughter. 'Who on earth's that?'

'I told you, Mam. His name is Michael O'Hara and he lives over Beechmount. He's a carpenter and I like him very much.'

'Where did you meet him?'

'In the shop. He came in to buy chocolates for his mother when our Eileen was there. She knows him and she introduced me to him.'

'What will Brian Muldoon say about this? Or have you finished with him? Brian seemed very serious to me.'

'Mam, it's none of Brian's business. I told you . . . me and Brian are just good friends.'

'Huh!'

'Listen, Mam. I've only just met Michael. I admit that I find him very attractive. But who knows? It might just fizzle out.'

'I think you're making a big mistake. You'd have all your wants if you married Brian.'

'Mam, I don't intend getting married for a long, long time.' Picking up two cups of tea, Claire could not resist adding, 'Although, mind you, Michael has predicted that we're destined to marry.'

The astonished look on her mother's face caused Claire to laugh aloud as she led the way back into the living room.

Sarah prompted Michael about his parents and his work. He good-naturedly answered all her questions. His father was dead. He had one brother and two sisters, and he had a good job and made enough money to support a wife. He smiled fondly at Claire as he talked and she smiled back.

When at last Michael rose to his feet and bade them good night, Claire said she would walk him to the gate. When the door closed on them Sarah turned to Mick.

'What do you think of that carry on then?'

'I think Michael's a very nice young lad, I prefer him to Brian Muldoon. Brian is too evasive for my liking. I always get the impression he has something to hide. You've got to admit that Michael answered all your questions without any sign of resentment. I'd like to see you get away with questioning Brian like that! You'd never dare try it, would you?'

'You're right, Brian is very reserved, but I like him.'

'I suppose the fact that he's a solicitor doesn't come into it? Mmm?'

'Believe it or not, no. That doesn't enter into my feelings for Brian. I think he'll make some girl a fine husband.'

'But not our Claire. I think you can forget all about having a solicitor for a son-in-law, Sarah. I think she's in love with this Michael.'

'But where did he suddenly spring from? You'd think that with him living over Beechmount we'd have seen him around at some time or other.'

'Beechmount covers a large area, Sarah, so it's not surprising that we don't recognize him. Besides, when were you last over there?'

Sarah sighed. 'You're right, of course! I only hope she doesn't rush into something she might regret later on.'

'She couldn't be much quicker than us. We'd only known each other about five months when we got married,' he reminded her.

'Ah, but that was different.'

'I know. You were pregnant!'

'Ah, now, Mick. That was a dig below the belt,' Sarah accused him.

Pulling her down on to his knee, Mick kissed her soundly. 'I'm only pointing out to you that you should mind your own business. You didn't take kindly to advice from Maggie, remember?'

'But this is different,' she insisted.

Mick decided not to argue with her. Sarah had a knack of twisting things around to suit the occasion. Pushing her gently to her feet, he said, 'Come on . . . let's get to bed.'

'I think I'll stay downstairs a while longer.'

'You just want to ask Claire all sorts of questions, don't you, nosy?'

Sarah laughed. 'You know me only too well,' she admitted, and proffered her face for a kiss. 'Just in case you're asleep when I come up.'

Sarah waited some time before at last sleepiness forced her to retire.

Mick was sitting up in bed reading. 'Well?' he greeted her.

'She's not in yet!' Sarah was worried; she was remembering that Eileen had managed to become pregnant to someone they had never set eyes on and how Johnny was blamed for it. Now she appealed to Mick: 'Do you think she's all right? I mean . . . we don't know this young man and she seems terribly attracted to him.'

'Sarah! What can possibly happen at the front gate?'

'They might not be at the gate.' Going to the window, she discreetly lifted the corner of the curtain. To her embarrassment, Claire waved a hand in acknowledgement to her. At Claire's gesture, Michael also glanced up. Raising a hand in farewell to Sarah, he kissed Claire on the cheek and strode off up the street.

Noting his wife's red face, Mick teased her, 'So they caught you snooping?'

'They were at the gate. I'm mortified! They'll think I was spying on them.'

'Never! Never in this wide world would they think a thing like that,' Mick chided her. 'As if you would do such a thing, Sarah.' He chuckled, and ducked as a pillow came sailing through the air in his direction.

So enthralled was Claire with the day's events, she climbed the stairs in a dream and passed her parents' bedroom door without calling out good night, as was her habit. She lay for a long time reliving the magic of the evening. Remembering the touch of his lips, pondering on the strength of the new emotions Michael had awakened in her. She was beginning to understand just what Beth had meant.

Sarah sat at the dressing table brushing her long

chestnut hair. Mick watched her and marvelled at how young she still looked. At forty-four she could easily pass for a sister to her four daughters. Not one single grey hair could he see as the hair rippled under the brush. As her arm rose and fell a full breast came and went from view, shining white through the sheer material of her nightdress. Aware of the effect she was having on her husband, Sarah prolonged her preparations for bed, creaming her face and throat with long sensuous strokes; wiping the cream off slowly and carefully. She was glad that after twenty-seven years of marriage she could still arouse him. Becoming aware that a show was being put on for his benefit, Mick laughed aloud and threw back the bedclothes. In one bound he was out of bed and standing behind her. She sat very still as they gazed at each other in the mirror. Then he sank to his knees behind the low stool and cupped her breasts in his hands. Burying his face in the thick burnished hair, he muttered, 'I love you, Sarah.'

Twisting round, she wrapped her arms around his neck, 'I know you do.'

'Sarah . . . perhaps I shouldn't ask . . . but did you ever regret not running off with Gerry Docherty that time?'

She held him close. She knew what had aroused these fears. Mrs Docherty, her mother's next-door neighbour, had died a few months earlier and the house was lying empty. Mick was probably worrying in case Gerry decided to return from Dublin to live in Belfast.

'No, Mick. Not for one second did I regret it. I was young and foolish, and the sun must have gone to my head. Remember how glorious the weather was that year? Why, we haven't had a summer like it since!'

'Thank God for that!' Mick said fervently, and Sarah laughed.

'I have often thanked God for not letting me ruin all our lives,' she confessed.

'Ah, Sarah . . . Sarah, my love.' Rising to his feet, Mick

pulled her up and over towards the bed. 'Now you're going to pay for putting on that shameless display, you wanton hussy. Come here!'

She was only too willing to obey.

The following weeks were the happiest Claire had ever known. Every spare minute was spent in Michael's company. She simply glowed with love and everybody remarked on how radiant she looked. Mick and Sarah got on well with Michael, and if Sarah regretted that Claire was in love with a carpenter when she could have married a solicitor, she was nevertheless glad to see her favourite daughter so happy.

Even Brian Muldoon seemed to take it very well. He congratulated her on her new appearance and teasingly said she must be in love. These remarks were made openly in the office and everybody remarked what a nice person he was to have taken it so well. Claire did not agree with them. There was a cold depth to his gaze that she did not trust. Pushing her uneasiness aside, she decided to take him at face value and thanked him for his kind wishes.

There was, however, one blot on the young couple's landscape. Michael's mother Maisie did not appear to be so happy about their relationship. The first time Michael invited Claire into his home, Maisie was warm and friendly. But as the evening progressed, Michael noticed a coolness creep into his mother's attitude towards Claire. At a loss to explain the reason for this, he was glad that Claire seemed unaware of the tension. He was annoyed with his mother! How could she possibly find fault with a lovely girl like Claire?

Maisie O'Hara was heart sore. Why, out of all the girls in Belfast, did Michael have to fall in love with Claire Ross? Each day she prayed that the young couple would tire of each other. That the affair would fizzle out. But she prayed in vain. She was aware that Michael was puzzled by her attitude, but how could she tell him the truth?

She couldn't bear to see this big son of hers hurt, so she prayed that some other girl would catch his eye. After all, Claire Ross was not his first girlfriend; please God she prayed, don't let her be the love of his life. Maisie was cool towards Claire. She talked constantly about Michael's previous girlfriends and acted as if she was blind to the deep love they obviously felt for each other.

Unable to bear it any longer, Michael decided to have it out with his mother; clear the air once and for all.

He waited until they had the house to themselves, then tackled her. 'Ma, I don't understand you! How can you possibly find fault with Claire?'

'Whatever gave you the idea that I don't like Claire? I just think that you're too young to be taking things so seriously. Take your time, Michael. Look around you before you settle down.'

'Hah! That's rich coming from you! Didn't you marry Donald's father when you were seventeen?'

'Aye, I sure did, and I lived to regret it. Donald was the only good thing that came out of that marriage.'

'Look, Ma,' he appealed, 'I would be obliged if you'll give Claire a chance. She's the girl for me and you're trying to come between us. I intend to marry her one day, and I hope you will welcome her as a daughter-in-law.'

'Ah, Michael, you haven't proposed, have you?' Maisie gasped in dismay.

'I haven't exactly got down on my knees and asked her to marry me, but it's understood between us. It's only a matter of time, Ma.'

'Ah, Michael . . . Michael, you don't understand what you're doing! You're opening Pandora's box.'

'What on earth do you mean, Ma?'

'Never mind, never mind. I've said too much already.' With a determined step Maisie headed for the stairs. Completely bewildered, Michael watched her climb them. He heard her bedroom door close firmly, then muffled sounds brought him to stand at the foot of the stairs, ears pricked. Was his mother crying? He stood some moments longer but all was quiet. He decided he must have been mistaken. After all, what had she to cry about? She should be very happy that he was going to marry a beautiful, sincere girl like Claire Ross. Claire was such a good person. There were no back doors in her. His mother was wrong to interfere in their affairs. Shaking his head, Michael slumped into a chair and thought long and hard on his mother's words. Pandora's box? What on earth had she meant?

Chapter Six

As Christmas approached Eileen noticed a change in Claire. Gone was the happy carefree air that had surrounded her sister since meeting Michael O'Hara. Now Claire was morose and nervy. Concerned, Eileen decided to find out what was wrong, even if it meant being nosy. They were working on accounts one Monday night when she tentatively questioned Claire.

'Claire, I don't mean to pry ... but I can see that something's worrying you. Have you discovered that you don't care as much as you thought you did about Michael? Remember, he's your first love and sometimes it just peters ...' Her voice trailed off at the look Claire bestowed on her.

'My feelings for Michael will never change!' Claire vowed. 'I love him so much I ache when he's not near. I never knew that I could feel so intensely about anyone, or anything, for that matter. Why, if anything happened to Michael, I wouldn't want to live.'

'Well then, why so glum? Lately you're the picture of misery. Have you two quarrelled?'

'No! No ... I wish that was the reason. You couldn't quarrel with Michael, even if you tried. He can always see the other person's point of view. Makes allowances for even the hardest cases. He makes me feel so humble, he's such a good person. There's no malice at all in him. Actually he reminds me of me dad, he's so easy-going. No, there's nothing wrong between Michael and me.' A deep sigh accompanied the next words. 'It's his mother.

When he first took me home to meet her she couldn't have been nicer. She made me more than welcome, and we got on like old friends. But then, almost overnight, she changed. At first I didn't worry, I know that some women are jealous of their son's girlfriends and I thought she would change. But she hasn't and now I hate going there, to be tolerated. I'm expected to sit and smile while she rants on about Michael's former girlfriends.'

To Eileen's dismay tears started to run unheeded down Claire's cheeks and she wailed. 'I feel so miserable, Eileen.'

Going to her sister, she gathered her close. 'Why didn't you say something before now?' she chastized her. 'You shouldn't bottle things up inside you like this.'

'I didn't say anything because I was so hurt. I hoped she would change, I've tried so hard to make her like me, but it doesn't make any difference. What's wrong with me, Eileen? Why can't she like me?'

The great silent sobs, that had been suppressed so long but now racked Claire's slight frame, tore at Eileen's heart and brought a fierce resentment against this unknown woman, Michael O'Hara's mother. 'Hush, love, hush. This woman must be a fool. There's nothing wrong with you!' she retorted. 'Anyone in their right mind would be glad to have you for a daughter-in-law.'

'Well, Maisie doesn't like me.'

'What has Michael got to say about all this?'

'It's tearing him apart, too! He can't understand his mother's attitude. He questioned her, but she just said she thinks he is too young to marry.'

'Well, I know it's nice if you get along with your in-laws, but it's not the end of the world if you don't! After all, it's not them you're marrying. As long as Michael loves you, that's all that matters. I take it you do intend to marry him?'

'Eventually. We were planning to get engaged at Christmas. But now I don't know what to do. We aren't in any hurry, so I suppose a ring can wait. We're saving up the deposit on a house. And it's not as if we're rushing into anything. That's why we can't understand her attitude. Still, I would like an engagement ring.'

'You let Michael buy you one! Don't worry about Mrs O'Hara. Did she behave like this when his brother got married?'

'No. That's why Michael's so puzzled. Donald was only twenty-one when he got married and there was no question of his being too young. And . . . we're starting from scratch. Both of us, until now, have been careless with money. It will be a couple of years at least before we can afford to get married. That's why Michael can't understand his mother making such a fuss.'

'Oh, well, in a couple of years time she'll probably love you,' Eileen jested, and was glad to see a smile tremble on Claire's lips. 'Come on . . . no more tears! Wipe your face. I think we have a drop of gin somewhere in the house. Widow's ruin, they say . . . but sure, we're not widows. I'll go dig it out.'

When Eileen returned with the drinks she found her sister composed and dry-eyed once more. Claire smiled at her wryly. 'Thanks for letting me rant on, Eileen. It's what I needed, to get it off my chest. To get things into perspective. I don't like to keep mentioning it to Michael, he's already so worried. He even suggested leaving home . . . getting a flat somewhere, but I wouldn't let him. He's devoted to his mother.' She turned a worried glance on Eileen. 'Deep down inside of me, I have this awful feeling that one way or another, she's going to come between us, and it frightens me.'

'Put that idea out of your head. You're becoming paranoid about it. If you and Michael really love each other, nothing will be able to come between you. Tell me, what about his sisters? Do you get on all right with them?'

'Yes, Bridget and Patsy are smashing! So are Donald

and his wife. They're all as mystified as Michael. I suppose I'll just have to grin and bear it. Obviously the woman just can't help disliking me.'

'Well, just you remember, it's not her you're marrying, so don't let her get you down.'

'You're right, Eileen! I'll try to ignore her attitude. In fact, if I can manage it I'll not go back there, because I always come home feeling so miserable.'

True to her word, Claire refused to go where she was not really welcome. Michael was hurt but put no pressure on her. In his heart he didn't blame her. He was in a quandary, didn't know what to think. What on earth was wrong with his mother? This was their first serious disagreement and that it should involve the girl he loved, caused him great distress.

Maisie O'Hara was relieved when Claire stopped visiting her home. She hoped it meant the end of her son's relationship with Mick Ross's daughter. Unwilling to question Michael, she watched and waited for signs that the couple had broken up. However, it soon became apparent that Claire was still a very important part of her son's life. When Michael informed her that he had asked Claire to marry him and that they planned to get engaged at Christmas, despair drove Maisie up the Falls Road to the corner of St James's Park. Her first husband, Sean, had worked at the 'Yard', and her eldest son Donald now worked there, so she had a fair idea what time Mick Ross would finish if he was on the day shift. She decided to try and intercept him. However, after waiting half an hour, and beginning to feel conspicuous, she decided he must be on a different shift and was about to move down the road towards Beechmount when she saw him hop off a bus.

When Mick Ross swung off the trolleybus there was joy in his heart. That afternoon he had been singled out for promotion and couldn't get home quick enough to tell Sarah the good news. This would mean a wage rise. They would be able to afford to run a small car. Sarah would be delighted!

He was passing the woman standing at the corner of the street without a glance, when she stepped forward and spoke to him.

'Hello, Mick.'

It took him some moments to abandon the plans he was making in his head and focus his attention on the small woman standing before him.

When he recognized her a smile split his face and he reached for her hand. 'Maisie! Maisie Simpson, How are you? But sure, I needn't ask. You look marvellous!' His eyes scanned her face. 'Time has been good to you, Maisie.'

'You're being kind, thank you. I must talk to you, Mick.'

'Of course, Maisie.' He hesitated, then asked tentatively. 'Would you like to come down to the house?'

In spite of the anguish she was feeling, a wry smile twisted Maisie's lips at the very idea of her arriving out of the blue with Mick. She could just imagine the look on Sarah's face! It was over twenty-two years since she had stood in their house in Waterford Street and confronted Sarah Ross, demanding that she make up her mind whether or not she wanted her husband back. Maisie had taken a gamble that time and she had lost. Sarah had sent for Mick and he had gone back to his wife, leaving Maisie. If she dwelt long enough on the past, Maisie could still feel the pain caused by Sarah's disdainful treatment of her. However, that was all long ago. It was now that mattered.

'I don't think that would be a very good idea, Mick. Will you walk with me? Just to the gates of the park will do. I know you're just coming home from work and probably hungry, but this won't take long.'

'Of course, Maisie.'

Changing the holdall from his left shoulder to the other side, he ushered Maisie to the inside of the pavement, suiting his step to hers and walking up the road in the direction of the Falls Park. It was chilly and he tightened the muffler at his throat, and pulled the collar of his donkey jacket up around his ears. Memories were flooding back to him and with them came feelings of guilt. He really should have kept in touch with Maisie over the years. She had been more than good to him when he had been at a very low ebb. If it hadn't been for her and her young son Donald, he'd have hit the bottle for sure, and God knows what would have become of him. He really should have kept an eye on her welfare. It was very remiss of him not to. Well, it was too late now for regrets; he hadn't kept in touch, and Maisie's reappearance was bringing justifiable feelings of guilt. Given the choice he would have kept in touch, but fear of what interpretation Sarah would put on his actions, had she found out, had forced his hand, and he had cut all ties.

With a sideways glance he studied Maisie. He had spoken the truth when he said that life had been good to her. Her hair was still like pale gold and bounced about her head as if electrified, bringing back memories of how the light used to catch it and make it look like a halo around her face. Her skin was still smooth and unlined, and even the thick winter coat she wore failed to conceal her curves. To his amazement a picture of her in a short see-through nightie crossed his mind, bringing a blush to his cheeks. She had been a lovely girl. Now she was an attractive woman. He wondered what friends and neighbours would think if they saw them walking together. He was sure some would have noticed already. Word would soon get back to Sarah. It was as well that this was an innocent meeting.

Maisie smiled slightly when he courteously walked her to the inside of the pavement. He had always been such a gentleman. He had changed little. A mite stouter perhaps, and his hair was almost completely grey, but he still managed to look handsome. How would he react to the bombshell she was about to drop? They had walked for some minutes and still Maisie could not find the words to break the contentment she could feel radiating from Mick.

He smiled happily down at her. 'Well now, Maisie. What can I do for you? Are you in some kind of trouble?' he asked kindly.

In spite of herself Maisie's voice was bitter when she answered him. 'Do you really think I'd come to you for help, Mick? You salved your conscience with a bottle of perfume and a toy twenty-two years ago, then walked away. Do you really think I'd come to you if I had any other choice in the matter? No, Mick. If I could help myself I wouldn't be here.'

'Ah, Maisie,' he cried defensively. 'Honestly, I thought it was for the best. You'd met another man. I was back with Sarah. It would only have complicated things if I had kept in touch.'

'To be truthful, Mick, at that time I agreed with you. I loved you, but I knew that you would never leave Sarah. I was very lucky to meet Matthew. He was a good man. He looked after me well until he died three years ago. But now I wish that you had made it your business to see how life treated me. I really cared for you, we were lovers. Was that asking too much?'

'No, Maisie, I'm sorry that I didn't. I admit I was in the wrong. But why bring all this up now?' They had reached the main gates of the park. Mick motioned across the road towards them. 'Do you want to go in and sit down?'

'No, Mick. You're the one who'll need to sit down. Brace yourself! I married a man named Matthew O'Hara.'

Mick gaped at her in bewilderment. Why on earth had she sought him out to tell him this? Was she going through that difficult period some women encounter, the time when some of them aren't accountable for their actions?

He looked so perplexed, Maisie wanted to shake him. 'Mick, listen to me! Michael O'Hara is your son!'

The penny dropped slowly. Then Mick was dragging deep breaths of the frosty night air deep into his lungs to help him hold on to his senses.

Maisie watched him and smiled grimly. 'Yes, that's how I felt when I first realized Claire was your daughter. Gobsmacked! Come on, you need to sit down.'

Leading the way across the road, she entered the park and made for the nearest bench. The grass crunched under her feet and the bench was coated with frost. Not a healthy place to be sitting but they wouldn't be there long. In a daze, Mick followed her. When they were seated he turned to her and entreated, 'Ah, Maisie . . . Maisie, tell me I'm dreaming? Tell me this is all a nightmare?'

'I wish I could, Mick . . . how I wish I could! But as sure as I'm sitting here, it's the truth!'

'Why on earth didn't you tell me you were pregnant?' he accused. 'Good God, woman, I'd the right to know!'

Maisie's voice was angry when she retaliated. 'Would you have wanted to know? Eh? Ah, no, Mick. Think about it! You were back with your precious Sarah and nothing else mattered to you. You were glad to sever all connections with me. When you came bearing gifts that Christmas you should have noticed that I was pregnant. You had eyes in your head! It was plain to be seen. I knew that Sarah was pregnant too, with Claire. I was further on than her . . . and you didn't even notice.' Maisie shook her head in disbelief. 'Or did you just assume it was this new man friend of mine who was responsible? Did you think I jumped into bed with anyone? Is that what you thought of me, Mick?'

He was flabbergasted. 'Maisie, I swear I didn't know! Do you think I wouldn't have tried to help out. Ah,

Maisie, do you really believe I knew you were pregnant?'

'No, in my heart I didn't believe you'd walk away from your responsibilities, Mick. There must be some truth in the old saying that there's none so blind as those who don't want to see. If Matthew hadn't been so willing to marry me and claim the child I was carrying as his ... I would have had to upset your and Sarah's lovey, dovey world.'

At the mention of Sarah, Mick cried. 'Oh, dear God! How am I going to tell her?'

Maisie grimaced. Sarah! Always Sarah. Well, she was in for the shock of her life. It was about time Sarah realized that the world didn't revolve around her. That her husband had feet of clay. With a wave of her hand Maisie dismissed Sarah and reminded him, 'More important still, Mick, how are we going to tell Michael and Claire?' In spite of the tight rein she had kept on her feelings, at the mention of her son, Maisie broke down. 'They're so very much in love and we've spoilt it for them, Claire is such a lovely warm caring girl, and I've turned her against me in my endeavour to part them. I hoped that they need never know. I prayed they would fall out. But no, Michael says he's buying Claire an engagement ring at Christmas.' She wiped her eyes with the handkerchief Mick thrust at her. 'They have to be told the truth.'

He put his arm around her shoulders to comfort her and she burrowed close. He couldn't think straight. 'Oh, Jesus, Maisie! What are we going to do?' he wailed.

Pity overruled all the bitterness Maisie was harbouring. 'Take your time, Mick,' she said softly, as she wiped away more tears. 'Think about it, and then let me know what you decide to do. Remember ... it's not a case of *if* we tell them ... it's a case of how and when. And the sooner the better. Now let's go home before we freeze to death.'

Before rising from the bench, she paused to allow a young girl coming down the path towards the gate, to pass by. As the girl came level with them Maisie drew back in dismay. It was Claire. She stopped in her tracks and stared at them in bewilderment. Her eyes took in the fact that Mick's arm was around Maisie's shoulders and she noted her tear-stained cheeks. Maisie sat very still and stared at the girl her son loved. The glorious chestnut hair framing a pale oval face. Big dark-lashed green eyes clouded with sorrow. High cheekbones pink with the frosty air. A girl she knew to be kind and considerate and whom she had hurt by her apparent dislike. A girl she would have welcomed as a daughter-in-law in any other circumstances. When the look in Claire's eyes turned to contempt, hot colour burned in Maisie's cheeks and she felt tears of self-pity sting her eyes.

Claire turned her attention to her father. 'Dad? Dad? What are you doing here?'

Mick opened his mouth but words failed him. He realized how guilty they must look. What could he say to his daughter? What on earth must Claire be thinking?

Claire was confused. How on earth did they know each other? Her father had never mentioned knowing Michael's mother but it was obvious that they were far from strangers. They both looked so embarrassed at her intrusion that without another word, Claire turned on her heel and hurried on down the park. What on earth was going on. Why was her father in the Falls Park with Michael's mother? Was this why Maisie disliked her so much? Could her father possibly be having an affair with Maisie?

Mick was never able to recall how he got home that night. He couldn't remember the walk down the Falls Road again with Maisie. He was in a daze. At the corner of St James's Park Maisie reminded him that she still lived in the same house, and that he must let her know his intentions. Then she gave him a gentle push in the direction of his home. Once in the house Mick hurried upstairs to the bathroom before Sarah could apprehend him. Promotion and pay rise were forgotten as he thrust his head under the cold tap. He descended the stairs with feet that dragged. He dreaded entering the dining room. What would Claire do? Would she question him in front of her mother? He hoped not. He needed time to think. At last he forced himself into the dining room and was relieved to find it empty. He sat at the table and played with the plate of food Sarah placed in front of him.

'Where is everybody?'

'You're late! Everyone else has eaten and gone,' Sarah informed him. 'Claire dined early. She's away up the Glen Road to deliver some papers for Eileen, and Emma's over in me mam's.'

Well, that answered all his questions. Even the one he had been asking himself. What was Claire doing in the Falls Park? On her return from her errand for Eileen, she had obviously decided to cut through the park. It was more pleasant to walk there than the road.

Sarah watched him push the food about his plate and was bewildered at her husband's lack of interest in his dinner. He usually wolfed it down. 'Is that why you're so late? Have you been eating elsewhere?' she challenged him.

'No, Sarah. I'm just not hungry. I don't feel very well.' He smiled wryly at these words. Talk about an understatement. He felt devastated. 'Perhaps I'm coming down with a bug. I'll go on up to bed now. Try and sleep it off.'

Mick was not one for complaining unnecessarily so Sarah fussed over him; insisted that he take a stomach powder. When she retired for the night she gave him some aspirin and a hot drink, saying it would make him feel better. Mick wished the aspirin could make him feel better; work a miracle. Unable to sleep, he tossed and turned so much that at last Sarah cried out in exasperation and pulled the bedclothes back around her for the umpteenth time.

'I'm sorry, Sarah. Look, love. I'll take a pillow and blanket and sleep downstairs on the settee. It would be silly, both of us losing our sleep.'

Sarah, at the end of her tether, agreed that this was a good idea and warned him that if he was no better in the morning she would send for the doctor.

Downstairs Mick walked the floor. As he paced up and down he could see no way out of the dilemma into which Maisie had plunged him. Everybody must be told the truth. His past had caught up with him. At first all he had worried about was Sarah's reaction to the news, but now he thought of Claire and Michael, so very much in love. This news was going to break their hearts. It could split the family! He blamed Maisie for not telling him the truth at the time. If she had done so, all this could have been avoided. He would have known that he had a son. And a fine strapping lad at that! A son he could be proud of. But at what cost? All those years ago, how would Sarah have coped with the news that Maisie was also pregnant? It was because of Sarah's jealousy that he had led her to believe that the friendship between him and Maisie was platonic. He had been afraid to tell his wife the truth then, but he would have to tell her now.

To be fair, hadn't he honestly believed that his wife intended to run off with Gerry Docherty? Wasn't that what all the indications were? Wasn't it Sarah's fault that when she asked him to leave the house, in his misery and loneliness he'd turned to Maisie for solace? Hadn't Maisie said that she understood? Hadn't she stressed that they were two lonely people and that they were hurting no one? She had promised that there would be no ties. If Sarah had decided to run off with Gerry Docherty he would have been damned glad of warm, passionate, kind Maisie. It was Sarah who had put *him* out of the house. It was her fault. His wife was in no position to cast stones. However, he knew better than to think that she would take this lying down. He'd be the villain; she'd be the saint!

And he *had* deceived her. She had confessed that nothing had happened between her and Gerry, bar a few kisses. She had waited for him to confess likewise and although he had not put it into words, he had led her to believe he also was blameless; let her believe that Maisie was just a friend. If he had been truthful then, this wouldn't come as such a shock to Sarah. What a fool he'd been. And now, here he was, blaming everybody but himself. He was also a yellow coward! This was something that he would have to face up to. Would Sarah forgive him?

Morning came all too soon for Mick. Before the family was awake he locked himself in the bathroom and dunked his head under the cold tap to wake himself up before facing Sarah. One thing he didn't want, and that was to stay at home today. He had to put on a show of feeling better or she would call the doctor out. He couldn't allow that to happen! He needed to get away from the house, to plan the kindest way to break the news to Claire and Sarah.

Claire came into the dining room when Mick was forcing himself to eat his breakfast. At the sight of the dark shadows under his daughter's eyes he felt like weeping.

Sarah greeted Claire with concern. 'Are you feeling ill as well?'

'As well?'

'Yes, your dad was poorly last night. There must be a bug going about. Perhaps the two of you should stay at home today, then you won't be accused of spreading your germs.'

Both father and daughter reacted strongly to this suggestion.

'I feel fine now, Sarah,' Mick stressed.

Claire avoided her father's eye and assured her mother, 'There's nothing wrong with me, Mam.'

'You could have fooled me. You both look like death warmed up. Don't they, Emma?' she asked her youngest daughter.

Emma had her nose in a book as usual. She was finding the work at St Dominic's hard going but was determined to make the most of it. She wanted to become a schoolteacher. Now she examined the faces of Claire and her father. 'I have to admit that you two do look washed out,' she agreed with her mother. 'But then, Claire never has any colour in her face.'

'Thanks! Thanks a lot. We can't all be robust like you!' Claire retaliated.

With a shrug Emma returned her attention to her breakfast and book.

Claire lingered over her breakfast, not wanting to leave the house at the same time as her father. She could not bear to walk to the corner with him and travel down the Falls Road in the same bus. What on earth would they talk about? Usually he was away long before now. Was he waiting to waylay her?

Grateful that Claire was not questioning him in front of Sarah, Mick did indeed want to get his daughter alone to thank her for her consideration. God knows what interpretation she had put on seeing him in the Falls Park with his arm around Maisie the night before, but anything was better than the truth. When Claire could delay no longer without fear of being late for work, father and daughter left the house together, with a warning from Sarah ringing in their ears that they were to come home if they felt no better during the day.

Claire walked in silence, avoiding her father's eye. Mick watched her covertly. He wished now that he had encouraged Brian Muldoon; made him welcome. Then perhaps Claire would have got engaged to Brian and

Michael might never have appeared on the scene. If that were the case, today he'd be in his glory, basking in his wife's admiration as they planned what to do with the extra money his promotion would bring each week.

With a sigh of regret, he broke the silence. 'Claire, I owe you an explanation – but later. I'll explain later, love,' he muttered, greatly embarrassed. 'And thanks for not mentioning seeing me with Maisie. You must be puzzled and confused, so I appreciate you not saying anything in front of your mother.'

Claire threw him a resentful glance. 'Are you having an affair with Michael's mother? Is that why she dislikes me so much?'

'An affair?' he cried, aghast. 'Ah, no, Claire! You've got it all wrong. I knew Maisie a long time ago. But honestly, until last night I haven't set eyes on her for years. And she doesn't dislike you. She was saying what a nice person you are.'

It was obvious that Claire didn't believe him. To escape travelling to town in the same bus as her father, and having to indulge in inane conversation, she headed towards Rockmore Road and her grandfather's shop. She would probably be late for work and receive a reprimand, but no matter! Anything was better than travelling down the Falls Road in the same bus as her father.

'I'll see you later, Dad. I want to have a word with Granda,' she lied. Without another glance, she hastened across the road.

It was a long slow-moving day for Mick. His haggard appearance and late arrival at work were put down to the fact that he must have been celebrating his promotion the night before and was now suffering from a hangover. As they heard about his good news, mates from other departments came to congratulate him. He thought his face would crack, he had to smile so often and tell lies about how thrilled Sarah was about his promotion. At the end of the day he was no further forward. He had racked his brains and could think of no way to soften the blow he was about to deal his family. All hell was about to be let loose.

If only he had someone he could talk it over with, someone who would understand. Get it sorted out in his mind by talking about it . . . Maggie! She had been aware of Sarah's infatuation with Gerry Docherty. Wasn't it she who had put him wise to what was going on? He would talk to Maggie.

Hoping Sarah wouldn't see him going by on the far side of the street, Mick passed his own house and entered Maggie's driveway. Going round the side of the house to the back, he entered the kitchen. He was dismayed to hear voices coming from the front of the house. He thought Maggie was always alone at this time of the evening, as the shop didn't close until eight. Then he realized that it was Wednesday. The shop closed at one every Wednesday. He was about to slip out again, when Maggie's voice reached him.

'I'm sure I heard the back door close, Barney.' Before Mick could escape, Maggie caught sight of him and cried back over her shoulder: 'Barney . . . I was right! It's Mick. What brings you here at this time, Mick?' Concern furrowed her face. 'Is anything wrong?'

'Everything is fine, Maggie,' he lied. 'I just wanted a word with you.'

'Come into the sitting room, Mick. There's a nice big fire there. And you'll never guess who's here. Gerry Docherty!'

Gerry rose to his feet to greet him. Observing Mick's haggard appearance, his apparent embarrassment at seeing him, Gerry made his excuses. 'It's nice seeing you again, Mick, but I was just leaving.' He turned to Maggie. 'I'll call in and see you tomorrow, Maggie. Good night, Barney.' With a nod at Mick, Gerry left the room and silence reigned until they heard the front door close

231

on him. Barney had also noticed that Mick was in a state and said haltingly, 'Perhaps you would like to talk with Maggie alone, Mick?'

'No . . . I'm in trouble.' He nodded towards Docherty's house and grimaced. 'And it looks like another ghost from the past is here to haunt me. There's going to be an almighty uproar and I'll not be able to keep it quiet, so you may as well hear about it now, Barney. It's Sarah I'm worried about. I just don't know how to tell her . . .'

'Take off your coat, son.' When Mick declined, saying that he wouldn't be staying long, Maggie took his arm and urged him towards the armchair beside the fire. 'Sit down, son. Barney, is there any drink in the house?'

With a nod, he left the room, and Mick turned in anguish to Maggie.

'Maggie . . . what would you say if I told you I had a son?'

Shocked, she groped for a chair and sat down. 'Mick . . . are you telling me you've got some girl in trouble?'

'No, no . . . well, not lately.' In spite of the seriousness of the situation Mick found himself smiling slightly at the idea that he was capable of getting a girl into trouble. He had never even thought of another woman since Maisie. 'Maggie, do you remember Maisie Simpson?'

Maggie started to shake her head slowly from side to side. The name seemed familiar but she was unable to put a face to it. Mick prompted her.

'The widow I lodged with when Sarah put me out of the house, remember? The time Sarah thought she was in love with Gerry Docherty?'

'Ah, yes, I remember now.'

'Well, Maisie bore me a son all those years ago. Maggie, I swear I didn't know anything about it. I didn't even know she was pregnant. She never meant me to know.'

Maggie was sceptical but held her tongue. Obviously Mick had enough to worry about without her chastizing him. She remembered, all those years ago, how Mick had led her to believe that Maisie was just a friend and all he wanted was for Sarah to take him back. Now she questioned him. 'How did you find out?'

'Maisie was waiting at the corner for me last night when I got off the bus. She told me then.'

Maggie shook her head in bewilderment. 'Excuse me if I appear stupid, but didn't you say she never meant you to know? Why is she suddenly telling you all this now? Is she threatening to tell Sarah?'

'No! Yes! No! You see, Maggie, she had no choice.' Mick paused for a moment, then dropped his bombshell. 'Michael O'Hara is my son.'

During this conversation Barney had returned to the room and stood silent. Now he thrust a glass into Mick's hand. 'Here, drink this! You need it.'

There was a stunned silence and Mick gulped at the whiskey Barney had given him, feeling the welcome warmth course through his body.

'Maggie, how am I going to tell Sarah?'

'Sarah? Never mind Sarah! Given time she can weather the storm, but what about Claire and . . . and Michael? I can't take in the fact that he's your son.'

'Listen, Maggie. I've been racking my brains all day and I thought . . . now . . . it's just an idea that came to me.' He leant forward entreatingly. If only they would agree with him! 'Supposing Maisie had died? Mmm? No one would have known the truth. Michael and Claire could have married in good faith and no one be any the wiser. Do you follow my reasoning, Maggie . . . Barney? I'm sure it's happened before! Now suppose we didn't tell them. Would that be so wrong?'

'Mick! How can you even harbour such a thought? What about their children? Eh? Have you thought about that? You're just looking for a way out, Mick, but there isn't one. You *do* know Michael is your son! They must be told.'

'I just thought I could spare them the heartbreak of knowing the truth,' he lamented.

'And maybe end up with a whole different kind of heartache? No, Mick! They must be told. You can't take the chance that handicapped children may be brought into the world because of your neglect. I'm sorry if I'm not telling you what you want to hear.' Maggie turned to Barney. 'Don't you agree with me, Barney?'

'I'm afraid I do agree with Maggie. You'll have to tell them, Mick. There's no alternative.'

He drained the glass. His hand was shaking. 'You're right! In my heart I know you're right. It was just a forlorn hope. Thanks for listening to me.' He nodded towards the empty glass. 'And for the Dutch courage. I'm going to need it. I'll go home now. Sarah will be wondering where I am.'

Maggie accompanied him to the back door. Full of compassion for this big man who wouldn't knowingly hurt a fly, she took him in her arms and gave him a bear hug. 'I know you won't believe me, Mick, but it will all sort itself out. It has to!'

'I hope you're right, Maggie. God, but I hope you're right! Thanks. Thanks for everything.'

Mick was right. Sarah was indeed wondering where he was. She met him at the door. 'Where on earth have you been? That's two nights running your dinner's been ruined. It's been in the oven for a hour. Don't you dare complain to . . .' As Mick moved further into the room, the light fell full on his face and the sight stopped Sarah in mid-sentence. 'Good God . . . you look awful! What's the matter?'

'Where is everybody?'

'Emma's away back to school for a while, they're rehearsing a Nativity play, and Claire is away up to Eileen's. She works there on a Wednesday night, remember? She was in a terrible hurry tonight, gobbled up her dinner so quickly she's sure to have a tummy ache. Why? Why do you want to see them?'

'Sarah, come into the living room and sit down. I've something to tell you.'

'Eat your dinner first.'

'No, Sarah. That can wait. I've a bit of bad news, I'm afraid.'

'That sounds ominous, Mick.' He just nodded and Sarah continued, 'You're frightening me.'

Mick took her by the arm and gently led her into the living room.

When Sarah was seated, her husband stood at the mantelpiece and tried to find words to confess his sin. Gerry Docherty came to mind and he found himself blurting out words that had no bearing at all on what he should be saying. He was just delaying the evil moment. 'Did you know that Gerry Docherty was home?'

Sarah gaped at him. Was this the reason he looked so awful? Had he heard Gerry was home and was worried how she would react to his return? She was surprised that Mick was still so jealous of Gerry after all these years. She decided to be honest. 'Yes, he called over to see me this afternoon. Is that what you're so upset about?' She rose to her feet and moved closer to her husband. 'He's not coming back to live next door to me mam and Barney. His son Danny . . . you remember young Danny? Well, he's a journalist now, and he's going to live there for a time. See what he thinks of Belfast. Gerry means nothing to me, Mick. And that's the truth.'

Mick reached for her and she willingly entered his arms. He sank his face into the softness of her hair. She smelt lovely and her arms clasped him close. There was a warm glow inside Sarah that Mick could still care so much. Her nose picked up the aroma of alcohol and she drew back and gazed up into his face. 'You've been drinking!' she accused.

Mick nodded. 'Dutch courage, Sarah ... I've something to tell you and no matter what you may think, please believe that I love you. That I've always loved you. Even if my actions may seem to say otherwise.'

'What on earth are you talking about? Mick, if you have bad news for me ... spit it out! Stop beating about the bush.'

'You're going to be very angry.'

Exasperated, she cried, 'Oh, Mick! Get it over with ... tell me!'

'Last night I discovered that, years ago, I fathered a son.' Sarah began to draw away from him but he clung on to her.

'You have a son?' Her voice was low, subdued. The calm before the storm?

Mick nodded and watched different expressions flit across his wife's face. Shock, disbelief, fear.

'Mick, if this is some kind of a joke, it's not funny!'

'I wish to God it was, Sarah. Twenty-two years ago, Maisie Simpson had my son.'

'Maisie?' Her voice came out in a squeak of disbelief. 'But you said ... you told me ...'

'I know, Sarah. I know what I led you to believe all those years ago and I was wrong to deceive you. But we were back together again, and I was so happy I pretended that I'd never slept with Maisie. I was afraid to tell you the truth. But I swear I didn't know Maisie was pregnant.'

With a vicious thrust of her fists and knees she was out of his arms and standing arms akimbo. At the back of her mind a voice was whispering: Maisie did what you could never do. She gave him a son. There were tears in her eyes when she asked, 'Why are you telling me this now, Mick? Is Maisie making demands?'

'No, Sarah. She never meant me to know. She's every bit as upset as we are. She had to tell me. You see, Sarah, Michael O'Hara is my son.'

Stunned, she sank slowly down on to the settee, her

mind grappling with this awful news. Her eyes were wide and he saw fear in their depths. Her first thought was for herself. What a tit-bit of scandal this was for the neighbours to feast on. 'So ... it's all going to be common knowledge?' Then she remembered her daughter. How much Claire loved Michael. Good God, they were about to get engaged! 'And Claire! What about poor Claire?' she ranted. 'Oh, dear God, what a mess.'

'I know. That's why I was in such a state. How am I going to tell her?'

'Is anything wrong?'

Neither of them had heard Emma enter the house. Now she stood in the doorway looking from one to the other in surprise.

It was Mick who answered her. 'No, love, no. There's nothing wrong.'

These words brought Sarah to her feet and her fury erupted. 'No, Emma. The arse has just fallen out of my world ... and your da says nothing's wrong! But then he would, wouldn't he? Since it's his sin that has found him out!'

'Sarah! There's no need for that kind of talk. Emma will learn soon enough.'

'For heaven's sake, stop treating me like a child. I'm fifteen years old!' Emma cried in exasperation. 'What's wrong? Is Claire pregnant?'

Sarah and Mick gaped at each other in horror. It was Sarah who muttered, 'I hope not. I sincerely hope not.' The glare she directed at Mick was full of hatred. 'Your father has something to tell you, Emma.' As she passed Mick on her way to the door, she stabbed at his chest with a finger. 'Tell her, you stupid bastard. Go on, tell her! She has a right to know! Is there only one bastard or have you any more skeletons in the cupboard for later on, eh?' she hissed.

'Sarah!' Mick made a grab for his wife's arm to detain

237

her. Deftly she eluded him and with a final glare at him left the room.

Emma was flabbergasted. Her mother swearing? 'What does Mam mean, Dad?'

Mick looked at his youngest daughter, so innocent to the ways of the world, and found he could not tell her the truth. 'Later, Emma. Don't worry, you'll hear all about it. I've to go out now for a while. See you later.'

Emma went over in her mind all she had heard but could not make head nor tail of it. The best thing to do was ask her mother to explain. She climbed the stairs but at the door of her parents' room she paused, undecided. She wasn't sure but she thought she heard muffled sobs coming from inside. Perhaps it would be better to wait until her father returned. Yes, that would be the best thing to do. He had promised to tell her later, so she would wait; not disturb her mother.

Mick strode down the Falls Road, aware that he should have stayed and comforted Sarah. But he couldn't bear to be derided in front of Emma. Better to let Sarah get used to the idea, then maybe she would listen to reason. After all, it was twenty-two years ago that he had committed adultery, not last week! Now he was going to see Maisie and Michael. That big, lanky, kind-hearted lad that everybody was so fond of, was his son. In spite of all the misery it would cause, he couldn't help feeling proud that Michael was his. But, how would Michael take the news? Oh, God, it was all such a mess!

It had been a long time since she'd heard it, but Maisie still recognized Mick's step approaching the house. With a worried glance towards where Michael sat reading, she hastened into the hall and opened the door before Mick got a chance to knock. With a finger to her lips, she ushered him into the kitchen.

'Well?' she whispered.

'I've just broken the news to Sarah.'

'How did she take it?'

'Bad . . . very bad.'

'And Claire? Have you told her?'

'Not yet. Have you told Michael?'

'No, I was waiting to see what you were going to do.'

'Is he here?' At Maisie's nod, Mick said, 'Shall we break the news to him together?'

With a sigh Maisie turned and led the way into the living room. When they entered the room, Michael rose to his feet, a hostile look on his face. Claire had told him about seeing his mother with Mick in the Falls Park the night before and it had taken all his self-control not to question his mother about the episode. However, Claire had asked him to wait and see what Mick would do and he had given in to her wishes. Now he eyed Mick warily, but it was his mother he addressed.

'Ma, how come you never ever said that you knew Mick Ross?'

At the mocking tone of Michael's voice, Mick raised a hand to stop any further remarks. 'Your mother did what she thought was best. I've come to explain, Michael.'

There was hostility in the look Michael directed between them. 'So you are having an affair, is that it? Well, Claire and I want no part of it. If you've come to ask me to keep silent, you needn't have bothered. We wouldn't dream of hurting Sarah by being the bearers of such bad news. I suggest you both catch yourselves on, before you do some irreparable damage.' His expression softened a little as he eyed his mother. 'I'm surprised at you, Ma. I know you miss Dad, but still . . . I'm surprised.'

'Sit down, Michael. I've some bad news for you,' Mick said.

Slowly, Michael sank down onto the edge of the settee, arms resting on thighs, hands linked. Mick turned to Maisie. 'Would you like to leave us alone?'

'No, I'll stay, Mick. I am as much to blame as you.'

She sat on the opposite side of the settee from her son and Mick chose a chair facing them.

'Michael, there is only one way to say this and that's straight out. Twenty-two years ago Sarah and I separated for a time and I lodged here, in this house, with your mother and Donald.' He smiled kindly at Maisie. 'Your mother was very good to me and we became very close. You are the result of that closeness. I knew nothing about this until last night. Maisie didn't want me to know. She has been distracted since you started dating Claire and of course she had to tell me . . . so there you are. Claire is your half-sister. You can never marry her. You're my son!'

Michael listened in stunned silence to this disclosure. He took in all the words but forbade his mind to digest them. When Mick finished speaking, Michael rose slowly to his feet. He felt calm and in control but he knew he was going to hit this big man he had come to like so much. He knew he shouldn't touch him, but still felt the greatest satisfaction when his fist crushed into Mick's nose, drawing blood.

Totally unprepared, the force of the blow crashed Mick's head back against the hard wood of the chair, stunning him. In a rage he staggered groggily to his feet, ready to retaliate. However, before he could get his bearings, another blow caught him on the jaw, knocking him back down on to the chair again, sending both him and it crashing to the floor.

The shock that had held Maisie frozen, passed, and she was on her feet, hanging on to her son's arm as he waited, clenched fist raised, for Mick to rise. 'Michael . . . please, son! Don't do this awful thing. I beg you, don't hit him. He really didn't know about you. Nobody knew but me and Matthew. And you didn't suffer because of it. Matthew loved you like you were his own flesh and blood.'

She flinched at the scorn in the look Michael bestowed

on her. 'You should have told me the truth, Ma. You're bound to have known that I had half-sisters running about. That I could meet them anywhere, any time. You should have warned me, Ma! Now what is going to happen? How will I be able to live without Claire?'

With one last glare at Mick, he grabbed his coat and left the house. All the while his mind repeated over and over: How will I be able to live without my lovely Claire? Did she know yet? He couldn't wait until she stopped work at nine. He'd have to go up to Eileen's now and find out if she had been told this awful news.

He discovered that Claire did not know. He broke the news to the two sisters, and from the circle of Michael's arms Claire rounded on Eileen and cried, 'I told you, didn't I? I told you she was going to come between us!'

Eileen was flabbergasted at the revelation that her father had committed adultery. It incensed her to think of the way he had treated Johnny because he thought he had seduced her. Why, the hypocrite! The bloody hypocrite! He had made her feel so ashamed.

Pity for her sister overwhelmed her, blocking out all other feeling. She had been so sure that nothing could separate Claire from the man she loved, and now, to hear this! 'Ah, Claire, Claire, what can I say? What can I say to you?' she lamented.

'Nothing. Nothing can change this terrible thing.' Claire pressed closer to Michael and looked long and deep into his eyes. 'Will this make any difference to us?'

He cupped her face in his hands. 'Not unless you want it to, love.'

As he bent to kiss her, Eileen quietly left the room. This was private business. The decision was theirs and theirs alone. But what about any children they might have?

Claire could not bear the thought of going home to

face her parents. She realized that her poor mother must now know the truth. Sarah would be in an awful state, but Claire knew that she could be of little comfort to her. They would only end up crying on each other's shoulders. Eileen offered to put her sister up for the night and assured Claire that she would be welcome to move in and stay for as long as she wished. Gratefully, Claire accepted her sister's offer. She needed time to think; to sort things out in her mind. The three of them sat for a long time discussing the implications of the confession from the past, speculating how it had come about. The two girls found it difficult to see their father in the role of adulterer. For as far back as they could remember, he had always appeared a loving husband and devoted father, whereas Michael was convinced that his mother must have been seduced. Michael and Claire were, however, emphatic on one point. It would make no difference whatsoever to their plans to get married.

Eileen listened in silence, knowing that when they had time to think more logically they were bound to see that it would be wrong to marry; even supposing that Mick and Maisie kept quiet and the church married them, unaware of their relationship to each other. It was nearly midnight when, declining Eileen's offer of a bite of supper, Michael at last bade them good night and thanked Eileen for sharing their troubles. Claire said she needed some fresh air and would walk to the corner with him. When they had gone, Eileen made up the bed settee and prepared a pot of tea and set out some crackers and cheese. Johnny, who had been working on some drawings upstairs during the evening, now joined them for a late snack. He quickly perceived that something was amiss but in the face of Claire's obvious distress, did not ask any prying questions. Talking easily and lightly in an attempt to ease the tension, he even managed to bring a reluctant smile to her lips with his silly jokes.

In bed that night Eileen related all the events of the evening to her husband. Johnny's reaction to the news upset her somewhat. He actually showed compassion towards her father.

'This is a terrible blow to Mick at his time of life. He should have been told the truth all those years ago. Now this woman's silence could ruin your parents' lives as well as Claire's and Michael's.'

'Hah! My dad's a hypocrite! Look at the way he . . .' Aghast at the words trembling on her lips, Eileen turned aside and pretended to sneeze. She had been about to say, 'Look at the way he treated you because of our shotgun wedding.'

'Bless you! You were saying?' Johnny prompted her.

'I forget what I was going to say now.' Eileen laughed softly and in an endeavour to divert his thoughts, snuggled closer to him. 'That sneeze knocked it right out of my mind.'

Johnny was persistent. The sneeze had not rung quite true to him. He pushed her gently away from him and looked into her face. 'You said: "My dad is a hypocrite, look at the way he . . .".'

'Oh, yes . . . yes, I remember now, I said my dad was a hypocrite because, well . . . he was always so good-living. I thought he was beyond reproach. I placed him high up on a pedestal! To me, he was next-door to a saint . . . and to discover that he was an adulterer? Well, it's just too hard to take in.'

Johnny noted her heightened colour and frowned. Why was she so agitated? 'Your father should be pitied, not criticized,' he said. 'That woman should have told him she was pregnant. It's like a slap in the face, coming out of the blue like this, after all these years. Especially in these awful circumstances. Maisie O'Hara deserves to be horse-whipped.'

'Aren't you being just a wee bit hard on her?' Eileen had no intention of letting her father off the hook so

243

lightly. 'After all, it takes two to tango, if you see what I mean! It wasn't all her fault, you know.'

This accusation gave Eileen food for thought, though. It didn't really take two consenting adults. Hadn't she been taken against her will? Hadn't her brief encounter with Billy Greer resulted in a child being conceived? Still, although her father had fallen a notch or two in her estimation, Eileen could not imagine him forcing himself on a woman. He was far too gentle for anything like that; much too considerate. Too considerate? Confused at her line of reasoning, she brought her attention back to her husband.

'I couldn't be hard enough.' Johnny was adamant. 'This woman's actions could cause a permanent rift between your mother and father. And another thing! Michael had the right to know who his real father was. He should have been told as soon as he was old enough to understand. Why, this Maisie woman probably palmed him off on to Matthew O'Hara as his own son. She sounds to me as if she is capable of doing almost anything, she is so devious. That's the worst thing a woman could do to a man. Palm another man's child off as his own. You can always be sure who the mother is, but a man has to depend on the integrity of his wife.'

Fear settled around Eileen's heart. What would Johnny do if he ever found out about Paul? It didn't bear thinking about. He would leave her, that was for sure. How would she manage without him? Life without Johnny would be one big empty void. But then, who would be malicious enough to tell him? Certainly not her mother or grandmother. And Kate? Kate would never betray her trust. Neither would Madge. What about Phillip? He might thoughtlessly let it slip out sometime. But sure, Phillip was living over in England and thankfully they saw very little of him these days. Too many people knew for Eileen's peace of mind. That was the trouble. She may as well have advertised it on the front page of the *Irish News* or the *Belfast Telegraph*! She shivered at the threat hanging over her like the sword of Damocles. Would Johnny ever find out?

He gathered her close. 'You're shivering. Are you cold, love?' he asked solicitously.'

'No! Somebody must have walked over my grave.'

'I'll soon chase the ghosts away,' Johnny vowed, and as he made love to her, fear lent more fervour to Eileen's responses. He marvelled that she could be so wanton, yet never say the words he so longed to hear. Over and over, he whispered, 'I love you, Eileen. So much that it hurts!' He waited patiently, hoping she would reciprocate. As usual, he waited in vain. Eileen thought that there was no need for words. Wasn't she showing him how much she loved him? Didn't actions speak louder than words? Johnny had to content himself with uneasy thoughts that she must love him. Surely lust alone could not arouse so much passion in her?

Sarah soon made it clear to Mick that she had no intention of forgiving and forgetting. When he arrived home from Maisie's, he found that his wife had relegated him to the settee. He climbed the stairs, determined to have it out with her, but the bedroom door was barred. Sarah refused to answer his whispered pleas for her to talk to him and at last, in despair, he descended the stairs again. Next morning, after a restless night, he discovered that Claire had not come home, and to make matters worse, his wife did not put in an appearance at the breakfast table. As he and Emma prepared breakfast he managed to fob off his young daughter's attempts to find out what was wrong. He had decided not to tell Emma the truth until forced to do so. He did not want to see condemnation in her eyes too.

Before leaving for work he wrote Sarah a long letter. In it he expressed the great sorrow and regret he felt at having brought so much shame to her and the family.

He apologized profusely for the pain he was causing her and begged her forgiveness. He also told her about his promotion, and begged her not to let this terrible tragedy mar the pleasure they should be experiencing as they planned how best to use the extra money; whetting her appetite with the suggestion of a small car. Ending the letter with vows of undying love, he placed the envelope in a prominent position where Sarah could not fail to see it, and left for work in a happier frame of mind.

That night, when Mick arrived home for his evening meal, he found the house dark and cold. His letter had not been opened and Sarah was nowhere to be found. There was, however, a note telling him to go over to Maggie's. Mick crossed the street to his mother-in-law's house convinced that he would find Sarah and his youngest daughter there. Perhaps she felt the need for her mother's support as they thrashed this out. That suited him fine. He knew Maggie would point out all aspects of the affair and surely Sarah would see that she was not without blame? Emma was in her grannie's, sitting at the kitchen table tucking into her favourite meal of fish and chips. Sarah was nowhere to be seen. When Mick entered the room, Maggie turned from the stove to greet him.

'Hello there, Mick. Take off your coat and go up and have a wash, son,' she said kindly, her expression sympathetic. 'I've made you some dinner. Beth is pregnant again and Sarah is going to stay with her for a few days.'

When Mick would have challenged this announcement, his mother-in-law gave him a warning look and nodded slightly in Emma's direction.

'Thanks, Maggie. I'm grateful to you. How are you today, Emma?'

'I'm all right, Dad. I've got to go back to school for a while for another rehearsal.'

'Hey! You'll be a big star before very long.' His

hand ruffling her hair brought forth cries of resentment.

'Ah, Dad ... I've just brushed my hair and you've wrecked it!'

'Sorry, love. Sorry.'

As Mick washed, his mind was in a turmoil. Was Beth really pregnant or was it just an excuse for Sarah being away from the house without causing any unnecessary gossip? Did Tommy and Beth now know all about his infidelity? Imagine this happening just when he was looking forward to a more comfortable life style now that they would have extra money to play about with. With the girls all grown up now, he and Sarah could come and go as they saw fit. He had to admit that she had been a wonderful wife and mother. Money had always been tight, what with taking on the mortgage for a big house and with four children to clothe and feed. There had been no proper holidays. A caravan at Islandmagee or Bray for a week had been the highlight of their year. But they had considered themselves fortunate to get away for a week. A lot of their friends could not afford any holidays at all.

Sick with worry, Mick forced himself to eat the steak and chips that Maggie had prepared for him, so as not to offend her. It was rump steak, thick and succulent, the dinner he most relished, but it may as well have been a piece of old boot leather for all the enjoyment he got out of it. With an effort he managed to clear his plate and thanked Maggie for all the trouble she had taken for him.

Shortly afterwards Emma left the house to return to school for the rehearsal of the Nativity play. She was glad to escape from the strained atmosphere. She had a feeling, that in spite of a barrage of questions to anyone who would listen, she was not going to be made any the wiser. The idea that Maggie was putting forth of

Beth's fourth pregnancy being the cause of all the unrest insulted Emma's intelligence. Did they think she was daft? She could imagine Beth being annoyed . . . but to suggest that everyone else was in a tizzy over her sister's pregnancy was ludicrous. Now if it was Claire who was pregnant, that would be a different matter entirely! She wasn't married and the fact that she had not been home at all last night gave food for thought. Emma was glad of the opportunity to return to school and normality for a couple of hours. If Claire was pregnant it wouldn't be a secret for long. Emma did not know a lot about sex but she did know that it could result in a baby being born, whether you were married or not. She had only recently deduced that not all mothers were married.

Once his daughter was safely out of the house, Mick questioned Maggie. His mother-in-law informed him that Sarah intended to stay at Beth's until she decided what to do next.

Mick was distraught. 'Do you think she'll leave me, Maggie?' he asked fearfully.

She could offer him no comfort. 'To be truthful, I don't know, Mick. You know what Sarah is like. She's a very proud and stubborn woman. The thought that the neighbours might have cause to gossip about her, even though she is apparently the innocent party, will infuriate her, and she will vent all her spleen on you.'

'She has every right to! It's all my fault.'

Maggie showed anger at these words. 'Mick, listen to me and pay heed. Shouldering all the blame is the last thing you must do. Remember Gerry Docherty? All this started because Sarah was infatuated with him. If you take all the blame . . . Sarah will let you, and she will be hell to live with. Don't be soft with her Mick or believe me, you'll live to regret it.'

'I'll put up with anything, Maggie, if only she doesn't leave me. Or worst still . . . ask me to leave the house! Where would I go?'

'There will always be room here for you, Mick. Remember that. But take my word for it, you'd be wrong to let her put you out of the house. Give her a few days to brood and see what she comes up with.'

'Is Beth really pregnant, Maggie?'

She smiled grimly. 'Yes, she is, and Tommy is in the doghouse because of it. You'd think to hear her ranting on about it, that she wasn't on the other end of it! Beth and her mother will be good company for each other at the moment. They will be able to cry on each other's shoulders, at just how badly done by they are. Give it a few days, son, and see what happens. While Sarah is away I've offered to cook you and Emma your evening meal so come here every night until things get sorted out.' Mick looked so dejected, Maggie placed a comforting hand on his shoulder. 'I know it's easy for me to say this, son . . . but try not to worry. Everything will work out all right in the end. You'll see.'

Mick knew that Maggie meant well, but how could he not worry? Sarah was so unpredictable. He was afraid to hazard a guess as to just what his wife might do. Thanking his mother-in-law for her kindness, he took his leave. He wondered if Michael would be at home. Should he risk calling down to see Maisie? Remembering the last time he had sought comfort from her, he decided against going down to Beechmount. Hadn't that comfort resulted in today's predicament? And what would Sarah think if she found out he'd been down there again? Maggie was right. Better wait and see what Sarah intended doing. His heart was heavy as he let himself into the cold empty house.

Eileen was wrong. Having had time to think it over made no difference to Claire and Michael, and it came as a terrible shock to all concerned when the couple announced that they still intended to marry. Everybody who knew of the circumstances was told to hold their tongues. This scandal must remain within the family circle. Emma was greatly affronted when told to keep quiet. Keep quiet about what? No one had ever told her anything! They were driving her round the bend with all their secret whispering. When she asked once again if Claire was pregnant, she was told not to be so silly. It infuriated her that they all insisted on treating her like a child. What if she announced that she was pregnant, eh? That would soon make them sit up and take notice of her; make them realize that she wasn't a child any more.

Maggie voiced her concern to Eileen. 'It's not right, Eileen. No good can come of it.'

'I know that, Grannie. But when I put myself in their position, I can understand how they must feel. And, Grannie, I'm sure it's happened many times before, I mean ... from what I hear, incest does go on in some families.'

At Maggie's horrified expression, Eileen threw back her head and laughed.

'What's so funny?' Maggie asked indignantly.

'I'm laughing at the expression on your face, Grannie. If anyone had told me that you had gaped, I would not have believed them. Yet I have just seen you do so with my own eyes.'

Maggie smiled. 'Your suggestion is enough to make anyone gape! But to be serious ... I'm afraid that I disagree with you where Michael and Claire are concerned. No matter how often it has happened before, it is morally wrong. It's against all the laws of nature. Have you ever seen what the children of incestuous couples look like? Not all of them, mind, but some. Even if they look normal, they can be mentally retarded. Would you wish anything like that on your sister? No, Eileen, it's wrong. You are closer to Claire than the rest of us. Talk to her! Try and make her see reason.'

Eileen became very serious. 'To be truthful, Grannie, I

think that they are taking a stand. I believe they just want to frighten me dad and Maisie. I could be wrong but I think they both know their love is doomed. They're just delaying the moment when they must surely part.'

'You could be right, Eileen.' Maggie sat silent for some moments. 'Yes, . . . yes, I think you probably are right. We'll just have to wait and see what happens.' She lapsed into silence once more, then sighed. 'It's going to be an awful Christmas! Everybody is so ill at ease and unhappy. Sarah is devastated! I thought she would have rallied round by now, but no. I tried to make her see reason but in vain. I hope she returns to the house before Christmas. If only Mick had told her the truth all those years ago she would have been better prepared to weather this storm now! As it is, she is making herself sick with worry. It's always better to be truthful, because, in the long run, your past has a habit of catching up with you.' She raised a brow at Eileen. 'Does Johnny know?'

Sadly, she shook her head. 'I wish he did. Since this bit of scandal befell the family, I feel as if a great black cloud is hanging over me, ready to burst. You see, Johnny has surprised me by his reaction to this bad news. He actually came out on Dad's side. He thinks Maisie is the lowest of the low. Condemns her for not telling Dad when she fell pregnant. He says he wouldn't be surprised if she had palmed Michael off on to Matthew O'Hara as his own son. After all, he said, Matthew isn't here to dispute the fact!' Eileen leant across and gripped Maggie's hand. 'Grannie, Johnny thinks that the worst thing a woman could do is dupe a man into thinking that a child is his when it is not . . . You can guess how I feel. I'm frightened, Grannie, I'm very frightened.' Tears glistened in her eyes. 'I couldn't bear to lose Johnny! Not now.'

Returning the pressure of Eileen's fingers, Maggie tried to console her; share her worries. 'I told you not to tell him and now I see I was wrong to do so. I thought I was advising you for the best, Eileen. I mean . . . Paul's father is dead and his only sister can't have children, so you are safe as far as that is concerned. History can't repeat itself there. Now I wish I'd advised you otherwise.'

'Grannie, don't you feel guilty! It was my choice. I'll just have to live and hope that he never finds out.'

'There is no reason why he should,' Maggie consoled her granddaughter.

Eileen just nodded. She didn't want to confess that she herself had almost let the cat out of the bag. Furthermore, if Maggie knew that Phillip was aware of Eileen's deception, she would not be so confident that her granddaughter's dark secret was safe.

Maggie eyed her closely, then ventured to voice her thoughts. 'Tell me, Eileen, why are you so bitter against your father where this episode is concerned? To my knowledge, you have not been down to see him and he could do with a bit of support. You mustn't take sides. There are always two viewpoints to every story, you know.'

'Do you blame me, Grannie? Do you really blame me? Look at how he reacted when Johnny and I were getting married. He treated Johnny like dirt! He still does, for that matter. Yet Johnny pities him! And to think that me dad had committed adultery ... Is it any wonder that I'm bitter? Just let me catch him looking askance at Johnny again. I'll soon let him know what I think of him! I've lost all respect for him, Grannie.'

'Ah, Eileen, Eileen ... don't be so bitter. It wasn't so much that he thought Johnny had seduced you. Ah, no, you judge Mick wrongly. Had you been a happy bride, he would have given Johnny his blessing. Mick was grieving because you looked so unhappy. We could all see your misery. How Johnny didn't twig on I'll never know. I guess he was blinded by his own happiness. You and your father were so close, he could feel your pain too. He knew you were desperately unhappy. You were pregnant! Those in the know thought it was Johnny's child. Can you blame Mick for thinking Johnny was the cause of your unhappiness? Besides,' she finished grimly, 'your mother is not so lily white in this latest affair.'

As she digested her grannie's words, Eileen felt guilty. She knew that Maggie was right. Her father had grieved for her. Now she bowed her head in shame. 'I'll call over on my way home and have a wee chat with him,' she promised. Words spoken by Maggie came back to mind. 'Grannie, you seem to know more about this bit of scandal than you're letting on. What did happen? How can you put any blame on Mam?'

'Eileen, all this happened a long time ago. The way I see it, the least said the better. I'd rather not discuss it any more, if you don't mind.' With a final comforting squeeze of Eileen's hand, Maggie sank back in her chair and changed the subject. 'I had some news today,' she confessed. 'Whether good or bad depends on how you look at it. Bernard has a son. Emily gave birth to a six-pound baby boy last Thursday. In his note Bernard wrote that he has no idea how his father will take the news, but he felt it only right to let us know that we have another grandson. What do you think of that, Eileen?'

'Ah, Grannie, I think it's wonderful news. How do you feel about it?'

'I am going to phone and ask Bernard to bring the child over. I shall also extend my invitation to Emily.'

'Oh! What has Granda Barney to say about that?'

'He understands that I want to see my grandson, but says he will not be here when they arrive. He can't forgive Bernard for marrying without even letting us know. Especially in a Register Office. It's such a shame really. Barney loves you all as if you were his own grandchildren, but this baby will be his first blood grandchild. I wish he would forgive and forget. Life is too short to harbour grudges.'

'I hope you succeed in changing Granda's mind, but I must admit I'm not very hopeful. He is so straight and decent himself, he expects others to be the same. He expects too much of Bernard. Still, I hope Bernard visits you before Christmas! It would cheer us all up. It's not a bit like Christmas this year. I never get the proper feel of it until the tree and decorations are up, and with Claire in the house, I don't like to start decorating.'

'Why ever not?'

'I don't want to appear to be celebrating with her in the house. It just doesn't seem right.'

'Don't be silly, Eileen! Claire would be upset if she thought she was spoiling your children's Christmas. Ask her to help you decorate the tree. I'm sure she will be only too happy to do so.'

'You reckon?'

'I reckon. Just act natural. After all . . . that's what Claire and Michael are doing.'

'You're right as usual, Grannie. You can always be depended on to put things into proper perspective. I'll ask Claire to help me decorate the tree tonight, and if she does get engaged at Christmas, I'll wish her well. After all, it's none of my business.'

'Nor mine,' Maggie agreed ruefully. 'And I must remember to curb my tongue if they do get engaged. As you say, it's none of our business. Could I ask a favour of you, Eileen?'

'Of course, Grannie. Fire away.'

'When I find out just when Bernard is coming, and if you are not too busy, will you come down and lend a bit of moral support?'

'Busy or not, Grannie, I'll be here. See a new baby? I wouldn't miss it for all the tea in China!'

'It's a pity Beth doesn't think more like you do.'

Eileen had the grace to look ashamed. 'Well now, Grannie, I actually meant someone else's baby not another one of mine. Beth really is upset, and I for one don't blame her. Poor Beth! I hope she has an easier pregnancy than she did with young Elizabeth.'

'She's young and healthy. They're comfortably off. So she shouldn't complain,' Maggie answered curtly. 'Meanwhile ... if I let you know when Bernard is coming, will you come down?'

'You can count on it, Grannie.'

'Thanks, love. I know I can always depend on you.'

Enough was enough! Mick's fist thumped the arm of his chair as he came to a decision, causing Emma to rear back in surprise.

This would be Sarah's third night away from the house and Mick had failed to contact her in spite of several attempts to do so. She just refused to speak to him. Tonight, however, he would not take no for an answer. He would demand that she see and talk to him. She must decide what she intended doing! He had to know where he stood. He rose from the table and addressed Emma. 'I'm going up to see your mother.' At the look of pity on his daughter's face, he bawled, 'You can stop looking like that! Tonight I'll force her to see me, so help me, then maybe this house will get back to some kind of normality!'

The door banged behind him with a resounding slam and Emma sighed. Her father must be awfully upset or he would never have slammed the door. What on earth was going on? Why was her mother staying at Beth's, and why was Claire living with Eileen? If only someone would tell her what was going on. Even her grannie, who could usually be depended on to be open and above board, was evasive when questioned. Well, perhaps tonight all would be revealed. She debated whether or not to miss rehearsals then decided against it. After all, her father had attempted to talk to her mother last night, and the night before, and failed. Why should tonight be any different?

When Beth opened the door to his knock, Mick quickly put his foot in it. 'I want to see your mother.'

She looked down at his foot in amazement. 'Dad, don't do that! Anyone would think you were a tick collector, and I was keeping you out. As far as I'm concerned, you're very welcome in my home. It's just that Mam won't agree to talk to you. I've tried my best to make her see reason, but she won't listen to me.'

Beth was obviously distressed and Mick's expression softened. 'It's all right, don't you fret. This is between your mother and me. Tonight I'd like to come in, please.' Beth willingly stood to one side and Mick entered the kitchen in time to see his wife disappear through the scullery out into the bathroom that Tommy had built on to the back of the house.

'Sarah! Come here! We must talk,' he bawled.

When Mick turned to speak to Beth, he found Tommy helping her into her coat. Then, lifting his own coat, Tommy addressed Mick. 'You're right, Mick. It's better to get it all thrashed out. We'll be gone an hour. Good luck, mate.'

'Thanks, Tommy. You're a pal.'

Tommy raised his eyes towards the ceiling and warned, 'Remember the kids are asleep, Mick.'

'I'm sorry for shouting, Tommy. I'll make sure they aren't disturbed.'

Knowing that Sarah would be well aware that Beth and Tommy had left the house, Mick waited a few minutes for her to put in an appearance. At last, he made his way to the bathroom and knocked gently on the door.

Sarah's voice whispered, 'I'm in the bath.'

'Come off it, Sarah! I've seen you in the bath before. Open this door . . . or so help me I'll knock it off its hinges,' he threatened.

Slowly the door opened and she stood before him, fully clothed.

'That was quick,' he taunted.

Ignoring his sarcasm, she gestured to show him that she wanted to pass him. He stood aside and then followed her through the scullery and into the kitchen. She stood with her back to him, gazing into the glowing embers of the fire. 'I have nothing to say to you.'

'You don't have to say anything . . . just listen. You are disrupting four homes with your stubbornness: Beth's, Eileen's, Maggie's and your own.'

Sarah swung round and glared at him. Mick's heart sank at the hatred he saw directed at him. He wondered if she would ever look kindly on him again. 'Are you trying to put the blame for all this misery on me?' she challenged him.

'No, I'm not. I accept full responsibility, so I am now going to try to put things right. I'm moving out of the house. That will leave it free for you and Claire to come home. It will also give Eileen and Beth the freedom of their own homes and relieve Maggie from the burden of cooking my dinner every night. Not that I couldn't have coped on my own with Emma's assistance . . . but Maggie insisted. I guess she felt sorry for me.'

Sarah didn't move. Her eyes held his as she questioned him, 'Dare I ask where you intend to stay?'

'I honestly don't know, Sarah. I just know that we can't go on like this any more.'

'I suppose the fact that Maisie's been widowed again has nothing to do with it?' she taunted.

'To be truthful, that never entered my mind, Sarah.'

'I don't believe you!'

'I'd hardly be likely to go there with Michael nursing a grievance against me, would I?'

Sarah's nostrils flared and Mick knew that she was fighting to keep control of her anger. He could see that she was absolutely seething with resentment. 'Do you expect me to believe that you are not aware that Michael is staying with his married brother? Have you not already been down comforting the obliging widow? The very obliging widow!'

Glad now that he had not given into the temptation

to go down and see Maisie, Mick defended her. 'Sarah! I will not let you belittle Maisie. I . . .'

'I'll belittle her . . . and you . . . as much as I like!' she angrily interrupted him. 'How dare you stand there and tell me what I can and can't say about your fancy woman? The little tart!'

'Sarah, Maisie is not my fancy woman. And there is no need for that kind of language.'

'How do I know that? Eh, Mick? How can I be sure that you are not sleeping with her? You told me once before that you had never slept with her. Yet she gave birth to your son. A virgin birth? That must have taken some doing!' Oh, how it hurt to know that Maisie had been the one to give him a son, and a wonderful son at that! 'I've been living in a fool's paradise all these years . . . thinking you loved me.'

'I *do* love you. I've never loved anyone else! And that's the truth, Sarah. I was lonely, and convinced that you were about to run off with Gerry Docherty. Remember, it was you who put me out of the house. Maisie took me in . . .'

'And you loved me so much you jumped straight into bed with her? How could you, Mick? How could you do this to me?'

'Good God, Sarah! It was twenty-three years ago, not last week! Catch yourself on, woman. Since you persist in throwing the past in my face, what about you and Gerry Docherty, eh?'

This reprimand brought hot colour to Sarah's cheeks. Chin high, she advised him, 'I think you had better leave, Mick.'

His hand reached out appealingly towards her but she flinched away from him.

'Go to her, Mick. You go to her, and I'll come home and look after my daughters.'

'I'll go home now and pack, Sarah.' His voice was forlorn. 'When I leave the house in the morning, I won't come back near it. That is ... if you promise to return there?'

Sarah defied the tears to fall as she nodded her head. It hadn't taken much coaxing to make him leave. Maisie must be waiting for him. Well, when this scandal became public knowledge, she at least would be able to hold her head high. She was not the one who had sinned. But that was cold comfort. She was the one who would lose the most.

After he had gone, Sarah sat for a long time debating what to do next. By offering to leave the house, Mick had put the onus on her. If he left on condition that she return there, the blame would be put on her if he went to stay with Maisie. She would be accused of driving him into another woman's arms, and that would never do. Why should she be placed in that wrong? Besides, if he did go to Maisie there was no chance whatsoever that he and she would ever come together again. This thought startled her. She had no intention of taking him back. Indeed she had not!

When Beth and Tommy returned they found Sarah packed and ready to leave.

'Thanks, Beth ... Tommy, for putting up with me. Mick has made me realize what a nuisance I've been making of myself. I'm sorry you had to be involved in all this sordid mess. I just didn't know where else to turn.'

'Mam, don't be silly! You were far from being a nuisance.' Beth moved closer to her mother. 'Don't go unless it's what you really want to do. You are quite welcome to stay here as long as you like.' She turned for support from her husband. 'Isn't she, Tommy?'

'Of course you are, Sarah. But then, we don't have to tell you that. You know that you're always welcome here. But I do think that you are doing the right thing going home. You must be very uncomfortable sleeping on that settee and it's obvious that Mick is lost without you.'

'Huh, that I don't believe! Nevertheless, I'm going home.'

'I'll walk you down, Sarah.' Tommy was wondering if all was well. Why hadn't Mick waited to carry Sarah's suitcase?

'Thanks, Tommy. It is quite heavy. Will you call down tomorrow, Beth?'

'Yes, Mam, in the afternoon. You know I'm not fit for anything these mornings.' These words were accompanied by a resentful glance at Tommy.

'Maybe it will be worth it, love. You might get a boy this time,' Sarah consoled her. 'See you tomorrow.'

At the side of her home, Sarah thanked Tommy for his assistance. She watched until he reached the gate and waved farewell, before going round to the back and letting herself in. She passed through the kitchen, and as she entered the hall, Mick came out of the living room.

'Sarah!' He couldn't believe his eyes. In his wildest dreams he had not imagined her coming home while he was still in the house.

'I am here on one condition, Mick.'

'Anything, Sarah. I'll agree to anything you say.'

'I want you to move into Claire's bedroom. She has no intention of coming home again.'

'She'll come round, Sarah. Given time, Claire will come home.'

'No, Mick. You're wrong. She and Michael still intend to get married. What do you think of that?'

'I don't believe you!' he gasped in dismay.

'Nevertheless, I speak the truth.'

Mick felt gutted. He stood in the hall and watched Sarah climb the stairs. At the top she could not resist one parting sarcastic shot. 'What about their children? Eh, Mick? How will you live with that?' Entering her bedroom Sarah shut the door with a resounding click.

*   *   *

260

Bernard chose Saturday afternoon to visit his mother. He did not expect a welcome from his father, so by choosing Saturday, and with Christmas Day just five days away, Maggie had a legitimate excuse for Barney not being there. The shop would be very busy with customers cashing in their Christmas clubs in exchange for goods. Emily had agreed to accompany him, and Bernard was proud and pleased to draw up to his mother's door in his newly acquired second-hand Ford Prefect car.

Eileen came out to greet them, followed more sedately by Maggie. Emily had been a bit apprehensive of meeting Bernard's family, but Eileen won her over immediately by hugging her and by her obviously genuine admiration of the baby as she took him gently from his mother's arms.

Bernard hugged Maggie close. There were tears in his eyes and he muttered gruffly, 'I've missed you, Mam. I've really missed you.'

Blinking back tears, she chided him, 'I'm sure you did!' Then, pushing him gently away, she went forward to greet Emily. 'Welcome to my home. I wish the circumstances could have been different . . . but that's life.' With a slight shrug of regret, she ushered Emily indoors and turned to Eileen.

'Now, Eileen . . . may I please see my grandson?'

'Oh, I don't want to part with him. He's gorgeous!' She said as she relinquished her hold on the baby.

Maggie cradled the baby close to her breast and gazed down on him. 'He's the picture of you, Bernard. I must hunt out some old photographs I have of you at this age to prove I'm right. Sit down, Emily, make yourself at home. Eileen . . . will you let Sarah know that they have arrived? She wants to see the baby.' At Eileen's surprised look, Maggie assured her, 'Your mother knows that Bernard is coming this morning. Go and fetch her over.'

So her mother had returned to the house? Bemused, Eileen left the room and Maggie inquired after Emily's mother. They had attended the same school and it helped break the ice that they had been acquaintances once. As the afternoon wore on Eileen was drawn more and more to Emily who was a girl after her own heart. No nonsense about her. Bernard was a changed man. Emily had obviously worked wonders where he was concerned. Gone was the lad preoccupied with only his own needs, and now a mature attentive young man had taken his place. Eileen placed the credit for this at Emily's door. The first chance she got she informed her grannie how she felt. Leaving Sarah to hold the fort, they were preparing tea. Maggie was quick to agree with her granddaughter.

'If only Barney would agree to speak to Bernard. See for himself how changed he is.'

'Will I go up to the shop and ask Granda to come down for a few minutes?'

'Oh, no. He would be very angry if we put him on the spot. Perhaps the next time Bernard visits me, Barney will agree to be here. We can but wait and see.'

'When did me mam come home?'

'Last night. I don't know what happened but your dad is still in the house so Sarah must have decided to stand by him. Thank God for that! With them both under the same roof, surely they will be able to resolve their differences now?'

'Perhaps Christmas won't be so bad after all, eh, Grannie? Last night Claire told me that she and Michael had decided to delay getting engaged. They don't want to spoil Christmas for everybody by flaunting a ring about. What do you think of that?'

'I think it is wonderful news. Yes, wonderful, Deo Gratis.'

Chapter Seven

It was with relief that Eileen started to remove the decorations from the Christmas tree and pack them away for yet another year. So much for the season of goodwill! The festive season had been so awful that if it had been up to her the tree would have come down on New Year's Day. However, Johnny advised against this. He said she would be spoiling the children's fun to dismantle it so soon. She had been of the opinion that Paul, Louise and Marie were too young to understand, but her husband pointed out to her that they would be sure to see Christmas trees still displayed in other people's windows and wonder why theirs had disappeared. Young children had a habit of saying the unexpected. She had teased him and said that he was superstitious, thinking it bad luck to take down the tree before the twelfth day of Christmas. To her delight he had actually blushed and admitted that perhaps she was right. Maybe he was just a wee bit superstitious. Greatly amused, she had given into his wishes.

Now it was Tuesday 6 January, the Feast of the Epiphany. This morning in church the children had stood wide-eyed in front of the crib and gazed in wonder at the camel and the statues of the Three Wise Men bearing gifts for the baby Jesus. They had apparently arrived overnight and it had taken all of Eileen's ingenuity to explain just how they had managed to get into the church. She had also explained to the children that their Christmas tree would have to be returned to the forest to grow again for another year and that it would be returned to them next Christmas. That would help to explain its disappearance in the morning. Now, to her great relief, it was at last the twelfth day of Christmas, time to put away the decorations and get rid of the wilted tree.

As she sat on the floor, amongst the dry prickly fallen pine needles, wrapping baubles carefully in fine paper before packing them into boxes, Eileen let her mind wander back over the festive holiday. It had been a disaster from start to finish. Sarah had expected them all to gather in her house on Christmas night as usual. In spite of great misgivings, just to please her they had. Maggie and Barney, with the help of the excited children, had helped to make things appear normal but the atmosphere between her parents had been electric. Eileen had felt heart sore for her father, he was so worried and haggard-looking.

Claire, in an endeavour to appear normal, had been acting too perkily; talking non-stop in a high-pitched voice that grated on the nerves. Michael had been the opposite to Claire. He was very quiet and appeared depressed. Sarah had acted as if everything was fine, gushing over the smallest thing and trying to please everybody except her husband. As for Mick, he had hardly opened his mouth; only speaking when directly addressed. And poor Emma! In the dark as to why everybody was acting so strangely, she had tentatively asked if she could spend the night with her best friend – a request that in ordinary circumstances would have brought howls of protest from her parents. To be away from her own home on Christmas night would normally be unheard of. To Emma's great relief, this time her mother had nodded her consent. Eileen had been amused at the alacrity with which her youngest sister had left the room to go upstairs and pack an overnight bag when granted leave of absence. It must all seem so strange to her, as if everyone was acting out some kind of pantomime.

To crown it all Phillip had arrived home on Christmas Eve. He had not been expected and Eileen was dismayed to be embraced in a bear hug and kissed under the mistletoe when they arrived at Madge's for Christmas dinner with her. During the meal Eileen was embarrassed and uncomfortable to find Phillip covertly giving her sympathetic glances. She wished he would catch himself on and behave! She had sat on tenter-hooks all afternoon, afraid Johnny would notice and question his brother's behaviour. That would surely start another row between them. She had been glad to get away from Madge's home; relieved to escape from her brother-in-law's attentions. Thus her nerves were already stretched to the limit even before entering the tense atmosphere of her mother's house.

'A penny for them?'

Eileen gave a little start of surprise. She had not heard Johnny enter the room. 'They're not worth a penny,' she confessed. 'I'm just thinking back over the Christmas Day fiasco.'

'It was rather traumatic, wasn't it?' he agreed, 'But at least nothing untoward was said outright. Everybody minded their own business and held their tongue. And it was just as well they did! One word out of place and the whole house would have exploded. It was like sitting on a keg of dynamite.'

He sat down on the settee, and with a deep sigh Eileen draped an arm across his thigh and rested her head against it. 'Still . . . the undercurrents were awful. You were marvellous, Johnny,' she praised him. 'You steered the conversation away from danger points many times. I was very proud of you.'

'You noticed?'

'Of course I noticed.' The look she threw him was full of surprise. 'So did me dad! I could see he was grateful to you.'

'I felt sorry for your father. He was afraid to open

his mouth, poor man. Your mother never once spoke directly to him. Not once! At least not when I was present. Imagine . . . Christmas Day, the season of goodwill, and your mother never addressed your father once. I wouldn't have believed that Sarah could be so cruel.'

'I suppose it depends on how badly hurt you are. Mam must feel devastated or she would have put on some kind of a show of friendliness in front of the family. She is very proud and all for keeping up appearances! If she had been able to do so, she would have pretended everything was all right between her and Dad. So she must be feeling very hurt . . . and lonely. She has no one to confide in, seek comfort from, without losing face. It must be awful for her. My heart goes out to them both. I dread to think what will happen if Claire carries out her threat to marry Michael. This thing is driving Mam and Dad apart.'

Johnny's hand was gently tousling her hair and she pressed closer still against the warmth of his body. It was wonderful to be alone with him, the children in bed and sound asleep. They didn't often get time to themselves these days, Claire and Michael seemed to want to be in their company as often as possible and it put a restraint on their conduct. Even when they were in bed at night they were aware of Claire downstairs in the room below theirs. Johnny was really being very considerate about it all. Not many men would be so understanding. Now Eileen raised her arms and swept her thick hair back from her face, knowing full well that this brought the cleavage that her low-cut cardigan exposed into Johnny's view. He responded to the unspoken invitation, his hands gentle, while his cheek caressed the auburn tresses. Slowly, Eileen turned and her arms crept up around his neck as her lips sought his. Gently he drew her up on to his knee. He eluded her searching mouth while all the while his lips trailed her face and throat and his hands caressed her, seeking to arouse her passion.

As usual Eileen willingly abandoned herself to her

husband's love-making, until fear of Claire's returning caused her reluctantly to try to push him away. 'Claire might come in.'

Johnny resisted her efforts to withdraw from his arms. 'Let her!'

'Oh, Johnny, no! Why, I'd die of embarrassment if she walked in on us.' Eileen was now feverishly trying to stop his endeavours to undress her.

'She won't walk in.'

'How can you be so sure? She has a key, remember!'

'I barred the door. She'll have to knock.'

Eileen relaxed against him. 'You planned all this,' she accused.

'Mmmm. Did I do wrong? Shall I go out and take the bar off the door?' he asked with a smile.

She shook her head and allowed him to remove her cardigan. 'No . . . you did right.' The garment fell to the floor followed by her brief camisole and brassiere. His hands tenderly caressed her and, passion mounting, all else was forgotten as she hungrily responded to his advances.

A half hour later when Claire arrived with Michael the door opened easily when she turned her key in the lock. They found her sister and brother-in-law kneeling on the floor wrapping the Christmas tree baubles.

With a wave in the direction of the sorry-looking tree, Claire said, 'For the first time in my life, I'm glad to see the end of Christmas. I'm usually sad to see the tree bare and bedraggled . . . but not this year! It's been so awful, hasn't it?' Her glance embraced them both and Johnny and Eileen nodded in agreement.

'Eileen . . . Johnny . . .' Claire reached for Michael's hand and gripped it tightly before she continued speaking. She was not sure that they were doing the right thing. 'Michael and I have talked things over and we've come to a decision.' Her look at Eileen was pleading. She hoped her sister would understand. 'We have decided to elope to Gretna Green and get married.'

Slowly, Johnny rose to his feet, Eileen was too astounded to move. To her relief her husband took command of the situation. 'Sit down, both of you. Will you have a beer, Michael?' he asked. Receiving a grateful nod, Johnny turned to Claire. 'There is some wine left . . . will you have a glass?'

'Yes, please.'

While Johnny was fetching the drinks, Eileen brushed the pine needles from her skirt and sat beside Claire on the settee. The look she turned on her sister was anxious. 'Are you sure you're doing the right thing? I mean . . . in the eyes of the church you won't really be married, you know.'

'We know that, but what else can we do? We intend to marry, and this way, at least in the eyes of the law, we'll be married. That's better than living openly in sin,' Claire lamented. 'Think about it! I can't see me dad and Maisie keeping quiet if we try to get married in church. They are both too virtuous! How they ever came to commit adultery is beyond me. And the church will never give us permission once they know we're related, we know that! So one way or the other we'll be condemned. No! We've looked at the situation from every angle and we really have no alternative.'

Eileen's even white teeth nibbled at her bottom lip in agitation. 'When are you going?' she asked apprehensively, fully aware of all the trouble their elopement would unleash.

'The sooner the better. You have to reside in Gretna Green for at least three weeks before the Registrar will marry you.'

Eileen was quick to grasp at this chance to have Claire at home alone. Perhaps she would be able to make her sister see how wrong it would be to marry Michael? 'Only one of you has to reside there,' she pointed out. 'Why not let Michael go on ahead and then join him later?'

He was quick to agree with this suggestion. 'I want to go over first, Eileen, but Claire won't hear tell of it.'

'Oh, don't be silly, Eileen!' Claire chastized her. 'I don't want to wait here on my own. I want to be with Michael.'

'And when you return, how will you explain your marriage to the neighbours and your workmates?' Johnny, returning to the room with a tray of drinks, asked this question.

Accepting a glass of beer, Michael answered him, 'That is something we'll have to give a lot of thought to. We will probably say we were carried away on a romantic notion. Couldn't wait to save up enough money for a grand wedding here.'

'But your friends and neighbours are sure to expect you still to take your vows in church?'

Michael shrugged and sighed. 'To be truthful that's the least of our worries. We will meet that hurdle when we come to it.'

'What about Mam and Dad? Eh, Claire? Will you not at least tell them that you're going to Gretna Green? They'll be worried sick!'

'Talk sense, Eileen! How can we? They and Maisie are the reason we're going over there! We're afraid that they'll try and stop us. We hope that once the damage is done, they'll all hold their tongues.'

'Ah, Claire, Claire . . . I feel for you, I really do! But I honestly think you're doing the wrong thing,' Eileen lamented. 'Would you not try parting for say six months . . . and see how you feel about each other then?'

Claire gaped at her sister in amazement. 'Are you daft or something? We couldn't bear to be separated for six days, let alone six months. Besides, it wouldn't make any difference.'

'It might! You know the old saying: "Out of sight, out

of mind". And you existed quite happily before you met him.' Eileen flashed Michael a rueful smile. 'Sorry, Michael, but that's the truth. She would probably have married Brian Muldoon and lived happily ever after.'

'Hah! Lived happily?' Claire cried in amazement. 'You must be joking! I was only half alive before I met Michael . . . I just didn't know it then! I could never marry anyone else now. And you don't really believe that load of old rubbish about out of sight, out of mind, do you?'

'Actually, I do.'

Claire turned an appealing glance on Michael. 'Tell her! Tell her how wrong she is.'

'I don't know what to say, Claire. I'll do whatever you want. If you want a trial separation, I won't object.'

Claire was scandalized. 'Michael O'Hara! How can you suggest such a terrible thing? I thought you loved me,' she cried in dismay.

'I do! I do love you. That's why I'll agree to anything you say. I want you to be fully aware just what you're getting yourself into. I'd die rather than cause you any unhappiness, love.'

'Well then, I say we should go to Gretna Green together and get married!' Claire declared defiantly.

In the face of such determination Johnny did not see any sense in trying to persuade them otherwise. Giving in graciously, he asked, 'How will you get there?'

'We'll go by ferry. It's cheaper than the plane. We can get a taxi to York Street Station and a train to Larne.'

'That won't be necessary, Michael. I'll drive you to Larne,' Johnny volunteered. He was very proud of the second-hand car he had purchased from a workmate in need of ready cash shortly before Christmas. It was an old car but had been lovingly cared for. He was only too glad to be of assistance to Michael and Claire. 'It'll take less than an hour by car and save a lot of bother and expense all round.'

'Thanks, Johnny. That's very kind of you, I don't know

how we would have managed without the support of you and Eileen these past few months. We'll never be able to repay all your kindness.'

'Just make Claire happy,' Eileen entreated. 'That's all I ask! Don't let her live to regret all this, Michael.'

'I'll do everything in my power to make her happy, Eileen, but as you well know, there are powers working against us.'

'You know, Gretna Green is down near the English border.' Johnny spoke tentatively. He didn't want to appear to be interfering. 'You don't have to travel away down there. You can get married anywhere in Scotland so long as you have resided there for at least three weeks. Why not Stranraer itself? That way you would save on travelling expenses.'

'We know that.' Claire smiled sadly. 'But we thought that if we couldn't have a church wedding, we could at least have a romantic one. So we will go to Gretna Green and get married over the anvil.'

Johnny raised his glass high. 'Well . . . since we can't persuade you to change your minds, here's to your future happiness.'

Eileen raised her glass in reply to the toast but as she sipped her wine her thoughts were bleak. She eyed Michael and Claire, so much in love, and sighed deeply. What did the future hold for them? Could they possibly live happily together, against all the odds? Only time would tell.

It was dark and cold, with a wind that nipped the ear lobes and reddened the nose. Huddled together, the four figures crossed the space from the passenger terminal to where the huge ship, all lit up like a Christmas tree, was waiting. They were the last to board. They had watched while lorries, trucks and cars had trundled aboard through the great gaping doors at the stern. Now it was the turn of the foot passengers. When non-travellers were forbidden closer access to the boat, Eileen held Claire close in a farewell embrace.

'I wish you all the very best, love. And . . . you keep in touch! Let us know how things go and when you intend to return, won't you now? Johnny will be only too happy to pick you up here again.' She turned to her husband for confirmation. 'Won't you, Johnny?'

He nodded his assent and Claire said gratefully, 'Thanks, Johnny. Of course we will keep in touch, Eileen! You will be my only contact back home here, remember. If we like Scotland and Michael can get a job, we might settle down over there. That way we won't be too far from home. Either way, we'll let you know what's happening. Now remember . . . as far as everyone else is concerned, you don't know where we are! You can tell them that we are fine, but not where we are or what we're doing. Once we're safely married you can tell everybody the truth, but until then, mum's the word. Promise?'

Eileen hated all this deception that she was being caught up in. Heaven knows, she'd had enough deception in her own life without abetting someone else's. But what could she do? This way, at least she would know what was going on. It would be better than waiting in the dark, wondering and worrying. She would be able to assure everybody that all was well. 'I promise,' she vowed, and turning to Michael warned, 'you look after her!' Then, eyes blurred with tears, she watched as Johnny hugged his sister-in-law close and then shook hands with Michael. Moving closer to Michael, Johnny pushed an envelope into his hand. 'It's not a lot, but I'm sure it will come in handy over there.'

Greatly embarrassed, Michael tried to return the envelope but Johnny moved quickly away and Michael pocketed the money. 'Thanks, Johnny,' he muttered. 'You're a real pal. It's only a loan, mind! I'll repay you one day.'

Johnny held Eileen close to his side as they watched

Michael and Claire climb the gangway that led the foot passengers on to the ferry. Eileen shuddered when she saw the gangway sway in the strong wind. With a final wave Michael hustled Claire out of sight and Johnny gently turned Eileen back towards the comfort and warmth of the passenger terminal.

'Let's have a hot drink before we head home, love. You're shivering.'

'It's fear that's making me shake. I don't know how our Claire can be so calm getting on that great big ship and it loaded with all those heavy lorries and cars! What holds it up in the water, that's what I'd like to know? And did you see how that walkway was swaying? I'd be terrified. I'd hate to be travelling on the water in this dreadful weather.'

Knowing that Eileen had never been on a ferry, Johnny tried to console her. 'It's not as bad as you imagine. It will probably be quite calm once they're out at sea. And they will only be on it for about three hours.'

'Rather them than me!'

Johnny pushed open the door of the terminal and once inside gave Eileen a gentle push in the direction of the waiting room. 'Take a seat, love, while I fetch some hot drinks.'

Eileen sat huddled in a corner, her mind full of doubts and worries. Had she been wrong to promise not to reveal the whereabouts of her sister? Her mother and father would be out of their minds with worry. And Maisie? What about Maisie? Her husband was dead. She had no one to comfort her. So far the rest of Michael's family were in the dark as to why he had left home. They thought Maisie had just taken an acute dislike to Claire. How could anyone in their right mind, who had met Claire, believe that anyone could dislike her? But then, they didn't know the full story. Besides . . . her own mother may as well be a widow for all the attention she was paying to her husband. She would be in an awful state as well. Where would all this end? And . . . horrible thought? What if her dad and Maisie still spoke out; forced an annulment? Would they be able to do that? Johnny's voice broke into Eileen's troubled thoughts.

'Here, love. This will warm you up.'

She clasped her hands around the hot cup of tea and looked at her husband entreatingly. 'Johnny, you think I shouldn't have promised not to tell Mam and Dad where Claire has gone, don't you?'

He shrugged his shoulders. 'The damage is done now, Eileen.'

'What else could I do? Eh, Johnny? This way, at least we know where they are. It would be worse if they had just suddenly disappeared without saying a word to anyone.'

'Don't worry about it, love. Remember, I didn't make any promises. If it comes to the crunch, I'll soon let them know what's going on.'

'You wouldn't!'

'Oh, but I would . . . if I thought it absolutely necessary.'

Somehow these words relieved Eileen's tortured mind. It was very comforting to be able to rely on Johnny in times of need. Not for the first time she realized just how lucky she was to have him for a husband. Smiling, she relaxed. She could, as always, safely leave matters like this in his capable hands.

Two weeks later Sarah arrived in Eileen's house in a temper. Refusing her daughter's invitation to sit down, she stood in the middle of the kitchen floor and, hands on hips, glared at Eileen. 'Where are they?' she cried aggressively. 'Eh? You have no right to keep this information from me, Eileen. I'm her mother, for heaven's sake!'

'Mam, I'm sorry, but I promised I would tell no one.' Eileen was determined that her mother would not bully her into breaking her promise to Claire. 'All I can say is that they are both fine and I think they will be home soon.'

'They've been away for two weeks now and not even so much as a card from them. Does *that* woman know where they are?'

'What woman?' Eileen asked, mystified.

'You know fine well who I mean.'

'Oh . . . Maisie! She does have a name, Mam.'

'I've called her a few in my time . . . does she know where they are?'

'No, Johnny and I are the only ones who know.'

'I could drop a word or two in Johnny's ear, remember?' Sarah threatened.

'Mam, how can you say an awful thing like that? That's blackmail, so it is.' Eileen was scandalized that her mother could even pretend about such a thing.

Sarah sank on to a chair at the table and slumped forward in defeat. 'I'm sorry, love. Of course I would never say anything to Johnny. Your secret is safe with me. I just don't know what to do or think these days.'

'Mam . . . as soon as I find out what they intend doing, you'll be the first to know. Until then, my lips are sealed.'

Going to Sarah, Eileen put her arm around her shoulders. 'Would it not be easier if you forgave Dad? Started treating him like a human being again? At least then you could share your worries. Remember, he must be in an awful state too. He will be blaming himself for driving Claire away.'

'And so he should! If he had behaved himself in the first place, all this wouldn't have happened. And do you know something, Eileen? He's trying to put the blame on me, so he is, for telling him to get out of the house.'

'Did you tell him to get out?'

'Yes . . .' Sarah shook her head distractedly. 'But that didn't give him the right to . . . you know . . .' She was embarrassed; thought she had said too much. 'Get his leg over,' she finished lamely.

Eileen hid a smile at her mother's choice of words and advised, 'I still think you should talk it over with him, Mam. You'll get nowhere if you don't talk to each other.'

'It's no good, Eileen. I've tried. Honestly I've tried hard to forgive him, but I can't. Every time I make up my mind to speak to your father I think of him and *her*, together. I just freeze! Can't make a move towards him at all.'

'Ah, Mam, it was all so long ago. Surely all these good years with Dad must cancel out his one fall from grace? Can you not just try and forget about it?'

'How can I forget? The result of his adultery is running about making life hell for us all.' Sarah looked Eileen in the eye. 'Do you know what I hate most about all this?' At Eileen's slight shake of the head, Sarah confessed, 'Maisie did what I couldn't do. She was able to give him a son.'

To Eileen's dismay, her mother spread her arms on the table and, putting her head down, cried as if her heart would break – great dry sobs tearing at her body. Going to her again, Eileen gently pulled her into her arms and soothed her. 'There, love. Don't cry. Everything will turn out all right, I'm sure it will.'

'I wish I could believe that, Eileen, but I can't. I've prayed and prayed for the strength to do what is right … and I still can't meet your dad halfway. It's not just pride, I hurt.' Sarah placed her hand over her heart. 'I really hurt deep inside. It's a great big constant ache. I really can't see things working out between us, ever again.' Rising to her feet, Sarah gave a rueful smile. 'Thanks for letting me cry all over your table. It helped. I needed a good cry and I wouldn't please your da by letting him see or hear me. I won't let him know how much he has hurt me.'

'Maybe you should, Mam? Give him a chance to make

amends. Have faith! Look at the way Granda Barney at last gave in and agreed to meet Emily and his lovely wee grandson. Now he thinks there's nobody like them. He's even trying to persuade them to move in with him and grannie! She says that was the result of prayer. So you see . . . miracles do happen.'

Sarah didn't agree with her daughter. 'You have to have faith for a miracle to happen and I just can't believe that things will work out, so I'd be foolish to expect a miracle.' With a final blow of her nose, Sarah sniffed, squared her shoulders and headed for the door. 'You'll let me know as soon as you hear anything, won't you?'

'I told you, Mam. You'll be the first to know.'

'I hope you hear from them soon. I'm living on my nerves these days.'

From the gate Eileen watched her mother walk down the street. The once brisk step was heavy and it broke her heart to see how her mother's shoulders had slumped again. Sarah had always been so upright. What would she do when she heard that Claire and Michael were married? It would probably be the straw that broke the camel's back. It could split her parents forever. With a sigh Eileen retraced her steps. Perhaps her worries were in vain. Maybe her sister would not go through with the marriage.

Since returning to work after the Christmas break Johnny had an aura of excitement about him. Eileen waited patiently for him to tell her the reason. Just when her patience was exhausted and she had decided to challenge him, her husband announced his good news. 'Listen, Eileen, I may have seemed a bit preoccupied lately but now all can be revealed.'

'Thank God for that! You've been like a cat on a hot griddle lately.'

'I've been promoted.' He paused to let this bit of

exciting news sink in. 'Departmental manager. What do you think of that?'

'That's wonderful news, Johnny! To be truthful . . . I never thought you'd get any further on in Short's. You've worked so hard you deserve promotion but I didn't think that I'd ever see the day it would happen. Not in Shorts', anyhow!'

'I applied for the job before Christmas. Then two weeks ago we were all interviewed. I did so well at the interview I felt that I was in with a good chance. That's why I was so on edge lately. Sam Wilson retired and George Patterson got his job. Willie Turner got George's job and that left his position vacant. Four of us applied for it. To be truthful, I was afraid to hope. You know how it is! That's why I didn't say anything to you. I didn't want to build up your hopes. It just shows how wrong you can be! Today I was told I was the best qualified for the job. I still can't believe it. I take up my new position on Monday morning,' he finished triumphantly.

'This is wonderful news, Johnny. Will it make much difference to us?'

'More money for a start. And a company car! Nothing flash but much better than our old banger. We will be able to sell that now. And I will also have an office of my own. Small, but my own. I'll be able to work without constant distractions. I can't wait to get started!'

'Will you have your own secretary?'

'I'll share Lorna Pollock with Willie Turner. Can I possibly detect a note of jealousy in your voice?' he jested.

Eileen was dismayed to realize that she did indeed feel a touch of unease at the idea of Johnny working in close contact with some other woman, but she had no intention of admitting it. 'Don't be silly!' she snorted. However she could not resist asking, 'Is she very pretty?'

Pleased that Eileen did appear to be jealous, Johnny

played down Lorna's good looks. 'She's tall and dark-haired.' He refrained from adding: And chased after by just about every unattached male in Short Bros.

Johnny drew Eileen into his arms, 'We will have to entertain now and again. You know, take clients out for a meal or a drink. You'll like that, won't you?'

Eileen's eyes lit up. At last she was going to have a bit of a social life. 'That's marvellous, I'll need some new style, mind. My clothes are a bit old-fashioned now.'

'You'll be able to dress to kill, my love.' He smiled happily down at her. 'I knew you would be pleased.'

'Pleased? I'm delighted . . . over the moon!'

'Well then, show me how delighted you are.'

'Now?'

'Yes, now.'

'Ah, Johnny, it's time I was starting the dinner.'

'It can wait.'

'The kids will be in soon.'

'Stop making excuses! They won't be home for another hour at least, and even I can't make it last that long. So come here.' He was drawing her over towards the settee.

'Upstairs, Johnny. Give me five minutes while I make myself beautiful and then come up.'

Johnny was high on excitement, every nerve end alive. To have so much at his age was a great achievement. He had everything he desired. The woman he loved more than life itself. Three wonderful children. A new job with unlimited prospects. He gazed around the comfortable but by now well lived in room. He would have to persuade Eileen to move house, in spite of her small business. They now needed a bigger place. In time, if he went any further up the ladder of success, they would have to entertain at home which would mean having to buy new furniture. So what! The sky was the limit. Realizing that more than five minutes had elapsed, he took the stairs two at a time, a smile of anticipation on his lips. The sky was indeed the limit!

The journey across to Stranraer was stormy, making the ship toss in the heavy swell, and Claire and Michael were glad to discover that they had strong stomachs and good sea legs. They even braved the strong winds, and arm in arm struggled along the deck, laughing as they hung on to the safety rail on the bulwark and battled against the wind. Michael's eyes kept returning again and again to the beauty of Claire's face. Green eyes shining with excitement laughed happily at him. Tiny droplets of spray glistened on her wind-swept hair. Cheeks bright red from the biting wind and lips rosy with colour invited kisses. Never had she looked more beautiful. Pulling her into the shelter of the deck structure he gave into the temptation to kiss her. Fingers entwined in damp tousled chestnut tresses, he kissed her brow, her cheeks, and finally claimed her eager lips. They embraced for a long time until at last he put her reluctantly away from him. 'Let's go inside, love. It's too lonely out here.'

Claire smiled slightly at these words. Michael was always so careful not to take advantage of her. How she loved him for it! Obediently, she allowed herself to be led into the ship's interior.

In the cafeteria, they sat side by side and planned their stay in Gretna Green. Michael took the envelope Johnny had insisted he accept from his pocket, and opened it. Wide-eyed, Claire silently questioned him.

'Johnny insisted I take it,' Michael explained as he leafed through the wad of one pound notes.

'That's an awful lot of money, Michael. I hope they aren't leaving themselves short. It really was very kind of them, and it'll come in nice and handy in Gretna Green.'

'Do you know something, Claire? I feel so stupid when I think of the money I have saved and me unable to touch it. I feel like I was a Mammy's boy, and it was nothing like that, it must be quite a tidy sum by now and we could sure use it.'

Claire squeezed his hand in sympathy. He had been so generous to his mother that she had banked some money each week in his name, vowing to give it to him whenever the need arose. Since they didn't want anyone to know of their plans he had declined to ask Maisie for the money. However, three weeks was a long time when you had to count the pennies. This money Johnny had given them was heaven sent. If the lodgings were not too expensive, they would be able to indulge in a few small luxuries.

It was still a dark afternoon, the sky laden with heavy snow clouds, when the ferry docked in Stranraer and they watched the lorries and cars roll down the great ramp and disappear into the gloom. Next it was the turn of the foot passengers. They made their way down the gangway and collected their luggage before walking along to the passenger terminal. Here they asked the times of the trains to Gretna Green. On being told that a train would leave shortly, they hurriedly made their way to the nearby railway station, followed by a cheeky shout of 'Good luck' from the knowing official.

It was late evening when they at last arrived at their destination. At the station Michael inquired about guest houses. The station master eyed them compassionately. 'Are you intending to get married?' he asked kindly.

Claire felt her cheeks redden, and nodded shyly.

'One of you will have to reside here for three weeks, ye know.'

Michael answered him. 'Yes . . . we know all about that. Do you know anywhere reasonable and clean?'

'Aye, I know that the Widow McCartan has a vacancy. Her guests got married only yesterday and moved on. She's supposed to be reasonable, and clean. And I have heard tell that she is also a great cook.'

'She sounds just what we're looking for.' Michael found himself grinning in reply to this small man's friendliness. 'Does she live nearby?'

'Just down that road a bit.' The man pointed ahead of them. 'Take the first on the left and then the next on the right. Mary McCartan's cottage is on the corner on the right-hand side. You can't miss it. There's a sign outside.'

They thanked him, and tucking Claire's hand under his elbow, Michael pressed it close to his side. Gripping their large suitcase in his free hand, he led her down the road, their heads bent into the biting wind.

Mrs McCartan was small, plump, and had a kind look in her eye. Claire took to her immediately. Unfortunately, there was only one bedroom to let. Seeing the look exchanged between Claire and Michael, Mrs McCartan was quick to ask, 'Is this a problem?'

'No . . . no problem.' Michael drew Claire to one side. 'I can sleep rough if necessary. You'll be all right here, love,' he whispered.

'We can share, Michael.' Seeing a refusal hover on his lips, she forestalled it. 'You can sleep on the floor, for heaven's sake!' She turned to their new landlady. 'Sorry about that, Mrs McCartan. We'll be very happy to take the room.'

'Good . . . good.' Leading the way down the hall, she said, 'I'll show you the room.'

It was small but spotless and Claire nodded her approval. 'It's lovely, thank you. It's just what we wanted.'

Reaching for the large delft jug that stood in a basin on the dresser, Mrs McCartan said, 'I'll fetch ye some hot water, and ye can freshen up and change out of those damp clothes before ye catch your death of cold. Since it's your first night here, I'll make ye a wee bite to eat.'

'Thank you. You are very kind.'

As they drank their tea and ate delicious home baked scotch pancakes, Mrs McCartan explained how most marriages were conducted in Gretna Green. First the couple must go to the Register Office and arrange to have the banns called. Three weeks later they would take their vows in the presence of the Registrar in front of witnesses.

Seeing Claire and Michael exchange an apprehensive glance, Mrs McCartan hastened to add, 'There are always plenty of young couples there willing to act as witnesses.' This was the legal ceremony, she explained. Next, if they were so inclined, they could walk along to the blacksmith's shop where they would once more take their vows over the anvil in a mock wedding ceremony. This was carried out in a warm romantic atmosphere and was called the 'wedding of the heart'. She also explained to them that if they were short of money a friend of hers who was a farmer might find some work for Michael, saying that he looked a strapping young man. When they had digested all this information, Claire and Michael bade Mrs McCartan good night and retired to their room.

Next morning as they tucked into bacon, eggs and black pudding, Mrs McCartan subtly questioned them. She had noted the sadness lurking in the eyes of the tall young man and wondered about it. Most couples who passed through her hands, although nervous or apprehensive, were in themselves apparently quite happy. Or in some cases the obvious pregnancy of the girls indicated the reason for a hasty marriage. However, she sensed that Claire and Michael were different. It was obvious that they were very much in love. In fact Mary McCartan would go so far as to say that Michael adored Claire, so why the sadness?

Being the inquisitive type she tried to find out. 'Did your parents not agree to you two getting married?' she asked as she placed yet more toast on the table.

Claire's answer was sad. 'No ... no, they think we should wait a while and see if we still feel the same towards each other. We've only known each other a few months and they think we might change our minds.' She smiled at Michael as she added, 'But we won't! We love each other very much.'

'My husband and I married three months after we met for the first time, and never regretted it. Unfortunately we never had any children and I've been very lonely since he died some years ago. That's why I do B&B. It gives me an interest in life. I get to meet different people. I could tell you a tale or two if I had a mind to, but the things I have been told in confidence will never pass my lips!' She looked virtuous. This was her way of letting them know that anything they said was safe with her. She paused a few moments but when it became obvious that no confidences were forthcoming, she continued, 'They come from all walks of life to marry here. Some of my guests still keep in touch with me. Some are happy ... but unfortunately some regret marrying in haste.'

Michael and Claire were still not to be drawn. Their landlady might not be so sympathetic if she learnt that they were blood relations. She would probably throw them out on their ears. Michael changed the subject. 'Tell us ... who were your most important elopers?'

Aware that she would learn no more from them, at least not for the time being, Mrs McCartan launched forth on stories from the past, some hilarious, some sad, and for the next half hour she kept them glued to the edge of their chairs as they listened to her every word.

Each morning, after they had fuelled up on the enormous breakfasts that Mrs McCartan cooked for them, hail, rain, or snow, Michael and Claire walked for miles exploring the Scottish countryside. Even in this bleak weather they could appreciate how beautiful it was and vowed to return in the summer and see it in all its glory. One day they took the train and visited Ayr, and another day they went to Glasgow. Claire fell for the beauty of Ayr but the city of Glasgow was too big and busy to appeal to her and she was secretly relieved when they discovered that suitable work would not be readily available there for Michael. Their evenings were spent dallying over one pint of beer for Michael and a fruit juice for Claire in one of the pubs frequented by couples waiting to take their marriage vows. Sometimes, for a change, they crossed the border into England to the hotel which an enterprising English gentleman had built. They made new friends and discovered that there were communal tents for those who were short of money. Michael offered to stay at one of these until their wedding day but Claire would not hear tell of it.

In spite of their good intentions, temptation had proved too strong and they were already sharing the bed so she could see no point in changing the situation. Michael was desperately worried that in spite of his trying to take precautions, Claire might become pregnant. She was not in the least helpful in this matter. She objected to birth control and was of the opinion that whatever would be, would be, saying that they must accept whatever God sent them.

The three weeks passed happily enough and at last their wedding day arrived. Claire dressed carefully in the new suit she had brought with her especially for the occasion. It was the 'New Look', short fitted jacket and calf-length straight skirt. Claire eyed herself in the mirror and was pleased with what she saw. The sloping shoulders of the jacket and pencil slimness of the skirt showed off her figure to advantage. The sombre grey of the suit was relieved by a frilly blue blouse and the black handbag had been borrowed from Eileen for the occasion. Something old, something new, something borrowed, something blue. She wasn't really superstitious but why take unnecessary chances?

Michael, looking handsome in a navy blue serge suit, thought Claire had never looked lovelier. Mrs McCartan, as was her habit, shed a few tears as she waved them off. Claire walked proudly by Michael's side, glad that the rain had abated for a time and she did not have to cover her suit with a raincoat for the short journey to the Register Office. There were quite a few couples waiting inside when they arrived. They stood patiently in the hall until their names were called and then entered the room where the ceremony was to take place. As she stood proudly by Michael's side in front of the Registrar, Claire tried to block from her mind the memory of Beth's wedding. Even Eileen's had been a grand affair compared to this bare room with no one present but strangers. But so long as she had Michael, what else mattered? Two of these strangers, a young couple from Cornwall, had agreed to witness the service and in no time at all it was all over.

Outside again, Michael looked smilingly down at Claire. 'Well, Mrs O'Hara . . . you're saddled with me, for better, for worse.' He cupped her face in his hands. 'I hope you don't live to regret this day, sweetheart.'

'Of course I won't, Michael! I love you.'

'Do you want to go over to the blacksmith's, love?'

'Oh, but we must! It's all arranged. Besides I think we will enjoy it.'

Claire was right. The wedding of the heart, or anvil wedding as it was affectionately known, was performed tongue in cheek in the blacksmith's shop, a short distance up the road from the Register Office. It was a light-hearted romantic affair where Claire and Michael held hands over the anvil and reaffirmed their marriage vows. It concluded with the 'blacksmith' clanging his hammer resoundingly on the anvil to the spontaneous applause of the onlookers who had gathered to witness the ceremony. Blushing, and still holding Michael's hand, Claire gave him a quick kiss before rushing him from the blacksmith's shop and down the road in the direction of Mrs McCartan's cottage.

It had been the most wonderful day of Claire's young life and to finish it off Mrs McCartan had prepared a high tea in their honour. And they were now legally man and wife, Mr and Mrs O'Hara! What more could they wish for?

Rain lashed against the window panes as the wind howled around the passenger terminal. They had arrived in Stranraer in sleet and now, three weeks later, they were leaving in sleet, a gale was blowing out at sea. Claire peered out towards the wind-lashed dock and shivered.

'Michael, that wind must be gale force. Do you think the ferry will leave on time?'

Aware of the fear that Claire was desperately trying to hide, he answered with more confidence than conviction, 'They won't leave unless it is absolutely safe to do so. You see, it might be quite calm once we clear the loch. Nature works in strange ways, you know.'

The double doors of the terminal crashed open and wind swirled fiercely around the lounge, disrupting all in its path, blowing over paper cups and spilling their contents. Anything that wasn't secured was lifted off the floor and rubbish was strewn everywhere before the staff managed to close and bolt the doors. Young children were terrified and started to cry. Worried parents comforted them and tried to reassure each other. Claire moved closer to Michael and he put his arm around her.

'It's so dark out there you'd think it was night-time instead of seven in the morning. I wish we were home, Michael.' The look Claire turned on him was full of apprehension. 'Are you happy about our marriage?'

'Yes, love. My only fear is that you might live to regret it. You'll feel like a pariah because you'll be unable to receive the sacraments now. In time you might want a child . . . and how can we risk that, eh, love?'

'As long as I have you, I'll be more than happy. I love you, Michael. I love you so much I can't believe we were wrong to marry. So you stop worrying about it.'

A voice boomed over the loudspeaker and he listened attentively. 'That's our call, love. Time for foot passengers to board the ship.'

He helped Claire to her feet and led her towards the doors that the staff were struggling to hold open to let the passengers out.

Outside, the strong wind almost lifted Claire off her feet and she squealed in alarm. Michael tightened his grip on her and with his free hand grasped hold of a young lad whose mother had two children to carry. 'I'll keep hold of him. You concentrate on yourself and the baby,' he told the woman. 'Steer clear of that water, you might slip,' he warned, and she gave him a grateful smile. She had been walking with her head bent, protecting the baby in her arms from the fierce wind, and had not seen the big puddle. Now, struggling against the wind, she made a detour around the water.

Once on board it was no better. The huge ship swayed in the rough swell rising steeply to one side, then falling, before rising steeply on the other. Michael was sure that their departure would be delayed until the storm abated, but he was wrong. About ten minutes later the ship edged its way out of Stranraer and up the loch towards the open sea, lurching violently from side to side.

When they had left Loch Ryan behind it was worse. The North Channel was in the grip of a terrible storm and the ship was at its mercy. It was tossed about by mountainous waves as if it was a cork and it was obvious that everybody was worried. However, they were putting a brave face on. Those who had travelled during storms before tried to reassure the other passengers. Claire could not conquer her fear and her grip on Michael was like a vice. Was this their answer for flying in God's face? Don't be silly! she admonished herself. God was merciful. He certainly wouldn't sink a ship because of her and Michael's misdemeanour.

They managed to stagger and lurch their way to the corner of one of the bars but when Michael offered to fetch something to drink, Claire begged him not to leave her. Eventually, she calmed down and Michael fetched some drinks and sandwiches. Claire nibbled at a sandwich but was unable to digest it. Her stomach was in knots and she had difficulty holding down what was already in it. This was much worse than the trip over. As time passed, Michael became aware that they had been on the ship for at least a couple of hours. A glance at his watch confirmed this. It was a quarter past ten. They had been sailing for the last two and a half hours. Even allowing extra time for the storm, land should be in sight by now. 'We should be home soon, love.'

About thirty minutes later when there was still no sign of land an announcement came over the public address system. 'Your attention please. This is your Captain speaking. This is an emergency. I repeat. This is an emergency. Would all passengers put on warm clothing and go immediately to the nearest assembly point. You will be met by members of the crew who will give you further instructions. I repeat. This is an emergency. Would all passengers . . .'

Trying to appear calm, Michael reached for Claire's warm outer coat and held it for her while she slid her arms into it. He wrapped his scarf around her neck, and pulling the hood of the coat up over her head and ears, secured it tightly under her chin. He gave her a comforting hug before donning his own overcoat.

Suddenly the boat listed to one side. When it failed to right itself, Michael realized that something terrible was indeed wrong and that they were in dire trouble. Everybody was thrown across the lounge and anything that wasn't nailed down went with them. Miraculously, no one seemed badly hurt. Helping Claire to her feet he urged her towards the deck, away from the side of the saloon that lay dangerously close to the water. Grabbing tables, chairs, anything that was permanently fixed, he managed to coax and push Claire on a slow tortuous journey upwards and through yet another compartment until at last they were near a door adjacent to the boat deck where they had been instructed to assemble. By now the list had become so severe that the crew were securing life lines to enable passengers to clamber up to the higher side of the ship.

Life jackets were handed out by the crew and Michael managed to strap Claire into hers and helped some youngsters into their before struggling into his own. Stewards and stewardesses were attempting to wrap all the frightened children in blankets, before guiding them outside on to decks lashed by huge stinging waves. Michael and Claire helped all they could and after what seemed like ages the women and children were at last in a sheltered position against the deckhouse and the men were clinging to the ship's rails. They saw flares fired into the sky but they didn't rise very high and Michael guessed this was due to the severe list of the ship. However, the crew were reassuring, saying a destroyer was on its way and should arrive about one o'clock. The time came and went, and still there was no sign of help. The crew members assured them a mayday distress call was sure to bring help quickly.

The ship gave another violent lurch, and seeing a human chain being formed to help passengers who were still trapped in lower decks, Michael went to join them. It was as he returned to Claire's side that the signal to abandon ship was announced and he knew they were now in grave danger.

'Come on, love. Let's get you into a lifeboat,' he said. He was amazed at how calm everybody was, but then, wasn't help on the way? There was no need for panic.

Michael was dragging Claire forward to where a lifeboat

was being loaded with women and children. She could not make herself heard against the howling wind. She was exhausted, but with a great effort of will managed to grab hold of a gangway stanchion and, clinging to it, forced Michael to a halt.

He turned angrily on her. 'Claire, we must hurry or you'll miss the chance to get into a lifeboat.'

'I won't go without you, Michael.' She was amazed at how calm she was suddenly feeling. All fear had left her. 'Michael . . . can't you see? Maybe we are meant to die together. Let's leave our fate in God's hands.'

'Claire!' he cried out in exasperation. 'Listen to me! We are not going to die! Come on, move your feet, love.'

Claire obeyed him but she had no intention of getting into a lifeboat without this new husband of hers. Michael was to thank God for her stubbornness. The lifeboat he had tried to cajole her into was lowered down into the water but before it could right itself a monstrous wave caught it broadside on and sent it crashing against the side of the ship. It overturned, spilling its occupants into the freezing water. As he gazed down in horror at it, Michael gripped Claire close. He had surely almost sent her to her death. What chance had those poor women and children, floundering about in those treacherous waters so close to the ship?

Michael realized what he must do if they were to stand any chance at all of surviving. Desperation lending him superior strength, he lifted Claire bodily in his arms and jumped into the heaving water.

They hit the icy water together and it closed over their heads as they sank down, down, down a long way, but Michael retained his tight grip on Claire and with strong kicks of his legs started the fight upwards. At last they broke the surface of the turbulent water, spluttering and gasping for breath. They were both strong swimmers and once they had regained their breath, with strong strokes, Michael urged Claire away from the ship. From a safe distance away, through the swirling mist and spray and bobbing up and down in the heavy swell, they watched in disbelief as the *Princess Victoria* went under. They couldn't believe their eyes. It had all happened so quickly. One minute the huge ship was there, and the next she was gone.

Clinging to some debris, they somehow managed to stay afloat in the freezing water. A raft drifted by close enough to enable Michael, with the help of the occupants, to bundle Claire aboard. However, as he attempted to clamber aboard after her, a huge wave lifted him away and the raft was borne out of his reach. He saw Claire's mouth open in a silent scream when she realized that they might be separated and saw her struggle with the occupants of the raft, but they held her firmly and soon the raft had drifted out of sight. He had at least the consolation of knowing that she was safe and thanked God for this. If he could just hang on, surely help must arrive soon?

Thrown about by mountainous waves he was unaware how long he had been in the icy water but it seemed a lifetime. Attempting to keep himself afloat, he grabbed at any piece of wreckage that came his way. Strong though he was, each time he clambered on to what seemed his salvation, it was only to be swept off again into the cruel icy sea. From time to time Michael saw other survivors thrashing about in the water or hanging grimly on to rafts, whilst others appeared to have succumbed to the terrible freezing conditions of the channel. It was a terrible struggle to keep his head above the water and he tried in vain to avoid swallowing the filthy salt water.

Empty rafts passed within reach but he was too weary and cold to try and board one. He couldn't tell how long he was in the water but the numbness that had started in his hands and feet was spreading throughout his body and still there was no sign of rescue. His mind began to wander back over his life. Was this the beginning of the end? Wasn't it said that your life flashed before your eyes just before you died? His thoughts turned to Claire. Was he meant to die that she might live in peace? Would she survive these awful conditions or would she also perish from exposure? Would he ever see his beautiful bride again? Please God protect her, he prayed. If they should survive, would their parents forgive them for getting married?

He remembered the first time he saw Claire decorating the shop window. So young and fresh and beautiful. It all seemed so long ago! If only they had not been separated and he was able to hold her and comfort her it wouldn't be so bad. Awareness came to him. There was some one near him in the water! Was it Claire? He tried to move forward but his movements were sluggish and the waves relentlessly tossed him back. The figure in the lifejacket was washed away again. Still no sign of help. An empty raft brushed against him but his hands were too numb and his body too weak for him to pull himself aboard. With a last superhuman effort from his tortured body, he managed to hook his arms through the rope looped around the raft. Claire's face was vivid in his mind as he slipped into merciful oblivion.

Johnny usually worked on a Saturday morning but had taken time off to go to meet Michael and Claire from the *Princess Victoria*. The weather was so atrocious he had phoned to make sure that the ferry had left Stranraer on time and had been assured that it had left at 7.45 that morning. Kissing Eileen farewell, he set off for Larne.

Once Johnny left the house Eileen washed and dressed the children and made them their breakfast. When they were settled playing with their toys she decided to audit some accounts while awaiting Johnny's return with her sister and Michael. Secretly in despair that the couple had gone through with the wedding ceremony after all, she had informed her parents that they would be home today but not by which route they would travel. She had also refrained from telling her parents the unwelcome news. That was something Claire must do herself. As was her custom the radio played softly whilst she worked. So completely wrapped up in her books was she, she just caught the tail end of a newsflash. Something about the *Princess Victoria* . . . Wasn't that the ferry that Michael and Claire were travelling home on? Had it been delayed after all? Was Johnny away on a wild goose chase?

Patiently she waited for a repetition of the newsflash. It was not long before it was repeated. The newscaster's voice came on the air.

'We are interrupting this programme to bring you news of a ferry disaster. We have just received information that the *Princess Victoria* has sunk in the North Channel. Rescue is being hampered by bad visibility and gale force winds. Relatives wishing information about their family or friends should call the following number. Further bulletins will be broadcast on this station as the situation becomes clearer. The number to ring is . . .'

Glad that she had a pen in her hand, Eileen scribbled down the number. Within the next ten minutes she phoned numerous times but the number was always engaged. Unable to bear the uncertainty alone, she pulled on her boots and coat. Covering her head and ears with a woollen hat, she left the house and headed for St James's Park.

Halfway down the street she stopped in consternation. The children! Good God, in all the confusion she had completely forgotten about them. Running back up the street she cajoled them away from their toys and quickly scrambled them into their outer clothes. Promising that she would bring them home sweets when she returned, she hurried them down the street to their Grannie Cleary.

Madge Cleary gaped in amazement when Eileen rushed in, breathlessly. She explained that the ferry had sunk and would Madge please look after the kids for a few hours? Bewildered, Madge tried to stall her but Eileen was already on the move again. With an, 'I'll explain later,' she was off.

Madge followed her out as far as the gate and watched her racing at top speed down the street, barely pausing before crossing the busy Falls Road. What on earth was all that about? What ferry had sunk and why was Eileen so worried about it? Entering the house she questioned Paul but the child was unable to enlighten her. He did not know what was going on so Madge knew that she would probably have to contain her curiosity until Eileen returned.

Sarah looked at her daughter in amazement when she burst into the kitchen. The radio was on and Eileen gestured towards it. 'Did you not hear the newsflash?' she cried breathlessly, all the while wondering how her mother could be so calm.

'I did! Those poor souls. Their relatives will be worried sick.'

Only then did Eileen realize that she must break the news. A cold tremor coursed through her body as she dropped her bombshell. 'Mam . . . ah, Mam . . . Claire and Michael are on the *Princess Victoria*.'

Sarah gazed at her blankly. Then as realization dawned she groped for a chair and slumped down. 'Oh, sweet Jesus! They don't expect many survivors. We'll have to phone! They gave a number to ring.'

'Here! I have it!' Eileen thrust the piece of paper on which she had written the emergency number into her mother's hand.

Sarah rushed into the hall to the phone and Eileen's voice followed her. 'I hope you get through, Mam. Every time I tried it was engaged.'

After numerous attempts Sarah at last got through. She was informed that destroyers and lifeboats were in the vicinity where the *Princess Victoria* had sunk but that gale force winds and poor visibility were hampering rescue attempts. She was also told that any survivors and the bodies of the dead were being taken to Belfast and Donaghadee. No names were as yet available.

Sarah relayed this news to Eileen and grabbed her coat and scarf. 'Let's go! Survivors will be taken to the Royal and the City Hospitals.'

'How do you know where they will be taken, Mam?'

'Oh, talk sense, Eileen! They are the two biggest hospitals! Where else would they take them? We can be waiting! It's better than sitting here doing nothing. We can even go to Larne if necessary.'

'Johnny went to Larne earlier this morning to pick them up. He didn't know anything about the disaster. We should stay here. He's bound to ring . . . let me know what's happening. When he can't reach me at home, he is sure to ring here.'

But Sarah was already out of the door and, with a deep sigh, Eileen followed her.

Chapter Eight

Johnny arrived at Larne Harbour in howling winds about ten o'clock that morning, giving himself sufficient time to park his car before the arrival of the ferry. In the passenger terminal he discovered that the ferry would be late on account of the bad weather. He had been in such a rush out of the house that he hadn't had time to eat any breakfast in case of any hold ups on the road, so ordering a mug of tea and a couple of rounds of toast, he retired to a not too busy corner to await the announcement that the *Princess Victoria* had docked. The terminal was fairly crowded with people waiting to board the ferry for the return trip to Stranraer, or waiting for friends to disembark. It was a very noisy atmosphere, what with excited children chasing each other in and out of the tables and exasperated parents trying vainly to contain them.

The playful children brought to mind Johnny's own family. Young Paul was a proper little lad; dark and intense and always inquisitive. When not kicking a rubber ball about he was forever getting into lighthearted mischief. Whenever possible Johnny would take him to a football match or to the Falls Park to work off some of his exuberance. He had great plans for his son and daughters. He would do all in his power to ensure that his children got a good education. With a bit of luck his new position in Shorts' would enable him to be able to afford to send them to college and hopefully on to Queen's University to complete their further education. He sat for some time daydreaming about his family, oblivious to the hustle and bustle around him.

Time dragged slowly past. It was approaching one o'clock and still no sign of the ferry. It should have docked long before this. Occasionally a restless traveller would approach the inquiry desk and ask what the hold up was. Shouldn't the *Princess Victoria* have docked by now? The harassed staff pointed out that a severe gale was blowing out there in the channel. Perhaps the ferry had been blown off course or something. They must remain patient.

From his corner seat Johnny calmly observed all this commotion. As more and more people bombarded the by now worried staff with questions about the long delay, he sensed that they knew more than they were admitting. He was about to go over and add some questions himself. However, before he could rise a young man sitting at the adjacent table motioned to him with a sidewards nod of the head. They leant towards each other and with another shake of the head towards the portable radio beside him on the table and eyes darting furtively about the waiting room, the man whispered, 'The ferry's in some sort of trouble.'

Johnny stared at him for a few brief moments as if trying to comprehend what he had just been told. Then with one accord they rose quickly from their respective tables and headed for the exit doors. Pausing briefly to pull on caps and gloves, they left the cosy warmth of the terminal behind them. Outside, the driving sleet stung their faces and the fierce wind tore angrily at their clothes as they battled their way across to the harbour. In spite of the howling wind and icy sleet whipping around, the dockside was crowded. There were hushed groups of people standing huddled together against the wintry elements. Joining one of the groups, Johnny was immediately aware of the seriousness of the situation. He realized that these weren't just people meeting family and friends off the ferry. Most of these folk were from Larne and were accustomed to storms at sea. It took a lot more than gales and blizzards to bring them out in force.

The ferry service provided employment for a lot of the inhabitants of the town and bad news travelled like wildfire through this seafaring community. News that the *Princess Victoria* was in trouble had very quickly passed by word of mouth through the town, bringing worried fathers, mothers, husbands, wives, and other relatives and friends to the docks to render moral support to each other and anxiously seek news of loved ones. Fear hung over them like a tangible cloud but as yet no tears were shed.

These were strong men and women, only too aware how treacherous and cruel the sea could be. Their forefathers had weathered many a storm, but they had a strong gut feeling about this one. They seemed to sense that the worst was about to happen. Down through the years there had been tragedies at sea and their forebears had stood here on this very dock waiting for news. Now it was their turn to wait and worry. After some time had passed, a tremor passed like a wave across the waterfront and to Johnny's amazement most of the crowd moved as one away from the docks.

Disconcerted, he grabbed a man by the arm. 'What's happening? Where is everybody going?'

The look the man bestowed on him was grief-stricken. 'God help them poor souls out there in that storm,' he wailed. 'The *Princess Victoria* has gone down.'

This news sent Johnny racing back to the terminal. He must let Eileen know what was going on. As he was about to dial his home number he saw a member of staff come from an inner office and reach for a microphone. Johnny delayed while he listened to the official's announcement.

'Ladies and gentlemen, it is my unpleasant duty to inform you that the *Princess Victoria* has sunk in the

North Channel, and that rescuers in the form of a Royal Naval destroyer, lifeboats and merchant ships are already in the vicinity, picking up survivors. That's all I know at present but I will keep you fully informed of any further developments. Thank you for your attention.'

Pandemonium broke out, everyone jostling each other and shouting at the same time, asking questions. Did all the passengers and crew get off? Where were they taking the survivors? How long must they wait for news? However, with an apologetic shrug of his shoulders, the official was already retreating to the sanctuary of his office, with a promise to keep them up to date.

Fingers drumming impatiently on the wall beside the pay phone, Johnny listened to the monotonous ringing at the other end of the line. Where on earth was Eileen? She would be expecting him to arrive home with Claire and Michael at any moment. Suddenly a thought dawned on him. Eileen always listened to the radio while she worked. She liked to be kept up to date with the news. Perhaps she had already heard about the disaster on the radio! That could be one reason for her absence. His wife was probably at this moment over at her mother's, breaking the bad news about Claire and Michael being on the *Princess Victoria*. Quickly, he dialled Sarah's number. Again the phone rang on and on.

With an apologetic glance at the queue that had formed and was waiting impatiently behind him, Johnny next tried Maggie's number. He did not blame the people behind him for being restless or for the snide remarks being directed at him. He would be exactly the same in their position. Everybody was in the same frame of mind, wanting to reach those back home and explain the reason for the delay. Greatly relieved, Johnny heard Maggie's clear voice come over the phone.

'Maggie! It's me, Johnny,' he shouted breathlessly into the mouthpiece. 'Is Eileen there, by any chance? I've tried ringing her at home and at Sarah's but can't get an answer.'

'It's funny that you should say that,' Maggie cried in surprise. 'About a half hour ago I saw Eileen and Sarah rush up the street. It was obvious that something was wrong, but by the time I managed to find my shoes to go out and ask what the trouble was, they were out of sight.'

'Have you been listening to the radio this morning, Maggie?'

'Yes ... yes, I have.'

She sounded mystified and Johnny asked. 'Have you heard any mention at all of the *Princess Victoria*? You know, the ferry?'

'Yes, there have been a few news flashes! They say she's in trouble.'

'She sank a short time ago. I'm calling from Larne. I came here to pick up Claire and Michael. They are on that ferry.'

'Oh, no!' Johnny heard the fear in Maggie's voice; could picture a worried frown gathering on her brow. After a pause fraught with sorrow, Maggie resumed, speaking unsteadily, 'No wonder Sarah looked demented. But where can they have gone?'

'They might have heard where the survivors are being taken.'

'The obvious place will be the City and Royal Victoria Hospitals. Sarah will have gone down to the Royal! She never could wait patiently at home like everyone else.'

'Maggie, I'll have to go now. There's a big queue waiting to get on this phone. If you see them, will you tell them that I rang? Tell Eileen that I will stay here and find out all I can. Will you do that for me, Maggie?'

'Of course I will, son. You take care now.'

'Thanks! I'll ring back later and let you know what's going on here. Goodbye, Maggie.'

The staff in the terminal were besieged by the crowd

and in vain explained that, as yet, all they knew was that the ship had gone down. Grumbling with frustration, some of the people moved back out on to the harbour to watch for any sign of a lifeboat. Time dragged by and Johnny was in two minds what to do. Should he hang on here in Larne, or go home to await word of survivors? He dithered, and it was about half an hour later that the official reappeared to make another announcement. This time he was accompanied by two policemen.

'Ladies and gentlemen, your attention, please. We have just been informed that some survivors have been picked up by the Donaghadee and Portpatrick lifeboats and will be taken back to their respective bases before being transferred to hospital. The sergeant here would like a word with you, if you please. Thank you.'

The sergeant, a big burly man with a walrus moustache, took the microphone from the official. 'Ladies and gentlemen, I know you won't like what I am about to say, but I ask you to please go home and wait there for news of your family and friends.' Mutterings broke out among the crowd and the sergeant lifted his hand for attention. 'Believe me, I know how you feel! But if you all head for Donaghadee, you could hamper the rescue services by causing congestion on the roads. And we don't want that now, do we?'

It came as no surprise to him that his request fell on deaf ears. Most of the crowd had by now made a hasty exit and were heading for the car park. With a slight shrug the sergeant relinquished his hold on the microphone. He had not expected these people to take any heed of him, but it had been his duty to try and get them to see sense. In their position, after waiting patiently for hours on end for some news, he would have done exactly the same thing himself.

Donaghadee was about forty miles further down the coast from Larne. Johnny was fortunate to have parked near the entrance to the car park and avoided the chaos building up as drivers further back were blocking others' exits in their haste to make the journey south. To his relief the car started on the first turn of the key. He was soon leaving Larne and heading in the direction of Belfast. The condition of the roads was atrocious due to the weather. There was by now a fairly heavy stream of traffic leaving Larne and driving in convoy in the direction of Belfast, probably with occupants all on the same sad mission as himself. It was a slow, frustrating journey through the Belfast traffic and it was nearly two hours later when he at last arrived in Donaghadee. Johnny drove straight to the harbour and as he got out of the car was just in time to hear a loud cheer go up as the lifeboat was spotted. Hurrying over to the crowd around it, he watched the lifeboat dock. There was a great feeling of urgency in the air, and police officers struggled to keep the crowds at bay as survivors were quickly borne from the boat on stretchers and loaded into waiting ambulances. These immediately raced away with bells urgently clanging.

Johnny could not be certain but he doubted if Claire or Michael were amongst these survivors. He had peered closely as each stretcher passed by but he saw no one that vaguely resembled his sister-in-law or Michael among the groaning, blanket-shrouded survivors. He asked the police inspector in charge of operations if any of them had been identified, but was told, that as yet, no official list of names was available. He was further informed that the families and next-of-kin would be notified as soon as possible.

Next he watched as the bodies were taken from the boat. These were quickly placed in rows in an empty boathouse and guarded by two police constables. Boldly, Johnny approached the makeshift morgue and asked if he could view the corpses to see if he could identify any of them. However, the constable politely denied him entry, informing him that the bodies would soon be transferred to the Belfast hospitals and City morgue for formal identification by the next-of-kin. Johnny gave in gracefully. It would serve no purpose to stand arguing with the policeman, who, when all was said and done, was only performing his duty.

The weather had by now deteriorated and the freezing wind had turned the sleet into a sheet of solid ice on the windscreen of his car. It took Johnny some time to scrape it clear, but at long last he was back behind the steering wheel and on his way to Belfast once more. The trip to Donaghadee had been a waste of his time. With hindsight he realized that he should have stopped off at one of the hospitals on his route through Belfast. He could have made some enquiries there and maybe saved himself a fruitless journey. He drove slowly back, the windscreen wipers struggling against the thick wet sleet.

Reaching the outskirts of the city, he headed across to the Lisburn Road where his first port of call was the Belfast City Hospital. Tired and wet, Johnny made his way from the car park to the main reception area. There was still no let up in the weather. Standing at the enquiry desk, he calmly answered a barrage of personal questions before getting permission to see any of the survivors. Walking slowly down the ward that had been specially designated for victims of the tragedy, Johnny shuffled from bed to bed with an apologetic nod here and there at the glazed eyes returning his stare. They were all men but Michael was not among them.

Next he viewed the bodies lined out in the mortuary, brought here by the rescue services. Again there was no sign of Michael or Claire. Tears were streaming down his face and he didn't give a damn who saw them. The sight of these bodies, battered and broken from their ordeal in the water, would have brought tears from a stone. And the saddest part about it . . . an awful lot of the victims were children. With a shake of the head he acknowledged to the waiting attendant that he didn't recognize any of them. His next destination was the Royal Victoria Hospital. As at the City Hospital, the reception area was crowded with people milling around; genuine folk on the same tragic errand as himself, some ghouls who seemed to appear at every tragedy, and the usual handful of newspaper reporters with notebooks at the ready looking for an exclusive story. Johnny waited his turn at the reception desk, hoping that none of the latter would try and interview him. He was in no mood for any of that nonsense.

To his great delight, as he stood surveying the milling throng, Eileen's voice reached his ears above the incessant din.

'Johnny! Oh, Johnny, I'm so glad to see you, love.'

His wife flung herself into his open arms and her tears were wet against his cheek as he bent to hug her. He gathered her close. 'Hush, love, don't cry,' he comforted her, patting her lovingly. 'Have you heard any news yet?'

'Yes Michael is here,' she sobbed. 'He's upstairs in one of the wards. They've given him something to make him sleep. He has a broken arm, some cracked ribs, and is suffering from shock and hypothermia, but otherwise he's all right. The doctor said that he'll make a full recovery.'

Johnny couldn't help but smile inwardly at Eileen's turn of phrase; broken arm, cracked ribs, shock and exposure. And he was all right? 'And Claire? Is there any news of Claire?'

'No. We still haven't heard anything about her.' Eileen clung to him. 'Oh, Johnny, I'm so frightened. I've this awful feeling that Claire is dead. Me mam's demented. She's sitting up there at Michael's beside willing him to wake to see if he knows anything about Claire. Come on up and see him.'

Eileen took his hand to lead the way towards the

stairway but Johnny checked her. 'Eileen ... have you seen the corpses?'

Tears welled up in her eyes as she admitted, 'No ... I'm such a big coward! But Mam looked at them. Claire's not in the morgue.'

'Well, love, I've been to the City morgue and she's not there either ... so there's hope yet.'

When they got there the ward was packed with anxious relatives, and doctors and nurses scurried between the beds. They found a tearful Sarah sitting by Michael's bed. He was propped up on the pillows, white and drawn, looking very much like a corpse himself. There was an ugly gash over one eye that had been stitched and an arm was in splints ready to be set. He was wakened by the sound of Johnny greeting Sarah, and she at once gripped his good arm.

Gazing blankly at her for some moments, Michael tried to raise himself up on the bed only to sink back in obvious pain as he put his weight on his fractured arm. 'Claire? Is Claire all right?' he gasped, sweat appearing in little droplets on his forehead.

'We don't know yet! When did you last see her?' Sarah's voice was shrill as she dabbed at his sweating brow with a tiny handkerchief. It rankled her that Michael was lying here safe and sound while her daughter was still missing.

Michael's eyes glazed and a pained expression crossed his bruised face. They guessed he was fighting inwardly to collect his thoughts. They waited in silence. At long last he spoke. 'I remember pushing her on to a life raft. There were other people on it and they helped to pull Claire aboard. I tried to climb on after her but the sea was too rough. It carried the raft away from me. That was the last time I saw Claire. But she must be all right, she was on that life raft with other survivors, I saw her.'

'I pray to God she is!' Sarah was sobbing again. 'I gave

the officer in charge her name and description. He'll let us know if she's brought in here.'

'What name did you tell him?'

At these words Sarah gave him a sympathetic look. Poor Michael. He must be suffering from concussion. Couldn't even remember Claire's name. 'Ross, of course! Claire Ross . . . what else?'

Michael was struggling to get out of bed. 'She's called O'Hara now. Claire O'Hara. I'll have to go and tell them.'

'What on earth are you talking about? Surely you're not . . .' Sarah gaped blankly at him for a moment, then gasped, 'You can't be . . . married!'

'We were married in Gretna Green last Friday. That's why we were in Scotland. To get married!'

Sarah paled, and turned a wrathful look on Eileen. 'Did you know anything about this?'

At her daughter's slight nod, she erupted. 'And you let them go? You didn't even do anything to stop them?'

'Ah, Mam . . . talk sense! How could I have stopped them. They're not kids, you know.'

'You could have warned me or your dad. We'd soon have put a stop to all this nonsense, and we wouldn't be sitting here now, not knowing whether your sister's alive or dead!'

'Here, what do you mean?' Michael interrupted her. 'Claire must have been picked up. I tell you . . . she was on the raft with others. I saw her. She must be safe somewhere.' He turned in desperation to Johnny. 'Will you get my clothes for me? I must find Claire.'

'Look here, Michael, they won't let you out until your arm's in plaster and they're sure that you're all right.'

But Michael ignored Johnny's advice, and although obviously in pain he prized himself up and off the bed and was frantically pulling open locker doors in search of his clothes.

'Hold on a minute, Michael. Your old clothes will

307

hardly be in there. You'll need some clean ones. I'll bring some down for you later on.'

'Can I count on you, Johnny? There is nothing wrong with me! I can't just lie here not knowing what's happened to Claire. I must find out where they have taken her,' Michael pleaded, slumping down on the bed again.

'I give you my word. And I'll try and find out if there is any news of Claire. I'll also call in on your mother and let her know what has happened. She'll not have realized that you were on the *Princess Victoria*. I'll see you later. Are you coming, Eileen . . . Sarah?'

Eileen nodded her head and leant towards Michael, patting him tenderly on his good arm. 'See you later. I'll send down some of those clothes that you left at our house. Are you coming, Mam?'

Sarah, however, was not to be budged. 'I'm staying here.'

'Mam, you need some rest. And what about me dad? He'll be home from work by now and will be wondering where you've got to. He'll not know what's happening.'

'He's not paralyzed! He can make himself a bite to eat. Not that he'll have to . . . your grannie will see to that.' Sarah's voice was bitter. 'She always looks after Mick's welfare.'

'Look, Sarah . . . They'll be calling off the search parties soon, have probably done so already.' Johnny's voice was gentle as he explained what was likely to happen. 'It's too dark now. They wouldn't be able to see a thing out there, but I'm sure they'll start again first light in the morning.'

'You mean that my Claire could be out on that water all night?' Sarah wailed.

'No! No, Sarah. I didn't mean that. She's probably safe in another hospital. The best place for us to be right now is at home. That's where the police will call as soon as they know anything. Come on, Sarah, let's go home,' he coaxed.

. Sarah allowed herself to be helped to her feet but still she argued. 'Perhaps we should all go to Larne and see what's happening there.'

'Sarah, they are picking up . . .' Johnny stopped himself in the nick of time. He had been about to say 'bodies'. Instead he said . . . 'survivors all down the coastline. Claire could be anywhere. Come on, let's get you home and Eileen will make us something to eat.'

'Eat?' Sarah was scandalized. 'I couldn't eat a thing. The very thought of eating just now would choke me.' She still protested, but at least under Johnny's gentle persuasion she was on the move, allowing herself to be led from the ward.

It was on the journey home that Eileen realized how late it was. Caught up in the excitement of the day she had completely forgotten all about her children. She was glad now that she had brought them down to Madge. Although obviously puzzled, her mother-in-law had told her not to worry and that she would be only too happy to keep them for as long as was necessary, and that the children could stay at her house all night if need be.

They went straight to St James's Park and there they found Maggie, Barney, Beth and Tommy, with Mick and a distraught Emma.

Entering the house, Sarah threw her husband a look of scorn. 'I suppose it never dawned on you to come down to the hospital and see if you could be of any assistance, did it?'

Mick was quick to retaliate. 'I knew nothing about the disaster, Sarah! I'm not long home,' he protested. 'And then I went down to Beechmount to tell Maisie the bad news.' He knew immediately that he had made a mistake, mentioning her name.

Sarah picked him up on it right away. 'Oh, of course your precious Maisie would naturally be your first concern!' Her voice rose shrilly. 'Well, you can go back down to Beechmount and tell her your precious son is safe . . .

309

but that *my* daughter is still missing. In fact, you can stay down there, if you like!'

In the ghastly silence that followed this dreadful outburst, Mick, at a loss for words, turned on his heel and left the house. Only Sarah could wound him with a word or look, and by God she was excelling herself lately. Her tongue was like a razor and she used Mick to sharpen it on. It was bad enough at present but he dreaded to think what she would be like if Claire was to perish, God forbid! There would be no living with his wife then. Johnny followed him from the room and out of the front door.

'Mick, I'm going down to see Maisie to tell her that Michael is safe. She has the right to know. Would you like to come with me and give Sarah a chance to cool down?'

Mick smiled wryly. 'Down to Maisie's? Are you trying to get me killed?' Then with a shrug he added, 'Ah, well . . . to hell with it! I may as well be hanged for a sheep as a lamb. Let's go, Johnny.'

The following twelve hours were the most traumatic the family had ever experienced. Eileen and Johnny had decided to spend the night at Sarah's. Conversation was sporadic with everybody being careful not to say what they really thought Claire's chances of survival were. Not in Sarah's presence anyhow! When at last the rest of the family had departed to their own homes, Mick persuaded Emma to go to bed, promising to awaken her if they heard any news about Claire. The rest of them dozed throughout the night, sprawled out on the settee and armchairs, ears alert for the ring of the telephone, but daylight dawned without any further news. On the radio they learnt that at first light the destroyer *H.M.S. Contest*, the frigate *Woodridge Haven* and the lifeboats had put to sea once more to continue the search for survivors and bodies. Aeroplanes from Aldergrove and Coastal Command were directing operations from above.

Eileen and Johnny returned to their own house and Johnny quickly washed and shaved. With his arm now in plaster, and against the wishes of the doctors, Michael had signed himself out of hospital the night before. Johnny had promised to pick him up at his mother's house early this morning to go to Donaghadee and await the return of the lifeboats. Jim Rafferty had offered to drive Barney and Mick to Larne to await developments there. Very much against her will, Sarah had been persuaded to remain at home with the rest of the family.

After a quick soak in the bath Eileen dressed quickly and brought fresh clothes down to Madge's for the children. They were still asleep and her mother-in-law, who now knew all about the disaster and Claire's and Michael's part in it, shooed her off, telling her not to worry about the children and to help her parents all she could.

Eileen held Madge close in silent gratitude before hurrying on her way. Early though she was, Eileen found her mother's house crowded. All the close female relatives and friends had gathered to give support to the family and Kathleen Raferty, having taken over the kitchen, was making breakfast. When asked what they would like to eat, all said they just wanted a cup of tea. Kathleen ignored this and soon the aroma of bacon and eggs wafted about the house, making everybody aware just how hungry they were.

Sarah would not hear tell of missing Sunday Mass and Eileen and Emma accompanied her round to St John's church. However, when the priest asked the congregation to pray for the survivors and dead of the *Princess Victoria* disaster, Sarah collapsed and had to be carried from the church.

It was a cold but bright morning and on the clear roads

the journey across Belfast on the way to Donaghadee was covered in a very short time. Johnny found it hard to believe that just the day before, these very same waters that he and Michael were now gazing upon had been churned to an angry white froth by the fierce gales sending great rollers crashing into the pier and spray high into the air. Today the only sign of the storm was the mounds of seaweed that had been left behind. The harbour was not so crowded as the previous day and as they walked aimlessly up and down, Johnny was sad at his inability to persuade Michael to remain in Belfast and await news.

He had tried to reason with his friend that they would be better off going to the City morgue, but in vain. Since learning that Claire was still missing, Michael had been lamenting the fact that he had allowed her to be separated from him in the water. He said he felt closer to her here at the waterfront; was sure that somewhere, she was still alive.

Tentatively Johnny warned him not to build his hopes too high. Trying to prepare Michael for the worst, he stressed that it was highly unlikely that anyone could survive a night in the channel in those freezing conditions. He explained to him that they would not be allowed to view any bodies that might be brought ashore here. They would be taken straight to Belfast for formal identification.

Michael rounded on him in a fury. 'Claire is not dead! Do you hear me? Do you think I wouldn't know in here . . .' he placed a hand over his heart. '. . . if she was dead?' He was so distraught Johnny did not attempt to argue with him any more and they resumed their aimless walking about. It was late afternoon when Johnny managed to persuade Michael to return to Belfast. They went straight to the morgue. This time it was Michael who viewed the corpses. The instant he returned to the corridor, Johnny immediately knew by the colour and look on his face that Michael had at last found his young bride.

Collapsing on to the wooden bench against the wall, he wailed, 'Ah, Johnny . . . Claire's in there. She looks awful! God only knows how much she suffered. Dear Jesus, help me. What am I going to do? How will I be able to bear this?'

Johnny sat down beside him and gripped his arm in sympathy. 'Michael, Claire must have been in the water a long time. Maybe she didn't suffer as much as you think.'

Johnny knew the words he uttered were inane and would be of little comfort to the sobbing broken man beside him, but he could think of nothing better to say. With another sympathetic squeeze, he said, 'I'll phone home and let them know.'

It was Sarah who answered the phone on the first ring and Johnny found the words that would rob his mother-in-law of all hope sticking in his throat. He asked to speak to his wife.

Eileen approached the phone slowly; she had a premonition that she was about to hear bad news. Gripping the receiver tightly, she whispered, 'Hello.' No sound left her lips.

Puzzled, Johnny said, 'Eileen . . . Eileen are you there?'

This time she managed to find her voice. 'Yes, Johnny, it's me.'

'Eileen, love . . . I'm sorry to put the onus on you. I'm a big coward, so I am! I just couldn't break the bad news to your mother. Michael has just identified Claire's body at the morgue. He says she looks awful. For God's sake, whatever you do, don't let Sarah rush down here.' The silence down the line lengthened and Johnny asked, 'Eileen . . . are you all right, love?'

She wanted to laugh at his stupidity. Would she ever be all right again? She found herself nodding and when Johnny again asked anxiously, 'Eileen . . . Eileen, speak to me! Are you still there? Are you all right, love?' she managed to croak in the affirmative. A sob threatened to burst from her lips and she stifled it as she silently replaced the receiver. She felt the colour drain from her face and her lips quiver as she turned to face her mother, trying in vain to form words to break the awful news. To her great relief no words were necessary. Sarah's eyes fastened on hers and a terrible shriek rent the air.

'No, no! Please say it's not true! Please, Eileen, say it's not true!'

Across the room Maggie's eyes silently questioned Eileen and when her granddaughter nodded, Maggie went to Sarah and gathered her close. 'Hush, Sarah, love, hush. It's God's will.'

These words only incensed Sarah all the more. 'God's will? No! Oh, no! Don't put the blame on God. It's Mick's and that woman's sin that's the cause of all this. It's them who should be dead. My beautiful Claire ... Oh, my poor beautiful daughter.' She rose to her feet, hugging herself to contain her pain. Then looking wildly around, she cried, 'I want to see her. Who'll take me down?'

Remembering Johnny's words of warning, Eileen became agitated. 'No! No, Mam, you mustn't.' She looked frantically around her. Her mother must not go to the morgue. At last, inspired, she cried, 'We need the doctor! Somebody phone Dr Hughes, please. Hurry!'

Sarah was not to be pacified and they had forcibly to restrain her until Dr Hughes arrived and gave her an injection. She was still rambling as she slipped into merciful oblivion and even when she was completely unconscious, great sobs racked her shaking body.

It was Johnny who supported Sarah at the graveside. She would not let her husband anywhere near her, and to keep the peace Johnny accompanied her in the car to the cemetery. He stood, arm around her shoulders, by the side of the grave. Mick stood some distance from them, comforting a distraught Emma. From the top of the open grave the priest's voice droned on and on, but Mick was unable to take in a single word that he was saying. Different emotions were surging through his body. The greatest of these was anger! He knew that grief should be uppermost in his heart, and grief was there for the loss of his beautiful daughter, but it was anger that held sway, overruling all other feelings. He was angry that all these years Maisie had denied him the right to get to know his son. Now he and Michael could never be friends, Claire would always stand between them. So bitter was his resentment he had to fight the temptation to rush across to where Maisie stood and push her headlong into the open grave. At this moment he hated her for all the trouble she had unwittingly created. Since she had held her tongue all these years she should have continued to do so and taken her secret to the grave with her. Then his lovely daughter would still be alive and Michael would have become his son-in-law; next best thing to the son he had longed for.

Commonsense prevailed and Mick forced himself to calm down. Maisie had acted in good faith. She had thought that she was protecting Michael and him by keeping quiet. She must be in torment now, poor woman, wishing she had kept her mouth shut. Mick looked at his wife. Poor Sarah! Not a bite had passed her lips since Claire's body had been found. She looked old and haggard. Would she ever forgive him? He thought not, and neither did he blame her for all the terrible things she had said to him and the scorn that she had heaped upon his head. Wasn't he already tortured by guilt? This disaster would drive them apart! There was nothing surer. How could he ever make amends to Sarah? What would become of them? His thoughts swirled about a mind in turmoil.

A movement at the other side of the grave caught his attention. He looked up in time to see Michael hurriedly leave his mother's side. Saw Maisie reach out to detain her son. Poor Michael. Would he ever come to terms with this awful tragedy? Would he continue to live in Belfast or emigrate as he was threatening to do? Would he always hold it against Mick that a past sin had resulted in his losing the only girl he had ever loved? How could Mick expect Michael to forgive him? He couldn't forgive himself.

With an abrupt movement Michael pushed his way from the graveside, knocking away hands that would have stayed him. He could not bear to see the coffin being lowered into the earth. The idea of his beautiful Claire being covered with clay devastated him. He wanted to cry aloud at the injustice of it all. Why had his new bride been the one to die? She who had never done anyone any harm! A new grave had been opened for Claire, right on the edge of the meadow at the bottom of the cemetery. Very much aware of the pitying glances directed at him, he stumbled a short distance from the grave and gazed across the meadow.

Through the mist and rain he could barely make out the shape of the sprawling building that was Milltown Boys' Home. He remembered Claire telling him that her father had been an orphan reared there. He pushed the wet hair back off his brow and sighed deeply. He was glad it was raining. To have buried Claire in bright sunlight would have been unthinkable. No . . . it was only right that the heavens should grieve with him.

Shoulders hunched against the cold he gazed across the wet bedraggled meadow, a resting place for future bodies, to where it merged with the dark grey sky. Great molten clouds pushed and shoved at each other as if in torment; just as his mind was in torment and despair. Were the clouds always angry like this up here in the cemetery? Were they fighting for the souls of the corpses buried in the ground? No, of course they weren't! The soul left the body at death. He was letting his imagination run away with him. Where was Claire now? Did she know the great sorrow he felt? Tears ran unchecked down his cheeks. He closed his eyes and let the pain wash over him. Would he ever be free from guilt? If he had left Claire alone, she would be alive today. He should have cleared off when he found out that they were related. But he had loved her so much he had believed that nothing could go wrong. This was the result of flying in God's face! Was Claire in heaven or had he, with the great love he bore her, condemned her to an everlasting hell? He would never know! That was the worst part of it. To go through life not knowing.

Opening his eyes he saw that the sun, in an endeavour to get out, had lightened the clouds. A silvery patch emerged, becoming bigger and brighter even as he gazed at it. Suddenly the breath caught in his throat. There was Claire! Not the wet battered form he had identified at the morgue, the awful sight of which had haunted him ever since. No! There she stood in all her beauty. The wind moulding the flimsy white gown she wore to her slight figure and lifting the chestnut hair back from her face, the way he loved to see it. Head high, she smiled at him, her eyes seeming to tease. With lifted hand she pushed her fingers through her hair in that old familiar way. He glanced over his shoulder to see if anyone else was witnessing this miracle but the mourners were, one by one, shovelling earth into the grave.

Doubting his own sanity, Michael swung back towards the apparition. Claire was still there. For some moments she held his gaze as if trying to impart a message to him and he felt peace ease some of the pain from his mind. Then, with a wave of her hand, his beautiful young wife turned away. He started forward, anxious to catch a last glimpse of her, but the clouds were closing in again and the vision of Claire was gone.

Stunned, Michael's eyes continued to rake the sky but she had disappeared completely. He shook his head to clear it, realizing that his mind had conjured up a picture of Claire that he wanted to see. A picture of her at peace and happy. It had all been his imagination . . . or had it? Of course it had! A safety valve to keep him from losing his sanity. And it did help. He felt more at peace now; more ready to face the world again. The guilt and worry of being alive whilst Claire had perished had eased. Just a little, but it was a start. He was now convinced in his own mind that she was at rest, and that lightened the burden of guilt he carried.

Johnny supported Sarah back to the limousine. She was in a state of collapse; a dead weight on his arm. To his dismay, Maisie stepped in front of them and he was forced to stop, bringing Sarah to a halt by his side. In a daze and anxious to get home without breaking down, Sarah gazed unseeing at the small woman facing her. Vaguely, she observed the outstretched hand and heard the muttered condolences. When she realized just who was offering these condolences she wildly pushed the proffered hand away from her and turning to Johnny, cried, 'Take me home! Don't let that woman near me.'

Embarrassed, Maisie stepped quickly back and in her haste stumbled on the uneven ground. Michael had delayed at the graveside to say his final farewell to his wife, and the rest of the family were hovering about waiting for him, too distraught to notice their mother's predicament. It was Mick who stepped forward and, taking Maisie by the arm, led her away.

For their ears only, but telling nevertheless, Sarah's low voice followed them. 'Why don't you just stay with her? Eh? It's all you've ever wanted, isn't it?'

Deep colour clouded Mick's face and an angry frown knitted his brow, but he held his temper in check. This was neither the time nor the place for a showdown. Ignoring his wife's stinging taunts, he quickly led Maisie ahead of the other mourners. 'I don't think it would be wise for you to come back to our house,' he explained. 'Sarah doesn't know what she's saying at the moment. She's terribly upset and might create a scene. Shall I walk you home? Or perhaps you would prefer to go by car?'

'You're right, Mick, I'd better go on home. Although, mind you ... I don't blame Sarah for being bitter. I'm sure I'd feel the same in her position. If you don't mind, I'd like to walk home.'

The short journey down the Falls Road was spent in silence, each busy with their own troubled thoughts. When they reached Maisie's door, with a word of farewell, Mick turned to leave her.

'Mick, please come in for a while.' When he would have demurred, she pleaded. 'Just a few minutes ... please.'

Reluctantly, he followed her inside. He was aware that he should be back home helping to cope with the return of the mourners. No sense in upsetting Sarah even further. But how could he refuse Maisie five minutes of his time?

She shrugged out of her coat and hung it at the foot of the stairs. 'Take off your coat, Mick. I'll make a pot of tea ... or perhaps you would like something stronger? I have a little whiskey.'

'No, Maisie, nothing for me, thanks. I've got to get back. The family will wonder where I am.'

Reluctantly, she agreed. 'All right, Mick, I understand ... but will you come down some night? I need to talk to someone. I feel that Donald and the girls blame me for what has happened. You see ... they don't know the truth. They think that Michael and Claire went to Gretna Green because I wouldn't welcome Claire into my home. They think I didn't like her. How wrong they were! She was a lovely person, warm and kind. In normal circumstances I would have loved her for a daughter-in-law. It's awful the way things turned out. As for Michael ... I can't get through to

319

him at all, he's so wrapped up in guilt himself. I feel so alone.'

Full of pity for this poor distraught woman, without thought Mick reached for her and gathered her close. Gratefully she snuggled against him. Cheek against her hair, Mick consoled her. 'Don't you blame yourself, Maisie. These things happen. God alone knows why.'

Cheeks wet with tears, she gazed up at him. 'You will come down some time soon, won't you?'

Compassion tempted him to stay a while and comfort her. Resisting the impulse, he pushed her gently away from him, but promised, 'I'll be back. Some time next week.'

As he trudged back up the Falls Road Mick pondered on the wisdom of visiting Maisie. Better stay away from her, he warned himself. She is as lonely and unhappy as you, and you know where that could lead. Stay away from her. Concentrate on winning Sarah back. After all, in spite of the way she is treating you, she is still your wife. She had just cause to berate you.

But what about Gerry Docherty? Was he going to stay on the scene? Mick had noticed Gerry and his son Danny at Claire's funeral. He remembered that Sarah had said that Danny was coming up from Dublin to live in his grannie's house. For the past couple of days Gerry had been there as well, obviously helping his son to decorate the house. How long would that take? Mick had enough on his plate at present without Sarah's old skeletons jumping out of the cupboard and reminding her of the past. From the way that he looked at her, it was apparent that Gerry still carried a torch for Sarah. The sooner that man returned to Dublin the better. What if Gerry should decide to stay in Belfast? Stranger things had happened.

Gerry's wife had died two years ago and Danny was his only son. There was every reason for him to stay here, especially if Danny settled into his new job on the *Belfast Telegraph*. With the added inducement that Sarah and Mick were obviously at loggerheads, Gerry had every reason to consider returning to live here. If he was as good a solicitor as they made him out to be he would have no trouble getting a position in Belfast. The very thought of Gerry's coming back to live in St James's Park made Mick's stomach turn over. God forbid that he should return to haunt them again. Mick found himself sending a plea heavenwards. That was a laugh! Did he really expect God to make things easy for him, after the way he had behaved?

To his dismay, when he entered his driveway the first person Mick saw was Gerry Docherty. He must have stopped to smoke a cigarette before entering the house. Unaware of Mick, Gerry dropped the butt of his cigarette and crushed it under his heel. He then smoothed his hair back with gloved hands before entering the hall ahead of Mick. Slowly he followed Gerry down the hall, taking note of his appearance. He was as blond as ever, but then, his fairness would effectively camouflage any grey hairs that he might have. His pale fine features were barely lined and he actually suited the gold-rimmed spectacles that sat on his short straight nose; they helped to give him an air of assurance. He must be about forty-five or six now, but he could easily pass for forty. The dark Crombie overcoat that he wore made Gerry appear taller and broader than he actually was and Mick felt envious. This man had everything going for him!

As Mick watched, Gerry pulled quality fur-lined gloves from his manicured hands and, pushing them into the pocket of his overcoat, proceeded to unbutton it, displaying a snow white shirt and dark blue serge three-piece suit. He certainly looked as if he wasn't short of a quid or two. Mick glanced down at his own grey woollen gloves and well-worn Ulster, and grimaced. He had heard that Gerry had done well and that he was now a partner in a small law firm in Dublin. Now Mick could see for himself just how well. That Crombie overcoat alone would cost a packet . . . but then, a solicitor with just one son to rear and a wife who until her death had lectured at Trinity College, surely couldn't help but succeed.

The living room was crowded and Sarah sat on the settee surrounded by people offering their condolences. It was obvious that she had been weeping. Her red-rimmed eyes widened slightly as they met Gerry's, then darkened as she saw Mick standing behind him. The look of scorn she focused on her husband caused friends and neighbours alike to look askance at him. Mick wanted to flee from the room but he stood his ground and watched. With a startled glance over his shoulder at Mick, Gerry bent over Sarah's slight form and gripped her hand tightly in his. Mick could not hear what Gerry said but he saw fresh tears course down his wife's cheeks. Her other hand reached out to Gerry in supplication, and cupping them both in his Gerry leant closer and murmured words meant for her ears only. With a smothered exclamation Mick turned on his heel and left the room.

In the hall, friends and workmates had gathered to offer him their condolences. The last to approach him was Brian Muldoon.

'I'm awfully sorry for you and your family at this terrible time, Mr Ross. Claire was a wonderful girl.'

Mick looked into Brian's dark brown eyes, so full of concern, and was overwhelmed. If he had listened to Sarah and encouraged this young man and made him welcome in his home, Claire might be alive today. Why had he been so pigheaded? So sure that he was right and that Sarah was wrong? What had he ever had against Brian? If Claire had kept on dating him she might never have noticed Michael. Mick gripped Brian's hand and, overcome with emotion, muttered apologies and shouldered his way into the kitchen.

Brian gazed sadly after him. He could make a guess

at what Mick had been thinking and he wholeheartedly agreed with him. If Mick had been more affable, Claire and Brian might have married and Michael O'Hara wouldn't have had a look in. Brian had harboured a grudge against Mick for a long time but in the face of the man's great anguish, resentment against him slowly melted. With a deep sigh of regret for what might have been, he quietly left the house.

In the kitchen Mick found his three daughters, Maggie, and Kathleen Rafferty. They were arranging the buffet prepared earlier that morning by Kathleen and some other neighbours.

Maggie greeted him, 'Mick, come here, son.' She indicated an empty chair at the table and gratefully he slumped down and acknowledged his daughters and Kathleen with a nod. He was suddenly feeling very tired and lonely.

Eileen was at the stove and the look she turned on her father was full of compassion. She poured a cup of tea. 'Here, Dad, drink this. You look frozen. Where on earth did you get to? We were all looking for you.'

'I walked Maisie O'Hara home. Your mother would have nagged on and on at her if she had come here, so I walked her home. I couldn't just put her in a car. That would have been too heartless. Somebody had to do it, Eileen, and there was no sign of Michael. Where is he?'

Aware that Kathleen was all ears, Maggie hastened to change the course of the conversation. Close friend that she was, there was still no need for Kathleen to know their dark secret. Now Claire was dead the knowledge that she had married her half-brother could die with her. 'You did right, son! Michael is still at the graveyard, poor lad.'

Mick knew that he should not ask questions in front of his daughters and Kathleen, but he could not help himself. After that display in the living room, he had to know. 'Maggie . . . do you know if Gerry Docherty will be staying on in that house?'

She squeezed his shoulder in a comforting gesture, guessing what was worrying him. 'No, Mick, I have no idea. I do know that he is on an extended holiday . . . but for how long, I just don't know. I imagine he will stay until the house is decorated and young Danny has settled in.'

'What difference does it make how long he stays?' Eileen asked, curiosity edging her voice.

Not wanting to whet Eileen's curiosity unduly, Maggie answered the question with an indifferent shrug. 'It doesn't matter how long he stays. I think your father is just glad that Danny has managed to get a job in the *Telegraph* office. He's a nice lad and will be good company for Emma.'

Not quite satisfied with this answer, Eileen nevertheless nodded in assent. She at least agreed with Maggie that Danny seemed to be a nice lad but thought that at twenty-one he was a bit long in the tooth for Emma who had only turned sixteen. Danny was very mature for his age. He would probably consider Emma a child. Besides, Eileen could not see her father pairing them off, especially at this particular time. Matchmaking was not one of his weaknesses and certainly at this present time, it would be the last thing on his mind. No, there was something else . . . something not quite right here, but for the life of her, Eileen could not fathom what could be wrong. Pushing all thoughts of it from her mind she returned to her chores at the stove. Anyway, she was probably imagining things.

Life goes on and slowly things returned to normal . . . at least as normal as could be expected in the circumstances. After settling up his affairs Michael decided to return to Scotland and try to get a job there, where he and Claire had been so happy together. Before he left he sought

Mick out and promised to keep in touch with him. He explained that at present it would be too painful to try to get to know his father better, but that he hoped some time in the future they could become close friends.

His words warmed Mick's heart. Now if only Sarah would forgive him, perhaps they could get on with their lives and make some kind of a go of it. They spoke to each other . . . but rarely. Only as acquaintances would; without any great interest or warmth, and Sarah, only when absolutely necessary.

Time passed slowly for Mick. To take her mind off things Sarah had offered to help Danny Docherty decorate the house next door to Maggie's, the house he had inherited from his grandparents. She had also roped Emma in and most evenings Mick found himself sitting alone in an empty house, from tea time until he retired to his lonely bed.

It was during these long, lonely hours, when he was most vulnerable, that he was plagued by thoughts of his dead daughter. Throughout the day he could concentrate on his work with unnecessary energy and blank out the guilt that dwelt within him. But at times like this, when he sat alone in his empty, loveless house, he was overwhelmed with remorse. If only he had done this . . . If only he had done that . . . Claire might be alive today. The very thought of his precious daughter was enough to bring tears to his eyes. Although his grief for the loss of Claire was profound, he was dismayed that he couldn't offer up even a short prayer for the repose of her soul. During these darkest hours, wallowing in the depths of despair, Mick even entertained dark thoughts of joining his daughter. He needed his wife's forgiveness to lift him out of his despair. If only Sarah would just sit down and talk to him, then perhaps they could at least ease each other's mental torture.

He was aware that Gerry Docherty had not yet returned to Dublin and jealousy was eating away at him like a cancer as he pictured Sarah and Gerry working side by side. He pictured Gerry trying to seduce Sarah. In her present state of mind would she succumb? The knowledge that Emma and Danny were also there did not ease his pain in the slightest. Nor had age lessened the strength of his jealousy! Indeed, no . . . the pain was every bit as intense as it had been all those years ago when they were young. In his misery he took to going out most evenings. Sometimes he went to the pictures or baby-sat for one or the other of his daughters. Of an odd night he went down to the Bee Hive bar where he knew most of the crowd. Anything to break the monotony.

He was lonely and sad, and the knowledge that Maisie would probably welcome him with open arms played on his mind. One thing he was sure of . . . if he ever decided to escape these lonely walls and seek Maisie out, this time in spite of the scandal it would cause, he would stay with her. He would never use her in that way again. He would burn his bridges and settle down to a new life with her.

Eileen smoothed the straight black pencil-slim skirt down over her hips and her sigh was a purr of pure pleasure. She reached for the jacket and slipped her arms into it. The collar draped softly across her shoulders and the wide lapels reached almost to her waist where the jacket was secured by one large button. She turned slowly in front of the full-length mirror, admiring herself. Oh, it was lovely! Beautiful! The most glamorous suit she had ever possessed. It had cost a small fortune but when Johnny had seen it on her in the shop, he had insisted that she buy it; had said that she looked like a million dollars in it. With gentle hands she carefully eased the ruffles of the white silk blouse into place along the lapels of the jacket. The soft sheen of the silk made her eyes glitter like diamonds and showed off the creamy texture of her skin and the bright auburn glow of her hair. It was

Easter Saturday and tonight she was meeting Johnny's workmates for the first time. They were all to gather in the International Hotel for a drink, and later on a meal. She had felt a bit nervous at first, but now in this beautiful outfit she felt poised and confident.

For a moment guilt swamped her, taking the edge off her pleasure, as thoughts of Claire surfaced in her mind. It was hard to comprehend that her sister had been alive and well just a couple of short months ago. Her mother still held it against her that she had not tried to prevent Claire from marrying Michael. But how could she? They were both adults, and very much in love. There was no way she could have dissuaded them. It was their decision to go to Gretna Green. No! In this instance her mother was wrong. Eileen's conscience was clear as far as that was concerned. Still, if only they hadn't gone to Gretna Green. If only Claire was here to share her pleasure. Claire would have loved this suit; would probably have borrowed it if going anywhere special, as they both wore the same size. She missed her sister desperately. They had been so close. Much closer than Beth or Emma.

The only times Eileen saw Beth these days was when she made a point of visiting her. Beth had only been in Eileen's home once since the day Claire was buried. Although she had not said so, was Beth, like her mother, harbouring a grudge against her? Did she also blame Eileen for not making a bigger effort to stop Claire going to Gretna Green? But then, Beth was going through an awkward pregnancy. She was having just as bad a time as she had experienced with Elizabeth. Perhaps Eileen was misjudging her sister and she would see more of her once the baby was born.

Eileen sighed and pushed the guilt from her mind. Claire would be the first to say, 'Whatever will be, will be. Life must go on.' She'd had such a philosophical outlook on life. If only they could convince her mother of that. She was still making life hell for Mick: treating him like a lodger in his own home; choosing to forget all the good times they had shared together. One good thing had come about because of the disaster; her father and Johnny were becoming very close friends, and this pleased Eileen. She often teased them about it, saying, 'You two will be getting wee hats the same.'

Even as she thought of Mick she heard a knock on the front door and guessed it would be her father. Johnny let him in and Eileen heard the noisy scramble of the children as they rushed to greet their beloved grandfather. Realizing that she was wasting too much time admiring herself and lamenting the past, she quickly put the finishing touches to her make up. Lifting the black suede clutch bag that matched her new black court shoes, she surveyed herself one last time. Pleased with what she saw in the mirror, she descended the stairs, a smile playing on her lips. From the hall Johnny and Mick watched her, eyes full of admiration.

'You look lovely, Eileen. Doesn't she, Johnny?'

'She sure does. I'll be the envy of every man in the room tonight.' Moving closer to Eileen, Johnny whispered, 'I wish we didn't have to go out. I wish we could go back upstairs and I could slowly remove all these grand clothes and . . .'

Aghast, she hurriedly interrupted him. 'Johnny . . . behave yourself!' Over his shoulder her eyes met her father's teasing glance and she felt colour stain her cheeks, aware that he had heard Johnny's whispered suggestions.

Johnny smiled at her embarrassment. 'Sorry, love . . . sorry. I got carried away, you look ravishing.' He was dismayed to find that he felt apprehensive about introducing his beautiful wife to all his workmates. Silently, he warned himself. Be careful, you fool! It was a long time since they had been anywhere special. He must not, under any circumstances, let anything spoil this evening. He must conquer his awful jealousy and trust Eileen completely, or he would ruin the close relationship that had developed between then.

A toot on a car horn heralded the arrival of their taxi and Johnny warned the children, 'You kids be good for your granda! Do whatever he bids you. Do you hear me?'

'Don't you worry about them, Johnny. They're the best behaved kids I've ever known. They are a credit to you so they are. And don't worry about coming home late either. I can stay all night if need be. I've no one waiting up for me.'

'Is Mam still being awkward, then?' Eileen asked sympathetically.

Annoyed at laying himself open for this question and tired of being the recipient of pity, Mick retorted, 'Ah, don't worry about me, Eileen. I'll wear your mother down or die in the attempt, so help me. Go on, get yourselves away out. Think of me very time you bend your elbow, Johnny,' he jested.

'Every time I down a pint I'll think of you, Mick . . . that's a promise! If by any chance we should be late, will you make up the bedsettee in Eileen's office? You know where everything is kept, don't you?'

Mick nodded, and with a final farewell Johnny hustled Eileen away from the children and out the front door.

They were about the last of the party to arrive at the International Hotel. When they entered the cocktail bar where they had arranged to meet, Johnny was aware that every man in the room was eyeing his wife. A rush of pride was quickly followed by dismay as his boss, known as a ladies' man, moved forward to greet them.

'Good evening, Johnny.' George Patterson addressed Johnny but his eyes scanned Eileen from head to toe, and he nodded his approval.

Quickly Johnny made the introductions. 'Eileen . . .

this is my boss, George Patterson, George, this is my wife, Eileen.'

She murmured, 'Pleased to meet you,' the colour deepening in her cheeks as George held her hand much longer than was necessary.

Smiling at her embarrassment, George kept a restraining hold on her hand. 'Come over and meet my wife,' he said, and drew her forward. As they crossed the floor he dropped her hand and put an arm across her shoulders. With a shrug Eileen rid herself of his hold. He didn't take offence, just smiled benignly down at her. His antics were watched by his wife. Margaret Patterson was small and plump. She greeted Eileen with a friendly smile.

'Hello, love. Don't pay any attention to my husband. He's harmless, wouldn't hurt a fly! It's all a big act. When you have been introduced to everyone else, come back and sit here.' She patted the empty chair beside her. 'We'll have a nice wee chat.'

With a mock sigh, George turned to Eileen. 'I must warn you that my wife is a very nosy person. Don't tell her anything you don't want repeated. If you want to spread a rumour . . . tell Margaret a secret.' George winked at Eileen and laughed loudly at his own wit. 'If you know what I mean.'

By the way Margaret's lips tightened, Eileen could see that she was annoyed at her husband's remarks and waited for an outburst of temper. Margaret controlled herself, and Eileen silently applauded her when with a smile she managed to join in the laughter directed against herself. Once all the introductions were over Johnny led Eileen back to the empty chair beside Margaret Patterson.

'What would you like to drink, love?'

'A Tom Collins, please.'

'And you, Margaret?'

'What's a Tom Collins like, Eileen?'

'Long and cool with a gin base.'

'Oh, that sounds nice. I'll have one of those as well, Johnny.'

He went to join the queue at the bar, and Eileen listened raptly as Margaret pointed out different people and explained their positions in the firm. Eileen was just about to inquire about Lorna Pollock whom she had yet to meet, when a stir at the door brought all eyes to it. A tall dark girl had entered on the arm of a very distinguished-looking gentleman, and had paused for effect. Eileen guessed that this was Lorna Pollock. 'Tall, with dark hair,' was how Johnny had described her. That was an understatement, if ever there was one! A cloud of thick raven hair framed a face that was a perfect cameo, and dark brown eyes fringed with long thick lashes surveyed the room. Statuesque, Lorna, like a Greek goddess, was very much aware that she was beautiful. Even her figure, poured into a crimson velvet suit, was perfect. George Patterson immediately swooped down on her like a vulture, and after greeting her companion, whisked Lorna away.

A snort brought Eileen's attention back to Margaret. 'That's Lorna Pollock,' she grunted. 'A menace if ever there was one. She's a real siren! Chases after all the men in the office, whether or not they are married. Look at her now, monopolizing George.'

Eileen followed the direction of Margaret's gaze. George had manoeuvred Lorna into a corner and now blocked her escape. The only way Eileen could describe the look on George's face was lewd. He was absolutely leering at Lorna, like a dog slobbering over a juicy bone. She appeared very uneasy, and anxious to escape.

With another disgusted snort, Margaret rose to her feet. 'Excuse me, Eileen. I had better go and rescue George from that vamp before she gets her claws into him.'

As Margaret moved away, Eileen saw Johnny leave his tray of drinks on the bar and move towards the couple in the corner. She saw him speaking to Lorna and nodding

331

in her own direction. Then, with a nod at George, he placed a hand on Lorna's arm and led her towards his wife. Eileen watched them cross the floor towards her and thought how handsome they looked together. Johnny was only slightly the taller of the two and his bright red hair was an eye-catching contrast to Lorna's dark good looks.

When the couple reached Eileen, Johnny took his wife's hand and said proudly, 'Lorna, this is my wife, Eileen . . . this is Lorna Pollock.'

The two women eyed each other and Lorna was the first to speak. Thrusting a hand towards Eileen, she said, 'I'm very pleased to meet you. Johnny is forever singing your praises.'

Gripping her hand, Eileen replied, 'I'm happy to make your acquaintance.'

'Look, I'd just love to sit and have a chat, Eileen, but you'll have to excuse me, I must get back to my partner. He will be absolutely lost without me, poor lamb.' Lorna leant forward and whispered confidentially, 'He's my step-father, you know. But I want everybody to think that he's my sugar daddy, so mum's the word. With a bit of luck it'll keep the *wolf* off my back.' She nodded in the direction of George and grimaced. 'Perhaps we can have a chat later on, Eileen.' Her eyes held Johnny's in a long lingering look. 'Thanks for coming to my rescue as usual, Johnny. You're a pet! I don't know what I'd do without you.'

To Eileen's surprise she saw Johnny actually blush and his eyes were appreciative as he watched Lorna cross the floor to her partner. Eileen brought him back to attention. 'I think you had better collect our drinks, Johnny,' she said softly.

At his wife's wry tone of voice, Johnny swung round and eyed her closely. Surely she couldn't be jealous? 'I had to rescue Lorna,' he explained. 'George can be a right pain in the ass, especially where Lorna is concerned. Every chance he gets he's sniffing around her.'

'I understand, Johnny, really I do. She's lucky to have you to look out for her. But our drinks are ready and waiting,' she insisted.

Without another word Johnny strode towards the bar. There was a warm glow in his heart at the idea that Eileen might just possibly be jealous.

It was a wonderful night and Eileen enjoyed herself immensely. She was very aware of the admiration directed at her and remembering how Johnny had championed Lorna, was pleased to bask in all the attention. Everybody was so friendly, especially George Patterson. Johnny had been spot on when he said that George was a pain in the ass; it had taken all her tact to keep him at arm's length without giving offence. Nevertheless it was with reluctance that near midnight they made their farewells and climbed into a taxi to go home. On the journey back Johnny held Eileen close and kissed her soundly. 'Did you enjoy yourself, love?'

Eileen was tipsy and snuggled closer still. 'Very much . . . very much indeed. It will be great to have a bit of a social life. I'm so glad you were promoted.'

Although it was after midnight when they finally arrived at Rockmore Road they were surprised to find that Mick had not retired for the night.

'Dad, you must be dead beat!' Eileen cried, 'Why didn't you go to bed?'

'I wasn't a bit sleepy, Eileen. And besides . . . with tomorrow being Easter Sunday I want to go to an early Mass, and somehow when I go to bed early, I tend to sleep late the next morning. Tell me . . . did you enjoy yourselves?'

'Oh, Dad, it was wonderful! Just wonderful. The meal was delicious. Four courses and each one mouth watering. It was a marvellous night.'

Mick smiled at his daughter's enthusiasm and eyed

his son-in-law. 'And you, Johnny? Did you enjoy yourself?'

'Very much, Mick. Will you join me in a drink before you go . . . or maybe you would like to stay here tonight?'

'Thank you, Johnny, but no. I always prefer to sleep in my own bed.'

He rose to his feet but Johnny was not taking no for an answer. Pushing him gently down on to the settee again, he insisted, 'You will at least have a whiskey before you go.'

Soon a large Jameson's was thrust into his hand. Raising it, Mick toasted them: 'To you, Eileen, and to Johnny. May you have a long happy life ahead of you. Oh, and by the way, thank you for your anniversary card.'

'I didn't know whether or not to mention your anniversary, Dad. It can't be very pleasant for you . . . or Mam, the way things are.'

'Your mother and I were married twenty-eight years today.' The whiskey was loosening Mick's tongue and bitterness crept into his voice. 'Do you know something, Eileen? Your mother didn't even bother to open the wee present that I bought her. Said that I should have more sense than to expect her to celebrate, so soon after Claire's death.'

Johnny and Eileen exchanged worried glances. Sarah was carrying things too far! Where would it all end? Going to her father, Eileen kissed him on the cheek. 'I'm sorry, Dad. I hope Mam comes to her senses soon.'

'She had better, Eileen. I'm getting to the point where I couldn't care less. If she wants me out of the house, I'll go! Digs would be better than coming home to that house every night.' Once more he raised his glass and with a wry twist of the lips, said, 'Happy Easter.' He drained his glass and rose to his feet.

'Have another one, Mick, before you go. It'll help you sleep.'

When Johnny reached for his empty glass, Mick stopped

him. 'No! No more, thank you. I'd better go on home now, before I get tipsy and say too much. Thanks all the same, Johnny. By the way . . . the kids showed me their painted Easter eggs. They said that if it's good tomorrow you're taking them to Bellevue to trundle them down the hill. If you decide to go, can I tag along? It's a long time since I've been up the Cave Hill.'

'Of course you can, Mick. We will be glad of your company,' Johnny assured him. 'If it's not raining in the morning, we'll pick you up about twelve. Is that all right with you?'

'Any time suits me. Weather permitting, I'll be ready and waiting.'

From the door they watched him out of sight and then locked up for the night.

'What's going to become of him, Johnny?' Eileen asked fearfully. 'How can Mam be so unreasonable?'

'We will talk about it in the morning. I have more pressing things on my mind at the moment.'

'What? What is so urgent at this time of night?' Eileen asked, eyes wide in wonder.

'This and this . . .' Johnny nibbled at her ear and his hand cupped her breast. 'First we are going to look in on the kids, and then, my love . . . we are going to bed.' Arm around her waist, Johnny led his wife up the stairs, suppressing her half-hearted objections with his lips.

Striding down St James's Park Mick noted that the Dochertys' house was lit up like a Christmas tree. Except for the small lamp in the hall, his own house was in darkness. This surprised him. Since Claire's death, Sarah had difficulty sleeping and usually read a book until the small hours of the morning. He opened the door and let himself into the hall, taking care to make as little noise as possible. The first thing he noticed was a sheet of notepaper propped against the hall lamp. As he read the words written on the paper, rage welled up inside him.

The note informed him that Gerry Docherty had come over just after he had left the house (How convenient! had he watched him go?) to invite the three of them over for a drink. A thank you for all the hard work that Sarah and Emma had put into decorating the house for Danny.

Mick stood clenching his fists and swear words that he would never normally even think of swirled about in his head. He could think of nothing bad enough to call Gerry Docherty. As for Sarah! Why, her actions hurt him abominably. How could his wife be so cruel? To refuse his gift and then go over and spend an evening drinking with Gerry Docherty. That man had spent the month of February in Belfast. A month that had been torment for Mick as he observed the change in his wife during the time she spent in the house across the road. And now Gerry was back. When had he returned? How long did he intend to stay this time? Oh, there was a P.S. 'Come over when you come home from Eileen's. Gerry says you will be very welcome.'

A china figurine stood on the hall table beside the lamp. One of Sarah's treasured possessions. Mick's hand closed around the figure of a shepherdess and he gazed down at it. He'd show Sarah just how much he cared about her antics! He raised his arm in the air to smash the ornament against the wall, then he hesitated. Ashamed of his childish actions, he carefully replaced the ornament. It would be pointless to spoil a thing of such beauty. However, this was the last straw! He'd had enough! He had been forced to come to a decision. Once Easter was over he would find some digs and leave this house of misery.

Voices and laughter outside alerted him that Sarah and Emma were on their way back. With swift steps he quietly climbed the stairs and when his wife and daughter entered the house, except for the hall light, it was dark and silent.

'Your dad mustn't be home yet,' Sarah said, as she closed the outer door. 'Ah, well, maybe it was better that he didn't come over to Danny's. He would probably have put a damper on a wonderful evening. Did you enjoy yourself, love?'

'Yes.' Emma was subdued. She wished her mother would speak more softly. She had a feeling that her father was upstairs and did not want him to hear her mother's cutting remarks.

'Well, I'm away on up to bed,' Sarah yawned. 'I feel so relaxed, I think I shall probably fall asleep the minute my head hits the pillow, for a change.'

'That's all that brandy and Babycham you drank over there,' Emma said dryly.

Sarah grinned widely. 'You could be right, Emma. I've got to admit that you probably are. God, but it's good to feel almost human again. Good night, love.'

'Good night, Mam. I'll be up soon.'

Mick had heard Sarah's cruel remarks. Well, he would not intrude for much longer where he was obviously not wanted. At least this time he would not have to go to the Salvation Army, and for this he was grateful. He never had got around to telling Sarah about his promotion. The opportunity had never presented itself, so each week he had banked the extra money. Now he had a tidy amount saved. He would stay in some guest house until he found a suitable flat somewhere well away from St James's Park.

Next morning, Mick somehow managed to control himself as he ate his breakfast, whilst Sarah and Emma discussed the previous night. It had obviously been an enjoyable occasion.

'Dad, you should have come over,' Emma admonished him. 'You would have enjoyed yourself. Grannie and Granda came in for a while, and Mr and Mrs Rafferty called in on their way to visit some friends. They stayed about an hour. Why didn't you come over?'

337

'Sure he was up in Eileen's until late,' Sarah reminded her daughter.

'No, I wasn't.' Mick's voice was mild. 'I heard you come in.'

Sarah looked a bit taken aback. She bit on her lip as she recalled her remarks of the night before. Had he heard her? She had not meant to be unkind. Not deliberately. It was just that lately she could not find anything nice to say about her husband. She resented all the trouble that he had brought down on their heads. She blamed him for the loss of her beautiful daughter and could find no pity in her heart for him. Still . . . she was not normally a vindictive person and now she felt guilty. Had Mick heard her? She was very aware that the brandy had loosened her tongue the night before. She eyed him closely but his eyes were on the slice of toast that he was buttering and his face was inscrutable.

Tentatively she asked, 'Why didn't you come over?'

Slowly Mick lifted his head and held Sarah's eye. 'And spoil your night out, Sarah?' he taunted, and had the satisfaction of watching a dark red blush rise in his wife's face to reach her hairline. 'Ah, no, Sarah . . . I'd never purposely do that. Not deliberately, anyway.'

Flustered, she rose from the table. 'Would you like another cup of tea?' she asked, trying in vain to keep her voice steady.

Watching her, Mick suddenly felt very weary; tired of putting on a charade in front of Emma. His daughter might be young, but she wasn't stupid. She must by now have figured out that all was not well between her mother and father. Abruptly, he rose from the table. It was another dry day, he'd go on up to Eileen's, save them the bother of collecting him. 'No, I don't want any more tea, thank you. I'm going out now, and don't make me any dinner. I don't expect to be home until late.'

When the door closed on him Sarah stared at it through narrowed eyes, Mick had deliberately refrained from saying where he was going. He never bothered to say where he was going these days. Was he seeing Maisie? Quite probably! Where else would he go? Would he make her remarks of the night before an excuse to get up to his old tricks again? Well, if he did ... if he dared and she heard tell of it ... it would be the finish of their marriage.

'I wish someone would tell me what is going on in this house. I know that Claire is dead. but surely that should unite us as a family, eh? Instead you and Dad are putting on one big act after another. If it's for my benefit, don't bother! Do you think I'm an imbecile or something? I know that things are terribly wrong. Mam, please tell me the truth. What's going on between you two?'

Emma's plaintive cry brought Sarah back from her musing. Forcing a smile to her lips, she turned and faced her daughter. 'You're imagining things, love. It's just that Claire's death has been a very traumatic time for us all. Everything will get back to normal eventually. Now ... what would you like to do today?'

'I had intended going to Bellevue with some of the crowd from school, but if you are going to be on your own, I'll stay here and keep you company.'

'Oh, no! You go on to Bellevue, love. It's too good a day to miss a visit to the zoo. Especially as it's Easter Sunday.'

'Are you sure, Mam? I don't mind staying at home.'

'Of course I'm sure. You might even see Eileen and her clan at Bellevue, I think they intend going there today. I'll go up and visit Beth. See if the kids are enjoying the Easter eggs I bought them. I'll get a bite of dinner there. Save me the trouble of cooking a meal, since your dad won't be home.'

Kissing her mother affectionately on the cheek, Emma hurried upstairs to prepare for her date. She had deliberately neglected telling her mother that some of the crowd she was joining were of the opposite sex. Lately she omitted to mention boyfriends in front of her parents. It only resulted in a barrage of questions. Who is this boy? Where does he live? Would we know his parents? Emma resented this intrusion into her private life and couldn't remember her sisters being subjected to an interrogation every time they were going out on a date, so diplomatically she just didn't mention boyfriends.

The weather turned out bright and sunny with a warm wind and Bellevue was packed with holiday makers. All the parents in Belfast seemed to bring their kids to visit the zoo and trundle their Easter eggs down the Cave Hill. Mick enjoyed going round the zoo with the kids, taking delight in their awe of the lions and tigers; their shrieks of joy in the monkey house. He was like a kid himself when they eventually settled on a gentle slope of the Cave Hill for a picnic lunch. When the kids had rolled their eggs, amidst squeals of laughter, Mick rolled his grandchildren one by one down the slope after them. The weather held out and an enjoyable day was had by all. Afterwards, Johnny dropped Mick off at the top of St James's Park.

'Are you sure you don't want to come over for a bite to eat, Dad?' Eileen asked. 'Mam might not be at home. After all, it is Easter and she might be over in Grannie's or somewhere else.'

'Get away with you, Eileen! You had enough in that picnic basket today to feed an army. I seem to have been eating all day long. Why, I'm bursting, so I am. Thanks for everything, love. You too, Johnny. It's been a wonderful day.' He stooped low and peered into the back of the car to where the three children were asleep. 'Give the kids a big kiss for me. I'll see you all soon.'

He waved the car off and turned down the street. As they often did these days, his feet dragged as he approached the house. In the midst of all the enjoyment today he had been plagued by doubts; was having second thoughts about leaving home. Almost twenty-five years ago he had left Sarah to the charms of Gerry Docherty. If Maggie had not been so ill after Bernard's birth Sarah might very well have run off to Dublin with Gerry, but Maggie's illness had kept his wife tied to home long enough for her to have second thoughts. This time if Mick left there was nothing to hold Sarah here. He would be giving her an excuse to go. The girls were all grown up and his wife would probably be glad to leave the house that held so many memories of Claire. He decided to have one last try to get Sarah to talk things over with him. If he could get his wife to go out with him tomorrow he would manage to manoeuvre her to a garage and look at some second-hand cars. Surprise her with his good news. Try to persuade her to take a holiday with him. Tour the South. That's what he'd do! Try to get Sarah to go out with him. Make her realize that they still had a lot going for them if only she would give him a chance. With these thoughts his step quickened and his heart was lighter when he entered the house.

He found her in the living room, sitting by the fireside, her feet on the hearth, reading a magazine. Without looking up she asked, 'Shall I make you something to eat?'

'No. No, I'm not hungry.' Mick eased his long frame into the armchair facing Sarah and eyed her intently. The soft light from the table lamp beside her turned her hair to a bright cloud and shadowed her high cheekbones. In repose the tight discontented droop to her mouth was gone and she looked beautiful. If only they could turn the clock back; return to how it was before Claire met Michael. They had been getting on so well until Maisie had dropped her bombshell. It saddened Mick to note that his wife was wearing a new outfit. It brought home to him just how far apart they had grown. Before this trouble all new clothes had been eagerly displayed to him and exclaimed over the moment she entered the house, and then donned for his approval and admiration. Now she wore a fine wool twin set that he had never seen before. Of the palest green, it clung to the curves of her breasts, still high and firm. The new black skirt she was wearing with it was long but must have a split in it, because her slim silk-clad legs were exposed to halfway up the thigh. She was still attractive enough to turn any man's head. He could also see that she had put on some make-up; shadow darkened her eyelids and pale pink lipstick glistened on her wide sensuous mouth, making him long to kiss her. If only he dared! Would he ever kiss her again? Was she at last coming to terms with her grief? Was there hope for him yet? He leant forward, arm outstretched to touch her. Without removing her eyes from the magazine, she flinched slightly. He stayed his hand, warning himself to be careful; not to rush her.

'That's a nice outfit. New, isn't it?' he said as he sank back in his chair, searching for the right words to open the conversation.

'Yes . . . yes, I bought it last week when I was in town with Beth.'

To his dismay she sounded defensive and he hastened to reassure her. 'I'm not being critical. I'm glad you're going out and about at last. That colour suits you, Sarah.' He waited and at last her eyes met his. Bright green pools that told him nothing. 'Listen, I want you to come out with me tomorrow . . .' His voice trailed off. She was already shaking her head in refusal before he had even finished speaking.

'No, I can't. Gerry Docherty came over this afternoon. He came to invite us both out for a drive tomorrow. He suggested going along the Antrim Coast and stopping off at Ballycastle for a meal. What do you think?'

Mick's thoughts were unbearable. Resentment, jealousy and hatred all vied for supremacy. So that was why his wife was all dolled up! Lover boy had been over. And just how long had he stayed?

Spots of angry colour flared in Sarah's cheeks as she watched the different expressions flit across her husband's face. 'Look at you! I can read you like a book!' she cried. 'You're wondering what we got up to, aren't you?'

Slowly Mick rose to his feet and stood towering over her. 'No, Sarah. Obviously you feel guilty, that's why you're so angry. Well, I will not go out in that man's car and watch him ogle you. And furthermore, I forbid you to go with him.'

In a flash, she was also on her feet, glaring balefully at him. '*You* forbid me to go? Since when do you decide what I do, eh? And just where were you all day? That's what I'd like to know! Well, let me tell you something . . . whether or not you come with us, I intend going to Ballycastle tomorrow. So put that in your pipe and smoke it!'

Mick was taken aback. Could Sarah really think he was seeing Maisie? 'Just where do you think I was today?' he asked softly.

'With *her!* You were with Maisie O'Hara, weren't you?'

'No, you've got it all wrong, Sarah. I wasn't with Maisie. I haven't seen her since the day Claire was buried.'

'Do you expect me to believe that? Why, you are out nearly every night of the week, so you are.'

'Why do you think I go out so often, eh? I go out because when you are not across the street in that house, you sit here like a deaf mute. *That's* why I go out!'

'I don't believe you. I trusted you before, remember? And look what happened.'

Sadly, Mick shook his head. 'No, I don't expect you to believe me. Nevertheless it's the truth. But you're only looking for an excuse for your own conduct and no matter what I say you'll find one.' Once again he pleaded, 'Sarah . . . please don't do this. Don't go out with Gerry Docherty. Come out with me tomorrow. I want to show you something. Explain something to you.'

Her chin rose defiantly in the air and her voice was unyielding. 'I have already told Gerry I will go with him, and I'm not going back on my word.'

'Sarah, don't do this. Tell him you've changed your mind. Please?'

Mutely she shook her head, and with a smothered exclamation Mick turned on his heel and left the room. He had tried and he had failed miserably. Sarah's mind was already made up.

Slowly, Sarah sank back down on to her chair. She had handled that all wrong. She wanted to go out in Gerry's car tomorrow. However, she was aware that with a bit of tact she could have persuaded Mick to come along with them. It would be safer if he accompanied them, but she didn't really want Mick to come. Didn't she want to be alone with Gerry? Was it true that Mick was not seeing Maisie? How could she believe him? He had lied to her before. Still, Mick had been right when he had accused her of feeling guilty. She moved restlessly in the armchair when she recalled Gerry's visit that afternoon. But they hadn't done anything. Only one kiss! And what was a kiss against Mick's carry on with Maisie? Still, they had come close.

She had been in the kitchen when Gerry entered the house by the back door. He would never have dared to come round the back like that if Mick had been at home. He must be watching their movements. This idea threw her for a moment. She did not like the idea of being spied upon. Just what had Gerry in mind? Dressed in grey flannel trousers and an open-necked sport's shirt, he'd looked handsome. He had sat at the kitchen table and she had made a pot of tea. As usual, talk flowed easily between them as they spoke of the past. Soon she was engulfed in a warm cloud of intimacy, as she basked in his admiration. Happily she agreed to go for a drive the next day.

Time ·passed quickly and it was when Gerry moved

to go home that the atmosphere became charged with emotion. As he wordlessly moved towards her, eyes bright with passion, Sarah became flustered. She was aware that they could be seen through the kitchen window. This had caused her to move slowly into the hall, still keeping eye contact. Gerry had followed her. Back against the wall, she had waited breathlessly in the passageway for him to reach her. He had faced her but made no further advances towards her.

'Are you sure, Sarah?' His voice, low and charged with passion, had sought to seduce her.

She wished that he had not spoken. His words broke the spell that he had managed to weave around her, blocking out reality. Now he had made her realize how cheaply she was behaving. She moved restlessly, and as if aware that he should have held his tongue, Gerry hastened to make amends. His arms circled her waist and he gathered her close against him. The kiss was long and deep and satisfying, making her long for more.

The sound of the back door opening and closing penetrated their passion and they sprang guiltily apart. When Emma had entered the hall Sarah was opening the front door and showing Gerry out, glad that she'd had the sense to move out of the kitchen. What if Emma had seen them? Shame reddened her cheeks at the very idea of it. Gerry however, was quite unperturbed. He had gripped her hand and said softly, 'Tomorrow, Sarah?'

'Yes, tomorrow, Gerry,' she had promised. A warm glow enveloped her now as she relived that moment in his arms. She had felt wanted, desired. It was a long time since she had felt any deep emotion. Dare she go for a drive with him? They would be alone all day in that big comfortable car. Dare she? Yes, in spite of the danger, she would dare! She couldn't help herself.

Mick remained in his room the next morning. He heard Sarah humming as she prepared for her date with Gerry and his heart was like lead in his breast. When at last she left the house, he rose from the bed and watched from behind the net curtains as she crossed the street to where Gerry was waiting. She looked wonderful, dressed in the black skirt of the night before that opened when she walked, displaying long legs set off by low-heeled black court shoes. Mick smiled grimly. Sarah preferred high heels; the flat shoes would be because she was aware that she and Gerry were about the same height. This time the skirt was teamed up with a white frilly blouse and dark green cardigan and he knew that the colour of the cardigan would make her eyes shine like emeralds. He saw Gerry say something, obviously complimentary, and Sarah throw back her head and laugh delightedly. When next she spoke Gerry glanced over towards the house and Mick guessed that she had told Gerry that he would not be accompanying them. A wide grin split Gerry's face and he quite literally hopped around the car to open the passenger door. He took his time settling Sarah in the seat and Mick was aware that a show was being put on for his benefit. Then Gerry climbed in to the driver's seat and without a backward glance they drove off.

A short time later Emma also left the house. She had knocked lightly on his door and asked if he would like some breakfast in bed. Pleading tiredness, Mick told her he would lie on for a while, make some breakfast when he got up. He would miss Emma; she was a good girl and obviously bewildered by the antics of her parents. Their home had always been such an open and friendly place but now the tension that existed was also putting a strain on her. Would she think any the less of him for leaving without saying goodbye? He hoped not! He was going to miss all his family.

An hour later he had packed all his clothes in two big suitcases. Not a lot to show for twenty-eight years of marriage. When he got a flat, he would come back for some bits and pieces that were exclusively his. Sarah could have the rest! Of course if she went to live in Dublin he would be free to return here. After all, the house was in his name. But . . . would he want to come back? He thought not.

Maggie gazed down in surprise at the small box Mick had just placed in her hand. 'For me, Mick? What is it?' she asked in wonder.

'I must admit that it wasn't originally bought for you, Maggie. It was Sarah's anniversary present, but she didn't want it and I couldn't think of anyone else I'd rather give it to than you.'

With a bewildered look at him, Maggie opened the box. Her gasp of pleasure was genuine and she fingered the string of pearls. 'But . . . but I don't understand. Sarah has always wanted a string of pearls and these are beautiful. Why did she refuse them?'

'She didn't know I was giving her pearls. They were gift wrapped and she refused to accept them. Said it was too soon after Claire's death to celebrate.' He watched Maggie closely and had the satisfaction of seeing her jaw drop slightly with amazement.

'She said that? She had a cheek! I'm ashamed of her, the way she's carrying on with him next door. I noticed him and her taking off this morning again. I don't understand why don't you put a stop to it, Mick?'

'I tried, Maggie. Believe me, I tried. But of course Sarah just threw my affair with Maisie in my face and said she could never trust me again. I suppose she's right too. Everything is such a mess. I'm at my wit's end, Maggie. I don't know which way to turn, so I've decided to move out.'

'Ah, son, you can't do that! Why, you will be throwing them into each other's arms.'

'I think they are already there without any help from me, Maggie.'

'Well . . . don't make it easy for them. That's your home

over there. You've worked hard to have it so lovely! Stay and fight for it.'

'Maggie, I'm fed up to the teeth. Do you know something? Every night when I'm coming home from work, my feet drag. I delay all I can to shorten the time I spend in that strained atmosphere over there. I thought that maybe over Easter it might get better, but if anything . . . it's worse! I'll be better off somewhere on my own.'

'Then you don't intend moving in with Maisie?'

'Maggie, I haven't set eyes on Maisie since the day Claire was buried.' He could see that Maggie was having difficulty believing him and he smiled grimly. 'No, Sarah didn't believe me either. To be truthful, I'm ashamed I haven't been down to see her. She's lonely. But you see, Maggie, I'm lonely too, and Maisie is a warm caring woman. I couldn't risk going down to Beechmount. I still had hopes that my marriage could be saved. However, once I'm away from home, it will be a different matter. I'll see whoever I like then. I've just turned fifty . . . there's plenty of life in this old dog yet.'

'Of course there is, Mick. You're a lovely decent man and my Sarah is going to live to regret her actions.' Once more she fingered the pearls before thrusting them towards him. 'I'm sorry, Mick, but I can't accept these, I can see that they are expensive. I can't take them. Take them back to H. Samuels! I'm sure they will refund your money.'

'Maggie, if you don't take them, I'll bring them down to Maisie.'

'You wouldn't . . .' Her voice trailed off as he nodded his head. 'Ah, son, don't do anything rash.'

'Will you accept them then, just to please me?'

With a sigh Maggie carefully removed the pearls from the box. Holding them to her throat, she turned her back to him. 'Will you clip them on for me, Mick? I'll treasure them always, so I will.'

'Thanks, Maggie. I'm going to miss you.' He gathered

her close and their tears mingled. 'Goodbye, Maggie.' Pushing her gently from him, he turned on his heel and hurried from the house. Soon Maggie saw him load his cases into a taxi and climb in beside the driver. He looked over and, seeing her at the window, raised his hand in a final farewell. He was still not sure that he was doing the right thing. However, he'd make the break and only time would tell if he had made the right decision.

Chapter Nine

It was Wednesday before Eileen heard about her father's departure from the house. They awoke that morning to bright sunlight and Madge arrived about eleven o'clock and offered to take the three excited children down to Willowbank Park to play in the sand pit and paddling pool there, leaving Eileen free to get her work squared up. She was forever grateful to her mother-in-law for her thoughtfulness. It was awkward trying to work when the schools were closed. Paul, Louise and Marie were very active children and hard to keep occupied. With not having a back garden, they had to be taken to the Willowbank playground or Falls Park to be entertained in the fresh air and Madge was always quick to offer to take them out when the weather was good.

Once her letters and invoices were sorted out, the sun lured Eileen outside. It was on days like this that she wished she had a garden out the back. Still, it would not be long now until they would be in a position to look at new houses. Eileen hugged herself as she thought of the joyful future she saw ahead of them. Oh, life was wonderful at the moment! Still, there was no joy in sitting in a back yard surrounded by brick walls dreaming of what might be. Donning a cardigan, she locked up the house and headed for St James's Park. It was Good Friday since she had last seen her mother or grannie, and she was glad of the chance to visit them and sit in one or other of their gardens for a good old gossip without the children there to interrupt them.

Her mother's back door was unlocked, but repeated calls from the hall failed to bring a response so she left the house and crossed the road to her grannie's. As she walked down the side of the house Eileen could hear voices raised in heated conversation. She was not surprised to find her mother in her grannie's company. Maggie was sitting on a deckchair, a cushion at her back, and her feet propped up on a small stool. As always, Eileen thought how lovely her grannie looked. Since Bernard's return to the fold with his wife and new baby son, David, Maggie had blossomed. Today her auburn hair, now highlighted with silver, was caught back from her face in an old-fashioned bun at the nape of her neck and the purity of her skin brought attention to her high cheekbones and soft luminous grey eyes. Seeing her mother and grannie together, Eileen was aware that they could very easily be mistaken for sisters.

Although a blanket lay invitingly on the grass, Sarah was sitting upright on the bench that ran along the wall under the kitchen window. Eileen could tell by her mother's grim expression that she was in a right old temper.

'Is anything wrong?' she asked tentatively. She hadn't come out on a nice day like this just to get caught up in other people's arguments.

Sarah's chin lifted defiantly in the air and she glared at her daughter. 'Wrong? What on earth could be wrong? Your grannie just can't mind her own business, that's all!'

Eileen eyed them both. She was in two minds whether or not to stay. She did not want to intrude. 'Would you two rather be alone? I can come back tomorrow,' she offered hesitantly.

It was Maggie who answered her. 'Hello, Eileen,' she said, and her voice held a warm welcome. 'It's lovely to see you,' she assured her. 'Sit down, love.' She nodded towards the blanket spread out on the neatly cut lawn.

Removing her cardigan, Eileen thankfully obeyed her. Propped up on her elbows, she watched and waited. It was her mother who next broke the silence.

'I suppose you also think that I'm to blame, eh? Well, before you start giving off, I don't want any advice from you either! After all, it was your father who walked out of the house . . . not me. And no matter what Mam may think, my conscience is clear. I know that I was a good wife. Let me tell you something. I've put up with a lot during my marriage and . . .'

Speechless with surprise, Eileen could only sit and gape at her mother. Why was she ranting on like this? Had she finally cracked up?

Quickly Maggie interrupted her daughter. 'No more so than any other woman. Sarah. In fact, you were luckier than most.'

Sarah held up a hand for silence. 'Hear me out! No one tries to see my point of view . . . I was desperately unhappy but no one wanted to know! Mick got all the sympathy. I was the cruel uncaring wife. Well, so far as I'm concerned, Mick being Michael's father was the last straw. If Claire hadn't died, maybe . . . just maybe . . . we might have made a go of it. But I'll always blame him for her death, so perhaps it's just as well that he has gone.'

Puzzled, Eileen turned her mother's words over in her mind. What on earth was she talking about? 'I don't understand. What do you mean? Has Dad left home?' she asked in bewilderment.

'Hah! Are you telling me that you didn't know?' Seeing Eileen's blank expression, Sarah continued more slowly, 'Oh, yes, your father packed his bags and went down to his beloved Maisie O'Hara when I was out of the house on Monday. What do you think of that?'

'I don't believe it! Why, he spent Sunday with us at Bellevue and he never said a word about moving. No, I don't believe you! What did you do? If he left, something awful must have happened. What did you say to him?'

These words threw Sarah. 'Your dad was with you on Sunday?' she said, eyes wide with disbelief.

'Yes. He came to our house shortly after eleven and we dropped him off at the corner of your street about eight o'clock on Sunday night.'

'He was with you all day Sunday?' Sarah could only repeat, unable to hide her surprise.

'Yes! Where did you think he was?'

With a harsh laugh Maggie forestalled her daughter. 'Oh, she thought he was with Maisie O'Hara! Isn't that where you thought Mick was, Sarah? Putting him in the wrong as usual. Salving your own conscience.'

They could see Maggie had hit the nail on the head. Sarah blushed deep red and jumped to her feet in a fury. 'I'm not staying here any longer to be criticized. I was a good wife and mother. Can any of you deny that?' she demanded.

They both shook their heads and Sarah looked mollified, but not for long. Maggie had to spoil her satisfaction by saying. 'I have never denied that. But everyone is human, and that goes for you too, Sarah. Just remember that Mick was a good husband and father. If Claire hadn't met Michael O'Hara and opened a Pandora's box, you would have been sitting here happy and contented with your lot. Or . . .' Maggie gave her daughter a subtle look. '. . . would you? Are you using Mick's one lapse from grace as an excuse for your own recent behaviour? Eh? Is that what you're doing, Sarah?'

'Look, Mick's the one in the wrong. It's him who has left the house and gone to join his fancy woman, but I'm the one who's getting all the blame, so I am. It's just not fair!' Sarah wailed, and they could see that tears threatened to fall.

'Sarah! You don't know that Mick has gone to live with Maisie,' Maggie chastised her.

'Where else would he go? Eh? Tell me that!' Feeling her composure slip, and not wanting them to see her in tears, Sarah reached for her cardigan. 'Oh, I'm away! I'm not listening to any more of this nonsense.' And cheeks ablaze with anger, she quite literally ran from the garden.

Mesmerized, Eileen gaped after her mother's retreating figure for some moments and then dragged her gaze back to Maggie. 'What on earth was that all about, Grannie?'

'So you really didn't know that your dad had gone?'

'No! I had no idea. He was with us all day Sunday and never once said a word about leaving home. I know he was fed up at the way Mam's getting on, but any man would be the same. In fact, I think he's been very tolerant. Mam treats him like dirt.'

'I know she does,' Maggie agreed. 'At the moment she thinks she is self-sufficient. But mind you, I believe she will be lost without Mick.'

'I personally don't blame him for moving out, Grannie. But what good will it do, eh? It's all such a mess. Something must have happened when he got home on Sunday night. Mam must have said something dreadful to him, to upset him enough to make him walk out. And if he couldn't bear it any longer, why didn't he come up to me? He knows he is always welcome. Did you see him, Grannie?'

'Yes, yes I did. As a matter of fact he came over to say goodbye before he left on Monday morning?'

'And did he not give any reason for going?'

'No, not really. Sarah had gone off for a drive in Gerry Docherty's car and I think your father had asked her not to . . . well actually he ordered her not to go and she defied him. So he packed his bags, came over here to say goodbye and away he went. I did try to reason with him but his mind was made up and he would not be swayed.'

Memories of Mick's visit on Monday morning reminded Maggie of the pearls. Eileen was too preoccupied to notice them about her neck and Maggie refrained from mentioning them.

She had worn the necklace today for Sarah's benefit. To give her daughter a jolt and waken her up a bit. She had not been disappointed! They had caught her daughter's eye right away. Sarah's distress when she learnt that Mick had given Maggie the pearls had been painful to watch. She had obviously put two and two together and realized that she was looking at her own anniversary present. And a beautiful expensive present at that. Now Maggie unobtrusively pulled the neck of her blouse up closer around her throat. She did not want Eileen to notice and comment on them. If Mick and her daughter managed to sort out their differences she would gladly return the pearls to their rightful owner. Until then she must put them safely away.

'I can't take it all in,' Eileen lamented. 'Dad played with the kids all Sunday afternoon and when we dropped him off, he said, "See you soon." Something awful must have happened when he returned home on Sunday night to make him take this drastic step.' Once more her eyes questioned Maggie. Eileen had a feeling that her grannie was not telling all she knew, but Maggie remained silent. She had said all she intended to say regarding Gerry Docherty. If Mick returned he would not appreciate any gossip about his wife and Gerry Docherty swanning about together. If the family learnt anything, it would not be from her. What Sarah saw in Gerry Docherty, Maggie would never be able to fathom. Gerry never had and never would be able to hold a candle to Mick Ross.

To Maggie's surprise her granddaughter blurted out, 'I wouldn't be a bit surprised if Gerry Docherty had something to do with all this. He's always sniffing around Mam . . . and she doesn't try to stop him! In fact, I think she encourages him. Imagine! At her age she should have more sense! Instead, where he's concerned, she acts like a young girl.' Eileen's nose wrinkled with distaste. 'To me,

Gerry is a bit of a pansy. He's too sweet to be wholesome.' Suddenly alert, she held her grannie's eye. 'Is that what you meant when you spoke of Mam's behaviour? Is she having an affair with . . .' Her voice trailed off. 'No, of course Mam would never be so stupid.'

'Now, Eileen, that's careless talk! And remember, your mother is still a very attractive woman. If she is responding to Gerry's advances . . . now I'm not saying that she is, mind, so don't go getting any ideas into your head . . . but if she is encouraging Gerry, it is because she is hurt. Maisie O'Hara gave your father a son! That is something Sarah always regretted, the fact that she never had a son. She's not thinking straight at the moment. I've tried to make her see reason, but she is determined to make your father suffer, one way or another.' Maggie fell silent for some moments before continuing, 'Of course, although Sarah will never admit it, she is very jealous of Maisie. To be truthful, I'm very worried about her. I'm afraid that she will do something stupid. She could cause such a rift that your father will never return.'

'Dear God, it doesn't bear thinking about! Just wait until Johnny hears about all this! He will never believe me.'

'No, I'm sure he won't. Him and your dad have became very good friends lately, haven't they? Does that not worry you, Eileen?'

She gazed at Maggie uncomprehending. Then she laughed aloud. 'Good gracious, no! Why should it? My dad doesn't know anything about our Paul . . . at least, I don't think he does. Besides, me dad would be the last person to mention it, even if he did know. He's far too decent a man to say anything that would cause trouble between me and Johnny.'

'You're right, of course,' Maggie agreed. 'I'll make us a cool drink and then we will talk about something more pleasant for a change.' However, as she poured the drinks an old adage passed through her mind: 'There's many a slip 'twixt cup and lip'. Mick would never intentionally cause harm . . . but tongues could be loosened when men drank together. Whilst in the kitchen she carefully removed the string of pearls and going into the hall, she placed them carefully back into their box and into the drawer in the hallstand. Tonight she would put them safely away upstairs. Sarah had looked dismayed to hear that Mick had spent Sunday at Bellevue with Eileen and her family. She had obviously thought that he was with Maisie. Maggie hoped this assumption had not led to her daughter's doing anything silly. Sarah was always saying what a gentleman Gerry was. Was her daughter blind? Could she not see that all Gerry wanted was to bed her? And besides . . . a real gentleman would never try to seduce another man's wife.

Alone in the garden Eileen let her thoughts dwell on her father. Poor man . . . what was going to become of him now? Was there going to be a scandal? Would he go and live with Maisie O'Hara? Perhaps he already had, but she sincerely hoped not! She could not imagine her father living with another woman. Especially one who lived just a stone's throw away, down the Falls Road. Oh, the disgrace it would bring to all the family! Surely her mother and father would come to their senses before it went that far? They just had to!

Blinded by tears, Sarah stumbled across the road and into the sanctuary of her own driveway. Her next-door neighbour hailed her but she pretended not to hear, and hurried down the side of the house and out of sight. At the moment she was in no fit state to converse with anyone, let alone hawk-eyed Mary Matthews. Mary was a kind woman but a bit of a gossip, and Sarah didn't trust herself not to break down and pour all her woes on Mary's accommodating shoulder. Her private affairs would become common knowledge soon enough, now that Mick had left home.

Once inside the kitchen she rested her back against the door and let the tears flow freely. Had she been wrong about Mick after all? Was he really not seeing Maisie? Then where was he spending all his spare time lately? He was out nearly every night of the week. He blamed her! Said he went out because she ignored him. What did he expect, after the way he had betrayed her? Still, she had been so sure that he had spent Easter Sunday with Maisie O'Hara. She was convinced that he was spending all his spare time down at Beechmount. He had denied it of course when challenged, and was very indignant when she chose not to believe him. But then, he would deny it, wouldn't he? Why was she being so stubborn? Did she really fancy Gerry Docherty after all? Why had she acted so foolishly?

She wished now with all her heart that she had not gone with Gerry to Ballycastle on Monday. Exactly what had she hoped to gain from it? Certainly Monday had been a disaster. But then . . . maybe it was just as well that it hadn't panned out as planned. Because of her guilt and shame, the events of Monday had preyed constantly on her mind these past two days. Step by step and with aching heart, she relived it all over again.

The drive along the coast had been lovely and she had sat enthralled watching the beautiful scenery pass by. The car, a dark green Rover saloon, was large and comfortable. It would be lovely to own a car; Mick would be in his glory if he owned one like this. She pushed thoughts of her husband away and brought her attention back to the view. Occasionally, they were forced to a crawl by a tractor in front of them on the narrow winding road, as farmers took advantage of the fine weather. Sarah did not mind. She rarely got out for a drive and the slow pace gave her plenty of time to take in all the famous landmarks. They had stopped at Carnlough and, hand in hand, had walked along the beach. She had left young and carefree, her worries forgotten for a time. In a small cafe near the seafront they had lingered over tea and hot scones drenched in butter and home made jam. They were completely at one with each other.

Then suddenly, to Sarah's dismay, into this intimacy, a well of sorrow so great she was unable to suppress it, rose in her breast. Gerry's kindness unleashed all the pent up grief and pain that she had suffered and had managed to contain since the death of her beautiful Claire. During the past couple of months she'd somehow managed to keep her emotions under control, occasionally venting her spite on Mick. He deserved it, didn't he? Her husband was the cause of all her sorrow. Yet none of the family could comprehend her feelings, implying that she should forgive and forget. Not one of them tried to see her point of view, so she had put on a bold front. To outsiders she must appear cold and uncaring, not mourning the loss of her daughter. How could they know any better? Now to her dismay tears spilt over and ran unchecked down her cheeks. At once an anxious Gerry was on his feet and around the table. 'What's the matter, Sarah?'

'I'm sorry, Gerry,' she spluttered, dabbing at her eyes with a handkerchief. She was glad that they were seated at a corner table and he was able to shelter her from prying eyes. 'I don't know what came over me, but suddenly the loss of Claire became so unbearable. I think it's all your kindness that unleashed these tears.' She gave him a watery smile. 'You see . . . Claire and I were so close. God forgive me, but I loved her more than the others.' Her gaze became compelling. 'Do you think that was why God took her from me?'

Gerry squeezed her hand gently. 'Now, now, Sarah, that's foolish talk! These things happen. Think of how many others died that day. It was God's will.'

The urge to confide in him, to tell all the details of Mick's infidelity and about Michael being his son, became overbearing. Surely Gerry at least would not expect her

359

to forgive and forget? The words were on the tip of her tongue but common sense prevailed and she bit them back. The fewer people who know their dark secret the better. Touching his hand gently, she said, 'Thanks, Gerry. Thanks for being so understanding. Now I think we should continue on to Ballycastle.' Without more ado he rose and led her from the cafe.

Gerry, however, was somewhat perplexed. It seemed to him that Mick was not comforting Sarah in her obvious bereavement. Whatever thoughts Gerry might be harbouring about Mick Ross, he was well aware that the man adored his wife. Nevertheless, from Gerry's point of view things could not be going any better even if he had orchestrated them himself. In Sarah's melancholy state, if he played his cards right, the plans he had in mind for today might just come to fruition. After all, one man's loss was another man's gain and Gerry intended to make the most of the situation.

Gerry was everything she had imagined him to be. The perfect gentleman. Treating her with gentleness; never overstepping the bounds of decency. Just the odd touch of his fingers along her cheek and those deep passionate looks that thrilled her to the core. She had quite literally basked in his adoration and everything had been wonderful. That was, until they had reached Ballycastle.

They had stopped at the best hotel there and ordered dinner. Such a posh hotel . . . Sarah had never been in so grand a place in her life before. Afraid of putting her foot in it, she had asked Gerry to order for her. The meal, iced melon and strawberries for starters, followed by roast lamb with all the trimmings, was rounded off with apple pie and fresh cream. It was delicious, and afterwards Sarah sat sipping her coffee, feeling cosseted by all the attention lavished on her. Gerry certainly knew how to treat a woman. But then, in his profession he probably dined out often, and all this was wee buns to him.

Afterwards she had excused herself and gone to the ladies' room to spruce up. Here everything was grand as well. The thick carpet under her feet and the concealed lighting gave the room an air of opulence. In the tinted mirror, by the glow of the soft lighting, Sarah's face appeared young and fresh, without a sign of wrinkles. She powdered her nose and as she combed her hair, smiled at her reflection and sighed contentedly. She could very easily get used to dining out in posh hotels like this one. It was a whole new way of life to her. All this grandeur must be costing Gerry a quare penny. What was he likely to expect in return? Now she was being cynical! Gerry was a gentleman . . . he would not expect anything. For a moment this thought saddened her. Startled, she examined her reasons for feeling this way. Did she actually want Gerry to chance his arm? Good God, no! Of course she didn't!

It was by now early evening and when she returned to the dining room Gerry suggested that they sit in the lounge overlooking the seafront and have a drink. Eagerly she agreed. She revelled in all this grandeur and attention. She wished this day could last forever and she did not have to return home to face all her worries. Sitting on a two-seater sofa, at a table by the window, Sarah gazed out over the sea. Uninvited, thoughts of Mick came to mind. If he was here with her, she would suggest they stay the night, and they could walk along the beach at dusk. It must be marvellous to sit here at breakfast and see the sun rise over the water, in the morning.

It was when he was about to order a second round of drinks that Gerry's intentions became quite clear. Tentatively she had questioned the wisdom of another drink since he was driving. 'Gerry, is it not a bit dicey you having another drink? Should we not be heading for home soon?'

To her surprise Gerry left the chair he was sitting in facing her and joined her on the sofa. It was just big

361

enough for two, but still a tight fit. In the confined space he was too close for comfort, the length of his body pressed against hers; shoulder to shoulder, thigh to thigh. She squirmed a bit and glanced around to see if anyone was watching them. To her great relief the other people in the lounge appeared to be interested only in each other, so she relaxed. The intimate closeness brought to Sarah's mind the time Gerry had tried to seduce her, all those years ago. And he had very nearly succeeded. She had a cheek really, putting all the blame on Mick! If she had not made life unbearable for her husband at that time, he would never have had an affair with Maisie O'Hara.

Gerry's hand on her thigh startled her back to reality. She moved restlessly, and he removed his hand and covered hers where it lay on her lap. His face was so close she could see the fine texture of his skin and feel his hot breath on her cheek. Not once in all the time she had known him had Gerry ever looked as if he needed a shave. Mick was the opposite! A few hours after he had shaved a fine stubble shadowed his face. Once more she pushed thoughts of Mick from her mind and gave her full attention to Gerry. What was it about Gerry that attracted her to him? Was it the idea of his money, a lifestyle so different from her own? Or was it just because he happened to be there when she was lonely? She had never really given it that much thought. Had never really questioned the whys and wherefores. She could honestly say that she had never harboured any regrets about sending him on his way, all those years ago. Her life had been full and happy until Michael O'Hara appeared on the scene and Mick's betrayal had been exposed. Now Gerry's hand squeezed hers and his lips trailed her cheek. She trembled slightly, a premonition of what was to come filling her mind. She was nervously wondering what could be next on Gerry's agenda.

Gerry was also nervous. Sarah was so unpredictable!

She appeared to be ripe for the picking, but once before he had thought she was his, and she had sent him packing. He had been very bitter about her rejection of him for a long time. Until he met and fell in love with his late wife, in fact. The knowledge that Sarah had once again managed to twist him around her little finger bothered him. Would today be any different? Would she succumb to his advances? He had no idea what had caused the terrible rift between her and her husband. As far as he could see there was no hope of a reconciliation between her and Mick, and he cared enough for Sarah to make her a proposition. In the eyes of the church they could not marry but he would care for her, if she gave him the chance.

Taking the plunge he whispered in her ear, 'Sarah, I hope you won't think me forward, but . . . I have booked a double room.'

She sat petrified. Was she hearing right? 'What? You've done what?' she cried aghast. How could he be so presumptuous? Booking a room without so much as a by your leave from her. And just when had he booked it, that's what she'd like to know! It must have been when she had gone to the ladies' room.

'Listen, Sarah . . . I don't expect you to spend the night with me. I know that would be out of the question. Just a few hours. We don't want any gossip, do we? No, I realize that you won't want to be away overnight, but we've come a long way these past few months and this is too good an opportunity to miss. Don't you agree with me, Sarah?' he asked coaxingly, his hands gently caressing hers.

Robbed of speech, she gazed down at their hands. Why did she feel so indignant? Wasn't this what she wanted – a commitment from Gerry? But . . . was it a commitment? She thought not! What Gerry appeared to be offering her was a bit on the side and she recognized it for what it was. That's why she felt so cheap! Funny, in spite of all the deep sensual emotions this man could arouse in her, she always ended up feeling cheap. Perhaps that was why, in spite of the urges he could trigger off, she had never taken the final step with him.

'Sarah, tell me I'm not mistaken. Please tell me you care for me.'

Suddenly all his arrogant bravado was gone. His voice was hoarse and pleading. He sounded like a bewildered boy and Sarah's indignation eased. After all, what else could she expect? She was a married woman and she had encouraged him. Tongue tied, she sank back into the depths of the sofa and pressed her body even closer against his, letting body language answer for her. After all . . . where was Mick at this moment? Probably with the irresistible Maisie O'Hara. Well, two could play at that game! She deserved some fun too, and now that it was being offered to her on a plate, she would be a fool to refuse it. Whilst a jubilant Gerry left to fetch the key to the room, Sarah took the lift to the third floor. Number thirty-two was the room she was looking for. It was almost facing the lift and she felt conspicuous as she waited for Gerry to come. It being Easter, the hotel was very busy. With the weather being so good she was surprised that there had been a vacancy in the hotel, because Ballycastle was very popular at holiday times. Other guests greeted her in a friendly manner as they passed along the corridor. Cheeks ablaze, she returned their greetings, convinced that guilt must be written all over her face.

What was keeping Gerry? The lift had been up and down numerous times and still no sign of him. She wished he would hurry up. At last the lift doors opened yet again, and there he stood, grinning from ear to ear, a bottle of champagne in one hand and two glasses in the other. To Sarah's dismay the other occupants of the lift were smiling benignly at them. Well, if folk had not already guessed what they were up to, they certainly would now! Gerry was acting like an excited schoolboy.

Embarrassed, Sarah cried in exasperation. 'Where is the key?'

'In my pocket.' The laughter and happy expectancy slowly died on Gerry's face as Sarah scowled at him. He gestured towards his jacket pocket.

Annoyed, she dug roughly into the pocket of his jacket and retrieved the key. At the third attempt her shaking hand managed to open the door and she stormed into the room. Gerry stood in the doorway, watching her beneath narrowed eyelids.

'Will you for heaven's sake close that door!'

'Sarah, loosen up a bit! Enjoy yourself!' he urged, and entering the room, pushed the door closed with his foot. Placing the champagne and glasses on the small table beside the bed, he slowly approached her. 'No one knows us here, Sarah! Relax. There is nothing to worry about.'

'Oh, no?'

He reached for her but she backed off and he cried in exasperation. 'No! You can safely let your hair down, Sarah.'

'How do you know that no one knows me, eh?' she challenged him. 'It's all right for you! You can go back to Dublin and no one you know will be any the wiser. Just remember I live in Belfast and could easily run into someone who knows me.'

Gerry was contrite. The idea of possessing her had blinded him to all else. He should have been more discreet. 'I'm sorry, love. I wasn't thinking straight. I got carried away with all the excitement, but I promise to be more discreet.' He was warning himself to be careful. He had a feeling that Sarah was having second thoughts and he could not bear to be rejected again, now that he had come this far. He was not going to blow this second chance with her.

She stood at the window, with her back to him, gazing out over the hotel grounds. The rays of the sun slanted in, highlighting the burnished copper of her hair. Trembling slightly, he put his arms around her and buried his face in her hair, cupping her breasts in his hands. They were fuller than he remembered them to be and he gently massaged them. Sarah waited expectantly. All the good feelings that had buoyed her up downstairs had dwindled away. Now she wished that she was at home in St James's Park. If only Gerry would throw her on the bed and make mad passionate love to her; make her forget everything, including the picture of Mick that plagued her mind, perhaps she would be able to respond. Gently, he nuzzled her hair aside and kissed the nape of her neck. A tremor coursed through her body and quickly she turned in his arms and feverishly offered her lips. Thankfully Gerry claimed them, and drawing her away from the window, edged her over towards the bed.

She went willingly and made no objections when he started to undress her. She was very much aware that her figure was still good, with firm high breasts and flat stomach. She could see by the look in Gerry's eyes that he was pleased with what he saw. Gerry was in his glory; could not believe his luck. He was worked up to a hundred. He had always loved Sarah, and now at last she was to be his. His marriage had been happy, but Sarah was his first love and he had never forgotten her. He had waited a long time to possess her, and as he gazed down on the beauty of her, he trembled as desire threatened to boil over. Aware that in his present excited state he might spoil things, he released her and stepped back from the bed.

'Shall we have a glass of champagne first?'

Sarah opened her eyes and gaped at him in amazement. Here she was, in spite of thoughts of Mick tormenting her, poised to give her all and Gerry wanted to drink champagne. Was he daft? She felt deflated; couldn't believe her ears.

Whilst he poured the drinks, Sarah sat upright in bed and pulled the covers up to her chin to cover her nakedness. Trust Gerry to make a mess of things. Here he was behaving like Cary Grant in one of those romantic movies, when she wanted a dashing knight in white armour to sweep her into his arms and out of her mind with passion.

He stood stripped to the waist and she eyed him covertly as he poured the drinks. In spite of being so slight, he had a little belly. Now Mick was still as flat as a pancake . . . Oh, forget about Mick! she chided herself. He obviously had conveniently forgotten her when he had bedded Maisie O'Hara. Be fair! her conscience cried. That was almost twenty-four years ago. Almost a quarter of a century. And remember, you were partly to blame. They had both been young and impetuous then, and there had been an excuse for Mick. Seeing the little pot belly being pulled in and shoulders being squared, Sarah realized that Gerry was aware of her scrutiny and, hiding a smile, she looked away.

'Thank you.' She accepted the glass of champagne from him and when he sat down on the bed, she squirmed over and made room for him.

'To us, Sarah.' He held up his glass.

She raised her glass and clinked it against his. 'To us, Gerry,' she replied, and took a sip from the glass, wrinkling her nose as the bubbles tickled her nostrils. To her surprise, Gerry knocked his drink back in one quick gulp and turned to her.

Taking the nearly full glass from her hand, he placed it on the bedside table. 'Right! We've wasted enough time already, Sarah. Come here!'

Thankfully she leant towards him. She wanted this over as quickly as possible so that they could be on their way home. She was aghast at this terrible thought. Wasn't she supposed to be enjoying this? Why then had she let it go so far? She had no idea just what had possessed her. Gerry's flattery had been a balm to her sore heart and wounded pride. She had wallowed in his admiration.

Now it was too late to back down. She pressed close to him and some of the tension eased as he kissed her urgently. This was more like it! Now at last they were getting somewhere! His lovemaking became more intense and she was lifted along on a wave of passion. Blocking all else from her mind, she let her emotions take over. Perhaps it would be worthwhile after all. This was a new experience for her, she had never been with any other man but Mick. Would it be very different or were they all the same between the sheets?

The kisses, nice though they were, seemed to go on forever and were leading nowhere. She opened her eyes slightly and examined his face. There was such a look of consternation on it she felt sorry for him. Obviously it was not going as he intended. Human frailty was letting him down. The spirit was willing but the flesh was weak. At last he buried his head in the hollow of her breasts and moaned, but not, alas, with pleasure. 'Sarah . . . I'm so sorry. It's been so long. I just can't seem to . . . you know? Ah, Sarah, forgive me please.'

Stifling the urge to laugh out loud at his antics, she hugged him close instead. She was experiencing a vast feeling of relief. In spite of all her endeavours she had not managed to commit adultery. She was aware that she had done an awful thing going to bed with another man, and was grateful that it had amounted to nothing more than kissing and clumsy petting. Oh, the intention had been there all right! If Gerry's flesh had not proved his undoing, adultery would have taken place. Relief mellowed her feelings towards him. After all, he had eased some of her guilt, and saved her from the ultimate betrayal.

'It's all right, Gerry. Never mind. It could happen to anyone,' she consoled him.

'It's never happened to me before,' he lamented.

'What do you mean? Have you known many women?' she asked reproachfully. Why had she assumed that the only other woman in his life had been his late wife? Because she was a naive fool, that's why! She'd imagined everybody was like herself.

He was unruffled and answered her honestly, 'Quite a few. But they have never meant as much to me as you do. That's probably why I failed. I do so want to please you. Maybe if we were to try again, Sarah?' His voice trailed off. She was already out of bed and heading for the bathroom. 'Sarah?' At the bathroom door she turned and faced him. His eyes ranged over her body; the high firm breasts and long slim legs. She really did look wonderful for her age. Desire surged through him again. Should he risk it? Still smarting from his recent impotence, he decided not to. 'Perhaps another time?'

'Who knows, Gerry? The opportunity may not present itself again. It's not often you can obtain a hotel room at such short notice, especially during the holidays and without any luggage.'

'We could book in advance. I booked this room a week ago,' he admitted.

At these words Sarah slowly advanced towards the bed. 'You were so sure of me?' she gasped, completely taken aback. 'What if Mick had accompanied us, eh? What would you have done then?'

'I was pretty sure he wouldn't. I mean . . . his stupid pride would not allow him. I'm really surprised he let you come along on your own with me,' he confessed. 'Don't look so surprised, Sarah. Any fool can see that things are not well between you two. You can't really blame me for booking the room on the off chance. You are attracted to me, you know that, Sarah. We had some unfinished business all those years ago. It was on the cards we should come together again.'

Sarah was speechless, but only momentarily. All pity for him flew out of the window and she attacked him mercilessly. 'You're a gag, Gerry Docherty! Just who do you think you are, lying there predicting we should come together again? To my everlasting shame, you actually managed to get me into bed, and naked into the bargain . . . and what happened? You couldn't manage it. But now I thank God for that! I don't know what I was thinking of. I must have had a brainstorm or something! I always thought you were a gentleman . . . Hah! Some gentleman you turned out to be.' In her wrath she was spluttering. 'Another thing, don't you ever dare talk about Mick Ross in that tone of voice again. Why, you couldn't hold a candle to him.'

'Now wait a wee minute, Sarah. You led me on! Why, if Emma hadn't come in when she did yesterday, it would have been plain sailing. 'Cause you were all for it! Don't you deny that, Sarah Ross.'

Sarah felt uncomfortable. She knew that he was right, but she wasn't going to admit it. She was too old-fashioned in her outlook for these secret trysts. This was all Mick Ross's fault! If only he hadn't fathered Michael O'Hara she would never have consented to accompany Gerry to Ballycastle today. This was her way of paying Mick back for the way he had treated her, and it had backfired on her. Now she had an irate Gerry to contend with too. Her worries seemed to be multiplying.

All anger left her and once more she turned towards the bathroom. 'Let's just call it a day, eh, Gerry?' she said sadly. 'I just want to go home.'

For some seconds he glared bitterly at the bathroom door. He had blown it! There was no way he could foresee Sarah ever consenting to come out with him again. He'd had his chance and failed miserably. If ever she succumbed to his advances again, it would have to be on the spur of the moment, before she had time to think. She was too strait-laced. She wanted him, and at the same time didn't want him. She was afraid to take a chance, that was what was wrong with her. With a deep sigh, he rose to his feet. He may as well get dressed. Their adventure was over, for today anyway.

They arrived back at St James's Park without exchanging half a dozen words. With a curt good night, Sarah quickly left the car and entered her house. Gerry sat for some moments deep in thought. Coming to a decision, he eased the car across the road and into his son's driveway. Tomorrow he would return to Dublin. He must let the dust settle on this episode before he dared face Sarah again. he couldn't understand why he had failed. It must have been because he was over eager. However, he could not bear to see the scorn in her eyes, so he must get away for a short while. He had by no means given up hope. Indeed, no! He still had every intention of seducing his first love.

In the hall Sarah stood quietly with head tilted, listening for signs that the house was occupied. Silence! A glance at her watch told her that it was only half-past nine. She could be in bed and apparently asleep by the time Mick or Emma came home. On the journey back home in the car she had come to a decision. She intended talking things over with Mick. Giving him a chance to plead his case as he had been begging her to. They could take it from there. She wanted to thrash this business of Maisie out with him; see where she stood. It wouldn't be easy admitting that she had been a fool, but she would. But not tonight. Mick could read her like a book and he would guess that she had been up to no good!

Although not much had actually taken place between her and Gerry, she nevertheless felt guilty. The intention had been there all right and that was sin enough. Mick must never know just how close she had come to committing the ultimate sin. With a deep sigh she kicked off her shoes; Emma would be home soon and since she didn't want to face her daughter either, she had better get herself up to bed. However, her mind was overactive and sleep eluded her. She tossed and turned. She heard Emma come home at eleven and sleep still proved elusive. It was the early hours of the morning before she finally dropped off; her last thought was of Mick. It was very late, where could he be? With Maisie? She sincerely hoped not, but where else could he be? A sudden thought startled her. Had he met another woman? If he had, she had no one to blame but herself. That night her dreams were troubled.

On Tuesday morning her suspicions of Mick's having another woman were intensified when she discovered that he had not come home at all the night before. Thinking that he had overslept, she had knocked on the bedroom door. Receiving no answer she had entered the room, to stand aghast. She knew at once that he was gone. The wardrobe doors stood ajar and she could see that it was empty. The alarm clock and the few personal belongings that he kept by his bedside were gone. There was no need to look in the chest of drawers, she knew that it also would be empty. Feeling the colour drain from her face and her legs grow weak, she sat on the edge of the bed and closed her eyes. Where had Mick gone ... or rather to whom had he gone? How long had he been planning this? Had he been looking for an excuse to leave her? Had she, by going off to Ballycastle with Gerry Docherty, given him that excuse? How would his leaving affect her? A week ago, with the state of mind she had been in, she would have been glad to see the back of him, confident that she would find comfort in Gerry's arms. A letter she had found in the hall that morning put paid to that idea. In the letter Gerry informed her that he was on his way back to Dublin but that he would return in two weeks' time to see her again. Besides, Gerry had been a great disappointment to her. Just let him come near her in two weeks' time! She would give him a piece of her mind. Indeed, yes! He would feel the wrath of her tongue, sneaking off like that.

Slowly she had descended the stairs, dreading breaking the news to Emma. Was it right to keep her in the dark about all that had happened? Emma was family. She had the right to know the truth. She was sixteen now and must know that these things happened. Sarah decided that she would tell her youngest daughter that Michael O'Hara was her half-brother. However, she never got a chance to tell Emma the truth. At the breakfast table, when she acquainted Emma of her father's departure, Sarah was unprepared for her daughter's outburst.

'This is all your fault!' Beside herself with grief, Emma poured out all her pent up anger on her mother. She had been dreading something like this happening! Now she accused her mother: 'If you had treated him with a little more respect, there is no way Dad would have left home.'

'Here, hold on a minute, girl!' Sarah bellowed. 'Who do you think you're talking to? Eh? It's not my fault that your dad has gone.'

Angrily Emma cried, 'Oh, no? Whose fault is it then? You're the one who has made his life unbearable. Since Claire died you've made this house a place of misery. Anyone would think that Dad had murdered her! I don't know how he put up with you for so long, the way you've been treating him.'

Taken aback by all this venom being spat at her, Sarah said sadly, 'It's all your father's fault, so it is. But then, I don't suppose you will ever believe that.'

It was soon apparent that her daughter did not believe her. With a withering glare Emma pushed her chair back from the table and left the kitchen. A few minutes later the front door slammed behind her.

With a start Sarah realized that she was still leaning against the back door. A sigh of regret escaped her as she pushed herself away and straightened her cramped limbs. She wished that it was Good Friday again and she could relive the past few days. With the knowledge she had now, she would certainly act differently. Wiping the tears from her face, she made herself a pot of tea; cure for all ills. After Emma had stormed from the house the day before, Sarah had remained indoors all day, hoping against hope that Mick would have second thoughts and come home, then the neighbours need be none the wiser. Why did she always worry about the neighbours? It was a long lonely day. The schools were still closed and Emma did not return to the house until near midnight and then went straight to bed without any kind of acknowledgement to her mother.

Fed up being on her own and not knowing what kind of reception to expect, Sarah had nevertheless that morning crossed the road to her mother's house. She had not really expected to receive any comfort there. Just as well! She didn't get any. The final slap in the face was learning that the beautiful string of pearls around her mother's neck had been given to her by Mick. She had guessed at once that she was looking at her own anniversary present and it hurt . . . how it hurt . . . to learn that Mick had given them away. He must really hate her. Eileen's arrival had not made things any easier. Indeed it only intensified her loneliness. It was obvious that they all blamed her; they were all on Mick's side. No one cared to see her point of view. You would think it had been she who'd had someone else's child!

With hindsight Eileen realized that she should have known that her father was very unhappy. At Bellevue whilst cavorting with the children he had seemed ordinary enough. However, in repose he had sat, arms around knees, gazing blankly out over the lough. She had been too wrapped up in her own bubble of happiness to pay much heed to him. The dinner at the International Hotel had been a huge success and on Sunday she had still been sated with the pleasure of it all and never really took much notice of her father. She had just been glad that he had been there to help occupy the kids. Therefore it came as a terrible shock to learn that he had left the house. Never in her wildest nightmares had she dreamt that it would come to this. And why hadn't her dad come up to her? Her grannie said, for the same reason he would never consider staying at her house: they were too close to home.

That night when Eileen heard her husband's key turn in the lock she ran to meet him in the hall. 'Johnny, what do you think? Me dad has left home!' she wailed.

To her surprise Johnny just nodded his head.

'You already knew?' she gasped in dismay. 'And you never let on?'

'Here now, hold your horses, Eileen. I only found out today. Mick rang me at work and told me the bad news. He was surprised that we didn't already know.' Having removed his coat and hung it at the foot of the stairs, slowly but surely, Johnny was manoeuvring his wife along the hall towards the kitchen. 'I'm starving! Let's eat. We can talk about this later.' Realizing that the house was unusually quiet, he asked, 'Where are the kids? Have they had their dinner yet?'

'Your mother has had them all day. She took them down to Willowbank Park and she's giving them their dinner at her house. She will bring them home shortly.'

Suddenly alert, Johnny asked, 'How shortly?'

'I don't know. Soon, I should imagine. She didn't say any particular time. Why?'

'Get my dinner on the table . . . quickly! Go on, scoot! If you hurry we might get a half hour to ourselves, and wouldn't that be nice? Think about it, woman! Does that not put ideas into your head, Eileen? Eh, love?'

She demurred. 'Oh, be serious, Johnny.' Nevertheless she quickly dished the dinner onto the waiting plates and was soon sitting facing him across the table.

'Listen, Eileen . . . I was never more serious! How long is it since we've been alone?'

'Saturday night,' she answered him dryly. 'You've a short memory.'

Johnny was not to be thwarted. 'Ah, but that was the exception to the rule.'

Unable to wait any longer, Eileen entreated, 'Tell me, Johnny, what did Dad have to say?'

With a sigh, he replied, 'Not much. He just wants me to meet him for a drink down in Mooney's on Cornmarket, tomorrow night after work.'

'Did he not give any inkling just why he left home?'

'No, but you don't talk about things like that on the phone. I'm sure he will tell me everything tomorrow night. And I don't for one minute doubt that he will have plenty to say. You know the way your mother has been behaving lately where he is concerned. I don't know how he stuck it for so long.'

'Still, Johnny, he has put up with so much, giving Mam plenty of time to come to her senses. So why go now? It doesn't make sense! I mean, he was with us all day Sunday and he never mentioned anything about leaving the house. Something awful must have happened to drive him out.' Her eyes were fearful when she put the next question to him. 'Do you think he has gone to live with Maisie O'Hara? That's the one thing Mam would never, ever forgive.'

'I don't know, Eileen, but I'm sure he will tell me the full story tomorrow. We will just have to wait and see.' Johnny scooped the last of the gravy on to a piece of meat and potato and polished it off. 'That was delicious.' He eyed her expectantly. 'Is there any desert?' At her nod of assent, he asked, 'Will it keep?'

'No, it will spoil if we don't eat it now.'

'Well then, stop wasting time, love. What are you waiting for? Inspiration? Wouldn't you like a bit of time to . . .' His voice trailed off as a racket at the door reached his ears. 'Ah, well, that puts paid to my plans. You can take your time, Eileen. We've already missed the boat.'

*   *   *

Mick sat sideways on a stool at the crowded bar in Mooney's pub, one eye on the door. He was early. When you are in digs and you have somewhere to go, you get out as quickly as possible. There could surely be nothing worse than sitting in a bedroom staring at the wallpaper. He was lodging with the sister of one of his workmates. A fine woman, but to be truthful she frightened him. Widowed two years previously, and childless, she had that look in her eye that spelt trouble. The last time he had left Sarah, he had lodged with another widow, Maisie O'Hara, and look where that had landed him. Two lonely people confined under the same roof could easily lead to more heartache, and that he could certainly do without right now. Rosie McCann was an attractive woman, some years his junior, and without any ties. To keep out of trouble he spent all his spare time in his bedroom.

His self-imposed imprisonment managed to keep any temptation at bay, but in the solitary confinement of his single room, and with little or nothing to do, he had too much time to ponder over the past.

In his loneliness he was tormented with thoughts of his daughter, Claire; the only reason he was in lodgings this day and not at home with his wife and family. Why in the name of heaven, had she to go and fall in love with the only lad in Belfast whom she could never marry? Yet she had and in spite of all their protestations she had run off and married her half-brother. And look where it had all ended; Claire in her grave, Michael in exile, and himself in another woman's home. Hardly a day went past that he didn't spare a thought for his beloved daughter and remorse was eating away at him. If he had a place of his own perhaps he could get on with his life. Not that he wanted to forget Claire . . . she would always be part of him. But as things stood he was becoming more and more depressed.

If only he could find a small furnished flat somewhere!

He was finding it difficult to get any kind of reasonable accommodation. The flats he had looked at were out of the question. The rent they were asking would soon deplete the money he had managed to save out of his last pay rise, and the furnished rooms that he could afford, and where he was expected to share a bathroom, he couldn't bear the thought of living in. Seeing Johnny enter the bar, Mick rose to his feet and with raised hand caught his attention.

The two men shook hands and Johnny eyed his father-in-law closely. 'How are you, Mick?'

Mick's smile was twisted when he replied, 'Oh, not too bad, Johnny. What will you have?'

'Mine's a Guinness, Mick.'

When the pints were drawn Mick gestured towards an empty table. 'Shall we sit over there, Johnny? It'll be a wee bit more private.'

Once seated, Mick leant across the table and addressed Johnny. 'I hope you didn't think me presumptuous, phoning you at work and asking you to meet me here?'

'Catch yourself on, Mick, it's always a pleasure to talk with you. Although, mind you, I wish it was under happier circumstances. Where are you living now?'

'I've got a room over on Templemore Avenue. It's handy to the shipyard, and well away from the Falls.'

'Well, that's a relief. Eileen and Sarah are convinced you're living with Maisie O'Hara.'

'Maisie O'Hara is a fine woman,' Mick exclaimed. 'She is nothing like what Sarah makes her out to be, and I admire her very much. If Sarah and I can't come to some arrangement where we can live under the same roof in some kind of harmony, I'll probably woo Maisie. That's if she will let me. Now, she's a woman who knows how to keep a man happy.'

Johnny listened to all this in silence. If Sarah wasn't careful she would lose Mick forever. 'You know, Mick, me and Eileen feel as guilty as hell. We feel we should have noticed that you weren't your usual self at Bellevue last Sunday.'

'Oh, but I was all right on Sunday.' Mick grimaced at this expression. 'Or at least as right as I've been for a long time. No, me and Sarah had a disagreement on Sunday night when I got home, and to be truthful, it was the last straw. I just had to get away and get some breathing space. How is she?'

'Eileen was down at Maggie's yesterday and Sarah was there. I'm afraid she is as defiant as ever. Eileen got an awful shock when she heard you had gone. And I hear that Emma is taking it badly too. She hasn't spoke to Sarah since she found out.'

'That's my Sarah! She can sure get everyone's back up.'

'Mick, are you happy in these digs? You know you can come and stay at our house for as long as you like. I'm sure you'd be more at home with us, and we'd be glad to have you.'

'Thanks, Johnny but it would be too close to Sarah. I'd probably be crawling down every night begging her to take me back.'

'The way I see it, she should jump at the chance to have you back,' Johnny assured him. 'If you don't mind my saying so, Sarah doesn't know when she is well off.'

'Ah, well now . . . I can't put all the blame on her, we were both at fault. Remember, I did have an affair.'

'But, Mick, that was nearly twenty-four years ago!'

Mick held Johnny's eye as he asked the next question. 'If you and Eileen were to part for any length of time and she had someone else's child, would you forgive her?'

Mick could see that his son-in-law was shocked at the very idea of it, and he laughed softly. 'You see, Johnny, it works both ways. That's why I was giving Sarah plenty of time to come to terms with it. You see, I betrayed her trust and she can't find it in her heart to forgive me.'

Johnny looked shamefaced. 'I see what you mean,

379

Mick. I suppose I would be very bitter if it happened to me. But what about the rest of the family? We all miss you, especially the kids.'

'And I miss them too! That's what I want to see you about, Johnny. Can we come to some arrangement so that I can see the kids now and again? And I'll have to see Beth and her lot. How is she?'

'As far as I know she is keeping all right.'

Mick sighed and stared down into his Guinness. 'I don't know how I'm going to stick this . . . cut off from all the ones I love.'

'Would you be willing to stay in our house every weekend? Sarah need never know, and we would be so glad to have you.' Johnny laughed gently as he warned, 'Mind you, I have to admit, you might get roped into a bit of babysitting. Shorts' are having a dinner dance in two weeks' time. How about it, Mick?'

'You've just made my day! Nothing would make me happier, Johnny.'

They sat over a couple of pints of Guinness each, and talked for almost three hours. It was Mick who made the first move to go. Reluctantly he rose to his feet. 'I'm keeping you away from your wife and family, Johnny.' Reaching for his son-in-law's hand, he pumped it up and down. 'I appreciate everything you've done for me, son.'

'You will come on Saturday, then?'

'I will, Johnny. I'll order a taxi. What time would you like me there?'

'Come in time for your dinner. Eh, Mick? Round about five o'clock. I can pick you up if you like?'

'No, Johnny, that won't be necessary. The Glens are playing at the Oval on Saturday, so I might just go and watch them. It'll pass the afternoon in for me. All being well, I'll come up straight after the match. Thanks again for coming down here tonight.'

'No problem, Mick. It's nice to get out on my own for

a change. By the way, I didn't know you were a Glentoran supporter.' He poked Mick playfully in the ribs and gave him a broad smile. They parted outside the pub; Mick cutting across towards High Street to catch a bus and Johnny heading up to Castle Street to do likewise.

Eileen was bathing Marie when she heard Johnny arrive home. 'Johnny, I'm in the bathroom. Come on up.'

Leaning against the bathroom door he grinned down at the smiling face of his youngest daughter. Marie giggled and slapped the bubbles with both hands. Dropping to his knees beside the bath, Johnny splashed water over the delighted child. Eileen waited patiently for him to speak.

Unable to contain herself any longer, at last she cried in exasperation, 'Well then . . . what happened? What did Dad have to say?'

Eyes twinkling, Johnny laughed. 'I wondered how long you could be patient. It must have been all of two minutes.'

'Johnny, don't tease. Put me out of my misery, for heaven's sake.'

'Your father seems fine.'

'Where is he living?'

'He has a room over on Templemore Avenue.'

'Thank God for that! Did he mention Maisie O'Hara?'

'Her name did crop up in the course of the conversation, I have to admit.'

'What do you think will happen now?'

'First I think we should get this young lady out of the bath. Are the other two sleeping?'

'Yes . . . Marie was sick all down her pyjamas, so I decided to give her a bath. I hope she's not sickening for anything. Measles is doing the rounds.'

Johnny held up the bath towel and Eileen lifted the dripping child out of the bath. Wrapping the towel around his young daughter, Johnny carried her into their bedroom and placed her on the bed. Once the now drowsy child was dried and powdered, and dressed in fresh pyjamas, Johnny kissed her good night and descended the stairs. He was soon joined by his wife.

'Do you think Marie will be all right?' he asked anxiously.

'She seems to be now. She's in her own bed and fast asleep. Perhaps she just ate something that didn't agree with her. You know what a glutton she is. By the way ... did you get a good lunch today, like you said you would?'

'I did, love. I went to the canteen and had steak and kidney pie and all the trimmings. I'm not hungry, so come here and sit down.'

Although the weather was warm during the day, it still got chilly at night time and Eileen had lit the living-room fire. From her favourite position at her husband's feet in front of the hearth she leant her arm across his knees and looked up at him.

'Well ... tell me everything that happened,' she ordered.

Johnny recounted all that Mick had to say. When he finished speaking Eileen said, 'That was a brilliant idea, Johnny, asking him to stay here at weekends. It means we will be able to keep an eye on what he's up to.'

Johnny grimaced with distaste. 'Eileen, don't talk like that! I for one don't intend to spy on him.'

Eileen was aghast at the very idea of it. 'I didn't mean it like that! You know I didn't!' she cried resentfully.

'I know you didn't love. It just sounded awful. However, there's one good thing about it ... it does mean that we will have a babysitter in two weeks' time.'

'Why? What's happening in two weeks' time?'

Gently Johnny broke the good news to his wife. 'It was up on the noticeboard today. Shorts' are having a dinner dance.'

He was pleased at her response. 'Oh, Johnny, that's

wonderful!' Eyes aglow she inquired, 'Is it formal?' When he nodded, she warned him, 'I'll need a long dress, mind.'

He drew her up on to his knee and kissed her. 'You can have two new dresses if you like,' he assured her. As always she responded eagerly to his advances, as if she could not get enough of him. As passion mounted he told her how much he loved her. Eyes closed he prayed silently, Please let her say it. But no, although Eileen pressed against him with abandon she remained silent. Then she was on her feet and urging him to his.

'Let's go to bed.'

'I need to check the doors . . .'

'Later, Johnny. You can come back down later and see to all that. I want to go to bed, now!'

Pride kept Sarah from inquiring into Mick's whereabouts. He had been out of the house almost two weeks now, and still she had no idea where he was staying. Although she was sure that both her mother and Eileen knew where he was, no one volunteered information. Everybody seemed to have conspired to keep her in the dark unless she asked direct questions, and that she wasn't prepared to do. The previous weekend Mick had sent her some money by post. He had enclosed a short note saying he would not be able to send her as much money every week, as he hoped to have a place of his own very soon. Sarah read and reread the words. So abrupt! Just headed 'Sarah', and signed 'Mick'. No return address. She was terribly worried; it sounded so final. Without Mick's wage coming in she would have to look for a job and there was no way that she would be able to afford to keep Emma on at school. She would have to see Mick and talk things over with him and come to some sort of financial arrangement. But who to ask regarding his whereabouts, without losing too much face? That was the question. Eileen . . . she would call up and see Eileen. Relieved to have come to this decision, she immediately put on her coat and left the house. She could not afford to let pride interfere with what had to be done.

Eileen greeted her coolly. 'This is a surprise.'

Her daughter's attitude immediately got Sarah's back up and she went straight on the attack. 'Oh, so that's why you haven't been down much lately? Am I not welcome here any more? I bet you don't greet your father like that. Surely by now his halo must have tarnished just a little? Eh?' she taunted.

'I'm sorry, Mam, It's just . . . Well, I've wanted to go down and see you, but I knew I would only end up begging you to take Dad back . . . and he won't hear tell of that. He has warned me off! Says that he doesn't want anyone fighting his battles for him. He's every bit as stubborn as you are.'

At these words Sarah's throat went dry and fear entered her heart. Nevertheless she tossed her head, and answered disdainfully, 'He needn't worry on that score. I'll not coax him to come back.'

'You'll wait until it's too late, Mam! That's what will happen! Dad is a fine attractive man, and I'm sure there is many a woman who would be glad to accommodate him, only he is not that way inclined.'

'What do you mean . . . not that way inclined? Eh? You forget that he fathered Michael O'Hara! That was no virgin birth.'

'Ah, Mam, now you are being crude! And anyway . . . that was all so long ago. Can't you just forgive and forget? You're not getting any younger, you know. Do you want to spend the rest of your life a grass widow?'

Sarah's patience was coming to an end. She had not come here to receive a lecture on morals and she still had not found out where Mick was lodging. 'Enough of that, Eileen! Let's clear the air once and for all, shall we? Is your dad living . . . or, as he would discreetly put it, lodging with Maisie O'Hara?'

384

'No, he's not! He has a furnished room over on Templemore Avenue.'

Sarah successfully hid her relief. 'Could I have the address then, please? I need to speak to him about some money matters.'

'Why not come up here on Saturday night and see him? He is baby-sitting for us. We are going to a dinner dance.'

'Will he be here alone?'

'Of course! Bar the kids. Wait until about eight . . . then they will be in bed and you will be able to talk to him without any interruptions. That is if you can talk rationally without getting into another war of words.'

Sarah turned towards the door. 'OK, I'll come up on Saturday night. Thank you,' she said curtly.

Eileen watched her walk along the hall in amazement. Was her mother not going to stay? 'Mam! What's the big rush? Are you not going to have even a cup of tea?'

Slowly, Sarah turned and faced her daughter. 'I didn't hear you offer me one. I got the distinct impression that I wasn't very welcome here any more.'

'For goodness sake, Mam, catch yourself on! Of course you're welcome here, any time. Take off your coat and sit down. The kids will be back any minute now and they will be glad to see you. They are always asking for their Grannie Ross.' As she passed back into the kitchen, Eileen squeezed her mother's arm sympathetically, 'Mam, we all love you. That's the truth! But don't you think it's about time you asked Dad to come home? Eh?'

'How do I know that he is willing to return? Has he not met anyone else?'

'No, of course not . . . but I hear tell the widow that he is lodging with has her eye on him. He is near dead to get away from her, but he can't find any other reasonable digs. We're worried sick about him. Please, Mam, ask him to come back to you. Surely the two of you can live together in some kind of harmony?'.

Hearing that her husband was lodging with yet another widow, Sarah's heart sank. Perhaps Eileen was right. She had better get a move on; try to make amends. 'That remains to be seen, Eileen. I'll come up on Saturday night then, and talk things over with him. I promise to listen to his side of the story. Now, don't you tell him that I'm coming! I want to surprise him.'

Gladly Eileen promised not to say a word to her father. She thought her mother's visit was more likely to be a shock than a surprise, but she was happy just to get them together under the same roof. At least it was a beginning. It would be up to them to thrash out their differences and hopefully come to an amicable conclusion that would make them all one big happy family again.

Chapter Ten

On Saturday night Eileen prepared for the dinner with care. The emerald green gown, bought from a small select shop in the town centre, left her shoulders bare, then clung to the curves of her body, to flow gently from the top of her thighs in soft folds that swirled around slim ankles. Normally she would never have dreamt of looking in the small exclusive boutique in Fountain Lane, well aware that their price tags were way beyond her pocket, but there had been a 'Sale' notice in the shop window. With Kate Madden by her side for moral support, she had dared to enter the premises. To her great delight she found just what she had in mind. Kate was profuse in her admiration, and egged on by her friend Eileen decided to buy the evening gown. Even at the sale price it was still very expensive, but once having seen how she looked in the dress, she could not resist buying it. If she made do with the black suede court shoes and handbag she had worn to the last dinner, she felt justified in spending so much money on one dress.

It was great to have Kate home again! Alone, Eileen might not have dared enter the boutique, and she would have missed out on owning such a classic creation. Kate had arrived to stay with her mother the previous weekend. Seven months pregnant, she had decided to return to Belfast for the arrival of her first child. She wanted to be close to her mother for the birth. Eileen had been delighted to see her. It was like Claire had returned. She and Kate had always been as close as sisters. In fact, Eileen confided in Kate things that she would never dream of revealing to anyone else. They had been inseparable since Kate's arrival from Dublin.

'You look beautiful.'

Eileen had not heard Johnny enter the room and now she swung round to face him. 'As long as you think so, that's all that matters to me, Johnny.'

'Is it, Eileen? Is it really?' Crossing the room he stood close to his wife and gazed on the beauty of her, but did not dare touch her. The deep cleavage and creamy shoulders rising above the dress were exciting him. Never had she looked more beautiful. He was aware that if he once put a hand on her he would have to take her and even though she would probably enjoy it, she would not be very happy about it as it would smudge her make-up and disarray her hair. Besides, he warned himself as the longing for her grew, and he was tempted, Mick would be arriving shortly.

Bewildered, Eileen gaped at him. 'What's that supposed to mean? Of course it's what you think that matters most to me. I don't care what anyone else thinks.' She leant forward to kiss him but he quickly turned away.

'You had better not, love. Your father will be here any minute now, and we don't want to start something that we can't finish . . . eh?' He held up a finger for silence and cocked his ear. 'I think I hear Mick now. I'll nip down and let him in.' He drew back and his eyes slowly scanned her from head to toe. He nodded his approval. 'You really do look beautiful, love. That dress was worth every penny. The taxi will be here soon. Hurry down, won't you?'

Eileen gazed after her husband for some moments, a slight frown creasing her brow. What on earth had Johnny meant by that? Surely, after all this time, he didn't still doubt her love for him? Hearing the children joyously greeting their grandfather, she quickly put the finishing touches to her toilette and descended the stairs. Her father was already enthroned in an armchair beside the hearth, a book of fairy tales held open before him, and was reading in a low voice. Paul and Louise were perched, one on each arm of the chair beside him, and Marie was on his knee, all listening attentively to him. The children had been bathed and were dressed in their pyjamas. With a bit of luck they would be in bed and fast asleep by the time her mother arrived. From the doorway, Eileen eyed her father. Although he had lost some weight lately, dressed in a blue casual shirt, open at the neck, and dark trousers, he looked quite handsome. She hoped that she was doing the right thing, springing her mother on him unawares. At least he was well groomed. She was glad that her father was still taking care of his appearance. Some men went to the dogs when they separated from their wives, but thank God her father was not one of them.

As if sensing her presence, Mick lifted his head and met her appraising look. 'Is anything the matter, Eileen?' he asked, a frown furrowing his brow.

'I'm just thinking that you look quite handsome for a man of your years. Have you got your eye on anyone yet?' she jested.

'What do you mean, a man of my years? I can still pass myself with the best of them, you know,' Mick retorted. 'And no, I haven't got anyone else yet . . . but I haven't given up hope,' he teased back. 'That's a lovely dress you're wearing. You look wonderful in it, Eileen.'

'Thanks, Dad. It cost a bomb but I do feel great in it. See you in the morning, kids, and you had better be good!' she warned. The children, patiently waiting for their grandfather to resume reading, all chorused, 'Good night, Mammy,' and waved her off. With a final farewell to her father, Eileen left the room.

Johnny was waiting in the hall and to her great delight, instead of her coat, he was holding a black stole threaded with silver, ready to wrap around her shoulders. 'Courtesy of Mam,' he said, grinning at her obvious pleasure.

389

Eileen allowed him to wrap it around her, and fingering the cobwebby softness of the crocheted wool, exclaimed, 'She is too good, so she is! She spoils me.' They were concerned about Madge's health at the moment. She was losing a lot of weight and although she had been sent to the hospital for tests, the doctors could find nothing wrong with her. 'How is she today, Johnny?'

'She looks a good deal better. When she first suggested crocheting this stole for you, I tried to put her off, thinking it would be too much for her. However she soon put me in my place. She said, and I quote her exact words, "I'm not dead yet! So don't you try to bury me. It will give me an interest. Take my mind of myself." So I gave in gracefully. There's our taxi, love, let's go.'

Once again the dance was being held in the International Hotel. As before, they all met in the cocktail lounge and Eileen was aware that her arrival caused a stir of approval. After greeting those nearby, Eileen's eyes scanned the room. She saw that Lorna Pollock was once more being escorted by her step-father. The minute Lorna caught Eileen's eye, hand in hand with her companion, she crossed the floor towards them. Once again Lorna was dressed in red; a bright figure-hugging velvet creation that left nothing to the imagination, and very little room for walking. Eileen guessed that the dress was every bit as expensive as her own. She detected a hint of surprise in Lorna's eyes as they scanned her from head to toe and was pleased to be so elegantly attired. She was also glad that Johnny had insisted after all that she buy new silver-coloured dance shoes and matching purse to complement the dress to its best advantage. She felt every bit as confident as Lorna looked.

'Hello, Eileen, it's lovely to see you again.' Lorna's smile deepened as she turned her attention to Johnny, giving him a brief kiss on the cheek. 'Hello, Johnny.

What do you think? We are seated beside each other at the dinner table.'

Johnny's grin was wide as he chided her, 'Now I wonder how that came about, eh?' With a laugh, he turned and confided in Eileen, 'Lorna was in charge of the place names.'

Ignoring the kiss, Eileen smiled and greeted Lorna and James, her chaperone. It crossed Eileen's mind that Lorna's mother must be very sure of her husband to agree to his squiring his beautiful step-daughter about. How come Lorna had no special boyfriend? Was she too choosy? Eileen was also asking herself why she felt uneasy in Lorna's company. Actually, she would have much preferred to sit with Margaret Patterson. Even if her husband George was a bit of a wolf, at least he seemed harmless enough. Eileen did not for one moment regard Lorna as harmless. There was something about this girl that she did not like. Was she jealous of her striking good looks. Or . . . and Eileen was inclined to think that this reason was more likely, was it because Lorna openly flirted with Johnny, and seemed to enjoy watching Eileen, tongue in cheek, to see how she was reacting to her advances? Did she enjoy playing cat and mouse games with people?

The meal was delicious and the service was excellent. James was the ideal companion and he kept Eileen and the matronly lady on his left-hand side, amused between courses. Across the table, Lorna was also entertaining Johnny, with whispered remarks, obviously meant for his ears only. Soon the tables were cleared and pushed to one side along the walls and the quintet, who had set up their instruments on the raised dais at the top of the room while the meal was in progress, started off the dancing with a waltz. To Eileen's dismay, James turned to her.

'The waltz is the one dance I pride myself on, so may I have the pleasure of the first dance, please?' he asked.

Eileen glanced uneasily at Johnny. Would he agree to

her dancing the first dance with this handsome man? Observing her glance at her husband, James hastened to add, 'That is of course if Johnny doesn't mind? Johnny?'

He broke off his conversation with Lorna, and raised an inquiring eyebrow. To Eileen's great surprise, at the repeated request he waved them off with a smile and a nod.

James had not exaggerated when he said that he could waltz. He twirled Eileen in and out of the steps like a professional ballroom dancer; weaving in and out of the less adept dancers with grace and poise. Eileen gave herself up to the joy of the music and they danced as one. As the music drew to a close, James bowed deeply before her, with old world charm.

'Thank you, my dear. I enjoyed that very much, indeed. May I have another waltz later?'

'I enjoyed it too, and of course you may have as many waltzes as you like, James.'

They found that Johnny and Lorna had retired to more comfortable seats in a small foyer, just outside the main banquet room. They had obviously not danced and were sitting close together, deep in conversation. What on earth were they finding to talk about? As Eileen and James approached the table, Lorna threw back her head and laughed aloud at something Johnny had said. Even white teeth gleamed and dark eyes caressed his face. Eileen was aware that the laughter and the flirtatious look were all part of an act, put on for her benefit. Even Johnny seemed a mite perplexed at Lorna's delighted response to whatever he had just said. Once again Eileen noticed just how much they complemented each other. Dark tresses against bright red. They certainly made a striking pair.

Becoming aware of their presence, Johnny jumped to his feet. 'That was quick.' He smiled. 'What would you like to drink, love?'

'I'll have a Tom Collins, please.'

Lorna asked for a gin and tonic, and James and Johnny headed for the bar. Lorna left the double seat by the window that she had shared with Johnny, and joined Eileen at the other side of the table.

'You are a very lucky girl, Eileen. Johnny Cleary is one hell of a guy.'

'Tell me something I don't already know,' she retorted.

Mouth agape, Lorna gazed at her. 'Did I say something to offend you, dear?' she asked, looking bewildered.

Ashamed at herself, Eileen apologized. 'I'm sorry, it's just that you were stating the obvious.' Afraid of letting her tongue run away with her, and saying something that she might later regret, she excused herself. 'Will you excuse me, please, Lorna? I must go and powder my nose.'

The cloakroom was packed; the women all vying for a position in front of the mirrors. Eileen locked herself in a cubicle and took stock of her reaction to Lorna. Was she just being silly, or was Lorna making a play for Johnny and wanted her to know it? Well, if war had been declared, Eileen was more than ready. No one was going to steal Johnny from under her nose. Not without one hell of a fight.

When she left the cubicle, the cloakroom was quite empty. Eileen washed her hands and paused in front of the mirror to powder her nose and renew her lipstick. Margaret Patterson entered the cloakroom and joined her.

'I'm glad that I'm having a bit of a respite tonight, while Lorna is making a pass at your Johnny.' Margaret's voice was low, to keep their conversation private. 'Don't give her an inch or she'll think she's a ruler,' she warned. 'You know, it's only because Johnny has been promoted that she is making a play for him. Remember, Eileen, I've been through it all! She can cause havoc to a marriage, so be on your guard against her. That vamp will try and come between you and Johnny! She will cause all kinds of unrest, if you let her.'

Eileen digested these words. She remembered that at the last dinner here a few weeks ago, she had pitied Margaret Patterson; had thought her a silly woman who was imagining that Lorna was making a play for George. It had appeared to her then, that George was doing all the chasing. Had she been wrong? Was George seeking Lorna out that night because she had been flattering his ego, but now had grown tired of her conquest? Eileen forced herself to laugh and appear carefree. 'Oh, I'm not afraid of any competition from the likes of Lorna Pollock,' she assured Margaret.

Margaret examined the beautiful face reflected beside her own homely countenance in the mirror and sighed. The dark auburn hair caught the light and glowed with health and vitality. The creamy skin was flawless, and wide-spaced eyes returned her look from between long dark curly lashes. 'No,' she agreed. 'You probably have no need to fear any woman, especially as Johnny is so besotted by you. Nevertheless, love, be on your guard . . . even the best husband in the world can be flattered by the attentions of a beautiful woman, and Lorna certainly knows just how to go about it. She is the most capable woman I know, but all the men in the office think she is an innocent little thing.'

Knowing that Margaret meant well, Eileen said softly, 'I'll bear your warning in mind.'

Keeping the smile on her face, she left the cloakroom with Margaret, and they walked towards the banqueting room together. In the foyer, before leaving her, and with a wrathful glance towards the table occupied by Lorna, Margaret repeated her warning, 'Remember what I said, Eileen.'

Eileen assured her that indeed she would. She had been dismayed to learn that it was apparently obvious to all, that Lorna was making a play for Johnny. It was thus reasonable for her to suppose that Lorna was paying Johnny a lot of attention at work as well. Just how far was she succeeding? For instance ... normally Johnny would never have waved her on to the dance floor to dance with another man, without a backward glance. A tall handsome man, at that! Even if he was old enough to be her father. And Johnny and Lorna had been sitting very close together when she and James had joined them after the dance ... Eileen gave her head a little shake to clear it. What on earth was she thinking about? Was this not the very attitude she dreaded Johnny taking up? She should be glad that her husband was not watching her like a hawk. When she arrived back at the table, she remained standing and addressed her husband.

'Shall we dance, Johnny? It's a slow foxtrot.'

He rose to he feet at once, excusing himself to the others, and taking her by the hand, led her out and on to the dance floor. They danced in silence for some moments and then Eileen asked, 'Does Lorna not have a steady boyfriend?'

'Not at the moment. She says that men all get the wrong idea about her. They think that she's a bit of a girl.'

'I wonder why?' Eileen's voice was dry.

Johnny pushed her gently away from him and gazed down into her eyes. 'You don't like Lorna!' he exclaimed, in surprise.

'Am I supposed to?'

'No. But tell me, why don't you like her? She was just saying that she hopes you and she can become close friends.' Johnny sounded bewildered. 'She likes you!' he finished triumphantly.

'Well, she is certainly not my cup of tea, and I am very thankful I don't have to see much of her! I'm afraid I don't find her as intriguing as you do.' Johnny once more pushed her away from him so that he could see her expression. Eileen smiled sweetly up at him. A fair imitation of the smiles that Lorna had been bestowing on him all evening. She was pleased to note that he got the message. 'Do you think we could excuse ourselves and get away from them for a short while? You know, circulate a bit ... go over and have a chat with the Pattersons or some of your other friends? I don't like sitting out there on our own. It isn't very polite, ignoring all the others.'

'I suppose you're right, but Lorna won't be very pleased.'

'Johnny, it has nothing whatsoever to do with Lorna! Tell me something, are you afraid of offending her?'

'No, of course not!'

'Well then, bully for her! I have as much right to enjoy myself as she has,' Eileen said firmly. 'And I don't want to spend the entire evening in her company. Don't worry, leave it to me. I'll make our excuses.'

Johnny grimaced down at his wife. 'I've a confession to make. I've invited her and James to meet us here, in the cocktail bar, for a drink next Saturday night.' He sounded sheepish. He was aware that he should have discussed this with Eileen first. He had not meant to issue an invitation, but somehow it had just come out without his thinking.

'You've done what?' Eileen gasped.

'I know, I know!' Johnny sought to placate her. 'I should have asked you first. But somehow or other the invitation just slipped out. I'm sorry, love. really I am.'

Eileen hid her dismay. It was obvious to her that Lorna was indeed using all her wiles to hook Johnny. Well, it was up to Eileen to make sure that she didn't succeed.

As far as Eileen was concerned, the dinner dance was not as successful as the previous occasion. Everyone else seemed to think it was a wonderful night, and Eileen had to admit that if she and Johnny had been in the company of anyone other than Lorna, she might have agreed with them. True to her word, Eileen had made their excuses, saying they must circulate or Johnny's other friends would think them standoffish, sitting out here in the foyer all night. This had left them free to mingle and Eileen had received a nod of approval from Margaret Patterson when they joined her and George for a drink. However, at the beginning of the evening, Lorna had confessed to having two left feet and had asked Eileen if she would mind dancing the waltzes with James, who just loved to dance, she said. So every time a waltz was played, no matter whose company Eileen and Johnny were in, she swooped down on them, urging Eileen to partner James. He was all for it, and Johnny did not seem to mind, so Eileen gave in gracefully and every waltz was danced with James whilst Lorna entertained Johnny. To her dismay, as she and James circled the dance floor, Eileen found herself watching Johnny and Lorna, their heads close together in conversation. They had so much to say to each other! Johnny must be really impressed with Lorna. True he danced all the other dances with his wife. But still, Eileen felt apprehensive.

At the bottom of Rockmore Road, Sarah hesitated. She was a bundle of nerves. What kind of a reception would she receive from Mick? No! Almost wailing aloud in despair, she turned tail. She just could not face him! Greatly agitated, she quickly retraced her steps across the Falls Road and hurried down St James's Park again. Back in her own house she forced herself to relax. Standing in front of the hall mirror, she critically examined her face. She had too much make-up on. Mick would know at once that she was putting on a show for him. What if she failed to impress him anymore? She sighed as she examined her reflection. She looked old. The lines around her mouth and eyes seemed more pronounced than usual. Would Mick find her unattractive? Stop this nonsense, she warned herself. Whether he found her attractive or not, must not enter into it. After all, it was her husband and not some fancy man that she was meeting. She had to face him . . . find out if they could come to some arrangement whereby they could afford to keep Emma on at school. It would not be fair if she was the one to suffer most, because of their shenanigans. If only Mick would offer to come back home she would endeavour to put the past behind her and keep him happy, and perhaps everything, might just work out all right.

Emma was rebelling against the conduct of her parents. She was running out every night, and returning late. She was refusing to tell her mother where she was going, or who she was with. Sarah knew that her words of warning were falling on deaf ears, and feared that her disturbed young daughter might get into some kind of mischief. Mick was needed at home; Emma needed his restraining hand. But would he offer to come back? Sarah could never ask him to return. After her antics with Gerry Docherty? The very idea that she had lain naked in bed with Gerry now made her squirm with repugnance. No . . . she would die of shame if anyone should ever find out. What if Mick was to question her about Gerry? Why, if she told him the truth, he would surely disown her, and that she could not bear. If she lied to Mick, he would know right away and would read more into her actions with Gerry than had really taken place. She was in a fix. She realized now just how foolish she had been, but was it too late to win back her husband?

Taking a handkerchief from her pocket, she carefully wiped the lipstick from her mouth, and also the slight touch of rouge with which she had shadowed her cheeks. Her hair was freshly shampooed and soft about her face the way Mick liked it. Gathering it back, she secured it with a hair slide at the back of her neck. There, now he would not be able to scoff her efforts to appear alluring. Now she looked dowdy. But . . . did she want to look dowdy? It was the lesser of two evils. She could not afford to appear to be grovelling. What if Mick had met and was now interested in another woman? The chances

398

were that he had. A handsome man like Mick? With one last despairing glance at her reflection, Sarah once more headed for the door. No matter what the result may be, she had to go up and see Mick. She really had no other choice in the matter.

Reaching the corner, she quite literally raced across the Falls Road and up Rockmore Road, afraid that if she delayed any longer she would once more renege. This was something that had to be done, and the sooner she got it over with, the better! Outside Eileen's door Sarah once more braced herself. Taking a deep breath she raised her hand and lifted the knocker. She knocked louder than she had intended and stood aghast as the sound echoed on the still night air. To her dismay, she could also hear it reverberate inside the house. Oh, please don't let the children awaken, she prayed silently.

Mick was in the scullery making himself a cup of tea when he heard the knock on the door. That's someone in a hurry, he thought. It was loud enough to waken the dead, no matter about sleeping children. An angry scowl puckered his face and he paused to listen at the foot of the stairs before going to answer the knock. All was quiet. Nevertheless he pulled the front door open abruptly, words of rebuff on his lips that remained unuttered. To say that he was surprised to see his wife standing on the doorstep would be putting it mildly.

They gazed at each other for some seconds in silence, and then Sarah cried out in exasperation, 'Can I come in for a minute, please?'

Silently Mick stepped aside. Passing him, Sarah entered the hall and headed for the kitchen. Mick quietly closed the door and slowly followed her down the hall. He was warning himself to be careful; not take anything for granted. In the kitchen she turned to face him.

'I'm glad I didn't waken the kids. I didn't mean to knock so loud.' Mick nodded at her apology but remained silent. Sarah swallowed the lump in her throat.

Her husband was obviously not going to make it easy for her. 'I suppose you're wondering why I'm here?' she mumbled through trembling lips.

'The thought had crossed my mind.' His voice was dry, his expression inscrutable.

'I want to talk to you about Emma. Is there any way we can afford to keep her on at school?' Sarah bit on her bottom lip in vexation. She had meant to lead the conversation around to Emma gradually. Now it looked as if that was all she cared about. But wasn't that the only reason she was here? Confused at the turn her thoughts were taking, she hurried on, 'She is doing so well at school . . . at least she was, until you left. Now she is running out every night, God only knows where. She will tell me nothing. Where she goes or who she's with.'

Mick heard her out in silence. Disappointment was a hard knot in his chest. Well, you surely didn't think she had come looking for you, did you? Oh, yes, you did! You fool, you stupid vain fool, he chastized himself.

His face gave away nothing of his thoughts. 'I've the tea pot on the boil. Take off your coat and sit down.'

Sarah removed her coat with trembling hands and folded it over the back of a chair. She now regretted coming here. Mick was so distant she didn't think she would get much joy out of him. She also regretted removing her make-up and tying her hair back. Mick looked so handsome. She felt old and plain. Although he was six years her senior, looking at them together now, no one would guess it. He had always suited that shade of blue. Had he worn it to impress her? Had Eileen told him that she was coming? Surely some other woman had her eye on him? He had certainly not been over the moon to see her. Far from it! However, she had not expected him to fall into her arms. Then why was she so disappointed? It was Emma's plight that had brought her here. She must bear that in mind. Her own personal feelings must not enter into it. She accepted the cup of tea Mick eventually brought to her, but refused any of the biscuits he offered, afraid that she would choke on them, she was so filled with emotion.

His wife was sitting on the settee but Mick avoided the seat beside her and sat on one of the armchairs opposite. He examined Sarah; the pale face and hair scraped back behind her head told him a lot. She couldn't care less just what he thought of her. Otherwise, she would have titivated herself up a bit. He remembered the morning that he had lain in bed and listened to her prepare to go to Ballycastle with Gerry Docherty. That morning, she had hummed and sometimes burst into song as she got ready for her outing. And she had looked ravishing as she crossed the street to Gerry's car. He remembered the new black skirt with the split up the back; the way her long slim legs were exposed when she walked. Her hair had been loose and flowing . . . and all this had been in Gerry's honour. It was very obvious to Mick that it was money, or rather the lack of it, that had brought his wife up here tonight! He must bear this in mind and then he would not be disappointed. The silence was deafening as they sipped their tea.

At last Mick broke it. 'Tell me, Sarah . . . just what do you really expect from me?'

'I just want to know where I stand. I'd hate Emma to suffer because we can't get on together. It wouldn't be fair to her, Mick.'

'You should have thought of that before you went gallivanting off to Ballycastle with your fancy man!' he snorted.

For a second hurt flitted across Sarah's face. How could Mick be so cruel? He was putting all the blame on her. She quickly gained control of her emotions. The expression had been so fleeting that Mick thought he had imagined it. Sarah's head rose in the air and her nostrils flared with disdain.

'Where I went, or who I went with, doesn't enter into

it, Mick. We were already at each other's throats long before I went to Ballycastle. Remember that! And it's not Emma's fault. None of this is Emma's fault. We're the ones to blame, not her. So why should she be the one to suffer?'

Ashamed at himself, Mick said, 'You're right, Sarah. Emma mustn't suffer because of us. I'll do all I can to help out, but you must understand . . . when I get a flat . . . and I hope to get one soon . . . I'll have two homes to support out of one wage packet. Of course I'll pay the mortgage and I'll help out all I can, but it won't be all that much. Remember, Sarah, I've got to live as well.'

'Every little helps, Mick. I just don't want Emma's education to suffer. I intend to get a job, but it might take some time. If I can't get into the weaving shop, I'll have . . .'

Appalled, he interrupted her. 'Ah, Sarah, you can't go back into the mill. Why, it would kill you at your age.'

She smiled slightly. 'As you well know, Mick, the only other thing I am capable of is cleaning, and there's not much money at that. I really don't mind going back to the mill, as long as Emma gets her chance. Besides, I'm not all that old. I'm sure I could still manage three looms. If I can get started in the Blackstaff or the Falls Flax, I'll be all right. There will be more money to be earned at the weaving than cleaning. However, I can understand that you will need to support yourself. I'm not thinking straight or I would have realized that.'

While she mouthed these words, her mind kept repeating: What about Maisie? Will you not be moving in with Maisie? But pride would not let her voice this awful thought. 'If you could help out for a while, Mick, I would be grateful.' She rose to her feet and carefully set the cup and saucer on the table, glad that her hand was steady enough now to prevent them rattling about. 'I'll have to go now. Sorry I butted in on your privacy.'

Mick blocked her way to the door. They were so close

her perfume wafted about him and the urge to hold her close was overwhelming. It had been so long since he had held her and he ached for the want of her. Again he warned himself to tread carefully, not to make a fool of himself. Sarah had certainly given him no indication whatsoever, that she might still care a little for him. In spite of all the resolutions he had made to himself not to inquire about Gerry Docherty's intentions, he blurted out, 'What about Gerry Docherty? Has he not offered to help out?'

It was on the tip of Sarah's tongue to spill the beans and get it all off her chest, but she caught herself in the nick of time. Pride would not let her admit that she had made a fool of herself. If Mick had shown more compassion, she might have thrown herself against his chest and confessed that she wanted nothing more to do with Gerry, but her husband was so distant, she felt like she was talking to a complete stranger. The awareness of him in the confined space was filling her with pain. She longed to be in a position to put her head against this chest and weep all down his nice blue shirt, sure of his love and understanding. However, she had forfeited all right to that. Afraid of the strong emotions that surged through her, she spoke abruptly, 'I don't know anything of Gerry's plans. He has been down in Dublin on business, but he's due back in Belfast tomorrow.'

Mick mulled over these words silently. He had been aware that Gerry had left for Dublin early on the Tuesday morning of Easter Week. Fool that he was, Mick had dared to hope that Sarah had sent the man packing. But no . . . Gerry was due back tomorrow. Just what had they both in mind? Would Gerry ask Sarah to go and live with him? Would she do so? If she did, would Mick ever be able to go back and live in the house, so full of memories, alone with Emma? Undecided, he watched Sarah shrug into her coat and followed her down the hall in silence. There were questions that he wanted to ask, but he was afraid to voice them. The answers would surely kill off any hopes he had of a reconciliation. At the door, he came to a decision. He would ask Sarah if she would like him to return to the house; thrash out their differences under their own roof. That way she would not have to commit herself right away. She would have all the time in the world to think about it. Perhaps he might even persuade her to give him another chance to see whether or not they could make a go of it. Before he could open his mouth, Sarah spoke.

'Sorry for disturbing you, Mick.'

'Sarah, I've been thinking,' he said hesitantly.

Pride kept Sarah's head high, her voice light as she lied, 'Don't you worry yourself, Mick. These problems are of my own making. I'm sure that Gerry and I will be able to work something out between us. Good night.'

Without a backward glance she closed the gate behind her and strode off down the street, her head high, her step firm. Mick watched her for some moments, tears in his eyes. He was aware that he had handled the meeting all wrong. If only Sarah had given him an opening, perhaps they could have come to an understanding. So great was his frustration, he thumped his fist against the wall, causing pain to shoot up his arm. Ah, to hell with it! There was no way he was going to try and compete with the likes of Gerry Docherty . . . a younger man, with plenty of money. The way Sarah felt towards him at the moment, he didn't stand a chance. He had waited long enough for his wife to show that she still had some feelings towards him. Now it was time to try and shape some sort of a future for himself. His thoughts turned to Maisie O'Hara. Many a time this past few weeks, in his great loneliness, he had longed to seek Maisie out to bask in the warmth of her friendship, but he had deliberately refrained. He wanted no complications should Sarah hold out an olive branch. Once he started seeing Maisie that would herald the beginning of the end of his marriage. He had unknowingly hurt Maisie in the past but he would never deliberately hurt her now. First, he must see Emma; find out if he could be of any assistance to her. Since leaving the house, he had already phoned Emma at school a few times, incurring the displeasure of Sister Bridget, in the process. He had begged Emma to meet him. His young daughter had been abrupt with him, and had refused to meet him in town. There was only one thing for it, he would have to go to the house. He agreed with Sarah: it was wrong that Emma should be the one to suffer because of their misconduct.

At the bottom of the street Sarah turned up the Falls Road. She could not bear the thought of spending yet another evening alone in that big empty house. Tears blinded her as she recalled how handsome Mick had looked. Was he seeing Maisie? Even if he wasn't, he would have no bother getting some other woman to care for him. What was going to become of her? Gerry had sent her a postcard saying he would be in Belfast for the weekend and asking her to meet him for a heart to heart talk. She did not want to see him, but what other choice had she? Mick had obviously washed his hands of her. If she encouraged Gerry, he might just offer some financial arrangement by which Emma could be kept on at school. Her future must be the first priority. If Gerry proved to be serious about her, maybe Sarah could, given time, learn to care for him. After all, she had considered herself in love with him many moons ago, and less than two weeks earlier she had been attracted enough to get into bed with him. But what about Mick? Was he really lost to her? In spite of the long tiring walk, Sarah found that sleep was still hard to come by that night. After a restless night she awoke bleary eyed and tired the next morning.

On the journey home from the dance, Eileen's thoughts

turned to her father. Had her mother visited him as she'd said she would? Had they come to some kind of agreement? Tentatively, she confessed to Johnny that she had arranged for her mother to come to their house tonight to see her father. To her dismay he rounded on her in anger.

'You did what? Are you crazy? Isn't this the very reason that Mick will not come and live with us?'

Regretting her decision to confide in Johnny, Eileen cried defensively, 'Mam really needed to talk to him! I thought that if she came to our house when we were out they would have some privacy to sort things out between them.'

'Well, at least you should have warned Mick of her visit! He will be convinced that we are conniving to get them back together again.'

'That's not a bad idea! I'd do anything . . . if I thought it stood a chance of helping them see sense.'

'Eileen, when a marriage flounders, it is only the two people involved that know all the ins and outs of it. They alone can put it back together again, nobody else! Do you not think that maybe your father has had enough? I personally think he is just waiting a reasonable length of time before he starts seeing Maisie O'Hara. She is a fine-looking woman, and it is obvious that she cares for him.'

Eileen's eyes closed with dismay at the very idea. 'You don't really think that, surely?'

'Why not? Eh, Eileen? Sarah has made no attempt so far to contact Mick. If she doesn't want him, why should he hang about waiting for her? Eh?'

'I think you're wrong. I think they will come together again,' Eileen said stubbornly.

With a shrug Johnny further showed his disapproval by withdrawing to his side of the taxi in a huff. He was angry at his wife for setting up a meeting without his father-in-law's knowledge. Needing some warmth and reassurance, Eileen threw him a pleading glance and tentatively lessened the space between them. Johnny made no move to hold her and she·retreated in hurt silence. What news would be awaiting them when they got home? Hopefully, her mother would still be there and her dad would accompany her home. Then she would have the satisfaction of seeing Johnny eat his words.

The taxi drew up to the door and almost before it had stopped, Eileen hurried from it, incurring a reprimand from her husband. Impatiently tapping her foot she waited while he paid the taxi driver. She refrained from knocking in case her father had retired for the night, as he had said he might do. A slight smile on his face, Johnny deliberately kept her waiting further while he slowly rummaged through his pockets for the key to the door.

Once inside the house, it was obvious that Mick had gone to bed. The bottom of the house was in complete darkness. In the kitchen Eileen turned a worried look on Johnny. 'What do you think happened?'

'God knows! Perhaps your mother didn't come. Or maybe they have agreed to differ. We shall probably hear all about it in the morning. Now, let's go to bed.'

At breakfast next morning, Eileen waited in vain for some sign that her mother had visited the house the night before, and all was well. She was disappointed. Her father was quieter than usual, but affable enough. Although Eileen gave him a few openings he was not forthcoming.

'Did everything go all right last night, Dad?' she inquired softly.

'Yes, why wouldn't it?'

'The kids behaved themselves, then?'

'Of course! Don't they always? They were in bed before eight.'

'Did you stay up very late?'

'Till about eleven.'

Eileen hedged about some more but was not enlight-ened by her father and fell silent in despair. She would just have to contain herself until she saw her mother. She admitted to herself that it did not look very promising. If her mother had visited him the night before, and they had overcome their differences, surely her dad would be unable to hide his delight? In fact, why should he even try to? No, it definitely didn't look good. It appeared that Johnny was right and would not have to eat his words after all.

Sarah's visit had unsettled Mick and he had not slept very well. Now Eileen's not so subtle questions made him aware that his wife's visit the night before had been planned. Why hadn't Eileen at least warned him? If she had, then he would have been prepared and things might have worked out differently. He refrained from chastising his daughter. What good would it do? Why couldn't they all mind their own business, and let him get on with his? Changing the subject, he inquired after her evening.

'Now that the third degree is finished, Eileen, tell me about your night out! What was the meal like?'

'It was lovely, Dad. Even better than the last time . . . if that was possible.' Eileen was aware that her father was deliberately being evasive, but she let him get away with it and went on to describe in detail the events of last night. It was no use flogging a dead horse. She would just have to contain her curiosity until she saw her mother.

On the way home from church the next morning, Sarah fell into step with Maggie. She had scoured the church for a sign of Mick but in vain. He had probably gone down to St Paul's to avoid running into her. She brought her attention back to her mother.

'Sorry, Mam. What's that you said?'

'I said Gerry Docherty's car has just turned down into our street,' Maggie repeated dryly.

'Oh, has it?'

They rounded the corner and Maggie gestured down the street to where Gerry was removing a suitcase from the boot of his car. Looking up he saw them and waved a hand in acknowledgement, hesitating, before entering his son's driveway.

Sarah turned a pleading look on Maggie. 'Mam, will you come in with me for a while? I need to gather my wits about me before I face Gerry. He is sure to see you come in, and he won't come over while you are with me.'

Maggie followed her daughter around to the back of the house and watched her unlock the door in silence. Sarah had lost weight! She was getting quite gaunt-looking. Once inside Maggie sat down at the kitchen table and motioned for her daughter to do likewise.

Sarah looked at her mother in bewilderment. 'Would you not like to go into the living room, Mam? We would be more comfortable in there.'

'Let's just sit here for a few minutes, Sarah.' Slowly she sat down and faced her mother across the kitchen table. When she was settled, Maggie addressed her. 'I've been meaning to speak to you, and now is as good a time as any, I suppose.'

At her tone of voice, Sarah grimaced. 'Mam, believe me, I'm in no mood for another sermon.'

'I don't intend preaching to you. However, I would like you to answer a few questions. Just bear in mind that I am not just being inquisitive, Sarah. Hmm?'

Sarah eyed her mother in silence for some moments, then said, 'All right, fire away.'

'You are still a young woman, Sarah, just what do you intend doing with the rest of your life?'

Sarah sighed, but answered readily enough, 'To tell you the truth, Mam, I haven't a clue. I just don't want Emma to suffer because of me and Mick. She is taking

409

all this very badly and I'm afraid I won't be able to keep her on at school. If that happens, I don't know what will become of her. You know that she's near dead to become a teacher, and she has the ability! It would be a shame if she couldn't complete her studies.'

'Tell me . . . where does Gerry Docherty come into all this?' Maggie's voice was quiet but her eyes were alert as she studied Sarah's face.

'Mam, I know you don't approve of me seeing Gerry, but if I need him to keep Emma on at school,' Sarah's shoulders rose in an eloquent gesture, 'then I'll do what has to be done, Mam, no matter what anybody thinks. I owe that much to Emma.'

'What about Mick? Remember that Emma is his daughter! Does he not have any say in her future?'

'Apparently not.'

'I suggest that you see him and find out how he feels about all this,' Maggie insisted.

'I saw him last night.' Sarah's voice was becoming cool, she did not want to discuss her meeting with Mick with her mother. The hurt still rankled.

'You saw Mick last night?' Surprise made Maggie's voice shrill.

Sarah smiled grimly. 'Yes, I found out that he was baby-sitting for Eileen, so I dandered up and had a word with him.' Sarah smiled inwardly at the idea of her dander. She should have said, I scurried up.

'What did he have to say about Emma?'

'He's talking about getting a flat of his own. If he does, he will have two places to keep up, and it is understandable that he will not be able to help financially.'

'Just what exactly did Mick say, Sarah?'

'I told you! He said that he will help out, you know, pay the mortgage, but other than that, he would not be able to afford a lot.'

'Mick said that?'

'Not in so many words, but that's what he meant,' Sarah assured her.

Maggie frowned. She found it hard to believe that Mick could act so callously. 'Don't you want him back?' she queried.

'That's beside the point, Mam. He has made a new life for himself now, and that's that!'

Maggie sat silent, gazing down at her hands clasped on the table in front of her for so long Sarah felt compelled to prompt her. 'Mam . . . what did you want to talk to me about?'

Maggie raised her head and her eyes held Sarah's for some seconds, seeking reassurance that she was doing the right thing. As if coming to a decision, she straightened up in the chair and asked, 'Do you remember anything about my mother, your Grannie Pierce?'

Sarah frowned with bewilderment. What on earth was her mother on about? She knew rightly that Sarah had never met her Grannie Pierce. Hadn't Maggie's mother disowned her when she married Sarah's father, a Roman Catholic? Sarah decided to humour her mother.

'I don't remember Grannie at all. I do, however, remember that when I was fourteen you landed me down to an interview for a job in Robinson Cleaver's. The girl who interviewed us turned out to be a friend of yours. She told you that me grannie had remarried and emigrated to New Zealand. If I remember correctly, you were awfully upset about it at the time?' Sarah smiled at the memory. Her mother upset? She had been devastated! Sarah had had to run to keep up with her on the trip round to the tram stop, such was her anguish.

Maggie nodded. Even after all this time, she could recall that feeling of desolation very clearly. 'I remember it as if it were only yesterday,' she agreed. 'From that day to this I have had no contact whatsoever with my mother. Not even a postcard to let me know that she was still alive. As for the man that she married . . . I never

411

met him at all. Still, it seems that blood is thicker than water. My parents were well off. When my father died, Mother inherited everything. My parents had disowned William and me years earlier, when we went against their wishes. Me for marrying Paul Mason, and William for not following Father into politics.'

'Well, some months ago I received a letter from a firm of solicitors in Londonderry. It informed me that my mother had died ten years ago. It appears that her will was quite intricate. Her second husband was much younger than her. When Mother died, this man returned to live in Londonderry, where he died only last year. To cut a long story short, all Mother's money was tied up in property. Her second husband had the right to live in one of the houses Mother owned, and the income, rents etc from the other properties, during his lifetime. On his death, all the property was to be sold and the money divided between your Uncle William and me.'

Mouth slightly agape, Sarah heard her mother out in silence. Then she gasped in anticipation. 'How much is it?'

'Twenty thousand pounds each.'

'Twenty thousand each? That's a fortune, so it is!' Sarah whispered in awe.

'I have not yet received the money ... there have been some last-minute holdups. Normally, I would not mention this to you until it was all signed, sealed and delivered. Still, the solicitors assure me the money is as good as in the bank.' Maggie leant forward and stressed, 'I am telling you this so that you will not do anything foolhardy. Two thousand pounds would give you a bit of independence, wouldn't it?' She leant back and continued, 'I have talked this over with Barney and that is how much I intend to give you and Bernard, two thousand pounds each and to each of my grandchildren, I will give one thousand pounds.'

To Maggie's surprise, Sarah burst into tears. Concerned, Maggie left her chair and going to her daughter, held her close. 'There, there, now. You are supposed to be happy,' she chided.

Wiping her eyes with the handkerchief Maggie thrust at her, Sarah blew her nose and confessed, 'It's the relief. Ah, Mam, you have just taken a heck of a weight off my mind. You will never know just how much this means to me. Now I can send Gerry Docherty packing, if I have a mind to.'

'Have you a mind to, Sarah?' Maggie sounded hopeful.

'I don't know, Mam. You see . . . I can't picture myself living on my own for the rest of my life. This past couple of months have been awful for me. I just don't know what to do for the best.'

Maggie gazed at her daughter in amazement. 'What about Mick Ross? Why not take him back? Or do you honestly prefer Gerry Docherty?'

'Mam, that is neither here nor there. You seem to think that all I have to do is snap my fingers and Mick will come running back to me. But it's not like that! He has apparently made a new life for himself. He will never come back here to live. And why should he after the way I have behaved? To be truthful, I don't blame him! I've been a real bitch, so I have. As for Gerry, only time will tell. But at least I don't have to throw myself at him. I can bide my time now.' Sarah hugged Maggie close. 'Thanks, Mam. Thanks for giving me some independence. It will have a great bearing on my future.'

Maggie placed her hands on Sarah's shoulders, and her voice held a plea. 'Listen, Sarah, I still think Mick would return if you were to ask him. Why don't you? Eh? At least give him a chance to say no. Don't let pride stand between you and a chance of happiness.'

'Mam, I couldn't! You don't understand. It's not just pride.' Sarah could not meet Maggie's eyes, such was

413

her shame. There was certainly no way that she could ever confess to her mother about her fling with Gerry Docherty. 'Don't ask me why, Mam, but believe me . . . I honestly can't ask him to come back. Too much water has passed under the bridge for a reconciliation.'

With a sigh, Maggie headed for the door. 'I think you are being very foolish. Give some consideration to what I've just said. I really do think that Mick would come running, if you gave him even the slightest hint that he would be welcome.'

Sadly Sarah shook her head. Her mother didn't understand. She would never have the courage to confess her capers to Mick, so how could she ask him to come home?

Sarah had been right in the assumption that Mick wanted to avoid her at church. He went down to St Paul's that morning, hoping that he would not run into Maisie, whom he knew went there every Sunday, although in bygone days she had gone to an early Mass. Not wanting to take any chances, he stood at the back of the church so that he could make a hasty exit should he see her. During the sermon, he let his mind wander over the previous evening. Imagine him being stupid enough to think that Sarah might have come to Eileen's last night to ask him to return home. He should have had more sense! Laying himself open to so much torment. Thank God Sarah had been unaware of the true state of his feelings. One thing that he didn't want was her pity. He had been unable to sleep all night. Wondering what if he had said this, or done that, would things have worked out differently? By the way Eileen had talked at breakfast, he guessed that they all knew that Sarah only wanted to see him to ensure that Emma's education was not interrupted. He would go up to Sarah's afterwards and see if he could talk some sense into his daughter. From what Sarah had said, Emma was not studying for her exams. Last night he had thought long and hard about her. If he stayed in his present lodgings, he would be able to afford to see her through college. Once she passed her exams, she would be well qualified to get a good job, and he would be free to look for a flat. Would he be able to bear to continue to live in the same house as Rosie McCann, for God knows how long? The thought of it depressed him, but he would just have to!

Turning the corner of St James's Park, he hesitated a moment when he saw Gerry Docherty's car parked outside Danny's house. He dithered for a while then, squaring his shoulders, continued down the street. What did it matter if Gerry was with Sarah? The idea of her with another man was something he would have to get used to. He went around to the back door and was surprised to find it locked. Using his own key, he quietly entered the house. The smell of the Sunday joint filled the air, and pots containing cabbage and potatoes bubbled on a low light on the stove. So Sarah can't be far away, he thought. Then another thought brought him to a standstill. What if Gerry and Sarah were up in the bedroom? That would explain the locked door. Abruptly, he turned to leave the house. The idea of finding them in a compromising position filled him with disgust. What about your worldly acceptance that you would have to get used to Sarah living with another man? he reminded himself. Well, he would at least take a look downstairs, and if she was not about, he would go away without looking any further. To his great relief he found Sarah in the living room seated in one of the armchairs, her feet up on a stool, fast asleep.

For some seconds he stood looking down on the woman he loved above all others. He recalled how she had looked twenty-eight years ago when he had first met her. Slim of body, with wonderful chestnut hair and bright green eyes. They had met at a gig in a barn of a hall down in Hastings Street. He had asked her to dance with him, and had admired the flimsy green dress that made her eyes shine like emeralds. He would never forget that first encounter. He was completely bowled over by her beauty. By the end of the gig he was head over heels in love with her. Later, when he had discovered that she was barely seventeen, he had tried to break off with her; put her out of his life and mind. But Sarah was having none of that. Then one night, to his great shame, he had taken her, and the result had been a pregnancy.

He came to with a start when he realized that Sarah was awake and watching him through hooded eyes. Embarrassed, he retreated a few steps and said, 'I'm sorry. I didn't mean to disturb you. I've come to have a wee word with Emma and try to talk some sense into her.'

Slowly, Sarah sat up straight in the chair. She was trying to comprehend the expression on Mick's face before he became aware that she was awake, but it had been all too fleeting.

'I didn't hear you come in, Mick.' She smiled wryly. 'I didn't sleep very well last night and I was having forty winks before dinner. Emma's not here at the moment, but she will be back soon for her dinner. She's over seeing Kate Rafferty. She bought some matinee coats for the baby yesterday. I suppose you know Kate is expecting a baby soon?'

'Yes, Eileen did mention it. I hope everything goes all right for her.'

Tentatively, Sarah asked, 'Will you stay for dinner, Mick? There's more than enough for all of us.'

He shook his head. 'Sorry, but I can't. Eileen will be expecting me back at her place for dinner.' A great sadness was encompassing him. Sarah looked so different from the night before. Her hair was a loose soft chestnut cloud about her face and in spite of a bad night her eyes were a clear sparkling green. Rouge shadowed her high cheekbones, and there was the remains of pale pink lipstick on her mouth. Had Gerry kissed the rest of it off? he wondered. She looked contented sitting there; as if a weight had been lifted off her mind. All this must be due to Gerry's influence. His rival had succeeded where he had failed. It looked as if he had lost her forever.

'Mick, I'm sure that Eileen would understand. You could give her a ring.'

Sarah saw by the surprised look on Mick's face that he was puzzled by her persistence. Was she making a fool of herself? In spite of these misgivings, Sarah insisted. 'That would give you plenty of time to talk to Emma,' she urged. Inwardly she was asking herself why she wanted him to stay? Wasn't she just prolonging the agony? Maggie's promise of two thousand pounds had made a big difference to her outlook. She didn't need financial help from Mick any more . . . or from Gerry for that matter. Gerry had been at the back door earlier but she had ignored his knock. She had not made up her mind just how she was going to handle him and until she did, she preferred not to see him. She had better not delay too long. After all, did she not still need his companionship? Or was she just keeping her options open?

Emma's coming in the back door saved Mick from having to make the decision. His daughter hesitated when she saw him, then without a word of greeting went to the fireside and sat down, gazing at her feet in tight-lipped silence.

'Hello, Emma. Are you not going to speak to me, love?' he asked softly.

She was the only one of his daughters to resemble him. Unlike her sisters, she had inherited his thick straight black hair and deep blue eyes. Now eyes so like his own, flashed scorn at him. 'Why? Why should I? When was the last time you spoke to me? You don't care what becomes of me. Sure you don't. You just packed your bags and went, without so much as a goodbye.'

'Ah, now, Emma, that's not fair! You know rightly that

417

it wasn't entirely my fault that I left the house when I did. I had a lot on my mind. I wasn't thinking straight.'

'You could at least have said goodbye, so you could!'

Mick slowly approached his young daughter. He could see she was deeply hurt and it was all his fault. Primed for rejection, he was amazed when Emma suddenly rose from her chair and, hurling herself into his arms, buried her head against his chest and sobbed as if her heart would break.

'Dad, come home . . . please come home,' she spluttered through her tears. 'Don't you love me any more?'

'Of course I love you. You are very dear to me.' He pushed her gently away and gazed down at her. 'Now . . . you know that! Don't you?'

Emma gazed back at him from eyes like drenched violets. 'Was it because of her you left?' Her head jerked in Sarah's direction and Mick was aware that his wife cringed from the scorn in her daughter's voice.

Gently he cupped his daughter's tear-streaked face in his hands and gazed lovingly down at her. 'Go wash your face, love. I'm staying here for dinner, and then we must talk. You mustn't blame your mother, Emma. It wasn't all her fault either. We were both to blame. Go on, wash your face! We'll talk afterwards.'

Mick made the necessary phone call to Eileen to apologize for not being able to make it back for dinner. He resisted her tentative question as to where he was and said he would see her later on in the afternoon. Silently, he helped set the table and then assisted Sarah in the kitchen, and soon dinner was laid out on the table. As they worked side by side, Sarah tried to form sentences that would encourage Mick to offer to stay, but they remained unspoken; his silence an unbreachable wall between them. Mick, for his part, was trying to think of a way that he could be close to his daughter, without upsetting Sarah's plans for the future. The preparations for dinner were accomplished in continued silence.

During the meal Emma sat close to her father and Mick worried as to how he could be of help to her. It was obvious that so far as Emma was concerned, money did not enter into it. She only wanted him to come back and live at home, no matter what. But what about Sarah?

When dinner was finished and the dishes were washed and put away, they all retired to the living room.

Emma sat on the arm of Mick's chair, an arm around his shoulders. She smiled sadly. 'You know something, Dad? That's the first time I've really enjoyed my dinner in a long while. Everything has seemed tasteless since you left, so I hope you're going to stay.' Her voice was confident. She was sure the battle was over.

'It's not as easy as that, Emma. First of all . . .'

In a flash she was on her feet, ready for flight. 'I knew it! I knew you were having me on. You'd rather live over Beechmount, wouldn't you?'

'I'm not living over Beechmount, Emma. Whatever gave you that idea?'

'Oh, I heard them whispering! Nobody tells me anything around here. You'd think I was about seven years old. Everybody is sure you are living with Maisie O'Hara! Where are you staying, then?' she asked in bewilderment.

'That's neither here not there.' During this discourse Sarah and remained silent. Now Mick turned to her. 'Sarah . . . I've been thinking. If I forgot about a flat and stayed on in the lodgings I now live in, we could afford to keep Emma at school until she finishes her studies.'

'It's all right, Mick. I don't need any assistance now,' she assured him.

'You needn't worry about keeping me on at school,' Emma interrupted them. 'I have no intention of going back! I haven't been to school since before the Easter break.'

At these words both their heads swivelled towards her.

'I'm telling you the truth. I've no intention of going back to school, so I haven't! I'm going to get a job in Woolworths.'

'Don't be silly, Emma. You can't possibly work in Woolworths.' It was Sarah who gained control of her voice first. 'You can't let all that good education go to waste.'

Mick backed her up. 'Your mother is right, Emma. If you pass your exams you will be able to go on to college. Think of it! By September you could be at college, and one day you will be in a position to look for a teaching post. Isn't that what you've always wanted, love? You have just got to be sensible about this, Emma.'

'Sensible? With you two for parents, how could I be sensible? You're both driving me round the bend, so you are.' With these words she flounced from the room and they heard her thump up the stairs.

Mick's shoulders rose and fell in a gesture of defeat. 'I'm sorry, Sarah. I did my best. I don't know what else I can do.'

She eyed him forlornly. It was obvious to her that even for Emma's sake he had no intention of coming back home, or surely he would have made a bigger effort?

She sighed deeply. 'It's all right, Mick. Maybe I will be able to change her mind.'

'I will remain in digs, Sarah, and contribute all I can to her schooling.'

'That won't be necessary. I'll be able to manage.'

'I don't want you to go out to work, Sarah.'

'I won't have to go out to work after all. I'll be able to make my own arrangements now.'

A frown knotted Mick's thick brows, giving him a belligerent look. 'But last night you said . . .'

Sarah interrupted him. 'I know, Mick, but last night was different. Circumstances have changed since then. I'll be able to manage now.'

Anger coursed through Mick's whole body. Gripping

Sarah angrily, his fingers digging cruelly into the soft flesh of her arms, he shook her. 'It's that git across the street who's supplying the money, isn't it?' he ground out through clenched teeth.

'What's it to you? Last night you acted as if that git across the street, as you call him, should be helping out. I just don't understand you at all, Mick.'

Realizing that she spoke the truth, he slowly released his hold on her and turned away. With one last disdainful glance, he grabbed his coat and left the house.

'Mam! Go after him.' Sarah turned her head to see Emma hanging over the banister. She had obviously been eavesdropping. Her daughter's voice was fraught with urgency. 'If you let him go now, he'll never come back. Please, Mam. He will stay if you ask him.'

Sarah shook her head. 'He hates me!'

'He doesn't! Are you blind? He loves you! Go after him, Mam! Please! Go on.'

Sarah's reluctant feet were leading her out of the door and down the path. At the gate she stopped. Mick was almost at the top of the street. Forcing herself out through the gate, she stood on the middle of the pavement and shouted in a loud voice. 'Mick!' He showed no sign that he had heard her. Suddenly Sarah realized just what she was doing. She felt exposed, aware that, alerted by her shouts, Gerry and a lot of neighbours were probably watching from behind net curtains. She started to retreat but some instinct urged her on up the street. Suddenly convinced that Mick would be lost to her for good if she didn't hurry, she broke into a run.

'Mick! Hold on a minute, Mick,' she shouted again in an even louder voice.

This time her husband heard. He stopped and quickly swung round to face her. He couldn't believe his eyes. His proud Sarah out on the pavement in her apron and slippers, shouting her head off. And on a Sunday at that. They stared at each other for what seemed ages. Then, heart beating like a trip hammer, Mick slowly retraced his steps towards his wife. Sarah had stopped, and now waited with bated breath.

He stopped just short of her, and Mick could see that his wife was agitated. She was actually wringing her hands; twisting her apron into knots. 'Mick . . .' Her voice trailed off in embarrassment.

'Yes, Sarah? he prompted warily.

'I . . . I don't want you to go.' The words came out in a gush and her face was red.

She could see that Mick was flabbergasted and repeated lamely, 'I don't want you to go. Please, Mick?'

'Sarah . . . I can't just come back for a couple of days, to please you and Emma. I'm only human, you know.' His hands came up in despair. 'Can't you see the suffering I'm going through? Are you trying to break me completely, Sarah?'

She relaxed slightly at these words. It seemed that her mother and daughter just might be right after all. 'Listen, Mick. I know that I've been very foolish. When you hear what I've done . . . you might not want me, but will you at least come back to the house and talk about it?'

He turned her words over in his mind. He had to be sure that Sarah was sincere. 'What about Claire? She will always be between us, you know that.' He watched closely for her reaction.

'I've laid her to rest, Mick, some time ago. It was you and Maisie I couldn't bear the thought of. The very idea that she had succeeded where I had failed! She gave you a son.'

'Ah, Sarah . . . I was delighted with my four daughters. As for Maisie, I keep telling you that there is nothing going on between us! You just won't believe me. Although, mind you I've been sorely tempted, so I have.'

Sarah stepped closer to him. 'I'm sorry. You didn't deserve the way I got on. Let's go back inside and talk.

Eh, Mick? I can feel dozens of eyes boring into us.' She smiled slightly. 'They will be talking about this for the next month, so they will.'

Still he held back. 'To hell with the neighbours! And Michael? What about him, Sarah? He's my son, and given the chance I intend getting to know him better.'

'I understand, Mick. Whatever you say goes.'

Still he made no effort to move. He was bewildered; couldn't understand his wife's sudden change of heart. 'What about Gerry Docherty?' he asked, his eyes watchful.

Sarah steadily returned his look. 'I don't give a damn about Gerry Docherty, I'm ashamed of myself. I was only using him to hurt you, and then it all went wrong.'

'Mind you, Sarah, if he ever so much as looks at you again, I won't be responsible for my actions. I'll knock his friggin' head off, so help me. I hate that smug little bastard! I should have filled him in years ago.'

Sarah smiled slightly at Mick's strong language. It was so unlike him. But still, it fitted the situation perfectly and she loved him for it. 'I wish you had, Mick,' she said softly. 'Then all this probably would never have happened.' She moved closer to him, almost touching. 'Mick . . . I can't bear this any longer. Come inside, please.'

'Before we go in love, let's give the nosy neighbours something else to talk about.' Grabbing Sarah, Mick hugged her close and kissed her. Then, with one arm around her waist, he led her back towards their home. He was in a state of euphoria as he followed her through the gate and down the side of the house. In the kitchen she turned and swiftly entered his arms. Her heart was full of joy. She knew now what the expression in Mick's eyes had been. Yearning! Yearning for her. Well, he need yearn no more. He was home again, to stay.

Three spectators of this moving display were Emma, Maggie and Gerry Docherty. Maggie wiped a tear from her eye as she moved away from the window. Thanks be to God, her prayers had been answered. In the adjoining house, Gerry was not so pleased. He stood riveted to the spot, a scowl puckering his face. He regretted losing his chance with Sarah. Now it looked like he wouldn't get another. But philosophically he shrugged his shoulders. Some you win and some you lose. He was still a young man, and there were plenty more pebbles on the beach.

Meanwhile, Emma was happily rearranging her plans for the future, while Mick was on the phone telling Eileen that he would not be up that afternoon after all as he had more pressing matters to attend to at home.

Chapter Eleven

The reunion of Mick and Sarah brought great relief and happiness to all the family. Using it as an excuse for a family gathering, Maggie invited them all to her home three weeks later. It was a Saturday afternoon and all the great-grandchildren were also invited.

As they strolled down Rockmore Road Eileen questioned the reason for this gathering of the clan. 'I wonder what is really behind this wee do?' she mused.

'Eileen, my love, I never in my entire life met anyone as impatient as you. In about five minutes flat we will probably know all there is to know. Can't you, just this once, wait and see?'

'I'm just wondering out loud, Johnny! Surely that's not a crime?' she cried, deeply affronted. 'I mean . . . if me grannie intended throwing a party, why not at Easter, eh? That would have been more appropriate! So why wait until now?'

'Tut, tut,' Johnny clucked his tongue and chastised his wife. 'Because Mick and Sarah were separated at Easter. Have you forgotten already?'

'I suppose you are right, Johnny. Still, I think there is more to this wee do than meets the eye. I personally think that Grannie is just using Mam and Dad's reunion as an excuse to get us all together at the same time.' Mention of her parents brought a huge grin to Eileen's face. 'Isn't it great that they are back together again? And acting like two love-birds. I suppose we will never know just exactly what happened between them.' She cocked an eyebrow at him. 'I don't suppose Mr Knowall happens to know anything about it, eh?'

Johnny grinned back at her roguishly and confessed, 'No, I don't! And I tell you once again, woman . . . it's none of our business! God, but I'd hate everybody to be delving into my private affairs. So long as they are back together, that's all that matters. So let's just leave it at that, eh?'

'It's smashing all the same, isn't it? And me dad's got a wee car now. He's over the moon with it, so he is. He'll be washing all the colour out of it, if he keeps on the way he's going. I've never saw anybody as delighted as him. It's his pride and joy! And me Mam is every bit as thrilled, although she acts as if she couldn't care less. But I wonder where they got the money for the car? It's not just an old banger, so it's not. It must have cost a packet.'

Johnny sighed deeply as his wife continued to express her nosiness. 'Mick told me he got a pay rise some time ago,' he admitted. 'He had been putting the extra money away, for a rainy day, so to speak.'

Eileen's head swivelled in his direction and Johnny saw her mouth gape. Snapping it shut, she gasped in disbelief. 'He told you that? And you never let on to me?'

Exasperated with her inquisitiveness, Johnny cried, 'As I said before, Eileen, it's none of our business. I don't tell you everything, you know. At least, not every single wee detail.'

'Oh, don't you, now?'

To Johnny's relief they arrived at Maggie's driveway and Eileen had to shelve her curiosity for the time being. The shrieks of excited children came from around the back of the house, and their three rushed forward to join the throng. Johnny and Eileen followed at a more sedate walk, Eileen wondering just what else he was neglecting to tell her.

They were the last to arrive but they had a good

excuse. Johnny worked every Saturday until five o'clock, but today his wife had insisted that he stop at eleven, to come to Maggie's gathering with his family. Still, by the time he got home and had changed into casual clothes, it was a close thing. The 'do' was to be a buffet luncheon and was to start at twelve. They were actually just on time, with a few minutes to spare. Even Bernard and Emily were there before them and they lived at the other end of town. Emily, very much at home now with her in-laws, was sitting on a stool, young David on her lap. She greeted Eileen with a warm smile. Of all the family, she felt most at ease with her. Reaching for the child, Eileen lifted the chuckling bundle up into her arms and cradled him to her chest.

'He almost puts me in the notion again,' she jested. 'Almost, but not quite. I think I'll wait another while. My, but he is getting heavy.' Eileen's knees buckled as she pretended to be weighed down by the child. 'What weight is he now?'

'Sixteen pounds,' Emily answered proudly. 'Will you hold on to him for a minute, please, Eileen? I want to heat a bottle for him.'

'I'll be only too happy.' With a smile of thanks Emily entered the house.

April had been a terrible month with constant rain. Showers had continued through into May, and it was a dull day, but nevertheless warm. Maggie and Barney had decided to risk the weather breaking and have the party outdoors. That way the kids could run wild without any danger of damage to Maggie's antiques and carpets. The grass being damp, chairs and benches and stools were arranged around the garden. High hedges sheltered them and offered privacy.

After greeting the rest of the family, still nursing David, Eileen chose a chair next to Beth and sat down. 'How are you keeping?' she asked solicitously.

Her sister·turned a pale drawn face to her and grimaced. 'Not too bad. I'm just so tired all the time, and my back is aching.' Her hand reached out and chucked the baby under the chin. 'Isn't he a beautiful baby? I hope I get a boy this time,' she said wistfully. 'That would make it all worthwhile.'

'So long as the baby is all right, that's all that matters.' At her sister's nod of agreement, Eileen asked, 'How long have you to go now?'

'Seven weeks. It seems like a lifetime. I can tell you one thing! There will be no more. I have made my mind up on that score. This is definitely the last. If Tommy doesn't like it, he can lump it. Or he can go in for the operation.'

'But . . . he couldn't! It's not allowed.'

'It's entirely up to him. Four kids are enough for anybody.'

Tentatively, Eileen inquired, 'Did you not try the rhythm method, then?'

'How do you think this happened?' Beth glanced down at her bump and eyeing Eileen's slim figure, threw her a derisive look. 'Obviously it doesn't work for everyone.'

'What would you two girls like to drink?'

Eileen was glad of Johnny's intervention and turned to him in relief. She now regretted confiding in Beth that she and Johnny used the safe period, as it was commonly called. She had a feeling that Beth blamed her for her present condition, which was quite stupid really.

'What is there to drink, Johnny?'

He leant forward and whispered confidentially, 'To be truthful, there are quite a few bottles of champagne in the fridge, but Barney said that they are for a toast later on. What do you make of that?' His eyes teased Eileen, whetting her curiosity. 'Something else for you to wonder about, eh, love? Meanwhile, you can have wine, red or white. Gin, vodka, drambuie, whiskey, or soft drinks.' He looked kindly at his sister-in-law. 'Barney says perhaps you might like a Guinness, Beth. There's plenty of iron in it.'

'Oh, no, thank you, Johnny. I know the doctor says that a Guinness a day would help to build me up, but I couldn't face one just now. Tommy went off to fetch me a cup of tea some time ago. He must have gone to milk the cow! Would you see if he is in the kitchen, and tell him to hurry up, please? Before I pass out.'

'Drambuie?' Eileen queried in surprise. 'Grannie is really splashing out! It must be a very special occasion. I'll have a Drambuie with some lemonade and ice, please, Johnny.'

With a nod of acknowledgement, he headed towards the kitchen and Beth turned to Eileen. 'What's all this in aid of, then?'

'I've no idea. I've been wondering about that myself, so I have. It's all very mysterious.'

'Don't be coy, Eileen. You and Grannie are as thick as thieves. She tells you everything.'

'Not this time, she hasn't! I'm as much in the dark as you are.'

'Huh! Tell me another.'

'Here you are, Beth.'

Tommy had arrived back with a cup of tea and plate of savouries on a tray for Beth. Relieved to escape her sister's acid tongue, Eileen, eyed the plate and said, 'Oh, I think I'll have to have some of that.' She rose to her feet. 'Here, Tommy, you can have this chair. This wee fellow is getting restless. Besides, I want to go and get some grub. I've been starving myself all morning for this. Grannie sure knows how to put on a nice spread.'

'Would you like me to hold David?' Tommy offered.

'No, it's all right. Here's Emily coming out now. She will be wanting to feed him.'

Barney came from the kitchen and eyed the sky. It was overcast, but a light wind was keeping the clouds on the move. 'I think we will take a chance and put a table out here for the food, then everyone can help themselves. Will you give me a hand, Mick?'

Relinquishing his hold on Sarah's hand, Mick rose at once from his seat. 'Of course, Barney.'

Eileen sat down on the chair vacated by her father, and eyed her mother closely. Since the return of Mick she looked happy and contented with her lot. Sarah wore a deep green vee-neck sweater that darkened the colour of her eyes and showed to advantage her pale luminous skin. Eileen could not fail but notice the string of pearls that adorned her mother's still smooth neck. 'Oh, Mam, those pearls are lovely.' She reached out and gently touched the beads, so smooth and well matched. Even in her ignorance of such matters she could tell that they were expensive. 'Did Dad buy them for you?'

Fingering the pearls lovingly, Sarah agreed, 'Yes, they are lovely, aren't they? And yes, your father did buy them for me, for a very special occasion.'

Sarah had no intention of telling her inquisitive daughter the little bit of history attached to the pearls. She smiled inwardly when she recalled how Maggie had returned the necklace and told Mick to give it to its rightful owner. She had then warned her daughter not to mention that she was aware that Mick had given them away. When presented with them, Sarah had thrown herself into her husband's arms and wept with joy, as if seeing them for the very first time, confident that her secret was safe with Maggie.

'I bet you're delighted with them. They look awfully expensive.' With an envious sigh, Eileen changed the subject. 'Well now, Mam. Tell me, do you know what all this is in aid of?'

Eileen's voice intruded into her mother's private happy musings.

'All will be revealed soon,' Sarah assured her daughter with a teasing smile. 'Just be patient for once.'

'So you do know, then!' Eileen exclaimed.

'Yes, but I'm not telling you. I knew some time ago, but your grannie swore me to secrecy.'

'Could you not give me just a wee hint, Mam?'

'Don't you dare, Sarah! Let her sweat it out like everyone else.'

Eileen laughed aloud at these words from her husband. 'You're determined I shall be kept in the dark. Aren't you, Johnny?'

'And why not? You are no different from the rest of us.'

Still Eileen persisted, 'Is it worth waiting for, Mam?'

'Eileen!'

'All right. Johnny, all right. I give up! I won't say another word.' She accepted the drink he passed to her with a loving smile. 'Thank you, love.'

Sarah smiled fondly at her daughter and admitted, 'I can tell you this much. It will be a very pleasant surprise to you all.'

They had not much longer to wait. Soon all had eaten their fill, and loosened by the abundant alcohol, tongues were wagging and all were at ease and happy. Once the table was cleared of excess food, Barney, with a slight nod of the head, motioned Mick to follow him into the kitchen. Soon they reappeared carrying bottles of champagne and then returned for glasses. Rising to her feet, Maggie took up position at the table, facing her family.

She smiled faintly as she began to speak. 'I am aware that you have all been speculating as to the real reason for this get together. And some more than others.' She smiled fondly in Eileen's direction, and unabashed Eileen nodded her agreement. Some embarrassment was apparent as the others squirmed in their seats or shuffled their feet as the case may be. It was Eileen, forthright as ever, who answered for them all.

'Yes, Grannie, you have whetted our appetites long enough. Now put us all out of our misery and tell us why we are gathered here today.'

'I have invited you all here together because I have some good news to impart that indirectly concerns you. To put it in a nutshell . . . I have inherited some money from my late mother.'

Silence reigned for some moments. They were all aware that Maggie's family had been wealthy but thought that she had forfeited any right to her share by marrying against their wishes. It was Beth who broke the silence. 'Is is much, Grannie?'

'A little over twenty thousand pounds. With some more, I don't know how much, to come later. Some building or other still has to be sold.'

A gasp of astonishment rippled around the garden and then they were all speaking at once, sincere in their congratulations to Maggie.

She thanked them. 'I know that you are happy for me, but I intend to share my good fortune with you all. Barney . . . Mick . . . please hand out the envelopes.'

Sarah, Bernard, Beth, Eileen and Emma were each handed a long white envelope. Eileen fingered hers. It was quite thin. She could not guess what it might contain. She glanced at her grannie. Maggie nodded in her direction as if giving permission for Eileen to open hers. With a smile of anticipation on her lips, Eileen eagerly tore open the envelope. Her hand covered her mouth and she gasped in amazement when she removed the contents. A cheque made out to Eileen Cleary for the grand sum of one thousand pounds. Overcome with emotion, she stared first at Johnny and then at Maggie.

Recovering her composure, in one bound she was across the garden and hugging Maggie. 'Oh, thank you, Grannie. It's a fortune. Thank you very much indeed.'

The rest of the family had silently watched this display. Now with urgent fingers they hastened to tear open their own envelopes in eager anticipation. There were shouts of joy and Maggie was hugged and kissed, until she cried out for mercy. Next Mick, Johnny, Tommy and Emily were each handed an envelope. These turned out to contain fifty pounds each and once again Maggie was embraced with profound thanks.

It was Bernard who took it upon himself to make the official thank you. He left his chair and went to stand beside his mother. Putting an arm around her shoulders, in a voice charged with emotion, he said, 'Mam, I know I speak for everyone here when I say thank you from the bottom of my heart. You have made the future a lot rosier for us all.' His eyes sought Emily's. 'I'll be able to go to night school after all, love.'

Flushed and happy, Maggie confessed, 'It has been my pleasure, son, and I am glad to hear that you intend going to night school. It would be a shame if you let your education slip, with the brains that you have.' Her eyes met Barney's and she smiled lovingly at him. 'Barney . . . I think we can break open the champagne now.'

Eileen practically skipped on the way home, she was so excited. Johnny was carrying Marie who had fallen asleep at Maggie's. He smiled down at his wife as she tugged at his free arm. 'Well now, your mother was right!' he teased her. 'It certainly was a surprise worth waiting for. Eh, love?'

'I can't believe it. And did you notice that me Mam and Bernard got two thousand each, and even young David got a cheque for a thousand pounds, to be invested in his name.'

'Well, it stands to reason that Sarah and Bernard would get more. After all, they are Maggie's own two children. As for David, like yourself he is a grandchild.'

'Oh, I'm not complaining! Heavens, no! I'm delighted with my thousand pounds,' Eileen declared. She was still overawed at the idea of having so much money. 'Oh, isn't Grannie good to us all? What shall we do with it, Johnny?' she asked excitedly. 'Why, with the savings we already have we could probably buy a house outright. We could put a big deposit down, and still have plenty left over for new furniture and carpets. Wouldn't we?' Without waiting for an answer, she babbled on, 'I know! Why not put it in the building society and let it grow for a while? Then when we see a house we fancy, we can just go out and buy it.'

'That's a very good idea,' he agreed. 'If that's what you want to do. But remember, it's your money! Do whatever you like with it.'

He was pleased when she stressed, 'No, Johnny, it's our money!'

Rain started to fall; large drops spattered them, bringing squeals of delight from Paul and Louise.

'Come on, kids.' Holding the two older children by the hand, Eileen left Johnny's side and started to run up the street. Quickly opening the door, she ushered the children inside, just as the heavens seemed to open. Johnny was hard on her heels. He followed her down the hall and into the living room. Depositing Marie gently on to the settee, he glanced at his watch. 'Look, Eileen, I forgot to bring some papers home from the office with me. I'll nip down now and get them.'

She gaped at him in amazement. 'You can't drive the car. You've been drinking all afternoon.'

Placing his hands on her shoulders, Johnny gave her a little shake. 'There is such a thing as a trolley-bus, remember? These papers are important, love. I can study them over the weekend.'

'But it's half-past four! You'll never make it before the office closes.' Eileen remonstrated. 'Besides, look at that rain! You'll be soaked,' she persisted.

'I have my own key, and I do possess a raincoat.' Johnny planted a quick kiss on her lips to silence any further arguments. 'I won't be long,' he promised.

'Can I come with you, Dad?'

'No, Paul, it's too wet. You stay and help your mammy.'

And fondly ruffling his son's hair, Johnny shrugged into his raincoat and quickly left the house.

After all the excitement at her grannie's house, Eileen felt a little deflated by Johnny's quick departure. When he had been promoted, she had not dreamt that he would be working all day Saturday. Most offices closed half day. He only really saw the kids on a Sunday now, and Eileen felt cheated, she had so little time to herself these days. Well now, she admonished herself, you have to take the bad with the good. Hadn't they more money coming in, and a company car? Wouldn't they be able to afford to buy a house soon? Especially now they had this windfall from her grannie. Yes, really she should be counting her blessings instead of fault finding! Nevertheless she still felt hard done by.

One of the things she missed most because of Johnny's working all day Saturday was her trips into town. As the days passed and she worked hard keeping her business up to date and the house clean, as well as looking after the kids, she became resentful. It was all right for Johnny! When he came home at teatime all he had to do was put his feet up and pore over his eternal papers. She was lucky if he was home early enough to spend a short time with the kids. She was especially resentful this particular week. The thirty pounds that Johnny had insisted she take of the fifty that Maggie had given him was burning a hole in her pocket. What was the use of having extra money if she couldn't go out to spend it? She just had to get out shopping! On Wednesday she decided to phone and ask Emma to baby-sit on the following Saturday afternoon, and was delighted when her young sister agreed.

Saturday dawned bright and sunny, but there was still a tendency for showers, somebody up above had sure got the months mixed up, and rain had been forecast for later on in the afternoon. Before leaving the house Eileen decided to phone Johnny and ask him to leave the office early and pick her up somewhere in town to drive her home. It was George Patterson who answered the phone. She recognized his voice at once.

'Hello, George, it's me . . . Eileen Cleary. Can I speak to Johnny, please?'

'You have just missed him, Eileen. He left at twelve, as usual. As a matter of fact you are lucky you caught me. I'm the last to go. I was actually on my way out when the phone rang. Was it anything important?'

'Oh, no, sorry to keep you, George. It isn't all that important. I'm sure Johnny will be home soon. Thank you, and goodbye.'

Laughing, she went into the kitchen where Emma was baking gingerbread men, helped by Paul and Louise, while Marie was lying down for a nap. 'Oh, I am pleased! It looks like I'll have company in town after all,' she announced. 'Johnny stopped at twelve today. He must be on his way home now.'

Forty-five minutes elapsed and realising that, even allowing for heavy traffic, Johnny must have other business to attend to or he would be home, Eileen decided that she would wait no longer. 'Emma, tell Johnny when he comes in that he has missed out on a shopping spree with me.'

'I'm sure he will be all annoyed,' Emma answered dryly. It was the subject of many jokes that all the men connected with their family were noted for their lack of interest in shopping.

'Aye, I suppose you are right. See you later . . . and thanks, Emma.'

The city centre was crowded and Eileen eagerly hopped off the bus at the bottom of Castle Street. Her first port of call was the London Mantle Warehouse on the corner of Chapel Lane. Finding nothing suitable there, she made her way down to Castle Junction and joined the throngs on Royal Avenue. She wished that Kate was with her, but on Thursday she had been admitted into hospital. There was cause for concern as her blood pressure had risen. Eileen had visited her in the Royal Maternity the night before and had found her looking wonderful, but since the baby was overdue, they were keeping her in until after the birth. If Kate had been with her Eileen would have tried the more exclusive shops in the hope of getting a bargain, but alone she hadn't the nerve. She was looking for something nice, not too expensive but nice. Once again Johnny had put his big foot in it. Although their previous Saturday night out with Lorna and James had not been very successful, to Eileen's chagrin her husband had arranged once more to meet them for a drink in town the following weekend. Eileen was annoyed, but had agreed to go this last time. She was not keen on Lorna Pollock and did not see why she should pretend to be, just to please Johnny. Meanwhile she intended to be tastefully dressed when in her company.

After visiting many shops and trying on numerous skirts and dresses, she at last found just the type of thing that she had in mind, in the Co-op store on York Street. Nothing flashy! A dark grey pleated wool skirt and a white Courtelle twin set that looked classy on her. Tired but happy, it was late when she at last joined the long bus queue at the bottom of Castle Street. She was glad that the weather men had once again got it wrong and the fair weather had so far held out. Under the impression that Johnny would be home early from work, she was not worried about the time, which was almost six o'clock. After a ten-minute wait the bus at last arrived and Eileen thankfully clambered aboard. It stopped at every stop on the Falls Road to let people off or pick others up, with the result that it was well after six when she got off it at the top of the Donegall Road. Crossing the Falls Road she was halfway up the street when the car passed and Johnny tooted the horn at her. Completely mystified, she stopped in the middle of the footpath, gazing after it. A few seconds later, Emma left the house and raced down the street towards her.

Seeing Eileen, Emma slowed to a walk and approached her apologetically. 'Sorry to rush off like this, Eileen, but I have a date tonight,' she greeted her.

'I'm sorry, Emma I could have been home sooner but I thought that Johnny would be here long ago. Instead it appears he is much later than usual. Is he only getting home now?' Eileen couldn't hide her bewilderment. At Emma's abrupt nod, she queried, 'He wasn't home earlier on and went out again?'

'No, he has just this minute arrived. Look, I'll have to run, Eileen. I'm going out on a special date tonight and I have a lot to do,' Emma confessed. She hesitated, trying to gauge what kind of mood her sister was in. Her pocket money didn't stretch to the latest fashions and she wanted to borrow one of Eileen's suits. Eileen did not like lending out her best clothes and Emma didn't blame her. She would be the first to admit to being accident prone. 'Eileen, is there any chance of your lending me your good black suit? I promise to take great care of it.' She held her breath as she awaited Eileen's reply.

Still preoccupied, her sister answered absently, 'Of course! Come back up with me now and I'll give it to you.'

'Oh, smashing! Thank you, Eileen. You won't regret it,' Emma assured her as she turned and retraced her steps.

Entering the house, Eileen headed straight for the stairs. In the bedroom she threw her purchases on the bed, and taking the black suit from the wardrobe, matched it up with a couple of blouses. Placing them carefully over the jacket on the hanger, she descended the stairs again.

'Here, Emma. If you like you can wear one of these blouses with it. Take them home with you and see which one you prefer. And remember, I want them back in mint condition!'

'Oh, thanks, Eileen. I will take great care of them. On my honour! Tonight is special for me and I know I will feel good in these lovely clothes.' Emma draped the clothes over her arm and, grinning broadly, went happily on her way.

Johnny was in the kitchen preparing tea for the kids. He threw her a warm smile. Eileen stood straight-faced, in the doorway watching him. 'You were late today. Where were you?' she asked casually.

Her husband turned a surprised look on her and then a frown puckered his brow. 'I'm not that much later than usual. I had a bit of business to attend to.'

'Oh, I see.' To hide her confusion Eileen turned away and leant over the table where the kids were arguing as usual. 'Paul ... leave Louise alone! You're a big boy now, and you shouldn't tease your little sisters.'

Paul gave her a scowl but behaved himself. Eileen turned to leave the kitchen. She needed space to think things out. Johnny's voice stayed her. 'Don't you want any tea?'

'No, I'm not hungry. I had a bite in town,' she lied, and without another glance left the kitchen. Something was niggling in the corner of her mind. Something didn't ring true. But what was it? Ah, now she knew what was bugging her. She recalled that George Patterson had said that Johnny had left the office *as usual* at twelve. At the time, she had thought it was a slip of the tongue. But supposing George was right and the office closed at twelve every Saturday? After all, why not? Most offices closed at midday. Where then was Johnny spending his Saturday afternoons, while she sat at home twiddling her thumbs? She must tread carefully she thought, and not jump to any conclusions. She needed to get things straight in her mind before she started bawling her head off, demanding to know just where her husband was spending his free time, and why he was lying to her.

After much deliberating, she decided to wait and see

how Johnny and Lorna behaved towards each other on the following Saturday night. Surely if he was seeing her on the sly, there would be some indication of it? The week passed slowly and Eileen found it hard to be her usual self towards Johnny. Not a patient person at the best of times, it was with difficulty that she managed to control her tongue. However, her patience was to no avail. Their date with Lorna and James did not materialize. On Friday afternoon Madge collapsed and was rushed into hospital. Johnny at once postponed the arranged meeting. Madge did not respond to treatment and on Saturday morning an operation was performed on her for appendicitis. It was too late! The appendix had burst and peritonitis had set in.

For a couple of days Madge's life hung in the balance and Johnny was worried out of his mind. 'Do you think that I should send for our Phillip, Eileen?'

Eileen gazed down on the woman who was like a second mother to her and whom she had come to love. Madge looked awful. Tubes sprouted from her mouth, nose and side, and blood was being fed intravenously into her arm. Eileen's voice was hesitant. 'The doctors say she will pull through. But . . .' Madge's bloodless face rivalled the sheets she lay on, and slack jowls drooping from her chin made her appear older than her sixty years. She looked to be at death's door. '. . . to be on the safe side, yes, Johnny, I do think you should send for him. It's better to be safe than sorry.'

A phone call had Phillip on the next available plane out of Manchester. Johnny picked him up at Aldergrove airport and an hour later he was at his mother's bedside.

Gazing fearfully across the bed at his brother, Phillip cried, 'God, but she looks awful! What do the doctors say? Will she pull through?'

'They say she will. But I thought you would want to be here, just in case.'

'You thought right! Never delay sending for me any

time you think I am needed.' His eyes held Eileen's, giving this statement added meaning, and she was glad that Johnny's gaze was fixed steadfastly on his mother. It would be a happy day for Eileen when Phillip got married and settled down. He still had the power to make her feel terribly uneasy.

It was the third day after her operation when Madge regained consciousness, and raised a laugh when she informed the nurse that she was hungry. Soon she was declared out of danger, and to Eileen's relief Phillip returned to England. She had enough worries on her plate at the moment without his intrusion. Even on the Saturday that Madge was operated on Johnny had made an excuse about some important papers he needed and had departed for the office. He was only away a short time, but as Eileen admitted to herself, if he was up to no good, it wouldn't take very long. During the time Madge was in hospital Johnny continued to be absent from home on Saturdays. Numerous unanswered telephone calls had convinced Eileen that indeed the office was closed in the afternoons, so where was her husband spending his time? She hazarded a guess and did not like what came to mind. She was filled with foreboding and a great sense of powerlessness. Should she confront Johnny?

Slowly but surely Madge rallied round and was soon discharged from hospital. She refused to go anywhere but her own house and reluctantly, Johnny had to submit to his mother's wishes. Eileen was only too glad to attend her mother-in-law daily. Until Madge was better, she brought her meals three times a day, and kept the house shipshape. In the evenings Madge's many friends visited her.

It was after one such visit from Sarah and Mick that Eileen noticed a sudden change in Johnny. It had started out an enjoyable evening. Her dad had suggested a game of gin rummy, and Madge had been all for it. They played for pennies and Madge, much to her delight, somehow managed to win every game. Calling a break for supper, Eileen had to laugh when her mother-in-law teasingly accused her of trying to break her lucky streak. Eileen retired to the kitchen and on the pretext of giving her a hand, Johnny followed her. Closing the door, he had leant his back against it, and secure in the knowledge that they could not be taken unawares, had taken her in his arms and gently kissed and caressed her. Eileen had returned kiss for kiss, caress for caress. It was a long time since Johnny had felt the need to show that he cared. He had been very preoccupied lately and Eileen had worried about their relationship, more than ever convinced that he was seeing Lorna. Now, in the warmth of his embrace, she was ashamed of her doubts.

When he became more ardent, she withdrew reluctantly from his arms. 'Not here,' she chided him. 'They'll be wondering what's keeping us with the tea. We will have all the time in the world when we get home.'

'Spoil sport!' Johnny chided, but he sounded annoyed. 'It is the thought we might be caught on that makes it so exciting,' he argued. 'Don't you think so?'

'No, actually, I don't. I get all the excitement I need at home.'

'Ah, Eileen, I wish I could believe that.' The words came out on a sigh and she gazed at him in amazement.

Johnny relinquished his hold on her and Eileen was surprised at the sadness that veiled his eyes. What was wrong with him? It was on the tip of her tongue to challenge him. Ask the question that was always on her mind: where did he spend his Saturday afternoons? Clear the air once and for all. Afraid of finding out some dreadful truth that she might be unable to bear, she managed to swallow the words.

'Tell you what!' she suggested. 'Why don't you and Dad go down and get some fish and chips? I feel quite peckish. Your mam might even eat some. Her appetite hasn't been very good since she came out of hospital and it would be great if we could tempt her with a fish. Go on, you and Dad go down while I make a pot of tea and butter some bread.'

Thinking of the delicious fish suppers made by the chippy at the corner of the Donegall Road, Johnny felt his own mouth water. 'That's a very good idea. You're making me hungry just talking about fish and chips. I'll get Mick to accompany me. We shouldn't be too long.'

Eileen was preoccupied as she worked. Had she imagined the sadness in her husband's eyes. Did their marriage lack excitement for him? Was he flirting with danger because the idea of being discovered excited him? Surely not? No! Johnny was not the type to risk a bit on the side just for the fun of it. He would have to be serious to take that kind of risk. There was only one thing for it. She couldn't go on like this much longer or she would end up in Purdysburn. Tonight she would have it out with him. Find out what he was up to. After all, perhaps she was wrong about him and Lorna. Maybe things were not working out as he had planned in his new position at Shorts'. Was he unhappy there? She had never questioned him about his work, secure in the knowledge that he was very capable and apparently more than able to cope with his new duties. Had she been too complacent? Or was it nothing to do with work? Had he allowed Lorna to get her hooks into him good and proper, and now he couldn't wriggle free? Well, he was in an amorous mood! Tonight, in the comfort of his arms, she would broach the subject and try to talk things over, husband to wife.

The men returned and supper was served. To Eileen's surprise, shortly afterwards Mick and Sarah made their good nights and left. The meal had been lovely, and Eileen was surprised when her mother rose to leave. She was aware that her mother-in-law had anticipated another few hands of gin rummy and would surely be disappointed. However, conversation had flagged and it was like flogging a dead horse trying to keep it going. When the men had returned from the chippy, Eileen had at once sensed a change in the atmosphere and soon realized that Johnny was the instigator. He was withdrawn and surly; barely answering her parents when they tried to keep the conversation going. Such a change from an hour ago in the kitchen! What on earth had got into him? It reminded her of the early days of their marriage when he had been at logger heads with all and sundry.

On the way home from Madge's, Mick was abstracted. Giving his arm a slight shake, Sarah inquired, 'What's the matter?'

Mick smiled down at her. 'Nothing, really.'

'Come on now. I know that something is bothering you.'

'I'm just a wee bit perturbed,' he admitted. 'Did you notice the change in Johnny?'

'I sure did! What a transformation. That's why I couldn't get out of there quick enough. We've had enough trouble of our own lately without getting mixed up in their affairs. There is something wrong between him and Eileen. Remember how long they were in the kitchen, and then Johnny came out and asked you to go to the chip shop with him? Well, they must have had an argument or something. When the two of you came back, he hardly said a civil word to Eileen. Or to any of us for that matter.'

To Sarah's surprise, Mick actually squirmed a bit. 'I'm afraid I can't agree with you there. He was in great form on the way down to the chip shop. Full of beans.' Mick gripped Sarah's arm closer to his side, and his next words sent a chill coursing through her. 'I've a feeling that somehow or other, I've managed to put my big feet in it.'

'What on earth do you mean, Mick?'

'Well, you know Johnny was very good to me when you and I were separated? He couldn't do enough for me. It filled me with so much guilt and shame that he could be so caring after the way I treated him when he married our Eileen. Remember how nasty I was to him?'

Sarah closed her eyes and whispered, 'Ah, sweet Jesus, Mick, what have you done?'

The fear in her voice brought Mick's eyes sharply to her face. 'Oh, it's all right, Sarah! I just apologized for the way I got on. I confided that you and I also had a shotgun wedding. I hope you don't mind me telling him that?' At her sad shake of the head, Mick continued, 'To tell you the truth, Sarah . . . I was sorry I bothered. He must have been very embarrassed about it. He just waved my apology away and changed the subject. I felt a right idiot.'

Arriving at their own door Sarah waited until they were inside before she broke the bad news to her husband. In the living room, she slowly turned to face him. 'I think you had better sit down, Mick. Before you hear what I have to say.'

At her husband's baffled expression, she repeated, 'Go on, sit down.'

Slowly, he sank down on to the settee, all the while eyeing her apprehensively. Sarah sat down beside him and taking his hand between her own, gripped it tightly. 'Johnny had no idea that Eileen was pregnant when they got married, Mick.' As her husband continued to stare at her, uncomprehending, Sarah dropped her bombshell. 'Paul is not Johnny's son.' Had she consciously played for effect, she would have been gratified at the result of her words.

Mick's face sagged in disbelief, draining of all colour, and he cried out in dismay, 'Ah, no, Sarah. Ah, no! In the name of God, what have I done?'

'You have opened a hornet's nest! That's what you've done, Mick.'

'But he must have known she was pregnant?' he argued. 'Johnny's no fool. He's far from stupid. He must have known, Sarah!'

'You're wrong, Mick. Johnny was very much in love and didn't want to know.'

'Did *you* know?' he barked at her.

Sarah was taken aback at his anger. 'No! I was as much in the dark as everyone else. It was when Paul was born that I found out the truth. I can tell you . . . it came as a terrible shock to me. How Johnny didn't twig on I'll never know. Eileen somehow managed to convince him that Paul was premature. Imagine, an eight pound, two ounce baby supposed to be almost two months premature! He didn't doubt he was the father. It's just as well he had no experience of newborn babies, or he would surely have guessed. Still, Eileen managed to pull the wool over his eyes and nobody else remarked on it. At least, not in Johnny's presence. But then, as you well know, most of the family knew, and the rest guessed that she was pregnant though we all thought it was Johnny's.'

An expression of distaste spread over Mick's face as the implications of what he had just heard penetrated his stunned brain. 'But then . . . why, that means Eileen was playing around, and she was only eighteen,' he gasped. 'I find that hard to believe, Sarah!'

'No, I don't think she was playing around. I think there was just the one boy.'

'How come we never heard tell of him?'

'I don't know, Mick. That's the truth. From the date of the birth, I deduced it must have happened shortly before our Beth's wedding day.'

Thinking back, Mick recalled how unhappy Eileen had been at the time. How he had tried to get her to talk to him. Well, obviously he had not tried hard enough! He was swamped with guilt at the idea of his failure. Now he had dropped Eileen right in it. He turned to his wife in despair.

'I should have been told the truth as soon as you found out. If I had known, this would never have happened,' he lamented.

Sarah was only human and could not help but get her dig in. 'Now you know how I felt when I learnt that Michael was your son,' she said softly. 'If I had been told the truth about your affair with Maisie, I would have been better prepared.'

Mick hung his head in shame. 'I'm sorry, Sarah, truly sorry about that. You know that, don't you?'

She nodded sadly, and continued, 'Mick, I wanted to tell you the truth about Paul but Eileen wouldn't hear tell of it. She said you would never be able to put on an act in front of Johnny, and she was right. This only happened because you felt guilty about the way you treated him.'

'I suppose you're right, Sarah. No doubt you are right. What do you think will happen now?'

'I don't know.' Sarah shook her head sadly. 'Johnny is very jealous of Eileen. And he really is very good-living. In his eyes you're either good or bad. There is no middle road as far as he is concerned. I don't know what way he will take it. I just hope you haven't done anything irrevocable.'

Mick put his arm around Sarah and they sat clutching each other, seeking comfort. Sarah was determined, that if she could help it, their new found happiness would not be jeopardized. Eileen and Johnny would just have to work things out between themselves. She intended that Mick and she would travel a bit, now they had a car and a bit of money in the bank. But, supposing Eileen felt compelled to leave Johnny? Where else could she go, except back to her parents? And then what would happen to all their plans and their cosy nest when young children started running about the house? As much as she loved her daughter and grandchildren their invasion would certainly upset the plans that Sarah hoped to put into operation.

* * *

Eileen's soul-searching talk with Johnny fell by the wayside. Although she still brought her mother-in-law down her meals, once Madge was mobile again she demanded to do everything else for herself. Johnny had slept in his mother's house for the first week after she was discharged from hospital to keep an eye on her, but then she told him to go home to his family. So that night, once her mother-in-law was settled in bed, Eileen prepared to go home. To her great surprise, Johnny elected to remain where he was. He said his mother looked a bit off colour and he would feel better if he was nearby in case she needed anything. Madge looked all right to Eileen, and she could see that her mother-in-law was as surprised as she, but neither of them questioned his determination.

Johnny had not looked Eileen straight in the face since he returned from the chip shop earlier on with Mick. Now as she shrugged into her coat he glanced at her, his eyes reaching no higher than her chin and his tightly compressed lips parted just enough to mutter, 'Ask Emma to stay overnight and keep you company.'

Eileen's chin rose in the air and her voice was disdainful. 'I don't need company! And since you obviously can't bear the sight of me, you can just stay here,' she hissed vehemently. Calling out a final good night to Madge, she literally ran from the house.

Johnny sank down on the edge of the settee and gripped his head in his hands, a great well of misery engulfing him. What was he going to do? How would he be able to bear this terrible desolation? This awful sense of betrayal. He wished that Mick had kept his mouth shut; he had been happy living in ignorance. His mother's voice broke through his despair. They had brought a bed down into the parlour for Madge to save her having to climb the stairs. Now Johnny went to the door and stood looking in at her.

'Come here, son. Tell me what's troubling you?' Her voice was filled with compassion.

Slowly he approached the bed. He didn't want to discuss his private affairs with his mother. Had she not tried to warn him? The very first time Madge had met Eileen, she had actually asked him if she was pregnant and he had taken offence. But then, he had thought his mother was actually accusing him of putting Eileen in the family way. Had she guessed the truth then? Probably! Hadn't he himself felt some reservations when Paul was born? Did everybody know the truth? Everyone but him? How could he have been so blind?

He stood at the side of the bed, and Madge patted the patchwork quilt for him to sit down.

'What's wrong, son? What's troubling you?'

Johnny remained standing. He was not in the mood for a tête-à-tête. 'I'm just a bit upset, Ma. I really don't want to talk about it.'

'Sometimes it is better to talk,' Madge said gently. 'You know what they say? A trouble shared is a trouble halved.'

'Not this time, it isn't, Ma. Can I get you anything before I go up to bed?'

She detected the deep misery that engulfed her son and her heart cried out for him, but she did not insist. 'No, Johnny, I don't need anything. Good night, son.'

Eileen raced up the street as if the devil was chasing her. She was breathless as she let herself into the house. Emma met her in the hall, combing her mane of dark hair into place with her fingers. 'You're home early,' she greeted her, obviously perturbed. 'I didn't expect you back for at least another hour, so I didn't.' She sounded peeved by her sister's unexpected return.

Eileen, still seething over her encounter with Johnny, snapped back, 'What's up with you? Surely I can come and go in my own house as I see fit . . .' Her voice trailed off as a young man left the living room to stand, looking a little shamefaced, beside Emma. Jolted out of her misery at the sight of him, Eileen cried, 'What on earth's going on here?' To her knowledge, Emma had never before entertained a man friend while she baby-sat. That it was Danny Docherty knocked all the wind out of Eileen. What on earth was Emma playing at?

'You already know Danny.' Emma was abrupt. Her secret was out. If her father heard that she was seeing Danny Docherty, there would be hell to pay.

'Of course I know him to see,' Eileen, regaining her breath, answered shortly.

'Danny Docherty at your service.' He grinned, looking much younger than his twenty-one years.

A large hand was thrust at her. Already halfway on the road to hysteria, Eileen had to stifle the laugh that sought to escape from her lips as she gazed at the figure before her. Unlike his father, Danny was at least six feet tall. Dark hair was swept back at the sides and combed down in a quiff at the front, in teddy boy style. He didn't have the long sideburns, or the suit with long draped jacket, but he did have the drain pipe trousers that were all the rage amongst some of the younger generation at the moment. Eileen got the distinct impression that he was trying to emulate the teddy boy look. Suddenly, she became aware that he was silently laughing at her reaction to him. When he winked and said, with a nod downwards that brought her attention to his feet encased in blue suede shoes, with soles about two inches deep, 'I'm almost there,' she warmed towards him. She also became aware that Emma was very annoyed. At once Eileen sought to make amends. Gripping his hand, she said formally, 'I'm pleased to meet you, Danny. There is no need for you to rush away. Would you like a cup of tea before you go?'

Danny nodded agreement but Emma, declining, reached for her coat. 'No, we had better get a move on. I'll see you tomorrow, Eileen.'

Danny once again reached for Eileen's hand and shook it. 'Thank you for the offer.'. He smiled wryly at her. 'Even if I was not allowed to accept it. I hope to see you again soon.'

His eyes were admiring as they smiled down into hers and Eileen became aware that he was very attractive. Not what she would call handsome, but attractive, with twinkling blue wide-spaced eyes set in a rugged tanned face. So unlike his father, she again thought.

'Good night, Eileen.' Emma sounded impatient. 'Come on, Danny, let's go.'

When the door closed Eileen pondered on them. How long had Emma been dating Danny? Eileen had gathered that their relationship was not platonic. One thing was sure, her father would not be very happy to hear about it. Irritably, she pushed all thoughts of her sister from her mind. She had enough problems of her own to worry about. As she locked and barred the outer door and then checked the back door and all the downstairs windows, her misery returned in great waves. This was Johnny's nightly routine and the pain deep within her surfaced again. Something awful was wrong but for the life of her she could not fathom what. There was despair in her heart as she wearily climbed the stairs to bed. It seemed her world was falling apart and she did not know how to cope with it.

The next morning Kathleen Rafferty phoned Eileen to let her know that Kate had given birth to a little girl at two o'clock that morning. 'Oh, Kathleen, that's wonderful news. I'm sure you're pleased since it's your first granddaughter.'

'I have to admit that I am. It's nice to have grandsons, but after four I admit that I have been hoping for a wee girl. Will I tell Kate you will be down today?'

'Just try and keep me away. Is Peter here yet?'

451

'Yes. He arrived last night. He's over the moon, so he is.'

'I'm sure he is. I'll see you down at the hospital this afternoon, Mrs Rafferty. Goodbye for now.'

Johnny came into the house while she was on the phone. He passed her without any sign of acknowledgement and climbed the stairs.

When she had finished her telephone conversation, Eileen followed her husband up the stairs. A suitcase lay open on the bed and Johnny was carefully arranging some of his clothes in it.

Stunned, Eileen watched him for some moments in silence. Then she asked, 'What on earth are you doing, Johnny?'

He looked her straight in the face with cold bleak eyes. 'You're not stupid, Eileen! What does it look like I'm doing?'

'But why are you packing?' She was bewildered. What had she done last night to deserve this drastic action? 'Where are you going?'

'I'm moving in with my mother until I decide what to do.'

'What to do about what?'

Johnny's hands grew still and he stood motionless, gazing down blankly at the open case for long seconds. Then slowly he turned to face his wife, needing to see her reaction to his next question. Then he would not be able to doubt his own senses; neither would he be able to kid himself that everything was going to be all right. Nothing could ever be all right again.

'Who is Paul's father?' he asked curtly.

His words were a bolt from the blue. Eileen felt the blood drain from her face and her knees actually buckled as fear coursed through her. Gripping the door for support, she managed to whisper, 'I don't know what you mean.'

He moved threateningly towards her and thrust his

face close to hers. 'For heaven's sake, Eileen, stop lying. Give me credit for having some sense. Has it not sunk into your thick skull yet that I know the truth? I know that Paul is not mine!' Suddenly all anger left him; his shoulders slumped and wearily he turned back to the bed. As he resumed packing, he finished lamely, 'I think I always knew, but I've been such a bloody fool, I didn't want to believe it.'

Mind in a turmoil, Eileen cried, 'I tried to tell you, Johnny, I did! Honestly, I really did. I tried to tell you a few times.'

He swung back towards her, face convulsed with rage, and ground out through clenched teeth, 'Well, obviously you didn't try hard enough, did you? Just tell me this, Eileen. Who the hell is the father? You must have been skulking about with him while you were dating me. All the while I was showing you respect, he was . . . you were letting him . . .' His voice broke at the very thought of it, but quickly regained control. 'That hurt, Eileen. That really hurt. Is he a married man? Does he live around here? I'm going out of my mind thinking about it. It's Kevin Rafferty, isn't it? Have you two been at it behind my back all these years? You must think me a right mug.'

Aghast, Eileen cried out in anguish, 'No, Johnny! No, you've got it all wrong! Paul's father died before he even knew about him. He was killed in an accident.'

Eileen was devastated; her mind racing to find the right words to explain. She had thought that the chance of Johnny's finding out the truth about Paul had diminished with each passing year. To have it thrown in her face now, without warning, floored her. Who had told him? Madge? Just what did he know? Johnny was speaking again.

'I nearly died last night when your father told me.'

'Me dad? But me dad didn't know,' she blurted out in bewilderment.

'He knew more than I did! He knew you were pregnant when we got married and that was enough for me. Who else knows the truth, Eileen? Eh? Did everybody know? Is that why they all treated me like dirt? And do you know what hurts most? You actually let them! You knew I was the innocent party and you let me be blamed. I'll never forgive you for that as long as I live. God, but my mind boggles when I think how stupid I was.'

'Johnny, only me mam, dad, and grannie knew that I was pregnant when we got married. They all thought you were the father.'

'Is that all who knew?' he mocked. 'Just your grannie, mother and father?'

Eileen's voice faltered, but she decided that this time he must be told all the truth. Gamely she admitted, 'Kate Rafferty knew the whole truth right from the beginning. I had to confide in someone, and she knew Billy.'

'Billy?'

'Yes . . . Paul's father.'

Johnny had heard enough. He couldn't bear to hear any more confessions. Slapping the case shut, he fastened it and swung it off the bed. 'I can't stand listening to any more of this crap. I'll get the rest of my stuff later.' He stopped in front of her and sneered, 'This will make you laugh! I actually thought you cared for me. I even hoped that some day you would learn to love me. Isn't that funny? Doesn't that make you want to laugh? I thought you might learn to care, and all you married me for was to hide your shame!'

Her hands reached out and gripped his lapels. 'Johnny, I do love you! You mean the world to me. Please believe me.'

The contempt in the look he gave her made her cringe inside. 'Love me? That's a gag. All these years you never once said those words. Not once! And you expect me to believe you now? Tell me, did you love me when you married me?'

Eileen could not lie to him. She had lied enough to last a lifetime. He saw the truth in her eyes. 'Well then, don't mock me, woman.' With these words he twisted round, freeing himself from her grasp, and roughly shouldering past, headed for the stairs.

Stunned into silence by the ferocity of the attack on her, Eileen stood mute for many moments. Then she sprang into action and hanging over the banister yelled after him, 'And that's it? The past seven years don't count?' Her fury was every bit as intense as his. 'I've worked my fingers to the bone looking after you and the kids, as well as running my wee business. Believe me, it wasn't easy coping with your tantrums. For years I did everything you wanted. It's only lately that I've had any kind of a social life. Now you're just going to walk out on me, all because of your injured pride?'

Johnny was amazed at her audacity. 'Injured pride? Is that what you call it? I have just found out that you cuckolded me and you actually expect me to stay here, all lovey, dovey and forgiving?' he fumed. 'Just what kind of a bloody idiot do you take me for? Eh?'

'Why not? Why shouldn't you stay? I'm still me. I haven't changed overnight. And I won't molest you, you can count on that. I won't try to compete with your beautiful Lorna. You're the wronged husband. You have everything going for you. Why, you can even feel justified now while you're entertaining her on a Saturday afternoon. You can just lay all the blame at my door.'

Confusion blanked all other expressions from Johnny's face. 'I don't know what you're talking about.'

'That's my line, Johnny! Remember, you're supposed to be the injured party. Did you really think I believed you were working every weekend? Eh? Did you really think I was that stupid? Even the day your mother was operated on, you stole away for a couple of hours with Lorna, and you've the cheek to blame me for being unfaithful! Is she like a drug to you? Can't you bear to be away from her? Oh, you hypocrite! You bloody hypocrite!'

Johnny's horrified expression brought Eileen's tirade

to a halt. All the fight went out of her, and she slumped against the banister.

'Are you going to stand there and tell me that you work every Saturday afternoon? Well, don't bother Johnny, because I won't believe you. Go on, get out. Your precious Lorna will be waiting for you. But what about that pride of yours, eh, Johnny? Will you be able to hold your head up in the office? Have you thought about that? The scandal it will cause? Since appearances are so important to you, have you given that any thought?'

He heard her out in silence. Now he mounted some steps and thrust his face close to hers. 'You're mad! I don't know what you're talking about, but I'm not even going to try and justify what I have been doing on my afternoons off. I don't have to explain anything to you ever again. I only wish to God I didn't have to see you again.'

When the door slammed behind him, bringing the children running sleepy-eyed from their rooms, Eileen gathered them close. At least she had her children. Just let Johnny try to interfere where they were concerned! She fought back tears. She must not break down in front of the children. To keep a hold on her emotions, she concentrated on what she was doing and blocked all else from her mind. First, feed and dress the children. Next, go down to church and smile at everyone she met. Then to her mother's house to see if someone would be willing to look after the kids while she went down to the hospital to see Kate and her new baby. She warned herself that she must not cry. Not even in private; a blotched face wouldn't help her any. She must remain calm and keep her faculties about her.

Back from church, she sat in her parents' kitchen and talked brightly about different things. Sarah watched her, a perplexed frown on her face. It was Mick who tentatively broached his betrayal, as he now thought of it.

'Eileen, I've a confession to make. I think you should know that I've let the cat out of the bag where you are concerned. I told Johnny that you were pregnant when you got married. I didn't know the truth, love, or I would have kept my big mouth shut!'

It was Sarah who answered him. 'She already knows, love. Eileen . . . what happened? Did Johnny say anything to you?'

Only then did Mick realize that his daughter was sitting bent over her cup of tea, with great silent tears streaming down her cheeks. Relieving her of the cup, Mick lifted her bodily from the chair and gripped her close. 'Ah, don't, love . . . don't go on so! Nothing is that bad.'

Against the comfort of her father's best woollen pull-over, Eileen sobbed and wailed convulsively. The children paused in their activities, to stand wide-eyed, gazing at their mother. Quickly, Sarah ushered them out of the kitchen and left father and daughter alone to their grief. Mick rocked Eileen gently in his arms until at last the sobs dwindled away and she pushed herself out of his comforting embrace.

'Thanks, Dad. I sure needed that.' She grimaced and with his handkerchief mopped up her tears. Then she wiped the back of her hands wearily across her eyes. 'I must look a sight, and I told Kathleen Rafferty that I would go down to the hospital today, to see the new baby. How can I go down, Dad, looking like this?' She glanced at her father and then cried aloud, 'Ah, Dad, don't you look so worried. Johnny had to know, and I suppose it was better sooner than later. I've been living in a fool's paradise.'

'Eileen, I would cut out my tongue rather than hurt you. You know that, don't you?'

'Yes, Dad, I know that. And I'll be all right. It's just . . . I've had so much on my mind lately, this was just the last straw. But don't you worry, I'll overcome it.'

'What if I had a word with Johnny. Eh, love?'

At these· words Eileen turned a horrified face to her father. 'No, Dad, you must not! Promise me you won't interfere?' she entreated. 'I'll sort this out in my own good time.' Distracted, she sought her mother. 'Mam? Mam?'

Sarah came running from the living room in answer to Eileen's urgent summons, an enquiring look on her face. 'Yes, love?'

'Mam, will you do me a favour? I promised Kathleen Rafferty that I'd go down to the hospital to see Kate this afternoon. Will you go and make some excuse for me? Tell Kate that I'll be down tonight. Will you do that for me, Mam?'

'Of course I will, love. I intended going down anyhow. Look . . . . leave the kids here and you go home and have a bath and a long rest. You will feel all the better for it.'

'Can I do that, Mam? Who will mind the kids?'

'Your dad will look after them while Emma and I go down and see Kate. He won't mind. He'll be glad of an excuse to give the hospital a miss. Go on, get yourself away up home.' She turned to her husband. 'Mick, you walk her up.'

'There is no need for Dad to come,' Eileen protested.

'I know that you will find this hard to believe, Eileen, but your dad can be quite diplomatic at times. If anyone wants to stop and talk to you, he will just kinda shoo them off. Go on, leave the rest to me. Oh, and by the way, don't bother cooking a meal. I'll feed the kids and I'll keep a bite over for you.'

'Thanks, Mam. Thanks a lot.'

Eileen found that a bath followed by a long rest did do her a world of good. She even slept for a while and woke refreshed. With her hair freshly shampooed and face carefully made up she looked all right. Only a very close inspection would show signs of her recent breakdown. No one looking at her would guess that her heart was breaking. It was a fine evening and as she walked down to her mother's house she felt her spirits rise. Perhaps all was not lost. If she was patient Johnny might return. After all was said and done, nothing had really changed. Once he had time to think, surely he would realize this? He could take all the time in the world as long as he forgave her and came back home. Please God, let him forgive me, she silently prayed. She felt a bit awkward when she passed by her mother-in-law's house, wondering if Johnny was watching from behind the curtains. To her dismay the door opened and Madge appeared on the doorstep and hailed her.

'Eileen, come in a minute.' When she hesitated, Madge said, 'It's all right. Johnny is out.'

When the door closed on them, Madge cried, 'In the name of God, Eileen. What's wrong between you two? Johnny's getting on like a bear with a sore arse. What happened last night?'

'He found out about Paul.'

Madge's hand covered her heart and her eyes closed. She stood silent for some seconds. 'How did he find out? Who would be that mischievous?'

'Me dad told him.'

'Mick? Never!'

She sounded so scandalized, Eileen actually smiled, albeit faintly. 'He didn't know that Johnny wasn't Paul's father but he did let it slip out that I was pregnant when we got married. That, of course, was enough for Johnny.' Eileen stepped closer to her mother-in-law. 'Madge, I didn't play around, honestly. It only happened once. I want you to know that.'

Madge's work-toughened hand reached out and clasped Eileen's arm. 'I believe you, love. I believe you.' And all the while her mind asked, But will Johnny?

'Thanks, Madge. I'll have to go now. Mam has the kids. I'll get a bite to eat there and then I'm off to the hospital to see Kate Madden's new baby. Did you hear that she had a wee girl this morning?'

'No. No, I never heard. Give her my regards, Eileen.'

'I will, Madge. Goodbye.'

Eileen closed the gate and turned down the street and was dismayed to see Johnny walking towards her. Her step faltered for a moment, but she squared her shoulders, raised her chin, and continued on down the street.

Johnny's eyes flicked over her. She looked beautiful. There was no sign whatsoever that she was pining for him. He paused as she drew level with him. 'Are the children all right?'

Afraid to trust her voice, Eileen nodded.

'Where are you off to then?' Johnny spoke without thought and could have bitten his tongue out he was so angry with himself. What was it to him where she went? After all, he couldn't trust her; she was no concern of his any more. Nevertheless he found himself hanging on her reply.

'I'm going down to the Royal. Kate had a baby girl this morning.'

Surprised to see relief flicker across his face, Eileen was irritated. Where did he think she was going? Did he think that she had someone all lined up ready to run to?

'I'll have to hurry, Mam is keeping me some dinner.' With these words Eileen continued on her way. Johnny's hand reached out tentatively, as if to stop her, but Eileen was unaware of it. Tears were once more threatening and she was determined that Johnny would not see them. Furiously she blinked them away. She had shed all the tears she intended to shed. One way or the other she intended getting on with her life. If Johnny returned home, great! If not, so be it!

A week passed slowly. Johnny put in an appearance now and again to see the children, but he remained distant with his wife. Eileen made a few futile attempts to get him to talk things over but it was like coming up against a brick wall. Eventually, she gave up and became as distant as he, and they conversed like polite strangers in their own home. Eileen bore it all bravely and smiled when she felt more like weeping. She was glad that she was busy. Her work and the children kept her occupied throughout the day and in the evenings she visited Kate in the hospital. Kate had questioned her a couple of times about Johnny's whereabouts, but then, as if sensing that something was amiss between them and that her friend did not want to speak in front of others, she did not pursue the subject.

Now, today, Kate was home from hospital and sitting across the hearth from Eileen. It was Saturday afternoon and she had called in on her to discuss the christening which was to be the following day. Eileen was elected to be godmother and Kate had hoped to persuade Johnny to be godfather, but there was no sign of him and she sensed that something was radically wrong. She eyed her friend closely, noting the unhappy droop to the fine sensual lips, and the dark shadows under the big haunted-looking eyes that Pan-stick failed to camouflage.

'What's the matter, Eileen?'

She wanted to scream. She had been asked this question so many times during the past week. Kate received the same answer as everybody else.

'There is nothing the matter with me. I'm just tired. I really must go down to Dr Hughes and get a tonic, since everybody appears so concerned about me.'

'Eileen Cleary . . . this is Kate Madden you're talking to. Not some simpleton! Now tell me, just what the hell's wrong with you?'

Without more ado, Eileen said quietly, 'Johnny found out about Paul.'

Kate gasped, but did not waste breath on platitudes. 'What does he intend doing about it?'

'He moved out a week ago. I've hardly seen him since.'

'Where is he staying?'

'At his mother's.'

'Phew! Thank God for that! He hasn't moved far. It's only natural that he's upset, but he'll be back,' she said with conviction.

Glad to have someone she could trust enough to confide in, Eileen impulsively blurted out, 'You don't understand! There is someone else. At least, I am almost sure that he is having an affair with a girl at work.'

'Johnny Cleary having an affair? I don't believe it!'

'She is very beautiful and apparently our marriage won't be the first to suffer because of her.'

'Let me get this straight.' Kate was leaning forward in her chair. 'Just why did Johnny leave the house?'

'I've already told you why! Me dad let the cat out of the bag about me being pregnant when I got married. That's why Johnny left.'

'Well then, . . .' Kate shook her head as if to clear it. 'What makes you think that he is interested in another woman?'

Relieved to get it all off her chest, Eileen explained about Johnny supposedly working every Saturday afternoon. Kate watched her through narrowed eyelids but heard her out in silence, broken only by an intermittent 'tut'.

When Eileen had finished her narration, Kate said, 'You didn't tackle him about it, then?'

'I intended to, but then Madge took ill and we were all so worried about her. But . . .' Eileen's eyes were bleak as she gazed at her friend. 'Even on the very day Madge was operated on, and even though he was out of his mind with worry when he saw how awful his mother looked, Johnny supposedly went into the office for a few hours. It was a Saturday. Now on top of what I already knew . . . well it confirms my suspicions.'

'I'm flabbergasted, Eileen! This doesn't sound like you at all. I've never known you able to hold your tongue.' A puzzled expression flitted across Kate's face and she said, 'Hey, hold on a minute! Didn't you tell me earlier that Johnny has taken the children out for a walk? If he's supposed to be seeing someone every Saturday afternoon, how come he's taken the children out today then?'

'I don't know. You could have knocked me down with a feather when he arrived about an hour ago and said he was taking the kids out for a breath of fresh air.'

'You missed your chance there, didn't you? You should have asked him why he wasn't at work, so you should. God, this isn't at all like you, Eileen Cleary.'

'Kate, when he first challenged me about Paul, I was taken completely unawares. I mean, after seven years, I was sure I was safe and when he suddenly asked me who Paul's father was . . . I nearly died. It was like a bolt from the blue! I tried to bluff my way out of it and he went mad. I was so afraid of losing him, I never mentioned Lorna. It was the next day when he came to pack his belongings that I threw her name in his face.'

'And what did he say?'

'Well, he never denied it. That's guilt enough for me. I love him so much, Kate, but he doesn't believe me.'

'It's about time you realized his worth!' Kate admonished her. 'Still, I think you're wrong, Eileen. Have you made any attempt to explain to Johnny just how you became pregnant?' At her friend's slight shake of the head, Kate continued, 'Well then, you should. He deserves an explanation, and after all, what have you got to lose?'

'He won't give me a chance. He's so cold and withdrawn, it's like talking to the wall. And you must admit that it's not something you can just blurt out of the blue. Remember, even you . . . my best friend . . . had difficulty believing that it only happened the once!'

Kate well remembered her reaction when Eileen had told her she was pregnant and looked shamefaced. 'I know! I know how I got on at you, but you have got to make him listen! When will he be back?'

'Soon, I imagine.'

'Would you like me to have a word with him?'

Eileen looked amazed. 'Are you daft? That's one of the things he hates most about all this . . . the fact that so many people know.'

Kate nibbled on her lower lip for some seconds and her eyes were anxious. 'Well then, you will have to tell him. And the sooner the better! There is too much at stake here for you to dither about. You must bring it all out into the open and then you will know where you stand. Tell Johnny the truth, Eileen.'

The front door opened and closed quietly. Eileen rose to her feet, an enquiring frown furrowing the smoothness of her brow. It could only be Johnny; he was the only one to have a key, but the children must not be with him. It was too quiet for that. They always created a racket when they came in.

She mouthed over at Kate, 'It's Johnny.'

They heard him pause in the hall and guessed that he was taking a peek at Kate's baby daughter who was asleep in her pram.

When her husband entered the room, Eileen greeted him. 'Where are the kids?'

Without looking at her, Johnny replied, 'Mam has them. That's a bonny baby you have there, Kate. What did you name her?'

'Eileen, after my best friend.' Kate was on her feet. 'I was just leaving, Johnny. She will need a feed soon and no doubt a change of nappy.' If Johnny had got shot of the children for a while it was obvious that he wanted a quiet talk with Eileen without being interrupted. Kate was determined not to play gooseberry. 'Eileen, I'll see you tomorrow. By the way, Johnny, is there any chance of you being godfather tomorrow? Eileen is going to be godmother.'

Eileen waited, expecting a polite refusal, but to her surprise Johnny quickly accepted the honour. 'I'd be delighted to, Kate. I've never stood for a child before. It's something I've always wanted to do but no one ever asked me.'

'That's marvellous, Johnny. It's after eleven o'clock Mass in the morning. I'll see you both tomorrow then.' Kate winked knowingly at Eileen and gave her a nod of encouragement as she made for the door.

Johnny helped Kate manoeuvre the pram over the doorstep and out of the gate on to the pavement. They both waved her off and then together returned to the living-room, Johnny first of all closing the outer door, and locking it.

Eileen remained standing. She did not invite Johnny to sit down, but from her stand at the mantelpiece, eyed him gravely.

Her husband stood, head bent, gazing at the carpet and shuffling his feet uncomfortably, apparently embarrassed by what he was about to say. Then clearing his throat with a low cough, he spoke. 'Eileen, we have to talk.'

When his wife remained silent, he flickered his eyes upwards and meeting her intent gaze quickly looked away again. 'I was thinking that perhaps we could live under the same roof ... for the children's sake, that is?' As Eileen turned the implications of this over in her mind, he added into the pregnant pause, 'It will also stop people gossiping about us.'

'You have obviously given this a lot of thought, Johnny, so spit it out. Put me in the picture. What exactly have you got in mind?'

Flinching slightly at the harshness of her voice, he sighed before saying, 'Like I said ... I will move back in. I will of course sleep on the bedsettee in your office,' he quickly assured her. 'I won't make any demands on you.'

465

'Oh, well, that's a relief,' she cried sarcastically. 'And what about your Saturday afternoon outings? Hmm? Will they continue as normal?'

He reddened slightly, but admitted, 'Yes, I'm afraid they will.'

'Oh, will they, indeed? And just why should I be so accommodating? Eh, Johnny? Or could you possibly mean that I'll be free to fly my kite, should the notion take me?'

She saw Johnny's face actually blanch, but his voice remained calm when he replied, 'If you are so inclined, I will certainly not stand in your way.'

So he really didn't care about her any more. Lorna was all he was interested in. A great feeling of desolation swelled within Eileen, threatening to overwhelm her. However, pride came to her aid, and head high, she mocked him. 'How come you are free today then? Is Lorna tied up with her step-father again?' How could he put up with this web of deceit? And how come Lorna's mother is so lenient towards her daughter and husband?

His shoulders lifted in a slight shrug. 'I hadn't much on today, so I took the opportunity to take the kids out.'

'Now . . . I want to make sure that I am picking you up right. Do you mean that we will live under the same roof but go our own separate ways? Is that what your mean?'

'If that's what you want, Eileen.' Sadness tinged his words.

Eileen was indignant. There he was, shifting the blame on to her. How dare he! 'No, Johnny, I don't appear to have any say in the matter,' she cried. 'You're the one who is laying down the rules. You seem to have it all figured out.' Realizing that she was bawling, she swallowed to regain control of her temper, and continued more quietly, 'However, for the children's sake I'll agree to go along with you. Just don't blame me if it doesn't work out. All right?' With these words she brushed roughly past him. 'You had better go. I have work to do.'

Johnny returned late on Saturday night with the belongings he had taken from the house over the course of the week. Bidding Eileen a curt good night, he immediately retired to her office and the bedsettee. On Sunday morning they prepared for the christening in silence. Eileen dreaded what lay ahead. She was aware that those in the know would be avidly watching and speculating. If Kate had not asked her to be godmother she knew that she would have found some excuse to be absent. To her surprise, before they left the house Johnny put a hand lightly on her arm, saying, 'Don't worry, Eileen. Everything will be all right.'

This she found hard to believe; so far as she could see, nothing would ever be all right again. However, true to his word, Johnny put on such a convincing act that even she was tempted to believe that all was well between them, and relaxing, she played along with him. From the benign looks directed at them by her parents and Kate, Eileen knew that everybody was hoodwinked, and felt happier than she had for a long time. If only Johnny had not become infatuated with Lorna Pollock he might have found it in his heart to forgive her. Instead, as things stood, he now had a good excuse for his own infidelity.

It was a wonderful day. The Raffertys laid on a slap-up feed and the drink flowed freely. Johnny even managed to be affable towards Kevin Rafferty and Eileen hoped that this was a foretaste of what the future held. If Johnny continued to behave like this, surely at some future date they must bury the hatchet and come together again as husband and wife?

That night, once the children were in bed and asleep, Johnny once more bade Eileen good night and headed for her office.

'Johnny, there is no need for you to spend all your time in the office.' She spoke tentatively, unsure how he would respond. 'Surely we can be a bit more friendly towards each other? Eh? Sit in here. Can I get you anything? A drink maybe ... or perhaps you would like a cup of tea?'

Slowly Johnny crossed the room and sat down in the armchair facing her. 'A wee whiskey would be nice ... if there's any left?'

'Of course there is! Who do you think was drinking it? Me?'

Johnny rose to his feet. 'I'll get it myself. Will you join me?'

'No, thanks all the same, I've had enough for today. But I'll have a small glass of orange juice, please.'

Johnny sipped at his whiskey and watched his wife covertly over the rim of the tumbler. She appeared to be deep in thought and he was tempted to offer her a penny for them. However that would never do. He was tipsy and if Eileen was any way nice to him he was likely to forget the promise he had made, not to make any demands on her. Quickly draining his glass he rose to his feet. 'I'll see you in the morning, Eileen.' He made his way to the kitchen and, rinsing the glass under the tap, put it to one side to drain.

Eileen gazed blankly at the doorway. So much for her intentions to try and act normal. Her husband was scurrying off to bed like a scared rabbit. When he passed through the living room again she kept her eyes averted. Let him run on! She didn't need him. Johnny paused in front of his wife and gazed down on the beauty of her. Thick auburn hair caught the light and long lashes fanned pale cheeks as her downcast eyes avoided his gaze. He had thought her so pure! Why had she deceived him? After all this time, did it really matter? These thoughts brought him up short. What was he thinking of? Of course it mattered! She had fobbed him off with another man's child. Suddenly he realized that staying under the same roof was not such a bright idea. He wanted her! After all she was his wife, but . . . he had promised not to molest her. In spite of urging himself to get out of the room before he made a fool of himself, he leant closer.

'Eileen . . . I know you think I'm an ignorant fool, and I promised that I would not make any demand on you. If I stay in the same room as you I might . . .' He shrugged. 'You know . . .' his voice trailed off lamely. Her eyes slowly lifted and met his. The look in them caused him to mutter, 'Ah, Eileen, Eileen.' As if without volition his arms hovered towards her. Swiftly Eileen rose to her feet and entered them, and he pressed her close. It had been a long time since he had held her. She felt soft and welcoming against him and her perfume wafted around them. He wanted her! He wanted her fiercely. The blood was pounding through his veins for need of her. His fingers threaded her hair and he pressed her closer still. As passion mounted Eileen drew his head down to hers. Once their lips met, all Johnny's promises to stay at arm's length flew out the window. Sweeping her up in his arms, he quickly climbed the stairs and laid her on the bed.

It wasn't exactly how she would have wished it to be. He kept apologizing and repeating that he had promised not to make demands on her, and here he was doing just that. He kept saying, how could he forgive such deceit? Kept asking why couldn't she love him? Was he so obnoxious? She assured him that he was not in the least obnoxious and that she did love him dearly. When at last he fell asleep, she cradled his head on her breast and sadness engulfed her. She knew that all her declarations of love were in vain. Even in his drunken state, Johnny had not believed her, but given a chance she would do all in her power to convince him. Tonight was a step in the right direction.

Awareness came slowly to Eileen the following morning.

She lay with closed eyes, at peace with the world. It was a long time since she had felt like this. Nowadays she was reluctant to face each new dawn without Johnny. Slowly she opened her eyes and turned towards her husband; the bed was empty. A glance at the clock showed her that it was half-past five. Much too early for Johnny to get up to prepare for work. Where was he? She smiled wryly; she could make an educated guess. Slipping her feet in to her slippers and shrugging into her dressing gown, she left the room. The bathroom door was open and he was not there. Slowly she descended the stairs. Quietly making her way along the hall to her office, she gently turned the doorknob. Johnny was sprawled across the bedsettee, snoring his head off.

In the kitchen Eileen made herself a cup of tea, and sat down for a good think. It was obvious that Johnny had regretted his weakness last night. He had no intentions of forgiving and forgetting, or he would not have left her bed. She had been vulnerable and he had used her. Tears stung her eyes as she remembered her actions and entreaties of the night before in an endeavour to make him believe that she loved him. And all in vain! Bitter resentment rose like bile in her throat. To think that she had let him reduce her to that state. Oh, but she hated him! Hated and detested him! It was just a pity that hatred was so akin to love. Her lips clamped tightly together, and her hands gripped the cup convulsively as she fought for control. How would she be able to look him straight in the face? She must! For the sake of her self-respect, she must face him without tears or reprimands. Her pride must see her through this latest episode of the charade her marriage had become. She had been such a fool! He had made her feel so dirty. One thing was certain: Johnny would never again use her like that. The next time Lorna was away, he could seek his favours elsewhere. She would never, ever, let him touch her again, she vowed.

* * *

The following weeks were strained. A mediocre June slipped lazily into a scorcher of a July. Eileen was sad as the weeks passed slowly by. June had seen the birth of Beth's son, and now that her confinement was over, she was directing her attentions towards buying a new house. Listening to her sister's plans to buy one of the new houses being built near the Broadway cinema saddened Eileen all the more. Johnny and she should have bought and by now been settling into a new house while the good weather held out. They had the money, but he showed no inclination to look at houses, and she didn't dare suggest it. They were in a rut! If she shed the odd tear at the unfairness of it all, no one was aware of it, least of all her husband. Her mother seemed to realize that although Johnny was back living at home, all was not well between them, and questioned her daughter. Eileen adroitly averted the conversation and Sarah inquired no more. She knew that she had been politely put in her place.

Kate had remained in Belfast with her mother for some weeks after the birth of her baby. While her friend was at home, Eileen managed to spend most of her spare time with her, especially in the evenings when she wanted to escape the silent intrusion of her husband. With Kate she did not have to put on an act. She could be her old self without worrying about letting her private affairs slip out. Kate, seeing the weight drop off her friend, worried about her and begged her to tell Johnny the truth. Eileen, still smarting from her husband's behaviour, was adamant that he must approach her first, and show her a bit more respect, so she resisted Kate's pleas. Although the June weather had not been great, on good days, together with the children, they had made their way up the mountain loney as far as Kate's pram would allow, and picnicked by the small waterfall. They also travelled as far afield as the Botanic Gardens and spent an afternoon in those colourful surroundings. One day when Kevin Rafferty was off work, he ran them to Bangor and spent the day there with them. Eileen had left a salad supper ready for Johnny and her conscience was clear when they arrived home in Kevin's car. They were living as strangers, and she felt that she owed Johnny no consideration. Still, when she saw the misery on his face when Kevin left her and the children off at the door, she felt like weeping. If it still distressed him to see her with Kevin why didn't he forgive her and forsake Lorna? Surely if he had some feelings for her there was still hope? Then she admonished herself not to live in a fool's paradise! Johnny didn't care or he would spend all his spare time at home with his family. As far as she could make out, he thought more of that woman than he did of his wife and children.

The morning that Kate was travelling back to her patiently waiting husband in Dublin, she visited Eileen. 'I've come to secure a promise from you,' she stated.

'Secure? What a very posh word. It sounds ominous,' Eileen laughed. 'But if it is in my power I will oblige you.'

'I want you to bring the children down to visit me for a couple of weeks . . . say, about the middle of August? Will you do that, Eileen?'

'Oh, Kate, that would be great, but isn't your family all going down during the summer? Won't you be fed up with visitors? And what about Peter? Won't he mind?'

'Yes, some of the family are coming down. Some I will be happy to see, but others I could see far enough, but you . . . you I will always be glad to see, and Peter is all for it. He likes you! So will you come?'

'All being well, Kate, I'll be down. That's a promise!'

Holding her close, Kate said, 'I look forward to it. See you then. I'd better run now. Kevin is getting out of work for a couple of hours to run me to the station. Goodbye, Eileen. And keep in touch, won't you?'

'Goodbye, Kate, and thanks for all your help. I don't know how I would have got by these past weeks without your support. See you in August. I'll give you a ring as soon as I know just when I can come. Away you go now, or Kevin will be wondering where you've got to.' With a gentle push, Eileen sent Kate on her way.

The twelfth fortnight was approaching. They had often grumbled about the way all the big firms closed for the same two weeks in July every year, which meant that everybody was booking holidays away at the same time. Eileen had hoped that Johnny would suggest they go away somewhere for a week, but no, holidays were not mentioned. It was the Wednesday before the twelfth when he approached her, and she could see that he was nervous. She waited breathlessly. Was her husband going to suggest that they go away together?

'I've probably left it too late to ask you, but . . . well, the usual crowd are meeting on Saturday night for a farewell drink before we break up for the holidays. Would you care to join them?'

Eileen successfully hid her disappointment. She was a fool! All Johnny wanted was to keep up a front at work; pretend that he was still a happily married man. She eyed him closely. He too was losing weight and looked quite gaunt. She was aware that she herself didn't look the picture of health, and queried the wisdom of going out into company. 'Would that be wise, Johnny? Don't they know all about you and Lorna at the office?'

'No, they don't know anything about me and Lorna at the office,' he barked in exasperation.

Quickly, she retaliated. 'I had to ask! I really don't think that it would be wise to go.'

'Surely you could put on an act for a few hours?' he taunted her. 'I did it for you!'

473

'Oh, yes, I could. And I know for a fact that *you* can! But will you? That's the question. Lately, you look as if you've forgotten 'how to smile.'

In spite of himself, Johnny felt his lips twitch. 'If I promise to smile all evening, will you come with me, please?'

'Is it just an informal get together? Not a dinner dance?'

Johnny nodded. 'Just about eight of us. It will only be for a few hours.'

'All right. If I can arrange a baby-sitter, I'll come.'

'Thanks, Eileen.'

It was a change of venue on Saturday night. Instead of the cocktail bar in the International Hotel they met the others in the lounge in the Deer's Head pub on Lower Garfield Street. To Eileen's delight, Lorna and James did not put in an appearance. She had been all keyed up to watch for any sly exchanges between Johnny and Lorna. When the couple failed to arrive she breathed a sigh of relief and was able to relax and enjoy herself, though she did wonder if Johnny was disappointed. If he was, it did not show. In fact, there were no innuendos from anyone. Knowing that Margaret Patterson would not have failed to drop her a hint if there was any gossip in the office, Eileen assumed that her husband and Lorna must be very discreet indeed. The outing was successful and Johnny seemed at ease with himself. He had drunk very little and it was Eileen's turn to be a bit tipsy. As they travelled home, she vowed that tonight would not see a repeat of the last fiasco when it was Johnny who was the worse for drink. She silently vowed to keep a tight rein on her emotions.

While Johnny paid off the taxi, Eileen entered the house. Tonight she wasn't surprised to find Danny Docherty in the company of Emma. Tossing her coat over the banister, Eileen smiled at them. 'Can I get you anything before you go?'

'Thanks all the same, Eileen, but we have just had a bite of supper.'

'Thanks, Emma. You too, Danny. We are much obliged.'

If Johnny was surprised to see Danny Docherty in his home, his face was non-committal. Thanking them both, he politely showed them out and locked and barred the door.

'Would you like anything to eat, Johnny?' Eileen's voice was hesitant. Not wanting to linger in his company, she hoped he was not hungry.

'No, no. I'm ready for my bed.'

Relieved, she said, 'Well then, good night, Johnny.' She was at the bottom of the stairs when his voice reached her.

'Eileen?'

Slowly she turned and faced him. 'Yes, Johnny?'

'I . . . I was . . .' She saw him swallow convulsively and waited patiently. She had no intention of encouraging him. 'Can I? I mean . . .' His voice trailed off.

Eileen knew only too well what he meant. She stood silent, waiting.

'Ah . . . it doesn't matter.' Again he hesitated, then said sadly, 'Good night, Eileen.'

'Good night, Johnny.' Seeing his shoulders slump as he headed for her office, she hardened her heart. Had she not vowed that he would not use her again?

The children slept late the next morning and for this Eileen was grateful. She remained in her room until she heard Johnny leave the house. Once awake he did not hang about and she smiled grimly at his haste to get away. He was afraid to face her, after her rejection. When she eventually descended the stairs she found an envelope propped up against the kettle. Eyeing it for a long time, she wondered, What's he writing to me about? Has he decided to leave again? Had he been trying to tell her so last night, and she, fool that she was, had thought he wanted to sleep with her?

The envelope was thick! Fingering it inquisitively she reached for the bread knife and slowly slit it open. It contained money and a brief note: 'Eileen, I have booked you and the kids into a boarding house, address above, in Bray for a week, starting tomorrow. Please forgive me for pestering you last night. I was an absolute boor! Johnny.'

He had booked her and the children into a guest house! No mention of himself. Where would he be while she was in Bray? And with whom? That was the burning question. Did he take her for an imbecile? Was he trying to get her out of the way for a week, while he was off work, so that he could gallivant about with his precious Lorna? Well, he was not going to succeed. Or was this to have been her reward for favours received had she responded last night? Whatever the reason, she wanted no part of it. It gave her great pleasure to tear the money and note into shreds. She replaced them in the envelope, and going into her office, wrapped them in the bedclothes where Johnny could not fail to notice them when he opened out the bedsettee that night. Then she folded the bed away. One of Johnny's chores was tidying the bedsettee before he left for work each morning. It showed how great was his hurry to get away that morning that he had neglected to do this.

The twelfth fortnight was a time of misery and pain for Eileen. She avoided Johnny like the plague; leaving him to attend to his own meals and washing and ironing. She had done her last chore for him. She had no intention of becoming his skivvy. He had asked to return for the sake of the children. To put on a front for their sake and to allay the curiosity of family and neighbours. Well, from now on she would devote her life to the children and Johnny could go jump in the lough for all she cared. It was at times like this that she most missed Claire. Her sister had been such good company. Would go anywhere at the drop of a hat. Emma was kind but she didn't like trooping about with the children, so Eileen did not try to involve her. As for Beth, unlike Kate she preferred to stay at home with her baby son. Besides, Eileen was sick to the teeth listening to her sister's plans for her new house. During the day, weather permitting, she took the children to the seaside; one day to Bangor, another day to Helen's Bay, or else they visited one of the many parks that were abundant in Belfast. On days when the weather was not so good they went to the pictures or visited her grannie or mother. Anywhere just to keep a distance between her and Johnny. Not that he was about much. But still, she did not want to be in the house with him sulking about, tripping over his bottom lip. The visits to her family were a terrible strain as she had to maintain a happy front. The money and planned trip to Bray were never mentioned again. Neither did Johnny volunteer any information as to where he spent his days, and pride forbade her to ask. He certainly did not offer to accompany her and the children on any of their trips, and her resentment towards him grew and grew, like a cancer eating away at her.

The second week of the holiday period was even worse! Phillip came home from Manchester for two weeks and between dodging him as well as her husband, Eileen thought that she was going round the bend. She even considered moving out of the house, but decided against it as she had too much to lose. Besides, where would she go?

At long last the holiday fortnight came to an end, and Johnny returned to work. For the first time in two weeks Eileen relaxed. She was so exhausted, she was actually glad when Phillip came and offered to take them all out for the day. She declined to go herself, but said that she would be forever grateful if he would take the kids off her hands for a few hours as she had a lot of work to catch up on. This was the truth. She had allowed for some free time off, but not two full weeks. Now the work had piled up and she must make up for lost time. To make it worthwhile for Phillip she offered to have a meal ready for him when he returned. Saying that he would call in and warn Madge that he would not be home for tea, he piled the excited children into the hired car and set off.

Eileen prepared a beef casserole and put it in the oven before retiring to her office where she attacked the backlog of paperwork with unnecessary energy. Then, satisfied with her labours, she prepared the vegetables and set the table. Having the house to herself, she even allowed herself the luxury of wallowing in the bath. With her hair shampooed and face carefully made up, she thought that she looked presentable.

Phillip, when he arrived back, told her that she looked beautiful. He had Marie in his arms fast asleep and across the child's head, his eyes spoke volumes. 'Louise is also asleep in the car,' he informed her. 'And Paul's not far behind. They had fish and chips about an hour ago, Eileen. I suggest you put them straight to bed and bathe them in the morning.'

'That's a good idea, Phillip. Will you carry them upstairs for me? I'll join you in a minute when I've put a light under the pots. You go on up the stairs with Uncle Phillip, Paul.' She gave her young son a hug and placed him on the bottom stair. 'I'll be up in a minute to tuck you in, love.'

Phillip helped Eileen get the children into their pyjamas and soon they were tucked up in bed and fast asleep. When they descended the stairs Eileen was very aware of Phillip's admiration and it was like salve to her bruised pride. She told him to pour himself a whiskey and take a seat while she finished off the dinner. He poured himself a drink and followed her into the kitchen.

On his way through the living room he had eyed the

table, set for two. Now he asked in a nonchalant tone, 'Is Johnny not joining us, then?'

Eileen had her excuse ready; she must not give Phillip any leeway, or he would pester her. 'He warned me that he might not be home until late. If he should come in there is enough for us all.'

He leant against the door frame and ran his eyes over her slim figure. 'Eileen, I can't help but notice that you have lost a lot of weight since I last saw you . . . are you on a diet?'

'You're letting your imagination run away with you, Phillip. Don't you know that it is fashionable to be slim?' she chided gently. She herself was worried about her weight loss. This was far and beyond the fact that she was unhappy. It was how her body chemistry first reacted to pregnancy. With each of her pregnancies she had lost weight before putting it back on again. So far there was no sign of morning sickness, but it was early days; with Marie she had been in her third month before sickness prevailed. Daily she prayed that she had not conceived. The idea of another pregnancy, with relations between her and Johnny at breaking point, filled her with dread. How would he react? He would probably accuse her of playing around again, such was his opinion of her. She kept her smile bright as she teased Phillip, and to her relief he did not pursue the matter.

Eileen opened a bottle of wine with the meal and under Phillip's admiring glances and humorous conversation, she mellowed and her whole demeanour changed. Seeing the transformation, Phillip cursed his brother. He would give his right arm for the chance to make Eileen happy.

Johnny arrived just as they were finishing their dessert and Eileen was on the defensive again. She looked her husband full in the face and he knew that he was being warned to put on an act for Phillip's benefit.

'Oh, so you got away earlier than you thought?' she

479

asked with a smile. It was obvious to both men that the smile was laboured. It evoked pity in one, and annoyance in the other.

Johnny eyed his brother with displeasure but followed Eileen's lead. 'Yes, I got finished sooner than I expected.'

'I saved you some beef casserole. You lift it for yourself. There's some potatoes and turnip as well.'

When he returned to the table with a laden plate, Johnny asked his brother, 'What are you doing here?' As he sat down, his eyes noted the empty wine glasses and the whiskey glass. It looked like his brother had been enjoying himself.

Before Phillip could reply, Eileen spoke out. 'Phillip very kindly took the children out for the day to let me catch up on my backlog of work.'

'Did he, indeed? How kind of him.'

Johnny's surly manner put a stop to any further pleasantries and when he had drained his after dinner cup of tea, Phillip rose to leave. 'I'll take the kids out tomorrow again if you like, Eileen. It will give you a break.'

'Thanks, Phillip. That will be a great help. I'll see you out.' At the gate she apologized for Johnny's behaviour.

'How can you put up with the like of that, Eileen?' he cried in bewilderment. 'Why don't you leave him?'

'You just don't walk out when something upsets the applecart, Phillip.' Voice very low, she explained, 'He found out about Paul.'

Phillip stepped back and gaped at her in amazement. 'I'm surprised you're still alive!' he exclaimed.

'He took it very badly.'

'Ah, well . . . I suppose any man would,' Phillip agreed.

'I must give him time to come to terms with it. I'm asking you to please respect my confidences and don't ever let him know that you are aware of the truth. Please, Phillip. Can I depend on you?'

His smile was sad and he shrugged slightly. 'Well, since

I can't persuade you to leave him, I can at least assure you of my trustworthiness. My lips are sealed, Eileen.'

'Thanks, Phillip. Thanks a lot. I appreciate all you've done for me.'

Suddenly he gripped her arm with great urgency. 'Let me do more, Eileen! Let me take you away from here. I love you!' When she drew back in alarm, he said, 'It's all right. It's all right. Don't look so scared. I'll behave myself. I'll see you in the morning, about ten. Good night, love.'

Still trembling at the force of his outburst, Eileen whispered, 'Good night, Phillip. I'll have the kids ready.'

Johnny had the table cleared and was in the kitchen washing up. Joining him, Eileen lifted a glass cloth and started to dry the dishes.

'It took you a long time to say good night, didn't it? What were you two talking about?'

It was on the tip of Eileen's tongue to tell him to mind his own business but she bit the words back and said mildly, 'We were arranging about picking the kids up in the morning.'

'And it took you ten minutes to do that?'

Furiously she rounded on him. 'Are you actually timing me, now? You! Who never tells me where you go or who you talk to? Don't you dare talk to me in that tone of voice, Johnny Cleary. Remember . . . you're the one who laid down the rules here! If I want to talk with someone else, I will! I don't need to ask your permission. I did warn you that you might not like the consequences. remember?'

Johnny stood gripping the edge of the sink and Eileen could actually see him fight for self-control. He won!

Swinging away from the sink he strode to the door. 'You're right, of course. Good night, Eileen.' Without waiting for a reply, he left the kitchen. She heard the office door close and with a sigh resumed drying the dishes. It seemed she was always in the wrong no matter what she did. Perhaps she should seriously think of leaving Johnny. This was no kind of life. It was easy to fool the children now, but as they grew older they would be bound to notice that their parents were anything but civil to each other. At least her job had made her financially independent and the money her grannie had given her was some security. She would wait until she returned from Dublin, before making up her mind.

The next morning she had a phone call from Kate. 'Eileen, what do you think! Peter got the chance to rent a cottage in Bray for a month, starting this Saturday. We went to view it at the weekend and it's a beauty. Right on the sea front! Would you be able to come down for the first two weeks? Peter is doing a bit of private tutoring and won't be able to get away. Could you possibly come, Eileen?'

'Oh, that would be lovely, Kate, but I would have to check my workload first and see if I can afford to take time off. What if I can only make it for one week? Would I still be welcome?'

'Of course! That would be better than nothing. Do your best, won't you? Let me know as soon as possible. Oh, there's the child crying! I'll have to go. 'Bye, for now.'

Since Claire's death, Eileen had employed a young trainee accountant, who was on maternity leave, to help out now and again. Anne Murray could be depended upon. If she had nothing better to do, she would be glad of the extra money. Eileen was sure that, if possible, Anne would oblige her. She was very competent and Eileen would be able to go to Bray with a contented mind if Anne was in charge. A few telephone calls and soon it was arranged. Anne Murray would take on Eileen's workload for the next two weeks. All excited at the idea of joining Kate in Bray, Eileen set to work with a will. Besides clearing up the backlog, she had only three days to get all the children's best clothes ready. She was grateful that Phillip had them away to the Zoo for the day, but there would be no meal waiting for him when

482

he returned this evening. It would be too dangerous! She was lonely and vulnerable, and Phillip made her feel attractive and desired. Hopefully, he would understand. If not . . . tough!

She was excited when she broke the news to Johnny that night. It would do them both a world of good to get out of each other's hair for a while. They were both functioning on a short fuse at the moment. To her dismay, she apparently set Johnny's fuse alight. Her husband rounded on her in a fury.

'Do you mean to tell me that you are going to Bray, relying on someone else's charity? And to a rented house, at that! Exchanging one sink for another. And you threw my offer of a week's full board back in my face?' he spluttered vehemently.

'I didn't want to go on my own with just the kids for company,' Eileen retaliated, angrily.

'You could have asked me to join you! Was that expecting too much? Or would it have spoilt things for you?' he yelled back.

Open-mouthed, Eileen gaped at him. 'You wouldn't have come with us!' She was not so sure of herself now. 'Would you?'

'Since you chose not to invite me, you will never know the answer to that now,' he yelled back even louder.

He watched indecision fight confidence on Eileen's countenance. Confidence won. Her look turned derisive and her head tossed. 'No, no, Johnny! You wouldn't have come. Why, you didn't even take us away for a single day's outing when you were off work. You were too busy flying your kite, you had no time for your own children.'

'My own children! How can I be sure they *are* my children?' The words came out without thought and he immediately regretted them. Eileen's face crumpled and he could see tears threatened.

'Eileen, I'm sorry. I didn't mean that. Of course I know the girls are mine!'

'Are you sure, Johnny? You seem to think of me as a trollop, so how can you be so sure the girls are yours? Eh?' She tried to sound defiant, but the words came out in a whimper, she was so shaken. Rocking gently back and forth, she hugged herself as if for comfort.

'Eileen ... I spoke out of turn. I was in a temper. I didn't mean what I just said.' Tentatively, he reached for her, wanting to soothe away the hurt that was so apparent. She cringed back from him and his arms flopped helplessly to his sides.

'Please forget I spoke! I honestly didn't mean it.' His arms stretched wide in a futile gesture and he headed for the door. Suddenly he swung round again. 'Tell me one thing. How do you intend getting to Bray? Eh? Don't you dare ask our Phillip to take you, or there will be hell to pay!'

Eileen's mind went blank for a moment; she had indeed intended asking Phillip to run her and the children to Bray. Now she fabricated. 'Me dad will be only to happy too run me down to the station, and I'm sure Peter Madden will pick me up at the other end. So you needn't bother your arse about us.'

Ignoring her unbecoming language, Johnny hissed through clenched teeth, 'I'll take the day off and run you to Bray in the car. And I don't want any more arguments about it!'

On these words he turned on his heel and left the house. Eileen stared after him in confusion. Lately, he was acting like a complete stranger. She never knew just what next to expect from him, but after this exchange her resolve to leave him was strengthened.

Bright fingers of sunlight, poking through a chink in the blinds, awoke Eileen on Saturday morning. The children were all excited and breakfast was a makeshift meal. Paul and Louise were too excited to eat and their high spirits rubbed off on Marie. Eileen could not persuade her to eat either. Johnny ate his breakfast in instalments between journeys from the house to the car, loading up the boot. He had surprised Eileen the night before by approaching her and asking for a truce; saying that he didn't want to spoil her holiday. Now he appeared to be in quite a genial mood. She wished that things could be like this always, and they were like any other normal family going on holiday together.

The journey was pleasant enough. There were no problems finding their way through Newry and Dundalk but they came unstruck in the big city. They entered Dublin during the busy period when the roads were choked with cars, buses, and more bicycles than they had ever seen in their lives before. It was the latter means of transport that caused Johnny most concern, cyclists recklessly threading their way in and out of the traffic. More than once he had to brake hard to avoid hitting one of them. Such was his concentration, he failed to see the road sign to Bray. Eileen was no help at all as she sat watching the Dublin life go by and gazed in fascination at the large department stores. Eventually, he managed to pilot the car in the right direction. After a few wrong turnings on the strange roads they at last arrived at the cottage. Kate was watching at the window and came rushing out to greet them. She was obviously pleased to see Johnny, and assumed that he intended to stay. 'Johnny! Peter is coming down later today, to stay overnight. He will be delighted to see you. But you will have to bunk down on the settee, mind. Will that be all right?'

To Eileen's surprise, he accepted with alacrity. 'That will be fine, Kate. I can only stay one night as well. There's no rest for the wicked,' he jested. Eileen gazed at him nonplussed. Her husband would never cease to amaze her.

The cottage was large, comfortable and modernized. It belonged to a friend of Peter's, and Kate was delighted to have it for a whole month. As she had said, it was right on the seafront and they spent the afternoon and early evening on the beach with the children. After supper, Johnny asked Eileen if she would like to take a walk along the promenade before retiring for the night. Hiding her surprise with great difficulty, Eileen said that she would love to. A blush warmed her face as under Kate's knowing eye she threw a cardigan across her shoulders and followed her husband from the house. Strolling along with the warm sea breeze fanning their faces, Eileen had the overwhelming desire to tell Johnny that she was pregnant again. It would be great to throw caution to the winds and confide in him. She stifled the urge. After their last war of words she was afraid of what he might say. In a way, their last encounter had been like a one night stand and Johnny seemed to doubt that one could conceive just like that. Besides he was making such an effort to be pleasant that she was afraid of disrupting the peace that bound them.

Pulling her arm companionably through his, Johnny pressed it close to his side. 'Eileen, I'm sorry about last night, really I am. I couldn't sleep for worrying about it. I don't for one minute doubt that the girls are mine. Do you forgive me?'

She nodded her head silently, and he continued, 'Listen, Eileen, when you and the kids return, we will have to make a greater effort to live in harmony. I know I have not been the nicest person in the world lately, but . . .' He slanted his eyes at her profile. 'You must admit that I have had just cause.'

Words of rebuff sprang to her lips but she swallowed them. Why bring Lorna Pollock's name up now? No, it would only spoil what had turned out to be a wonderful day. She brought her attention back to her husband, as he continued.

'I've been thinking, Eileen. We have three lovely children.' Her heart warmed at these words. That was one way she could not fault him. His attitude towards

Paul had never altered; he still treated him as his own flesh and blood. Johnny really was a good person. All their troubles had stemmed from her deceit. Now she listened attentively.

'I'm sure you will agree with me that three children is enough, so why can't we have a marriage of convenience? Be there for our children. Give them every chance we can. We could even go on holiday together. Live like any other ordinary couple except for . . . you know.' He shrugged negatively, as if sex was of no importance.

Eileen couldn't believe her ears. He didn't want a proper marriage any more. But then, he had Lorna! But what about her? What about her needs? And what about the baby she now knew for certain was growing inside her? Tearing her arm roughly from his grasp, she put the width of the walkway between them.

When she spoke her voice was shrill. 'I'm sorry, Johnny, but I can't agree with you there. I happen to want more children. I would like another two. So you see, a marriage of convenience wouldn't suit me at all. What will you do now? Ask me for a divorce?'

'Hush! There is no need to let the whole country know what we're talking about. And don't be so silly! You know rightly, that we can't get a divorce.' He looked perplexed, and his confusion came across to her. 'I don't understand you, Eileen. I've thought long and hard about this, and I really believed that you would find my proposition appealing. After all, you have made it quite clear that you don't want me . . . you know . . . in that way. Well, that's your prerogative. But . . . don't you even like me any more?'

'Oh, Johnny!' Eileen was utterly exasperated. How could she ever get through to him? 'What's the use? You never believe a word I say. I may as well talk to the wall as talk to you.'

Much to her relief they arrived back at the cottage. Leaving his side, Eileen quite literally flew down the

487

path and indoors. By the time Johnny negotiated the length of the path and entered the cottage his wife was nowhere to be seen. Everyone else had retired, so with a heavy sigh he arranged the blankets and pillow that Kate had left folded on the settee. He was beginning to despair of ever understanding his wife again. There were times when she seemed like a complete stranger to him. The way she was acting, you could be forgiven for thinking that he was the one in the wrong.

Next morning when the house awoke, Johnny had gone.

Two weeks later, it was with reluctance that Eileen packed her bags and prepared for the homeward journey. In spite of morning sickness, she had enjoyed herself immensely. Kate sat on the edge of the bed and watched her pack.

'I'm sure going to miss you, Eileen.'

'Once Peter arrives tonight, you won't have time to miss me.'

'Will you promise me one thing, Eileen? Promise you will tell Johnny about the baby.'

'Mmm.'

'Eileen, you must! You need his support and help. Good God, you have to tell him. He has the right to know.'

Eileen sat down beside her friend. 'Kate, I've told you everything else, so I may as well tell you – Johnny doesn't want any more children. He only wants a marriage of convenience.'

'Never!' Kate's eyes were round with surprise. 'You mean . . . you told him you were pregnant and he said he didn't want another child?'

Eileen's head swung slowly from side to side, and she explained. 'No! He doesn't know I'm pregnant, but he does want us to live together as friends . . . you know what I mean? So I am going to ask him for a separation.'

Kate turned these words over in her mind and Eileen

488

continued, 'It's all right for him. He has Lorna! But what . . .'

'Here, hold on a minute, Eileen,' Kate interrupted her. 'After seeing the way Johnny Cleary looked at you when he thought no one was watching, I don't believe for one second that he's having an affair. Besides, I've known him as far back as I can remember and he has always been the same. He's too decent a man to get involved with another woman!'

'Where then is he spending his Saturday afternoons? Eh? And where did he spend his time when he was off work for two weeks? He was out every day, Kate, and he never once said where he was or what he was doing!'

'For heaven's sake, Eileen, why don't you ask him where he was? Put yourself out of all this misery. You're changed a lot, Eileen Cleary. It's not like you not to face up to things. Don't beat about the bush! Ask him straight out, for heaven's sake. If what you say is true, then you can get a separation!'

'You've got to be joking! I couldn't ask him! My pride wouldn't let me.'

'Ah, Eileen. I think you are being awfully foolish. How will you manage with four young children? Where will you go? Eh? You won't be able to survive on pride alone.'

'I'm going to play on Johnny's sympathy. I'll ask him to move out. He can live with his mother. Or Lorna . . . for all I care.'

Their conversation was brought to a close as shouts from the children heralded the arrival of Johnny. Once the car was loaded, and they had eaten a bite of lunch, Kate waved them off. Her heart was sad. She had been tempted to take Johnny to one side and have a quiet word in his ear. However, if that hadn't worked out Eileen would never have forgiven her, so she had resisted the temptation. Why were they being so pigheaded? It was obvious to her that they loved each other. Why couldn't they see it?

*   *   *

489

If the truth were known, Eileen was very disappointed when she returned home. For weeks she had thrown Johnny all sorts of hints, that this could do with a coat of paint, and that needed a lick of varnish, and wouldn't the girls' room look lovely with pink wallpaper? Her hints had fallen on deaf ears. The house was exactly as she had left it. Oh, it was clean and tidy but no decorating whatsoever had taken place. But then, she reasoned, she was a fool to have expected anything else. It was just another sign of her husband's indifference. Johnny had better fish to fry. It strengthened her resolve to ask her husband for a separation.

Still, for another few weeks Eileen dithered. It was such a big step that she was contemplating. She would miss Johnny! Even if they were not all that close, he was at least there in the house in times of need, and she felt safer because of it; especially as her husband appeared to have turned over a new leaf. He was attentive, helpful, and trying so hard to be affable. He was even spending his Saturdays at home now; taking the children out from under her feet. Leaving her free to go shopping. If she had not been pregnant she would have waited to see what the outcome of his endeavours would be. But she was pregnant, and soon she would be unable to hide it. What would Johnny's reaction be? Would he accuse her of playing around? That, she would be unable to bear. If he dared accuse her of that, she would never ever forgive him. She would throw him out of the house! A great well of bitterness assailed her. Was she to suffer for the rest of her life because of one unforgettable experience in the dark grounds of the Floral Hall with Billy Greer? She must tell Johnny about the baby before she became noticeable. Still, she wavered. What was she waiting for, she asked herself, a miracle?

Standing in front of the full-length mirror, Eileen examined her image. She was beginning to put on weight. Her breasts were more rounded and her waistline thicker. She could not afford to dither about any longer! It was time to tell Johnny; time for a showdown. Her condition would soon be apparent to all. He glanced up when his wife entered the living room and his eyes stayed on her. She was worth looking at! Weeks in the sun had threaded her hair with bronze tints. It now reached her shoulders and was a mass of unruly curls. Her skin was honey-coloured and her eyes were pale and glittering like diamonds. Standing there in her white cotton dress she looked about eighteen. There was an aura about her. He examined her intently and suddenly the truth hit him like a sledge hammer. She was pregnant! There was no mistaking that soft ethereal aura. Dragging his eyes away from her, he gazed intently into the fire, fighting for composure. He had delayed too long; she had met someone else. Rising abruptly to his feet, he brushed past her. He needed some time to himself! Time to think how this would affect all his carefully laid plans.

'Johnny! Where are you going? I need to talk to you.'

His reply was muffled, as he opened the outer door and left the house. If Eileen had not known otherwise, she would have sworn he was drunk. She had been unable to make out a single word he had just said, his voice had been so slurred. Slowly she sank down on to the settee. There was no hope of saving her marriage. Johnny could not even bear to stay in the same room as her. He was as changeable as the weather. Tears gathered in her eyes and she let them flow. There was no one to put on a brave front for. She very much doubted that her husband would be home again that night.

Johnny found himself in St John's church. At this time of night the church was almost empty. Just two other people were there; one man kneeling deep in prayer, and a woman alternating between the sacristy and the altars with vases of fresh flowers. Johnny knelt in the front pew and gazed blankly at the tabernacle. Was there really a God there? Just when he had come to terms with Eileen's betrayal, here she was, pregnant again. Well, if she had strayed, he had no one to blame but himself! Who did he think he was ... some kind of saint? He may as well be, the way he was behaving. Holier than thou, that was Johnny Cleary. He had acted as judge and jury. He had eventually convinced himself that he must forgive and forget if he was ever to know peace again. However, the way Eileen was behaving, he had been unable to tell her of his change of heart. Their future was all laid out as far as he was concerned. He had worked so hard these past months, but by doing so had neglected his wife. She had been vulnerable; left open to temptation. While he had been working towards a better future, Eileen had been lonely. He should have let her know what he was up to. Now it looked like she had met someone else. She would probably want to leave him. And he deserved it! Oh, yes, he would be the first to admit that he deserved it! He had been a surly bugger these last few months. It was a wonder that Eileen hadn't moved out before now. He should have held out the olive branch long ago, then she would not be pregnant today. What did it matter that she didn't love him? He loved her! Could not imagine life without her.

The question that he had been avoiding came to the fore in the muddled layers of his mind, and he acknowledged it. Who was the father? Phillip? Oh, God, no! Not his brother! How could they get round that? He could not bear the thought of it! The very idea sickened him. But suppose Phillip was the father? Would he still want to hold on to Eileen? Yes, he would fight Phillip for her, or any other man, for that matter. He loved her and could not bear to let her go. But to rear another child that was not his own? Could he bear it? Burying his head in his hands, he prayed long and earnestly for guidance.

Half an hour later, quietly letting himself into the house, Johnny made his way along the hall and entered the living room. Eileen was curled up on the settee fast asleep. In sleep she looked so young and vulnerable. He could see that she had been crying. Her head was tilted back against the arm of the settee and tear streaks ran from the corner of her eyes into her hairline.

Kneeling by her side, he gently touched her face. Her eyes shot open and she started up in panic. 'It's all right, Eileen. It's only me.'

When she would have sat up he placed a hand on her shoulder and gently stayed her. 'I want to talk to you. I've a lot of apologizing to do.'

'Johnny ... before you start, there is something that I have to get off my mind. I've been trying to tell you ... I'm expecting a baby.'

'I know.'

Her eyes widened and her mouth opened. 'You know? How do you know?'

'I realized it tonight. You have that look about you.' He grimaced and added, 'I have to admit, it knocked the wind out of me.'

'I'm sorry. I know you don't want any more children, but it just happened. We strayed from the safe period, remember? And this is the result.'

Johnny was stunned. Her words were going round and round in his head. We strayed, and this is the result. *We* strayed ... what did she mean? To hide his confusion and give himself some respite, he sank his head onto her breast. Could the child possibly be his?

Still uncertain – after all had she not duped him once before? – he lifted his head and met her eyes. 'Why didn't you tell me?' he asked in bewilderment.

'I only found out for certain shortly before I went to stay with Kate, and you were never here. I saw very little

493

of you.' Her voice was accusing and he bowed his head abjectly. 'Then, that night on the promenade, just when I had plucked up enough courage to tell you . . . what did you do? You said you didn't want any more children. You wanted a marriage of convenience!'

'I only said that because you wouldn't let me anywhere near you, Eileen. I thought you couldn't bear me to touch you! I didn't want to lose you, so I convinced myself that as long as we shared a home, it would be all right.' He gripped her hands tightly and gazed beseechingly at her. 'I'm truly sorry, love. I admit I've been a right bastard. Can you ever find it in your heart to forgive me? Please?'

'Can *you* forgive and forget, Johnny? Devote yourself to me and the children? That's what I want to know. I won't stand for any more nonsense. I want a proper marriage. I want a man who is here when I need him. Not just when it suits him.'

'Just give me one more chance, Eileen . . . please?'

Her eyes searched deep in to his for a long time. Solemnly, he held her gaze until at last she nodded. He had not mentioned Lorna Pollock. Well, only time would tell if he had severed all connections with her. It would be difficult for him, she realized, since he worked in close proximity with the girl. Meanwhile, Eileen could only take him on trust.

'What about the baby?'

'Eileen, . . . remember when we were first married, I said let's take all God sends? Well, if we want to give our children a good start in life,' he cupped her face in his hands and held her gaze, 'I think another two will be quite sufficient. Don't you agree?'

Joy lit up her face like a spotlight and she whispered, 'Yes, Johnny.' She could not believe her ears. She expected to wake up and discover it was all a lovely dream. 'Oh, Johnny, I do love you so.'

He was unable to believe his ears – the words he had always longed to hear had finally come. But he could not doubt his wife's sincerity. He was filled with a warm glow.

'Really, Eileen? Do you really and 'truly love me?' he whispered hoarsely.

'Yes, I do, I love you very much. But before we go any further, I must explain about Paul.'

At once Johnny checked her. He was afraid he would not be able to cope with the intimate details. 'There is no need, Eileen.'

'Oh, but there is! I want to be able to bury the past once and for all.'

She shuddered at the memory of that unforgettable night and went on to describe how in all innocence she had left the lighted ballroom and gone out into the dark grounds of the Floral Hall with Billy Greer. In a voice that trembled, she explained how Billy had been too strong for her.

'The bastard!' Johnny interrupted.

Eileen shouldered part of the responsibility. 'I should have recognized that he was drunk. Then I would never have gone outside with him. I should have known better.'

'I wish you had told me this sooner, Eileen.'

'I tried, God knows I tried! But you always picked me up wrong.'

'Why didn't the bastard marry you?'

'He was killed in a road accident ... the very next night.' She tugged playfully at his hair and inquired, 'Besides, would you have believed me?'

With a wry smile he admitted, 'I really don't know. As you well know, I'm a jealous bugger. Can't bear to picture you with anyone else.' He was glad that Eileen had forestalled his apologies. He shuddered to think of her reaction if he had jumped in feet first and assured her he would willingly take on yet another man's child rather than lose her. That would have been unforgivable. She would surely have asked him to leave.

495

Silence reigned for many moments. It was Eileen who broke it. 'Do you know what I think, Johnny? I think it was all meant to happen. You see, I don't think I would have married you otherwise. I mean . . . I was very fond of you, but I thought you were too old for me. I never dreamed that I could ever fall in love with you, and now I love you so much I can't imagine life without you, ever.'

Gripping her by the arms, Johnny hauled her down on to his lap. 'I can't believe what you're saying, Eileen. When did you discover that you loved me?'

'To be truthful, I honestly don't know. You just gradually grew on me. And then, when I thought for sure that you didn't love me, I was really worried out of my wits. I thought our marriage had come to the end of the road. You see, Johnny, I couldn't bear the thought of going on as we were. Tonight I was going to suggest a separation.'

He kissed her soundly and vowed, 'Everything will be different from now on, you'll see. I will spend the rest of my life making you happy, love.'

'Really?' she asked mischievously. When he nodded, she added, 'Well, if you really mean that, you can start by doing a bit of decorating. This house needs brightening up. It's beginning to get on my nerves, so much needs doing.'

His nose wrinkled with distaste. 'Ah, Eileen, you know how much I hate painting and papering.'

Laughing happily, she pushed herself to her feet. 'Don't worry . . . I'll give you a hand with it.' She stretched out a hand towards him. 'Come on, let's go to bed.'

Bounding enthusiastically to his feet, Johnny gripped her close. 'Yes, that's the best offer I've had today.'

Next morning he brought Eileen her breakfast in bed. The three children crowded into the room after him. Louise and Marie each presented her with a small posy of violets, and Paul solemnly brought her the morning paper.

'I see someone's been down to Grandad's shop bright and early. Thank you, darlings, they're beautiful. Come on . . . give us a big hug.'

As they clambered on to the bed beside her, she eyed Johnny over their heads. 'What's all this in aid of?' she asked suspiciously. 'Don't you think for one minute that you're getting off the hook this easy! Today we're going down to Christie's for some wallpaper and emulsion. OK?'

'Whatever you say, love. Now, kids, get off the bed so that I can set this tray down before there's an accident.'

When the children scrambled down off the bed and raced noisily out of the room. Johnny placed the tray carefully on her lap and, bending, kissed her. A long satisfying kiss.

Breathless and pleased, she chastised him, 'My breakfast will be getting cold if you don't knock off.'

'I'll let you get on with it, love. As soon as you are ready we'll go out.'

'Where? Where will we go, Johnny?'

'I thought you wanted to go shopping,' he cried in astonishment. 'Have you changed you mind already?'

'You mean, your are actually taking me out shopping?' She pretended to faint. 'I expected you to cry off. What about the kids?'

'We'll take them with us. Don't look so surprised, Eileen.' Johnny laughed aloud at his wife's expression. 'Remember, I'm a changed man. Your wish is my command. So hurry up and get a move on.'

An hour later they all piled in to the car and set off. At the corner, instead of turning left down the Falls Road towards the city centre or across and down the Donegall Road, another route to town, Johnny turned right and pointed the car towards the upper Falls.

'Johnny . . . where are you going?'

'I want your opinion on something. It won't take too long.'

When they approached Milltown Cemetery, where the road forked, he chose the road to the right; the Glen Road. They travelled some distance up into the countryside where new houses were in various stages of construction and completion.

At last, entering a driveway, Johnny drew to a halt in front of an impressive-looking new detached house.

'I want your opinion on this house. Maybe we could afford to buy one like it in a few years time . . . if you really fancy it, that is.'

Slowly, Eileen got out of the car. A house as grand as this would surely be beyond their means? To her mind, it was a mansion. Even the children seemed subdued as they tumbled from the car and stood looking about them in silence, as if trespassing on someone's private property, waiting for the inevitable angry shout. But not for long! Spying a tree with low-hanging branches down the side of the house, Paul ran towards it, followed by his two faithful disciples. The garden was partially landscaped and a man was raking over the new soil in one of the flower beds. He lifted his hand in a knowing greeting, but Johnny barely acknowledged him; he was busy searching Eileen's face for response.

'Well, what do you think?' His voice held an edge of boyish excitement.

Eileen was in a trance. Her eyes were roaming all over the front of the beautiful house. It was more than she had ever dreamed of. Double-fronted, the bay windows were wide with a lead diamond pattern. The door was a shining dark mahogany with a half lead-light; a beautiful scene with three mallards rising in flight, in all their glorious green and blue and purple and white plumage. It was also adorned with the very best of brass furniture. Slowly Eileen advanced and gingerly fingered one of the mallards. 'It's beautiful, Johnny.' Her voice was soft as if she was afraid of breaking the spell that bound them. A deep sigh escaped her lips. 'However, I don't somehow or other think that we would ever be able to afford anything as splendid as this.'

'If we could . . . would you mind living up here? It's pretty far out, mind. No corner shops and no running down to your mam or grannie when you feel like it.'

'That wouldn't matter! In a house like this, I'd be in my glory. I wouldn't want to leave it.'

Digging into his jacket pocket, Johnny fished out two shiny door keys on a ring and proudly handed them to her. 'Open the door to our new home, Eileen.' His eyes were bright with unshed tears as he watched her reaction to his words. All the pain he had suffered, all the innuendos about his behaviour with Lorna, were forgotten at the expression of wonder on his wife's face. All his lonely labours spent over the past months were now brought to happy fruition.

'You mean . . . Surely you can't mean this is *our* house?'

'Oh, indeed I do! And a terrible time I had trying to keep it a secret. I wanted to surprise you and my reward is the look on your face at this very moment.' He kissed her briefly on the lips and gave her a little shake. 'Come on . . . hurry up and open the door, or don't you want to see inside?' he teased. Over his shoulder he addressed the gardener. 'Hi, Jack, will you keep an eye on the kids for a couple of minutes?' Receiving his affirmative, Johnny quickly followed his wife into the house.

Eileen stood in the hall and gazed around her in wonder. It was a large square hall with three doors opening off it. The smell of new plaster and fresh paint hung pungently in the air. On the bare wall facing the front door hung a small framed tapestry with the embroidered motto: 'WELCOME HOME, EILEEN'. She stared speechless at it, and then at Johnny, tears glistening in her eyes. Throwing her arms around him, she gave him a long, fierce hug. Regaining her composure, she pushed him gently away and walked towards the door to her left, high heels clicking on the black and white hexagonal tiles beneath her feet. The door opened on to a magnificent room with a great slate mantelpiece above a cream-coloured tiled grate.

Johnny followed her. 'This is the lounge, Eileen. I know you like Maggie's fireplaces, so I felt safe choosing this one. Did I do right?' Sensing a withdrawal on the part of his wife, he was quick to add, 'Mind you, it can easily be changed if you don't like it!'

'Mmm. No, no, it is beautiful, Johnny. It's out of this world,' Eileen assured him, at the same time warning herself: Now be careful! Don't let resentment spoil everything. Let him have his big moment. Nevertheless, she found that she could not shrug off the bitterness that threatened to consume her. She was hurt that he had planned all this alone; had kept her in the dark. Did he not realize that she would have wanted to share in all the preparations? Or had the house originally been meant for Lorna Pollock? Aghast at this unwelcome thought, she turned away.

Unable to understand the sudden change in his wife, Johnny gently guided her down the room towards a door at the bottom. 'Come through here and see the kitchen, love.'

He threw the door open with an exaggerated flourish. His spirits were dampened; he felt cheated. He was not getting his just reward for all the planning and supervising he had put into this house. Eileen should be ecstatic. Instead, her brief silent glance took in the fitted cupboards, the shining enamel sink, the black and white stove, and an open door looking into what was surely the dining room. Without a single word of appreciation, she went to the back door and inserted the key in the lock. Opening the door she stepped outside and stood staring forlornly at the back garden with unseeing eyes.

The doubts she was harbouring were overwhelming her. Just where did Lorna Pollock fit into all this?

Suddenly Johnny became aware that she was crying. Great silent tears springing from a well of uncertainty gushed unchecked down Eileen's cheeks.

Hastily going to his wife, he gathered her close. 'What's wrong, Eileen? Don't you like the house?'

Gazing intently up into his face she replied with more anger than intended, 'Of course I do, and what kind of fool wouldn't? But was this house really built for me, Johnny? Eh?'

Uncomprehending, he stared at her in confusion. 'What on earth are you talking about?' he asked, completely baffled.

'I mean ... did you build it for Lorna Pollock? Eh, Johnny? Did she turn you down?'

His jaw dropped in amazement for some seconds, then he was thrusting her away from him in anger. 'I don't believe I'm hearing all this. How can you even think such a thing?'

'Well, just you look at it from my point of view, Johnny Cleary! For months and months I've been in the depths of despair. Miserable and lonely while you have been enjoying yourself up here. If you were building this house for me ... why didn't you include me in your plans? Or did you think I wasn't capable of making a decision?'

The enormity of what he had done hit Johnny like a thunderbolt and he hurried to make amends. 'I intended to! Honestly! Once the blueprints were ready I intended that we would sit down and plan the interior together ... then I found out about Paul. Can't you imagine how I felt, Eileen? Here I was, working my fingers to the bone to build you a dream house, and all the time you had been deceiving me! To be truthful ... at that time I made up my mind that you would never set foot in it. I planned to sell it once it was completed. Then as time passed the thought of life without you brought me to my senses. I couldn't visualize a life that didn't include you. Even if it meant only sharing this beautiful house with you, so long as I was near you, that was all that mattered to me.'

Overwhelmed by this confession and his declaration of love, Eileen wailed, 'Ah, Johnny. I'm sorry. Now I've spoilt your lovely surprise. I'm so very sorry.' Tears continued to fall and he thrust a handkerchief into her hand. 'Here now . . . wipe those tears away. There will be no more crying.' In spite of himself, there was a touch of exasperation in the way he led her back to the house. Trust Eileen to throw a spanner in the works!

In an effort to appease him, she gushed, 'I still can't believe it. It's just . . .' Her outstretched arm encompassed the kitchen. 'It's beautiful, so it is. And to think this was where you have been spending all your spare time.' He nodded and she sobbed, 'And I was so beastly to you. But you see, I thought . . . I thought . . .'

'I know exactly what you thought. You thought that I was having it off with Lorna Pollock. Didn't you?'

Eileen hung her head in shame and nodded. Gently Johnny tipped her tear-streaked face up to his. 'How could you be so silly, Eileen? Can't you get it into that thick skull of yours, that I have never needed anyone but you, as sure as God is my judge.' Kissing her briefly, he led her through a third door leading from the kitchen back into the hall again, saying casually, 'By the way, you might be interested to know that Lorna married James a couple of months ago.'

'But . . . but . . . he's her step-father,' Eileen gasped.

'Nevertheless, they are married and have emigrated to Canada. It was a quiet affair. Nobody from work was invited.'

'But what about her mother?'

'I don't think she'll mind too much. She died about two years ago.'

'You never said anything about it to me. You let me think . . .'

'I didn't know, Eileen. I just assumed that Lorna's mother didn't like socializing. Lorna told me her mother was dead the same day she told me she was marrying James. And remember, I did say there was nothing going on between me and Lorna but you wouldn't listen.'

Still doubtful, a vision of bright red and jet black curls close together flitted through Eileen's mind. Tentatively she asked, 'You're not sorry?'

Cupping her face in his hands, Johnny held her eye. 'Not in the slightest.' He edged her towards the last door off the hall, adjacent to the staircase. 'This is the living room, love.' He nodded towards the stairs. 'And you won't have to worry about the children running up and down the stairs with dirty feet, destroying the lovely carpet I'm sure you are already picturing in your mind, because there is a fair-sized cloakroom under the stairs, complete with toilet and wash hand basin. Mind you, Eileen,' he confessed, 'I've spent most of our savings getting this house just the way I want it. If I had just put down the bare deposit it would have been the same as the rest of the new houses on the road. That's why I spent all my spare time up here supervising the work. I wanted to make sure that I got my money's worth. However, I certainly didn't touch your wee windfall from Maggie, so you will have a good start towards carpets and furniture.'

'I can't wait to get started! Oh, Johnny . . . that staircase is beautiful. I can just picture how it will look once it's carpeted.' She stood and gazed upwards. The staircase was wide. Three steps led to a shallow landing with a large window looking out on to the side garden. Eileen paused there to look out at the children playing before continuing up the main stairway. At the top of the stairs she stood and looked down into the grand hall. Hurt still rankled but she contained it

503

and smiled bravely, determined not to cause any more discord.

Seeing she still needed reassurance, Johnny moved closer to her and gripped her hands. Holding them tightly against his chest, he said earnestly, 'I meant to tell you! I swear I meant to tell you, Eileen! Once it began to take shape I intended bringing you along to get your opinion on everything. But when I found out about Paul I was very hurt and angry. It took away all the pleasure that I was experiencing. For a long time the pain embittered me. Then I realized that I just could not exist without you. That night we walked on the promenade in Bray I was going to tell you about it . . . ask you at least to live in the same house as me. Remember what happened that night? Mmm?'

Eileen smiled faintly at the memory. 'It seems we were at cross purposes,' she said sadly.

'You can say that again. Let's be glad that at last everything is sorted out and we can begin to enjoy ourselves without any more bickering.' He kissed her; a long searching kiss that asked forgiveness. At last, as the feeling of depression slowly evaporated, she responded and he smiled down at her. 'Come on now, love, let me show you the rest of our domain.'

The three main bedrooms were big and spacious and Eileen had no difficulty expressing her pleasure at them. She immediately earmarked a small box room for her office, and as she so aptly put it, the bathroom was out of this world. Regaining her former happiness, with stars in her eyes, she cried, 'Now, Johnny, when can we move in?'

'Whenever you like! It's ours! Lock, stock and barrel.'

'Well then, let's get back down to Rockmore Road and start packing. This is the first day of the rest of our lives and I don't intend to waste one single minute of it!'

Before they left the house, Eileen stood in front of Johnny and gazed up at him mischievously. 'I'm glad

I confessed how much I love you, otherwise you would have thought it was this lovely house that bound me to you.' Becoming serious, she asked, 'You do realize now how much I love you, don't you, Johnny?'

'Yes, Eileen, I believe you. You have made me the happiest man in the world.' He hugged her close for a long time, then opening the door said, 'Come on, the past is over and done with! Let's get on with the rest of our lives.'

Playing With Fire

I dedicate this book to my daughters-in-law,
Debbie and Helen, and my sons,
Con, Paul and Edan.

Acknowledgements

I would like to express my sincere gratitude to
Shelagh Peacock of Darlington, Cath Holden,
also of Darlington, and Sue & Billy McDowell from
Belfast, whose special assistance was invaluable.

Author's Note

The geographical areas portrayed in *Playing With Fire*
actually exist and historic events referred to in the course
of the story are, to the best of my knowledge, authentic.
However, I would like to emphasise that the story is
fictional, all characters fictitious and any resemblance to
real persons, living or dead, purely coincidental.

Chapter One

Nervously Susan Cummings followed her friend up the stairs that led to the Club Orchid dance hall. Each Sunday night saw them outside the Club Orchid on the corner of King Street where they met for their weekly venture into modern ballroom dancing. In the small cloakroom Ruth Vernon met Susan's eyes in the mirror and asked excitedly, 'Well? Did he turn up?' Receiving a brief nod, she hurried on. 'Well, what happened? Was he nice? Are you going out with him again?'

'Yes, he was very nice. A perfect gentleman, if you must know. But . . . I don't think I'll be seeing him again.'

Ruth's eyes went round with surprise and her mouth gaped slightly as she probed. 'Why on earth not?' Bewildered, she cried, 'I don't understand. Did you not fancy him after all?'

Oh, if only that were the case, Susan lamented inwardly. But the simple truth was he hadn't asked her for another date. They had gone to the Ritz Cinema but she couldn't remember much about the film; just that it was a western and Jim seemed to have enjoyed it. He had held her hand throughout the film and she had been so aware of the pressure of his arm against hers, sending tingles through her body, that she lost all interest in the film and sat in a well of happiness. He had been a perfect gentleman all evening. After the film they had walked up to Johnny Long's and each had one of his famous fish suppers. Sitting in one of the booths they had talked for ages. She had been enchanted. No long pauses punctuated the conversation, like they usually did when she was talking to the opposite sex.

At the corner of the street where she lived, Jim had seemed taken aback as he eyed the wide avenue with its opulent houses. He made no attempt to find out which of these houses was her home. He had already realised his mistake and was content to make his good night at the corner of the street. 'Posh, eh?' he said and a wry smile twisted his lips. Her heart had turned a somersault when he placed his hands on her shoulders and looked down into her eyes. With all her might she willed him to kiss her, but in vain.

'Susan, I've really enjoyed myself tonight. You're wonderful company. Thanks for coming out with me.' His voice was full of emotion and the back of his hand sensually trailed her cheek, but as she moved her lips towards it, it was quickly withdrawn. 'Good night, Susan.' To her amazement, with a light peck on the cheek he had turned tail and was gone before she could voice her concern.

Tears pricked her eyes as abruptly she answered Ruth's question. 'He didn't ask for another date.'

'Didn't ask? You're having me on! It's obvious he fancies you. Good heavens, he never takes his eyes off you. Even when you're both dancing with different partners.'

'Well, he didn't ask me, so there!' Susan cried, her frustration showing. 'He was a perfect gentleman, so he was. He gave me a peck on the cheek and thanked me for going out with him. And that was that! He must just like dancing with me,' she added forlornly. 'Or perhaps he found me too boring.'

'Don't be silly! It's obvious that he cares for you. He was probably afraid of you turning him down.' Ruth shot a concerned look at her. 'Were you snooty with him? You can sometimes be very snooty, you know, Susan. You take after your mam in that respect. Still, he will be here tonight, you'll see. The minute we enter the ballroom he'll be there like a flash, asking for a dance.'

Susan fervently hoped her friend was right. She certainly hadn't been uppish with him. She saved that for people she didn't like. And she liked Jim. More than liked him. In fact, to her great consternation, she thought she was in love with him. Could these feelings possibly be love? They had danced often these past six weeks ever since they first met. She had been thrilled to bits when he had at last asked her for a date. And this was the outcome: sadness and despair.

Fluffing her soft, dark-brown hair loose around her face, she renewed her lipstick and eyed her reflection in the mirror. Big, dark, grey eyes, set in long thick lashes, gazed mournfully back at her.

'Don't look so glum,' her friend advised. Then, seeing the big eyes cloud with tears, Ruth added more gently, 'You really do like him, don't you? Never mind. Let's hand in our coats and go and give tonight's talent the once-over.'

Inside the ballroom they made their way over to the side of the dance floor where all the girls gathered. A quick glance across the floor to where the men stood and Susan felt her heart drop. Jim Brady was tall, easily identified in a crowd, and it was obvious that he was not present. Ruth squeezed her hand in sympathy. 'It's early yet. He'll come,' she whispered. 'Don't worry about it.'

The music started up and two young men who had been eyeing the girls up, and slowly edging closer, approached and asked them to dance. The evening entertainment had begun. The girls were extremely good dancers and popular with the regulars. New patrons soon noticed and the girls seldom sat out a dance. The time flew past and, in spite of Jim's non-appearance, Susan enjoyed dancing to her favourite records.

At the intermission, while their current partners were in the pub below the dance hall getting them drinks, the girls climbed the stairs to the cloakroom to powder their noses.

'For heaven's sake cheer up, Susan. I don't know how you're managing to get any partners tonight! You've a face as long as a Lurgan spade.'

Susan rounded on her in anger. 'Don't exaggerate, for goodness sake!'

Then, catching sight of herself in the mirror, she had to agree with her friend and giggled ruefully.

'That's better. Forget Jim Brady and enjoy yourself. Maybe it's just as well he's not here if you care so much for him. He's probably got more sense than you and doesn't want to start something that can only end in tears.'

'What do you mean?'

'He's a Catholic, isn't he? Imagine·your dad's reaction if you dared bring a Catholic home. Eh? Why can't you be like me and love them and leave them? Enjoy yourself! You wouldn't catch me getting involved with a Catholic.'

They were descending the stairs to the dance hall when Susan saw Jim cross the lower landing and enter the hall. Seeing the joy on her companion's face, Ruth followed the direction of her gaze and sighed. 'Really, Susan, you would be better off without him,' she warned. 'I didn't realise that you were so keen on him.'

'Oh, don't be daft. I just like him.'

Dismayed that she had allowed her current dance partner to monopolise her time, Susan trailed reluctantly behind Ruth to join the two lads. Jim's swift glance quickly found her and their eyes locked. He nodded in acknowledgement. His glance also noted that she and Ruth had obviously paired off with the two young men. He eyed the unattached girls still gathered in a group to one side of the dance floor and, when the music started up again, he had already chosen his partner: a tall, willowy blonde, who entered his arms obviously delighted at the chance to dance with him.

They passed each other often on the crowded floor, but Jim studiously avoided looking her way. Susan was annoyed with herself. She should not have allowed this stranger to stake a claim to all her dances. She might have guessed that Jim could possibly arrive late. Still, he had never been late before, so how was she to think otherwise? As the evening wore on Susan tried to think of a way to get rid of her partner without offending him, but he just would not take the hint.

Meanwhile Jim danced all the dances with the blonde and Susan noted that the tall girl hung on his every word. Was he not going to ask her to dance with him at all? But how could he, when her partner never left her side? As the last dance was announced, and knowing that Jim would never encroach on another man's territory, Susan was tempted to excuse herself and, leaving her partner, ask Jim for the last dance. She was saved from the embarrassment this would undoubtedly have caused by seeing Jim leading the blonde on to the dance floor at the first bar of the final waltz. Blinded by tears and seeking comfort, Susan let her partner hold her closer than was necessary. Jim made her aware of the wantonness of this action by the disdainful sneer he directed at their bodies.

Bewildered, she pressed closer still. How dare he! How dare he look at her like that, after ignoring her all evening. To her great shame she suddenly realised the effect her actions were having on her partner. Gazing up into his dazed eyes, she pushed him away. 'I'm sorry. Very sorry.'

'No, it's me who should be sorry. I apologise. I couldn't help myself.'

Breaking from his grasp she pushed through the dancers and left the ballroom. In the cloakroom she powdered her flushed face and, retrieving her coat and Ruth's, waited impatiently for her friend. She was one of the last to arrive and, pushing through the other girls, confronted Susan.

Edging her into a corner for some privacy, Ruth whispered furiously, 'Just what do you think you're playing at? Leaving that poor sod standing on the dance floor.'

'Oh, I'm so sorry, I didn't mean to offend or embarrass him.'

'I don't know how you manage it, but in spite of everything he still wants to see you home.'

'Oh, no!' Susan was aghast. 'I don't want him to see me home. I just want to be alone.'

'Catch yourself on! Jim Brady will probably be seeing that blonde home. Show him you couldn't care less. Anyway, I'm afraid you have no choice. I accepted for you. And I think it's the least you can do, after the way you behaved. They will both be waiting outside for us.'

Ruth started back in amazement when her friend gripped her arm. 'Tell him I've already gone. Please, Ruth. Here, I've got your coat for you. You go on now and I'll stay here as long as I can. Give you all a chance to get on your way.'

Ruth looked at her friend's flushed, distressed face. Heavens above, she was actually trembling. 'What's got into you, Susan? You've been leading him on all evening. It's not like you to deliberately hurt someone.'

'I don't want to hurt him, but I will not be pressurised into his company. Not in the state I'm in at the moment.'

'Oh, all right then! I'll give you a ring tomorrow afternoon.' Ruth peered intently into her friend's eyes. 'Will you be okay on your own?'

'Of course. Just get me off the hook, please.'

Oblivious to the curious looks and whispers of the other girls, Susan waited patiently until the cloakroom emptied and she was alone. Then, stretching her limbs to relieve some of the tension from her body, she slowly left the cloakroom, knowing the staff would want to lock up as quickly as possible.

Downstairs, she cautiously stepped on to the pavement and breathed a deep sigh of relief. The crowds had thinned out and there was no one she knew in sight. It was a beautiful evening; a time for lovers, and she felt sad as she made her way down to the bus stop. As she hurried along she became aware that someone was close behind her and glanced anxiously over her shoulder. Jim lengthened his stride and quickly joined her.

'Is it all right if I see you home, Susan?'

A quick disdainful lift of the head accompanied the derisive retort. 'Huh! What happened to the beautiful blonde you danced with all night?'

'Janet? She is attractive, isn't she?' He grinned and glanced sideways at Susan's glum face. 'However, I had no desire to see her home. I hung about outside in the hope that you wouldn't let that big ape you were dancing with take you home.'

'He's a very nice person, so he is,' she defended her absent partner. Turning a suspicious look on him, she frowned. 'I didn't see you outside.'

'Well, I saw Ruth and the two lads head towards Castle Junction, but I stayed out of sight in case someone else was with you.'

She stopped and rounded on him in anger. 'What do you take me for? Eh? Do you really think I would dance all evening with someone and then go home with another man?'

Gripping her by the elbows, he shook her slightly.

'Then why isn't he here with you now? The way you were dancing together I could see he thought he was on to a good thing.'

'How dare you! If you followed me just to hurl insults, please leave me alone.' With these words she wrenched herself free of his hold and stormed down Castle Street.

Jim gazed after her for a few seconds, then with an exasperated sigh set off in pursuit.

When he reached her, he was dismayed to see tears rolling down her cheeks. Drawing her into the doorway of the Bank Buildings, he thrust a handkerchief into her hand and gathered her close.

'Here now, don't go on like that,' he said gently. 'I didn't mean to upset you. It was just my jealousy getting out of hand.'

Surprise stopped the tears and she gaped up at him in disbelief. 'You were jealous?'

He frowned. 'You sound surprised.' A quick glance at his watch caused him to exclaim. 'Look, if we don't hurry we'll miss the last bus. I'll explain later.'

Taking her hand, he pulled her arm through his and hurried her down into the town centre and towards her bus stop. Ashamed at her outburst and thinking that she must look a sight, Susan stood in the bus queue, head bent, wishing Jim would explain what he meant. Had he really been jealous? It was hard to believe. He had appeared to be enjoying the blonde's company. Still, the girl had looked as if she would gladly have let him escort her home, but obviously he hadn't asked. Janet! Even her name was different – sophisticated.

The bus arrived and the queue moved forward. At the entrance she turned sadly to wish Jim good night.

To her amazement he hustled her aboard, asked for two fares and guided her upstairs to the upper deck. They sat on the back seat and he put his arm around her.

Aware that he lived on the Upper Falls, the opposite end of town from her, she reminded him, 'You won't get another bus back into town at this time of night.'

'I'm well aware of that,' he said resignedly. 'Still, it's a beautiful night and the walk back will do me good. I can go to a late Mass in the morning. You do realise that I'm a Catholic? Don't you?'

She nodded and the silence lengthened. She willed him to speak, but he remained deep in thought throughout the journey. They had left the bus and were making their way to the top of her street before he spoke again.

'I didn't intend going to the Club Orchid tonight, you know.'

'Oh?' Her eyes searched his face. She sensed that she wouldn't like what he was about to say.

He continued slowly, as if choosing his words carefully. 'But then, I couldn't help myself. I'm vain enough not to want you to think too badly of me, so I came to explain.' He grimaced. 'I didn't expect the jealousy that overwhelmed me when I saw you stuck against that guy like a sticking plaster. Was there any need for that?' She writhed with shame and he smiled and assured her, 'I didn't really think him a big ape. You could probably do a lot worse. He seemed a nice enough lad, but that didn't make any difference. I still didn't like it one wee bit.'

They had arrived at the corner of her street and he threw his arms wide as his eyes roamed over the detached houses set in their own grounds. 'Believe me,

Susan, I was gobsmacked when I saw all this opulence the other night. I hadn't realised you were so well off. I nearly died when I saw all this.'

'What difference does it make?'

'Are you kidding? Of course it makes a big difference. Had I known, I wouldn't have asked you out in the first place. Can't you see? We don't move in the same circles. I'm surprised that your parents allow you to frequent the Club Orchid.'

'They don't know! Anyhow, I don't honestly see what difference it makes. After a few dates we would probably be bored stiff with each other. Do you know what? I think you're a coward, Jim Brady. That's what I think.'

His arms circled her waist and a smile softened his features. 'You don't really think that,' he disagreed. 'Or you wouldn't be attracted to me. You *are* attracted to me, aren't you, Susan? I'm not wrong about that, am I?'

His lips were tantalisingly close and she trembled in his arms. 'A little,' she confessed with a slight smile and pressed closer. 'It can't do any harm to see each other now and again. Can it?' she added persuasively.

Framing her face with his hands, he whispered against her lips, 'Do you really believe that? You won't be disappointed when we have to part? Because we will have to part, there's no doubt about that. You won't say that I led you on? You see, there really is no future for us to share, Susan.' .

'No, I won't hold it against you. Let's give it a try and see what happens. Mm?' Her lips parted in invitation and all his good intentions went out the window as he claimed his first kiss.

* * *

Rachel Cummings sat at the breakfast table after her husband had left for work and eyed her two daughters in concern. They were out every night of the week and her husband had insisted that she find out just what they were up to. She hated to pry into their affairs, but Trevor was right. They were both young and impressionable, Susan having just passed her twenty-first birthday and Alison nineteen. It was their duty as parents to keep a close eye on them and make sure they didn't get into any trouble.

Why did Trevor leave everything up to her? she lamented inwardly. On the other hand, he could be so forthright that the girls would probably take offence and there would be one hell of a row. So, determined to keep the conversation amicable, Rachel said in a teasing voice, 'Your father and I were just saying last night that we don't see much of you two lately.'

The look of amusement that the sisters shared and then bestowed on her showed her plainly that they were not fooled.

It was Alison who spoke first. 'Ah, me dad has asked you to find out what we're up to. Is that right, Mam?'

An embarrassed flush crept up Rachel's face. 'If you could be a wee bit more open about your affairs we wouldn't have to pry,' she declared. 'But no, you disappear every evening dressed to kill and we don't know where you are or who you're with. When I ask where you've been, all I get is "Out!" You can't blame us for being worried. We do right to worry about your welfare. Some of the young ones are so permissive these days.'

'Well, since you put it that way, if you must know,

I'm seeing a very nice bloke. Shall I bring·him home for you and Dad to run your beady over?' Alison asked and laughed as alarm registered in her mother's eyes.

'It must be serious if you're willing to bring him home,' she cried. 'Do be careful, Alison. You're young and have your whole life ahead of you.'

'You can't have it both ways, Mam! Do you want to meet him or not? It's not serious. At least not as far as I'm concerned. I had no intention of inviting him to tea, but if it sets your mind at rest I'll bring him home on Saturday. I know you'll like him. I just hope it doesn't give him any ideas.'

Rachel looked more alarmed than ever. 'Ideas? What kind of ideas?'

'He might think I'm keen on him since I'm bringing him home to meet the family. You know, getting his feet under the table, you might say.'

Susan rose to her feet and, to avoid any awkward questions being directed at her, said, 'Do bring him to tea, Alison. Let's have a look at him.'

Alison looked sternly at her mother. 'I'll invite him to tea as long as you promise he won't be given the third degree. All right?'

'I can't speak for your father, Alison, but I will have a quiet word of warning in his ear before the lad arrives.' Rachel turned to her other daughter before she could escape. 'What about you, Susan? Would you like to bring your young man home on Saturday, as well? Make a night of it?'

Trying to appear nonchalant, Susan asked, 'What makes you think I've got a young man?'

'Haven't you? Where do you go every night, then?'

'I'm with Ruth a lot of the time, and now and again I go out with a boy. Nothing serious.' She wept inwardly. Four months of dating had not lessened her feelings where Jim Brady was concerned and she was sure he felt the same. It was serious; very serious. She just had to persuade him that they were meant for each other.

'Will you be here to meet Alison's young man on Saturday night, then?'

'Yes, I'll be here to tea, but I'll be going out shortly afterwards,' she warned.

'So will I!' Alison cried in alarm. There was no way she was going to sit in on a Saturday night. 'I'll bring Graham to tea, Mam, but I'm not staying in all evening. Do you hear that?' She emphasised, 'I'll be going out as well.'

No matter what her mother said to try to convince her otherwise, Alison made it clear that she had no intention of sitting in the company of her mother and father on Saturday night, and Rachel had to give in gracefully.

Trevor straightened his tie and patted his thinning hair into place before turning to his wife. 'Well, will I do? Although why we have to dress up to meet some lad we don't even know, I'll never understand.'

'We want to make a good first impression, just in case he turns out to be Mr Right.' Rachel smoothed her hands over her hips and wiggled the material of the pale-grey crêpe dress she was wearing into position. It was a long time since she had worn this dress and she was dismayed to find that she had put on a little weight. She hoped Trevor wouldn't notice.

He did, and in his usual blunt manner remarked on it, running a critical eye over her body and exclaiming, 'You've put on a bit of weight, girl. Don't let it get out of control. You know I can't stand fat women.'

Rachel smiled wryly as she watched him pull his tummy in. He was so conceited he would never admit to being overweight. 'I could say the same about you, Trevor, if I was as tactless as you, that is.'

He buttoned his jacket, patted his stomach and smiled smugly. 'There you are. Look at that.'

'I advise you to keep your jacket open or that button will pop the minute you sit down,' Rachel warned. 'Let's go downstairs. He'll be here any minute now.'

Graham was already standing on the doorstep gathering the courage to ring the bell. It had come as a great surprise to him when Alison had invited him to tea. He cared deeply for her. Did this mean she cared for him? It was up to him to make a good impression. Straightening his shoulders and fidgeting with his tie, he reached for the bell.

It was Alison herself who opened the door. She looked good enough to eat, dressed in a short white dress of clinging material that left little to the imagination. Her hands reached for his and drew him inside. 'Hello, Graham. I might have guessed you'd be on time.' As she spoke she was slowly leading him towards the lounge. 'Don't look so scared,' she whispered. 'They won't bite.'

Her parents rose to their feet when Alison pushed him gently ahead of her into the lounge. 'Mam, Dad, this is Graham Robson.'

Her father eyed him and apparently liked what he saw. But then Alison had expected him to, hadn't she?

Graham was every parent's idea of a suitable suitor for their daughter. Grasping his hand, Trevor said, 'Welcome, son. What would you like to drink before the meal? Sherry? Whiskey?'

'A small whiskey please, with plenty of lemonade.'

Rachel's mouth gaped slightly. She couldn't believe her ears. Imagine Trevor offering Alison's boyfriend alcohol. But then this was no young lad, this was a mature young man. A frown furrowed her brow. Surely he was much too old for Alison?

Aware of her surprise, Graham cleared his throat and turned to her. 'I'm very pleased to meet you, Mrs Cummings.'

Still a mite perturbed, Rachel smiled briefly at him. 'Take a seat, Graham. I'll see how things are going in the kitchen.' Leaving the room, she quickly crossed the hall and entered the big modern kitchen that was her pride and joy. A far cry from the little scullery in the house she had been reared in on the Shankill Road. Stretching the length of the house, it had the latest in modern equipment.

At times like these, to leave herself free when entertaining someone new, she called on the assistance of two sisters who ran a small catering business. For a nominal fee they could be persuaded to cook a meal in your home for anything up to twelve people. Their cuisine was always mouth-watering and Rachel had no doubts that everything would be just fine. 'How's it going, Evelyn?'

The smaller of the sisters greeted her with a smile. 'Everything's fine, Mrs Cummings. We're ready to serve any time now.'

Rachel drew in a deep breath of appreciation. 'Mm, it smells delicious. Give us another ten minutes, then serve it. Is the dining table set?'

A nod of the head confirmed this. 'Everything's in order, Mrs Cummings. Just leave it to us.'

'Good! Ten minutes then.'

As she crossed the hall again, Susan came down the stairs. 'Well, is he presentable enough for Father?' she whispered.

'Hush!' Her mother gave her an anguished look. 'He might hear you.'

'For goodness sake, Mam, these walls are thick. There's no chance of being overheard. What's he like?'

'Very nice. But . . .' The doubt in her voice caused Susan's brows to rise in query. 'He looks much older than I anticipated.'

'Really?'

'Yes. Come see for yourself.'

Trevor and Graham were deep in conversation, while Alison, looking bored, was leafing through a magazine. Graham rose courteously to his feet when they entered the room.

'Have you met my other daughter, Graham?'

'No, Mrs Cummings, I have not had that pleasure.'

'This is Susan, my eldest daughter.'

'I'm very pleased to meet you, Susan.' A charming smile, exposing even white teeth, accompanied the words, and Susan was surprised to feel the colour rise in her cheeks as his eyes openly admired her. He really was charming, but then, she agreed with her mother, he was much older; old enough to have acquired such charm. Where on earth had Alison met him?

'Likewise, I'm sure.' She returned his greeting with a warm smile.

Graham proved to be a great conversationalist and kept them entertained during the meal. Afterwards they retired to the lounge and Alison became alarmed when her father offered Graham another drink. 'No, Dad. If Graham takes another drink he won't be able to drive.'

'Well, he can get a taxi home and pick his car up tomorrow. Is that all right with you, Graham?'

'I'd like that, if Alison doesn't mind?' With raised brow he awaited Alison's reaction.

'Alison does mind, as a matter of fact! She minds very much.' A baleful glare was bestowed on him. 'You promised to take me to the Orpheus tonight.'

'Orpheus? What's the Orpheus?' Trevor cried in bewilderment.

'It's a ballroom, Dad. It's above the Co-op, in York Street. This will be my first time there. Graham, you promised! You know you did.'

Graham smiled wryly at Trevor. 'I did promise, Mr Cummings, and I'm a man of my word. It was lovely meeting you and Mrs Cummings. The meal was delicious. I really enjoyed it. I hope we will get to know each other a bit better in the future.'

'Feel free to visit us any time you like.'

Alison had shrugged into her coat and, grabbing her handbag, tugged at Graham's arm. 'Oh, come on, Graham, or we won't get in.'

Seeing that Susan had also donned her coat, Graham asked politely, 'Can we give you a lift into town, Susan?'

'Yes, please, Graham.'

On the short journey to town Susan sat in a daze.

Every Saturday night for the past few months she and Jim had frequented the Orpheus. It had come as a shock to her to hear Alison say they intended going there tonight. She always met Jim in the foyer, but now she asked Graham to drop her off at the corner of Donegal Street. When the car stopped Alison twisted round in her seat. 'Where are you going tonight?'

'I'm not sure yet. Thanks for the lift, Graham.'

Before any further embarrassing questions could be directed at her, Susan jumped from the car. What on earth was bringing them to the Orpheus tonight?

She waved the car out of sight on its way to the car park, then set off along York Street.

Jim Brady watched Susan hurry towards him and a wave of tenderness washed over him. She was so beautiful and such a lovely person. He felt guilty wasting her time. They couldn't go on as they were. The longer they continued to meet, the harder it would be to break up and the more hurt Susan would be. The attraction between them was too strong. It was becoming increasingly hard to hold his emotions in check. He wanted her with a desire that put everything else from his mind. If only there was a chance that one day they could wed, he would be the happiest man in the world. But marriage was out of the question and anything less was not good enough for her.

Her eyes lit up when she caught sight of him and a smile of pure joy wreathed her face. She stopped, breathless, in front of him. 'Hi there,' he whispered and his voice throbbed with passion. They gazed at each other for some moments, then he took her by the arm and led her towards the lift. 'Let's get up to the ballroom. I want to hold you close.'

In a daze, she had been following his lead. Now she stopped in her tracks and tugged frantically at his sleeve. 'Jim, Alison and her boyfriend, Graham, are coming here tonight. Can we go somewhere else instead, please?'

He stopped and stood lost in thought for a short while. 'Does it matter if your sister sees us? After all she's bound to guess that you are seeing someone.'

Susan stood undecided and he leant closer. 'Let's stay. I'm just aching to hold you close, more than anything else in the world. Mm?'

Encouraged by these words, she ventured, 'We could go somewhere where we could really be alone.'

He drew back instantly. His passion was too raw to seek solitude somewhere. Afraid of wavering in his resolve, he cried abruptly, 'That's out of the question, and you know it! Come on, let's dance the night away.' And without further ado he took her arm and led her towards the lift from where the strains of 'Misty' could be heard drifting down from the floor above.

Agog with excitement, Alison stood at the entrance of the grand Orpheus ballroom. Used to Sammy Leckie's small dance hall, she was bemused by the size of the Orpheus. And tonight there was an orchestra playing. Imagine dancing to live music instead of records. Her eyes rose to the ceiling, where a huge silver ball slowly rotated, throwing slivers of light on to the swirling bodies below.

A sigh of contentment escaped her lips. She turned to Graham. 'Isn't it marvellous?'

He laughed at her excitement. The band was playing a waltz and the couples on the floor twirled gently to its beat. 'Let's join them.' Without another word he swept her into the swaying mass.

Graham had plenty of practice and was a competent dancer. He twirled her in and out of the other dancers and she closed her eyes and gave herself up to the magic of the music. As the waltz drew to a close, she reluctantly opened them again and was amazed to see her sister and a tall man dancing close by.

Susan hadn't seen her. How could she? She was gazing spellbound at her partner and had eyes for no one else. Not that Alison could blame her! Oh, no. She would be the first to admit that he was a very handsome fellow. Grabbing her sister by the arm as she was about to move off, Alison cried indignantly, 'Susan! Why didn't you say you were coming here?'

Embarrassed, Susan lied. 'I wasn't sure where we would finish up tonight.'

The men shared a perplexed glance and edged their partners to the side of the dance floor. They waited expectantly to be introduced.

The silence lengthened and Alison said, 'Well . . . aren't you going to introduce us?'

Reluctantly, Susan did so.

Shaking Alison and Graham by the hand, Jim – always the gentleman – said cordially, 'Grab a table and I'll fetch some drinks. What would you ladies like?' Fruit juices were ordered and Jim raised an eyebrow at Graham. 'What's your poison, Graham?'

'I'll come to the bar with you. You won't be able to carry them all, and I know from experience that trays are like gold dust in here.'

The bar was crowded and as they waited their turn the two men eyed each other. Graham was wondering how come Alison had no idea that her sister was courting. It was obvious to him that Jim and Susan were very much in love. It was in the air all around them. It was he who spoke first. 'Have you met the girls' parents yet?'

A crooked smile twisted Jim's mouth. 'No, and I don't think I'm likely to.'

'Oh . . .?'

'I'm from the wrong side of the track, you see.'

'But surely, in this day and age, things like that don't matter?' said Graham with genuine surprise.

'My mother's a widow and I've two younger sisters to keep an eye on. My wage is needed every week. Can you see her father welcoming me as a suitable husband? Especially as I'm a Catholic.'

'Hmm, I see what you mean.' After a short pause Graham continued, 'You seem very attracted to each other. I wish Alison would look at me like that.'

Embarrassed, Jim was non-committal. 'It's where it all ends that counts. But there's no future for us.'

'I'm sorry. Forgive me. I should mind my own business.'

'No harm done. Here, grab a couple of these glasses.'

The two girls sat at one of the small tables that dotted the sides of the dance floor. Alison's eyes glowed as she looked around her. 'It's wonderful here. I suppose you come all the time?'

Stretching the truth a bit, Susan confessed, 'Most Saturdays.'

'You're a dark horse, Susan.' Alison's voice was accusing. 'Jim's gorgeous. Why are you making a big a secret of him?'

Susan smiled slightly at her sister's obvious admiration. 'He is gorgeous, isn't he?' she agreed. She had a feeling that her sister would want to stay with them the rest of the evening and she was thinking of ways to put Alison off. She wanted Jim to herself. 'Graham is also very nice. I could see Mam and Dad were impressed with him.'

'I'm sure they'd like Jim, too. Why didn't you invite him to tea?'

'I'm afraid I can't agree with you there. He wouldn't get much of a welcome in our house, I can assure you of that.'

Alison's eyes widened, then closed for a few seconds as comprehension dawned. Her voice was full of pity. 'Of course. How stupid of me. With a name like Jim Brady he has to be a Catholic.'

'Here you are, Susan,' Jim handed her a glass of juice. 'Graham is coming with yours now, Alison. He stopped to talk to someone.'

'I'm here.' With a flourish, a glass of juice was set on the table in front of Alison. 'Cheers.' Graham raised his glass.

A chorus of 'Cheers' was followed by a brief silence as they quenched their thirst.

To Susan's consternation, after a few minutes of desultory conversation Graham asked her to dance with him. With a startled glance at Jim, she reluctantly followed him on to the dance floor.

Alison looked expectantly at Jim and he responded. 'Shall we?'

As they circled the floor Alison gazed up into Jim's face. 'Have you and Susan been seeing each other for a long time?'

'Not very long. Why do you ask?'

'You look very lovey-dovey together.'

A wide grin split his face at the audacity of her remark. 'Do you think so?'

'I do indeed!' An insinuating look accompanied the words.

His deep-blue eyes crinkled at the corners when he smiled and she thought how handsome he was. 'Just what are you suggesting, Alison?'

She shrugged. 'I don't know. But I'd hate to see Susan get hurt.'

'She's a big girl. She knows the score.'

'Are you sure? She believes everything she's told. She's very trusting. Not like me.' Alison tossed her blonde curls. 'I take everything with a pinch of salt.'

He laughed – anyone would think she was the older sister. 'Believe me, she knows the score.'

'Are you planning to marry, then?'

'If you don't mind my saying so, I don't think that's any of your business. Are you going to marry Graham?'

'Who knows? It's early days.'

'Has he asked you to marry him?'

'No.' She laughed aloud. 'But he will,' she added confidently.

They were passing Graham and Susan, who were covering the floor in silence and noting the ease with which Alison was engaging Jim in conversation. Susan remarked, 'Our Alison would feel at. home in the company of the Queen. I wish I had her personality.'

Graham grimaced. 'She's not always so forthcoming with me.'

'Really?'

'Yes, really. And there is nothing wrong with your personality. I think you're charming, and it's obvious that Jim is besotted with you.'

His admiration was apparent and Susan coloured slightly under his gaze, receiving the compliment graciously. 'Thank you.'

They smiled at each other and she thought what a nice person he was. Her sister was a lucky girl. Over her shoulder, Graham watched Alison laugh and flirt with Jim and his eyes were bleak. Why couldn't she tease him like that? Did she care about him at all? Surely she must, or why ask him home to meet the family? If only she were more like her sister.

Susan's earlier premonition proved right. After the next dance Alison and Graham sought them out and it was taken for granted that they would share a table. The two men got on like a house on fire and Susan had to admit that she enjoyed the light-hearted banter. Her only fear was that Jim would insist that she go home in Graham's car. These fears were unfounded, however. At the end of the evening Jim politely but firmly turned down Graham's offer of a lift home. He said he was taking Susan for a bite of supper.

'What a good idea,' Alison cried delightedly. 'Why don't we join them, Graham?'

Graham stood silent. He could understand Jim's

dilemma. If he accepted, Jim and Susan would have no opportunity to be alone.

They were standing outside the Orpheus and, to her delight, Jim reached for Susan's hand and tucked it beneath his elbow. 'If you don't mind, Alison, we would like to be alone for a while. Mm?'

'Oh, I see.'

Noting her disappointment, Jim suggested gently, 'Perhaps we could all join up again next Saturday night?'

Afraid that Alison was going to insist on joining them for supper, Graham quickly agreed. 'That's a great idea, Jim. I look forward to meeting you again. Good night. Good night, Susan.' With these words he propelled a protesting Alison along York Street, leaving Jim and Susan alone.

'That puts a stop to our Saturday nights together at the Orpheus,' Susan mused.

'Why? I think it's a good idea that we meet up. I enjoyed their company.'

'So did I,' Susan admitted. 'But I thought you liked being alone with me,' she added peevishly.

They were cutting through Smithfield Market area and he pulled her into the doorway of a pet shop. 'I do. I love being alone with you, so that I can do this.' His hand caressed her breast.

Her eyes lit up and she lifted her face for his kiss. The kiss was long and satisfying and their passions rose.

'You see? This is what happens when we're alone. I can't keep my hands off you.'

'But I want you to touch me,' she cried in bewilderment. 'We were meant for each other, Jim. Surely you can see that? Don't!' He had removed his hand and she tried to pull it back. 'Don't push me away like this, Jim. I love you.'

Reluctantly he widened the space between them even more.

'We can't go on like this, Susan.'

'I know! I know we can't. We could get married quietly, and go somewhere outside Belfast to live.'

'Ah, Susan. Susan.' He shook his head in despair. 'I told you there was no question of us marrying. Remember? It isn't just our religious differences. You know that. I've explained to you that my mam's a widow. I've to provide for her and the girls. You said you wouldn't hold it against me when the inevitable happened and we had to part.'

'Are you saying that you don't want to see me any more?' she cried aghast, fear sending a shiver down her spine.

'No, of course I'm not saying that, but we can never marry.'

'Well, then, whatever you like, Jim. I don't care what people say. I'll live with you.'

Resting his hands on her shoulders, he gazed at her beseechingly. 'Susan, I love you and I will never use you in that way. Now, can we continue to see each other without any strings attached?'

Left without any choice, she nodded glumly, the tears threatening to fall.

'Then let's go get something to eat. I'm starving.'

The idea of eating anything made her feel sick. How could he even think of food? Nevertheless she managed to nibble at a sandwich and drink a few sips of tea while she talked brightly to him. She would tolerate anything just to be with him.

Jim watched the effort she was making and thought how unfair life was. It must soon end; it could only get harder. But not yet, his heart cried. Not just yet. Surely he deserved some time with her? He loved her so much.

To Susan's deep regret, Saturday night at the Orpheus became a regular foursome. Oh, she loved the company, but she missed the intimate moments between dances when Jim sat with his arm around her shoulders whispering sweet nothings in her ear. In spite of sulks from Alison, Graham never again offered them a lift home. There was an unspoken agreement that they part company outside the Orpheus, and this pleased Susan no end. Then, one Saturday night a few weeks later, it was absolutely pouring down when they left the hall after the dance. There had been a slight drizzle when they arrived, but now the rain was literally bouncing off the pavement. They eyed it in silence for some moments.

Graham diffidently offered them a lift. 'I know you would prefer not to, but that rain looks as if it's in for the night.'

Jim drew Susan to one side. 'I think it would be a good idea if you went home with Graham and Alison tonight. I'll get a taxi.'

'No, Jim. I want to stay with you for a while. We haven't had a minute alone all evening. I'll get a taxi home later on.'

'Be reasonable, Susan. Even if we go for a bite of supper, we'll be soaked to the skin by the time we get there. If Graham gives us a lift to the café, Alison will want to join us and it would be churlish to refuse her.

It would become a habit, so it would. Do you want that?'

She could see his point of view and shook her head glumly.

'So please accept Graham's offer of a lift.' Jim tilted her face up to his and kissed her. 'See you on Tuesday night as usual.'

Graham had tactfully led Alison out of earshot to give them more privacy. Now he moved forward as Jim turned towards them, an inquiring look on his face. 'We'd be very grateful if you would give Susan a lift home, Graham. And I'll see you both next Saturday.'

Jim hurried along Royal Avenue and turned up Castle Street hoping to catch the last bus. He was lucky and caught it by the skin of his teeth. Nevertheless, he was already soaked to the skin. But he begrudged paying for a taxi home. He needed to be careful with his money if he was to entertain Susan twice a week. Money was no real problem to her and she didn't understand. He stared at his reflection in the bus window. His hair was plastered to his head and his eyes had a bleak look. Susan's annoyance at his decision to send her home with her sister rankled. After supper every Saturday night he always got a taxi to her street to make sure she got home safely. Then he walked home, but that was out of the question tonight; surely she understood that?

Another problem had cropped up. His youngest sister Louise was due to leave school soon and Sister Vincent, the head nun at St Vincent's School, had sent for his mother and asked her to consider sending

Louise to St Dominic's College for further education. His mother had been against the idea, saying that they couldn't add to the burden Jim already carried, but with his other sister May already at St Dominic's, how could he deny Louise her chance? It was the penalty of having two clever sisters. But with all these commitments, when would he ever be in a position to get married?

It felt as if he carried the worries of the world on his shoulders. He felt like a man who had been married for years. Susan thought that religion was the only stumbling block to their marrying; if only she were right. Why, if that was the case, he would defy the Church and her father, and marry her no matter what the cost.

It was a month later when the bottom fell out of Susan's world. The Saturday night started off as usual. Susan arrived with Alison and Graham, and Jim was waiting in the foyer for them. Greetings were exchanged and they made their way to the ballroom. Soon, however, alert to every nuance where Jim was concerned, Susan became aware that something was wrong. As they circled the floor he held her with a desperation that was very apparent to her.

'What's up, Jim? What's bothering you? Do you feel ill?'

He shook his head in denial. 'I'm perfectly all right.' After all, a breaking heart was not considered an illness.

'Jim, come off it! I know something's wrong.'

His lips trailed her face and a sigh escaped his lips. 'We will talk about it later.'

He would say no more and she had to curb her

impatience and wait. The other two seemed unaware of anything out of the ordinary and the evening passed slowly.

As usual, they said good night to Alison and Graham outside on the pavement. It was a cold night and, arms entwined, they hurried to their special café, where they always sat at the table in the corner and talked and talked. Tonight Jim was silent, locked in his own deep thoughts. Her patience, which had been sorely tried all evening, suddenly snapped.

'All right, Jim, I can't stand the big silence any longer. Let's hear all about it.'

'First things first. What would you like to eat?'

'I'm not hungry, thank you.'

These words brought a reluctant smile to his drawn face. 'You're always hungry.'

'Not tonight, I'm not. Food would choke me.' The waitress had approached their table and Susan gave her order. 'Just coffee for me, thank you.'

'Make that two coffees, please,' Jim seconded her.

He reached across and clasped her hands in his. 'Susan, you know I love you, don't you?'

Sensing bad news, her heart started racing and her nails bit into his hands. 'Yes. What is it, Jim, what's the problem? Is your mother ill? Can you not see me for a while?'

'Not for a while,' he said slowly. 'In fact, I think it's time to call it a day.'

She swallowed deep in her throat, hurt beyond measure. 'What do you mean, call it a day?'

'You know what I mean, Susan. It's not fair to you, to go on as we are.'

'I'm not complaining.' Her lips twisted in a wry smile. 'Well, not often anyhow.'

'You're a young, attractive woman, Susan, and I can't waste any more of your life.'

'What are you suggesting, Jim?'

'I think it's time we parted.'

The waitress arrived with the coffee and Jim released her hands. 'Thank you.'

Susan felt bereft without his touch. This is how she would feel if she never saw him again. 'Just tell me this, Jim. Have you met someone else?' she whispered fiercely.

'Don't be daft! I could never look at another girl while I have you.'

'Well, then, I can't see why we can't keep on meeting. We're certainly not doing anything wrong. Your priests could certainly find no fault in our relationship.'

His lips tightened and an angry colour crept up his face. 'And how long do you think I can stand this? Think, Susan. Do I have to spell it out for you? I'm a man! I can't bear to be with you and not have the right to show my feelings.'

She leant eagerly across the table and whispered urgently. 'But we can show our feelings. I feel the same. You know I do. We will just have to be careful, Jim.'

Her heart sank. He was shaking his head before she had finished speaking. 'I've too many commitments. As you know, our Louise is starting at St Dominic's College. I've already spent the few savings I had tucked away for a rainy day. She needed uniforms, books and other bits and pieces. I've actually had to go into debt. Then there will be extra bus fares. If we had stayed in Spinner Street instead of moving up the Falls, we wouldn't have had a mortgage and the girls could have walked to college. But we did move! It seemed a good idea at the time, but that was before I met you. As things stand, I can't see any hope for us at all.'

'I'll wait, Jim. I'll wait as long as necessary. I didn't realize that you were so worried about money. Why, that's no problem. I can pay for our outings.'

'Do you think I'd let you do that? No. I've made up my mind about this. Lord knows it wasn't an easy decision, but we can't keep on seeing each other.'

Their coffee grew cold as they argued, but he was adamant. In the taxi on the way home, Susan was all over him. She would make him realise just how wonderful life could be, whether or not they were married.

In the shadowy corner shielded by tall hedges, where they usually said good night, she went wild, full of passion and offering her all. To her delight, instead of pushing her gently away, as he normally did when she got worked up, he lost control. Gripping her tightly, he pounded his body against hers, his mouth savagely devouring hers. Feverishly, she clung to him, egging him on. Her heart was singing. At last he was going to be hers. She was wise enough to know that once Jim took her, in his eyes they'd be as good as married. It wasn't the way she would have planned it, but what did it matter if it was here on the corner, so long as it meant he was committed to her?

Suddenly she found herself flung back against the hedge as he turned his back on her. 'Jim?'

For some moments he stood, shoulders heaving, fighting for control. Then he swung round and lashed out at her. 'Stop tempting me, Susan. Can't you see any further than your nose? You're being very unfair.'

'I only want to show you how much I love you,' she whispered. Her arms reached out appealingly to him. 'Come on, Jim. We won't be hurting anyone.'

He shook his head sadly and moved away. 'I'm sorry, Susan. More sorry than I could ever say.'

Without a backward glance he left her. She stood there, petrified, watching him out of sight, unable to believe it was all over.

For some time she remained where she was, trying to come to terms with his rejection. Surely if he had any feelings at all for her he would not have turned down her offer in such a crude way. She felt like a prostitute who had not come up to expectations. Shame sent a hot flush washing over her body as she relived her wanton actions. It abated, leaving her icy cold and shaking all over. There was a sick feeling in the pit of her stomach. Tears rolled down her face and she brushed them angrily away. She would show him, so she would. He'd never get another chance to reject her.

Nerves ragged, she made her way up the street and entered the driveway to her home, all the while muttering angrily to herself. Dismay brought her tirade to a halt as she saw Graham leave the house and head for his car. She turned and hurried down the drive again, hoping to elude him, but he caught sight of her and started towards her. 'Susan . . . Hey, there.'

Forced to retrace her steps, she was glad of the shadows; hoped he wouldn't look too closely.

Peering anxiously at her, he asked, 'Susan, is anything the matter?'

An involuntary shiver passed through her body. He put an arm round her shoulders in concern. 'Come on, let's get you into the house where it's warm.'

'No. No! I can't go in just yet. I can't face anybody at the moment.'

He was in a quandary. He couldn't leave her out here in this state, but what else could he do?

His eye lit on his car and, taking her by the arm, he said, 'Let's sit in the car until you feel better. It will be a lot warmer there.'

I'll never feel better again, she thought bitterly, but allowed herself to be helped into the back seat of his car.

He clasped her cold hand between his and tried to rub some warmth into it. 'You're frozen, Susan. Tell me what's wrong. Have you and Jim quarrelled?'

Suddenly his kindness made it all too much to bear and harsh sobs tore from her throat.

Aghast, Graham gathered her close and murmured words of comfort in her ear. 'It'll be all right. Why, Alison and I also had a tiff tonight. All couples disagree sometime or other. It's human nature.'

Her mouth yawned wide in protest. 'Uh-huh. It's worse than that. He doesn't want to see me again.'

'Don't be silly! He loves you.'

Pressing her forehead against his chest, she burrowed wildly against it, wailing away. 'He doesn't. He doesn't. You don't understand! I made such a fool of myself. I'm so ashamed. I offered myself to him and he pushed me away in disgust.' She drew back and gazed up at him, to see his reaction to her words. 'Would you turn Alison down, if she wanted to . . . to . . . you know what I mean.'

In the dim light he smiled wryly. Turn Alison down? Chance would be a fine thing. She kept him firmly at arm's length. Alison took all she could get and gave nothing in return. He was having second thoughts where she was concerned. Meanwhile he couldn't believe that any full-blooded man would turn a girl like Susan down. Over the weeks he had found himself very attracted to her. She wasn't as pretty as her sister, but she had more between the ears. He had been amazed at how much he looked forward to his dance with her every week. Now here she was, in his arms, and every nerve in his body was aware of her.

'I bet he wasn't disgusted,' he said gently. 'You've misunderstood, so you have. Why, it's obvious Jim loves you.'

His fingers entwined in her hair and he gently drew her head back so that he could see her face. 'No man in his right senses would turn you down, Susan. No man. You're lovely.'

Her eyes widened into great dark pools of mystery and her lips trembled at his words of admiration. He warned himself to be careful; she trusted him and didn't realize how tempting she was being.

'Let's get you inside. Your parents have retired and I'm sure Alison will be in bed by now. Come on, I'll make you a nice cup of tea before I go.' He put her gently from him and turned to leave the car. She was so vulnerable; he had to get away from the temptation, before his body betrayed his desire for her.

Relieved to hear that her parents were in bed and she wouldn't have to face them, Susan relaxed. 'Give me another couple of minutes, Graham. If Alison is still awake, she'll ask all kinds of questions. She won't give up until she hears the truth, and I couldn't bear that.'

He left a space between them and turned in his seat to watch her.

Her eyes searched his face, seeing the sadness there. Momentarily distracted from her own misery, she asked gently, 'Why did you and Alison quarrel tonight, Graham?'

'Oh, the usual. Nothing important. To be truthful, we've quarrelled quite a lot lately.'

A cold hand reached out to cover his. 'I'm so sorry to hear that. You're a very nice person.'

He covered her hand with his. 'You're still freezing.' She moved closer and his arm circled her waist as she snuggled against the warmth of his body and gazed up at him. Her lips were so close. Too close for comfort. Should he risk a kiss? No, it would be too dangerous!

He could never figure out who made the first move, but her lips were soft as velvet and moved beneath his with a hunger that matched his own. Passion mounted as his hands caressed her body; soothing the hurt and pain of rejection away, all thoughts of Jim and Alison were forgotten.

In a daze, Susan groped for the handle of the car door and stumbled out on to the drive. She gaped in confusion at Graham as he followed her. What had she done?

'Susan, I'm sorry. I got carried away. Can you forgive me?'

She tore her eyes away from the anguish in his. 'Just go home, Graham. Please go.'

'No!' He couldn't just leave like this, as if nothing had

happened. He had to make her understand that he really cared for her; had meant no disrespect. The fact that she had been a virgin floored him. 'No. We must talk.' He stepped towards her. 'Let's go inside.'

'No. Go home! Do you hear me? I don't want to talk to you.'

Hearing the hysteria rising in her voice, he hesitated. Then he opened the car door and climbed inside. 'All right, I'll go. But we must talk about this, Susan. It can't be ignored.'

She turned and climbed the steps to the house, fumbling in her handbag for the key as she went. Glad that the house was silent, she quickly climbed the stairs and entered the bathroom. For some time she sat on the edge of the bath reliving the events of the evening. How could she have done those terrible things? Flinging herself at one man and then eagerly succumbing to another man's advances. After Jim's rejection, Graham's lovemaking had been balm to her hurt feelings. And she had enjoyed it! Every single moment of it. Even the sharp pain had only enhanced the pleasure. She hadn't expected to enjoy intercourse, especially in the back of a car of all places, but she had and now she felt sated.

Stripping, she entered the shower cubicle and ran the water as hot as she could bear it. Her body still glowed with the aftermath of passion and she allowed herself to revel in it. It was wrong, her mind cried. You are the lowest of the low, encouraging the man who may be your sister's future husband to make love to you.

Why not? her heart cried. No one need ever know. Graham certainly wouldn't broadcast the fact that he had seduced his girlfriend's sister. And I might never know anything like it again. Tears poured down her cheeks; why couldn't it have been Jim? Jim . . . Jim, how can I live without you? But no, it had to be her potential brother-in-law. She wished she had never been born.

Chapter Two

The train shunted to a halt and Susan rose wearily to her feet. She had been travelling since early morning and every bone in her body ached with fatigue. With each passing hour she had become more depressed. Rushing off to visit her Aunt Edith had seemed the answer to her problems – a chance to sort out her affairs – but what if she sent her packing? What would she do then? She would be stranded in a strange town with little money and nowhere to go. Not that her aunt would just show her the door! No, she wasn't like that. However, she might try to persuade her to return home, and that Susan couldn't do.

Early that morning she had left Belfast in a positive frame of mind, determined to put the past behind her and make a new life for herself over in England, but as the day progressed doubts had set in. Without Aunt Edith's help she would have to return home and face the music. Her heart quailed at the thought of the reception her news would evoke in her parents. Their wrath would know no bounds! Her father would never again be able to hold his head high, would never be able to preach what his daughter was obviously not practising.

Though why he should be held to account for her failing, she would never understand. She supposed it was all in the mind. As for her mother, although kind and gentle, Rachel was such a proud woman, and her daughter's news would absolutely devastate her.

The journey over on the ferry from Larne to Stranraer had been stormy and Susan had felt quite ill, bringing up all she had eaten that day but feeling no better for it. Terrified that she had perhaps put the baby at risk and was about to lose it there and then, she had sent prayers heavenwards. To her great relief they had arrived in Stranraer without further mishap. Once on *terra firma* her heaving tummy had settled and after a short wait she had boarded the train to Carlisle in a better frame of mind. On the journey down through Scotland the still-breathtaking autumn scenery of fiery red and orange hues – especially when mirrored on lochs, doubling their beauty – had absorbed her full attention, lulling her into a sense of calm. Surely in such a wonderful world it was wrong to despair? Life must be worth living, no matter what the hardships might be.

At Carlisle she had changed trains and soon found herself in Newcastle. Here, she knew from past experience, there would be a long wait for the connection to Darlington. She checked and found that her memory had served her right: there was indeed a long time to wait before her next train was due. She did some window shopping, but eventually the sharp wind sent her in search of warmth. Entering the cosy atmosphere of a small café, she ordered some sandwiches and a pot of tea to pass the time. To her surprise she discovered she was quite ravenous and devoured the sandwiches, which were unexpectedly tasty.

Now, at last, she had reached Darlington, her destination. Soon she would know her fate. Her Uncle Billy was meeting her at the station. From there they would go to Albert Hill, known as 'Little Ireland' because so many Irish people had settled there over the years. It was five years since Susan had last been over on holiday. Then she had been a carefree young girl; now here she was, back again, a woman scorned. A woman scorned was indeed a terrible thing. It made one want to lash out at anything and everything. Look what she herself had done when Jim Brady had refused her wanton offer. Shame washed over her as she recalled his words. Gentle, kind words, but rejection nevertheless. Well, in her misery she had encouraged another man and certainly made a mess of things. Now she must pay the price.

She had been a gangly teenager the last time she was in Darlington. Although she had grown little, she had filled out and knew that she looked quite different. Would Billy Devine recognise her now? Straightening her shoulders, she grabbed her suitcase and left the train to stand on the platform amongst the bustling crowd. She had enjoyed her last stay in Darlington and it was every bit as busy as she remembered it. Even at this late hour there was a lot of activity. Anxiously she scanned the faces of those obviously waiting for their family or friends. She saw Billy at once; he stood head and shoulders above the crowd. His eyes examined her face and passed on. Smiling slightly, she gripped her case with both hands and approached the big man. Placing her case to one side, she tentatively touched his arm. He frowned down at her and then his face lit up and he cried, 'In the name of God, Susan, but haven't you grown up. You were this height . . .' a large hand gestured a ridiculous height, 'the last time I saw you!'

Some of the tension left her body as she laughed aloud at the very idea that she had been so small just five years ago. 'I was a bit bigger than that, Uncle Billy. I really haven't grown all that much. I've just filled out,' she laughed gaily.

He reached for her hands and pulled her into a bear hug. 'You look wonderful, love. Let's get a taxi and get you home. Edith is so excited. She can't wait to see you.'

Susan hesitated, not wanting to put him to the expense of a taxi, and said haltingly, 'Can we not walk, Uncle Billy? If I remember correctly it's not very far.'

'Not in a taxi, it's not, and I'm certainly not trailing you through the streets in this freezing weather. Besides, I can afford it, so hold your tongue. Is this your suitcase? Well, then, let's get a move on.'

He was right. In the taxi it was just a short journey from the station through the town to Albert Hill. Her Aunt Edith had the door open and was on the narrow footpath before the cab stopped.

Gripping her by the hands, she gazed into her niece's pale face. 'You look tired, love. But then, sure you've been on the go all day.' Pulling her close, she cried, 'Oh, it's good to see you again. But what am I thinking of, keeping you standing out here in the street? Come on inside where it's nice and warm.'

The house seemed smaller than Susan remembered it. Only the knowledge that her cousin Jack, their only son, had gone to work in London had encouraged her to seek asylum with them. Would she be too much of a burden?

'Take off your coat and hang it behind the door, Susan. Then sit yourself by the fire while I lift the dinner. I've a nice casserole simmering away here. Billy, put that suitcase upstairs and entertain her until I'm ready.'

Billy quickly did as he was bid and, descending the stairs again, took the armchair facing her. He smiled fondly as his wife's excited voice shouted questions from the kitchen. 'She's been like a cat on a hot griddle all week preparing for your arrival,' he confided.

He eyed his niece keenly. She looked worried. He had a feeling this was to be no short visit and it bothered him. Had she fallen out with her da? If they had plenty of room, it wouldn't matter in the slightest how long she stayed. Edith would revel in her company. However, although there were three bedrooms in the house, the smallest was used for storing all those out-of-date bits and pieces too precious to throw out, and the other room was Jack's. If things didn't work out for Jack in London, what then? His son must have a room to return to.

Pushing his worries to one side, for after all he could be wrong, he asked, 'How's your mam and dad, love?'

'Well. Very well.'

A smile cracked Billy's long, solemn face, sending it into a wreath of wrinkles. 'Is your dad still holding up a pillar of the church, then?'

She smiled in return, her heart warming to this big man. Her father never could understand what had possessed his good-looking sister-in-law to run off with

Billy Devine. A married man who had given up a good job with a good pension attached to it, to run off with Edith. He had also left behind a very embittered wife. Edith had been pretty enough to turn any man's head, but what had she seen in him? Ugly as sin and as common as muck, her father had often said of Billy whenever his name cropped up in conversation, which it did often enough over the years. The fact that he was a Catholic hadn't helped matters much.

'And what about Alison? Is she still as lovely as ever?'

'She is indeed. She's courting, you know?' At his shake of the head Susan laughed and said, 'How could you know? But yes, she is. I expect an engagement will soon be announced.' It saddened her to think of Alison marrying Graham. She was so offhand with him. Treated him like dirt. He deserved better. She smiled inwardly. Imagine her defending the very man who was responsible for her present predicament. Wonders would never cease.

Nevertheless, Alison would soon be walking down the aisle on the arm of her proud father. And Trevor would be very proud; anything his youngest daughter did was all right by him. She was the apple of his eye and apparently never put a foot wrong. In his opinion, Graham was a great catch. Would she herself ever walk down the aisle? She doubted it. She doubted it very much. What man in his right mind would settle for second-hand goods?

Edith's voice reached them from the kitchen. 'You can move over to the table now. The dinner is ready.'

They sat at the pine table and Susan sniffed in appreciation as Edith removed the lid from the steaming casserole. 'That smells delicious, Aunt Edith.'

Smiling her thanks at the compliment, her aunt informed her, 'It's lamb, well, I suppose I should say mutton, but the best taste for a casserole comes from mutton, and the vegetables are from the market. Did I hear you right, there? Is Alison about to become engaged?'

'She is indeed. In a few weeks' time – at Christmas, I imagine – she will get engaged to Graham Robson.'

Dishing ladles full of the thick casserole into the bowls that were sitting ready, Edith handed Susan one and eyed her with raised brow. 'She's a bit young, isn't she? The vegetables are in that dish and the potatoes are in the small one.'

'Thank you, everything looks delicious. Alison isn't all that young. She was nineteen in May.'

'Still, that's not very old. And what does my dear sister Rachel think of all this?'

'Actually, she's quite pleased. Graham is a staunch Protestant and manages a big car showroom in the city centre for his father. He's an only child and the business will be his one day. He's also quite handsome. He's a bit older than Alison, but I suppose that's all to the good, as she is a bit of a scatterbrain. Anyway, the parents are thrilled to bits.'

'Huh! And what about you? Any sign of you tying the knot?' Edith watched in amazement as bright colour swamped her niece's face.

'Me, get married? Never! Who would have me?' 'Now' hovered on her lips, but she bit it back.

Edith frowned. 'A bonny girl like you? Why, many a man would consider himself lucky to get you.'

'You're very kind, Aunt Edith, but I don't think so.'

'You're talking nonsense! And you know it.'

Determined to put an end to this embarrassing conversation, Susan quickly piled turnip, carrot and potato on her plate and tucked into the thick casserole. 'Mm . . . this is delicious.' If only she were getting married, she lamented inwardly. Then her problems would be non-existent and she certainly wouldn't be sitting here in Darlington. How could she have been so foolish? Just because Jim Brady had scorned her advances, she had thrown caution to the winds, and look where it had got her.

There was jam roly-poly and custard for dessert and then Edith rose to her feet and started to clear the table. 'You sit over by the fire, love, and I'll make you a nice wee cup of tea.'

Pushing back her chair, Susan objected. 'Oh, no. I'll clear up. You sit down, Aunt Edith.'

'Do as you're told. Tomorrow you can do your share of the work.' She turned to her husband. 'Billy, away down to the club for an hour or so. Susan and I will be having a good old natter. You'd probably be bored to tears listening to us women.'

Glad for the excuse to get out for a pint, Billy grabbed his coat from the rail and, giving Susan a big wink, left the house.

Slowly Susan sank into the armchair, hands clenched tightly between her knees to stop them trembling, and gazed into the fire. Now for the reckoning. Her aunt was bound to ask her reason for visiting them, out of the blue like this, so near Christmas. How much should she tell her? Not everything, that was for sure. She was too ashamed to admit the whole truth. But she would have to tell Aunt Edith about the baby. What would she think of her niece's fall from grace? Would she be disgusted and send her packing? Or would she let her stay here until after the birth? Dear God, please let her be understanding, Susan prayed inwardly.

She sat rehearsing her words, discarding this explanation in favour of that one. To her great relief her aunt thrust a cup of tea into her hand, patted her consolingly on the shoulder and took the initiative. 'Don't look so worried. You're in trouble, aren't you?'

Tears brimmed over and she dashed them away with the back of her free hand. 'Yes, how did you guess? And I'm so ashamed. Oh, Aunt Edith, sure you won't sent me home?'

Taking the armchair facing her, Edith pulled it closer so that their knees were almost touching. Gazing earnestly into her niece's face, she said, 'Tell me all about it, love.'

Susan shrugged resignedly. 'There's not much to tell. I was foolish and now I must pay the penalty.'

'What about the man? Is he not willing to marry you?'

'He doesn't know!' Her voice rose shrilly. 'And anyhow, he can't marry me.'

'Is he already married?'

'No. But he would never marry me. It was just a one-off. We were both feeling low and, well, it just happened. He'd had a tiff with his girlfriend and I'd had cross words with a friend and was feeling very down. I should have known better, Aunt Edith. I liked him, but it wasn't as if I really fancied him. Later he was so ashamed. It was painful when I had to face him again. I just wanted to curl up and die. When I realised I was pregnant, I couldn't tell him. Can't you see? He wouldn't have wanted to know. It would have put him on the spot. Besides, I'm in love with someone else, and so is he. That would be no basis for a happy marriage. I was so stupid! I never thought that there might be consequences and I suppose neither did he. As I said, it all happened on the spur of the moment.'

Edith was incensed at the idea that a child had been conceived because they had both been feeling low. What was the world coming to? She wanted to chastise her niece, give her a good shaking; but, controlling her temper, she said, 'But . . . if he's free, he has a right to know. Surely you can see that, Susan? It's his child as well as yours. He might want to give it his name.'

To Edith's distress her niece became even more distraught, great sobs rasping from her throat and tears rolling down her cheeks. Going to her, Edith gathered her close.

Susan clung to her. 'He must never know. Why do you think I ran away?'

'There now. There now. You'll make yourself ill if you go on like this. Did your mother put you out?'

Stifling her sobs, Susan cried, 'She doesn't know. Oh, Aunt Edith, she mustn't ever find out. Promise you won't tell her.'

Pushing her niece back so that she could examine her face, Edith reasoned, 'Now Susan, she will have to know sometime. Surely you can see that? And the sooner, the better.'

'No! Please let me stay here until after the birth. Please, Aunt Edith. I've always been careful where money is concerned and I've a fair bit saved. Perhaps I'll be able to get a part-time job. Once the baby is born I'll work something out.'

Hearing hysteria rising in Susan's voice, Edith reluctantly assured her. 'Of course you can stay, love, if you really want to. But we will have to go into this more thoroughly and do what's best for all concerned. It's only natural that you're not thinking straight at the moment. Look, drink up your tea and then I'll show you to your room. You try and get a good night's sleep. We'll discuss this tomorrow.'

On his return from the club, Billy saw that his wife was perturbed. A glance around the room and into the kitchen showed him that Susan must have retired for the night. 'Has she gone to bed then?' he whispered.

'Yes, she was absolutely exhausted.'

His eyes narrowed at her expression. 'Why so worried, love?'

Rising to her feet, Edith faced him. She was aware that he was hoping their son would return from London any day, and that Billy would want his room left vacant for him. 'Billy, she's pregnant,' she said softly.

His face closed and he looked stern. 'Now, Edith, that's not our problem,' he warned. 'So don't be getting involved.'

'I know that, but can't we put her up for a while? I'll soon talk some sense into her, make her realise that her place is at home.'

'Did that bitch Rachel put her out?'

'No. Actually, Rachel doesn't know about the baby.'

'What? You'd think she'd be the first to know. Look,

much as I like Susan, she can't stay indefinitely. Jack might want to come home at any time.'

'You know that's not likely.'

'Still, he might!' Billy said stubbornly. 'We must keep his room ready for him.'

She shook her head sadly in disagreement, but went on, 'We'll work something out, Billy. Let's play it by ear. Eh, love?'

With a sigh he reached for her and gathered her close. How could he deny her? He would never be able to comprehend just what she saw in an ugly brute like him. Sinking his face in her soft, sweet-smelling hair, he muttered, 'Whatever you say, love. Whatever you say.'

After a restless night Susan awoke feeling listless. Her Aunt Edith had sounded as if she intended persuading her to return home. But how could she go home? How could she face her family and friends? And what about *him*? He was like part of the family now and, if she returned, he would be sure to guess the truth. She was so ashamed of herself; couldn't believe that she had been so foolish. If only she could wake up and discover it was all a bad dream, how different life would be for her. To think that because of a rejection from Jim Brady and a tiff with Alison, a child had been conceived. If she returned home what a predicament she would be in. Graham obviously loved Alison. How would he react? It would be enough to give him a heart attack. No, she couldn't go back! It would upset too many apple carts.

Slipping from beneath the blankets and thick patch-work quilt, she crossed to the long, narrow window, shivering when her feet left the small bedside mat and hit the icy-cold oil-cloth. Dawn was breaking and she gazed out over the back yards at the frost-covered rooftops with tears in her eyes. Back home she would be standing on warm carpet, gazing out over fields and hedgerows. Well, she had made her decision and she would just have to grin and bear it. That is, if her aunt allowed her to stay.

A glance at the watch her father had bought her for her twenty-first birthday six months ago brought more tears to her eyes. They had thrown a wonderful party for her. Life had been good then. She'd had a good job in Kennedy Construction, where she was personal secretary to the MD, and a beautiful house to call home. When she had met Jim everything had changed. Her love for him had blinded her to everything else. So what if he wasn't prepared to marry her. It wasn't the end of the world. She'd had nice friends and a good social life. How could she have been so blind? In the dim light the small luminous face of the gold watch showed her it was only five o'clock. Thankfully she tiptoed across the icy floorcovering and crept back under the bedclothes, but not to sleep; too many regrets plagued her.

At six o'clock sounds downstairs alerted her that her aunt and uncle had made an early start to their day. Dragging on her dressing gown, she hurriedly descended the stairs.

Billy was on his knees by the hearth of the small kitchenette grate, raking out the cold remains of yesterday's fire. On the hearth rolled-up papers, sticks and a bucket of coal were ready for today's heating. Quietly she approached him. 'Let me do that, Uncle Billy.'

Startled, he glanced over his shoulder at her in surprise, but before he could speak her aunt came in from the kitchen.

'In the name of goodness, Susan, what are you doing up at this hour? Away back to bed and I'll bring you up a cup of tea when the kettle has boiled.'

'You'll do nothing of the kind! I didn't come over here to be waited on hand and foot. Give me something to do, please.'

'I forgot to tell you last night. We have leased a stall in the market. We sell fruit and veg. Billy goes to the wholesalers early every day for fresh produce. However, there is no need for you to be up. I help him on the stall, but I don't leave the house until nine o'clock. So away back to your warm bed.'

'Please, Aunt Edith. Please let me do something to help out.'

'Susan, there is no need for you to rise at this unearthly hour,' Edith insisted. 'Go on, away back to your bed.' Seeing that her niece was about to argue, she relented, 'Okay, okay. Keep an eye on the porridge, if you must do something. Billy always complains that I make it too thick, so keep stirring it. Anyway, I want to talk to you before I go to work.'

Billy was long gone; the breakfast dishes were cleared away and the hearth was brushed and washed. Pouring another two cups of tea, Edith motioned Susan to take a seat by the blazing fire. Sitting facing her, Edith looked long and earnestly at her before speaking.

'Susan, I don't know what to do for the best. Our Rachel married well and, remember, I know the home

you come from. I'm sure you were never short of anything.
It will be entirely different over here, you know.'

'I know that, but I'll be forever grateful if you let me
stay.'

'Let's get this all sorted out first. Why all the secrecy?
You won't be the first girl to have a child out of wedlock.
It would be a nine-day wonder, and then your parents
would rally round. I admit our Rachel is proud and stiff-
necked, but she wouldn't let you down.'

'Aunt Edith, you know what me mam is like. She'd
die of shame. She wouldn't be able to hold her head up
in public again. I couldn't do that to her. I just couldn't!
And then there's Alison. The scandal would take all the
joy out of her wedding preparations. It wouldn't be fair
on them if I stayed at home.'

Struck by a sudden thought, Edith said, 'They do
know where you are, don't they?'

'Yes, I left a note.'

'A note?' Edith's voice was shrill. 'You didn't speak to
them? Won't they think that a bit strange?'

'No, Dad and I had an argument. You know how it
has always been between him and me. I can't do right
for doing wrong. And, lately, he can't look at me without
finding fault. I admit I've been a bit of a handful this
past year. You know – rebelling against everything.
Anyway, I threatened to leave home. He told me to go
and be damned, so I took him at his word and left.'
She gave a wry grimace. 'No, they won't be surprised.'

Dismayed at the animosity against her father that her
niece couldn't hide, Edith said, 'All families have these
falling outs. He probably regrets it now.'

'Huh!' Susan shook her head in disgust. As if!

Realising that she was making no headway, Edith changed tack. 'What about Christmas? It's not far off. They'll expect you home then!'

'I'll make some excuse. Say you need me here.'

'Your dad won't stand for that. His daughter away from home at Christmas? He'll come looking for you, you mark my words, girl.'

'Aunt Edith, please believe me, he won't care enough. He never has.'

'You're wrong! I'm not over-fond of Trevor Cummings myself, but I know he will be worried and hurt if you don't go home for Christmas.' Her frown deepened. 'When is the baby due?'

'June.'

'June? That's seven months away. Are you sure you're pregnant? You're not just late? I mean, you've just turned twenty-one. Your blood changes every seven years. Your period could come yet, Susan.' It was a forlorn hope, but Edith eyed her niece optimistically.

Her hopes were dashed. A harsh laugh escaped Susan's lips. 'Oh, I'm sure all right! I wish I weren't, but there is no doubt about it.'

'When do you think the wedding will be?'

'Alison confided in me that she would like a June wedding.'

'Surely she'll want you to be bridesmaid?'

'I know she does. But, even if I'm at home, I can't be a bridesmaid. How can I? I can't be fitted for a dress with a big belly. Now can I?'

'But if you're at home I'm sure Alison will give you a chance to get over the birth and settle for a later date, say in August. Eh?'

Susan stretched out her hands in despair. 'Can't you see? That's why I'm here. I don't want to upset everybody's plans. That's why I left home. Please let me stay here. Please,' she pleaded.

'How will you cover this all up, eh? Not going home at Christmas will be bad enough, but to miss the wedding as well . . .?' Edith threw her arms wide, a horrified look on her face at the very idea of it. 'Susan, it just can't be done,' she gasped. 'And after the birth, what then? Are you putting the baby up for adoption? Is that how you hope no one will ever know?'

'No, I'm not. I intend keeping this baby. To be truthful, I haven't planned any further than the birth. Look, let me stay until Christmas, then we can decide what to do. Just give me a chance to sort things out in my own way. Please, Aunt Edith.'

'What if our Jack wants to come home? What then? That's his room you're in. What if he wants to come home for the Christmas break? Which we sincerely hope he does. What then?'

'Well, surely there must be some convent or home over here that will take me in.' At the very idea of a home for unmarried mothers Susan was unable to control her emotions, and tears gushed from her eyes. 'I wish I hadn't been so foolish! Oh, how I wish I could die.'

Going to her, Edith gathered her close and rocked her gently in her arms. 'Hush, now, there will be none of that kind of talk in this house. We'll work something out,' she murmured, but her eyes were bleak. Her sister would never forgive her when she found out – as she was sure to . . . eventually.

* * *

It was with trepidation that Edith joined·Billy at the market stall. Although they rarely saw eye-to-eye, Billy thought the sun shone out of his son's backside. He would strongly object to Jack's room being occupied at Christmas.

It was Monday and market day in Darlington. Every Monday and Saturday stalls were erected in the square adjacent to the indoor market and – hail, rain or snow – a constant stream of people travelled from all the small towns and villages around in search of bargains. It also meant extra revenue for the indoor market. As was usual on such days, a steady queue of customers kept conversation between husband and wife more or less on a business level. It was lunchtime, when the crowd thinned out looking for some place to eat, before Billy got a chance to question her.

Unwrapping the sandwiches bought from a neighbouring stall, he asked Edith before biting into one, 'Well? How long does she want to stay?'

'Until Christmas.' Billy swallowed quickly and opened his mouth to protest, but she forestalled him. 'If we hear from Jack and he wants to come home, she has promised to move out.'

'And just where will she go, Edith?' he cried in disbelief. 'Eh? In her condition?'

'I don't know, Billy. She's adamant that she won't go home. Perhaps we could make enough space in the spare room for a single bed. It would only be for a few nights. Failing that, I'll get someone to put her up. In the meantime, can't we play it by ear, love? The chances of Jack coming home are slight. To tell you the truth, I'll be glad of her company. It will take my mind off him.'

He gazed into big, brown eyes filled with entreaty and once again was lost. In his heart he was aware that the chances of Jack coming back to Darlington were indeed slim. He wouldn't come without *her*, and surely she wouldn't have the gumption to show her face around here for some time to come. But what if she tired of Jack? She had, after all, dumped one man to run off with him. What then? To Edith's relief, he sighed and agreed. 'All right, love, if that's the way you want it, we'll play it by ear.'

Trevor Cummings looked up inquiringly from his plate of bacon and eggs when his wife entered the room sorting through the morning mail. He would never admit it, but he was sorry he had been so hard on Susan lately. But in the circumstances, who could blame him?

Meeting his eyes, Rachel shook her head. 'Nothing from Susan.'

From her place at the table Alison said plaintively, 'Mam, she has only been away a week. Give her a chance.'

'She doesn't deserve a chance,' her father said gruffly. 'What did I do that was so wrong, to justify her running off like that? We've had these rows before and she stayed put. What was so different this time? Eh? Tell me that. Your sister Edith has a lot to answer for, Rachel, taking her in like that. She should have sent her straight home.'

'Perhaps she got fed up listening to you, Dad.' Alison ventured to speak out on her sister's behalf. 'You did go on and on at her.'

Tentatively his wife intervened. She knew why Trevor had always been hard on Susan. 'Trevor, I agree with

Alison. You did come down rather hard on Susan lately. And for what? Voicing her opinion? Staying out late? Good heavens, she's a grown woman.'

Trevor's fist descended hard on the table, making his wife and daughter jerk in surprise. 'She should have known better than to answer me back,' he bellowed. 'Good Lord, you can't expect me to tolerate insolence from my own daughter. Can you?'

With a sigh, Rachel carefully mopped up the tea she had spilt. 'Now she's twenty-one we have no control over her. Remember that!' she warned. 'You could have been a bit more diplomatic. When she comes back you will have to bite your tongue now and again to keep the peace.'

'Huh! Chance would be a fine thing.'

'Now, you know you don't mean that. You want her to come home as much as I do.' She glanced quickly at her husband's dour face and said tentatively, 'Perhaps I should go over and try to talk some sense into her?'

'You'll do nothing of the kind! Let her make the first move.'

Clenching her teeth in frustration, Rachel cried, 'I do wish Edith was on the phone. Then I could at least talk to Susan, make sure she's all right.'

'What about me going over?' Alison offered brightly. She had an uneasy feeling that there was more to Susan's escapade than met the eye. There was something fishy going on. She had tried to find out what had happened between Jim Brady and her sister, but Susan had remained tight-lipped, insisting that their parting had been mutual, with no animosity on either side. Why, then, had she been so miserable?

'No, thank you. You'll stay where you are.' Rachel was aghast. 'What would Graham say if you were to go?'

'He would probably come with me. A wee holiday break.' Alison's eyes danced with mischievous glee at the very idea of it.

Her father fixed a stern eye on her. 'Don't even joke about going off alone with Graham until you're married.'

Alison turned aside to hide the smug look on her face. Parents could be so blind. She had no intention of making any mistakes. So far she had managed to keep Graham at bay. If he became too frisky, she would make sure that precautions were taken. Not that she thought he would. He had been quite cool lately and, come to think of it, marriage had not been mentioned between them for a long time. Could he be having second thoughts about marrying her?

It was a Wednesday evening that Susan rang her mother, confident that she would find her alone. She knew her father would be playing bowls. He was in the Churches' League and, when not playing in tournaments, he practised in the church hall every Wednesday night. Wednesday was also the night Alison went to Sammy Leckie's to learn advanced ballroom dancing. Susan was hoping for a private chat with her mother – a chance to assure her that she was all right, without her father giving off in the background. The continuous peal of the phone resounded for some moments. Susan pictured her mother setting her perpetual knitting carefully to one side, before leaving the lounge and crossing the hall to answer it. It saddened her to think that in the normal course of events her mother should be knitting for her first grandchild.

'Hello, Rachel Commings speaking.'

'Hello, Mam.'

Rachel didn't receive many evening calls and she had expected it to be someone leaving bowling fixtures for her husband. Her delight was therefore all the more obvious when she heard her daughter's voice. 'Susan! Thank God to hear your voice. Are you well?'

'Yes, Mam. I'm fine.'

'What on earth possessed you to run off like that?'

'Now, Mam, you were there. You heard me dad. He treats me like a five-year-old.'

'It's only because he worries about you. He's afraid of you falling in with the wrong company.'

The wrong company? If they only knew, she thought resentfully. In their eyes Jim Brady would be the wrong company, but she couldn't persuade him to lay a finger on her. Yet the *other* one had taken advantage of her vulnerability and seduced her. Thoughts of Graham suddenly crowded her mind, making her recall the warmth and excitement of their union. A feeling of desolation swamped her. It was her own fault; she should have known better.

'Susan? Are you still there, Susan?'

She stifled the tears that threatened. 'Yes, yes, Mam. I'm here.'

'Are you crying, love?'

'No. I've got a cold. You know, watery eyes and runny nose?'

'Do take care of yourself, love. You know . . . your father regrets speaking to you like that. We would be so pleased if you would come home.'

'I find that hard to believe, Mam. He's never really

shown concern for me. Alison is apparently giving him the ideal son-in-law, so I don't count at all. Ha-ha, that's all that matters. He couldn't care less about me.'

'Ah, Susan, you've always been so defiant. You get your dad's back up. He's terribly disappointed that you took the huff and ran off like that. Of course he cares and wants you to come home.'

'Mam . . . he isn't taking his spite out on you, is he?'

A silence met these words. Then Rachel cried, 'What on earth do you mean, Susan? Of course he isn't!' She was alarmed at how perceptive her daughter was.

Susan remembered the times her father's spiteful remarks had reduced her mother to tears; remembered the muffled weeping coming from her parents' bedroom, and did not believe her. 'I'm sorry, Mam, if I'm bringing you grief. Don't let him browbeat you.'

'You've got it all wrong, Susan.'

'Have I, Mam?' Wanting to change the subject, Susan asked, 'What about Alison? Is she engaged yet?'

'Not yet. I imagine a ring will be bought at Christmas.'

'You know, I envy her. She's two years younger than me, yet she can do whatever she likes! So long as she is with "Graham" she gets away with murder. Dad doesn't demand that Graham has her home by eleven every night. No, those two can do no wrong. Graham would never do anything ungentlemanly. Huh!'

Unable to understand her daughter's bitterness against Graham, Rachel said soothingly, 'Well, he is older than Alison. We trust him to respect her.'

'But you don't trust me?' Susan felt a hypocrite. Here she was, about to become an unmarried mother, and she was giving off about her parents' lack of trust. Why, they would probably disown her if they found out.

'We do trust you. We were just worried when you refused to bring your friend home. I think your dad was under the impression that you were dating a Catholic?' She waited hopefully for her daughter either to deny or confirm the accusation. Her words hung in the air for a few seconds, then sadly she continued, 'I've been wondering about your work, Susan. Did you ask for time off? Surely you didn't hand in your notice? Not knowing what you told them, I was afraid to phone the office. Is your position still open for you?'

Susan laughed; her mother never did wait for an answer. 'One question at a time, Mam. Yes, Mam, my job is safe. I've managed to get time off. One of the other secretaries will take over until I come back.' Susan wasn't really telling lies. Her boss was a very understanding person and would bring in a temp if required to keep her position open. Knowing it would go no further, Susan had confided in him and she had until after the birth to decide what she wanted to do. However, since she didn't know how long she would be away, she couldn't expect her job to be kept open indefinitely. But there was no need for her mother to know this.

Rachel's relief was obvious. 'Thank goodness for that. Well, you've made your point, so come home at once. I worry about you over in that small, cold house at this time of year.'

'Mam, anyone listening to you wouldn't believe you had been reared in a small kitchen house on the Shankill Road, with no hot water and an outside toilet,' Susan teased. She knew her mother didn't like to be reminded of her roots.

'That may well be! But *you* have known only the best. Will you come home?'

'I'm enjoying my bit of freedom, Mam, so I'll stay on here for a while. And the house isn't cold, it's like a wee palace. Edith and Billy have it lovely and comfortable. Don't worry about me.'

'I can't help worrying. I don't want you led astray.'

Susan sighed inwardly. 'Mam, believe me I have less chance of going astray over here than I had back home. Aunt Edith keeps a close eye on me. You can rest assured, I'm not in any danger of being led astray.'

'How is Edith?'

'She's wonderful, Mam. They are both so kind to me. They have a stall in the market now and sell fruit and veg. It's proving very profitable. I help out sometimes. I enjoy meeting the Darlington people. It reminds me of the market back home.' The pips sounded. 'Mam, I've run out of money. I'll phone you again soon. Give Dad and Alison my love.'

'Susan! Susan,' Rachel cried in distress, but the phone was dead.

The wind had strengthened while she was on the phone and icy gusts whipped at Susan's clothes, moulding them into the contours of her body as she left the phone booth, almost lifting her off her feet with its ferocity. She had eased the woollen beret up off her ears whilst phoning and, as the wind set her ears tingling, she made to pull it back down over her unruly curls, but was too late. The wind wrested it from beneath her hand and tossed it like a feather along the street. With a cry of dismay she raced after it and for some moments struggled against the wind in an effort to retrieve it. However, it eluded her efforts and an extra-strong gust lifted it far beyond her reach. She slowed down in frustration. There was no way she could catch up with it in this gale-force wind.

A figure suddenly sped past her, long legs quickly covering the ground. She watched as he effortlessly retrieved the beret and turned back towards her. As he drew near, to her surprise she recognised him. He and her cousin Jack were close friends. She had often trooped about with them on her last visit all those years ago. Would Donald Murphy recognise her again? With a flourish, he handed her the beret.

'Thank you. Thank you very much.'

At the sound of her Irish brogue he leant closer and dark-blue eyes scanned her face. 'Don't I know you?' One fist hit the palm of the other hand as recognition dawned. 'Ah, yes, you're Billy Devine's niece. I heard you were over here. We met some years ago, but I don't suppose you'll remember.'

'I remember perfectly,' she retorted, pulling the beret down over her ears and tucking her hair in under it. 'I'm not senile, you know,' she teased.

'I didn't mean to imply you were,' he replied stiffly.

She gaped at him in amazement. 'Touchy, aren't you? I didn't mean any offence.'

'No offence taken.' He swung away and then back again. 'I'll walk home with you.'

'There's no need.'

A slight smile curved his thin, sensitive lips. 'I'm going in that direction.'

They walked along in silence, the wind making

conversation difficult. He had grown quite a few inches and filled out since Susan last saw him. She was very aware of the bulk of him as they battled against the wind. He had certainly grown into a very presentable young man. She wondered if he was married. Stealing a glance at his brooding, dour looks, she declined to ask. In her opinion Heathcliff, her hero in *Wuthering Heights*, wouldn't hold a candle to Donald's sullen expression. Hark at her! Imagine thinking along those lines. Would she never learn?

To break the effect he was having on her, she shouted above the wind, 'This is some wind, isn't it? Is it usually this strong?'

'Yes, it is strong,' he agreed. 'Usually we're sheltered here in Darlington. It lies in a valley and we miss the worst of the snow and gales, thank God. Take Barnard Castle, for instance, it's just a few miles away and is not so lucky. It can be cut off for days at a time by snow and we would see nothing here in Darlington. To be truthful, I think we're in for some snow here, at the moment. It's certainly cold enough. However, when it does fall it doesn't lie long. How long are you over for?'

'I haven't made up my mind yet. I just came over for a short holiday.'

At the corner of the street she prepared to say good night, but to her surprise he continued walking around the corner and down the street.

Bemused, she followed him. 'There really is no need for you to come any further, Donald. I'll be quite safe,' she chided.

'Oh, but there is,' he assured her. When they arrived at her door she turned to him. 'Will you come in for a cup of tea? I'm sure Aunt Edith will be pleased to see you.'

'No, I'd better not. It's getting late. I've something to attend to and then I'd better get on home. Good night.'

'Good night, Donald. Thanks for walking me home.'

He lifted his hand in farewell and she watched in amazement as he took a bunch of keys from his pocket and, approaching the house next door, inserted one in the lock. It turned easily and he give her a big wink before disappearing inside.

As Susan entered the house, her aunt rose from her seat by the fire and came into the hall to meet her. 'You look frozen. I'll make us a cup of tea. Did you get through to your mam all right?'

'Yes. She was relieved to hear from me. She asked after you and Billy.'

'Is everything all right at home?'

'Mmm . . .' Hanging her coat on a hook in the hall, she said, 'Donald Murphy walked up from the phone box with me. I didn't realise he lived next door. I thought that house was empty.'

'It is . . . well, not quite empty. When his aunt died he somehow or other managed to get his name put in the rent book. When it became common knowledge there was a bit of an uproar at the time, as half of the street wanted it for someone or other. However, whether or not hands were greased – and they probably were – we will never know. But the landlord stood firm and his word was law. As far as he was concerned, Donald's name was in the rent book and that was the end of it.'

Edith fell silent as if undecided. Then she continued, 'Donald was engaged to a girl at that time and they intended starting married life there, but it wasn't to be. He doesn't live there himself, but comes up and stays a few days every month to keep it aired. I sometimes wonder if he expects her to come back to him.'

'What happened? Did they not get married then?'

'No. Apparently she fell in love with someone else.'

'So that's why he's so different. I can sympathise with him. He must have been very unhappy. If I recall correctly, he used to be such a happy-go-lucky sort of lad, and now he seems quite surly. I asked him to come in for a cup of tea, but he was in too much of a hurry to get back home.'

Edith sighed and her eyes took on an empty look. 'I suppose I may as well tell you the rest of it. He isn't very friendly towards us Devines.'

'Oh, why's that? Didn't he and Jack used to be best mates?'

'They were. That's why he avoids us when he can. You see, it was our Jack she ran off with.'

'Oh, no. How awful for him. He must have felt betrayed.'

'Don't put all the blame on Jack!' Edith tersely defended her son. 'These things happen. It nearly broke Billy's heart. This community is so close-knit, you wouldn't believe it! They all rallied round Donald, because he was the injured party and his family were here long before Billy and me. In fact, Donald was born over here. They said some awful things about Jack. Billy also turned on him. Railed at him about doing the dirty on a mate. That's why I don't think Jack will ever come back. I could tell he was hurt at his father's attitude. I suppose, knowing our own history

– how Billy fell in love with me and left his wife – Jack must have thought his father a right 'hypocrite. But there were extenuating circumstances. You see, Donna, Billy's wife, didn't love him, or I would never have agreed to come away with him.' Tears welled up and ran down her cheeks.

Reaching across, Susan gripped her aunt's hands tightly. 'Oh, Aunt Edith, don't upset yourself. I'm so sorry for you both. What an awful thing to happen. What was this girl like? Did you like her? If things had been different, would you have welcomed her as a daughter-in-law?'

'How can I say? I never really got to know her.' Edith's voice was sad. 'Her name was Margaret McGivern. I say was, because for all I know she might be Mrs Devine now. She was attractive all right. Not what you would call a raving beauty like, but attractive, with pale-blonde hair and great dark eyes. She came from the other end of town, Saltersgate. She and Donald were to be married at Christmas and Jack was to be best man. The three of them ran about together everywhere; to the dances and the picture houses and the clubs. They were inseparable. However, she was only in this house one time. If she and Jack were carrying on behind Donald's back, we weren't aware of it. I would never have tolerated it under my roof and neither would Billy.'

She fell silent and Susan waited patiently, convinced that more was to come. She was right, for after some moments of contemplation her aunt continued tearfully. 'The night she told Donald she was in love with Jack, Donald went berserk and came looking for him. They had one hell of a brawl out there in the street. It was awful. They beat each other from one end of the street to the other. No one else was allowed to interfere. Billy tried to separate them, but the men crowded round him and warned him to let them be. They near murdered each other. Margaret was hysterical, so I brought her inside. Somebody phoned the police and an ambulance, and both Jack and Donald ended up in casualty in the Memorial Hospital, under police guard. When they had taken statements and knew the full story, the police wanted Jack to press charges, on account of it being Donald who started the fight, but he declined. The next morning he and Margaret left for London. It was heart-breaking, so it was, watching them drive off for the station in a taxi. Jack's ribs were bandaged and his face was a right mess. He was obviously in great pain.' She paused, lost in unhappy memories. Her voice was bitter when she continued. 'Donald vented his spleen on us. You'd think it was our fault, the way he treats us. He never gave us the benefit of the doubt. It's awful annoying. He just can't be civil towards us. But we honestly hadn't a clue what was going on. As I say, she was only in this house that one time.'

Susan sat, head bent, as the implications of what she had just heard penetrated her brain. It seemed to her that, in the circumstances, Jack would be unlikely to come back to Darlington. Not to live anyhow. Not in this house, with Donald renting the house next door. She recalled the old adage 'Every cloud has a silver lining'. Did that mean there was hope for her? Would she be able to settle here and keep her shame a secret from those in Belfast? Oh, if only . . .

'What about her parents?' she asked tentatively. 'Will

they not be able to persuade her to return. Won't she miss her family?'

'Margaret's parents died young and she was reared by her grannie. She died about a year ago. There's nothing to bring Margaret back here. Nothing at all. Oh, God, why couldn't she have married Donald Murphy and left our Jack alone? She has ruined all our lives. You hear such bad reports about life in London. For all we know, they might be living on the streets,' wailed Edith.

'Have they any money?'

Edith nodded sadly. 'The money we had saved for a van – Billy insisted that Jack take it. He accepted it on the understanding that he would pay it back when he was able. And I know he will, but it wasn't all that much, it won't last for ever.'

'So long as they have some money, they'll find some kind of accommodation, and if they really love each other, they'll be happy no matter where they are. Jack has a trade, hasn't he?'

'He was a fitter in Cleveland Bridge, but will he be able to get that kind of work in London? I doubt it.'

'A fitter can do all different kinds of jobs, Aunt Edith. There's plenty of work in London. He will get into a factory or a garage. Have you not heard from him at all?'

'Huh! One miserable letter to let us know they had arrived safe and well. One miserable letter. Not a word of regret or sorrow for all the trouble he'd caused.'

'He's been too ashamed, so he has. I know how he feels. It's shame that keeps you from getting in touch. But he'll write again, Aunt Edith, when he has some good news to tell you. Just you wait and see.'

Edith wiped her eyes and said, 'I hope you're right. It's great to be able to talk about him. Billy won't let me mention his name in this house. He doesn't like me worrying about them. But I can't help worrying. It's what mothers do best.'

Rachel slowly replaced the receiver in its cradle, a worried frown on her brow. To her, Susan had sounded homesick, so why didn't she come home? As she crossed the hall to the lounge the headlights of a car flashed across the windows as it turned into the drive. She changed course and went to open the door for Alison and her friend, surprised that they had come home by taxi. It was a terrible extravagance. Young people these days were hopeless where money was concerned. You would think it grew on trees.

It was starting to rain. Rachel drew back the net curtain and peered through the window at the side of the door. Great spots splattered the car and she saw that it wasn't a taxi but a comparatively new saloon car that stood outside in the driveway. Through the gloom she was amazed to see her daughter lean forward and kiss her companion, a young man, on the lips. A slow, sensuous kiss. He made to gather her close, but she laughingly broke away from him and, leaving the car, dashed up the steps and turned to wave him off.

Rachel opened the door and Alison laughed. 'That was good timing, Mam.' She shook the loose raindrops from her short blonde curls and eyed her mother keenly. 'Are you all right, Mam? You look a bit pale.'

'Who was that?'

'Just a boy I dance with in Leckie's.'

'You kissed him!' Rachel accused her.

'Just a peck, Mam.'

'It looked more than a peck to me. I thought you were going to eat him. Alison, remember you're practically engaged to Graham.'

'Oh, for goodness sake. What he doesn't know won't harm him.'

'That's the wrong attitude to take when you're contemplating marriage to someone, Alison. I'm surprised at you.'

'Mam, things are different now from what they were in your day.'

'Huh! Not all that different. You had better be careful, girl, or you will lose Graham.'

'I couldn't care less, Mam. There are plenty more fish in the sea. It's Graham who's pressing for an engagement, not me. I'm willing to wait.'

Rachel looked at her beautiful, wilful daughter and could understand why Graham was in such a hurry. He was afraid of losing her.

'Why are you looking at me like that?'

'Hmm. I want to remember what a fool looks like when Graham says "Let's call it a day."'

Alison pulled a wry face and headed for the stairs. 'See if I care.' And she didn't! Life had suddenly become more exciting now that she was learning advanced ballroom dancing. Once she could go to the big ballrooms, the world would be her oyster. The young men were queuing up to dance with her as it was. But they were too young. She preferred the older, more sophisticated man. That was why she had started going out with Graham in the first place. He had prospects and money, but now he bored her. To be truthful, he didn't seem interested in her any more either.

Her mother's voice halted her. 'Susan has just this minute been on the phone.'

She turned, her voice full of regret. 'Oh? I wish I'd been here. How is she?'

'She seems well enough, but I thought she sounded a bit homesick. Probably wishful thinking on my part. She certainly has no intention of coming home just yet.'

'I don't blame her. She's probably having a whale of a time over there. I wish I had her nerve. Imagine taking off like that! I wish something exciting would happen to me.'

'Is getting engaged not exciting enough for you?'

'Catch yourself on, Mam! What difference will it make?'

'You will have an exciting time planning your wedding and looking for a house.'

'Balderdash! It will be years before we marry. Meanwhile, I intend to enjoy myself. Good night, Mam.'

'Good night, Alison.' Rachel watched her climb the stairs, a frown creasing her brow. 'Sweet dreams,' she whispered, 'And I sincerely hope they are of Graham.' Was their youngest daughter as innocent as they would like to believe? It was bad enough Susan proving difficult. Please God, let Alison behave, or life with Trevor would be unbearable.

Susan made her aunt a cup of tea and insisted on adding some of the precious whiskey set to one side for medicinal purposes.

'Oh, you really shouldn't, Susan. That's for emergencies.'

'This is an emergency. You need a good night's sleep, Aunt Edith. After all this reminiscing you won't be able to settle without a little help. Here, drink up.'

Edith sipped at the hot liquid and felt the warmth spread throughout her body, easing the tension from her limbs. 'You really are a blessing in disguise, Susan. I'm glad you came over. Although I wish for your sake the circumstances were different. Did your mother not demand that you go home?'

Susan grimaced. 'She did indeed, but I put her off.'

'I worry about you, Susan.'

'Don't, Aunt Edith. The last thing I want is to be a burden on you.'

'Never that, love. You'll never be a burden. I'm so glad you're here.'

They sat in silence sipping their tea and pursuing their own thoughts. The heat of the fire and the effect of the whiskey took their toll, and soon Edith rose to her feet, her eyes heavy with sleep.

'I think I'd better go to bed before I fall asleep here. I'll see you in the morning, Susan. And thanks for everything. If you're going to bed, love, don't bar the door. Remember Billy isn't home yet. It would never do to lock him out.'

Susan also retired early. She had a lot to think about. If she could just manage to stay here in Darlington until the baby was a few months old, she could claim that it was conceived over here. That way no one would ever guess who the father was. She was glad she had met Donald Murphy tonight. The subsequent conversation with her aunt had made her future look brighter. She hoped that Jack did well down in London and had no desire to return to Darlington. If he should happen to return for the Christmas break, then she would persuade Donald to rent the house next door to her.

Feeling more secure about her future, she fetched a writing pad and pen and, sitting propped up in bed, commenced to write to her friend Ruth Vernon. It was about time she let her best friend know her whereabouts. But she would not mention her reason for coming to England, oh no! If she could help it, no one would ever know the truth. Still, it would be nice to hear from Ruth and be kept up to date on what was happening back home. She bit on the end of her pen for some moments, sorting out in her mind what she wanted to say. Then, happily, she put pen to paper and soon had covered several pages, without giving any secrets away.

Chapter Three

A few days after posting the letter Susan received a reply from Ruth.

Dear Susan,
How mean of you to leave without letting me know. I always
thought of you as my dearest friend. I couldn't believe my ears
when I phoned and Alison told me you'd gone over to England.
I was devastated! However, I do understand and accept your
apologies. I know you were in the doldrums since you split up
with Jim Brady. You shouldn't have let him get to you like that!
There's no man worth all that emotion. By the way, he has also
disappeared from the scene. He isn't, by any chance, over there
with you? Eh? Only joking. Life over here is dull at the
moment. I sure as hell miss you and I'm looking forward to
seeing you at Christmas. Darlington sounds like good fun, but
don't you go getting too fond of it. Your place is back here in
Belfast, with or without Jim Brady. At the moment I'm seeing
Dougie Smith, remember him? He's all right, I suppose, but the
earth doesn't move when he kisses me. Is that important? Did it
move when Jim kissed you? Do people just drift into marriage,
Susan? Oh, how I wish you were here, so that I could discuss
all my problems with you, face-to-face.

> *Goodbye for now, please write soon.*
> *Your true friend*
> *Ruth*

Susan read the letter over and over and the tears rolled down her cheeks. There was no way she could have told Ruth she was leaving Belfast. Ruth would have wheedled the truth out of her, and no one – but no one at all – must know that the baby was conceived back home. How she wished that she was footloose and fancy-free like Ruth. She missed her friend dearly. Wait until Ruth heard she was not coming home for Christmas. She smiled grimly at the idea. The air would surely be blue. She would wait until nearer Christmas before answering this letter and send Ruth a small present. She folded the letter carefully and placed it under her pillow. It brought her best friend and the past close to her, and she had a restless night thinking of what might have been.

Edith was quick to notice Susan's pallor the next morning. 'Do you feel ill, love?' she inquired anxiously. 'I suppose it's time you saw a doctor. Shall I try and get you an appointment with Dr Allen today?'

'No. Time enough for that after Christmas, Aunt Edith. I feel fine, so I do.'

'Well, you sure as hell don't look it! You don't want to risk losing the baby, so you don't.'

Susan turned away to hide her expression. Didn't she just? If only she could miscarry, it would be relief beyond belief. She would do nothing to harm this baby, which at the moment she just knew was there. A couple of mornings of queasiness and a missed period had alerted her, and the pregnancy kit she bought had proved positive. But other than that it wasn't real to her as yet. If the baby was to voluntarily leave her body, she would look on it as an act of God.

However, she felt so well in herself that it was unlikely to happen. She explained to her aunt; 'That letter I received yesterday was from my best friend. It made me a bit homesick, that's all. But I'll get over it. Come on, we'd better get a move on or we'll be late for work.'

Still worried, Edith hesitated. 'Look, you go back to bed. I'll tell Vera you're feeling poorly. She'll understand.'

Shooing her gently towards the door, Susan assured her, 'You'll do no such thing. I'll be fine.'

At her newly acquired job, in the stall next to her aunt's in the market, Ruth's letter played on Susan's mind throughout the day. Ruth had said that Jim was also missing. But then Susan hadn't set eyes on him since he had rejected her advances and walked away, without even so much as a backward glance, so what was new? Was he involved with someone else? No matter! Even if he still cared for her, he wouldn't have anything to do with her now. As far as he was concerned, she had certainly burnt her bridges good and proper. She must look to the future.

A blanket of snow covered the ground as far as the eye could see, turning the town into a winter wonderland. In a happier frame of mind than she had been for some days, Susan picked her way carefully along the slippery footpath, along Albert Hill and on to North Road, stopping cautiously to look in the shop windows. There was nothing of particular interest to her in these shops and, after a lot of near tumbles, she arrived breathless on Northgate. Here the big-name stores were prominent and her attention heightened. The pavements seemed safer and she stepped out more confidently. She stopped at the windows of Marks & Spencer to admire their wares, before moving along to British Home Stores, which was vying with M&S in its endeavours to outdo their Christmas displays. She was looking for suitable presents to send home. Already some goods were marked down in price and she saw a couple of bargains that would come in handy, particularly a pink sweater that she knew would suit Ruth. During the week she would hunt down these bargains when her employer granted her the few promised hours off work. She bypassed John Collier and Alexandre, not being interested in the latest fashions for the male sex. There was no special man in her life to buy for, and the others would receive aftershave.

A glance down Crown Street showed there was nothing of interest to her there. At the General Post Office she crossed the road and backtracked a bit to view the fashions in the windows of Doggarts' store. She gulped at the price tags, which at the moment were well beyond her pocket. Still, it was a store that seemed to stock just about everything and she had heard good reports about the quality of their goods. She silently resolved to have a look inside when she had some spare time.

Reaching the junction of Northgate and Bondgate, Susan hovered close to the Midland Bank on the corner of Prospect Place, to shelter against the flurry of snow blowing down Bondgate. The heart of the town stretched before her, dominated by the market clock tower, and she paused to admire the view slumbering in a virgin-white mantle. Any other day and this vast white mass of snow would already be broken and slushy, but it was early Sunday morning and so far hardly a footprint marred the scene. Glancing behind her, she saw how her own isolated footprints were already obliterated beneath the fresh fall of powdery snow. It was as if she was in a world of her own. Even the sky was a thick white cover capping all this beauty. The snow muffled all sounds and a peaceful hush seemed to embrace the scene. A calmness settled in her soul at such tranquillity.

When she awoke early that morning and saw the thick layer of snow on the rooftops she decided that the time had come to do the window shopping she had been promising herself. The stall next to her aunt's in the market sold greeting cards and wrapping paper. The owner had bought in toys and novelties for the festive season and had been looking for someone to help out with the Christmas rush. Her aunt had put in a word for Susan and an interview was set up. To her great delight, the owner, Vera Crabtree, and she had hit it off right away and the job was hers.

The idea of earning some money and being able to pay her way without breaking in on her savings had come as a great relief. Also, she had not much time to brood and found that she was settling in nicely. It did, however, mean that her days were taken up – even Saturdays – and she had no time to do her Christmas shopping. Only two weeks to Christmas and she still hadn't bought all her presents.

She loved the snow and now, as she gazed at the scene before her, she realised how much at home she felt here. Darlington was an old Quaker town and the architecture of the buildings appealed to her eye. The Pearl Assurance building on the corner of High Row and Bondgate, in particular, was very imposing, especially this morning when snow covered its ornate domed roof and high chimneys, which towered above the roofs of the smaller buildings. Close by, Dressers, the stationer, also looked very attractive with its colourful name sign and posters calling attention to its wares. Jackson's Dry Cleaners and Dunns separated it from two more imposing structures housing the Yorkshire Penny Bank and Barclays Bank.

Standing majestically on an island at the junction, the statue of Joseph Pease stood in all its glory as he silently surveyed the town he had helped to fashion back in the 1800s. She had been reading a lot about this man in a book that her aunt had lent her. To all intents and purposes he had been a spectacular figure, becoming the largest coal merchant in the North-East and generously donating the land for South Park to be laid out for the pleasure and recreation of the people of Darlington. He became the first Quaker MP, entering the House of Commons in 1833 – a pursuit that he had carried on, in spite of opposition from his father and the Society of Friends, of which he was a dedicated member.

The statue itself was weather-beaten and today had a white hat of snow, becoming higher by the minute. This served to make Pease look very formidable. Becoming aware that her toes were beginning to go numb in her thin-soled patent boots, Susan stamped her feet and headed for the Saxone shoe shop on the far side of the road next to the King's Head Hotel. She was reluctant to trespass on the virgin-white carpet, but consoled herself with the knowledge that the falling snow would soon fill in the gaps. It would be trampled anyhow, by church-goers and the like, she reminded herself.

Having caught a glimpse of a pair of fur-lined boots in the window of the shoe shop on her way home from work, she now wanted a closer look. If they had thick soles and weren't too expensive she intended treating herself. At first she thought they had gone, but sighed with relief when she saw they had merely been moved to a higher place on the display shelves. To her great joy she discovered they had also acquired a 'Sale' tag and were a bargain. Tomorrow she would nip out and, if they had her size, she would buy them during her brief lunch break, before they were snapped up.

Pleased with herself, she crossed the main road and carefully climbed the few steps to High Row, pausing on the way for a closer look at Joseph Pease and reading the four bronze plaques around the plinth at the base of the monument. These illustrated important episodes in the great man's illustrious career: politics, education and involvement in the railways. On High Row itself, the shops were also trying to outdo each other in their Christmas displays. Suddenly struck by thoughts of home, Susan was overwhelmed by the memory of the decorations that would be lighting up Belfast city centre. The usual giant Christmas tree outside the city hall would be decorated and ablaze with hundreds of colourful lights, and Royal Avenue would be a sight to behold. Every year she and Alison went down town just to see the wonder of the lights being switched on. She supposed Graham had accompanied her sister this year. Discovering tears trickling down her cheeks, she brushed them away with a swipe of her hand. It was senseless moping over the past. If she could arrange it, this would be her home from now on.

Her mother had been astounded when Susan had told her she would not be home for Christmas. Angrily brushing aside her excuses, Rachel had demanded to know how she could put Edith before her own family, especially at this time of year. Susan was ashamed to use her cousin Jack's absence from home and her aunt's unhappiness as an excuse to stay here. God forgive her, she was building a web of lies and deceit that might one day strangle her.

Determinedly pushing all worries to the back of her mind, she paused at the bottom of Post House Wynd and glanced across to survey her place of employment, the indoor market. Dwarfed at one end by the magnificent town clock, which had also been donated by that generous man, Joseph Pease, the market stretched the length of West Row and was embraced at the other end by the town hall on Horsemarket. All looked splendid in their Christmas finery. Continuing on along High Row, she paused between shops to peer up into Buckton's Yard, Clark's Yard and the Mechanic Institute Yard. All these intriguing, quaint little entries contained a conglomeration of small shops, which she had as yet to explore. It would be something to do after Christmas when she had more time to herself. Who knew what treasures of the past she would find there? This must be how children felt as they anticipated Christmas, she thought, and promised herself that one day in the not too distant future she would explore all these intriguing yards.

She was gazing into Binns' store window when a voice close at hand startled her.

'What has you out so early? Could you not sleep?' Donald Murphy teased. 'Perhaps a guilty conscience?'

Startled, she spun round and gazed up into his dark, brooding face, lightened slightly by the hint of a smile. A fine dusting of snow covered his thick, dark hair and clung to the edge of long eyelashes. 'You frightened the life out of me, Donald Murphy! Creeping up on me like that.'

'Sorry. I didn't mean to alarm you. It's the snow muffling my footsteps. Normally you would hear me a mile off. And you haven't answered my question,' he insisted. He had been admiring the figure in the bright-red coat and knee-length white patent boots and was surprised to discover it was Susan. Why, she was lovely! How come he hadn't noticed earlier? Margaret McGivern must have dulled all his senses towards women. How he missed Margaret! He must have neglected her, for her to turn to Jack Devine like that. He wished he could turn back the clock, but it was too late now. However, this girl exuded sensuality. How come he hadn't noticed before? The white fur snood that Susan wore showed off to perfection her pink-and-white porcelain complexion, which glowed with health. Big, smoky-grey eyes, fringed with long, thick lashes, gazed at him from under exquisitely curved black brows, and her soft, sensuous lips were pink and enticing.

Aware of his admiring scrutiny, Susan blushed. What was he playing at? she thought angrily. Anyone would think he was seeing her for the first time! A pink tide of colour rose from neck to hairline, making him aware that he was staring. He apologised at once. 'Sorry for gawking, but I suppose you already know how pretty you are. Mm?' A light laugh accompanied the words and her embarrassment deepened. Taking pity on her, he let her off the hook by returning to his former question. 'Well . . . what are you doing out so early on this marvellous Sunday morning?'

Still acutely embarrassed by his admiration, she retorted, 'I could ask you the same question. What brings *you* out so early on a Sunday morning?'

'I'm on my way to Mass in St Augustine's.'

'Oh, sorry, I never thought of that. Well, I'm ashamed to admit that I'm not as clean-living as you. I'm just window shopping. I don't get a chance during the week.' She tilted her head and gazed up at him. 'I'm working now, in case you don't know.'

'Really?'

'Yes, Vera Crabtree – you know, she has the stall next to Aunt Edith's in the market – has taken me on to help during the Christmas rush. That's why I'm window shopping. This way I'll know just where to go when I do get a few free minutes.'

'I know Vera. She's a very nice woman.'

'I couldn't agree more. She's so easy to get on with.'

When Susan moved off, Donald fell into step beside her and, after a short silence, asked diffidently, 'Is Jack coming home for Christmas?'

'Not that I know of. Aunt Edith got a letter from him on Wednesday and he told her that Margaret's pregnant.' She watched him from under lowered lashes and felt heart-sore when she saw the raw misery etched on his face. It was obvious he still loved the girl. She could certainly appreciate how he felt. To lose the one you love and then hear she was expecting your best friend's child must be a traumatic feeling. It made everything so final.

He sighed. 'I suppose it's only to be expected. Are they married?'

'I honestly don't know very much about them. It pains Billy to hear Edith talking about Jack, so I just mind my own business. I don't want to upset them by asking embarrassing questions.' She and Donald had met a few times and indulged in casual conversation since her arrival here, but so far she had not ventured to mention Jack and Margaret. Now she said hesitantly, 'I'm so sorry about what happened, Donald. You and Jack were such good friends. It must have been an awful experience for you.'

He shrugged. 'Ah, it was! But it's all water under the bridge now.'

'Aunt Edith and Uncle Billy are heartbroken, you know. They not only lost a son, but a very good friend. Do you not think you should bury the hatchet?'

'That's easier said than done. They must have known. Everybody else did.' His face tightened and his voice thickened. 'They must all have had a good laugh up their sleeves at my expense.'

'I'm sure no one was laughing at you,' she said softly.

'Edith could have dropped me a hint, and perhaps things would have turned out differently. But then, it was their Jack who was the culprit. In their eyes he can do no wrong.'

'They honestly didn't know. It came as a terrible shock to them. Edith told me that Billy said some terrible things to Jack, and now he fears he will never see him again. They're hoping desperately that he will come home for at least a few days at Christmas. I feel guilty as hell, because I know how much they want him to come but I hope he doesn't.'

'Why's that?'

She laughed. 'Oh, all self-interest, I'm afraid. I'm occupying his room at the moment. I don't know where I'll end up if he comes home.'

'You don't intend going home to Ireland for Christmas, then?'

'No.'

Her tone and attitude should have warned him off, but he persisted. 'I hear you're married. What about your husband? Will he not expect you home?'

Her lips tightened. She had not wanted to pretend she was married, but Edith had produced a wedding ring that had belonged to Billy's mother and suggested that Susan wear it, saying there was no need for people to know her business. Thinking that perhaps, when she started to show, her condition might prove embarrassing to Edith and Billy and not wanting to bite the hand that fed her, Susan had agreed to wear the ring. However, the deceit bothered her.

'No!' Her voice was curt, her face closed. 'He won't be expecting me! And, if you don't mind, I don't want to talk about it.'

Donald longed to question her further; to find out how one so young and beautiful could already be separated from her husband. The man must be a fool. But in view of her attitude he decided to hold his tongue; at least for the time being! They had reached the corner where High Row meets Blackwellgate.

'Sorry. I didn't mean to be nosy back there. Look, I'd better not dally. I don't want to be late for Mass.'

Looking around her, the only spire that Susan could see was the one to the right of the three big coolers of the power station that dominated the skyline. This spire she knew belonged to St Cuthbert's Church, rising as it did beyond the roof of the market. 'Where is this St Augustine's Church, then?'

Donald smiled at her bewilderment and pointed ahead. 'Just up there on the right.' Impulsively he added, 'Come with me and see for yourself. It's a beautiful old church. Well worth a visit.'

She laughed aloud. 'I'm not a Catholic.'

'Oh . . . I thought you were. I saw you at St William's last Sunday with Edith and Billy.'

'Nevertheless, I'm not Catholic.'

'Come on, coax yourself. You'll love it.'

Still she hesitated. 'Tell you what. I'll come with you and pray that you will in the near future make your peace with Aunt Edith and Uncle Billy. What's the chances of that happening?'

For the first time since her meeting with him outside the phone box, she saw a real smile light up his face, dispelling the dour look and making it rugged and quite handsome. 'I think the chances are very good.'

'You're on then.'

Happily she walked beside him, unable to hide the smug look on her face. Edith and Billy would be very pleased. She was so lost in thought that it came as a surprise when Donald suddenly stopped at a wrought-iron gate. It divided a row of houses and a great big detached house on the corner of Larchfield Street.

He laughed as she glanced around in obvious surprise. 'We're nearly there.'

He ushered her through the gate and she could see by the trampled snow that others had been here before them. At the end of the narrow entry she saw St Augustine's Church for the first time. She was mesmerised at how a church so near the main thoroughfare could be completely hidden from view. When they left the short entry, on their right beyond a snow-covered lawn a sprawling building was obviously the parochial house. Donald soon confirmed her suspicions and said that the building now on their left was the junior school, the main entrance to it being in Larchfield Street.

The church itself was very old. They entered the porch and she watched as he dipped his fingers into the font of holy water and crossed himself. Nodding to stairs to the left of the door, she asked where they went and was informed that they led to a balcony along the back of the church, where the organ was and the choir gathered to sing the hymns. Donald pushed open the heavy inner door and ushered her through.

She paused inside and gazed around her in wonder. 'It's lovely,' she whispered and without any prompting from him made her way up the church, admiring the beautiful stained-glass windows on either side, as she went. She sat in a pew near the front and took in the intricate detail of the three altars. It must have taken years to perfect.

They were early, but soon the church filled up and the altar boys, followed by the priest, came through a door to the right of the altar and Mass began.

Susan found herself kneeling when Donald knelt and, as there was no choir at this early Mass, singing the hymns from the hymn book. As she participated in the solemn service, peace settled on her heart and she felt that things would surely work out for her.

The service proved all too short and soon they were on their way back through the town. The return journey showed how the beauty of the snow had already been impaired as people went about their business this lovely winter's morning. At the corner of Skinnergate Susan indicated that she was going in that direction to continue her window shopping.

Catching sight of the Pali sign up on the left-hand side of Grange Road, he was struck by a thought. Dare he? Would she go on a date with him? She could only say no.

To Susan's surprise, with a nod of the head across the road, he asked tentatively, 'I wonder . . . would you like to come to a dance with me at the Pali next Saturday night?'

She had heard of the Pali. It was a very popular dance hall. Her heart missed a beat. Go to a dance? How she wished she could. 'I'm sorry . . .'

'Look,' he interrupted hastily. 'I know you're married, and you know I don't want to get involved, otherwise I wouldn't dare ask. We understand each other. Can't we be mates? Enjoy a night out together?'

She pondered for a moment. He didn't know, of course, but it was the thought of her condition that was causing her to hesitate. She came to a decision. She wasn't showing yet, so why not? God knows when she would ever get the chance to go to a dance again. She could wear a loose top; hide her slight bump. Before she could change her mind she said, 'I'd love to.'

Again a smile transformed his face. 'Great! I'll pick

you up at seven-thirty then. It will give me a chance to bury the hatchet with Edith and Billy.'

He was gone before she could express her delight.

The news that Susan would not be home for Christmas enraged Trevor Cummings. He glared at his wife as she read extracts from the letter in her hand. 'Just who the hell does she think she is? What must that big galoot Billy Devine think of us, that our daughter prefers their company to ours at this important time? You write and tell her that if she doesn't come home now, she won't be welcome here ever again.'

'You don't mean that, Trevor.'

'Oh, but I do, Rachel. I mean every word I say, so you be sure to tell her that.'

'Dad, she might have a very good reason for staying in Darlington. Perhaps she has fallen in love with someone.' Alison was trying to keep the peace, but her father rounded on her in anger.

'If that's the case, she can stay over there! She won't be welcome here any more, the way she's carrying on.'

A worried look passed between mother and daughter. Rachel's chin rose in the air and she cried defiantly, 'Then I'm afraid you will have to tell her so yourself for a change. As far as I'm concerned, this is her home and she will always be welcome here.' With a pronounced flounce she left the room, to hide the tears that threatened.

'Dad! How can you be so hard?' Alison exclaimed. 'Susan's your eldest daughter. It could have been much worse, you know. If she had remained here she might have married a Catholic.'

Once more Trevor rounded on her in 'fury. 'So she was seeing a Taig. Was she?'

'I didn't say that.' Alison was dismayed at her slip of the tongue. 'I know she dated one for a time, but obviously it wasn't serious or she would never have gone over to England.'

Still glaring at her, Trevor asked in a soft voice that was more insinuating than a roar, 'Is there more to this than meets the eye? Eh, Alison? Are you keeping something from me? Did Susan go over to England because she has something to hide?'

Alison gaped blankly back at him. What was he getting at? Then, like a bolt from the blue, comprehension dawned and she gasped, 'How can you think a thing like that? If that were true she would have stayed here and got married.'

All the fire left Trevor and he slumped in his chair. He knew only too well how some men used young girls and then discarded them. 'Only if he was *willing* to marry her,' he said sadly. 'Only if he wanted her.' He reached a hand towards his daughter. 'Come here, love.' Hesitantly she approached him. Gripping her hand between his, he whispered, 'Ah, Alison, at least you are fulfilling my hopes. No one could ask for a better son-in-law than Graham.'

Alison looked at him in misery. She didn't want to fulfil his hopes. She wanted a life of her own. Tugging her hand from his, she turned on her heel and hurried from the room. Trevor gazed after her in amazement. What had he done now? Bloody women! He'd never understand them as long as he lived.

* * *

Graham listened in dismay as Alison ranted on about her sister's decision to remain in Darlington over the festive season. He had not had a chance to make his peace with Susan concerning his licentious behaviour. Each time he had been in the Cummings' home she had managed to elude him. Only once had he actually come face-to-face with her. A few days after the episode in the car he had arrived back from town with Alison, and Susan had been in the act of leaving the house. He had managed to block the doorway, forcing her to stop. Glad that Alison had continued on into the kitchen with her purchases, he had whispered urgently, 'Susan, can you ever forgive me?'

'Hush!' She looked furtively around to make sure they were alone. The shame that clouded his hazel eyes made her cringe. To think she had brought him to this. It was awful that she was the cause of his despair. 'Forget it! I have,' she hissed curtly.

Alison's voice hailed him from the kitchen. 'Will you kindly bring the rest of those groceries in here, Graham.'

'Coming, Alison.' Still he blocked Susan's path, whispering fiercely, 'We must talk. Let me at least give you a lift into town, please?'

Angrily she shouldered past him. 'No, thank you. I'll get the bus.'

He gazed after her in dismay. Remembering her hissed remark *'Forget it! I have'*, he squirmed inside. Had she really been able to forget what happened? He had found it the most wonderful experience, and she had participated with enthusiasm. He had never known such heights of passion until that night with Susan. Or was that because it was sweet, forbidden fruit? Was that why it had seemed so wonderful? He must try and get her to speak to him; discover if it really was all over between her and Jim Brady. If so, he would make a point of gradually breaking free of Alison and would pursue Susan. He was convinced that it was her he now loved, and given the chance he would do all in his power to win her. Had she really felt nothing that night?

To his great distress, in the following weeks Susan had continued to avoid him and, as things stood between him and Alison, his hands were tied. It came as a shock to hear that she had run off to stay with an aunt in Darlington. Was Jim Brady pestering her? Was she still besotted with him? Had she run away to avoid bumping into him? Graham determined that when Susan came home at Christmas he would have it out with her. Now Alison was saying that her sister was not coming home.

'Mam is so disappointed, and as for Dad, he's incensed. I don't know how she can do this to us.'

'What reason does she give?'

'Huh! She says Aunt Edith needs her, because my cousin Jack is away living in London. Do you know what I think, Graham? I think she has met some man over there. That's what I think! Why else would she stay away at Christmas?'

Graham's heart sank. 'If that's the case, why not say so? It's nothing to be ashamed of,' he reasoned. 'Does she say when she will be home?'

Alison shook her head glumly. 'One good thing! Aunt Edith is moving house in the New Year, and Susan says they'll be getting a phone installed. At least we'll be able to talk to her when we feel like it. Not wait until she deigns to go to a phone box.' Then she would find out whether or not what her father had hinted at bore any truth. She found it hard to believe that her sister could be so foolish, but she and Jim Brady had been very close. Susan had been besotted with him! Like putty in his hands. There was no denying that.

She mustn't mention these doubts to Graham. It wasn't fair to condemn her sister without proof. She moved closer to him and raised her face in invitation. It was beginning to annoy her that lately she had to make the first move every time they were alone. She recalled how keen he had been at the beginning. Kissing her at every opportunity. Trying to excite her with his body. Positively annoying it had been. Now they may as well be brother and sister, for all the attention he paid her. But then, hadn't she told him that they must wait? To be truthful, she was surprised that he had taken her rejection so much to heart. Also, there had been no pressure to get engaged lately. Had he changed his mind? Surely not! Everyone envied her, and kept asking when the big day was. Pressing closer, her eyes questioned him.

Reluctantly Graham embraced her. He was finding it more and more difficult to put on a show. He couldn't believe that he no longer desired Alison. At the beginning he'd had difficulty keeping his hands off her; in fact, just the sight of her small, firm breasts in the tight sweaters she wore had been enough to excite him. Now all his thoughts were of Susan. Memories of her fiery passion constantly plagued him. How he longed to see her again. He didn't for one moment think that Alison would be exactly heartbroken if he decided to call it a day. She cared little for him. He realised that he shouldn't let it drift on like this, but how could he keep tabs on Susan otherwise? Still, he was being unfair to Alison. It was time he broke off their relationship. Huh! If you could call it that!

To his dismay, Alison pressed closer still. The pressure of her body against his was obviously a come-on and shock gripped him at the idea. Surely he was mistaken? Alison had never before acted as if she desired him.

'Graham,' she whispered tenderly. 'I've been very unfair to you, darling, holding you at arm's length all this time.'

'Perhaps it's all for the best, Alison,' he said gently. 'To tell you the truth, I'm beginning to think that we aren't really suited to each other.'

Shock coursed through her body, but she smothered it. 'What do you mean?' she asked in bewilderment. It was unthinkable that Graham should let her down. She would be a laughing stock.

'Well, it's obvious that you don't seriously care for me . . .'

'What on earth gives you that idea?'

'Huh! The way you treat me.'

She pressed urgently against him. 'Oh, but I do. Indeed I do care. That's what I'm trying to tell you. I know now that I was wrong to keep you at arm's length. I care deeply for you.' Her mouth was urgent beneath his, her hands frantically caressing his body. Everybody was expecting an engagement at Christmas, and she had no intention of disappointing them. Dismayed at her actions, Graham tried to arrest the unexpected flow of passion. Somehow, it didn't ring true. To his great relief, he heard the doorbell sound and someone cross the hall to answer it. .

Talk about being saved by the bell. Thankfully he drew away from her. 'Somebody might come in and catch us.'

Her head tossed in the air and she glared at him. 'I hope you haven't been leading me up the garden path, Graham Robson. I think this weekend would be the right time to choose the ring, don't you?' she taunted daringly. What if he really wanted them to cool it? How could she face everyone? Her parents would put all the blame on her.

She watched anxiously as she put this ultimatum to him. Graham dithered. He knew he should take this opportunity to persuade her that they weren't meant for each other, and that it wouldn't work out between them, but he was too cowardly. He found himself nodding in agreement. After all, he reassured himself, engagements could always be broken.

It was Billy Devine who answered Donald's knock on the door on Saturday evening. Thrusting out his hand, he gripped Donald's and drew him into the house.

'It's good to see you, son.'

'You too, Billy. I've been a fool, so I have.'

There were tears in Edith's eyes when she hugged him close. 'You know, son, we really didn't have a clue what was going on.'

'I realise that now, Edith, and I'm sorry if I caused you a lot of grief. You had enough on your plate at the time.'

'You're here now, Donald, and that's all that matters. Sit down, son. Susan will be down in a minute.'

Hesitantly Donald said, 'Edith, I've been thinking . . . Perhaps the Pali isn't exactly the right place to take a girl like Susan. She strikes me as upper-class. Should I suggest somewhere else?'

Before Edith could answer him, Susan entered the room. He rose to his feet at once, his gaze admiring.

'You look wonderful,' he said softly.

A blush covered her face at the compliment. 'Thank you, kind sir,' she replied.

They left in a flurry of goodbyes, with Donald – at Edith's pleas to visit them more often – assuring her, with an admiring look at Susan, that he certainly would. After they'd gone Edith turned to Billy, her face puckered with worry.

'Billy, you don't think . . .?'

He put a finger gently to her lips. 'I'm not going to think anything, and neither are you, my love. They are adults after all, and they are both free.'

'She's pregnant, Billy! Do you think she's told Donald about the baby?'

'As I have already said, it's none of our business, Edith. At the moment all I can think of is the fact that for the first time in weeks we have the house to ourselves.' He was urging her towards the stairs; his mouth stifled her objections.

Pushing him away, she cried, 'All right! All right, there's no need to smother me.' And, with a girlish giggle, she preceded him up the stairs.

'I heard what you said to Edith about the Pali. Do you think I'm some kind of a snob, Donald? Is that how I come across to you?'

'No, not really, but the Pali is frequented by the soldiers from Catterick Garrison and can get a bit rough at times. It gets a bit of a name, but no one will bother you as long as I'm with you.'

'It sounds like the Plaza back home. That's where all the servicemen who come into Belfast go. I was only there the once with my best friend. I thought it was brilliant, all those men queuing up to dance with us. We had a great time.'

The Pali wasn't as spectacular as the Plaza. There was the same dim lighting, the big silver ball revolving in the centre of the ceiling, throwing fingers of light on to the white shirts and coloured dresses of the dancers; and the hushed, excited chatter against the throbbing music. There the likeness ended. The Plaza had bars where wine and beer was sold. Susan could see no bars here. After a visit to the cloakroom to leave her coat and change from her boots to her dance shoes, she returned to Donald.

Her eyes were glowing with excitement and he laughed as he led her on to the dance floor. 'I can see you're impressed.'

She nodded. Her happiness was apparent. 'It's a bit like the Plaza back home,' she repeated. 'I feel very daring being here.'

'Where did you usually dance?

'The Orpheus and Club Orchid.'

'With your husband?'

Her happiness faded. 'No.'

Annoyed at himself for putting a damper on her feelings, Donald cried, 'Look, forget I said that. I didn't mean to spoil things. Let's just enjoy ourselves.' With practised steps he swung her in and out of the dancers to the strains of a quickstep. They finished at the bottom of the hall as the music came to a halt and, seeing two empty chairs, he steered her over to them.

'That was wonderful, thank you. I can't believe my luck!' she sighed.

'What do you mean?'

'You being able to dance so well.'

He threw back his head and laughed aloud. 'Oh, so you thought I'd have two left feet, did you?'

'No! No, I'm only admitting I'm not much of a dancer and I need a good partner to lead me around the floor.'

'Aren't you being a bit modest? I bet you could dance with anybody in this hall,' he teased.

She just grinned happily at him and again he was struck by how lovely she looked. The first chance he got he would take Edith aside and find out what had gone wrong with her marriage.

The music started up again and he eyed her. 'Fancy a slow foxtrot?'

'My favourite dance,' she said as she slipped into his arms and was drawn close.

As he nodded to friends and acquaintances, Donald was aware of the envious glances cast in his direction and for the first time felt free of the hurt invoked by Margaret's betrayal. Susan was indeed a partner to be proud of. Her soft brown hair glowed with copper high-lights and her eyes were dark, mysterious pools. Although they knew she was with a partner, even the soldiers were cheeky enough to give her the eye. Very much aware of their interest, he unconsciously drew her closer still. Her head rose in the air and she gazed reproachfully up at him. Immediately, he loosened his hold. He mustn't give her the wrong impression. After all, it wasn't as if he was actually making a play for her. He still loved Margaret McGivern. No one else could ever take her place.

'Sorry, I got carried away. You're very lovely, you know.'

She blushed and stiffened in his arms and he regretted his actions. 'Don't look like that. I promise to behave myself.'

She remained stiff and unyielding for the remainder of the dance. When it ended he led her to the long table where soft drinks were sold. 'What would you like to drink?'

'Orange, please.'

The chairs were all occupied, so they stood to one side and sipped their drinks. Seeing a worried frown pucker her smooth brow, he leant towards her. 'Look, Susan, please don't be worrying. I didn't mean any harm. We can go home any time you like.'

'It's all right, Donald,' she sighed. 'It's just that I can't afford any more complications in my life. As things stand, I've enough to worry about.'

'I realise that, Susan, and I don't want to add to your troubles. I promise to be on my best behaviour from now on. I'll be the best mate you ever had.'

She still looked unconvinced, but nodded her head. If only she could believe him. It would be lovely to have someone she could go out with, with no strings attached; someone to depend on. But in her heart she thought it would be better if she didn't see him again. This must be their first and last date. It was too dangerous! Something about him reminded her too much of

Jim Brady and she wanted him to hold her close; she longed to close her eyes and pretend she was with Jim. She was lost for companionship, but Donald, like herself, was on the rebound. It could cause all kinds of problems.

In spite of the uneasy start, the night was a great success. They danced every dance and Susan felt happier than she had been for a long time. They walked home in the crisp, frosty air and she did not demur when he took her hand and tucked it beneath his elbow.

'I really enjoyed myself tonight, Susan.'

His voice was like a caress and she sighed. Was he going to start all that again? Her hand wriggled to get free, but he tightened his grip on it. 'I promise I won't overstep the mark again. I realise you're not free, but then in my heart, neither am I. I still love Margaret and I'll never change. Nevertheless I value your friendship. Please say you will come out with me again?'

'It wouldn't be fair, Donald. You know nothing about me. There might be talk.'

'Why would there be any talk? We're doing nothing wrong. I honestly don't see why we can't be friends,' he cried in bewilderment. 'It won't cost you anything. At least say you will come to the dance with me on Boxing Night. Please?'

It was on the tip of her tongue to tell him she was pregnant, but then he might not want to be her friend. He would know soon enough. 'All right. But, Donald, please don't expect anything from me. I admit that I don't know many people over here and I'm very lonely at times. I do need a friend, but I'm in love with someone else, and friendship is all there can ever be between us.'

His mind went blank, then rushed into overdrive. She was in love with another man? So that must be why her marriage was on the rocks. He wouldn't have believed it of her. Where was this other man now? Had the break-up of her marriage been in vain? Surprised and saddened at her situation, he was silent until they reached her door.

Susan made no effort to break the silence; just gently removed her hand from his now-loose clasp. Nor did she invite him in when they arrived home. 'If you still want me to come to the Pali with you on Boxing Night, just let me know. I'll understand if you don't. Good night, Donald.'

She unlocked the door and was through it before he could gather his wits about him. He stood dumbfounded, staring at the door. What was he thinking of? He had acted like an idiot. Of course he still wanted her to go to the dance with him on Boxing Night. He would call in during the week and make sure she understood that. More at ease in his mind now, he headed home. After all it was no concern of his if she loved in vain. Wasn't he in the same boat? It was a friend he wanted – a dance partner – and he couldn't think of anyone he would rather have.

To Susan's dismay, her aunt and uncle were still downstairs and sitting by the fire sipping cups of tea. 'I thought you'd bring Donald in for a cuppa. It would have given us a chance to talk,' Edith said.

'I thought you would be in bed and I didn't want to disturb you,' she lied convincingly.

'Never be afraid to bring him in, love'. Even if we have retired, you won't annoy us. Did· you enjoy the Pali?'

'It was great, Aunt Edith. I don't know if you were ever in the Plaza back home? It reminded me of there. Donald's an excellent dancer. I really enjoyed myself.'

'Pour yourself a cup of tea and sit down, love. You look frozen.'

With a resigned look, Susan did as she was bid and joined them by the fireside.

'We got some good news tonight.' Edith sounded nervous and Susan moved restlessly on her chair. 'You know Mrs Duggen down the street?'

'Yes. The woman who lives in the corner house?'

'That's right. Well she came for me earlier on. Our Jack had phoned her and asked her to fetch me. And . . . what do you think? He's coming home for Christmas after all.'

Slowly Susan set her cup shakily on the table, grateful that the tea didn't slop over the edge. She forced a smile to her face. 'Oh, I am pleased for you. You must be delighted.'

'We are. We're over the moon. But now, love, I don't want you to be worrying. We'll sort out somewhere for you to stay. They will only be here a few days. They said they'd come on Friday, stay over Christmas Eve, Christmas Day and Boxing Day, and leave on Tuesday. I'm so happy I could cry.' Without more ado she proceeded to do so.

Edith's tears blinded her to Susan's reaction, but Billy could see that, although his niece tried to show pleasure, it didn't ring true. He realised that she was worried and said, haltingly, 'Susan, we will make room for a bed in the spare room for you, if that's all right? It will only be for a couple of nights, after all.'

'That would be great, Uncle Billy, but won't I be in the way?'

'Don't be silly. You're family. Everything will be fine, so it will.'

Tears ran down Susan's cheeks as she lay in bed that night staring at the ceiling. She was glad she had managed to put on a good show in front of her aunt and uncle. She was also glad she had sent all her presents off to Ireland during the week. Although Jack wasn't coming until next Friday, her aunt would want to get this room ready for him and Margaret, and she would have to find somewhere to live right away. She didn't agree with her uncle. The spare room was out of the question. Oh, she didn't mind being in cramped quarters for a while, but it wouldn't work out. She would feel that she was intruding on their privacy. Jack would want to patch things up with his parents and he couldn't talk freely if she was there. Her aunt had agreed with her that the junk room, as she called it, was unsuitable, saying that she would see that Susan found somewhere comfortable to stay. God knows where she would end up while her cousin and Margaret were here. After the way she had treated Donald's overture to friendship, she could hardly now ask him to rent the house next door to her.

Her thoughts turned to Vera Crabtree, as she tried to remember if any of her family were still living at home. She must ask Aunt Edith. Poor Donald. His face appeared before her mind. He would be devastated, seeing the woman he loved pregnant by another man. And . . . what if her cousin decided to stay in Darlington? What would happen to her then? God alone knew the answer to that.

Chapter Four

While Susan was tripping the light fantastic around the dance floor in Donald Murphy's arms at the Pali, Alison was doing likewise at the Orpheus.

The dance was almost over when, to her surprise, she saw Jim Brady approaching their table. 'Look who's here, Graham,' she muttered.

Graham rose to his feet at once, hand extended in welcome. 'Why hello, Jim. It's good to see you.'

'You too, Graham. I've just arrived. Hello, Alison. I trust you are well?' His eyes roamed over the table noting that there were only two glasses. 'Is Susan not here tonight?'

'No!' Alison's voice was abrupt. She volunteered no further information.

Embarrassed, Graham said, 'We haven't seen you in a while, Jim. Where have you been hiding yourself?'

'I've been busy, Graham.' He smiled slightly. He wasn't going to admit that he'd been broke lately. Couldn't afford to go out. That was nobody's business but his own. Besides, these people wouldn't know the meaning of the word skint.

The music started up and he said, 'Graham, is it all right if I dance with Alison?'

'Be my guest.'

'Huh! Have I no say in the matter?' Alison cried, greatly affronted.

Both men grinned at her chagrin. 'Please may I have this dance, Alison?' Jim extended a hand and smiled disarmingly, sure of her reply.

God, but I'd love to turn him down, she thought angrily; wipe that smirk off his face. But she wanted to question him about her sister, so needs must. With a great show of petulance, she allowed him to lead her on to the dance floor.

Waiting until they were out of earshot of Graham, she looked up at him and demanded, 'What did you do to my sister that sent her scurrying over to England in such a hurry, eh?'

'Susan's in England?'

She could see that he was flabbergasted, but taunted, 'As if you didn't know!'

'On my honour, I didn't. I came here tonight looking for her. I've missed her terribly. I couldn't stay away any longer.'

'Well, I'm afraid you've left it too late. You've no chance of seeing her. She took off weeks ago and is now staying with Aunt Edith in Darlington. She's got herself a job and all. What do you think of that?'

Jim was dumbfounded; didn't know what to think. Perhaps it was as well. Now he wouldn't be able to ask her forgiveness and beg her to be friends again. After all, he could still not offer her marriage.

'Tell me something, Jim. Has she run away to hide something from us?'

She watched him closely. His brow furrowed and he

looked bewildered. 'I don't understand. Hide what?'

'Come off it. You know damned well what I'm getting at. Is she pregnant? Is that why you dropped her?'

His jaw dropped and his face stretched with horror. Then, grabbing her by the upper arm, he hustled her off the dance floor and into a corner. 'Explain yourself, miss,' he said tersely.

Flustered, she cried, 'My dad is convinced she ran away because she's . . .' The words refused to come. 'In the club.' She shrugged. 'You know what I mean?'

'Well, let me tell you something, Alison Cummings. If Susan is pregnant, it's not my doing.'

'Huh! You would say that anyway, wouldn't you?'

The urge to strike her accusing face was so strong that Jim turned on his heel and walked away. Her dad, with his filthy mind, was absolutely wrong. There was no way Susan could possibly be expecting a baby. He hadn't laid a finger on her and, as far as he knew, there had been no one else in the picture at the time. He lifted a hand briefly in farewell in Graham's direction and headed for the door. Tomorrow night he would go to the Club Orchid and find out what Ruth Vernon had to say. Susan and she had been as thick as thieves. If anyone knew anything about Susan, it would be Ruth. He would clear Susan's name once and for all.

Ruth Vernon was surprised when Jim, for the first time ever, asked her to dance with him the following night in the Club Orchid. 'This is a surprise,' she exclaimed. 'Where've you been?'

'Oh, here and there. Look, I've a favour to ask you. Could we sit this one out and talk?'

'I'm with Dougie Smith. If we sit out together, he won't like it. He'll wonder what I'm up to.'

Jim's disappointment was so acute that she asked, 'Is this about Susan?' He nodded eagerly and she pondered for a moment. 'Go down to the bar and get yourself a drink and buy me a Coca-Cola. I'll explain to Dougie what's happening and I'll meet you over there,' she nodded towards the door, 'in ten minutes. Okay?'

'Thanks, Ruth. I won't forget this.'

Ten minutes later they sat outside the ballroom, on the stairs that led to the ladies' cloakroom. Ruth touched her glass to his. 'Cheers.' She added warningly, 'If I'm very long, Dougie says he'll come looking for me.'

'This won't take long. Tell me, did you know that Susan was living over in England?'

Ruth nodded, but explained, 'Mind you, she went off without saying a word to me, or anyone else for that matter. Just took off out of the blue. I only found out when I phoned her house and Alison told me.'

'But why go to England? She must have hinted at something.'

Ruth's shoulders lifted in a shrug. 'I honestly don't know. I do know that she was terribly cut up about you, but I thought she was coming to terms with it.' She paused and reflected. 'To be truthful, I got an awful shock when I heard the news. Alison wouldn't even give me her address, but eventually I received a letter from Susan and she apologised for not telling me she was leaving.'

'And she didn't say why she went away?'

'No, not a word.' Ruth gave him a glare from her big,

brown eyes. 'But I think that's obvious, don't you? She was running away from you, so she was.'

Relieved to hear this, Jim said tentatively. 'Her father thinks she was hiding her pregnancy.'

'Mr Cummings thinks that?' Ruth gasped, her head swinging from side to side in denial. 'He's got it all wrong. She would have confided in me. She'd have needed someone to talk to.'

'Alison thinks that if her sister is pregnant, I'm the one to blame.'

'Well, that's understandable! You're the only one Susan was seeing. She was nuts about you.'

'She didn't see anyone else after we split up?'

'No, she was too heartbroken.'

'Then she's not pregnant. I never laid a finger on her. And that's God's honest truth.'

'I'm glad to hear that, Jim. It would have caused a lot of problems.'

'Will she be home at Christmas then?'

A sad shake of the head. 'I'm afraid not. I received a present from her yesterday morning and a letter. She says she won't be home.'

'Did she say why?'

'Some cock-and-bull story about not wanting to leave her aunt.'

'Ruth, can I please have her phone number?'

'Unfortunately her aunt isn't on the phone.'

'Her address, then?'

'Jim, I would have to ask her permission first. Give me your address and, if she says all right, I'll post it on to you. That's the best I can do. After all, she must have left to get away from you. What other reason would she have? And who knows, maybe she's met someone else.'

Jim searched his pockets and found an old receipt. Quickly he jotted down his address on the back of it. Ruth's remark that Susan might have met someone else dismayed him. 'Let me know as soon as you can, won't you, Ruth?'

'Sure. I'd better go now, Jim. See you around.'

Graham watched dumbfounded as Jim left Alison standing in a corner and, with a wave of farewell in his direction, left the room. He hurried to meet her. 'What was all that about?'

'Nothing.'

'Come off it, Alison. It's obvious something's wrong. Surely he didn't chance his arm?'

'Don't be silly!' She was silently debating whether or not she should tell Graham about her father's accusation against Susan. If Jim was telling the truth, and somehow she believed he was, it would be foolish to besmirch her sister's good name by repeating her father's insinuations. She decided against telling him.

'He wanted Aunt Edith's address and, when I refused to give it to him, he stormed off,' she lied, then asked tentatively, 'Did I do the right thing?'

Quickly Graham agreed with her. 'You sure did! She's better off without him. Still, you must try and persuade her to come home for Christmas. It's unthinkable that she should stay over there.'

'She phones me mam every Wednesday night, so I'll stay in this week and have a word with her. But, mind you, I don't think it will do any good.'

'It's worth a try. She should be with her family at this time of year.'·

'You're right! I'll do my best to persuade her.'

Donald strode along North Road trying to get his mind around the enigmatic puzzle of Susan Cummings. What age would she be? Twenty? Twenty-one? Certainly no more than twenty-two. And she had a failed marriage behind her. She had confessed to being in love with another man. Where was this other man? Had she left her husband, only to find out this man didn't love her in return? Or had he a wife he refused to leave? Was that why she had come over to Darlington? He really must make an effort to get Edith on her own and find out just what the situation was. Suddenly he realised he had no need to do that. He had no designs on Susan. They would just be good mates, and mates took each other on trust. He would make sure he was around when she needed him. If she wanted to confide in him about her past, she would tell him in her own good time. That would be a bonus; a sign of her trust. Meanwhile he must not pry into her private affairs. After all, he was in the same boat as Susan with a failed romance behind him. They needed each other, and he had certainly been no comfort to her tonight. What must she be thinking of his silent condemnation? That's what it had amounted to, condemnation. He was thoroughly ashamed of his attitude. At the first opportunity he would seek her out and put matters right.

The chance of earning some extra money for Christmas had encouraged Donald to work every night. It was

Friday, the day before Christmas Eve, when they had stopped for the holiday break, before he was in a position to call and ask Susan if she would still accompany him to the dance on Boxing Night. Who knows, perhaps if he played his cards right, she might even agree to go out to the pub with him tonight for a drink?

He sang lustily as he showered, causing his mother to eye him suspiciously when at last he put in an appearance. She had sorrowfully watched him nurse a broken heart and was fearful of him making another mistake on the rebound.

'What has you so happy?'

'Mam, I'm going to ask a very beautiful girl to come out with me for a drink and I'll be the happiest man in the world if she says yes.'

A worried frown gathered on Mary Murphy's brow. 'Now you be careful, son,' she warned. 'You know what happened the last time.'

'That's all in the past, Mam. This girl and I are just good friends. No strings attached. So you have nothing to worry about.'

'Do I know her?'

'No, but you'll have heard of her. She's Edith Devine's niece.'

'Jack's cousin?'

He nodded. 'You'll like her, Mam. There's no nonsense about her.'

'Will you never learn? Has that family not caused you enough heartache?'

'Mam, I've explained. We're just good friends.' He gave her a hug and an affectionate kiss on the cheek.

'Stop worrying about me and don't wait up, I might be late.'

'Donald, no matter what you might think, there's no such thing as platonic friendship between a man and a woman. Do you hear me? You take care!'

'I will, Mam, I will.'

His assurances rang in Mary's ears long after he had gone. She sent a prayer heavenwards. 'Please, dear God, don't let him be hurt again.'

It was almost nine o'clock when Donald eventually arrived at Edith's house. He stepped into the hall and raised his hand to knock on the kitchen door, but hesitated as animated voices reached his ears. They seemed to have company. One well-remembered voice stood out from the rest, causing a fist to close around his heart. 'That was a lovely meal, Mrs Devine. It's great to be home. Thank you for having us.'

'You're welcome, Margaret. I only wish you were home for good.'

Jack's voice came next, sounding worried. 'Mam, do you think Susan will be all right in that wee spare room?'

'Your dad got a mate to store all the rubbish he won't part with, and that single bed up there is very comfortable, so it is. I wanted her to go into a guest house, but she said she was all right. She's been sleeping there since Monday.'

Careful not to make any noise, Donald backed out on to the pavement and hurried down the street. He felt gutted. The old feelings of betrayal had returned to torment him. Why did they have to come back now, just when he was getting over her? But then, there was no need for him to see Margaret. He would make himself scarce until they left.

At the corner of the street he almost bumped into Susan. Seeing his distress, she gripped his arm in concern. 'You saw them, then?'

'No. I heard their voices.' A bitter laugh accompanied these words. 'That was enough to send me scampering away.'

'I'm sorry, Donald. I wish I could have prepared you, but I didn't know where you lived and I didn't want to ask Aunt Edith. It would have taken the joy out of their coming, if you know what I mean? She's sure to be worrying about the effect it will have on you. I hoped you'd come and see me before they arrived.'

'I've been working every night. It's you I was coming to see, but when I heard their voices I just couldn't go in.'

'They arrived this afternoon. I offered to stay behind and get the stall ready for tomorrow's last-minute rush. I wanted to give them some time alone. Get the awkwardness out of the way. I dread it, so I do. I'm going to be in the way, I know I am, but I couldn't find anywhere to rent and I've nowhere else to go.'

He nodded. 'I heard them talking about you. They were wondering if you would be comfortable in the spare room. I wish I could be of some help.'

She took the bull by the horns and cried, 'You can!'

'Can I?' he said in bewilderment. 'How?'

'You can rent me the house next door.'

He gazed at her blankly for some moments. Then the penny dropped. 'Of course you can stay there! How come I never thought of that?'

Relief made her voice shake. 'Oh, Donald, you don't know what this means to me.' She looked at him anxiously. 'Will you come back with me now? You could help me move my stuff in.'

He backed off a little. 'I don't think that would be a good idea, Susan. Look, here are the keys. I'm sure Billy and Jack will give you a hand with your stuff.'

She moved close and stared earnestly into his eyes. 'Does this mean I won't see you while they're here? I'm depending on your company, Donald.'

'Of course you'll see me. We can meet away from the house.'

'Donald, you will have to face them sooner or later. Please come back with me now and get it over with. I haven't much stuff. It'll only take a few minutes to move me into your house, and afterwards we can go out for a drink if you like? Mm, how about it?'

'I'm sorry, Susan, but I just can't face them.' With these words Donald turned abruptly on his heel and was off.

Susan pocketed the keys with a sigh. She could understand his reluctance to face the enemy, but she wished he'd been a bit stronger. It would be better in the long run.

She had almost reached the house when he again fell into step beside her. 'You're right, of course, Susan,' he said with a rueful smile. 'I may as well face the music and get it over with. You will help me all you can, won't you?'

A delighted smile brightened her face. 'Of course I will, Donald. But remember, I've yet to meet Margaret.' She stepped into the hall. 'Are you ready?' she whispered. He nodded and she pushed open the door.

Jack rose to his feet at once and came towards her, a welcoming smile on his face. The smile faltered when Donald followed her into the room.

It was Billy who broke the awkward silence. 'Come in, Donald, and pull up a chair. Would you like a beer?'

Relieved that there was no sign of Margaret, Donald replied, 'No thanks, Billy. Hello there, Jack. How's things with you?'

'Hello, Donald.'

Before tension could set in Susan quickly intervened. 'Donald has suggested I move into his house next door while Jack is here. He's come to help me move my stuff in.'

'That's a wonderful idea – you'll be more comfortable there than in the spare room. In the circumstances, it's very kind of you to offer, Donald.'

In the kitchen Edith and Margaret stood silently throughout this discourse. At last Edith whispered, 'Do you want to face him now or later?'

'It's best to get it over with.' Slowly Margaret dried her hands and headed for the door.

Donald felt his heart contract at the sight of her. Pregnancy obviously agreed with her. Light-coloured hair framed her head like a golden halo, her white skin gleamed like thick buttermilk and her sensual lips needed no make-up to enhance them. She positively bloomed. How come he hadn't noticed the way the wind was blowing and had allowed Jack to walk off with her?

'Hello, Donald, how are you?'

'I'm very well, Margaret.' He was glad that his voice sounded strong and confident. 'Susan here is going to stay next door for a few days. I've come to help her move in her bits and pieces.'

Jack hastened to introduce the two girls. 'Margaret, you've never met my cousin. Susan, this is my wife.'

'I'm very pleased to meet you,' Susan said formally. She could understand both men lusting after this girl. She had that spark that would always turn men's heads. 'I've heard all about you.'

'I'll bet you have.'

Taken unawares by the bitter note in the other girl's voice, Susan turned abruptly to Donald. 'Is there any bedding next door?'

'Plenty of blankets, but you'll need some sheets and pillowcases.'

Glad to escape the tension that was building up, Edith headed for the stairs. 'That's no problem. I'll fetch some.'

Remembering her promise to help Donald over this awkward situation, Susan said, 'Donald, if you come up I'll show you what I want moved.' And she followed her aunt upstairs.

Tentatively Jack offered, 'Can I be of any assistance?'

'No, no, you're all right. We'll manage.'

When Donald had followed the women, Jack went to his wife and took her in his arms. 'Don't you distress yourself,' he warned. 'Think of the baby.'

Fighting back tears, Margaret released herself from his embrace. 'I'll finish the washing up.'

'I'll help you.'

Left alone, Billy sank down on to the settee and buried his head in his hands. He was delighted to have his son home, but felt uncomfortable in the presence of Margaret. No matter how often he told himself it took two, he could find no fault in Jack. He was convinced that his son would not have seduced her behind his friend's back if he hadn't had plenty of encouragement from her. He placed all the blame firmly at Margaret's door. Donald was a good man, and she shouldn't have two-timed him. She should have been honest with both men. However, for Jack's sake he would do all in his power to make her welcome.

With a deep sigh, he rose to his feet and climbed the stairs to give Donald a helping hand.

Upstairs, Edith looked around the small room she had done her best to make comfortable. 'I got the impression that you were all right here, Susan,' she said accusingly. 'You should have said, and I would have found somewhere else for you to stay.'

'Oh, Aunt Edith, please don't be annoyed,' Susan cried in alarm. 'It is comfortable. Honestly! But can't you see? I'd be in the way. You need time alone with your daughter-in-law to get to know her. This way, we won't be falling over each other. You will have more time with your own family and won't be worrying about me.'

Edith remained tight-lipped and, going over to her, Susan whispered, 'Please understand. I wouldn't offend you for the world.'

Her aunt's expression relaxed. 'Promise me you'll come in for all your meals.'

'All except breakfast. I can manage to make that myself,' Susan teased. 'I will also be able to have a lie-in, if I feel like it.'

Edith frowned in Donald's direction. 'I know it's none of my business, but will he be staying there with you?'

'You can rest assured, I won't, Edith. I'll not sully your niece's good name.'

'Well then, let's move her stuff in next door.'

An hour later they smiled at each other across the pub table. 'That wasn't too bad, now was it, Donald?'

'No. As you said, it's better to get it over with. But . . . I'll tell you something. I'm glad she wasn't there when we went in to say farewell. I was all tied up in knots.' Susan remained silent and he eyed her covertly. 'What did you think of her?'

'She's very pretty.'

'Did you like her?'

'Ah, come off it, Donald! How can I tell? I only exchanged a couple of words with her.'

'I fell for her the first time I saw her.'

'Well, I'm not you. Whether or not she and I become friends remains to be seen.'

Last orders were called, and Donald appraised her. 'Do you fancy another one?'

'No, thank you. I've an early start in the morning.'

'Fine. I want to go back with you and make sure that fire I lit is okay.'

'There's no need for you to come back, Donald. I'm sure the fire will be fine.'

'I'm coming back.' His tone brooked no argument and she silently followed him from the pub.

The house was much warmer than it had been earlier on. 'It's lovely and cosy. Thank you, Donald.' Edith had insisted that Susan bring tea, sugar and milk in with her and now she said, 'I'll make a cup of tea and then we'll discuss the rent.'

'Get away with you! I don't want any money from you.'

'All the same, I'll feel better if I pay my way.'

'How about you making me a meal on Boxing Night before we go to the dance?'

'So you still want me to go with you?'

'Of course I do, Susan. I know how it must have looked to you last week. As if I was sitting in judgement. I didn't mean to. I promise to mind my own business in future. Can you forgive me? I need a friend more than ever now, especially if they decide to remain in Darlington.'

'Do you think there's any chance of that happening?' Susan asked in dismay.

'To be truthful, I can't see Jack staying in London. It's not his scene. I think they'll be back in the not-too-distant future. Margaret will want the baby born here.'

Handing him a cup of tea, Susan sat down on an armchair at the side of the fire. Donald took the only other chair in the room, facing her, and waved a hand vaguely around. 'As you can see, there's not much furniture. When my aunt died I got rid of most of her old stuff. I knew Margaret wouldn't want an old woman's bits and pieces. Mind you; I had plans. I would have worked my fingers to the bone to make it nice for her.'

'It could be made very comfortable indeed,' Susan agreed.

To her dismay, his head sank on to his chest and she knew he was fighting back tears. 'How am I going to get through this, Susan? I thought I was getting over her. Now look at me! A right bundle of nerves.'

Going to him, she put an arm across his shoulders

in sympathy. 'You'll get over her. Just wait and see. I'll help you all I can.'

Turning, he put his arms around her waist and sank his head on to her breast. 'I'm glad you're here, Susan.'

Gently she edged away from him. It would be so easy to become involved. She was also at a low ebb at the moment, but it wasn't a lover she needed – it was a friend. 'We'll help each other, Donald. Now it's time you were leaving, or Aunt Edith will be getting worried. She's probably taken up sentry duty behind the blinds,' she laughed.

Reluctantly he rose to his feet and reached for his coat. At the door she gave in to the temptation to give him a hug of comfort. Too late, she saw Jack unloading the car he had arrived in. He nodded in their direction and his eyes were full of speculation. Ah well, it would give him and Margaret something to talk about, she lamented.

At work the following morning Edith gave Susan a handful of mail. She smiled as she opened it. There were last-minute cards from her family and friends who had expected her home at Christmas. Ruth's contained a short letter explaining about her meeting with Jim Brady at the Club Orchid. The market doors were opening to the public and Susan put all her mail carefully under the counter to be enjoyed later, but Ruth's note played on her mind as she attended to her customers.

What could Jim possibly want to write to her about? It would be a waste of time corresponding with him. They could never meet again. He wouldn't want her now, in any case, if the truth ever came out.

Jack and Margaret stopped by the stall while doing some last-minute shopping and were greeted excitedly by Vera. 'Oh, it's lovely to see you again, Jack. Mind you, you were a naughty boy.' Releasing him from her bear hug, she turned to Margaret. 'You too, young lady. You know you broke poor Donald Murphy's heart when you ran away with this scallywag.'

Jack gave Susan a sly look. 'I wouldn't worry too much about Donald if I were you, Vera. He's already found consolation.' He drew Margaret towards him. 'You haven't been introduced to my wife, have you?'

'No, I haven't had that pleasure. And a bonny girl she is. I wish you all the very best, love.'

'Thank you. You're very kind.'

'Where's Mam?'

'She's just nipped out to get something for her lunch,' Vera informed him. 'And your dad has run out of tomatoes, so he's away to get some more. Here's your mother now.'

'Jack, Margaret! What are you doing here?'

'Just dropped in to say hello to Vera. We've been doing some shopping. Now we're off for something to eat.'

'I say. Excuse me,' Vera interrupted. 'Would you take Susan with you, please? She must be starving. She's been working like a trooper all morning.'

'Oh no, I couldn't,' protested Susan. 'We're too busy.'

'This is our slack time. I'm ordering you to take a break,' Vera insisted.

Susan threw an imploring look at her aunt, but no help was forthcoming from that quarter. Reluctantly she slipped her arms into her coat, which Vera held ready for her. 'I hope you don't mind, Jack? I don't want to impose.'

'Not in the slightest. We'll be delighted to have you join us, won't·we, Margaret?' But his wife had already moved away from the stall and her reply was muffled.

They had lunch in a small café in the Market Square. Conversation consisted mostly of Margaret trying to find out all about Susan's background and her relationship with Donald. Susan answered as best she could without giving away any secrets, but her patience was sorely tried and it took all her willpower not to tell this inquisitive girl to mind her own business.

When Jack left them for a short time, she made a point of turning the tables on Margaret. Pretending sympathy, she quizzed the girl on her own relationship with Donald.

'It must have been very upsetting for you to have had to choose between Jack and Donald?'

'Yes. It was. I was in an awful pickle at the time. Donald was so upset. I suppose you heard all about the big fight between them?'

'I did. But you can't blame him for being angry. After all, weren't you engaged to him? It must have come as an awful shock to discover that you were two-timing him.'

'It wasn't like that! It wasn't like that, at all. He shouldn't have taken me so much for granted. Had he paid more attention, we'd be getting married on Boxing Day.'

Susan was taken aback. 'I didn't realise a date had been set.'

'Huh! Donald will only tell you what he wants you to know. Are you in love with him?'

'I beg your pardon?'

'I suppose you are. He's hard to resist when he turns on the charm.'

Susan leant across the table. 'It sounds to me as if you're still in love with him?'

A dark flush covered Margaret's face. 'What gives you that idea?'

Susan remained silent, and just sat scrutinising the girl's embarrassed face. Jack, coming back to the table, put an end to the conversation, but Susan was convinced that this girl did indeed still carry a torch for Donald. So how come she had married Jack?

Quickly Susan finished her meal and rose to her feet. 'That was lovely. I enjoyed it. Thank you both for treating me, but you do realise I must hurry back, don't you?'

Her cousin waved her off. 'Away you go, Susan. We know you're busy. See you at dinner tonight.'

Smiling brightly, Susan hurried off. She had plenty to think about. If Donald found out that Margaret was still in love with him, it could cause all sorts of problems. What would he do? Would he try to win her back, or would he see her for the fickle person she was?

Jack and Margaret decided to go to midnight Mass with his parents on Christmas Eve and, wishing them a happy Christmas and promising to come in early the next morning, Susan retired to the house next door. Making herself a cup of tea, she carried it upstairs and, once snug in bed, settled down to read her mail.

In her letter Ruth didn't give any reason why Jim Brady suddenly wanted to contact her. But then, she probably didn't know his reason. Jim was the type of person to confide only in close friends. Should she write to him? No. There would be no point. It would just prolong the agony. They certainly had no future together. To take her mind off Jim, she recalled the conversation she'd had with Margaret. Was Jack aware of the risk he was taking in coming home? It was obvious that he loved his wife very much.

A loud knock on the door brought her slowly from her bed. Pulling the curtains slightly away from the window, she peered down into the darkness. It was Donald. What did he want at this time of night?

When she opened the door she could see that he was the worse for drink.

'Can I come in for a while, Susan?'

'It's very late, Donald. We don't want to start any gossip, do we?' she warned.

'I'll not stay long. I was on my way to midnight Mass when I realised that I was in no fit state to go.'

'Ten minutes! No longer, mind. Sit down and I'll make you a strong cup of coffee. It will help sober you up.'

He removed his coat and shivered slightly. 'It's cold in here. Did you not light the fire?'

'There was no need. I've been next door all evening. I was nice and warm in bed when you came.'

'I'm sorry, Susan. I shouldn't have come here, but I needed someone to talk to.'

'What about? As if I didn't know!' Susan said drily as she spooned instant coffee into the cup.

'I can't help myself. I can't stop thinking about her.'

The kettle boiled and she handed him the steaming mug of coffee. Sitting on the armchair, she pulled her legs up underneath her and wrapped her candlewick dressing gown tightly around her to capture some warmth. 'Remember, she's married now, Donald. And the Catholic Church forbids divorce, so don't start something you can't finish.'

'I know all that. And if she wouldn't have me before, why should she want me now, eh?' He looked blankly at her empty hands. 'Are you not having one?'

'I've just finished a cup upstairs. I don't really know much about what happened between you and Margaret. Why did she turn to Jack in the first place?'

He shook his head in despair. 'I honestly don't know! I thought we were so well suited. And . . . I respected her, mind! Never made a wrong move. Never once touched her up, if you know what I mean.'

Thinking of how she had longed for Jim Brady to touch her, Susan said, 'Perhaps she wanted you to touch her, show how much you cared?'

He looked scandalised. 'There was no need for that! She knew I loved her.'

Susan shrugged. 'Well then, why did she turn to Jack?'

'I wish I knew.' Putting his cup on the hearth, he moved over and knelt in front of her chair. Placing his hands on her thighs, he looked beseechingly at her. 'I want to ask you a favour, Susan.'

She could feel the heat of his hands through the towelling material and was filled with a longing for close bodily contact. Not sex, just contact with a strong male body. Pushing his hands away, she cried, 'Well? What do you want to ask me?'

He looked at the hands she had pushed away and was at a loss as to what to do with them. Steepling them as if in prayer, he said, 'While Margaret is here could we pretend we have something going between us?'

His nearness was unsettling her and, unfurling her legs, she sprang from the chair and moved restlessly about the room. 'That's impossible. For a start, no one would believe it.'

He moved to stand in front of her, his head bent so he could look into her eyes. 'I wouldn't take advantage. Just subtly give out the idea that we're seeing each other. Please? It won't cost you anything.'

'I can't do it. It wouldn't work.'

He put his hands on her shoulders. 'Why not? Who knows, we might even learn to care for each other.'

She gazed up at him, little knowing how vulnerable and appealing she looked. His mouth hovered over hers, but before he could claim her lips, she found the courage to push him away. 'It's time you were going. They'll be coming home from Mass soon and I don't want Aunt Edith to see you leave and get any wrong ideas.' She lifted his coat from where he had hung it on the floor and, thrusting it at him, pushed him none too gently towards the door. 'Remember, Aunt Edith has invited you to join us tomorrow night. Are you up to it, or shall I make excuses for you?'

He shrugged into his coat. 'I'll be there. Thanks for the coffee.'

'Happy Christmas. See you tomorrow.'

She closed the door on him and leant against it, trembling like a leaf in a storm. It had been too close for comfort. He must never realise just how close, otherwise he'd never be away from her doorstep. Tense and irritable now, she climbed the stairs, but her Christmas mail failed to hold her attention. She was remembering the great longing and need he had aroused in her. Was she forever to be unfulfilled?

There were a lot of people about so late at night. At first Donald was bewildered, then he remembered midnight Mass. These people must be returning from there. He recognised Jack's voice approaching and drew into the shadows, away from the street lights, not wanting to speak to him. Billy, Edith and Jack all passed by, but there was no sign of Margaret. Perhaps she had felt unwell and come home earlier.

He was about to turn the corner of the street when her laughter rang out. She was talking to two girls whom he recognised as old school mates. He was about to pass on when, bidding them all good night, she caught at his sleeve, bringing him to a halt.

'Hello, Donald. Walk me back up to the house, please. I want a word with you. Good night, girls, see you around.'

In spite of the speculative glance from the girls – well, they would have heard about her treatment of him – and surprised that she wanted to speak to him, Donald suited his step to hers and they dandered back up the street.

'I hope you didn't mind me stopping you like that, but I couldn't get away from them.'

So she didn't really want to talk to him; he was the lesser of two evils. Disappointment stabbed like a knife in his chest. She proved him wrong by stopping well before they reached Edith's door and drawing into the shadows. He followed her, trying to hide his bewilderment.

'Donald, I'm glad of this opportunity to apologise for all the hurt I've caused you.'

'Don't worry about it, Margaret. It's all in the past. The best man won.'

'Did he, Donald? I'm not so sure about that.'

Her voice was soft and caressing and he wasn't sure he'd heard her correctly. While he was still in a daze she moved close and raised her face to his. 'Happy Christmas, Donald.'

Her lips were inviting and, without thought, he drew her closer still and claimed them. The kiss went on and on as they swayed together and their passion flared. Before it could get out of control, she came up, panting for breath. 'Not here. Not now. Jack will come looking for me. Do you still think the best man won, eh, Donald? See you tomorrow night.' With a light laugh she left him standing there, gasping, his mind racing. What on earth was she playing at? Perhaps he would find out tomorrow night. His thoughts were in turmoil, but his step and heart were a good deal lighter as he headed home.

Christmas dinner was a leisurely affair stretching over a couple of hours. The starter, chilled melon and prawns, made the day before and kept refrigerated, was doused in crème de menthe and was mouth-watering. Billy was not a lover of turkey, so a large goose had been chosen to grace the table. Sizzling and crackling, it was perfectly complemented by dishes of fresh vegetables and creamed, roasted and delicious boiled small potatoes. Last but not least, a rich plum pudding tempted them to find room for it.

Praise for Edith was profound and she could barely conceal her pleasure. When everybody had eaten to bursting point, the table was cleared and they all lolled on the sofa and chairs, striving to keep their eyes open. Giving his head a good shake to dispel his sleepiness, Billy rose to his feet and announced, 'You girls are welcome to retire for an hour or two. Remember, we are entertaining tonight. I'll wash the dishes and clear up the kitchen.'

'I'll give you a hand, Dad,' Jack volunteered.

'Well, now . . . if you're sure you're up to it, I'll be glad to take you up on your offer, Billy.' Without more ado Edith headed for the door.

'I feel sated. If I don't lie down for a while I'll not be fit to see anyone this evening.' With a wag of her hand Margaret followed her.

Billy eyed Susan. 'What about you, love? Won't you go up to the spare room for an hour or so?'

'I'd prefer to go out for a stroll and get some fresh air, if you don't mind. I'll walk down to the phone box. I promised the family I'd ring today, but I hate leaving you two to do all the hard work.'

'Don't worry your head about us, Susan. You'll probably get roped into helping prepare the buffet for later on. Away and phone your folk. Give them my best regards.'

'Thanks. I'll do that. See you later.'

The wine had flowed freely during the meal and Susan felt quite tipsy as she made her way down the street, anticipating the conversation she would have with her parents. Would her father consent to talk to her? Perhaps, if he was cornered by her mother and sister, he would feel obliged to.

She dialled the number, smiling as she waited for someone to pick it up at the other end. A great sadness enveloped her as she listened to the phone ring on and on and on. A glance at her watch showed her it was four o'clock. She pictured the scene back home. It would be somewhat similar to the one she had just left. Her dad would be out for the count on the chair by the fire. Her mother would have gone to have a lie down, sure that she would hear the phone if it rang. But what about Alison? Probably she had gone over to see Graham's parents.

Tears blinded her as she hung up the receiver and left the phone booth. This was the loneliest she had felt since leaving home. Until now she had been too busy and had managed to keep her fears and worries at bay. Now she was swamped with unhappiness. Before she realised it, she was walking along North Road. On the opposite side, Northgate Park seemed like a good place to pull herself together.

It was bitterly cold and the trees lifted frost-coated branches towards the slate-grey sky. The grass crunched under her feet and an icy wind tugged at her clothes. The park was empty except for a couple of parents obviously there under pressure while their children tried out their new bikes and roller skates. A few men were walking their dogs. She was glad there was no familiar faces about; no need to put on a brave front. Snuggling deeper into the collar of her coat to keep out the chill, she walked quickly along the path until no one else was in sight. With no one to notice, she let the tears rain freely down her face. What had she to look forward to? A very lonely life, by the look of it. Would things be any

better if she had stayed at home in her own familiar –
if perhaps unfriendly – surroundings? Would her parents
have forgiven her by now?

Graham would most likely have realised the child was
his! Would he have cared enough to give up the woman
he loved to marry her? No, why should he? She had
been more than willing. The child was her responsibility alone. Besides, the scandal would have been too
great. Her parents would never have recovered from it.
She had done the right thing, she thought. Her place
was here, now. Wiping her face dry on the back of her
gloves, she turned for home. At least the tears had
released all the pent-up emotions she had been harbouring, and she felt better for it.

Her thoughts returned to Graham. Had he and Alison
become engaged today? And what about Jim Brady?
Should she write to him? She left the park and was
crossing the road, deep in thought, when a voice hailed
her. It was Donald Murphy. Realising there must still
be some signs of her recent breakdown, she waved,
silently willing him to go on. He appeared not to get
the message and waited for her to reach him and his
companion.

He eyed her closely, noted the sign of tears but held
his tongue. Turning to the woman by his side, he said,
'Mam, this is Susan Cummings. I've mentioned her to
you. Susan, this is my mother.'

The women silently greeted each other with a nod.

'I'm taking Mam to her sister's. She's spending the
next two days there. Are you stretching your legs,
Susan?'

'Yes. I tried to phone home, but apparently no one

was there, so I took a walk in the park to try and burn off some of the Christmas dinner calories before trying the phone again. If you'll excuse me, I'll give it another go. Nice meeting you, Mrs Murphy.'

Without waiting for an answer Susan walked away. She had been very aware of Mrs Murphy's disapproval and it annoyed her. Why was this woman finding fault in her? She didn't even know her.

This time the phone was answered on the third ring and an apologetic Alison made excuses for missing her earlier. Glad to hear her sister's voice, Susan brushed these to one side. The next forty-five minutes were spent talking to each member of the family. Even her father contrived to sound sincere as he wished her a happy Christmas. Then Graham came on the line. 'Hello, Susan. How are you? I hope you're enjoying yourself over there.'

The misery of earlier on had evaporated as she spoke to her family and she answered him truthfully enough. 'Yes, Graham, I'm enjoying myself. Alison has been describing her ring to me. It sounds lovely. Congratulations.'

He lowered his voice. 'Susan, have you forgiven me?'

Ignoring his question, she said, 'Graham, I wish you and Alison the best of everything.'

'When are you coming home? Everybody asks after you. Even Jim Brady went out of his way to inquire about you. Come home soon, Susan. We all miss you.'

'I'll phone again in the New Year, Graham. Happy Christmas.' Slowly replacing the receiver, she pondered his words. It was probably her imagination, but she'd thought he sounded as if *he* really missed her. That was nonsense of course! Hadn't he become engaged to her sister? And . . . Jim had been asking about her. Why? What could possibly have happened to make him inquire about her, after the way he had treated her?

Donald was waiting a short distance from the phone box. 'I thought I'd catch you. You look much happier now. Why the tears earlier on?'

'Oh, you know how it is. There was no answer when I rang home and I felt a bit homesick. You know what it's like at Christmas when you're away from home.'

'And now?'

'Now I feel much better.'

'Did you enjoy your Christmas dinner?'

'It was delicious. To be truthful, I was surprised when I heard we were having goose. Back home we always have turkey at Christmas and I didn't fancy the idea of goose. But it was mouth-watering. Aunt Edith made an orange sauce to complement it and I thought it was very tasty indeed.'

He smiled down at her. 'Edith would be pleased to hear so much praise of her cooking. Do you want to go for a walk?'

'No. I'm helping to prepare the buffet for tonight. I'll see you then.'

'I'll walk to the corner with you.'

She stopped at the top of the street. 'No need for you to come any further.' She paused. 'Tell me, Donald, why does your mother dislike me so much?'

His face coloured. 'She thinks anyone connected with the Devines is bad news as far as I'm concerned. I explained that we were just good friends, but she said there was no such thing as platonic friendship between a man and a woman.'

Susan grinned at his embarrassment. He sounded like a young lad. 'Then we'll just have to prove her wrong, won't we? See you later on.'

Chapter Five

Alison heard the phone ringing as the car drew to a halt in the driveway and, scrambling from it, she raced up the steps and into the hall. It stopped just as she reached it. Graham locked up the car and slowly followed her inside.

She swung round to face him with a grimace. 'That was probably Susan.'

'I imagine it was. I told you we should have waited until after she phoned.'

He was tight-lipped with anger and she gazed at him in amazement. 'It's no big deal. She'll ring back later. After all, she can't expect us to stay in all day waiting for her to ring. She should have given us a definite time.'

'Perhaps she can't make definite arrangements,' Graham said defensively on Susan's behalf. He was trying to keep a rein on his temper. He was so disappointed to have missed her, and all because Alison wanted to show off her ring to a friend. And he might not be here when she rang again, might not get a chance to speak to her. 'Remember, she has to get to a phone box and she might not be able to get away when she feels like it.'

'Well, that's just too bad then! After all, it was her choice to stay in Darlington. We certainly did our best to persuade her to come home.' Aware that Graham was still displeased and unable to fathom the reason why, but not wanting to spoil Christmas Day, she asked coaxingly, 'Would you like a drink?'

'Would I not!' he answered grumpily. 'But you know fine well we're going to Mother's for tea, and I'll be driving.'

'We can always get a taxi.'

'They'll be like gold dust today. But . . .' She waited patiently as he pondered. 'Dad doesn't usually drink during the day. Even Christmas Day. I'll phone and find out if he will be able to pick us up here. However, you'll have to stay the night at our house.' He held her eye, knowing she would not like this idea. Alison and his mother did not really hit it off.

'That's all right,' she agreed, all the while consoling herself that it wouldn't be too bad, for there would be other people there.

Mr Robson himself answered the phone. He said there would be no problem and he would pick them up about seven. They sat on the settee and, mollified, Graham raised the glass of beer she had poured for him. 'Happy Christmas.' He comforted himself with the thought that Susan would surely ring again before they left.

'Happy Christmas, and here's to our future together.'

The fact that Graham only half-heartedly returned this salute wasn't wasted on Alison. She couldn't understand him. She turned her left hand this way and that, examining the solitaire diamond ring on the third finger. It was beautiful and had cost a pretty penny. Surely he must care for her, else why go to the extent of getting engaged? She glanced across at her father, spreadeagled asleep on the armchair. He had certainly been as pleased as Punch, plying Graham with drinks and insisting that he stay over the night before. Already he was planning a New Year party in their honour. Her mother had been more subdued; her congratulations no less sincere than her husband's, but looking as if she had reservations. But then, didn't her mother think her the flighty type?

'I've been thinking, Alison . . .'

With a start she brought her attention back to Graham. He paused so long that she prompted, 'Well?'

'Why don't we go over and see for ourselves how Susan is?' At the look of amazement that she turned on him, he added hastily, 'It would be an excuse for a wee holiday.'

Still looking surprised she cried, 'Don't be daft! Me dad would never hear tell of it. You and me go away together?' Her eyes became suspicious. 'Anyway, how come you're so worried about our Susan?'

'Surely it's only natural? After all she'll soon be my sister-in-law. And I'm really being selfish. A winter break would do both of us the world of good and we would be killing two birds with one stone.'

Still she looked unsure what he was going on about. 'Well, anyhow . . . Dad would never hear tell of it.'

As if aware that they were talking about him, Trevor awoke with a grunt and a snort. He stretched his limbs and peered at them, bleary-eyed. 'Did someone speak to me?'

'No, Dad. But your name was mentioned,' Alison admitted.

Deciding to grab the bull by the horns, Graham said, 'Mr Cummings, I was wondering if Alison and I should visit Susan early in the New Year, just to make sure she's all right?'

'If you mean before you're married, the answer's no. At least, not with Alison, you won't! Once you're married you can do as you please, but to be truthful, I don't really think Susan merits your concern. She has shown very little for us.' Rising with difficulty from the deep chair, Trevor left the room, disapproval showing in every line of his body.

Alison shrugged her shoulders and sighed. 'I told you so'

Graham grimaced. 'Pity. A wee break would be very nice. Perhaps if we worked on his compassion?'

'My father doesn't know the meaning of the word. At least not where our Susan's concerned.'

'Oh, you never know. We'll keep plugging away at him.'

Alison turned away to hide her expression. She couldn't understand why Graham was being so persistent. Suddenly her demeanour brightened as a possible explanation developed. She was holding him at arm's length. Perhaps he was being devious. What if he really wanted to get her completely alone and was using a visit to Susan as an excuse to do so?

It was late, after nine o'clock, before friends and neighbours started to drift into Edith's home. This was usual, Susan was told. The effects of the Christmas meal were allowed to settle before any more food could even be considered. Soon the house was full to capacity, and still they came. It was ten o'clock before Donald eventually arrived.

Susan was chatting to Margaret when she sensed, rather than saw, her tense up. Following the direction of her look, she saw that Donald had entered the room. Seeking Edith out, he gave her a bottle of whiskey. Relieved of this duty, he scanned the room. Margaret was obviously waiting for his glance and their eyes locked.

Embarrassed at witnessing such naked longing in the girl's eyes, Susan swung her gaze to Donald. He had yet to notice her, but she could see he was taken aback by Margaret's reaction as well. Then he became aware of Susan and a grin split his face. Slowly he gently shouldered his way towards them, stopping to greet this one and that on the way. Margaret still stood galvanized to the spot and Susan looked frantically about for her cousin, afraid he might be witnessing this dramatic scene.

Fortunately, he was nowhere to be seen. Nudging Margaret with her elbow, she whispered furiously, 'Get a grip on yourself, Margaret. Do you want another brawl to start?'

Margaret blinked and gave her head a slight shake as if to free it from the hypnotic trance. Just in time! Jack was suddenly there at her side. 'Are you feeling all right, love? You look a bit pale.'

A blank gaze met these words and then Margaret seemed to become aware of her situation. She made her excuses in a whisper. 'It's a bit warm in here, Jack. Could we go outside for a few minutes for a breath of fresh air?'

'Yes, of course. I'll fetch our coats and we can go for a short walk. The air will do you good.'

He made his way out to the hall, passing Donald without a glance.

Arriving at their side, Donald avoided Margaret's intense gaze. 'Hello, girls, that's a smashing spread you have ready. I'm looking forward to it. Meanwhile, can I get you a drink?'

'The heat's too much for me at the moment, Donald. Jack and I are going for a walk. Perhaps you would like to join us?'

'Thanks all the same, Margaret, but I've just arrived. I warn you, wrap up well, it's freezing out there.'

'Here, love.' Tenderly Jack wrapped a thick woollen scarf around his wife's neck and helped her into her coat. 'Let's go. See you two later.'

Not once did he meet Donald's eyes. This led Susan to believe that he had indeed been aware of his wife's interest in her old flame. Dismayed, Susan sipped at her drink. Poor Jack. He must know how the wind was blowing. She eyed Donald covertly.

He was well aware of her sly glance and challenged her. 'What are you looking at me like that for?'

'I saw the way you two looked at each other just now, and it worried me,' she confessed.

'Just what did you see, eh? I was as taken aback as you.'

'She's still in love with you, Donald.'

'You're imagining things. She married the one she wanted.' The urgent kiss of the night before that had plagued him came to the fore again. The sheer intensity of it had excited him all day. Hadn't Margaret implied that Jack wasn't the right man for her after all? If that were the case, what did she intend doing about it?

Susan was eyeing him intently. The strains of a waltz came from the next room and he asked abruptly, 'Would you like to dance?'

'Donald, they're packed in there like sardines in a tin. There won't be room to move, let alone dance. Let's save our energy for the Pali tomorrow night, eh?'

'You're right. Let's try and find somewhere to sit.'

They made their way from the room and eventually sat crushed together on the lower stairs. She smiled at him. 'How long will the party go on?'

'There will still be some diehards here in the morning.'

'You're joking!'

'I'm not.'

'Thank God I can slip next door when I've had enough of it.'

'I wish I could come with you,' he said wistfully.

'You can always curl up in one of the chairs,' she offered. 'But I wouldn't recommend it.'

'You didn't think I was suggesting anything else now, did you?' he teased.

'I just don't want there to be any misunderstanding between us.'

'You know, I might just take you up on that offer.'

She shrugged. 'Feel free. After all, it's your house.'

They sat in silence for some moments, but at last, unable to curb her curiosity, she asked, 'If Margaret finds she still . . .' Her tongue faltered. She could not believe that 'love' was the right word to use here. '. . . fancies you, will you be pleased?'

He shrugged. 'I don't think "pleased" is the right word. Flattered, perhaps. But what difference would it make now? She married Jack.'

'Maybe she's discovered she made the wrong choice. What then?'

He smiled ruefully. 'You know, that's what *she* said last night.'

Susan's mouth fell open. Gently he put a finger under her chin and closed it. 'You may well look surprised. You could have knocked me over with a feather when she said it.'

'You said . . . last night? How come?'

'When I left you they were all coming up the street from midnight Mass. I managed to avoid them, as I thought, but when I rounded the corner, there she was talking to some friends. I walked back up with her.'

'Alone?'

'Yes, alone. Her friends were going in the opposite direction, so of course we were alone. She asked me to walk up to the house with her.'

'And she told you she had made a mistake?'

'Yes, she wished me a happy Christmas and . . . well, we shared a Christmas kiss.'

Susan could imagine how it had been and was disgusted at these revelations. 'I suppose you pushed her away and sent her home to her husband?' she cried scornfully.

Remembering his response to the kiss and the anticipation that had hovered just below the surface all day, he felt ashamed. He lashed out at her rebuke. 'It's none of your business. I'm not allowed to probe into your past, so why should I let you interfere in my mine?'

She was on her feet instantly, hissing into his face, 'Because this isn't *past!* This is *present.* And in case you've forgotten, she's my cousin's wife and I'm very fond of Jack!'

She swung away, glad the hall was now empty, as people had drifted into the kitchen to help themselves at the buffet table. He grabbed her arm and pulled her back. 'Is it just because of Jack you're so annoyed?'

Her brows gathered together in a frown. 'What do you mean?' Then comprehension dawned. 'Huh! You don't imagine for one minute I'm interested in you, do you? Hah! Chance would be a fine thing. Where women are concerned, you don't seem to be able to tell your arse from your elbow.'

He relaxed his hold on her and she was off in a flash. He winced at the sound of his front door slamming shut. Susan must be really fond of her cousin to be so upset. He remained deep in thought until the door opened again. He looked up, all smiles, thinking Susan had returned, if only to sample the buffet.

It was Jack and Margaret. Quickly she slipped off her coat and, handing it to her husband, sank down on the stairs beside Donald. 'You were right! It is freezing out there, but I enjoyed our walk. How about you fetching some grub now, Jack?'

Reluctantly Jack hung their coats on the hall stand. 'Would you not come and pick your own? There's such a variety in there, I'll not know what to get you.'

'Oh . . . just get me anything! I'm easily pleased, as you well know.'

'Is there anything in particular you'd like?' he persisted.

'A couple of slices of meat and something savoury will do lovely, thank you.'

Donald saw the worried speculation in Jack's eyes and felt sorry for him. 'Will you mind my place, Margaret, while I get something to eat as well? All this talk of food is making my tummy rumble.'

She rose to her feet at once. 'If you two think I'm sitting out here on my own, you can think again. I'm coming with you.'

They queued at the table and filled their plates. Donald made his way back to the stairs and was delighted to see they were still empty. Margaret was on his heels and sank down beside him.

'Where's Jack?'

'He was following behind us. He'll probably be out in a minute or two.'

Donald felt uncomfortable. Susan's words, 'I suppose you pushed her away and sent her home to her husband?' echoed in his ears. He shouldn't be sitting here in the hall, alone, with Margaret. But what excuse could he fabricate if he left her? And, come to think of it, why should he worry about Jack's feelings? Jack certainly hadn't worried about him when he was seducing Margaret.

Aware that she was looking at him, he avoided her eye. He was also very conscious of the pressure of her thigh against his on the narrow staircase. He stirred restlessly and she increased the pressure. 'Stop it, Margaret!' he said tersely. 'You're a married woman now,' he chastised her. 'Why couldn't you have been like this before?'

She gaped at him in disbelief. 'I tried. God knows, I tried. But you were such a goody-goody. You refused to be tempted. Why do you think I used Jack to try to make you jealous?'

He couldn't believe what he was hearing. 'I was showing you respect,' he muttered, glancing around to see if they could be overheard, aware this wasn't the place for an argument! What if Jack put in an appearance? The nervous state Jack was in at the moment, there could very well be another fisticuffs and he was having none of that. He rose to his feet. 'Look we can't sit here like this. What if Jack comes back? He might get the wrong idea.'

'I don't care. It's better to get it all out in the open.'

He gazed down at her in panic, in his agitation knocking over his can of beer. 'Now look what you've made me do. And listen, Margaret, as far as I'm concerned, there's nothing to get out in the open! After all, you married Jack! You're expecting his child.'

Flushed with temper, he left her and went to fetch something to mop up the spilt beer. When he returned, to his great relief she had gone.

When it became obvious that Susan wasn't going to return, he sought out Edith and explained, 'Susan went next door with a headache earlier on. I want to bring her in a plate of food, but I've no idea what she likes.'

'Oh dear, I'm sure she'll be starving. Look, I'll fill a plate and you fetch a couple of cans to bring with you.'

'Thanks, Edith.'

For some moments he thought Susan wasn't going to answer his knock, but at last the door opened a crack and she glared out at him. 'What do you want?'

He gestured to the covered plate and held up the cans. 'Peace offering, I didn't mean to offend you.'

Slowly the gap widened and she stood back to let him pass. 'I must admit I'm feeling peckish,' she said, closing the door and motioning him into the living room. A fire burnt brightly in the grate, affording the only source of illumination to the room. He reached for the light switch, but her voice stayed him. 'Don't put the light on, please.'

Placing the cans on the floor, he pulled the small table close to the chair by the fire and, unwrapping the plate, set it down. Taking her hands, he drew her forward and by the light of the fire examined her face. 'Am I the cause of those tears?' he asked gently.

'Donald Murphy, I wish you'd stop thinking you have any power over my emotions! I was crying because it's Christmas night, and I'm far from home and lonely, and nobody seems to care about me. So there! It had nothing whatsoever to do with you.'

'I'm glad to hear that, Susan.' His hands cupped her face. 'I hope I never cause you pain.' He brushed her lips with his and, before she could complain, assured her, 'Just a Christmas kiss. Now, sit down and eat up.'

He watched her eating, reaching over now and again to help himself to some titbits from the plate. Noting the sad droop of her wide mouth, again he pondered the reason why she had run away from her family and friends. Surely if the man she loved was over in Ireland, that's where she should be?

Finishing the last sausage roll, she licked her fingers and gave a contented sigh. 'I enjoyed that, Donald. Thanks for thinking of me.' She made to rise, but he was on his feet at once and gently pushed her down again. 'Really, Donald,' she demurred. 'I should be next door helping to keep the dishes cleared.'

'Just you sit there. Let Margaret pull her weight for a change.'

'You know,' she mused, 'I really do wish I liked Margaret. After all, she's family now, but somehow or other I can't warm to her.'

'Maybe you just need some time to get to know her?'

A sad shake of the head rejected this idea. 'I don't think so.'

He sat on the floor beside her chair and took her hand. 'Listen, Susan. I don't know what way things will go. Margaret keeps coming on to me, and I'm only human. Could you not pretend we fancy each other and I'll have an excuse to keep her at bay?'

She gently touched his face. 'Poor Donald. It's not fair the way she's treating you.'

'What do you mean poor Donald?' he cried indignantly. 'I should be delighted to know she still cares. After all, Jack seduced her from under my very nose. I can't believe I was so blind! I wouldn't be human if I wasn't pleased the tables are turned. But still, every time I look at Jack I feel ashamed. She's making mugs of us both.'

'I'm glad you can see that.'

'Mind you, it doesn't do my blood pressure any good when she flashes those big eyes at me. Believe you me, if we're ever alone I don't think I'll be able to control myself.'

'Do you really think it will help if we pretend to fancy each other?'

'I do. Then she won't be so ready to flaunt herself about.'

'All right then. I suppose I can pretend for a day or so. Meanwhile, I must go in and give Aunt Edith a hand.'

He helped her to her feet. 'First I'm going to heat the

two water bottles, belonging to my dear departed aunt, that are under the stairs,' he announced. 'You will then have a nice warm bed to come back to.'

'That's very thoughtful of you, Donald. You'll make some lucky girl a good husband one day. While you fill the bottles, I'll go and freshen myself up a bit.'

Margaret was sullen as she helped in the kitchen. Edith worked in silence alongside her. A neighbour was also helping out and conversation had been sporadic. It had now dried up. All the women turned with obvious relief to greet Susan when she arrived.

'Sorry I was away so long, but I had an awful headache.'

'How's your head now, love?'

'It's fine, Aunt Edith. I took a couple of aspirin and then Donald brought me in some food and now I feel great.' Her eyes became distressed when she saw the tired lines on her aunt's face. Her neighbour also looked as if she was on her last legs. How come some had to work so that others enjoyed themselves? 'You two take a break. Margaret and I should be able to manage in here.'

When the door closed on them, Margaret muttered, 'What makes you think I want to be stuck in here? Huh, some holiday break!'

'I didn't think you'd mind. Aunt Edith has been kindness itself to you, and she does look awfully tired,' Susan reprimanded her.

'It's all right for you to talk! You've had a break. I saw Donald go off with a plate of food. Did you enjoy your little tête-à-tête? Or was it more than that? He looks after you well. Better than he ever looked after me.'

Susan was astonished at the jealousy that emanated from this girl. Had she no pride at all? And what about poor Jack? As if he had been evoked, the door opened and Jack's head appeared.

Immediately aware of the tension, he asked tentatively, 'Need any help, girls?'

'You can take over from me. I seem to have been in here for ever. I need a rest,' Margaret whinged.

'Why don't you go on up to bed, love?'

'I'll go soon. I'll listen to the singers for a while. There's some good voices in there.'

Silence reigned for some time after Margaret had left. It was Jack who broke it. 'This isn't working out as I had hoped.'

'Oh . . .' Susan's voice was non-committal. She didn't want to hear his gripes.

'I hate London! I hoped if we came up here for Christmas I might be lucky enough to get a job when the factories open again. I'd still have to go back down for a while and work my notice, and stay long enough to get the bond money on the flat back, but I wouldn't mind. The thought that I was coming back here would make it all worthwhile.'

'Then you won't be going back on Tuesday?'

'To tell you the truth, Susan, I don't know what to do. Margaret doesn't want to go back down south at all, but where would she stay?'

'Don't worry about me, Jack. She can remain in your parents' house. Donald will let me stay next door for as long as I like.'

He gave her a sideways glance. 'Are you and him . . . ye know?'

Remembering her promise to Donald, but mindful of the fact that Jack thought her a married woman, she said vaguely, 'It's in the early stages yet. Who knows what will happen. And remember, we're both on the rebound . . . so we're taking it a day at a time.'

'So you and your husband really are separated?' She nodded. 'And you do like Donald?'

'Very much. He's a fine person.'

'I know he is. We were best mates once. I hoped he'd understand when Margaret and I fell in love.'

'Was that not expecting too much?'

'To tell you the truth, Susan, I don't know how it came about. Margaret was Donald's future wife, and I was just their friend. We went everywhere together. Then all of a sudden I was obsessed with her. I was actually jealous when she danced with Donald. I couldn't think straight. I had to have her, no matter who got hurt in the process.' He was silent for some moments. 'I've been thinking . . . What with my parents being caught up in the business, Margaret would be lonely and bored. Could she possibly stay next door with you? You'd be company for each other.'

Susan had no difficulty whatsoever figuring out how his predicament had come about. Margaret was a very devious person. Her refusal was swift. 'No! I'm sorry, but the answer is no. You'd be better taking Margaret away with you.' The very idea of living under the same roof as Jack's wife repulsed her.

'Don't just dismiss the idea offhand, Susan. At least give it some consideration.'

She opened her mouth to refuse again, but he forestalled her. 'Just think about it. Please?'

* * *

Donald saw Margaret enter the living room and was glad there was no empty space beside him. He kept his eyes averted and hoped that she would take the hint and stay away from him. She wasn't put off. Crossing the room, she sat on the arm of his chair. Quickly he rose to his feet and, with a smile, offered it to her.

'No, stay where you are. I'll be quite comfortable here.'

When he insisted, she sat down and patted the arm of the chair. 'Stay beside me, please. I know hardly any of this crowd.'

Reluctantly he joined her, glad that another singer had been called on to perform and that the strains of 'Danny Boy' rising in the quiet room made conversation difficult. When the applause had died down and another singer was being persuaded to do his piece, Margaret tugged at his sleeve. Donald bent low to hear what she had to say, very aware of the luminous skin, the shining hair. He fought down his rising emotions. What was keeping Susan? She had promised to help him.

'Donald, do you care for me at all?'

'Margaret, there's no use bringing that all up again. It's all over between us.'

'You like Susan, don't you?'

'Yes, I do! Very much.'

'Are you seeing each other?'

He nodded and she sighed.

'Then the baby is yours?'

He was very still as he digested these words. What on earth was she talking about?

'I must say I'm surprised,' she continued. 'You professed

to love me, but you held me at arm's length. Yet you must have jumped into bed with her as soon as she arrived in Darlo. What's she got that I haven't? Was it because of the way I treated you? Were you feeling rejected? Is that why you were so easily tempted? Was I that easy to forget, Donald?'

His endeavour to turn the conversation and question her was frowned upon, as a woman's soprano voice took off, filling the room with sweetness as she sang 'This is my Lovely Day'.

He was glad of the respite. It saved him from putting his big foot in it. His mind was in turmoil. Was Margaret trying to cause mischief, or was Susan really pregnant?

The door opened quietly and he saw Susan slip into the room. His eyes slid over her figure, but she wore a loose sweater that covered her well. But surely he would have noticed before now, if she really was expecting? Hadn't they danced together? Still, she might not be showing yet. He glanced down at the girl by his side. Her bump was small but noticeable; there was no doubt she was expecting a child. He saw Susan whisper to Edith and Billy and guessed that she was saying good night. The song finished and, amidst the applause, Susan used the respite to cross the room. Ignoring Margaret, she leant close and smiled into his eyes. 'I'm going home now, Donald. Want to come in for a nightcap?'

For the life of him he couldn't respond to her teasing invitation. He knew she was doing as he had asked and was pretending that they were on more than friendly terms, but his mind baulked at the idea that she might be expecting a child. Good God, would everyone think it was his?

'I think I'll stay a while longer and listen to the singers,' he eventually managed to answer her.

Shock blocked all expression from her face. She slowly straightened, her eyes raking his face with contempt. She shrugged. 'Suit yourself. Good night, Margaret. Looks like you win. Enjoy yourself.'

He half-rose to follow her, but Margaret had a vice-like hold on his arm and, as someone else was about to sing, he didn't want to cause a fuss. 'I'll see you tomorrow.' His voice followed her, full of apology, but Susan hardened her heart. He had warned her he would be unable to resist Margaret, but he shouldn't have let her make a fool of herself like that.

'Don't bother! I'll be busy.'

'What about the dance tomorrow night?'

She didn't deign to answer him, but Margaret was quick to ask, 'What dance?'

'In the Pali,' he said abruptly.

'I'll get Jack to take me. Why not join us?'

'I think not, Margaret. I'm sure I can persuade Susan to go. Will you excuse me, please?'

He collected his coat and muffler and left quickly. His house was in darkness and he knew better than to try to get Susan to admit him again. She had been angry! And no wonder. Hadn't he asked for her support and then, when it was offered, had refused it? But Margaret had taken him unawares. Was Susan really pregnant? If she was, why hadn't she told him? What would people think when she could no longer hide it? They were bound to think it was his. Well, what about it, he lamented inwardly, so long as those who mattered knew the truth? However, he found that it did matter! It mattered a lot. There had been enough gossip about him lately.

Tomorrow he would find out what she was playing at. After all, they were friends, not lovers. She didn't have to confide in him, he reminded himself for the umpteenth time. But she should have told him! Prepared him. After all, it would only be natural for people to assume he was the father.

Margaret watched him leave the room, a grim smile on her face. She had noted different expressions flit across Donald's face. She had seen the perplexed frown puckering his brow and drew her own conclusions. Susan had obviously not yet told him he was about to become a father. Now why was that? she mused.

It was lunchtime when he first arrived at Susan's door. Receiving no answer to his knock, he braced himself and banged on Edith's door. It was opened immediately by Margaret.

'Is Susan not in?' she asked, a hint of a laugh in her voice. 'Mind you, I thought she was. Come in.'

'It's all right. If she's not here, I'll call back later.'

'She'll probably come here for her lunch. Why not join us?'

Reluctantly he entered the hall and, to his dismay, the house appeared to be empty. 'Where is everyone?' he asked as he hung his coat on the rail.

'Edith and Billy went off to visit somebody and Jack has gone to see a friend about a job.'

His heart skipped a beat. They were alone. He shouldn't be here. 'So you aren't going back to London then?'

'Not if I can help it. For heaven's sake, stop hovering

about there and sit down. I won't bite you.'

Suddenly she gave a pleased cry and patted her stomach. 'Oh, the baby just kicked me. Look.' She moved close to his chair and he could indeed see her stomach moving. 'It's turning over. Feel!'

He cowered back in the chair with a grimace of distaste. She laughed in derision. 'You really are the limit, Donald. Imagine being afraid to touch a little baby.'

'I'm not afraid. It just doesn't seem decent. Besides, it isn't a baby yet.'

'It is, you just can't see it yet. Does Susan's move? How far on is she?'

He had decided not to let her guess he was in the dark regarding Susan's condition. 'I'm afraid you'll have to ask her that.'

She stared intently at him. 'I do believe she hasn't told you about it. Now, I wonder why? Can it be that she's not sure of you?'

She was bending over him, her soft blonde hair brushing his face.

'Eh, Donald? Why is she not sure? Could it be you still care for me, and she knows it?' Her breath fanned his cheek and he waited for the remembered soft feel of her lips against it. Instead she leant closer and her lips and tongue teasingly caressed the corner of his mouth. All the old yearning awakened and he turned his lips to meet hers. It was wonderful to be near her like this. The gentleness of the kiss intensified and he rose and gathered her close.

For some moments they devoured each other and then, dragging his mouth from hers, he cried, 'Margaret, where did I go wrong?'

'You didn't,' she wailed. 'It was my fault. All my fault. I was impatient and tried to hurry things on by making you jealous. Then it all went haywire and ran out of control. I didn't realise Jack was such a passionate man and we got carried away. After that, there was no going back. It was exciting, but it was you I wanted. I thought that perhaps, if I explained everything to you, you'd understand, but then before I had the chance to talk to you, you and Jack had that big fight. And then I had no choice – I had to go off with him.'

'And there I was trying to do things decent, managing to keep my hands off you, and you were letting Jack get his leg over. I don't understand! I wanted you to know I respected you. That's why I hung back,' he cried bitterly.

'I realise that now. But at the time I thought you were being offhand and didn't care enough.'

'Offhand? How could you think that?' Aware that his passion was getting out of control, he tried to put her from him, but she clung on.

'To be truthful, Jack's passion took me unawares. I never dreamt he could be so fiery. He's a wonderful lover, but it's *you* I love, Donald. I can't stop thinking about you. I should never have married Jack.'

Pictures of her and Jack together flashed before his mind and he felt repulsed. How could she have carried on like that with Jack if she loved him? 'It's too late, Margaret. Besides, what if I didn't come up to your expectations as a lover, eh? You'd be throwing away a good marriage for nothing.'

She pressed closer still and he groaned with desire. 'I don't think I'm likely to find you wanting.'

'Behave yourself, Margaret. Someone is sure to come in.'

'Meet me, Donald! Just say where and when and I'll make sure I'm there.'

His mind baulked at what she was asking of him. 'It wouldn't work, Margaret. I couldn't do that to Jack. We were best friends at one time.'

'He didn't consider your feelings when he seduced me, now did he? So why should you consider his? You want me! That's obvious. Come on, no one need ever know.'

'You're expecting a baby,' he cried, horrified.

'Do you think I could ever forget that? But there'll be no harm done, if that's what you're afraid of. It's not a sickness, you know.'

The doorknob rattled and then a loud, angry knock heralded the arrival of Jack. Margaret reluctantly withdrew from the warmth of Donald's embrace. Drawing a deep, steadying breath, she smoothed the hair back from her face and went to let her husband in.

'Why did you lock the door? You knew I wouldn't be long,' Jack said accusingly. He looked closely at his wife. 'Are you feeling all right? You look flushed . . .' For the life of him he couldn't describe just how she looked. His nostrils flared when he entered the living room and saw Donald sitting by the fireside, a newspaper open on his lap.

Jack's eyes darted from one to the other of them suspiciously. He hated the way his jealousy bounded out of control when he saw them together.

Donald rushed into speech. 'I'm waiting for Susan. You haven't by any chance seen her?'

'Yes. I've just walked up the street with her. She's just gone in next door.'

Donald wondered if it was safe to get up. Margaret guessed his predicament and, grabbing his coat from the rail, threw it at him. 'I told you she wouldn't be long.' She turned to her husband, keeping his attention. 'Well, any luck, Jack?'

Glad of the chance to escape, Donald said, 'I'll nip in and see her.'

Still Margaret detained him. 'Oh, before you go . . . Jack, there's a dance on at the Pali tonight. Donald's taking Susan – can we join them?'

'I don't think you're in any condition to go dancing, Margaret.'

'Why not? I won't be the only expectant mother there, you know. Besides, we're married. We've nothing to be ashamed of.'

From Jack's bewildered expression, Donald guessed he was not aware of his cousin's condition. Trying to retrieve the situation, he cried, 'Susan could very well refuse me. After all, she might just want a quiet night at home.'

'Then you can come with us. Can't he, Jack?'

Donald was out of the door before Jack could reply.

He walked the length of the street to give his emotions a chance to cool down. He really shouldn't let Margaret get to him like this. It was reckless the way she kept throwing herself at him, not caring who noticed. He would have to put an end to it once and for all. She was married and pregnant, and had already made a fool of him once before, and he had no intention of letting it happen again. Feeling much calmer, he approached his house and quietly knocked on the door.

Susan scowled at him. 'What do you want?'

'Can I come in for a minute? . . . Please?'

Reluctantly she moved aside and, passing her, he entered the living room.

'You will have to come into the kitchen. I'm making myself some lunch.'

'Margaret said you'd be going next door for your lunch.'

'Huh! After the way you behaved last night?' She tossed her head angrily. 'I wouldn't give her the satisfaction to gloat. She probably thinks I'm running after you. Besides, I can't stand that girl. She's always asking questions. Probing into my affairs. Why should I tell her any of my business?'

His eyes intently on her face, Donald said softly, 'You must have become quite pally at some stage, since you told her about the baby.'

Hot colour flooded her face and then receded, leaving her deathly pale. 'I told her nothing of the sort!' she whispered. 'What exactly did she say?'

'She asked me when *our* baby was due.'

Her hand clutched at her throat. 'Oh my God. What did you say?'

'I was gobsmacked. Didn't know what to say. I told her she would have to ask you about that. She could see I was flabbergasted and I think she surmised that you had not told me I was to become a father, so I didn't enlighten her.'

'I'm so sorry, Donald. She must have guessed. Probably because she's pregnant herself, she recognised the signs.

I know Aunt Edith would never have broken my confidence. But for her to accuse you? Why, that's monstrous, so it is. She's just jealous, that's what it is. Jealousy!'

He shrugged. 'It's what everyone else will be thinking once they know.'

'Don't worry, I'll soon make it clear you're not the father.'

Her voice was bitter and, his ego dented, he retorted, 'Thanks a lot! I'm not all that bad, you know.'

'Oh, for heaven's sake don't go seeing slights where there aren't any. You'd make a fine father, but we must keep the record straight.'

'Is your husband the father?'

She turned away. Should she admit there was no husband? No, that would only complicate matters further. Donald would think he was dealing with a nutcase. 'No, he isn't the father.'

His mind ticked over and slowly he voiced his thoughts. 'So the baby is the reason your marriage broke up?' She made no comment, just continued buttering bread. 'You must care very much about this other man, so where is he? Did he let you down?'

She turned and stared intently at him. 'I don't want to talk about this, Donald, so would you like to leave now, or stay to lunch?'

He saw that he was going to be none the wiser and replied, 'I'd like to stay for lunch.'

'Then take off your coat and make yourself useful, like setting the table for instance.'

Against Susan's better judgement she agreed to accompany him to the dance that night. Margaret had persuaded Jack to bring her along and it was no surprise when they joined Susan and Donald. Every dance, the minute the music started up, Donald hustled Susan on to the floor. Finding all this activity too much for her, she chided him, 'Much as I enjoy dancing, I'm afraid this is getting too much for me. I'm getting a bit exhausted.'

'You never complained before.'

'We did have wee breaks before . . . You know, like sitting out a dance for a chat or a drink?'

He looked crestfallen. 'I'm sorry, Susan. I just want to keep as far away from Margaret as possible.'

They were near the table where the drinks were on sale and she steered him towards it. 'I'm gasping for a drink.'

He smiled down at her. 'What would you like?'

'An orange juice, please. Oh, there's two seats. I'll grab them and you hurry, before they discover where we are.'

Their seats were screened from the dancers' view by the couples who were standing on the edge of the floor sipping their drinks. They relaxed, secure in the thought that they had some time to themselves.

'Do you know something, Susan? I'll be glad when Jack goes back to London tomorrow.'

'Even if Margaret stays behind?'

Donald jerked upright, spilling his drink down the front of his shirt. 'You can't mean that!' he cried, feverishly mopping at his shirt with a handkerchief.

'Oh, but I do. He asked me if I would let her stay with me.'

'*What?* Why you? Surely the obvious ones would be his parents?'

'I know, but he thought she might get bored, what with them working all day at the market. And it wouldn't do for Margaret to be bored, now, would it?' she added sarcastically.

'You surely didn't agree?'

'No, I certainly did not, and I made it quite plain to Jack. If she should agree to stay with Aunt Edith, can I remain in your house?'

Eyes bright with laughter fixed on her face and he said teasingly, 'Well . . . I don't know about that. You never paid your rent and I was considering eviction.'

Consternation widened her eyes. 'I forgot all about that. It's because I got such a shock at lunchtime. It went completely out of my head.'

A shadow fell across them. 'So here you are! Hiding away. You two must really be in love.' Margaret stood before them, hands on hips, disapproval apparent in every line of her body.

Reluctantly Donald rose to his feet and motioned her to sit down. 'Where's Jack?'

'He's getting me a drink.' The music was just starting another quickstep. 'How about giving me a dance, Donald? If I didn't know any better, I'd swear you were avoiding me.'

'Here!' A glass of lemonade was thrust into her hand, and Jack glared at her. 'I think you've danced enough for one night. Don't forget your condition. We don't want any accidents, do we?'

Her lips tightened and her nostrils flared in anger. How dare Jack speak to her like that in front of them. 'Susan is dancing just as much, if indeed not more than me. Are you not going to advise her to take it easy?' she retorted.

'What on earth are you talking about, Margaret?' His bewilderment was obvious.

Her smile was malicious. 'Has your dear cousin not confided in you then? She's also expecting a baby.'

Shocked eyes rested on Susan. 'Is this true?'

She rose to her feet. 'I can't see what business it is of yours, Jack, or anybody else's, for that matter. But yes, I am. Now if you'll excuse me, I'm tired and I think I'll go home.' Donald moved to join her, but she stayed him with a raised hand. 'There is no need for you to accompany me, Donald. Stay and enjoy the rest of the dance. I'll be perfectly all right on my own.'

'Oh, but I want to see you home. If I'm lucky I might even get something to eat,' he teased, trying to lighten the atmosphere.

To his relief, she laughed and agreed with a smile. 'You just might at that. Good night, Jack.' An abrupt nod was all she allowed herself in Margaret's direction.

It was a beautiful night; stars twinkled brightly against a dark sky. The air was crisp and their breath was like fine mist hovering on the frosty air as they made their way through the town centre towards North Road.

'Isn't it a lovely night?'

He glanced sideways at her. 'It certainly is, and so are you.'

She laughed aloud. 'Are you trying to boost my morale?'

'I'm trying to figure out what makes you tick. You married one man and are expecting another man's child. Why aren't they here fighting over you? I don't understand.'

'Because until Margaret opened her big mouth, no one but Edith and Billy knew about this baby. It's the best-kept secret. Certainly no one in Ireland knows, and that's the way I want it to stay.'

'Surely the father has a right to know?'

'He isn't free.'

. 'Ah, I guessed he must be a married man.'

'No, he isn't married. He is, however, engaged. Look, I'm talking too much. Please don't ask me any more questions on this subject. It'll only end in tears.'

'Just one more! Why not tell him? If you love each other, he will probably break off the engagement and marry you.'

'Ah, but you see, that's the snag. He doesn't love me.'

In spite of the fact that she felt far from laughing, the expression on his face brought forth a reluctant chuckle. 'It's all very complicated, Donald, and I'm too ashamed to tell you the truth. So can we just forget my problems and concentrate on yours?'

'I must confess mine are nothing compared with yours.'

'Take my advice and let them stay that way. Forget Margaret! She's nothing but trouble. You'll meet some nice girl one day who is free to return your love. Now let's change the subject. I'm going to keep my side of the bargain and cook you something tasty for supper. What do you think of that?'

'I think that's a very good idea.' He reached for her hand and drew it under his arm, quickening his step at the same time. 'I'm starving. Remember, I missed dinner today.'

She laughed aloud. 'You're not going to let me forget, are you?'

For the remainder of the journey they were locked in their own thoughts. Susan was very aware of his body brushing against hers. Through her own stupid fault she was missing out on so much. She warned herself to be careful. In her vulnerable state she might send out the wrong signals and, since this was to have been Donald's wedding day and he was missing Margaret, anything could happen. Why had she promised to cook him a meal? The rest of the evening could be fraught with danger.

Donald's thoughts were running along similar tracks, only he couldn't see what harm it would do if they comforted each other. Who knows, perhaps if he played his cards right, he might win her around to his way of thinking. He was humming softly, his nerves tingling with anticipation, when they at last arrived at his house.

Inside, he closed the door and drew her into his arms. In the semi-darkness she stood very still, her big, haunted eyes gazing up at him. His head bent and, receiving no resistance, he trailed his lips gently over the contours of her face. Aware that she should be stopping him before it got out of hand, she nevertheless pressed closer, savouring the sweetness of his caresses. Encouraged, he was slowly edging her towards the stairs, all the while seducing her with his mouth and hands.

Suddenly she twisted away from him. 'No, this is wrong!'

'Why? Why is it wrong? We're not trespassing on anyone else's preserves. We're two lonely people who are attracted to each other.'

'I don't want this. I want true love, not just a one-night stand.'

'Who knows where it might lead, eh? I do care for you, Susan. Once your divorce comes through, we might very well care enough about each other to marry.'

She grasped at this excuse. 'That might well be, but until I'm free I don't want to be used by someone who's running away from someone else.'

He stepped back as if stung. 'I wouldn't use you like that,' he protested.

'Oh no? What would you call it?'

'I was trying to comfort you.'

'Thank you very much, but I don't need that kind of comfort. I think you should go now. More than anything else in the world, I need to be respected.'

He looked incredulous. 'You think I don't respect you?'

'How could you, when you think I'm ready to jump into bed with you?'

Without another word he turned on his heel and left the house. She gazed at the door and then kicked it violently again and again. She wished she could kick herself; meanwhile she could only take out her frustration on the door. Struck by a thought, she smiled wryly. He must be starving. And she still hadn't paid her rent.

She was in the kitchen heating the kettle for the water bottles when there was a knock on the door. Convinced it would be Margaret thinking Donald would be here and wanting to invite herself and Jack in for supper, sharp words were hovering on Susan's lips as she wrenched open the door.

Donald stood there looking sheepish. 'I'm sorry.' He shrugged. 'I'm afraid I'll never learn, Susan. I do admit I was hoping to get you into bed, but I honestly didn't mean any disrespect. I really did think we could comfort each other.'

'Okay I understand, and I forgive you.'

She made no effort to invite him in and he grimaced. 'I suppose I've forfeited any chance of some grub?' She hesitated and he pleaded, 'I really am starving, Susan.'

'Oh, come on in then, but you had better behave yourself.'

'You can count on that. I've learnt my lesson.'

The engagement party arranged for New Year's Eve was a great success. Held in the Royal Avenue Hotel, the lavish buffet and constant flow of wine and beer ensured that everyone enjoyed themselves. Rooms were also available at a discount for those who wanted to stay overnight. Alison was flushed with triumph, and Graham had put all thoughts of Susan to one side and had convinced himself he was a very lucky man that such a lovely girl had consented to be his wife.

He eyed his parents chatting to his future in-laws. His father had been won over long ago by Alison's beauty and charming manner, but he knew that his mother still had reservations. She was not over-enthusiastic about the match. Not that it mattered. In her opinion no one would be good enough for him. She had hoped for someone better for her only son. A politician's daughter, for instance. And there had been little chance of that.

In spite of her family's ranting and raving, Susan had resisted all efforts to persuade her to come home for the engagement party. She sent Alison some good-quality towels for her bottom drawer, but Graham still thought it very heartless of her to let her sister down. Even if she couldn't face him, she could have avoided him, as usual. She was very good at doing that, he thought resentfully.

A June wedding was being suggested by his in-laws and he was glad that Alison didn't appear to agree with them, saying she was too young to start having babies. And that would be the next thing on the agenda, if their parents had their own way. Then why had she been so determined to get engaged at Christmas? For the life of him he could not understand how a woman's mind worked.

The atmosphere was wonderful and the crowd laughed and danced the night away. As midnight drew near, Alison and Graham joined those closest to them to see the New Year in. The only blot on the landscape had been Susan's absence. When all the excitement had died down and the New Year greetings were over, Graham drew Alison to one side.

'I know we have two single rooms booked, but can't we share one of them, eh, love?'

He saw dismay register in her eyes before she came up with an excuse. 'But my room is next door to my parents. One way or the other they would be bound to know.'

He gathered her close. 'Did no one ever tell you that where there's a will there's a way?'

'It would be too risky, Graham. I'd die of shame if we were caught. Look at how me dad treats Susan, and we aren't even sure she's pregnant.'

He drew back, brows gathered in a frown. 'Susan pregnant? You never said.'

'Well, we don't *know* that she is. And Jim Brady denies it. But why else run over to Aunt Edith and refuse to come home under any circumstances, if she has nothing to hide?'

Graham was flabbergasted. He felt all at sea, as if he had missed the important part of a film. 'How come you never mentioned any of this to me before?'

'It was me dad who first put the idea into my head. And then when she refused to come home at Christmas and for my engagement party as well . . . You have to admit it does look very suspicious.'

'But why did you not say anything to me?'

'I didn't say to anyone, except Jim Brady – remember that night at the Orpheus? I wanted to find out if he knew anything. But he denied all knowledge of it. Of course he might very well be innocent. If it does happen to be true, she could have met someone over there.'

'You should have told me, Alison.'

'What difference does it make?'

'I'm your future husband and you should tell me these things.'

He turned away and Alison watched him head for the bar, relieved that apparently he had given up the idea of sharing a room tonight. Time enough for all that when they were married, she thought.

At the bar Graham ordered a double Black Bush, and armed with his drink found a quiet corner. Lighting a cigarette, he mulled over the news he had just heard. He recalled that Susan had been a virgin the night he had taken her. Could she possibly be expecting his child? No! It was out of the question. She would have had no reason to hide. All she had to do was tell him.

Alison watched him head for a secluded corner table without so much as a glance in her direction and slowly followed him. He must be very annoyed since he didn't even offer her a drink. Absorbed in thoughts of Susan, Graham had completely forgotten her existence, but to his surprise suddenly Alison was on her knees beside him.

'Graham, have I offended you? I honestly didn't mean to.' She had decided to give in to his wishes and keep him happy. 'As you say, where there's a will there's a way, so shall I come to your room when I'm sure the coast is clear? Most people have already retired, so it shouldn't be too long.'

He looked into her lovely face and discovered that the passion he had felt earlier had completely evaporated. Placing his drink to one side and his cigarette in an ashtray, he cupped her face in his hands. 'It's all right, love. I respect your wishes. Let's wait until we're married.'

'You mean that, Graham?'

He brushed her lips lightly with his. 'Yes, dear. Now off you go to bed. I'll just finish my drink and then I'll be off, too. See you at breakfast in the morning.'

Feeling that she was in the wrong and he was dismissing her like an unruly schoolgirl, she repeated, 'Are you sure?'

'Yes, I'm sure.'

'Well, all right then. I'll see you in the morning.' Still apprehensive, she left him.

He sat for a long time after she had gone, going over and over again in his mind the few encounters he'd had with Susan after that fatal night. She had obviously been embarrassed and avoided him, but then it was an embarrassing situation. But surely she must have known he would stand by her. Still, she would have been considering Alison's feelings as well. If – and he very much doubted it – she was pregnant, it could still be Jim Brady's. There was nothing to prove that she had not been seeing him again. Or, as Alison had pointed out, she might have met someone over in England.

He sat on, imagining what it would be like for Susan to have his child. It would cause a scandal! No doubt about that. Could it possibly be true? Was that why she had taken off like that? Some time passed as he sat lost in thought, until the silence that had descended on the hotel made him aware of the late hour. A glance at his watch showed it was half-past four. He found when he rose to his feet that he felt very unsteady. Making his way to the lift, he pressed the button and was soon in his bedroom. Not bothering to remove his clothes, he threw himself on the bed. His last thought was of Susan. Somehow or other he must see her. But how?

Chapter Six

To his great joy, Jack was promised a job in Cleveland Bridge as soon as he could tie up all the loose ends in London. Margaret adamantly refused to go back down with him and, glad that her beloved son was going to be living close at hand, Edith agreed that she could live with them until he came back.

She was full of apologies to Susan, explaining that she really had no choice in the matter. Susan hastened to assure her that she was happy enough the way things were. She loved this time of day when she and her aunt could talk freely. Margaret never rose early and they were having coffee together, as usual.

'Billy has agreed to start looking at houses,' Edith informed her niece. Then we three can move and leave Jack and Margaret in this house. What do you think of that?'

'Aunt Edith, please don't worry about me. I think I can persuade Donald to let me keep on renting his house. That's a laugh. He won't take any money off me. But you know what I mean – he will let me stay. Once the baby is born, I'll have to think seriously about my future.'

'Susan, I can't help worrying about you. It's time you saw a doctor, you know.'

'Yes, I realise that. Can I join your doctor's surgery?'

'I don't see why not. I'll make an appointment for you to go and see him. I'm sure he will take you on. I'll make it for Wednesday, shall I?'

Vera Crabtree had asked Susan to continue working part-time: Fridays and Saturdays, so Wednesday suited her fine. 'That would be great, Aunt Edith.'

'Would you like me to come with you?'

A definite shake of the head accompanied her answer. 'No, that won't be necessary.' She smiled wryly. 'You've enough running about to do with Margaret, without me adding to your list.'

'Ah now, Susan, you know I wouldn't mind in the slightest.'

'I know you wouldn't, but I'd rather be independent. I'll keep you up to date on all matters, I promise.'

'I wish you and Margaret had hit it off . . .' Her aunt's voice trailed off and she looked appealingly at Susan. Getting no response, she added, 'You would be company for each other, you know, going to the clinic together.'

'Margaret has plenty of friends in Darlington, Aunt Edith. She'll be all right. I'm a bit of a loner. I prefer my own company.' This wasn't really true. She missed her own friends back home and Margaret would be a very poor substitute. She would rather do without than befriend someone like Margaret. 'I'm fine, really I am.'

Edith still looked worried, but Margaret was her daughter-in-law and must come first. Susan had asked her not to reveal that she was already pregnant when she arrived. Aware that Donald would therefore be regarded as the father, Edith had questioned the wisdom of this, but was assured that Donald knew which way the wind blew and was quite happy with the way things stood.

This was true, it kept Margaret off his back.

They looked at lots of houses and at last put in an offer for one on the outskirts of town in Cockerton Village. A semi-detached house, it had three big bedrooms, two reception rooms, a kitchen, bathroom and gardens at front and rear.

Edith was in her glory and, with shining eyes, confided in Susan that she had despaired of ever owning a house, and to her, this one was like a mansion. It required some work on it, but this was reflected in the asking price, and she and Billy would willingly work their fingers to the bone to get it just the way they wanted. They hoped to move in before Easter. Easter Sunday was early this year. It would fall on 6 April and Margaret's baby was also due around that time.

They had expected Margaret to be delighted to have a home of her own, albeit a rented one, but when Billy offered to get Jack's name put in the rent book she just shrugged indifferently, and agreed it would do until Jack arranged something better.

Jack had been spending weekends at home with his wife, finding it harder and harder to leave each Sunday evening. Eventually, at the end of January, he returned for good. It was soon obvious that he did not share his wife's view about living in a rented house. He was over the moon at the idea of getting his parents' comfortable home, saying that it would be long and many a day before they could afford to buy a house. Margaret was far from happy at this idea and an expression used back home came to mind as Susan looked at her dour countenance: 'She had a face like a Lurgan spade.'

Donald invested his savings in a second-hand Austin Mini. A cute little red number. The first time it drew up to the door they all gathered on the pavement to admire and exclaim over it. And not just the family! It was such a close-knit community that the whole street was out giving it the once-over; passing knowing comments on its good points and ignoring its bad.

Had it been a brand-new Aston Martin, Donald could not have been more proud. Every Sunday after Mass he collected Susan and introduced her to all the towns and villages round about. Places like Barnard Castle and Richmond, and Durham and York, where she was enthralled by the quaint cobbled streets in The Shambles and by great York Minster. She was aware that when he arrived each Sunday morning they were watched from behind her Aunt Edith's net curtains, and she could guess who was spying on them.

True to his word, Donald's conduct was beyond reproach. He was a real mate, helping her in every way he could, and she grew to depend on him. When her pregnancy started to show, he confided in her that he didn't care if everyone thought the baby was his, adding sadly that indeed he wished it was.

The car was another thorn in Margaret's side; something else to whine about. Why couldn't Jack buy a car and take her out and about? she lamented the first time they were alone.

'For the simple reason that we are still in debt to my

parents. When we clear that, then – and only then – will I consider going into more debt for a car.'

'But that could take years,' she gasped.

'So be it! There are more important things to consider than a car. Like, for instance, the baby.'

She scowled. 'You know, sometimes I wish . . .' Her voice trailed off.

'What, Margaret? What do you sometimes wish? That you'd never married me?' he said bitterly. 'Well, let me tell you something. Sometimes I wish I was footloose and fancy-free, just like Donald Murphy! He seems to be having a whale of a time gallivanting about in his new car, and maybe, just maybe, you would then look at me with cow's eyes.'

Fear entered her heart. He had never spoken to her like this before. Terrified that he might find her wanting and start to look elsewhere, she said quickly, 'I didn't mean that at all.'

'Didn't you?' With a scornful look he turned on his heel and left the room, glad he had given her something to think about. He was fed up to the teeth with her griping. She hadn't a kind word to say about anyone or anything these days. There was simply no pleasing her.

The house in Cockerton was pronounced habitable in the middle of March, in so far as the bathroom had been refitted and most of the kitchen cupboards replaced. It still needed a lot doing to it, but Edith and Billy couldn't wait to move in and decided to do so right away and refurbish as they went along. Susan was invited to move with them and, although she had vowed to stay where she was until the baby was born, she was glad of the opportunity to get away from the ever-simmering envy of Margaret, who made a habit of popping in to see her whenever she got the chance. The next week was spent carefully packing books and knick-knacks into cartons and tea chests in preparation for the move.

Donald immediately gave notice to the rent man that his house would soon be empty, much to the delight of Jack, who would be glad to see the back of the man who had once been his best friend. Susan, however, was dismayed when she heard, sure that Donald would regret his decision when he met and wanted to marry some girl. He assured her that he was glad not to have to visit the house any more. Nothing else was said, but Susan wondered just what Margaret had been up to, when given the chance, to make Donald so relieved to escape. She tried to pry, but Donald just tapped the side of his nose with a forefinger and would say no more.

It was near Easter when fate created an unexpected opportunity for Graham to visit England. The business was booming and his father was eager to open another car showroom. Something different, a completely new design. Graham, who that very day had been admiring the latest building designs in Newcastle, hastened to get the magazines to show him.

His father examined the pictures presented to him and exclaimed, 'These are in Newcastle, England. Why would we want to go and see them when we have fine architects here in Ireland?'

Seeing his chance to get across the water slipping away, Graham confided, 'Dad, I need a break. Just a few days away on my own.'

George Robson eyed his son closely. 'I've noticed you're not' yourself lately, something's bugging you. If you aren't happy about your engagement to Alison, son, break it off now. I realise you won't want to hurt her, but the longer you leave it, the harder it will be.'

'It's not that, Dad. There's something else I need to get sorted out in my mind and I need some space to think.'

'Mind you, you will only be going over to have a look.'

'I know that, Dad. But, you know, it wouldn't be a bad idea branching out. Newcastle, after all, is less than an hour away by plane.'

'You can get that idea out of your head, young man. Your mother hates flying.'

With a cheeky grin Graham said, 'Ah, but then, she wouldn't have to go.'

George returned the grin, glad to see his son looking more relaxed. 'Away and book your flight, before I change my mind.'

'Thanks, Dad. Thanks a million.'

There was nothing wrong with Alison's geography and when she heard his plans, she was quick to point out how close to Darlington he would be.

'You know, I didn't realise that,' he exclaimed. 'Tell you what. If I can find the time, and it's not too far away, I'll go and surprise Susan.'

'I wish I could go with you,' Alison lamented. 'It's not fair.'

Successfully hiding his dismay at her suggestion, Graham said, 'I know. But your dad would never hear tell of you coming along. Besides, I won't be free to entertain you. I'll be busy meeting different people and going out to look at buildings. You'd be bored stiff.'

'Not if you dropped me off at Susan's while you were carrying out your business. I'll have a word with Dad.'

However, Trevor was not so forthcoming, accusing Alison of following in her sister's footsteps. Disappointed, but knowing how much her mother was missing her eldest daughter and not wanting to cause any more friction than was necessary, she agreed to remain at home while Graham was away. Ashamed of the relief he felt, Graham was extra-attentive to her and promised to buy her a nice piece of jewellery while over in England.

Uneasy, but unable to figure out why, she clung to him as he was about to leave for the airport. 'Don't you go falling for one of those English girls,' she warned.

'Don't be silly! I'm going over on business, remember,' he admonished her. 'I won't have any free time to chat up the girls.'

'If you get a chance to see our Susan, try and get her to come home. Tell her how much we all miss her.'

'I will. I'd better go, love. I'll ring tonight. Okay?'

She nodded and lifted her face for his kiss. With a peck on the cheek and a quick hug, he put her from him.

'See you soon.'

She watched him drive off through a blur of tears. If only she had been more forthcoming at the beginning of their relationship there wouldn't be this invisible barrier between them. Now, try though she might, she couldn't get close to him. When had it all gone wrong?

At their engagement party. They had been so close that night; the closest she had ever come to feeling any passion for him, and he must have sensed it, but when he had proposed that they sleep together she had reacted like a Victorian lady. No wonder he seemed to have gone off her. When he came back she would make it up to him. But did she really want to start all that? Surely there should be more to marriage than two people taking vows. There should be passion, excitement, awe. Shouldn't there? Or was it just in books that passion throbbed and they couldn't keep their hands off each other? She certainly had no inclination to fondle Graham's body. Quite the opposite; the idea repulsed her. She had the greatest admiration for him, but he did not appeal to her in that way and sometimes this worried her.

From remarks made by her friends she gathered that most of them felt the same; not sure if they had met the right one, yet afraid to let them go and end up old maids. The first time she had met Jim Brady, that night at the Orpheus, before he and Susan had been aware of her, she had sensed deep emotions between them. It had been like an electric current in the air. She had envied her sister her good fortune. Yet apparently it had ended in heartbreak. What did one do for the best?

The move into the new house went smoothly. Billy's friends in the market rallied round and on Sunday, with a lot of vans and open-backed lorries available for transport, the contents of the old house were soon trans-ferred to the new home. Jack and Margaret had also helped out, as had Donald. The six of them were sitting amidst a jumble of boxes and crates having their first cup of tea on the new premises, when a knock on the door brought Edith proudly to her feet.

'I bet you that will be one of the neighbours to wish us well. Our first visitor. I'll answer it.'

Edith, who had visited the house regularly, painting and polishing, was already on nodding acquaintance with a few of her neighbours, but the man standing on her doorstep was not one of them. They eyed each other for a few seconds. He recognised Edith's resemblance to her sister. 'I'm looking for a Mrs Devine,' he said politely and she immediately recognised the Belfast brogue. 'I went to her old address and was directed here.'

'I'm Edith Devine.'

'I was told your niece, Susan Cummings, would be here with you?'

A frown gathered on Edith's brow. 'Who wants to know?'

'I'm a friend from back home. I'd business in Newcastle and thought I'd take the opportunity to call and see her.'

Jumbled thoughts filled Edith's mind. Was this the child's father? Had he somehow or other heard about her niece's predicament and come to claim her?

Back in the sitting room they sat with strained ears. They heard Edith open the door and the murmur of voices. Then Edith returned, a worried look on her face and a tall man at her heels. 'It's someone to see *you*, Susan. Someone from back home.'

Shock coursed through Susan's body and she went

deathly pale as she gazed in amazement at Graham Robson.

He could see that she was upset and rushed into apologies. 'I'm sorry for not letting you know, Susan, but I had business in Newcastle and thought I'd pay a flying visit.'

Susan swallowed to try to remove the lump that was lodged in her throat and rose slowly to her feet. With hand outstretched and a sickly smile of welcome on her face, she approached Graham. 'It's wonderful to see you.' His eyes swept over her, taking in her obvious pregnancy, and she thought he looked excited. But why? She rushed into introductions. 'Graham, let me introduce you. This is my Aunt Edith.'

Cordially Edith clasped the hand offered to her. 'I realise now who you are,' she exclaimed. 'You're Alison's young man. Welcome to my new home. We just this afternoon moved in, so you will have to forgive the mess.' To Susan's relief she took over the introductions. 'This is my husband Billy and son Jack. That girl is Jack's wife and this is a friend of the family, Donald Murphy.'

Donald could see how dismayed Susan was and, remembering how hard she had worked to keep the knowledge of her pregnancy from those back home, he shook Graham warmly by the hand. 'This is a pleasure. I've been looking forward to meeting Susan's family.' It was up to Susan now whether or not she wanted this man to think they were a couple.

She shot him a grateful look. 'He has indeed been torturing me to take him home to meet you all,' she agreed, with a fond smile in his direction. 'But I wanted to wait until the baby is born.'

Graham looked deep into her eyes. This conversation was ad lib. It didn't ring true. Before he could think of a reply, Edith cried, 'Look, we haven't even offered the man a chair. Sit down, son. Make yourself comfortable. I'll rustle up something to eat.'

'That won't be necessary, thank you. I would just like a word with Susan, if I may?' His gaze was pleading. 'Bring you up to date about things back home. I've hired a car. Perhaps you will come for a drive with me?'

'I'll just tidy myself up a bit. Excuse me, please.' On reluctant feet she climbed the stairs to the bathroom. What on earth had brought him here? How should she handle this?

A silence fell when she left the room. It was Edith who broke it. 'I hear you have just become engaged to my other niece, Alison. Congratulations, son.'

'Thank you.'

'May I second that, son. She's a lovely girl.'

Graham smiled at Billy. 'I'm a lucky man.'

This Alison was a very lucky girl, Margaret thought. Those shoes were hand-made and that suit and Crombie overcoat must have cost the earth. Besides, there was something funny going on here. How come Susan hadn't told her family about the baby? To her, it was obvious that they didn't know! This man had been gobsmacked, and something else . . . An elusive expression had flitted across his face; too swift for her to put a name to it.

When Susan returned she was dressed for outdoors. 'I'm ready, Graham.'

'Graham, I insist you come back here for a bite to eat before you go back to Newcastle.' He opened his mouth to make an excuse, but Edith was adamant. 'I insist. It won't be a feast, but it will fill the gap.'

'I don't want to be any bother.'

'I assure you, it will be no bother at all.'

He nodded. 'Thank you very much. I'd be glad to.'

In the car Graham turned to her. 'Which direction?'

'Turn up West Auckland Road and then straight on,' she said.

Soon they were out in the countryside, with trees and hedges flashing past on either side. It was a typical March evening, cold and blustery. Great dark clouds buffeted each other low in the sky, as if anxious to shed their heavy load. Susan gazed blindly out of the window, waiting for the interrogation she knew was to come. Graham was silent, trying to figure things out in his mind. He didn't want to put his foot in it. Where did this Donald fellow fit into all this?

Ten minutes passed and, unable to bear the silence any longer, Susan turned a reproachful gaze on him. 'Why did you come here, Graham?'

'I told you. I had to come to Newcastle on business, so I thought I'd kill two birds with one stone. Everybody's worried sick about you, you know, and it looks like they were right to be worried.'

'There's no need. I told them I was all right,' she said stubbornly.

His eyes fastened briefly on her stomach. 'You call *that* all right?'

'It's nobody's business but mine! I've settled in over here. If I was to go home, my dad would give me no peace. I'd be the lowest of the low.'

'Don't let Trevor keep you away from your family and friends, Susan. He has already guessed you're pregnant. Believe me, it would be a nine-day wonder.'

She gaped at him in horror. 'My dad thinks I'm pregnant?'

'I'm afraid so. Mind you, nobody believed him! Jim Brady danced with Alison one night at the Orpheus and he swore he never touched you.' But I did, he inwardly lamented. His teeth gnawed at his lower lip as he tried to frame the next question.

'Jim Brady knows I'm pregnant?' she cried, aghast. 'Ah no, no!' The very idea of him knowing filled her with a great sorrow. What must he be thinking?

In spite of her efforts at self-control, she started to tremble and low moans escaped her lips. Frantically he watched for a lay-by to stop the car in. To his relief one came up right away and he drew the car into it and turned to her. 'Susan, don't let it upset you so. No one knows you're pregnant. It was just an idea your dad came up with. A reason for you not coming home.'

Images of Jim Brady filled her mind, his dark, handsome face full of disgust at her downfall. What a low opinion he must have of her. All the same, he should find it easy enough to believe. Hadn't she thrown herself at him, and hadn't he pushed her away?

Graham reached for her hands and clasped them tightly. Blindly she turned to him for consolation. Then, with an exclamation of dismay, she pulled herself free, all thoughts of Jim fading from her mind at Graham's touch. The dark warmth of the car's interior brought to mind another time spent in similar circumstances – and look where that had led. Would she never learn? Still, how she longed for the comfort of his embrace. Anybody's 'embrace, for that matter. Just to be held by him would be wonderful. Just to be held by someone, with no strings attached, would be soothing to her tortured soul, but she couldn't take that chance. What if she blurted out everything into his sympathetic ear?

Feverishly she groped for the door handle. The heat in the car was stifling; she needed to get out of here, needed fresh air, or she was likely to faint. A heavy mist had descended and the air, with an agricultural taint, was far from fresh, but still she gulped great mouthfuls of it into her lungs. The cold dampness hit the back of her throat, making her splutter and cough.

He was out of the car and beside her immediately. 'Susan, please get back in the car. I'm not going to touch you.'

'You're dead right, you're not,' she gasped indignantly between coughs.

'Please, Susan, don't be so bitter. If only you knew how much I regretted that night. If only I could turn back the clock, I would do so. Can't you forgive me?'

'I forgave you a long time ago, Graham. It was just one of those things. We were both to blame.'

Instinctively her hand rested on her stomach and he was quick to notice. 'It was my fault! I knew you were vulnerable, but I couldn't help myself, Susan. You're very lovely, and so sensual. I was gobsmacked when I realised you were a virgin.'

Sensual? He thought her sensual? Why couldn't Jim have thought so? She pushed this thought away and latched on to the rest of his words. 'Why?' she cried accusingly. 'Why were you gobsmacked? Did I come across to you as an easy lay? Did you think I'd been sleeping around?'

'Of course not!' he retaliated, alarmed at her reaction. 'Just, you and Jim were so close I felt sure you must have been intimate.'

'Hah! I'll have you know he wouldn't so much as lay a finger on me. That's how intimate we were.'

'That's because he loved you.'

She was quick to note the past tense. 'You said "loved". Is there someone new in his life now?'

He shrugged his shoulders and spread his hands wide in frustration. 'How would I know? I never see him these days.'

She stood with bowed head and he sensed that she was crying, though not a sound came from her. He should go away and leave her in peace. But he had to find out the truth. A sob escaped her lips and, thrusting a handkerchief into her hand, he persisted in his quest. 'Susan, you were a virgin that night . . . Is this my child? I may as well own up, that's the real reason why I'm here this evening. The business in Newcastle was just an excuse to get over and see you. And I want a truthful answer.'

She recoiled from him in horror. How had he guessed?

'What on earth makes you think that?'

'Alison only let slip that you might be pregnant on New Year's Eve. She had never mentioned it before or I'd have been over here long ago. It struck me immediately that, if Trevor was right, I might be the father. I haven't been able to think of anything else since. Only, if it is, I can't see why you didn't tell me. Is it mine? Is it, Susan?'

'No! No, it's not yours.'

'Susan.' His voice was slow and deliberate. He must make his position clear. 'I'd be more than willing to marry you, you know. You need have no qualms about that.'

Willing to marry her. What a wonderful recipe for a happy marriage! Everyone talking and pointing the finger. A heartbroken Alison in the background. Even for the sake of the child he would be unable to hide his love for her sister. The child would have its father's name, but everything else would be a disaster.

Looking him straight in the eye, she said, 'Believe me, you are not the father.'

'Then who is? You have to tell me, so I can go home with a clear conscience.'

'Graham, listen to me. If I had wanted to wash my dirty linen in public, I'd have gone home. I'm not proud of the position I'm in, you know! Far from it, but it's nobody's business but my own and, if I can help it, it won't be talked about in the dance halls of Belfast. You can go home and marry Alison with a clear mind.'

Still unsure, he probed, 'Are you telling me the truth?'

'Yes. Now will you please take me back. I'm cold.'

She climbed awkwardly back into the car, but he knew better than to try and assist her. On the journey back she sat crouched against the car door, the picture of misery, and he regretted adding to her worries. Still, he had to be sure. After all, he was engaged to her sister. They were just drawing up to the house when the heavens opened and rain fell in a sheet.

The door was opened quickly. 'You just made it in time.'

Susan wryly examined her soaked coat and replied, 'I don't know about that.'

'Take off your coat, Graham, and hang it up there.' Edith nodded to a rack in the hall. 'I'll fetch you a towel for your hair in a jiffy.' She helped her niece off with her coat. 'Are you all right, love,' she whispered.

'I'm fine, Aunt Edith, just cold. My, you have been busy,' she exclaimed when she entered the sitting room. All the cartons and tea chests had disappeared, and the settee and chairs were in position against the wall and close to the coal fire that now burned brightly in the grate.

Billy laughed. 'You should see the state of the living room and kitchen. Meanwhile, we can be comfortable in here for the rest of the evening.'

'Where is everybody?'

'Jack and Margaret had made arrangements for tonight, so Donald offered to run them home. Donald's coming back for his tea. Sit over here, love, you look like death warmed up.'

Relieved to know that Margaret wouldn't be there watching every move with those inquisitive eyes, Susan sank into the armchair closest to the fire. Billy soon had a conversation going with Graham, and Edith disappeared into the kitchen. Susan sat and gazed into the leaping flames, her thoughts in a whirl. The cat was well and truly out of the bag now. When they heard about her predicament – shame or no shame – her parents would expect her to return home. No matter how hateful it might be to her father, he would demand that she come home and face the music. If she didn't, he would wash his hands of her for ever.

With a start of surprise she became aware of sounds coming from the kitchen. Rising to her feet, she addressed Graham. 'Will you excuse me, please? I must help Aunt Edith.'

Without waiting for a reply, she joined her aunt. 'Thank God you came in,' Edith greeted her. 'I'm standing here deciding what to do for the best. Do you want to be alone with Graham? Will I get Billy in here on some pretext or other, then you and Graham can have a good old chinwag?'

'No! I know I must try to persuade him to hold his tongue about me, but not at the moment. I'm too mixed up and weepy, and the last thing I want to do is bawl in front of him.'

Reaching for her, Edith held her close. 'You really should go home now, love,' she said gently. 'He will face a barrage of questions when he gets back. You can't expect him to cover up for you.'

'I can try.' She clung tightly to Edith. 'Why, oh why, did he have to come over? I was managing so well. Now what am I going to do?'

'What about trusting him? Eh, love? Tell him the truth. Explain who the father is and why you don't want anybody back home to know. Perhaps then he will cover up for you.'

Drawing away from her, Susan said, 'You don't understand. I can't do that.'

'You're being silly. You know what they say? A problem shared . . .'

Susan shook her head. 'You don't understand.'

'You can say that again. I've noticed you've taken off the wedding ring.'

'I'm wrapped up in so many lies and·half-truths that sometimes I don't know myself what's right·any more. But one thing's for sure – he's not going home with the idea I'm married. If I have to go home eventually, I'll have enough explaining to do, without everybody asking questions about an imaginary husband.'

'Mm, I see what you mean.' Edith nodded to the pots bubbling away on the cooker. 'I've had these simmering for ages. It's almost ready, love. Away and tidy yourself up a bit. We'll work something out between us.'

Graham watched covertly as Donald lavished care and attention on Susan during the very appetising meal Edith had managed to conjure up at such short notice. Later, as they sat conversing by the fire, Donald shared the settee with Susan, murmuring now and then into her ear. Not enough to be intimate, but just enough to make it obvious he cared for her.

The rain continued to pour down and the wind was gathering strength. He would have to make a move soon, but he still needed another private chat with Susan. In a dilemma, he flailed about in his mind for an excuse to be alone with her. It was Edith who gave him the excuse to extend his stay.

'Graham, that's a terrible night to be on the road. Can you not stay overnight? What time is your flight tomorrow?'

'I think you're right, Edith. I'm not too sure of the road back to the airport. I'd be more comfortable driving in daylight and my flight isn't until noon. When I was looking for your house earlier on, I noticed the Traveller's Rest Inn nearby. Perhaps they will have a room.'

'You can stay here!' Edith exclaimed. 'I know it's all a mess at 'the moment, but the settee is comfortable. Or, if you don't fancy sleeping here, I'm sure Donald will put you up in his house.'

All eyes turned on Donald. Not knowing what Susan would want him to say, he met her eyes. She give a slight nod. This way she would be able to see Graham before he left in the morning and beg him not to reveal her secret.

'That's fine by me,' he agreed.

To their surprise, Graham accepted Edith's offer. 'Thanks very much, Donald, but if it's all right with you, I'd be glad to sleep on the settee.' He looked towards Edith. 'If you're sure it's no bother?'

'No bother at all. While you were out in the car with Susan we put up the two beds, and I have left some bedclothes out for the settee.'

Billy rose to his feet. 'In that case I don't see why we can't have a drink. I refrained from offering you one earlier, Graham, because I thought you would be driving back to Newcastle tonight.'

'What about Donald? He'll be driving,' Edith exclaimed.

'He can walk down to the village later on and phone a taxi,' Billy pointed out reasonably, and leaving the room he returned with a bottle of whiskey and some cans of beer. 'Will you get the glasses, love? I've no idea which box they're in, and there's a bottle of wine somewhere for you, and maybe Susan will have a small glass.'

The drink loosened their tongues and the evening passed pleasantly. Susan questioned Graham about all her friends back home and listened in rapture as he related all about the engagement party. 'You should have been there, Susan,' he chastised her gently: 'You were sadly missed. Everybody was asking about you.'

'Ah well, you can see how it is.' Her hand patted her stomach in a futile gesture. Regret made her voice sad.

Graham looked at her and wondered, if she had come home in that condition, would the engagement have taken place? He was far from convinced that he wasn't the father.

At half-past ten, Donald rose to go home. 'It's been a long day and I'm sure you're all tired. I'll go now and let you get to bed. I'll call up tomorrow night after work and see if I can give you a hand with anything.'

'Thanks, Donald. We'll be glad to see you.'

He turned to Graham. 'You're sure you wouldn't prefer a bed?'

'No, thanks all the same, I'll be fine on the settee.'

'I'll run away on then.'

He held Susan's eye and she responded. 'I'll see you out, Donald.'

They opened the front door and gazed out into the torrential rain. 'You'll be soaked. Take my umbrella.'

He smiled wryly. 'I think not. It would be blown inside out in no time.' He moved close and lowered his voice. 'Did I do the right thing back there, letting him think we were a couple?'

'You did the right thing,' she agreed. 'And thank you.'

Before she could move he had his arms around her and, when she looked up startled, his mouth covered hers. She stood passive – after all, it was just a good-night kiss. However, he persisted gently and against her will her lips, as if of their own volition, moved hungrily under his.

Dragging her mouth away, she covered his with her fingers. 'This will never do, Donald. There is absolutely no need to put on an act out here.'

'It's no act! Surely you realise that I care?' She shook her head despairingly and he confessed, 'I have to admit I'm frightened, Susan.'

'Frightened?'

'Yes, there's something about the way that guy looks at you. As if he had a claim on you. Is he a friend of your husband's, by any chance?'

'You're imagining things, and no, he isn't a friend of my husband's. I wish you wouldn't harp on about my husband.'

'I can't help it. And there's nothing wrong with my imagination. He acts too possessive towards you. Don't let him persuade you to go home, sure you won't? Your place is here with us. Now, away in and close the door. It's freezing out here. I'll see you tomorrow night.'

The rain battered against the window panes and the wind was fiercely relentless in its buffeting pursuit of admittance. Tired and weary in body and spirit, Susan tossed and turned, but her mind was too active to let sleep claim her. No matter what direction her thoughts took, she could find no way to persuade Graham to cover up for her. At last, in despair, she left her bed and, donning her dressing gown, quietly descended the bare stairs to the kitchen. She was pouring herself a cup of tea when Graham's voice came to her.

'Is there another cup in that pot?'

Silently, she opened the cupboard door and lifted down a mug. Filling it with tea, she nodded to the sugar bowl and milk jug. 'Help yourself.'

He added a little milk and two spoonfuls of sugar, and then, wrapping his hands gratefully around the mug's warmth, held it to his cheek. She had so far avoided looking directly at him. Now, noting that he was stripped to the waist, she exclaimed in concern, 'You must be freezing. Can I fetch you an old shirt of Billy's?'

'It's okay, I'll be warm enough. I've plenty of blankets in there. I heard someone come down and hoped it was you. We must talk, Susan.'

'I know.' She led the way into the sitting room and he followed her. Without meeting his eyes, she said tentatively, 'Graham, I have a great favour to ask of you.'

His eyes were wary, but he said, 'Fire away.'

'Please don't tell anybody I'm expecting a baby.'

'You're asking the impossible, Susan. I can't do that.'

'Why? You say you came over here on business? Well, tell them you never got down to see me, then they won't question you.'

'But why, Susan? They have to know some time.'

She was sitting hunched over the dying embers of the fire. Now she rose and, placing her cup on the mantelpiece, approached him. 'It's very important to me that no one knows.' She placed a hand on his chest and gazed appealingly at him. 'Please do this for me.'

Placing his own cup on the mantelpiece, he rested his hands on her shoulders and gazed down into her eyes. 'Susan, even if I'm not the father, I'd be willing to take the responsibility and marry you.'

She gazed at him, startled, her mouth gaping slightly. 'Don't be ridiculous! You love Alison.'

Afraid to declare his love for her – after all, it would

look as if he was stringing her sister along, and wasn't he? he derided himself – and at a loss for words, he said weakly, 'I also care for *you*.'

She shook her head in bewilderment. 'You don't know what you're saying, Graham. I don't want your pity.'

'Pity? No, not pity. Far from it! I care deeply for you.' His arms slipped around her and, receiving no resistance, gently drew her close to his body. For the second time that night she found herself in a man's embrace. He clasped her closer still, one hand pressing her cheek against his bare chest, his lips ruffling her hair. Mesmerised, she stood immobile listening to the thudding of his heart; aware of his rising passion. The memory of the pleasure that this man's hands and body could do to her sent a wave of sensual longing through her. Her response to him was swift and sweet, and she savoured it and pressed closer still. Cupping her face gently in his hands, he raised it for a kiss. His lips were more urgent than Donald's and passion heightened swiftly between them. Dismayed at her fiery reaction, she tried to break away, but, weakened by longing, her effort was feeble and went unnoticed, and the kiss intensified.

They were on the settee when she came to her senses. What on earth kind of woman am I, she thought, aghast, that I could go from one man to another and respond so readily? It was because I was hungry for affection, that's why, she consoled herself. With a mighty shove she pushed him away. He rolled off the settee and, arms around his knees, sat gazing up at her, bereft. It had been wonderful holding her close, even with the child between them; it had felt like coming home. It strengthened his resolve. He was now more than ever convinced that the child was his.

'I'm sorry. I got carried away. Again! You have that effect on me, Susan. I do care deeply for you, you know.'

'It's infatuation, and it's wrong, Graham. You're engaged to my sister. She loves you!'

'Does she? I'm not so sure about that. And, as you well know, engagements can be – and often are – broken. You need me more than she does. Alison will survive. You know that as well as I do!' He was on his knees now beside the settee. 'And it's not infatuation. I think you care more than you realise, Susan, or you would never have lost control like that. I didn't force you.'

She turned away in despair. 'I'm aware of that! No need to rub it in. It's because I'm lonely. That's all it is.'

'I don't believe that. You wanted me as much as I wanted you.'

'Graham, I don't understand your reasoning,' she cried in frustration. 'We were never meant for each other. I never noticed you back home. I was besotted by Jim Brady; still am, as a matter of fact. And you know that's the truth. That episode with you was an accident. It should never have happened.'

'But it did happen! If the baby is mine, I want to . . .'

'Hold on a minute!' she curtly interrupted him. 'Get that idea out of your head once and for all. You're not the father.' Crossing her fingers out of sight, she lied, 'Donald is going to make an honest woman of me. I just don't want everybody back home to know until I have a ring on my finger. Then they need never know it was conceived outside matrimony. You know what

Mam and Dad are like. Will you do this for me, Graham? Please?' she pleaded.

'Susan . . . How can I tell your family a pack of lies?'

'At least think about it. Please, Graham. I'd be indebted to you. Come on, get up off that and let's finish our tea.'

They sat each side of the hearth and finished their tea in silence. At last she decided he'd had enough time to think and rose to her feet.

'Well?'

He had been trying to think of a reason to persuade her to go back home with him, and now raised a startled glance. 'Well, what?' he asked, a bewildered frown on his brow.

'Oh, men!' she cried and, forgetful of her sleeping aunt and uncle, she thumped up the stairs.

Edith and Billy left the house very early next morning and a sullen Susan prepared breakfast for Graham. Determined not to make any promises he might later regret, he ate the bacon and eggs in silence.

'There's plenty of hot water if you would like a bath,' she informed him.

'Thanks, but I'll have a quick shower at the hotel.'

'Do you not think it's time you were making a move?'

A glance at his watch brought him to his feet. 'You're right. I'll just visit the bathroom and then I'll be on my merry way.'

Dressed for the road, he stood tentatively in front of her. 'Have you had time to think what you intend doing?' she asked, her eyes beseeching him.

He shook his head. 'No, I'm afraid not. Is there any

way I can get in touch with you and let you know what I decide?'

'The phone is being installed today, but I've no idea what the number will be. Can I call you?'

'If you like. At the office, please.'

He wrote his number on the pad she handed him. 'Tomorrow morning. I'll go to the office in the morning.' He sighed. 'The die will be cast, one way or the other by then.'

'Thank you. And safe journey home.'

A quick hug and he left her standing at the door in tears.

The tears continued to fall as she cleared up the breakfast dishes. In the bathroom she brushed them angrily away. She must get control of her emotions; she had a job to go to, and customers expected a bit of pleasant chitchat. Time enough for tears if Graham blew the whistle on her and she had to return to Belfast.

Chapter Seven

Graham drove carefully up to Newcastle through the heavy mist and rain, struggling with his conscience all the way. He was sorry he had been unable to reassure Susan before he left that morning, but how could he deceive Alison and her parents? There was no way he could see himself telling lies about Susan's welfare. He would never be able to keep up the pretence and would trip himself up in the process. Her silent reproach had been unbearable. Those beautiful, big grey eyes had almost swayed him. However, he had managed to stand firm, although it had pained him to see her looking hurt and tearful. Did she not realise just what she was asking of him?

Suppose he did pretend not to have seen her, and something went wrong at the birth and she died – how could he live with himself? And these things did still happen, in spite of the advancements of medicine. On the other hand, he could see her point of view. If he kept his mouth shut, she could come over later in the year, married to Donald, and no one would dare question the date of their wedding. The very idea of her married to someone else was like a knife turning in his breast. One thing he had learnt from the meeting. It had been brought home to him in no uncertain terms that he could not possibly marry Alison. Not feeling as he did about her sister.

To his dismay, while he was showering, a knock on his door informed him that the flight was delayed due to severe weather conditions at Aldergrove. He was in a dilemma. He couldn't even phone Alison and let her know of the delay! She would be wondering why he didn't ring sooner, but if he did, she would be sure to inquire after Susan and he had yet to decide what to do. What a mess! He was beginning to wish he had never come over here; better to have lived in ignorance than have this decision to make. But it was too late for those kinds of regrets. What could he say to Alison? If only he knew what to do for the best. If he followed his instincts and spoke out, would Susan ever forgive him? He might just drive her into marriage all the quicker. Donald seemed a nice enough guy, but he couldn't bear the idea of her marrying him. Especially if, as he was inclined to believe, the child was his.

It was late afternoon before it was judged safe to take off and, after tedious hours prowling about the airport, he at last boarded the plane, still undecided. As usual, as they neared Aldergrove airport, the pilot told them what kind of weather to expect. They were warned to take care on the roads. Apparently there had been heavy snow during the night in Northern Ireland and the roads were treacherous.

It was dark when they eventually landed and, after picking his luggage up, Graham walked to where his car was parked in the long-stay car park. He cleared the snow from it and placed his suitcase in the boot. A Jaguar, the car was in perfect nick and the engine fired at the first turn of the ignition. Carefully he edged it out of the car park into the slow-moving traffic. As had been forecast, the roads were still treacherous and, to make matters worse, snow was starting to fall again.

His windscreen wipers were soon having trouble in their fight to keep a space clear for his vision. He sat hunched over the steering wheel, peering ahead through the swirling snow, carefully keeping a safe distance from the car in front. The needle never passed the thirty mark, but although impatient to get home, in these atrocious conditions he was not tempted to go any faster. To his astonishment he saw in his side-mirror a Mini car pull out to overtake him. On the brow of a hill? The man must be a lunatic. They both saw the headlights come over the top of the hill at the same time. In an attempt to avoid hitting the oncoming car, the Mini driver came close to the Jaguar, clipping the front wing. Graham swung the car towards the side of the road and automatically slammed on the brakes. The wheels locked and the rear swung sideways, hitting the Mini and sending it spinning into the path of the oncoming car. Then he crashed through a hedge. The trunk of a great oak tree came rushing to meet him through the snow.

Alison sat by her mother's bedside, gently caressing her hand and whispering words of comfort to her. 'The ambulance will be here soon, Mam. You're going to be okay.' Words her mother could not hear.

But was she? Alison was frantic with worry. Was Rachel going to be okay? What had brought this on?

She had heard her parents arguing in their bedroom but had been unable to distinguish what was being said. This was nothing new; her father had a nasty tongue sometimes and seemed to save its sharpness for her mother. Susan had been on the receiving end of it before going off to England, but she had been able to face up to him.

Two hours they had been waiting now. With the heavy snow there had been a pile-up on the motorway and some accidents involving broken limbs on the slippery footpaths, with the result the ambulance service was under acute pressure. When her mother had collapsed, the doctor had diagnosed a stroke. He made her as comfortable as possible before calling the ambulance.

Her father's voice, fraught with anxiety, reached her from where he hovered in the hall. 'They're here, Alison.'

'Thank God.' Poor Dad was out of his mind with worry; was probably blaming himself. What on earth would he do if Mam died?

Descending the stairs, she was in time to hear her father ask the ambulance man, 'Where are you taking her?'

'The Mater.'

'No, you are not! I want her taken to the Royal Victoria Hospital.'

'Look, mister. Sorry and all that, but the doctor was lucky to get her a bed anywhere. Believe me, this weather is causing havoc on the roads and the hospitals are stretched to the limit.'

Seeing her father was about to argue, Alison cried, 'Dad! Mam needs attention *now*. It doesn't matter which hospital she goes to.' With these words she pushed him aside and preceded the ambulance men upstairs.

Still unconscious, Rachel was lifted gently and carried downstairs. Trevor and Alison followed her into the ambulance. At the hospital they waited impatiently while she was put to bed and examined by a doctor. Alison sat huddled in a chair and Trevor paced the floor. At last they were allowed in to see Rachel.

She lay with eyes closed. One side of her face was slightly twisted. Alison reached for her hand, which also lay twisted on the bedclothes, and stroked it gently. Her eyes sought her father's. 'Do you think she'll be all right, Dad?' Her voice broke on a sob.

Trevor gripped his daughter's shoulder tightly. 'I hope so. Oh God, I hope so. How could we manage without her?'

It was some hours later and, having been assured that Rachel was in no immediate danger and that things looked hopeful for a full recovery, they agreed to go home and return next day.

The phone was ringing as they entered the house and Alison rushed to answer it. 'It's sure to be Graham, Dad. I expected him home long ago.'

Trevor watched her eyes widen and her face take on a shocked expression.

'When did this happen? Why didn't you let me know? Of course, I'm sorry. I've been to the hospital as well. My mother was taken into the Mater today. Dad and I are just home from there this very minute. Yes. Yes, of course I'll come right away. Bye. See you soon.'

She dropped the phone in its cradle and ran to her father. His arms held her close. 'What's wrong, Alison?'

'That was Mrs Robson. It's Graham. He's been in a car crash. He's in the Royal.'

'Is he badly hurt?'

'They don't know how bad his injuries are. I'm meeting his parents at the hospital in half a hour. Will you run me over?'

'You should have something to eat first, Alison.'

'I'd rather go now, Dad. Food's the last thing on my mind at the minute.'

He released her gently. 'All right. If that's how you feel, let's go.'

Susan replaced the public phone, installed at the bottom of the market, on its hook and hurried back to the stall with an apologetic look at Vera. This was the third time she had attempted to get in touch with Graham, but to no avail. Apparently he was on holiday and had not returned to work yet. But he had said he'd be in the office today. Perhaps he would be in this afternoon – she could try then, or should she leave a message?

It being Holy Week, Vera had asked her to work the full week. 'I'm sorry about this, Vera, but I did promise to phone and find out how things are.'

'Never worry. We're not exactly rushed off our feet at the moment. Feel free to phone when you get a respite.'

In spite of many more calls, the reply remained the same: Mr Robson had not yet returned from holiday. In despair, Susan asked for his home number, but was refused it on the grounds that the staff were forbidden to give out personal numbers. What was Graham playing at?

That night, on the pretext of letting her family know

their newly acquired telephone number, Susan rang home. One way or the other she had to find out if Graham had blown the whistle on her. Here she also had difficulty making contact. After numerous attempts, she finally got through.

The phone was answered by her sister. 'Where on earth have you been?' Susan asked, highly indignant. 'I've been trying to get hold of you for ages.'

'Susan? Is that you, Susan?'

'Of course it's me. Don't you recognise my voice?'

'I'm sorry. It's just that I didn't expect it to be you. We – Dad and I – were thinking of sending you a telegram.'

'A telegram? What on earth for? What's happened?'

'Mam's had a stroke. She's in the Mater hospital. Please come home, Susan.'

So this was probably the reason why Graham wasn't at the office. He had obviously decided to keep his mouth closed about her. Or . . . dear God, was the bad news he had disclosed the cause of her mother's stroke? No! Alison would not be so calm if that was the case. She would be ranting and raving. Graham had probably decided she had no choice but to come home now; that's why he was keeping quiet. Well, he was wrong! Unless her mother was in immediate danger she would stay put.

'Susan? Susan, are you still there?'

'Yes. I'm still here. Look, I'll ring you back tomorrow and find out how things stand. Okay? We're very busy in the market. I might not be able to get the time off.'

'Susan, how can you?' Alison was aghast. 'Mam's unconscious. We need you here.'

Susan had no intention of being rushed into doing anything hasty. There was too much at stake. 'I'll phone tomorrow night, when you have more news.'

'You should come home in the morning, if you have any decency in you at all. Don't you understand? Mam's had a stroke. You should get the first possible flight over here. How am I supposed to attend two hospitals every day? Eh? Tell me that.'

Alison's voice had risen hysterically. 'Hush, calm down. Two hospitals? I don't understand. Is Dad ill, too?'

'No . . . Oh God, didn't I tell you? Graham's car crashed on the way home from Aldergrove on Monday. He's in the Royal in a critical condition.'

Susan's knees buckled and she sank down on to the nearest chair, unable to believe her ears. 'Graham's injured? How badly?'

'He has concussion and broken ribs. He's unconscious and his spine is damaged, and God knows what else is wrong with him. They won't know for some time whether or not he'll walk again. It's awful watching him lying there. Oh, Susan, I'm going out of my mind with worry. Dad's useless. He blames himself for Mam's condition and he's fit for nothing. You've just got to come home.'

'And is Dad to blame?' Susan asked, an edge to her voice.

'Of course he isn't! They had an argument, but that's nothing new, as you well know. Susan, please . . . please, come home.'

Susan's lips tightened as she digested this information. She knew only too well how arguments went between her parents. Her mother was too soft! She let him bully and jeer at her and ended up in tears. Mam would need her. Whether she liked it or not, she had to go home.

'All right. I'll book a flight tomorrow and let you know what time it arrives. Good night, Alison.'

Alison stared blankly at the receiver as the disengaged tone purred. Susan hadn't even given her a chance to say good night. But then she must be terribly upset. Thank God she was coming home.

Trevor had come into the hall and listened to Alison's side of the conversation. 'Well? What had *she* to say for herself?'

'She's coming home tomorrow.'

Needing time to think before she blurted out her decision to Edith, Susan grabbed her coat and scarf from the rack in the hall and headed for the door.

'I'll be back soon, Aunt Edith,' she called out and was through the door before anyone had a chance to question her.

As she stormed along West Auckland Road anger was uppermost in her mind, followed closely by despair. She was angry that, after all her planning and plotting, the decision whether to go home or stay was being taken out of her hands. Then shame smote her as she pictured her poor mother lying ill in a hospital bed. How bad was she really? There was only one way to find out and that was to go over and see for herself.

And what about Graham? It would be awful if that fine man never walked again. She remembered the strength of his arms, the passion he had aroused in her, and felt like weeping. Life was so unfair. It would be

such a waste if he was crippled. He would need someone strong to support him. Would Alison be able to face
up to marrying a cripple? Her sister could be very selfish at times. Hopefully she would be a comfort to
Graham, but Susan had her doubts.

She walked for a long time, into the countryside. It
was a cold, crisp evening and in the comparative quiet,
calm entered her soul. Whatever lay in front of her had
to be faced up to. It was as simple as that. It wouldn't
be pleasant, but the decision had been taken out of her
hands, so . . . so be it. At last, with a deep sigh, she
turned tail and headed home.

Donald's car was drawing up to the kerb as she
approached the house. Deciding that she may as well
break the bad news to him first, she motioned him to
stay in the car and climbed in beside him.

One look at her face and he was all concern. 'What's
wrong, Susan? You look awful. Are you ill?'

She shook her head. 'Let's go for a short drive. I need
to talk to someone. Clear my brain. Just stop anywhere,
Donald.'

Once out of the built-up area, in the quiet of the
countryside, he drew the car to a standstill on the grass
verge and turned to face her.

'What's happened that has upset you so much?'

'I'm going home tomorrow.'

Reaching across, he gripped her hands. 'You can't! I
won't let you.'

'I've no choice! My mother's ill. She's had a stroke and
she'll need me. Our Alison will be absolutely hopeless
in a sick room.'

His grip tightened. 'Ah, Susan.'

Her eyes were bleak. 'I just hope when she sees this bump,' her gaze rested sadly on her stomach, 'it doesn't finish her off. As for my dad, he might very well show me the door. Then where will I go?'

'What about your husband? Is there any chance of you going back to him?'

He sounded so worried that she wanted to blurt out the truth, but what good would it do at this late stage? Donald might take her confession as encouragement – a sign that she cared for him – and she had enough on her plate at the moment without fending him off.

'There's no chance of that.'

His sigh was heartfelt. 'Thank God for that, at least!'

'Will you take me back now, please? I haven't told Edith yet.'

Edith and Billy were about to get into a taxi when they arrived back at the house. 'We didn't know you were coming up tonight, Donald, or you could have saved us the taxi fare,' Billy exclaimed.

'Jack phoned about fifteen minutes ago,' Edith explained. 'Margaret's in labour, so we're in a hurry down to Greenbank Hospital to lend him support. Will you keep an eye on the dinner, Susan? I put it on hold, not knowing where you'd run off to.' There was a query in the words, but Susan pretended not to notice. No need to upset Edith at the moment with her own bad news. 'Now you're here, you can finish off that pie in the oven. About another half-hour should do it. When it's ready, you have yours and give Donald some. There's plenty to go round. Just stick ours in the oven till we get back. I'll ring as soon as there's any news.'

'Give them my regards.'

'I will, love. Bye for now.'

Susan waved them off and entered the kitchen. A look at the steak-and-kidney pie and she too judged it would be another good half-hour before it was ready. The turnip was already cooked and strained and set to one side. She lit the gas under the potatoes.

Donald was watching her closely as she went about these chores. Her hands were shaking, and every now and then tremors passed through her body. Edging her gently to one side, he lowered the gas under the pots. Then, taking her by the arm, he led her into the living room. Pushing her into one of the armchairs, he poured some whiskey and thrust it into her hand . . . 'Here, drink up.'

She tried to push the glass away. 'I don't want . . .'

'Drink up.' He stood over her until she had drunk some of the whiskey, and then, taking the glass from her, placed it on a nearby coffee table. Pulling her up into his arms, he cradled her against the warmth of his body.

'I dread going home, Donald. My dad will do his nut when he sees me.'

'Then don't go!'

'I have to. I must go and find out just how bad my mother is.' Suddenly Graham entered her mind. 'I forgot to tell you. Graham was involved in a car crash. He's badly hurt.' She felt guilty. Imagine forgetting about Graham.

'Good God! When did this happen?'

'On the way home from the airport. It was snowing heavily at the time.'

'Poor Graham.'

'I know. And poor Alison. She was almost hysterical on the phone, and no wonder, with Mam and Graham both in hospital; she doesn't know whether she's coming or going. I'm afraid I was no comfort to her whatsoever. All I could think about was my own predicament.' He heard her out in silence. Glad of his understanding, she relaxed against him for some moments, then gently pushed herself free. 'I'll finish off the dinner and after we've had ours, perhaps you'll take me somewhere quiet for a drink?' He nodded and she continued, 'Edith will be upset when she hears the news. We'll let her get over the birth of her first grandchild before breaking it to her.'

Leaving a note for Billy and Edith, telling them their whereabouts, they walked down to the Traveller's Rest. In a quiet corner of the lounge Donald gripped her hand tightly. 'Listen, Susan, I've been thinking. How's about I go home with you, and you introduce me as your boyfriend. Then everybody will assume the baby is mine and your secret will be safe.'

She looked at this dear, caring man and wished with all her heart she could take him up on his offer. He would make a good, loving husband and father for some girl, but not for her. No, not for her. He deserved someone better. Still, to go home with him there to support her would be heaven. Squeezing his hand, she pushed temptation to one side. 'Donald, you really are a good man. But can't you see? That would only start up a new pack of lies. Besides, you have your job to consider.'

'It's coming up to Easter, I can easily get a few extra days off.'

'Thanks, Donald. I really appreciate your concern. But it wouldn't work out. If I have to . . . can I pretend we are close friends?'

'You don't have to pretend. We are close. I wish you were divorced, then I could propose to you – you know, put a ring on your finger.' He lifted her left hand and rubbed the ring finger. 'I've noticed you aren't wearing your wedding ring. Could that possibly mean your divorce is through and you're not saying?'

She was saved from answering him by the boisterous entry of someone through the lounge door of the pub. It was Billy. A wide grin on his face, he approached their table, obviously bursting with pride. 'I couldn't wait to tell you. It's a girl. Six pounds six. Our first grandchild. What do you think of that?'

Rising to her feet, Susan gave him a warm hug. 'That's wonderful, Uncle Billy, congratulations. And so quick, too! I'm sure Aunt Edith is thrilled to bits. Is Margaret all right?'

'She's exhausted, but glad it's all over. It wasn't all that quick. Seems she's been in labour since last night, but they knew we would be busy at the market and didn't want to worry us.'

Donald thrust out his hand and Billy gripped it. 'Congratulations, Billy. May you live long to enjoy your granddaughter. What would you like to drink?'

'Thanks, Donald, but if I start drinking now, God knows what time I'll get home and I've an early start in the morning.' He glanced at their almost empty glasses. 'Shall I wait for you? Are you ready to come back to the house?'

'Not yet, Uncle Billy. We have something to talk over.

We'll be up shortly. I'm sure you're hungry. Away and get your dinner before it's all dried up. The pie's delicious.'

'See you later, then.'

Later that evening, when all the good wishes for their little granddaughter were over, Billy fetched a bottle of fine wine. 'I've been saving this for an "occasion". And I think this is a big occasion.'

The wine was duly poured, but as they raised their glasses to toast the baby, Susan felt tears run down her cheeks. Donald put an arm across her shoulders and gave her a hug.

'What on earth's the matter?' Edith cried. 'You haven't started, have you?'

'No! No, God forbid I'd be this early.'

It was Donald who explained. 'I'm afraid Susan has had some bad news.'

A sob in her voice, Susan took over. 'Mam has had a stroke, Aunt Edith. She's in hospital. And Graham crashed his car on the way home from the airport yesterday. He's in a bad way, so you see I have to go home as soon as possible.'

Edith groped for a chair and sat down. 'Oh, my God. I can't take it in. Rachel's a young woman in her mid-forties. What on earth caused it?'

'I don't know.' The tears fell faster and the fear uppermost in Susan's mind rushed into words. 'Perhaps she was worrying about me.'

'Ah, don't say that, Susan. We all worry about our children.' Edith glanced at her husband. 'I'll have to go over with her, Billy.'

'But . . .' Billy stopped short. What he was about to say could not be said in front of Susan. It would sound so callous.

She smiled through her tears. 'It's all right, Uncle Billy. I know you can't do without her at a busy time like this. And Margaret will need her help with the baby.' She turned to Edith. 'Tell you what. You can come over later on in the year, when you're not so busy.'

'If she's very bad you'll let me know, won't you, Susan? I'll come right away, market or no market.'

'I'll phone and let you know how things stand when I find out for myself.'

'Billy.' Edith turned to her husband. 'Could you spare me for a few days when the market is closed after Easter?'

'I'll manage, love. But what about Margaret? Will she not need you?'

'Margaret will be out of the hospital by then. Once back home, she will be okay.'

Billy looked dubious but held his tongue. It was only right that his wife should go over and see for herself how her only sister was. Margaret was a young woman; she would manage. She'd just have to!

Susan booked a very early morning flight and Donald insisted on driving her to the airport. He was grim-faced as he helped her with her luggage. When the flight number was called, he gathered her close. 'Promise you won't do anything foolish.'

'What do you mean, foolish?'

'I don't really know what I mean. But don't think you're alone and be forced into something you don't want. Do you hear me? Remember I'm here if you need me. A phone call will have me on the move in no time.'

'I'll have to go now. Thanks for everything, Donald.' Gently she released her hands and with a final 'thank you' joined the queue heading through the security gate.

How she dreaded the next few hours. Would her father put her out? Her grandparents on her mother's side now lived in Enniskillen; they would be tolerant of her plight, but lived too far away to be of any use to her, while her father's parents were very strait-laced; they would frown on her wantonness, and that she could do without. She would need somewhere in Belfast to stay. Perhaps Ruth would be able to suggest somewhere. But that would mean everybody knowing her business. She would just have to play it by ear.

The flight to Aldergrove was short, but today it seemed shorter still. In no time they were told to fasten their seatbelts and soon they were taxiing along the runway and Susan prepared to meet her father's wrath.

Heart in mouth, she descended the steps from the plane. She hoped Alison would be with her father. What if her sister was unable to come? After all, she had two patients to visit every day. It must be a terrible strain on her. Susan dreaded this first meeting with her father. In her big, loose winter coat her pregnancy was not immediately obvious. She hoped they wouldn't notice until they were in the privacy of their own home.

The minute she entered the arrival lounge, Alison, with a cry of delight, swooped down on her and gripped her close. Her brows gathered together as she hugged her. Drawing back a little, she whispered, 'So it's true! You *are* expecting?'

'Yes. Be careful. I hope Dad doesn't notice until we get home.'

'Ah, Susan. He'll go berserk, so he will.'

'Do you think I don't know that? Why do you think I didn't want to come home in the first place? Hush now. Here he comes.'

Trevor nodded briefly at his eldest daughter and reached for her suitcase. Then, without a word, he led the way out of the lounge and headed for the car park.

Although he held the passenger door open and motioned for Alison to sit in front with him, she declined. 'I'll sit in the back with Susan. Bring her up to date on how things are.'

The car door closed with unnecessary force and Alison grimaced as she climbed in beside Susan.

'How is Mam?'

'She has regained consciousness and recognises us, which is a good sign. They say it's only a minor stroke and expect her to make a complete recovery.'

'Poor Mam. I can't remember her ever being ill before.'

'We popped in to see her before coming here and I told her you were on your way home. She looked so pleased.'

'What about Graham?'

'He has also gained consciousness, but he's in pain and they're keeping him sedated. He has hardly spoken at all. His parents are devastated.'

'And you? How do you feel?'

A tear escaped and ran down Alison's cheek. With a warning glance at the back of her father's head, she whispered, 'Not now. Later. We'll talk later.'

* * *

It was brought home to Susan, on the journey to Belfast, just how different her life had been for the last few months. She would miss Darlington! Over there she had been accepted for what she was; she had been taken at face value. Especially by Donald. He had been a true friend. Here tongues would wag and the finger would be pointed at her. She would be in disgrace.

She quickly left the car and hurried up the steps to her home. The confrontation with her father was imminent.

'I'll make a pot of tea and then we'll go and see Mam.' With these words Alison removed her coat and headed for the kitchen.

Slowly Susan followed her example and, hanging her coat in the cloakroom, went after her. The big clock adorning a prominent place on the wall showed it was still only eleven o'clock in the morning. 'Will we be allowed into the hospital this early?' she queried.

Alison glanced over her shoulder to reply, then swung round in amazement to gaze at her sister's bump. 'Oh, God. You're quite big, aren't you?' she whispered, her dismay apparent. 'I didn't realise . . .' Her voice trailed off. 'Dad will do his nut when he sees you.'

Not wanting to be reminded just how her father would react, Susan repeated tersely, 'Will we be allowed into the hospital this early?'

'We can visit any time we like at the moment. It's the same with Graham; although he's off the critical list now, we can still go in any time. His mother haunts the hospital. She disapproves of me because I don't do likewise. But I had Mam to think about and Dad to look after. I couldn't sit in the Royal all day. Besides, he slept most of the time and it frightened me to see him so helpless. It will be easier now you're here.' Her eyes were still fixed on the bump. 'Is it . . . is it Jim Brady's?'

'No! It's not, and I wish you'd give Jim a rest. I don't want to hear his name mentioned again.'

'When are you due?'

'I'm not sure. End of June or beginning of July.' Susan silently prayed she would go that length of time, but it was more likely to be early May. Hearing footsteps crossing the hall, she whispered warningly, 'Hush. Here's Dad.'

Susan turned to face her father as he followed them into the kitchen, a defiant tilt to her head.

His eyes raked her from head to toe and the look in them said everything. 'I knew it! You're nothing but a dirty wee slut.' He turned on his heel and left the kitchen.

'Oh, Susan, don't look like that. He doesn't really mean what he says half the time. He'll come round.'

Fighting back tears, Susan said, 'Well, that was short and sweet. I'm not really bothered what he says to me. It's those looks of his – he can make you feel so small. And as to him coming round? I don't care whether he does or not. I am only here because of Mam. He can go to hell for all I care.' A tear escaped and she brushed it impatiently away with the back of her hand. 'I suppose I should be glad he didn't order me out of the house. I'll have to watch my p's and q's and not give him any excuse to throw me out.'

At the hospital it was a quiet period. The patients had been prepared for the consultant's visit and the nurses were busy getting the wards ready for the great man's arrival. Rachel shared a small ward with an elderly patient. This woman was asleep, but Rachel lay, eyes fastened on the doorway, awaiting the arrival of her eldest daughter. Her eyes met and clung to Susan's when she at last came through the door.

Sinking to her knees beside the bed, Susan pressed her cheek against her mother's. 'Mam, Mam, I'm so sorry. Is this all my fault?'

Concern clouded Rachel's eyes and she gripped her daughter's hand tightly with her own good one and shook her head.

Glad that her mother's mind seemed unimpaired, and wanting her to know the bad news before her father arrived, Susan whispered, 'Mam, I've some bad news. I'm expecting a baby.'

Rachel's eyes sought Alison's. She understood and answered the unspoken question. 'Yes, Dad knows, and he isn't very happy about it.'

The grip on Susan's hand tightened and Susan cried, 'Don't you worry about me. I can handle Dad. Thank God, you're not as bad as I imagined you'd be. Once we get you home, we'll soon have you on your feet again. And what do you think? Aunt Edith is coming over to visit for a couple of days next week. Also, you are a great-aunt now! Jack's wife had a baby girl yesterday.'

Rachel smiled her crooked smile. It faded as she glanced over her daughter's shoulder. Turning her head to see the cause, Susan saw that her father had entered the room. Ignoring her, he bent over his wife.

'Are you feeling any better today, dear?'

She nodded, her eyes wary.

'No thanks to her!' Trevor continued with a glare at Susan. 'What do you think of all this, eh, Rachel? Our daughter's nothing but a common little slut.'

Rachel's hand clawed agitatedly at the bedclothes and, afraid he would upset her still further, Susan rose quickly to her feet. Kissing Rachel on the cheek, she whispered, 'It's great to see you, Mam. I'll be back later.'

Their next visit was to the Royal Victoria Hospital. Not waiting for their father to come out and give them a lift over, they walked down Crumlin Road to Carlisle Circus and caught a bus into the city centre. From there they got another one up the Falls Road.

During the journey, each remained lost in her own thoughts. It wasn't until they left the bus and were walking down Grosvenor Road that Alison spoke of her anxiety. 'You'll find a change in Graham. He's so thin, he seems to have shrunk, and I'm worried about the results of his X-rays.'

'What if it's bad news, Alison? What will you do?'

'I don't know. I'm terrified at the idea of being married to a cripple.'

'As long as you love him, you'll see it through.'

Panic in her voice, Alison cried, 'That's just it! I don't think I love him enough. What if I can't go through with it? What then, Susan? I'm out of my mind with worry.'

'Whatever you do, don't make any decisions yet,' Susan warned. 'Wait until you know how bad he is. You can't let him down now. That would be cruel. It could even set him back no end. He needs assurance that you'll be there for him.'

Blinking back tears, Alison led the way up some stairs and down a corridor. She motioned towards a doorway. 'He's in here.'

Graham had a small ward to himself. He lay flat on his back, his legs hidden by a blanket-covered cage, his arm in plaster. His bed was close by the high, narrow window and he was gazing blankly out at the heavy grey clouds that obscured the sky. His mind was as leaden as the sky. What was to become of him? His face in repose was very sad; a droop to the lips, thick eyelashes shadowing pale cheeks. He was unaware of them until Alison spoke. 'Look who's here to see you, Graham.'

His head swung slowly in their direction, and a smile lit his gaunt features when he saw Susan. 'You came home after all then?'

'I had no choice. I came because of Mam's illness, Graham.'

'Rachel's ill?' He looked askance at Alison. 'You never told me.'

'You were too ill! This is the first chance I've had. How do you feel, love?'

'Oh, not too bad, considering. I'll survive.'

'I'm surprised your mother isn't here.' Alison peered fearfully around as if expecting Alma Robson to pop up from nowhere.

Guessing the line of her thoughts, Graham smiled. 'She was! I made her go home. I know she means well, but she was driving me round the bend with her fussing.' He smiled at Susan. 'I'm glad you decided to come home, no matter what the reason. Your place is here with your family. You need their support at this time.'

Alison was indignant and showed it. 'You knew she was pregnant and you never said?'

'I never got the chance. Remember, I was out cold most of the time. But as I said to her, and repeat yet again. Your place is here with your family.'

'What about the baby's father? If it's not Jim Brady, who is it and why isn't he here to support her? That's what I'd like to know,' Alison cried.

Graham was quick to get his oar in. 'I'm sure the father would be only too willing to support her, given the chance.'

Avoiding his accusing eye, Susan retorted, 'I wish you'd all mind your own business! All will be revealed in due course.'

'Will it, Susan? The truth and nothing but the truth? We'll see about that. Is Donald with you?' Graham asked diffidently.

'Donald? Who's Donald?'

'A friend of mine,' Susan informed her sister. 'No, Graham. He wanted to come, but I put him off. He sends his regards, and so do Edith and Billy. Jack's wife has had her baby. It's a little girl.'

Relieved that Donald wouldn't be hanging around, Graham said, 'I'm glad to hear that. She seemed a nice girl.'

'Huh! That's a matter of opinion.'

'Graham, you have obviously met all these people, so why did you not ring and tell me about them?'

'That was my fault, Alison. I tried to persuade Graham to keep quiet about this.' She grimaced down at her stomach. 'I don't think I succeeded, though, did I?' She glanced in Graham's direction. 'You were going to blow the whistle on me, weren't you?'

'To be truthful, I really don't know what I would have done, Susan. I was in a dither, and once that tree came rushing at me, I was out for the count and remembered no more.'

'What's the latest news on your back, Graham?'

'I don't know, Alison. They took more X-rays, but they're more likely to tell my parents or you the results, than me. But enough about me. Tell me, what's the matter with Rachel?'

'The same morning you were tangling with that tree, Mam had a stroke. But thankfully, it's only a minor one and she's expected to make a full recovery.'

'Thank God for that.'

'Graham, we came straight from the Mater and I'm here empty-handed,' Susan confessed ruefully. 'Can I bring anything the next time I come to visit you?'

'I've everything I need, Susan. Just bring yourself, I'll be glad to see you.'

He was smiling foolishly at her, unable to hide his delight at her presence. Embarrassed, she glanced at her sister, but Alison seemed unaware of his reaction. Relieved, Susan said, 'It's been a busy morning, Graham. Now I've seen for myself that you're on the road to recovery, I'd better go back to the house and unpack. No need for you to come, Alison; stay and keep Graham company.'

To her dismay, Alison was on her feet in an instant. Susan had not wanted to take her away. Indeed, her intention was to leave them alone. 'I'll come with you. I've some shopping to do. You don't mind if I go now, do you, Graham?'

With a wry smile, Graham agreed, 'Not in the slightest, Alison. You'd be bored stiff sitting here. Goodbye, Susan.'

'I'll come back tomorrow, Graham. I hope you have some good news by then. So long for now.'

'Come with Alison tonight, Susan.'

'Will your parents be here?'

He nodded. 'Probably.'

She smiled wryly. 'I had better not.'

'You will have to meet them sometime, you know,' he said gently. 'After all, one way or another, we are to be related.'

She flashed him a warning look. One way or another! Was he going to make things awkward for her?

Unaware of the undertones, Alison assured him, 'I'll bring her with me tonight, Graham. We'll go to the Mater first to see Mam and then come up here. See you then, love.' She kissed him on the cheek and followed Susan out of the door.

Graham gazed bleakly after them. With each day that passed he was slipping further and further into despair. So far he had been able to hide his misery, but how much longer would he be able to conceal this terror that plagued his mind? Never to walk again? How could he bear it? To be confined to a wheelchair for the rest of his life. How could he tie a healthy young woman to a cripple? Would he now not be able to father a child? His mother was already lamenting the fact that she would probably never have a grandchild. Had the doctors hinted at this, or was she jumping the gun? Whatever the result of the tests, as soon as he was able he would release Alison from her promise to marry him. Even if he should recover completely, he knew he could not now marry Alison. No, it was Susan whose face was forever with him. If he recovered fully he would do all in his power to win her over. *If he recovered fully!* He wasn't very optimistic.

Susan and Alison decided to walk down Grosvenor Road into the town centre. Silence reigned for some time. A covert glance at her sister revealed the worry and tension that Alison had managed to hide so far. Pushing her own troubles to the back of her mind, Susan slipped her arm through Alison's and pressed it close to her side.

'Let's go round to the Ulster Milk Bar and have a cup of their wonderful coffee, and you can tell me all about it.'

Sensing her sister's urgent need to talk, Susan propelled her past the stores with their eye-catching window displays advertising their Easter wares, and straight to the milk bar on the corner of Castle Place. They sat at a secluded table and sipped at the frothy coffee. 'Come on now, tell me what's bothering you,' Susan said gently.

To her dismay, tears gathered in Alison's eyes. She blinked furiously to contain them. 'Oh, Susan, I'm devastated. I can't even sleep at night trying to picture how I'd manage to look after Graham. I'd be hopeless looking after an invalid. Bad enough if Mam was bedridden, although thanks be to God she isn't, but a *man*?'

'Aren't you being a bit premature? Graham might very well make a full recovery.'

'What if he doesn't? Eh? How will I manage?'

'He has money! He would build a house to suit his needs. Nurses would come daily to attend to him until he can look after himself. You're lucky it's only his lower limbs that . . .'

'Lucky? Are you daft?'

'I'm just pointing out that it could be a lot worse. Lots of people confined to wheelchairs live full, active lives.'

'I'd still have to help him to bed. Lie beside him every night. Would he expect to . . .' There was dread in the look she bestowed on her sister. 'You know? Indeed, will he even be able to?'

'You sound very selfish, Alison. Forget about your feelings for a minute and put yourself in his place for a change. You cared enough to become engaged to him so you must have some deep feelings for him.' Struck by a sudden thought, Susan asked fearfully. 'Have you met someone else?'

'No. There's no one in particular. To be truthful, though, before his accident I think Graham had also changed his mind.'

'I don't understand. If you were both in doubt, why get engaged?'

'It was my fault. I insisted. I knew Dad was expecting us to, and with you refusing to come home and him being so annoyed, I didn't want to disappoint him as well. Also . . .' she added shamefacedly, 'I didn't want to lose face where my friends were concerned, and they were all waiting for me to produce a ring. Mind you, Mam had reservations. I know she thought I was too flighty.'

'By the sound of it she was right. Just don't do anything rash, eh? Take each day at a time and wait and see what happens. If he recovers, your worries will be over, and if you're still in the same frame of mind, you can eventually break off your engagement later on. But until then, for goodness sake hold your tongue.'

The sensation that someone was watching her caused Susan to turn her head slowly and scan the café. Jim Brady was on his feet instantly and, leaving the tall stool at the bar, wended his way between the tables towards them.

'I thought I recognised the back of your head, Susan. When did you get home?'

'Hello, Jim. How are you?'

He leant closer. 'All the better for seeing you. You look wonderful! May I join you?' Without waiting for assent, he sat down, sure of his welcome, a delighted grin on his face. 'Hello, Alison.' The greeting was thrown in her direction without wasting a glance on her.

Alison acknowledged him with a nod. She was in a dilemma. Would Susan want her to stay put, or would she prefer to be alone with him? A slight shake of the head warned her not to go.

Jim leant across the table, his eyes devouring Susan's face. 'Are you just home for Easter or for good?' He couldn't believe she was here, sitting facing him.

'I came home because my mother is ill, Jim.'

'Oh, I'm sorry to hear that. So . . . you won't be staying?'

'That depends on circumstances.'

His attention was riveted on Susan, and Alison felt invisible. Perhaps she should go? His next words brought her to her feet. 'Susan, you will never know how I regret that last evening.' This was private! She had no right listening in on this.

'Look, Susan, I've something to do. It's two o'clock. I'll meet you at the bus stop at half past. Okay?' Susan looked at her blankly and Alison repeated, 'Right! Half an hour at the bus stop?'

The words sank in and Susan nodded. 'All right. I'll be there.'

At the door Alison looked back to wave, but Jim was gripping Susan's hands and talking earnestly to her. Neither spared her a glance.

Eyes aglow with happiness, Jim cried, 'I can't believe this is happening. I'm so glad to see you. No one would give me your address. They said you forbade them to. Why would you not let me write to you?' In his happiness the words tumbled out in a rush.

Susan couldn't take in what he was saying. If he had cared so much, why had he rejected her? Glad that the table hid her shape, she said, 'Because there would have been no point. We have nothing to say to each other. Remember, you yourself made that very plain, Jim.'

'I was stupid. A fool. Please don't make me suffer for my stupidity.' He swung his head from side to side at the memory. 'But I thought I had no choice. I couldn't see any future for us, and I didn't want to be wasting the best years of your life. But what do you think?' His eyes shone and his voice shook with excitement as he explained. 'Things have changed. Ma has got herself a fellow. Imagine! I couldn't believe it when she told me. Although why I'm so surprised I don't know. After all, she's still a young woman. She met this man just before Christmas. He's a widower with a comfortable income and they're to be married on Easter Monday. How does that grab you? He's a grand man and he's going to look after the girls' education. I'm free to do as I please.'

Her heart thumped wildly in her breast as she drank in his beloved features. At his words she smiled wanly at him. 'I'm very pleased for you, Jim.'

A puzzled look crossed his face; apprehension dampening his happiness, he stressed, 'Can't you see what this means? We can be married. I've always loved you, Susan. You must surely know that? I haven't changed. There'll never be anyone else for me. I'll marry you anywhere you like.'

A deep sadness engulfed her. If only she hadn't been so foolish, she could now have her heart's desire. 'Jim, you don't understand. It's too late for us. Much too late.'

'Have you met someone else?'

'No.'

'I don't understand. How is it too late?'

'I can't explain. Just take my word for it, it's too late. There's no going back. There's no *us* any more.'

He glanced at his watch and then out the window. 'Look, there's my mother waiting outside. I was here to meet her, but I was early, so I came in for a coffee. I couldn't believe my eyes when I spotted you. Ma's taking me to see her new home. Would you like to meet her? I'll call her in, shall I?'

'No! Please don't.' He had made to rise, but at the panic in her voice he sat slowly down again. He frowned, strong white teeth gnawing at his lower lip for some seconds, then he said softly, 'I understand. You don't want to meet her just yet. But you will see me again, won't you? Promise.'

Glad that he would be leaving the café before her, and wouldn't have to see her waddle out, she promised. 'Give me a ring and I'll meet you sometime next week. Go on. Away you go now.'

Reluctantly he rose to his feet. Still doubtful, he repeated, 'At home? Is it all right to ring you at home?'

'Yes. At home.'

Still uneasy, he repeated, 'You're not just putting me off? You will meet me, won't you?'

'Yes, if you still want me to, I promise to meet you. Look, your mother has spotted you. Go out to her.'

'There's something wrong, Susan. I know there is. Tell me, please.'

'I'll explain everything when I see you again. Okay? Please go.'

With an abrupt 'I'll ring you tomorrow', he left her.

She watched mother and son greet each other and then Jim took his mother's arm and, with a final glance over his shoulder into the café, led her away. Only then did Susan relax; his presence had kept the adrenaline pumping through her body, making her feel more alive than she had for many long months. He still had the power to thrill her. Now, his presence removed, she slumped down into her chair, a mass of quivering nerves.

She had hoped to avoid any contact with Jim while she was at home, but here she was, less than a day in Belfast, and he was one of the first people she bumped into. He obviously didn't believe she was pregnant. Why on earth had she promised to see him again? She couldn't possibly meet him in her condition. What explanation could she give him? She would have to make some excuse when he rang. How she wished things were different and they could take up where they had left off. Lost in thought, she sat on, imagining how it might have been; forgetful that Alison was waiting for her.

Chapter Eight

Alison had arrived at the bus stop at twenty-five past and now, twenty minutes later, she was stamping her feet and swinging her arms in an attempt to keep out the cold. What on earth was keeping Susan? At last, in despair she headed back to the Ulster Milk Bar, praying all the while that her sister wouldn't take a different route to the bus stop and that they'd miss each other. She needn't have worried. Susan was sitting where she had left her, the empty coffee cup in front of her and a look of misery on her face.

She came out of her reverie with a start of surprise when Alison stopped at the table. 'I'm sorry. Is it time to meet you?'

'Well past it.'

Susan started to rise, but Alison with a hand on her shoulder said kindly, 'Sit where you are. I'll get us another coffee.'

The warm liquid brought a little colour to Susan's cheeks and she apologised. 'I'm sorry. I completely forgot about the time.'

'What had Jim Brady to say for himself, and why did he leave you in such a state – and you in your condition? He should be horsewhipped.'

'You've got it all wrong! Thank God he didn't notice my condition.' She patted the table. 'This hid my bump. He was meeting his mother. When she arrived he wanted to introduce her to me, but I managed to put him off by promising to meet him next week.'

'Surely that wasn't enough to upset you?'

'No. He asked me to marry him.'

'Why, that's wonderful news . . .' The look of derision cast in her direction caused Alison to come to an abrupt halt. 'I . . . I thought you loved him!'

'I do. At least I think I do. But so much has happened I don't know whether I'm standing on my head or my heels.'

'But you will accept his proposal?'

'Don't be daft! How can I?'

A bewildered expression crossed Alison's face, then she said slowly, 'So he really isn't the father?' She smiled wryly. 'You know something? I didn't believe you.'

'I know you didn't. But now you know!'

'Then . . . who on earth is the father?'

'Look . . . if it becomes necessary, and only if it becomes necessary, I'll tell you who the father is. Until then you're wasting your breath asking.'

'Well, drink up. We'd better head home. Dad will be starving. Do you know something? That man won't even get up off his backside to make himself a bite to eat. Mam has him spoiled rotten. She waits on him hand and foot.'

'More fool she! Let's get going, then. We wouldn't want him to fade away to a shadow, now would we?'

* * *

Rachel was discharged from hospital on Good Friday, on condition that she rested completely. They had given her a brain scan and were pleased with the results. She was to return to the hospital for therapy twice a week. The stroke was a warning, the doctors tried to instil into her. She was very lucky, they said, that although still a bit shaky on her feet, she could walk. Speech therapy would in time probably give her full recovery of her voice, and meanwhile, although her speech was slurred, she could communicate quite well. The future looked very promising, but she mustn't take any unnecessary chances.

Glad to be home and in her own bed, she silently vowed to obey the doctors' orders to the letter. After all, she was soon to be a grannie and didn't want to miss out on that pleasure. Propped up on pillows, she smiled happily at her eldest daughter. 'I'm so glad you're home, Susan.'

Placing a tray across her mother's knees, Susan replied, 'I'm glad you're coming on so well. Now I want you to eat all your lunch. I'll stay with you in case you need a hand.'

Rachel's left hand was still very weak – almost useless – but as she was right-handed she was able to feed herself if the food was cut into small pieces. However, she soon indicated that she'd had enough and, pleased at the amount she had managed to eat, Susan removed the tray. 'I'll bring us both up a cup of tea and we'll have a nice little chat. I won't be long.'

This was their first time alone together and as they sipped their tea, Rachel attempted to question her.

'Mam, don't strain your voice. I know you must be

worried about me, but don't overdo it. I'll try and fill you in on how things stand. First, Dad acts as if I've been sleeping around, and I want you to know that I haven't. Honestly! I've only ever been with the baby's father.'

Although it was slurred, Susan had no difficulty understanding her mother's next question and answered as honestly as she could. 'No, I won't be marrying him. He's already engaged to someone else. Come on now, you've talked enough. Finish your tea. It's time you were having a nap. We can have another chat later.'

Rachel gripped her arm with her strong hand and managed to say in her slow, indistinct way, 'You'll stay at home, won't you?'

'Mam, that depends on a lot of things. As you can imagine, Dad's not exactly over the moon to have me here in this condition. He never speaks directly to me, and it will probably be worse when the baby comes. So let's just wait and see what happens. Okay?'

'I suppose so. You know, Susan, he can't help how he feels.'

'Oh, can't he?'

'One day I'll explain and you'll understand.' The tablets Rachel had taken with her tea began to take effect and her lids drooped towards sleep. Pulling the bedclothes over her mother's arms, Susan gently touched her cheek. 'Yes, Mam,' she whispered. 'I'll stay if I possibly can, and God help me dad if he annoys you,' she vowed. 'I'll swing for him.'

Susan examined herself in the full-length mirror and sighed. She was dressed for outdoors, but even the loose coat now failed to hide the fact that she was pregnant. Alison sat on the bed watching her.

'You should have warned him on the phone what to expect,' she chided. 'He's bound to get one hell of a shock when he sees you.'

'I tried to put him off, but he wouldn't take no for an answer.'

'He might have, if you'd told him the truth.' Alison tilted her head inquiringly. 'In your heart, are you maybe hoping he will say it doesn't matter and he still wants to marry you?'

'Huh! Chance would be a fine thing.'

'I still can't believe you let this happen to you. I would have thought you'd be the last person to let a man take advantage of you.'

A harsh laugh escaped Susan's lips. 'You'd be surprised how things can happen. Indeed, you would be very surprised.'

Agog with excitement, Alison pleaded, 'Well, tell me! I'm near dead to know! Help me to avoid the pitfalls.'

'That's just it. We can only look out for ourselves, and I failed miserably.'

Jim Brady was a bundle of nerves as he waited for Susan at the corner of Castle Street. When he had phoned on Wednesday she had done her damnedest to put him off. Offering all kind of excuses, from her mother's illness to needing time to herself. Only the threat that he would come to her home had made her relent and agree to meet him. He stood to attention when he saw her hurrying along towards him, dark curls lifting in the breeze and cheeks glowing pink with the cold. She looked wonderful. Absolutely wonderful. How he had missed her!

A frown puckered his brow as she drew closer; she had put on a lot of weight. Shock coursed through him as comprehension dawned. Good God! So it's true. She really is pregnant . . . his Susan.

Susan stopped in front of him and met his accusing gaze.

'Are you . . .' His voice trailed off.

She tossed her head and looked him straight in the eye. 'Yes, I am. Do you want me to pass on by, or are we going to the pictures as planned?'

At a loss for words, he simply looked her up and down in amazement. After bearing his scrutiny for some moments, she turned and started to retrace her steps. He was instantly beside her.

'I say . . . I'm sorry. You took me by surprise. Why didn't you tell me?'

She shrugged. 'Perhaps I wanted to see the shocked expression on your face when you finally got the message.' Her lips tightened and her eyes scorned him. 'I certainly wasn't disappointed.'

He took her gently by the arm and drew her to a standstill. 'If we're going to the Ritz, we're going in the wrong direction.'

'Are you sure you want to go?' She was at a loss now over what to do. 'I honestly never thought of the position I was placing you in. Suppose someone sees us and gets the wrong idea. What then?'

He shrugged. 'Too bad! I never was one to care what anyone thought, so let's get going or we'll miss the start of the big picture.' A grin showed his even white teeth.

'Now that would annoy me,' he assured her, and led her along Donegall Place in the direction of the Ritz.

She could feel him giving her covert glances but was unable to think of anything to say. His futile attempts at conversation petered out for lack of support and the journey across town was conducted in comparative silence.

They joined the queue that was already wending its way into the auditorium and were soon settled in their seats. In the darkness of the cinema he was very aware of the bulk of her sitting next to him. He remembered how slim she had been not so long ago. How he had slipped his arm around her and held her as close as the arm of the plush-covered seats allowed, revelling in the passion she could so easily arouse in him. Now he had no inclination at all to hold her. This attitude dismayed him. Was he being fickle? After all, this was the same girl he had courted and asked to marry him. The girl he still dreamt of every night. But, to be fair on himself, she *was* carrying another man's child, and by the look of her it must have happened shortly after she had offered herself to him. Had he had a lucky escape? Was she really that promiscuous?

Susan could imagine the drift of his thoughts and tears smarted her eyes for times lost. What had she done so wrong in her short life that one lapse had left her pregnant and her life in ruins? One mistake – one! – had ruined everything. In the dark, warm intimacy she longed for him to hold her hand, to show he still had some feelings for her, but he sat rigid, as if afraid of accidentally touching her arm.

The film seemed to go on for ever, but at last to her

intense relief it was over and they left the cinema. March was certainly living up to its reputation and going out like a lion, with sharp winds penetrating through to the very bone. Shivering, she pulled her coat closer around her and on the pavement faced Jim with a bright smile. 'Thank you for a lovely evening. I was glad to get away from the house for a few hours. As you can imagine, my dad is far from happy with me. To be truthful, I'm surprised he allowed me to stay at home.'

'He probably knows when he's on to a good thing. He knows you will look after your mother hand and foot.' He took her hand. 'Susan, I apologise for hounding you the way I did. I had no right! But I had no idea. Oh, I was told you might be pregnant . . . Indeed, Alison even accused me of being the father, but I couldn't take it in. I thought there must surely be some mistake. I just couldn't believe it was true.' He paused as if the enormity of it still confounded him. Then he asked tentatively, 'Do I know him? Have you set a date for the wedding?'

Ignoring the first question, she said, 'There isn't going to be a wedding. At least, not for me. Just think, Jim. I'll be the lowest of the low, an unmarried mother. Alison and Graham got engaged at Christmas, but they haven't set the date yet, what with Graham being in hospital.' She watched him digest these words. Which would catch his attention most? Graham's plight or her own? Graham won.

'Graham's in hospital?'

'Yes, he was involved in a car crash last Monday. I believe the weather was terrible here last weekend.'

'It was indeed. A lot of heavy snow! The road conditions were atrocious.'

'Well, Graham was over in England last week . . .'

'Visiting you?' he interrupted suspiciously.

Fear squeezed her heart. Hadn't she known Jim was no fool? 'No. Why would he visit me? As it happens, he was over in Newcastle on business and, on his return on Monday, on the journey home from Aldergrove his car was caught up in a collision with two other cars. I don't know the ins and outs of it, just that Graham and another man were badly injured and a man and woman were killed.'

'Thank God Graham survived.'

'Indeed! He was very lucky. The car was a write-off.'

'That beautiful Jag? That must have hurt more than the injuries.'

'Wrong again. They don't know if he'll ever walk again, let alone drive. He must be in a terrible state, but he's putting a brave face on it. Look, I'll have to go, Jim. Remember, times have changed.' Her smile was strained as she admitted, 'I'm in no condition to be running for the last bus.'

'Ah.' He sighed audibly. 'Those were the days, eh, Susan? I prayed they'd last for ever.'

'So did I,' she echoed sadly. 'So did I.'

'I'll walk to the bus stop with you.' Reluctantly she fell into step beside him, loath to prolong the agony, wanting to lick her wounds. After a short silence he continued, 'Do you know something? I also got promotion at work. I thought life was smiling on me for a change. I pictured us living happily ever after, but now this . . .' He gestured vaguely at her bump, then cried in anguish, 'Why, Susan? Why the big rush? Could you not have waited a while? Was that act so important to you? I thought you cared for *me!* I can't believe you rushed to someone else right away. By the look of you, you can't have waited any length of time.'

Hearing the hurt and bewilderment in his voice, she cried, 'I can't explain, Jim. It wasn't like you think. You wouldn't want to hear how foolish I've been.'

'Try me.'

She shook her head. 'Least said, soonest mended.'

'Why won't this guy marry you?'

'He has offered, but he isn't free. There would be a terrible scandal and I couldn't do that to my parents. It's bad enough as it is.'

They were nearing the bus stop, where a queue had formed, and he drew her to one side. 'A married man? I don't believe it!' he cried incredulously. 'You rushed into the arms of a married man? You would never be that stupid.'

Afraid he might put two and two together and guess the truth, she nodded. It was best if he thought a married man was responsible. 'These things happen, Jim.'

Jim pondered on her words. It saddened him to think that she must have been seeing this other man when she was dating him. There was no other explanation. 'And if he wasn't married, would you marry him?' he queried.

'If he was free I might, for the sake of the child. Look, here's my bus. Thank you once again for a lovely evening.'

Against his better judgement he gripped her arm. 'I'll come with you.'

'That won't be necessary,' she cried in alarm. Tears were threatening and she was determined that he wouldn't see her break down. He ignored her plea.

'I want to. To tell you the truth, I'm finding it hard to make the break.'

He paid the fares, but when he would have hustled her upstairs, she declined, saying the climb would be too much for her, and chose a seat near the front of the bus where private conversation would be impossible. He was finding it hard to make the break! These words warmed her heart and helped her get a grip on her shaky emotions.

At the corner of the street, in the shadow of the hedges, she cringed with shame when she recalled their last encounter there. She felt degraded. How could she have been so wanton? So shameless! But she had loved him. Was so sure her love was returned, she had thrown caution to the wind. Was he remembering too, and thinking she had loose morals? How could he think anything else, with her a short time later the size of a house! In a voice choked with emotion she said, 'Thanks again for a lovely evening, Jim. Now I really must go. Me dad will be wondering where I am.'

Once again a hand on her arm delayed her. 'Susan, we can't just part like this. I feel at a loss. Can't we remain friends? See each other at least now and again?'

Her heart raced wildly and her thoughts went into overdrive. If they could remain friends, then once the baby was born and she was slim and attractive again, perhaps she would be able to win him back. Was there hope for her yet? Common sense prevailed. It would be foolish for them to see each other again and give food for idle gossip. It wouldn't be fair to him.

She shook her head. 'It wouldn't work out, Jim. Who knows, perhaps once the baby is born and the dust has settled, we might run into each other again. Until then, it's better if we don't see each other. So please, Jim, let me go. I've enough on my plate without worrying about you popping up.'

Taking her face between his hands, he gazed into the beautiful, haunted eyes and whispered, 'I wish with all my heart that things were different. I can't believe we have no future, Susan, but I see what you mean. At the moment I would be an embarrassment to you. Perhaps later.' A gentle kiss was pressed on the trembling lips and he left her gazing tearfully after him.

Cold and windy though it was, Jim decided to walk home. His mind was in turmoil. If only he hadn't rejected her all those months ago, they would be in a position to marry now. But he had rejected her advances, and curtly. He would be the first to admit that it could have been handled better. But he had been afraid of taking advantage of her! Still, someone else had done just that, and obviously without taking precautions. If she had really cared for him, could she have turned for solace to someone else so quickly? No! She must have known this other man. They must have had some kind of a relationship going, whilst she was seeing him. There was no other excuse for her actions.

Did he still hope to marry her? He was still very much attracted to her, but did he want her for his wife now? He was too confused to tell. After the baby was born perhaps they could take up where they had left off. But . . . what about the baby?

* * *

To cool her emotions, Susan went for a walk along the silent avenues. The rain from the wet hedges blew on her face and she welcomed the coldness. She felt in a fever. Oh, Jim, Jim, what have I done? she lamented.

It was late when at last she quietly entered the house. Her father came out from the lounge and faced her. 'Where have you been?'

She wanted to tell him to mind his own business, but bit on her tongue, afraid to agitate him. 'I was at the pictures.'

'Till this time of night?' he cried in disbelief. 'Who with?'

This time her tongue would not be stilled. 'That's none of your business.'

His lips tightened and his nostrils flared. 'What you do while living under my roof is very much my business. For a start, you'll keep decent hours! You've disgraced us enough already.'

Again her tongue would not be stilled. Stretching her arms wide, she stuck out her stomach even further. 'Look at me, Dad! What do you think I was doing in my condition?'

'Huh! I couldn't make a guess. If I live to be a very old man, I'll never understand you. You're not in the least like your sister.'

The temper drained from her. She couldn't afford to antagonise her father any further. 'You're right,' she agreed sadly. After all, she was unlikely to be out late again, so why get her dad's hump up. 'I was out with an old friend. It was a one-off. It won't happen again. Is Mam asleep?'

'I doubt it! She's lying up there worrying about you.'

'Oh, I am sorry. I'll go up and say good night. Set her mind at rest.' She climbed the stairs, glad to have avoided a confrontation.

The worried look on her mother's face saddened Susan. She must watch her step where her father was concerned and not cause her mother any more distress. 'Can I get you anything, Mam?'

'No. Now I know you're home I can take my tablets and maybe get some sleep.'

'Mam, you're exhausted. You mustn't wait up for me.'

'I wouldn't normally, but your father has been acting a bit strange lately and I don't want you two at each other's throats.' Rachel struggled to raise herself on an elbow.

'Here, let me give you a hand.' Placing an arm gently around her shoulders, Susan tenderly raised her mother up sufficiently to put the tablets in her mouth and assisted her in washing them down with a drink of water sitting ready on the bedside table. Then, fluffing the pillows, she settled Rachel down for the night. 'Good night, love. See you in the morning.'

'Susan.' Rachel beckoned her down and, when she leant over, with her good hand gently touched her daughter's hair. 'Susan, I'm worried. You never talk about the baby – you do want it, don't you?'

'Of course I do.' Susan was nonplussed, but realised that her mother had hit the nail on the head. She never mentioned the baby. Indeed, she tried not to think of it. Time enough for that when it was born. She shrugged negatively. 'I suppose it's because I've had an easy pregnancy and so many other things to worry about.' She smiled reassuringly at her mother. 'I have made some plans, you know. I've a drawer full of baby equipment over in Darlington. I suppose, now I'm home, I don't want to rub me dad's nose in it.'

'You should see the doctor, Susan. After Easter you really would need to get booked into the hospital.'

'I'm already booked into Greenbank Hospital over in Darlington. After all, I don't know whether I'll be here for the birth.'

Alarmed now, Rachel cried, 'But you said you'd stay here.'

'I know, Mam. I know! Please don't get upset. I have to play things by ear. You know yourself that Dad's not too happy about me living here in my condition. It's bad enough now, but what will it be like when the baby comes along, eh? When the neighbours have an excuse to stop me in the street and inquire after its health and try to find out who the father is. If it proves too much hassle for Dad, I'll have to go. I wouldn't wish that on either of you. Aunt Edith really does make me feel at home, so you needn't worry. I'd be happy staying with her.'

'While there's breath in my body, you will always be welcome here. It is your home too, you know! I'll have a quiet word with your father.'

Hearing footsteps on the stairs, Susan whispered, 'But not tonight, Mam. Promise you'll leave it for a while. It will be better for all concerned.'

Seeing the wisdom of her words Rachel nodded her head. 'All right. Now away to bed.'

'Good night, Mam.'

Susan was never to learn what her mother said to her

father, but things took a sudden change for the better. Trevor didn't go out of his way to speak to her, but neither did he ignore her completely or constantly find fault and the atmosphere over Easter weekend was quite amicable.

Her mother insisted on talking about the baby. Lamenting the fact that she was unable to knit for her first grandchild, she phoned and arranged for an exclusive shop in town to send her a catalogue of all their baby clothes and nursery ware. From this many clothes were selected, until Susan cried out in despair that one baby would be unable to use so many outfits. A beautiful cradle was also ordered, and Susan gasped when she saw what it would cost and tried to talk her mother out of buying it, but in vain. Nothing would be too good for her first grandchild.

Names were often discussed and there was much laughter as some outlandish ones were suggested and then discarded. Susan was at last able to think of the baby she carried. It was great not to worry too much about the future; not with her mother behind her. Her only real worry now about having the baby in Belfast was . . . who it would look like.

To Susan's amazement, her father made no outward objections to all the plans her mother was making, and she began to look to the future. Should she ring her boss, Mr Kennedy, and find out how things stood at work, and whether there would still be a position for her after the baby was born? She decided it would be worth a try. It would be nice if she had a job to go back to.

* * *

Edith's arrival on the Tuesday of Easter week brought great excitement to the household. Ideally, Susan would have accompanied her father to the airport to meet her, but Trevor made it obvious that he would prefer Alison's company, so Susan remained at home to keep her mother company. However, the minute the car stopped in the driveway, Susan was there gripping her aunt close.

'It's wonderful to see you again, Aunt Edith. I've missed you so much. How's everyone back in Darlington?'

'And I've missed you too, love. Everybody's fine! They all send their regards.'

'Look here!' Trevor said tersely. 'I'll put Edith's case up in the spare room. Don't keep her standing in the cold, Susan, or your mother will be out here, too.'

Tired of waiting, Rachel had indeed ventured to the door. Edith quickly climbed the steps to the house and the sisters eyed each other at arm's length. 'You look great,' Edith exclaimed. 'I expected an invalid.'

'I'm coming along fine, except for this.' Rachel motioned towards her left arm.

'I'm glad to see you looking so well.'

'You look wonderful too, Edith. And how's that big husband of yours?' Rachel had always had a soft spot for Billy Devine. He had the ability to make her laugh – something Trevor seldom did.

'The same as usual. Wouldn't hurt a fly. By the way,' Trevor was descending the stairs and, with a twinkle in her eye, Edith informed him, 'Billy sends his best regards, Trevor.'

Knowing full well that she was taking the mickey, he

ignored her remark and growled, 'Will you all come inside and close that door before we freeze to death'.

They moved into the hallway and, closing the front door, Susan edged them towards the lounge. 'Let's get you two settled. You can have a long natter while Alison and I make some lunch.'

Sitting on the settee, Rachel said fondly, 'Susan tells me you have a stall in the market, Edith.'

'Yes, and we're doing very well, I'm happy to say.'

'I'm glad for you. Billy has the right disposition for dealing directly with the public. So do you, for that matter.'

'I was a bit doubtful at first, you know. Didn't want to risk using our savings, but Billy talked me round to his way of thinking. Now we're doing so well I'm glad he did. I'm sure Susan told you we've bought a new house?' Edith lifted an eyebrow and, receiving a nod of confirmation, continued, 'Well, we have also just last week invested in a brand-new van. What do you think of that?'

'That's wonderful news, Edith.' It was Trevor who answered her. 'About time Billy gave you some kind of a decent life.'

Greatly affronted, Edith cried, 'I beg your pardon? I'll have you know that I've never wanted for anything in all the years I've been with Billy Devine.'

'Are you trying to tell me you don't regret running off with a married man? Cutting yourself off from family and friends. Huh! For a Catholic into the bargain?'

'I can honestly put my hand on my heart and say I've never had a day's regret.'

'Hmm! Are you still living in sin, then?'

'Oh, don't be so old-fashioned! Besides, it's none of your business, Trevor Cummings, but for your information, Billy and I got married years ago, after the death of his wife.'

'Poor woman. You probably sent her to an early grave.'

In spite of herself Edith's voice rose shrilly. 'No. She died of cancer. We had nothing whatsoever to do with it,' she informed her brother-in-law with a glare. He was going too far!

During this discourse Rachel had tried to make her voice heard, but in vain. Trevor seemed determined to insult Edith. Catching sight of her sister's anguished look, Edith joined her on the settee.

'Don't pay any attention to us, Rachel. You know what we're like when we get together. It's just a bit of banter, isn't it, Trevor?'

Her brother-in-law had the grace to look ashamed as he became aware of his wife's distress. 'Of course it is! Don't upset yourself, love. Would you like a glass of sherry before your lunch, Edith?'

'That would be lovely, Trevor. How is your business doing in the present climate?'

'Not bad. Not bad at all.'

To the relief of all, Alison put her head round the door and announced that lunch was ready. In the dining room the tension eased as the conversation became general. Relieved, Rachel inquired about Edith's new granddaughter.

'She's a wee beaut, so she is. They have named her Angela because she looks like a wee angel.'

'Hah! There speaks the doting grandmother,' Trevor said drily.

'Just you wait and see. You'll be exactly the same when Susan's baby is born,' Edith assured him.

'I don't think so. It will be a wee bastard, after all. So how could anyone in their right mind be proud of that?'

Shock struck them all dumb. Susan kept her head bent over her plate to hide the tears that threatened to fall. She willed someone to say something. Anything to break the tension. It was her mother who broke the ghastly silence.

'Well, I for one will be more than proud to welcome my grandchild and it will live here in this house with its mother, as long as Susan wishes to stay,' she cried with a defiant look in her husband's direction.

Edith waited until Trevor looked up, and then, catching his eye, she upbraided him. 'Do you know something, Trevor? You are a nasty bully. You miss out on so much with your false puritan ways. Because we know you're not as good as you make out to be, don't we? You were a Jack-the-lad in your younger days. Weren't you?'

Colour flooded his face and a sneer twisted his mouth. 'No matter what you may say, this child is a bastard. There's no getting away from that!' Crumpling his napkin into a ball, he threw it on his plate and, pushing his chair away from the table, left the room.

Later that day, when Rachel was having her afternoon nap, Edith expressed the desire to take a trip into town to see all the changes that had taken place since her last visit. Declining a lift from Trevor, who was in the doghouse since his remarks at lunchtime, she and Susan headed for the bus stop. Alison accompanied them on her way to visit Graham.

'I was sorry to hear about Graham's accident, Alison. Coming on top of your mother's stroke, it must have been very traumatic.'

'It was, Aunt Edith. I can assure you, I didn't know whether I was on my head or my heels. You met Graham, didn't you?'

'Yes, and I found him a very nice young man.'

'Oh, yes, he's that all right,' Alison agreed with her. 'Every parents' idea of a perfect son-in-law. But I'm a bit annoyed with him. He never even phoned to say he had managed to get down to see Susan.'

'I think he got a bit of a shock when he did see her,' Edith said soothingly.

'No matter! We're engaged to be married. He should have let me know.'

They had reached the bottom of Castle Street, where Alison was leaving them to catch a bus up the Falls Road to the hospital.

'Will it be all right if I come up to see Graham, after we've had a walk round town? Would I be intruding?' Edith asked tentatively.

'Of course you won't be intruding. I'm sure he'll be glad to see you. Will you come too, Susan?'

'All right. You can wait with Graham and come home with us.'

'Not if his mother's there, I won't,' Alison said with a grimace. 'If she's there I won't stay long.'

They left her and headed for the big stores. As they went from shop to shop Edith tried to lift the gloom that had enveloped her niece since her father's remarks at the dining table. 'Don't pay any attention to your dad, Susan. He won't be able to resist the baby once it's born.

Nobody can resist a wee baby. Especially when it's their own flesh and blood.'

'Still, he's right in what he says. It's what everyone else will be saying behind my back. It's not fair to the baby, either, not having its father's name.'

'If it's going to worry you, love, come back to Darlington with me. Mind you, there will be those over there who will call it a bastard as well, you know. My daughter-in-law, for one, although I don't think you will worry about the likes of her.'

'I certainly won't. Has she been taking my name in vain then?'

'Only if Donald is there. She tries to make him admit he's the father and says he should make a honest woman of you before the child is born. She's just winding him up. However, she had better watch her step. I think our Jack's getting a bit fed up with the way she taunts Donald.'

'And what has Donald to say about all this?'

'He says he would be only too willing to marry you, but you won't have him.'

'Dear Donald, he's too kind for his own good.'

'He really cares about you, Susan.'

'I know he does. But we're just very good friends, that's all. We're not in love with each other.'

'Sometimes that's the best basis for a happy marriage.'

'Not for me and Donald. It wouldn't be fair to him. Does Margaret see much of him?'

'Not to my knowledge. But then I'd be the last to know, wouldn't I? Besides, where would she get the time, what with the baby and all?'

'She's still very fond of him, you know.'

'Yes, I'm aware of that. But thank God we both know where his interest lies. You could do a lot worse, Susan. He's more than fond of you.' Receiving no answer, she continued, 'I wish our Jack would put his foot down. Billy's forever warning me to keep my nose out of their affairs, but I don't want to see Jack hurt again.'

Susan wasn't too sure where Donald's affections lay. Without her as a buffer against Margaret's wiles, who knew what might happen? But she couldn't add to Edith's worries by mentioning this to her. 'I'm sure Margaret realises how very lucky she is to have you for a mother-in-law. She won't want to do anything to alienate you.'

'I can only do my best. Margaret isn't an easy person to get close to.' Recalling Alison's remarks about Graham's mother, Edith asked, 'Does Alison not get on with her future mother-in-law?'

'Well, I don't really know. I think it's them being confined in the hospital ward together for long periods. Alison has got a couple of weeks compassionate leave off work on account of Mam, so it will probably be easier when she returns to work. Graham's mother expects too much of her. He's an only child and his mother haunts the hospital. They're bound to get on each other's nerves.'

'It must be awful for his parents watching him lying there. How's he coming on?'

'I'm not sure. He seems to be progressing favourably, but they still don't know whether or not he'll walk. I'm sure he's worried sick, but you wouldn't think it to look at him. He puts a brave face on it.'

* * *

Later that afternoon it was with apprehension that Edith followed Susan into the small private ward now occupied by Graham at the Royal Victoria Hospital. The idea of a strong man like Graham lying helpless tugged at her heart strings. She was also wary of meeting his mother. The poor woman must be devastated. She could imagine how she would feel if it was her Jack. What did one say to his mother? A quick glance showed that Graham's mother wasn't present and she breathed a sigh of relief. But neither was Alison.

Clasping her hand between both of his, Graham cried, 'Edith! It's kind of you to visit me, and you only here for a few days.'

'It's a pleasure to see you, Graham. Billy and Donald sent their best wishes. Where's Alison?'

'She's nipped down to the hospital shop to get me a box of tissues. She won't be long.'

'Where is this shop? I wanted to buy you something in town, but Susan said you would be annoyed if I did. But I really would like to.' She flashed her niece a reproachful look. 'Is there anything in particular that you'd like, Graham?'

'I wouldn't mind a bottle of mineral water, Edith, if it's not too much bother.'

'Of course, it's no bother at all.'

'The shop is on the next floor up. You can't miss it, so I'm told. It's near the head of the stairs.'

'No doubt I'll find it. Is there anything else you need?'

'No, thank you.'

Edith quickly left the room and Susan looked at Graham in amazement.

'I know! I know what you're thinking, and normally

I wouldn't ask anyone to trek to the shop to buy me anything, let alone a visitor from England. But this is a God-sent opportunity. I couldn't let it pass. Do you realise I haven't had one minute alone with you since you came home? Please come closer, I want to talk to you.'

Slowly she approached the bed. Before she was aware of his intention, he reached for her hand and gripped it tightly. 'Susan, I can't stop thinking about you.'

'Graham, this will never do! You're upset. You don't know what you're saying. It's because you're lying here with all different wild ideas running through your mind. Ideas that have no foundation whatsoever.' She struggled to release her hand, but he clung on desperately.

'How come I don't believe you?'

'Well, it's the truth! And I've done all I can to convince you.'

'In vain, I'm afraid. I still don't believe you.'

At her wits' end, her voice rose shrilly. 'Nevertheless, it's the truth.'

'Susan, I should never have got engaged to Alison. It's you I want. Even if the child isn't mine.'

Angry now, she snapped, 'Let go of my hand. They'll be back any minute.'

Her tone of voice brought him to his senses and he relaxed his grip. 'I'll let go if you promise not to run away.'

Hearing footsteps approaching she whispered, 'I promise.'

Reluctantly he let go of her hand and she quickly put some distance between them.

The footsteps passed and he said softly, 'Alison told

me Jim Brady has asked you to marry him.' She nodded, but didn't bother to inform him that that was before Jim knew about the baby. He continued, 'Susan, please don't do anything rash. I feel so helpless lying here. I beg God every day to grant me the power of my legs that I might be in a position to pursue you.'

Alarmed, Susan whispered furiously, 'Graham, stop this nonsense! You have no right to speak like this.'

'Are you going to marry Jim?'

'What I do is none of your business. You're engaged to Alison! I don't understand why you're acting like this. But no, I'm not going to marry Jim, if it makes you feel any better.'

'Please don't be angry with me, Susan. I can't bear it when you're cross.'

'Well then, behave yourself!'

To appease her, he quickly changed the subject. 'What do you think? Dad has had his study turned into a bedroom for me. He's arranged for a therapist and a nurse to come in every day, so that I can go home. I'll be glad to get away from this place. They're letting me out on Saturday. You'll visit me at home, won't you?'

Beside herself with worry, she hissed, 'Not if you behave like this, I won't.'

'I promise to be good.'

'I wish I could believe you. Hush,' she warned as he opened his mouth to answer her. 'Here they are now.'

Edith came in first with a huge bunch of flowers and a bottle of mineral water.

Embarrassed, Graham chastised her. 'Edith, they're beautiful, but you shouldn't be spending all your money on me.'

'I'm glad to.' She looked vaguely around the room. 'What will I do with them?'

'I'll show you where the sluice room is,' Alison volunteered, and to Susan's dismay she was once more left alone with Graham.

'Susan, come a bit closer. I don't mean to annoy you, but I feel so helpless lying here.'

Remaining where she was, she said, 'Graham, keep your voice down, for goodness sake. How can you go on like this? You're not being fair to Alison. She's desperately worried about you.'

'I know she is! And I feel such a traitor. I've offered her her freedom, you know, but she won't hear tell of it. So what else can I do? As for keeping my voice down . . . How can I, when you insist on standing away over there? Come a bit closer.'

'If you're sure you don't love Alison, and it's not just this silly obsession you have, then make her listen to reason.'

'Can I tell her the truth? You know . . . about the baby? That would make her sit up and take notice.'

'Don't you start that nonsense again!' she cried, tears of frustration filling her eyes.

'Start what again?' Alison asked as she entered the room holding the flowers. Placing the vase on the bedside locker, she looked inquiringly at her sister. 'Mm?'

Susan's heart was in her mouth. Edith was eyeing her with a quizzical expression on her face. Just what had been said? What had they heard? She couldn't think straight. Graham came to her rescue.

'She was chastising me. I was going on and on about

hating this place. You will all be glad to hear they are letting me go home on Saturday. I think they're glad to get rid of me and my constant whining.'

Diverted, and with a gasp of relief Alison sat on the side of the bed. 'Why, that's wonderful news, Graham, so it is. But how will you manage?'

'Dad has had the study converted to suit my needs and the hospital is lending me a wheelchair. I want to buy one of my own, but they insist I wait a while. They seem to think it might not be necessary.'

'That's good news, Graham. It means they think you might be able to walk again. Oh, I can't tell you how pleased I am to hear this.'

He hit the top of his thigh with a fist. 'I find it hard to believe, with these two useless things lying here. But enough of that! Time will tell.' He gave all his attention to Edith. 'Susan tells me you have some snaps of Jack's baby. Did you bring them along to show me?'

Susan had told him no such thing and stood silent, amazed at his ingenuity.

'I sure did.' With a pleased smile Edith plunged into her large handbag. Alison leant forward to adjust the collar of Graham's pyjama coat, and while the two women were so occupied Susan took the opportunity to give Graham a warning look above Alison's head. He just gave her a cheeky wink in return. Obviously he thought he had the upper hand.

It was raining heavily when they left the hospital and they decided to take a taxi home. Whilst waiting for it to arrive, Susan was very aware of the speculative looks her aunt was giving her. She had been afraid that Alison might ask embarrassing questions, but was thankful her sister apparently had not picked up on Graham's remarks. Of Edith she was not so sure, but to her relief nothing was mentioned.

It dismayed her the attitude Graham was taking. He seemed determined to make her admit the truth. She wished with all her heart that she had not visited the hospital today. By her foolishness, she appeared to have set things in motion and who knew where they would end? It appeared that Graham was willing to throw discretion to the winds, and she couldn't take a chance. It looked as if she would have to return to Darlington. If she didn't, Graham would keep on trying to wear her down and a scandal would be unavoidable. It was her mother's health that worried her most. She must break the news gently to her. Rachel was doing so well; was avidly looking forward to the birth of her grandchild. What if it set her back or caused another stroke? It didn't bear thinking about! To have that on her conscience would be unbearable. But wouldn't hearing that the baby was Graham's be an even greater shock?

Susan decided to have a word with her father, get him to explain to her mother that she must return to England with her aunt. He would be glad to be shot of her. If it meant her leaving the house, she could depend on him to win his wife round to their way of thinking. It was difficult to get him alone, but at last the opportunity presented itself. After dinner that night, declaring, to no one in particular, that he must examine the summer house and see what would be required to make it habitable for the summer months, he left the house and headed for the bottom of the garden.

Waiting until the others were otherwise occupied, Susan saw her chance and, leaving the house via the French windows, stealthily made her way down to the summer house.

Trevor had examined the roof of the structure; no sign of leaks. It appeared in good condition and, with a pleased smile, he turned his attention to the windows. If he was surprised that Susan came seeking him, he managed to conceal it admirably.

He frowned in her direction and said, 'I think we'll get away with a lick of paint this year.'

'That's good news.'

There was silence for some moments, as he continued his examination. At last, satisfied that he was right and only very minor repairs were required, he smiled wryly at her. 'Come over here and sit down.' When she had obeyed, he said, 'I imagine you have a reason for following me out here?'

'Yes, Dad. I've a favour to ask of you.'

'Yes?'

'I would like to return to England with Aunt Edith, but I'm afraid of upsetting Mam. Will you break it gently to her?'

To her amazement his face flooded with colour and appeared to swell with anger. He actually stuttered when at last he attempted to answer her. 'Ho-w d-dare you! How dare you waltz over here and worm your way back into this house. Against my better judgement I allowed you to stay, and now you throw my goodness in my face. Why are you going back to England? I suppose it was that Edith who's persuaded you to leave here?'

Unable to hide her amazement, Susan cried, 'Aunt

Edith has nothing to do with my decision. She doesn't even know I'm talking to you.'

'Why then? Eh? Why are you going back with her?'

Completely confused at his reaction, Susan said, 'I thought you'd be glad to see me go.'

'Oh, don't think for one moment I wouldn't be glad to see the back of you! It's your mother I'm thinking of. This news could cause a relapse and she might not be so lucky next time.'

'I know. That's what's worrying me,' she said mournfully. 'That's why I want you to break the news to her.'

'Well then, if you're really worried, don't go. Stay! Have the baby here. Give her something to look forward to. She hasn't looked this happy since you left the house last year. Besides, the damage is done. Everybody now knows you're about to give birth to a bastard, so why go now?'

'Don't, Dad, there's no need to use that word. It sounds so awful.'

'I'm sorry, Susan, but you know I believe in calling a spade a spade, and I'm only speaking the truth. What I'm trying to say is, there's no reason for you to leave now that the cat is well and truly out of the bag.'

'I'd love to stay, Dad. But it's a bit complicated.'

'I suppose the father has shown up and is threatening to make himself known. Eh, is that the situation?'

Surprised at his intuition, she agreed, 'Something like that.'

Once again her father astonished her. Leaning across, he gripped her hand. 'Susan . . . can you not marry this guy before the baby is born and give it his name? You're not being fair to the child.'

'I can't! You don't understand. The scandal would be terrible.'

'Who the hell is he, then?' He turned aside in disgust and growled, 'A Taig, no doubt.'

'No, actually you're wrong. He's a Protestant.'

'What's the problem, then? Will he not have you?'

'He's not free,' she whispered.

'Ah, I see. A married man. How could you, Susan? How could you be so bloody stupid?'

Susan sat with head bowed, unable to defend herself. After a short pause, he continued, 'Ah, Susan, Susan. It breaks my heart to see you in this situation. You've spoilt your whole life, so you have.' To her great amazement he put his arm around her shoulders in a comforting gesture. 'Well, we will just have to make the best of it. But you must stay here. Your mother's welfare must come first. Okay?'

'Okay. If you think I should.'

'I think you should.'

Edith spent the next two days at Enniskillen visiting her parents. Thus she was able to curb her curiosity during the remainder of her stay and it was the morning that she was returning to England when, on the pretext of borrowing a pen, she cornered her niece in her bedroom. Susan looked at her, surprised at her request; there were pens lying about all over the place. Reaching for one on her dresser, she turned to find Edith closing the bedroom door and standing with her back against it.

'I want a few minutes alone with you, girl,' she declared. 'I've a question to ask you, and I want the truth, mind.' She lowered her voice before continuing. 'Is Graham the father of your child?'

Sinking slowly down on to the bed, Susan whispered, 'How on earth did you guess?'

'I heard! That day at the hospital I heard enough to make me suspicious. And now you have just confirmed those suspicions. How on earth Alison didn't twig that day, I'll never know. She is very naive, unless of course she doesn't want to face the truth. What on earth are you playing at, girl?'

'You've got to believe me, Aunt Edith. I wasn't carrying on with him! It's like I told you. It just happened on the spur of the moment.' She patted her stomach. 'And this is the result.'

'Does Graham know the truth, or . . .?'

'No. He guesses. When me da suggested that maybe I'd run away to England because I was pregnant, he put two and two together and came over to see for himself. But I convinced him he was wrong. At least, I put doubts in his mind. If I'm lucky enough to go over my time, he might be convinced I met someone over there and got carried away. That's why I didn't want to come home. I wanted to be in a position to lie, if necessary, about the baby's age. I don't want to cause a scandal. Especially now, with Mam being the way she is.'

'Would you not be better coming home with me then?'

'It's me mam. She's so looking forward to the birth of her grandchild. It's all she talks about. If I go she might have a relapse. And . . . believe it or not, me da wants me to stay.'

Edith's eyes stretched in surprise and she cried, 'Wonders will never cease.'

Susan grimaced and shrugged her shoulders. 'I know. I was surprised, too.'

'Is Graham in love with you?'

'At the moment he thinks he is. He's all mixed up.'

'Surely he won't marry Alison, in these circumstances?'

'He tried to break off the engagement, but she won't hear tell of it. To be truthful, she as good as admitted she doesn't love him, but she is probably feeling noble and feels she must stick by him.'

'Dear God, it's a vicious circle, isn't it?'

'You can say that again.'

'Well look, you know I'll always be there for you. You can come over to Billy and me any time. No matter what the circumstances. Remember that!'

They were in each other's arms, their tears mingling. 'Thanks, Aunt Edith. I don't know how I'd have managed without you these past months. I don't deserve your help.'

Embarrassed at all this emotion, Edith gave her a gentle push. 'Ah, get away with you. I must go and finish packing. Take care, love. And remember I'm there for you.'

Chapter Nine

Susan clasped her precious bundle close to her breast as she carried it up the two staircases to the attic rooms. Once she was certain she was staying at home for the birth, she had asked her parents' permission to be allowed to decorate these two rooms for herself and the baby. She was pleased with the result. Her bedroom was painted in cool shades of grey and lemon with a suite, consisting of wardrobe, chest of drawers and long elegant headboard, of pale ash toning in nicely with matching bedding and curtains. The nursery was decorated in various shades of blue, ranging from powder blue to a ceiling so brilliant it lit up the whole room. Watercolours of nursery rhymes adorned the walls and an assortment of soft cuddly toys were scattered about on shelves. She paused on the threshold, drinking in all this beauty, and couldn't believe how fortunate she was.

Rays of May sunlight seeped through the slats of the venetian blinds on the wide dormer window, giving the nursery a misty fairytale aura. Her shoulders heaved as she sighed with contentment. Crossing the soft carpeted floor, she laid her son in the brand-new cot presented by his grandfather (much to Susan's surprise). He was beautiful; the loveliest wee baby in the whole wide world. She laughed softly at the very idea. Didn't all mothers think that? Still, right from the beginning, except for the slight blue bruises on his temple where the doctor had delivered him with the aid of forceps, his features had been perfect; pale and interesting, with great big, dark eyes. Not in the least bit red and wrinkled like other babies she had seen.

Intently she examined these features now, but could see nothing of Graham – or herself for that matter – in him. Her mother was convinced he was the picture of Trevor and had hinted that he would be ever so pleased if the baby was named after him, but Susan shied away from this idea. Trevor was not one of her favourite names. Born a fortnight ago today, her son had been two weeks early, throwing all her conniving plans into disarray. She who had hoped to last until at least the middle of June had produced a baby two weeks premature. Her father had been sceptical, saying that the baby looked big enough to him and asking if there was any particular reason why she was claiming it was premature? Noticing her mother's discomfiture, Susan had indignantly cried, 'No, why should I? What reason would I have to claim he's premature if he was fullterm? Not that two weeks makes much difference.'

'In some cases it can make a lot of difference. I've heard tell some women do that to pull the wool over their husband's eyes. But then, you don't have a husband to deceive.' His shoulders were slumped as he left the room.

Susan glanced at her mother in bewilderment and

was amazed to see red spots of embarrassment in her cheeks. 'What was all that about?'

'Just a wee bee your father has in his bonnet.'

Digesting these words, Susan suddenly reached a conclusion. 'Was I premature?'

Rachel sighed. 'I suppose you may as well know. You're old enough now not to agitate your father by mentioning it. Yes, you were a couple of months premature.'

Again Susan took her time answering, sifting through the muddled thoughts racing through her mind. 'But . . . why would he be agitated?' Her eyes widened as comprehension dawned. 'Are you trying to tell me Dad thinks I'm not his daughter?'

'Just sometimes . . . Silly things, like baby William coming early, for instance, trigger off these doubts.'

Mesmerised, Susan gazed at her mother long and earnestly. It explained so many things. Why sometimes, out of the blue, her father suddenly seemed to dislike her without any justification. Why every now and again he was nasty to his wife.

'Is he . . .' She paused in confusion. This was delicate ground she was treading. She had no right to probe. Or did she?

With a harsh laugh Rachel anticipated her question. 'What do you think? It's mainly because you don't look like any of us. Never have! But that's not unusual in a family. Most times he believes, but every now and again I don't know what gets into him, but the doubts creep back. It can be very upsetting, I can tell you.'

'I'll bet it can. And you've had to put up with this torture all these years?'

'Mm, what else could I do?'

Going to her, Susan gave her a hug. 'Ah, Mam. Poor Mam.' It was only much later she realised her mother had neither confirmed nor denied whether Trevor was indeed her father.

Now that the child was born, Susan had time to reflect on the past months. She was amazed at the extreme lengths to which she had gone to hide her pregnancy. Disrupting everyone by running over to Aunt Edith, instead of facing the music at home. But if she had stayed, wouldn't Graham have guessed right from the beginning and let the cat out of the bag? Then all hell would have broken loose. Her father would most definitely have kicked her out on to the street for her betrayal of her sister, no matter what her mother said. Alison would have hated the very sight of her, and what about Graham? Would he have been so eager to claim responsibility at that time?

No, she had done the right thing and the father's name had remained her little secret. So long as it stayed that way, she didn't care about anything else. This was a wonderful feeling of release. What did it matter what people thought of her? Sticks and stones and all that! To think she had been daft enough to worry about the likes of that! All that mattered to her now was the welfare of this beautiful wee baby. Her son! She would work her fingers to the bone for him. If anybody got too nosy, she would tell them to take a running jump. No one could take this wonderful gift away from her. The only blot on the landscape at the moment was that a father's name would not appear on her son's birth certificate.

The doctor who had delivered him had been called Dr William McCartney and so, recalling her mother's hints and to avoid any arguments, Susan had said the baby would be christened William after this young doctor, who had relieved her of pain and delivered her son safely into the world. William was also her grandfather's name and so her mother wasn't too disappointed. William Cummings. She turned her mind away from what his name should really be, and the inheritance she was denying her child. In the circumstances, that couldn't be helped!

A shadow fell across the cot and she glanced over her shoulder as her mother joined her.

'Mam, I was so engrossed in William I didn't hear you come up. You shouldn't have climbed all those stairs,' Susan chastised her.

'I just wanted another little peek at him. I don't know why you want to keep him away up here, anyway,' Rachel said grumpily.

'Ah, Mam, you've been nursing him for the last half-hour. You still have to be careful, you know, not to over-tire yourself,' Susan reproached her. 'And you know very well why I chose these rooms – it's because I want him to disturb the household as little as possible. I'm very grateful that you and Dad are accepting him and I don't want any regrets. Up here, if he's restless at night you'll hardly hear him.'

Rachel hung over the cot admiring the pink chubby cheeks fanned by thick dark lashes. 'He's beautiful,' she enthused. 'Look at those eyelashes. And you know something, Susan, we don't expect him to be quiet for ever. It wouldn't be natural.'

'I know, but remember, Dad and Alison still have to get up early for work, so they need a good night's sleep. The less bother he is, the better for all concerned.'

'I suppose you're right.'

'Don't worry, you'll see plenty of him. We're still in the same house after all, not miles away, and he will be downstairs most of the day. You'll soon be sick of him.'

'No, never,' Rachel vowed softly. For some seconds they stood in silence and paid the baby homage. Then Rachel whispered, 'He doesn't look in the least premature. Are you sure he is? Perhaps you got your dates wrong?'

Susan shook her head sadly. 'He's premature all right. No mistake about it. I only wish he had hung on until sometime in June.'

'Why?'

'So that certain people wouldn't get the wrong idea.'

'Who? Who might get the wrong idea? Oh, Susan, why must you be so secretive?'

'Because you wouldn't understand.'

'You'd be surprised. Try me. You know I can hold my tongue when required. I've had plenty of practice over the years. You'd be amazed at the things I can't let pass my lips. I know a lot of secrets.'

Susan laughed. 'Well, this is one secret you won't have to keep, because I'm not telling you anything.'

'Ah, well, if that's how you feel. While he's sleeping, you take a wee rest. You'll need to build up your strength. After all, he is only two weeks old, and I agree with you, there's bound to be some sleepless nights ahead. So rest every chance you get. I'm so excited, Susan. I can't believe he's so beautiful. By the way . . .

Graham said he would be over tonight to see him.'

Knowing the dismay that she felt must be written all over her face, Susan bent and fussed over the cot, adjusting the blankets, to hide it. 'Is he well enough?' she asked.

'I forgot, you haven't seen him lately, sure you haven't?' This realization made Rachel frown. 'How come?'

'Oh, you know how it is. I felt large and ungainly and didn't fancy seeing his parents in my condition in case they thought I was flaunting myself. You know what it's like? I didn't want to start their tongues wagging.'

'The Robsons? Never! They're too refined for that kind of nonsense.'

Susan laughed aloud. 'Now, Mam, you know there isn't a woman on earth who can resist a bit of scandal, and I'm sure Alma Robson is no exception.'

Her mother smiled and said, 'I suppose you're right.'

'You can take my word for it.'

'Mm. Well, Graham is doing remarkably well and can get about on sticks now. It's like a small miracle. They say it was the shock to his nervous system that caused the paralysis, but in time he should make a complete recovery. But you must already know all this. You've surely heard us talking. You'll see tonight for yourself how well he's doing. Now take a lie down, and I'll keep an eye on William.'

'I don't feel in the least sleepy, Mam. I'm too tensed up. I'll connect the intercom and then come down and sort out those wonderful presents that arrived this morning from Darlington. People are too kind! Even Donald has spent far too much on William.'

'Okay, if that's what you want. I'll put the kettle on, and we'll have a nice wee cup of tea first.'

Feverishly now, Susan re-examined the features of her son. As far as she could see, there was nothing to cause anyone to exclaim and say, 'Doesn't he resemble Graham?' But then what was she thinking of? Why should they? They wouldn't be looking for signs of Graham in him. After all, he was engaged to her sister. Except for Graham, that is! He would certainly be looking to see if there was any family resemblance.

Entering her own room, she stood by the wide window and looked down on the garden. The borders were a riot of colour with May flowers, and the smooth, green lawn, mowed in opposing stripes, swept down to the newly painted summer house. Their house was set in beautiful surroundings. She could hear birds twittering in the hedgerows and a red squirrel scampered along the lower branches of the oak tree. Was she going to be forced to leave all this splendour and go back to Darlington just to avoid Graham?

She hadn't seen Graham since that fatal afternoon at the hospital; had made all kinds of excuses to avoid going visiting with Alison. She could imagine how he must resent her attitude towards him, but she had felt unable to face any more interrogations. Now tonight he was coming to see the baby. God grant that he would be reasonable and wouldn't make things awkward for her. Wouldn't make insinuations in front of the family. This was no bump any more! It was living flesh and blood; beautiful flesh and blood. Graham would be more determined than ever to lay claim to him. Given the chance, she must convince him once and for all that he wasn't William's father. But how? He was so stubborn.

Everything had been working better than she had dared hope. Her father was more affable towards her since the birth, and positively doted on his grandson, bastard or not. Her boss was saying that her position would be open for her so long as she didn't delay too long. The knowledge that she would be in a position to give her son a good life had gladdened her heart. At last she could see some kind of a future before her. A light at the end of the tunnel, so to say. She wasn't going to let Graham spoil her dream!

Her mother's voice reached her, bringing her out of her reverie. A last look at the sleeping child and she descended the stairs and joined Rachel in the kitchen.

'What kept you? Is William all right?'

'Yes. He's in a sound sleep. I just couldn't tear myself away.'

'I don't blame you. We'll have to start advertising for someone to help me look after him when you return to work.'

'Mam, there's plenty of time yet. I've another few months before I go back,' Susan exclaimed, a laugh in her voice.

'You may well laugh, girl, but not just anybody will do, you know. For a start they'll have to have good references, and those ones won't be hanging around waiting for you to advertise for their services. So the sooner we start looking, the better.'

'I suppose you're right,' Susan readily agreed. 'But let's wait another few weeks, eh, love?'

* * *

Susan stood beside her mother and looked from the window of the lounge as Graham's father assisted him from the car, watched anxiously from the back seat by his mother. He looked much better. In the six weeks or so since she had last seen him, he had put some weight back on and his face had lost its grey pallor. His father made to help him up the steps to the house, but Graham shrugged him aside and manoeuvred up the steps slowly and deliberately, but quite capably on his own, with the aid of his walking sticks. Alison stood waiting at the door for him, patiently curbing the urge to go and put a supporting arm around his waist to help him. His father declined her invitation for him and his wife to come inside. They were going to a business dinner, he explained, and would pick Graham up at about eleven o'clock.

Slipping an arm through Graham's, Alison tenderly led him slowly into the lounge. Trevor was on his feet at once and, offering his hand to Graham, exclaimed, 'Welcome, son. It's great to see you back on your feet again.'

When Alison would have guided him to the nearest chair, Graham resisted her efforts and, shrugging off her hand, walked slowly and obviously in some pain across the lounge to where Rachel and Susan hovered over the cradle. The reproachful look he cast in Susan's direction as he leant painfully over to gaze on the baby was not lost on Alison and she was quick to come to her sister's defence. 'Now, Graham, as I explained, Susan has been very busy, and with that little rascal coming early, she hadn't time to visit you. Anyway, she's under no obligation to you. So don't start giving off to her.'

Her words were lost on him. He was gazing avidly at the sleeping child. With his free hand he gently touched the soft pink cheek. 'He's beautiful.' He raised his head and met Susan's eyes. 'Congratulations, Susan.'

The emotion that gripped Susan as Graham looked on his son for the first time took her unawares. The enormity of what she was doing suddenly struck her and a great ball of pain gathered in her throat, threatening to choke her. She was depriving this man of the right to his son and heir. But what else could she do? It was out of her hands. If only things had been different, she silently lamented. If only Alison wasn't involved. But her sister must at all costs be shielded from their terrible betrayal. Swallowing the lump in her throat with difficulty, she mumbled, 'Thank you.'

Something of the anguish she was feeling must have been reflected in her face because his eyes clung to hers pleadingly. The silence stretched and, to her relief, Alison broke it. 'We all agree with you on that score, Graham. He is beautiful,' she said fondly. She put a hand gently on his arm to help him towards the settee. When he would have resisted, she insisted softly, 'Shouldn't you sit down, Graham? You mustn't overdo it. You know what the doctors said about doing too much too soon. Why take unnecessary risks?'

He waved her away. 'I'm all right.' His eyes once again met Susan's and saw the anguish there. With a sigh he allowed Alison to help him.

Once settled in an upright posture with cushions supporting his back, he said, 'You're looking well, Susan.'

'I feel great. Just tire easily. You're looking much better

yourself. It's wonderful to see you walking again. Can I get you a cup of tea or coffee? Or a drink?'

'A cup of coffee would be most welcome, thank you. And yes, I should be running about in no time.'

'That's if you do as you're told,' Alison warned. 'I'll make the coffee,' she volunteered and left the room.

'While you and Graham catch up on each other's gossip, I'll prepare some snacks – nothing too heavy,' Rachel said. 'Trevor, will you give me a hand and then see to the drinks for later on?'

He followed his wife from the room and Graham gave a rueful smile. It couldn't have worked out better if he had planned it. He and Susan were alone.

He patted the settee. 'Come and talk to me, Susan.'

Afraid to antagonise him, she reluctantly crossed the room and sat down.

His eyes scanned her face, taking in the bloom of luminous skin, the shining hair and worried eyes. No one would ever guess she had just had a child. He longed to reach for her but managed to control the impulse. 'Motherhood certainly agrees with you, Susan.'

'Thank you. Graham, I apologise for not visiting you at home but you wouldn't listen to reason and you're so wrong. So *very* wrong,' she stressed. 'I didn't want you giving everybody the wrong idea.'

'Am I wrong, Susan? Do you know what I think? I think you were afraid to come, in case the truth would leak out.' He lowered his voice. 'Am I right?'

She closed her eyes tightly and raised her face towards the ceiling in frustration. 'No, you're not right! Oh, Graham, how can I ever convince you?'

He reached out and covered her hand with his. An involuntary thrill ran through her and her eyes shot open wide in amazement. Jerking her hand away, she whispered, 'Don't do that!'

A triumphant smile lit his face. 'You see? You have feelings for me after all.'

'That's where you're wrong! To me, you're just my sister's fiancé. Nothing else!'

He spread his hands wide. 'Seeing is believing.'

Desperate now, she beseeched him. 'Don't do this, Graham. Don't spoil things for me. Don't drive me across the water again. Much as I like Darlington, I want to stay here.'

Fear plucked at his heart. Would she really run away again? Surely not. Still, he couldn't resist the temptation to find out the truth. He had to take the chance of maybe driving her away for ever. 'Susan, I can't just stand by and watch you ruin all our lives.'

A tear spilled over and ran down her cheek. Brushing it angrily away with the back of her hand, she whispered, 'You're being very foolish. My sister is a lovely girl. You should be delighted that she's going to marry you.'

'I know that! And God knows I wouldn't hurt her for the world, but it's you I want. Why can't you listen to reason? We could get this all sorted out. The scandal would be short-lived and then we could get on with our lives.'

Despair gripped her. So much for convincing him. He was as obstinate as ever. And could she blame him? To her great relief, William started to whimper and, glad of the respite, she rose eagerly to her feet. Graham reached out and gripped her arm. 'This isn't over, Susan. Not by any means. We must talk.'

Knocking his hand aside, she crossed the floor and lifted the child. 'He's hungry. I'll have to give him a feed.' Without another glance in Graham's direction she left the room.

As William nuzzled contentedly at her breast, Susan tried to analyse the effect Graham's touch had had on her. She had been amazed at the thrill of pleasure that had shot through her; had been taken completely unaware and been unable to hide her reaction from him. He had been surprised too, and how he had gloated! God, what a mess she was in. She would have to do something drastic, to put a stop to all this nonsense. She would confess that she intended seeing Jim Brady again, with marriage in mind. Not that she really thought marriage would be in his mind, but one never knew.

A large bouquet had been delivered to the hospital the day after William's birth, from Jim. How he had known, Susan had yet to find out. Probably through Ruth, whom she had been meeting every Wednesday in town on her day off from the supermarket where she worked.

Ruth had proved a staunch friend. As soon as she heard that Susan was back home she had phoned to make arrangements to see her. They met in the city centre and at that first meeting, when Ruth saw her condition, she wept openly in sympathy with her.

'Ah, Susan, Susan, my heart goes out to you.'

Susan shrugged and admitted, 'I've been foolish, but I'm not the first and I certainly won't be the last.'

'Ah, Susan. And to think I believed Jim Brady when

he denied all knowledge of it,' she cried indignantly. 'I really did!'

Susan shook her head in frustration. 'For heaven's sake don't you start.'

Ruth's eyes scanned her face, 'You mean it isn't his?'

'That's exactly what I mean.'

Susan had watched different expressions flit across her friend's face and could imagine the trend that her thoughts would take. She would be thinking back over the time after Jim and she had split up; would be trying to fit another face in the frame. Unsuccessfully, of course.

At last Ruth smiled ruefully. 'But . . . I don't understand. Who else was there?' she asked in confusion.

'Believe me, you wouldn't want to know,' Susan assured her.

'You're wrong! I do want to know. Every single gory detail.'

Linking her arm through her friend's, Susan said firmly, 'Well, you're not going to. So let's find somewhere we can have a coffee and you can tell me all your gossip.'

Ruth brought her up to date on all their friends and acquaintances. She shyly admitted that she was in love with Dougie and was hoping he felt the same and would ask her to marry him. A twinge of jealousy plucked at Susan's heartstrings at this news. Why had she been so foolish?

During the following weeks Ruth had tried to wheedle the father's name out of her friend, but eventually gave up in despair. She kept Susan up to date on all the gossip and casually mentioned that Jim Brady was on the scene again, but didn't seem interested in any one particular girl. Eventually Susan confided in her that Jim had asked her to marry him. Round-eyed with wonder, Ruth hung breathlessly on her every word. Susan told her of running into Jim in the Ulster Milk Bar, and of how the table had hidden her condition and he had proposed marriage. She made a big joke of how, later, when she gave into his pleas and met him to go to the pictures, he apparently changed his mind when he saw her big bump.

Ruth listened in silence to all these disclosures, tears in her eyes at the futility of it all. 'Ah, Susan. I'm so sorry. Why on earth didn't he ask you to marry him before?'

'There were family problems.' She shrugged. 'Or, who knows, perhaps it wasn't meant to be.'

They sat sipping their coffee, pursuing their own lines of thought, and then Ruth asked, 'How did your dad take all this?'

'Can't you imagine?'

With a grimace, Ruth said, 'Yes, I think so, but obviously he's come round or you wouldn't still be living at home. How is he now?'

'Not too bad. He thinks I've made a complete mess of my life.'

'You can't blame him for that,' Ruth said softly. 'Mm?'

'I know. You're right of course. Still, these things happen, but life goes on. I'll work something out.' Suddenly she bent over, clasping her stomach in obvious pain. 'Ouch! That was a funny sensation,' she gasped.

Ruth panicked. Rising to her feet, she shrieked, 'What will I do, Susan? Shall I call an ambulance?'

'Believe me, Ruth, even if it is starting, it will be a long time before anything really happens. Besides, I'm not due yet, I've weeks to go. Sit down and finish your coffee.'

Reluctantly Ruth sat down, anxious eyes fixed on Susan's face. When another pain gripped her friend and could not be ignored, she was on her feet again instantly. 'No buts about it! I'm phoning for the ambulance now.'

'No! Hold on a minute.' When the pain had subsided, digging into her handbag Susan brought out an address book. 'Here, look for my dad's office number and ring him. He'll come and fetch me.'

Fifteen minutes later she was on her way to the Royal Maternity Hospital. Ten long, torturous hours later, her son was delivered into the world.

Alone in the lounge, Graham rested his head back against the top of the settee and, closing his eyes, tried to recapture and put a name to the expression he'd caught on Susan's face as he looked at the baby. Pity? Compassion? But it had been too fleeting and had eluded him. However, her reaction to his touch hadn't been so elusive. It had been both startling and satisfying, and had filled him with great joy. Surely she must care to react like that?

Rachel wheeled a trolley into the room and Alison followed her, carrying a tray laden with a large coffee pot, teapot, sugar bowl and milk jug. Seeing the expression on his face she asked, 'What are you looking so pleased about?'

'Am I?'

'Yes. You're like the proverbial Cheshire cat with that

big, foolish grin on your face. I suppose it's William. He has that effect on everybody. One does tend to smile inanely when he's about.' She peered into the empty cradle. 'Where is he?'

'He was crying . . .'

'Never,' Alison interrupted him teasingly. 'Our William never cries.'

His grin widened. 'Well, whinging a little then, and Susan took him away to feed him.'

'Mm, yes, maybe a little whinge.' She poured him a cup of coffee and smiled tenderly as she handed it to him. Rachel asked him what he would like from the selection on the trolley.

'He really is a lovely baby, isn't he?' she said as she put the sandwich he asked for on a plate and handed it to him.

Graham readily agreed and did a bit of probing. 'Doesn't anyone know who the father is?' he asked tentatively.

Regretfully Rachel shook her head. 'No. Whoever he is, he's a fool. He doesn't know what he's missing.'

'Perhaps he doesn't know he has a son?' Graham suggested.

'Well, all I can say is, he must be very stupid not to have guessed.'

'Perhaps Susan is deliberately keeping him in the dark?'

Rachel's brows rose. 'Why would she, if he was free and willing to give the child his name? If he's married he definitely won't want to know.'

'Hush, she's coming back!' Alison hissed.

Susan was aware, by the sudden silence and embarrassed glances in her direction when she entered the room, that she had been the topic of conversation. Serenely she crossed the floor and gently laid the sleeping child in his cradle, then turned to face them all. 'That coffee smells delicious. May I have a cup, please Mam?' Thus setting them all at ease.

Alison helped herself from the trolley and settled next to Graham on the settee. 'Just think, Graham, if you hadn't been in that accident, we would be sitting here planning our wedding for next month.'

'Oh, if only you were. It would be great to be up to one's neck in wedding plans,' Rachel cried. 'Have you thought of another date yet?'

'No!' Graham said abruptly. 'It won't be this year, I fear. Not the state my legs are in.'

The look that Alison turned on him was full of amazement. 'But we talked about a Christmas wedding,' she cried. 'Your mam has her heart set on it.'

'I know! But to be truthful, I'd like to walk down the aisle completely cured. Not shuffling along on a stick. Surely you can't blame me for that? There's no big hurry, is there, Alison?'

Alison's shrug was dismissive. 'So long as you can convince your mother how you feel, it will be all right with me. But please get her off my back, Graham. She thinks I'm the one holding back.' With a disgruntled look on her face she pushed herself free of the settee and, with a muttered excuse, left the room.

Graham gazed after her in bewilderment and made futile efforts to rise.

'Don't you be getting up, Graham. I'll make sure she's all right.' Susan found her sister sitting at the kitchen table, head buried in her hands.

'Alison, don't think I'm interfering, but do you not think it better to wait until the spring to get married?'

Pushing her hair back from her face with a tired gesture, Alison cried, 'To be truthful, I've reached the stage where I don't care if we never get married. Since his accident Graham is getting on like a zombie. He never shows any affection. As for his mother! She's changed her tune. Before the accident I got the idea I wasn't good enough for her precious son. Now she can't get us married quickly enough.' She fell silent for some moments, then cried in a rush, 'Sometimes I wonder if Graham will ever be really well. Maybe he will be lame all his life. What if she knows something I don't?'

'I doubt that, Graham wouldn't deceive you.'

'But what if he doesn't know? Or, what if he does know and that's why he's postponing the wedding?'

'Nonsense! The doctors wouldn't keep him in the dark about anything that serious. As he said, he wants to be really fit before he gets married.'

Alison looked unconvinced. 'I don't know about that.'

Pulling a chair away from the table, Susan sat down beside her sister and gazed earnestly at her. 'Listen, Alison. If you're unsure of your feelings, if you feel you don't love Graham enough, take my advice and agree to a separation for a time.'

'Love? What's love? I'm very, very fond of Graham. I know we can make a go of it. So if we're going to marry, the sooner the better.'

Susan slumped in her chair, woebegone. She had thought that if her sister and Graham had a trial separation, Graham would have no excuse to frequent their home. But by the sound of it, he would soon be part of the family. He was no match for Alison *and* his mother.

It was a beautiful day, the middle of June and the sun shone brightly, throwing down a heavy heat. Cherry trees were in full bloom along the avenue where Susan was walking with her pram. She had been to the park and William lay spreadeagled, a parasol protecting his little arms and legs from the direct rays of the sun. Turning into the driveway she pushed the pram around the house to the back garden and parked it in the shade of the oak tree. Covering it with a protective net, she entered the house in search of a cool drink.

Her mother met her in the hall. 'Someone rang a short time ago. He said he would call back later.'

'Did he give a name?'

'Of course. How silly of me. He said to tell you that Jim Brady had called and would ring back later.'

Rachel watched as delight lit up her daughter's face with a rosy hue. 'Do you know him, then?'

'Yes, yes, I know him.'

'Is he . . .' Her voice trailed off.

Anticipating the question, Susan shook her head. 'No, he is not William's father.'

'Is he important to you?'

'He's just a friend, Mam, but I do like him a lot.'

Worry puckered Rachel's face. 'You will be careful, won't you?'

Susan laughed. 'Mam, it's only a phone call, so it is. And he probably just wants to ask after my and William's welfare.'

'Just be careful, love. Won't you?'

Annoyed at her mother's persistence, Susan answered curtly. 'Don't be silly, Mam. I'm not likely to make the same mistake again. What time did he phone?'

Rachel glanced at her watch. 'About an hour ago.'

Just then the phone rang and Susan hurried through the kitchen and into the hall to answer it.

'Hello?'

'Is that you, Susan?'

'Yes. Who's speaking, please?' As if she didn't know. But she intended playing it cool.

'Jim . . . Jim Brady. How are you?'

'Oh, hello, Jim. It's nice to hear from you. I'm fine. What about you?'

'I'm all right. I've been thinking a lot about you.' There was a pregnant pause as he waited for her to return the compliment. For the life of her she couldn't. What with caring for William and fighting off Graham, he hadn't been on her mind all that often, lately. 'Are you still there, Susan?'

'Yes. Yes, I'm still here, Jim.'

'Can we meet?'

'I'd like that, Jim. I'll have to arrange for a babysitter, of course. When suits you?'

'Let's make it Saturday night, shall we? There's a big band playing at the Orpheus and I thought we could go there. Is that all right with you?'

'Yes, sounds great. I'd like that. I'm sure my mam will look after William.'

'Smashing! I'll pick you up at half-past seven. Goodbye till then.'

'Pick me up?'

'Yes, I've got a car now, a Hillman Minx. Nothing

great, but it gets me from A to B. See you on Saturday then.'

'Right! Goodbye, Jim.'

Fearing the sensual feelings that his voice had aroused would be evident on her face, Susan hurried upstairs. She didn't want her mother to see and worry about her. In the bathroom she gazed at her reflection in the mirror and was surprised to find that, except for a brightness in her eyes, she looked no different. With a rueful smile she retraced her steps and went to join her mother.

'Well, was that your friend?' Rachel asked.

'Yes. Mam?' A raised brow invited Susan to continue. 'Jim has asked me to go out with him on Saturday night. Is there any chance of you babysitting? I promise not to be home late.'

'You know I'll be only too glad to look after William any time, Susan.'

'Thanks, Mam. Oh, I think I hear him. He'll be hungry. I'd better go out before he starts yelling the place down.'

Susan's milk was drying up and the nurse at the clinic had advised her to wean him on to the bottle, before it disappeared completely. Placing her crochet work to one side, Rachel rose to her feet. 'I'll make him a bottle. I'm glad he'll not be depending on you for a feed when you return to work. It will make it easier all round.'

Susan met Ruth as usual the next day, a Wednesday. Ruth was waiting at the bus stop to help her off with the pram.

'You're looking very smug today,' Susan greeted her friend as she adjusted the pram and, reaching for her son, settled him in it.

'Oh, he's lovely, and awake for a change. That's the first time I've actually seen his eyes.'

'Stop changing the subject. What's that look in aid of?'

A hand was thrust towards her displaying an engagement ring.

Susan gasped, delighted for her friend. 'Oh! It's beautiful! No wonder you look so smug. Congratulations. I take it Dougie bought it?' Her eyes twinkled teasingly.

'Of course! Who else would have me?'

'Oh, now, there are plenty who'd have you, and you know it. When's the big day then?'

'We haven't decided yet. Probably sometime next year.'

'That's an event to look forward to. Would you like to take a walk around the shops today, Ruth? I've decided to treat myself to a new dress.'

'Oh . . . for any special occasion?'

'Not exactly. However, I am going to the Orpheus with Jim Brady on Saturday night, and if I get something nice I'll wear it then,' Susan informed her casually.

Ruth's smile widened. 'You're joking me, aren't you?'

Susan suppressed a laugh at her friend's expression. 'Cross my heart and hope to die.'

'That's wonderful news, so it is.'

'Don't read anything into it. It's only a date, for heaven's sake.'

'Huh! He must still be keen all the same, or he wouldn't have bothered. What with the baby and all.'

Susan had been thinking along similar lines herself, but she wasn't going to let Ruth know her thoughts. 'Time will tell,' she said.

'I noticed when I passed on the bus earlier on, there's a sale on in the London Mantle Warehouse. Let's walk up there and see what they have to offer.'

'Good idea.'

They walked along Donegall Place and up Castle Street to the long, narrow shop with the grand name, which stood on the corner of Chapel Lane. Susan examined the window displays and was not impressed. 'That was a wasted effort. There's nothing there to lure me inside,' she decided.

'I know what you mean. It's all a bit old-fashioned-looking, isn't it? You want something special to make Jim sit up and take notice.'

'I wouldn't go as far as to say that. No, it's not just for Jim's benefit. Anything I buy I'll have to really like. It will have to last a long time. I can't afford to be extravagant any more. I've William to think of now.'

They headed back down towards the centre of town, stopping to look in shop windows along the way.

In Fountain Lane Ruth stopped in front of a small boutique. A solitary dress was displayed in the window, with no sign of a price tag. 'Isn't that classy, Susan?'

'It certainly is. Let's move on.'

'They've got a sale on.'

'Believe me, sale or no sale, it will still be too expensive for my budget.'

'It would suit you down to the ground, so it would.'

'That's neither here nor there. I simply couldn't afford it.'

'How do you know? It costs nothing to look.'

Susan looked intently at the dress. Draped against a black velvet background, its deep ruby colour seemed to glow; the design was simplicity itself, the material soft and clinging. With breast-feeding William and exercising to strengthen her muscles, she had regained most of her figure and could picture herself in this creation. Oh to be rich and not have to count the cost. Once she was back at work things would be different, but for now she must be careful with her money. There was always the chance Graham would make it impossible for her to stay in Belfast and she would need her savings to settle in Darlington. With a sad shake of the head she walked determinedly on. Reluctantly Ruth followed her.

They had afternoon tea in a café where there was room for the pram, the Ulster Milk Bar being too narrow and confined. Ruth was very quiet and Susan was worried about her. Lifting her friend's left hand, she examined the ring. 'Why so quiet, Ruth? Are you worried about getting married?'

'Don't be daft! Dougie is the best thing that ever happened to me. It's you I'm worried about. I want you to knock Jim Brady sideways on Saturday night. I want him to propose to you again.'

'And do you really think a dress will make all that much difference?'

'Not to Jim, but it will make you feel a lot more confident.'

Inwardly Susan agreed. Ruth saw her wavering and urged, 'Just try it on. If it looks awful then nothing's lost.'

'What if it looks good, what then, eh?'

'Just to please me, at least try it on.'

'Oh, come on then. But mind you, nothing will induce me to buy it if it's too expensive, okay?'

* * *

They retraced their steps to Fountain Lane and, with trepidation, entered the small shop. A tall, very thin woman hurried towards them frowning disdainfully at the pram. 'I'm very sorry, but prams are not allowed on these premises.'

Looking politely around her, Ruth asked in her best posh voice, 'And where does it say so?'

The woman's nostrils flared and she stretched taller still at the audacity of this young woman. 'It doesn't, but surely it's obvious that such a small establishment cannot cater for prams?'

Susan began to edge out backwards, but with a hand on the pram Ruth stopped her. 'As you can see, the child is sleeping. We shall not take up too much of your precious time.' With these words she headed towards the rear of the shop to a rail with a sale sign on it.

Flashing an apologetic look at the woman, Susan left the pram inside the doorway and followed Ruth. Only two dresses on the rail were her size. One she disliked immediately and quickly replaced. A glance at the price tag on the other one caused her to gasp aloud and make to hang it up again.

'Try it on,' Ruth whispered furiously. 'I won't please her,' with a nod in the assistant's direction, 'to let her know we can't afford her creations.'

'But I can't afford it! Besides, I don't even like it.'

'How do you know? It might look lovely on.'

'No!' Susan was adamant. 'I don't like the colour. It's just not me.'

'Oh, Susan!' In despair, Ruth approached the woman

and peered·at the name tag attached to her jacket. 'Ah, Lynette, what size is the dress in the window?'

'Twelve.'

'Is it in the sale?'

An abrupt nod confirmed it was indeed in the sale.

'Can my friend try it on, please?'

'I'm afraid I'm not allowed to interfere with the window display.' Lynette was looking down her nose from her superior height, causing Ruth's temper to rise.

'That's all right, I'll remove it for you.' She had the access door to the window display open before a horrified Lynette could intervene.

'Here, you can't do that.' Lynette grabbed her arm. 'Only Mrs Donovan can do that.'

'And who, may I ask, is Mrs Donovan?'

'The proprietor.'

'And where is she?'

'She's off work for a few days.'

'And are you not in charge while she's away?'

'I am, yes, but . . .'

Ruth interrupted her. 'If you're in charge, you can take that dress out of the window and let my friend try it on.'

Lynette's more-superior-than-thou attitude was quickly evaporating and she was practically wringing her hands with indecision. 'I'm afraid . . .'

'Well, don't be,' Ruth interrupted. 'If it doesn't suit I will help you to drape it round the stand again. And if it does suit my friend,' tongue-in-cheek she said, 'you will have made a cash sale and Mrs Donovan should surely be pleased.'

With more than a little reluctance, the dress was carefully taken from the window. Lynette took great pains to remove all the pins that kept it tucked into shape. Reverently she placed the dress over Ruth's outstretched arm. 'Please be careful with it.'

'We have tried on dresses before, if I may boldly inform one,' Ruth assured her in her continuing posh accent. 'And without any accidents, if I may add.' She motioned Susan into the small cubicle and, following her, drew the curtain across.

Quickly removing her blouse and skirt, Susan pulled the dress over her head and, smoothing it down over her hips, surveyed her reflection in the mirror. She was amazed at the transformation before her eyes. The dress was cut low at the front and even lower at the back. Her shoulders rose above it in creamy splendour. The deep ruby red of the dress darkened the grey of her eyes and her skin seemed to glow. Only the offending straps of her bra spoiled the effect.

Ruth gazed at her in awe. 'Take your bra off!' Susan tucked the straps out of sight and Ruth whispered, 'You look absolutely gorgeous. I told you it was you! You just have to buy it, Susan.'

'I'm afraid to look at the price,' Susan wailed. 'It's bound to be too expensive.'

The tag was hanging on the back of the dress and, with trembling fingers, Ruth turned it over.

'Well . . . it's not as dear as the other one,' she said. 'And it does look lovely on you.'

'Just give me the bottom line, Ruth, and get it over with,' Susan ordered, only to gasp in dismay when her friend told her.

Feverishly she started to remove the dress. 'Hold on

a minute, Susan. At least let me get another look at you before you take it off. You'll never look so lovely again.'

Gazing at her reflection in the mirror, Susan agreed with her. Twisting her hair into a knot on top of her head, she pouted and sighed at her image. 'I really do suit it, don't I?'

'You look absolutely gorgeous in it. Can you not possibly afford it?'

'It would take up a big chunk of my savings. I can't justify buying it. It would be a sin to waste all that money.'

'It's a pity, though. Jim Brady wouldn't be able to keep his hands off you in that outfit.'

'Can I be of any assistance to you ladies?' Lynette's voice reached them.

Pulling aside the curtain, Ruth gestured towards Susan. 'Doesn't she look wonderful, Lynette?'

Lynette clasped her hands together and gave out a suppressed exclamation. 'Oh, madam. Oh, madam,' she whispered.

Susan smiled wryly at her. 'Thanks for letting me try it on, but it's much too expensive for me.'

William started to stir and she hurriedly closed the curtain and quickly removed the dress. She put on her clothes and left the cubicle, handing the dress to Ruth. 'Help Lynette return it to the window, Ruth. I'll need to attend to William. Thanks again for letting me try it on.'

'Madam? If I may be so bold?'

'Yes?'

'That's last year's model. I have the authority to lower the price if necessary.'

Both girls gazed at her in wonder and at last Ruth asked, 'How much?'

'I can reduce it by a further twenty pounds for a cash sale.'

The two girls looked at each other. 'Susan?'

'Well, now . . .'

Her hesitation was enough for Ruth. 'She'll take it,' she cried, settling the matter.

Between them they managed to scrape up the required deposit and Susan arranged to collect the dress on Saturday morning. Outside the shop she gazed in bewilderment at Ruth. 'I can't believe I've just bought that dress! I must need my head examined.'

'You'll be glad on Saturday night when you see the look in Jim's eyes. He won't be able to resist you. He'll be fighting off all the single guys. You wait and see.'

Still undecided, Susan bit agitatedly on her lip and lamented, 'Perhaps I should go back and cancel it? Eh?'

'You'll do no such thing! You'll never get the chance to own a dress like that again. And it's so simple it will never date. Believe me, you got a bargain there, so you did. It's a real gem. You won't regret it.'

'I hope you're right. I feel guilty spending so much money.'

'Trust me. Everything will be all right. I might even get Dougie to give his beloved Club Orchid a miss and come and see the attention you get on Saturday night.'

Not at all pleased by this idea, Susan informed her, 'You can't! It's a ticket-only dance.'

Ruth was not to be so easily put off. 'It will run late then?' she queried.

'Midnight! But I won't be able to stay till the end. Mam will be babysitting.'

'Nevertheless I'll get Dougie to walk me round there after we leave the Orchid. Will that be all right with you?'

Still unhappy at the idea, Susan nodded her consent. It would be ungracious to do otherwise.

Chapter Ten

Saturday started out a beautiful day, bright and sunny with a light breeze keeping the heat in check. Susan spent the afternoon in the garden with William. He was becoming very aware of all around him and followed the toy that she dangled about in front of him, with big bright eyes and groping fingers. She had hoped his eyes would change colour, and become grey like hers, but they remained blue.

Rachel watched from her easy chair under the tree. To her great delight, she had discovered that therapy had strengthened her damaged arm enough for her to manage a crochet hook. She was now busy working on some matinée coats for her grandson. 'What time are you going out tonight, Susan?'

'Jim's picking me up at half-past seven.'

'After tea give yourself plenty of time to get ready. I'll see to William's needs.'

'Are you sure, Mam? I was going to bathe him before I got ready. What about your arm?'

'I'll manage fine, so don't you worry your head about me. It's surprising what I can do now. I've been very lucky, you know.'

'You have indeed, Mam! And we're all very pleased for you. I'll be delighted to leave William in your tender care. You're an angel, so you are. Thanks a lot, Mam.'

'My pleasure. I love having that wee rascal all to myself. I think Alison has persuaded Graham to take her out tonight too,' she mused. 'I'm so glad for her. She's young and has her whole life ahead of her. She should get out more often before she gets tied down to married life.'

'Oh.' For some reason Susan felt apprehensive. 'Did she say where?'

'No, she didn't mention it at all. I was in the lounge, but she was so delighted to be going out that she was shouting with excitement and I couldn't help but overhear. I wasn't eavesdropping, mind, so I didn't hear any particular venue being mentioned.'

Susan mulled over this information in her mind. One thing was sure: Graham, although walking with just the aid of one stick now, was still very shaky on his legs. Even he would hardly have the gumption to go to a dance in his condition. On the other hand, if her sister had mentioned that Susan was going to the Orpheus with Jim Brady, he would be contrary enough to do just that.

She gave herself a little shake and warned herself not to be paranoid about him. Besides, it was a ticket-only dance and even Graham would have difficulty obtaining tickets at such short notice.

After tea that evening her mother cradled her grandson in her good arm and shooed her daughter upstairs to get ready for her date. When Susan would have demurred, Rachel cried, 'Away you go! I can cope all right. My arm's not as bad as you think. Besides, if I need any help your father will be here.'

The dress, collected that morning, hung on a hanger from the back of the bathroom door. It had got slightly wrinkled, but the steam from the bath should soon resolve that problem. She still fretted about how much it had cost, and no way was she going to put an iron to it. With her luck she was likely to scorch it.

As she lay soaking in the bath, she eyed the dress. It really was beautiful; the material soft and clinging and the rich ruby suited her colouring perfectly. But . . . was this creation not meant to be worn for someone you cared dearly for? Someone you were committed to and were sure of? Someone you loved and who loved you in return? Did she want Jim to be so bowled over by her in it that he would be unable to keep his hands off her, as Ruth had suggested? Did they not need to take things easy, one step at a time; see how they felt about each other now that a child was involved? What if he did get carried away – would she be able to resist him? She certainly should! Once bitten, twice shy was going to be the motto of the day. However, it was so long since a man had held her and kissed her that she would be vulnerable. She would have to be very, very careful tonight.

Putting the finishing touches to her make-up, she was still undecided about the dress. Brushing her thick, freshly shampooed hair until it glowed with chestnut highlights, she secured it with clips on top of her head in a crown of curls, emphasising the geometry of her face: high cheekbones, widely spaced grey eyes, perfect nose and small, determined chin. She moved her head from side to side, pouting at her reflection, and her full, sensuous lips spread into a wide smile at the antics of herself. Next she turned her attention to the dress.

To avoid messing her hair she stepped into it and carefully wriggled the soft material up over her hips and into place over a strapless bra purchased for this very purpose. She had thought that perhaps it had been the dim, coloured lights in the shop that had made her look so good in it, but no! Here in the bright lights of her bedroom she studied her image reflected in the full-length mirror and felt and looked every bit as glamorous. There was still a slight heaviness about her hips, but the drape of the dress hid this.

She let out a long sigh and eyed her reflection apprehensively. It was make-up-your-mind time. Should she or shouldn't she wear it? After some thought she slowly removed the dress and hung it reverently on a hanger. It just didn't feel right to wear it tonight. It wasn't the right time. Perhaps if Jim and she became close she would wear it for him alone. She put a dustsheet over it and hung it at the back of the wardrobe, glad that she hadn't mentioned it to any of the family.

A shout from her father alerted her to the fact that Jim had arrived. Vexed with him for being early, she hurriedly changed her bra and, selecting another snug-fitting velvet dress, quickly pulled it on. She had meant to be ready to leave as soon as he arrived, and not give her father a chance to question him. She descended the stairs in a rush and crossed the hall, aware of voices coming from the lounge. Her father's deep tones were recognisable and she sighed. She had hoped to avoid this meeting. Her father would be giving Jim the third degree.

Surprise slackened her features as she entered the room. Both Graham and Jim were holding a conversation with her father. Jim gave her a broad grin of welcome, indicating that he was getting on all right with Trevor. Graham acknowledged her with a wave of his hand.

Alison hurried towards her and whispered, 'Do you mind if we accompany you to the Orpheus?'

The dismay she felt must have shown, causing Alison to continue quickly, 'I'm so sorry. Graham and I were going to the pictures, but when Jim arrived and said you were going to the Orpheus, Graham asked if we could tag along. Say you don't mind, Susan. Please? I'd be ever so glad to get out to a dance for a change.'

'But you can't! Didn't Jim mention it was a ticket do?'

'Yes! Jim did explain that, but Graham still wants to give it a shot. You know how it is. If any tickets are returned they sell them at the door. He thinks we stand a good chance of getting in.'

Susan had forgotten about being able to buy returned tickets. Still unable to hide her annoyance, she asked, 'Will he be able to dance? You'll be bored stiff if you have to sit and watch all evening.'

'He thinks he will be able to manage a few slow dances. And I hope you would let Jim give me a couple of dances. Ah, come on, Susan. I'd do the same for you, and you know it.'

Rachel appeared in the doorway, William cradled in her arms. He was rosy from his bath and dressed for bed. 'I just wanted to tell you not to leave the dance too early, Susan. Your father can carry William's cot into our room so that he can sleep with us tonight.'

Putting her arms around both her mother and child, Susan said gratefully, 'Thanks, Mam. Thanks, Dad. I'll phone later and make sure he's not playing up on you. I was going to come and see him before I went out.' She ruffled her son's wispy hair and planted a kiss on his cheek. 'Mam, have you met Jim yet?'

'No, I've been seeing to William. How are you, son?'

'I'm fine, and very pleased to meet you, Mrs Cummings,' he replied, rising quickly from his chair.

'Are you all going out together?' Rachel asked, surprised to see Alison and Graham still there.

'It looks like it.' Susan's voice was dry and her mother gave her a sharp look. 'I think it's nice to see you all getting out together,' she said softly. 'You know, a family affair? I'm sure you'll enjoy yourselves. Now, if you'll all excuse me, I'll take this little fellow upstairs.'

The others gathered round to kiss William good night. Only Jim hung back, looking ill at ease. At last Rachel was free to leave the room and, bidding Trevor and her good night, the four of them left the house and, with admiring comments about its make and colour, climbed into Jim's new car. Although he tried to hide it, Susan noticed that Graham was in pain as he eased himself into the car.

'Sit in the front, Graham, you will have more room.'

'No, thank you, Susan, for your concern, but I'll be fine here.' His voice was abrupt, causing her to take umbrage.

'Suit yourself.' He had no right going to a dance, and him hardly able to walk, let alone dance.

* * *

In the cloakroom at the Orpheus Alison turned to her sister in despair. 'Look at me! I'm not dressed for dancing. I should have nipped upstairs and changed my clothes before I came out.' She grimaced down at her skirt and blouse. 'I'm sure they'll all be dressed to kill in there tonight.'

Glad she had decided against wearing the new dress, which would have caused speculation, Susan smoothed her hands over her empire-line velvet dress and sadly agreed with her sister. 'No, you're not. But never mind. You won't be doing much dancing, will you? Tonight you'll just be a spectator. It wouldn't be fair on Graham if you were to dance with someone else and leave him sitting alone.' If she could possibly avoid it, she was determined not to sit out any dances keeping Graham company. She was in no mood for his snide remarks and subtle threats.

Alison looked at her sister through narrowed lids. 'You're still annoyed with me, aren't you? Why are you being so unreasonable, Susan? It's not like you.'

'Well, I'm sure you can appreciate that I would have liked to be alone with Jim. It's been a long time and we have a lot of catching up to do.'

'When Graham suggested we come along and Jim didn't raise any objections, I was so pleased to be going to a dance I wasn't going to argue about it. Even though I had an idea you might not want our company. I don't understand why, Susan. Surely it won't make that much difference whether we're here or not?'

'No? Well, that's neither here nor there. What's done is done, so let's join the men and make the best of it.'

Susan felt Alison's acute bewilderment at her attitude, but for the life of her she couldn't shrug off her displeasure.

They found their partners seated at a table near the edge of the dance floor. The bandsmen, resplendent in their dress suits and bow ties, were already in place and testing their instruments. Soon the first dance, a foxtrot, was announced. Jim rose immediately and with a slight bow asked Susan to dance.

She was so stiff in his arms that he frowned down at her. 'Is anything bothering you?'

'As if you didn't know,' she muttered. 'Did you have to ask them along?'

'I thought you knew all about it!' he cried defensively. 'The way Graham put it, I thought my say-so was already taken for granted. Do you think I wanted them along?' He gathered her closer. 'I've thought of nothing this past couple of days but having you all to myself tonight.'

Mollified, she relaxed in his arms. 'Just please don't leave me sitting with Graham, or I might say something to offend him. He had no right tagging along – and him hardly able to put one foot in front of the other.'

Jim frowned. 'You're putting me on the spot, Susan. I'll have to give Alison a few dances. Surely you can see that? It's only common courtesy to ask her.'

Knowing he spoke the truth, she replied mournfully, 'I know. I'm talking a lot of nonsense. It's just that I'm annoyed at his cheek, asking to join us. But let's make the best of it and enjoy ourselves.'

'Yes,' he agreed. 'We'll have plenty of time in the future to get to know each other again,' he whispered in her ear and let his lips trail over her cheek and neck, sending thrills of pleasure coursing through her.

They danced the next dance together and sat the next one out talking to Alison and Graham. The following one, with an apologetic glance at Susan, Jim asked Alison to dance. She was on the floor like a shot and Susan felt ashamed because she begrudged her sister a little bit of pleasure. Prepared to excuse herself and retire to the cloakroom, she glanced across at Graham. The excuse died on her lips when she saw the misery reflected in his eyes.

'Are you in pain?' she asked anxiously. 'Can I get you anything?'

'Hah, so you have decided to forgive me?'

Mystified, she queried, 'Forgive you for what?'

'For spoiling your reunion with your precious boyfriend. You haven't spoken directly to me all evening.'

Her lips tightened in anger. 'So it was deliberate, then?'

He shook his head as if weary of arguing. 'Not really. The occasion arose during the conversation and I couldn't resist it. You should have seen your sister's face when Jim said you were going to the Orpheus. I couldn't deny her the pleasure of at least watching the dancers, if it was at all possible. But you're spoiling it all for her, begrudging her a dance with Jim. I wouldn't have believed you'd be so selfish.'

Hot colour blazed across her cheeks at the insult and she glowered at him, nostrils flaring in anger. He thought she had never looked more lovely. 'What about me?' she cried. 'Eh? Doesn't it matter that my night is ruined?'

'And why is it ruined? Because I'm here?' His voice

was bitter and his eyes showed distaste. 'I never thought of you as a selfish person, Susan, but I'm getting an eye-opener tonight. Alison is a much better person than you'll ever be.'

'For once I agree with you! And you're a very lucky man that she's still willing to marry you, after the way you've been behaving lately. Getting on like a spoilt brat. Don't you realise that if she got an inkling of how we betrayed her trust, she would drop you like a hot potato?'

Suddenly alert, he leant forward only to fall back as the sudden movement caused a spasm of pain. 'Perhaps that's the best thing that could happen?' he hissed through clenched teeth.

'Oh, don't be ridiculous! You'd be spoiling everyone's happiness just because you can't accept the truth.'

He lapsed into silence and she waited breathlessly for his response. If only he would believe her.

She was silently urging him to speak and at last he did. 'Don't get me wrong, Susan, I'm still convinced William is my son. I can even see a likeness to my family in him.'

Fear gripped her heart. 'That's wishful thinking, and you must surely know it,' she cried in anguish.

'I don't think so. However, he was conceived in a moment of lustful madness that we've since regretted. We will both have other children, so forget I exist, if you must. I'll never trouble you again.'

Shame was consuming her, making her bitter in return. 'I'm glad you're convinced at last. Now maybe you'll get out of my life and leave me alone. I'm sick to the teeth of listening to your insinuations. Do you hear me?'

Tears blinding her, she rose from the table and hurried to the cloakroom. How dare he talk to her like that, she fumed inwardly. He was treating her as if she were some naughty schoolgirl. Whereas he was the one who was behaving irrationally. How dare he! Well, at least she was shot of him at last. Hopefully he would never bother her again. But would it spoil things for Alison? Did her sister really want to marry him? Would she be happy married to Graham? And how would it be to have him for a brother-in-law, constantly watching William grow up, with suspicious eyes.

Oh, dear God, it would be an awful way to live. But on the other hand of course, if Jim did ask her to marry him, she would be living at the other end of town. That should help matters. She repaired her make-up and, when she could delay no longer, made her way back to the ballroom.

At the table Jim rose to his feet and eyed her with concern. 'Are you all right, Susan?'

She nodded, aware that all eyes were on her. 'Can we dance, please?'

Wordlessly he led her on to the dance floor. Tenderly holding her close, he pressed his cheek to hers and was dismayed to discover that it was wet with tears. Drawing back, he looked down at her. 'What on earth's the matter?'

Thankful that the dimmed lights hid her tears from the other dancers, and ashamed that she was unable to control them, Susan buried her head against his chest and muttered, 'I'm sorry. It must be the aftermath of having a baby that reduces me to tears for nothing. Having a baby upsets the hormones, you know. I think maybe I'm suffering from postnatal depression.'

'Come off it. Baby or no baby, you're not stupid enough to cry for nothing. Did Graham upset you?'

'It doesn't matter.'

'Oh, but it does matter. What happened?'

'Forget it, Jim. Please? It was my own fault. I didn't try to hide the fact that I resented their company and Graham took exception to it and we had words.'

'But, he had no right . . .'

'Please, Jim, don't let me spoil our first evening back together. I just need time to get a grip on myself.'

'Okay. Let's stay away from the table for a while. Give you a chance to pull yourself together. Shall we have a drink?'

She nodded gratefully and he twirled her in and out of the dancers until they were close to the bar. While they waited to be served she felt calmer and her conscience began to plague her. 'Jim, I feel guilty leaving them sitting there.'

'They're not our problem, Susan. After all, we didn't invite them along.'

'Still . . . I feel I am mostly to blame. Can we bring them back a drink and let bygones be bygones?'

Undecided, he eyed her through narrowed lids. 'Are you sure that's what you want to do?'

'Yes.'

He shrugged, obviously still perturbed. 'All right! If that's what you want.'

'How do I look? Would you know I've been crying?'

Jim eyed her intently. 'No. No, you would never guess. Now take a deep breath and give me a big smile, then we can go back to them.'

Graham saw them approaching the table and his heart lifted. He thought he had blown it. He regretted his outburst to Susan. Watching her plastered against Jim Brady as they circled the dance floor had made him so jealous that he had lost control of his reason and, when given the chance, had lashed out blindly with his tongue. He had said some terrible things to her. Now he gratefully accepted the glass of beer Jim handed him. 'Thanks, Jim.' He raised it to Susan. 'Cheers.'

Susan raised her glass of orange juice in reply. Holding his eye, she asked, 'All friends again?'

Alison was looking from one to the other of them in mystified surprise. Deciding to give them a chance to resolve their differences, Jim placed his beer on the table and said, 'Would you like to dance, Alison?'

'Only if it's not going to upset anyone.' She looked apprehensively at her sister.

'Please, be my guest.'

Alone at the table, Graham and Susan eyed each other. 'Can we call a truce?' she asked apprehensively.

'With pleasure. But first I would like to apologise. I said some unforgivable things to you.'

'Yes, you did.'

'I'm very sorry, Susan. I realise now that I have been very unreasonable where William is concerned. I promise I won't harass you again. If at any time in the future you should change your mind and wish to talk to me concerning him, I'll be only too willing to listen. Meanwhile, he's your son and I wish you both the best of everything.'

Susan couldn't believe her ears. He was letting her off the hook. 'Do you mean it? No more insinuations?'

'I've been a fool. Instead of trying to win you over, I've driven you away. I realise now your heart belongs to Jim.'

'Can we be friends, Graham?'

He grimaced. 'That won't be easy.'

'What about Alison? If you marry her we will be family.'

He shrugged. 'I admit I'm very fond of her and intend marrying one day. So why not her? Believe me, if we do marry, I'll do all in my power to make her happy. She will want for nothing. But don't you worry about it. I'll keep out of your hair.'

The rest of the evening passed without incident, until near the end, when Ruth swooped down on them followed by an embarrassed Dougie. Stopping in front of Susan, she gaped in confusion. 'Dougie knows the doorman and he let us in for the last couple of dances,' she explained. Her eyes roamed over her friend's dress and then rose questioningly to her face.

Glad that Ruth had the sense not to question her openly in front of the others, Susan advised her friend, 'You had better get on the floor then and sample this great band.'

With a wry smile at them all, Ruth turned to her partner. 'Come on, Dougie, let's not waste any more time.'

During the course of the evening Graham had managed to dance a couple of slow waltzes with Alison. Now he gestured towards the dance floor and said, 'May I have this waltz, Susan?'

Silently she allowed herself to be led on to the floor;

it would be unkind to refuse, but she wished he hadn't asked. She entered his arms and he drew her close. 'I hope you don't mind me asking you to dance? It will only be a bit of a shuffle, you know.'

'No!' Her voice was curt and she repeated more gently, 'No, why should I?'

'Well then, relax. I won't bite you.'

She was afraid to relax in case she gave him the wrong impression. She was remembering how, when he had stayed overnight in Edith's house, she had got carried away at his closeness. But then, hadn't she that very same night almost succumbed to Donald's charms? It seemed she was just too easily seduced. He winced and, concerned, she asked, 'Does it hurt you to dance?'

He smiled wryly. 'Believe me, the pleasure is worth the pain.'

She glanced up and saw the dark shadows under his eyes; the pain he tried so hard to hide. 'Look, Graham, there's a couple of empty chairs over there along the wall. Let's sit down.'

'Promise you'll stay with me, not run away.'

'Of course I'll stay. What kind of a person do you take me for?'

He opened his mouth to speak, but closed it again.

'What were you going to say?' He looked so forlorn that she wanted to put her arms around him and press his head to her breast. Comfort him as she would a child. God, what was she thinking of? That was Alison's responsibility.

They reached the chairs and he sighed with relief as he sank carefully down on to one of them.

Undecided, she hovered in front of him. 'You look

awful! Can I get you anything? Some painkillers perhaps?'

He shook his head. 'Just sit down and keep me company for a wee while.'

She obeyed and asked speculatively, 'What were you going to say, back there?'

Before he could answer her question, Alison and Jim stopped in front of them. 'Are you all right, Graham?' Alison asked anxiously.

He shook his head. 'No, I don't feel so good. Sorry for spoiling your night, love, but I'd like to go home now. Please phone for a taxi.'

'I'll run you home.'

'You'll do nothing of the kind, Jim. The dance will soon be over.'

'I insist . . . In fact, I'm sure Susan won't mind if we all leave now?' He glanced questioningly at Susan.

Quickly Graham cried, 'I won't hear tell of it! I've been a big enough nuisance for one night. Please phone for a taxi, Jim. Perhaps you will be kind enough to take Alison home?'

'Of course.' Seeing that he was at the end of his tether, Jim said, 'I'll ring for a taxi now.'

'Thanks, mate.'

The rush of late-night revellers going home had yet to start and the taxi arrived in no time at all. Leaving Alison at the door to say good night in private to her fiancé, Jim and Susan bade him farewell and returned to the ballroom.

'He must love Alison a lot to suffer as he did tonight, just so that she could have a dance,' Jim mused. 'I'm not sure I'd have the guts to do it.'

'Mm, indeed he must.'

Her voice was tinged with irony and he questioned her, 'Do you know something I don't?'

'Such as?'

He shrugged. 'I can't even hazard a guess, but I know this much: something isn't right between you two.'

'Will you excuse me, Jim? Ruth has just left the room alone. She must be going to the cloakroom. I want to speak to her. I'll be back in a jiffy.'

In the cloakroom Ruth faced her friend in indignation. 'What on earth are you playing at?' she cried. 'What happened to that beautiful dress you bought?'

Hustling her into a corner, away from the other two occupants in the room, Susan hissed, 'Hush. Alison will probably be in here any minute. She's seeing Graham into a taxi.'

'You didn't show it to her?'

'No. As a matter of fact, I didn't show it to anyone.'

'How were you able to resist?'

'I only collected it this morning, remember?'

'Well, put me out of my misery! Why didn't you wear it tonight? Did you spill something on it? Is that it?'

'No. I'm saving it for a better occasion. Perhaps Christmas.'

Ruth's eyes lit up. 'He's proposed, hasn't he?' she gasped in delight. 'You're going to get engaged at Christmas and that's why you're saving it.'

'Do you know something, Ruth? You could write a book with that imagination of yours. Jim hasn't asked me to marry him and I'm not getting engaged.'

'Watch my lips, Susan. After paying all that money,

why are you not wearing the dress tonight? That's all I want to know.'

She shrugged negatively and confessed, 'I felt too grand in it. Overdressed, you know, for this kind of a dance. And I'm glad I didn't wear it. No one else is wearing an off-the-shoulder dress here tonight. I'd have stuck out like a sore thumb.'

'A very attractive sore thumb. If I looked half as good as you did in that dress, I wouldn't care about anybody else. I'd be in my glory. Showing off.'

'I'm different from you. I prefer to keep it for a special occasion. So there.'

Ruth glanced over Susan's shoulder. 'Hi, Alison. Did Graham get away all right?'

'Yes, the taxi came in no time. I shouldn't have asked him to come here tonight. It was selfish of me. It was too much for him. He's exhausted, poor dear.'

'Never mind. Did you enjoy yourself?'

'I did, Ruth.' Alison glanced at her sister. 'In spite of everything, I enjoyed myself.'

Sensing a mystery, Ruth looked from one to the other. Her mouth opened to speak, but Susan forestalled her. 'Come on, there must surely only be a couple of dances left. Let's not waste any more time in here in idle gossip.' She left the cloakroom and the others were obliged to follow, with Ruth silently vowing to get to the bottom of the mystery next time she met her friend.

When the car drew into the driveway, Alison, who had remained silent throughout the journey home, leant forward from her seat in the back, and patting Jim's shoulder, said, 'Thank you very much for the lift home and for tolerating our company at the dance, Jim. It was very kind of you.' Without a glance in her sister's direction, she said, 'Good night, Susan' and hurried from the car.

They watched her climb the steps and disappear through the door. 'She's still very annoyed at you,' Jim mused.

Tight-lipped, Susan argued, 'I'm the one who should be annoyed.'

'Yes, I suppose so.'

'What do you mean, *suppose*? I'm very disappointed in you, Jim. I thought you, at least, would be on my side.'

'Here! Hold on a minute. I'm not on anybody's side. My mind boggles just trying to make sense of it all.'

Realising that he must be bewildered at her attitude towards Graham, she apologised. 'I'm sorry. I didn't mean to spoil everyone's night. It's just that I'd been so looking forward to it and I'm afraid I couldn't hide my disappointment. It's as simple as that. No other reason. Anyway, thanks for putting up with me, Jim. Good night.'

She was out of the car so quickly that for a moment he sat, taken aback. Bounding from his seat, he caught hold of her at the bottom of the steps. 'Hey, hold on a minute. Why the big rush?'

'I thought you'd had enough of me for one night.'

'Don't be silly. Get back in the car, I want to talk to you.'

Fearful of eyes watching them from the house, she said, 'It's a lovely night, let's go for a walk.'

Obediently he followed her down the driveway. They

headed on up the Old Cavehill Road and he was amazed when, a few minutes later, the Cave Hill loomed before them.

She heard his gasp of surprise and agreed, 'It does come as a bit of a shock the first time you see it. This is what I call the gentle side of the hill. It's easier to climb than the rest of it.' He still seemed dazed and she teased him, 'You didn't realise I literally lived at the foot of the Cave Hill, did you?'

'I knew it was a long trek back the nights I walked home in the winter months, but I didn't realise you lived so far out.'

She slipped her arm through his and they climbed the twisting path until all the houses were out of sight. 'It's too late to climb any further. Shall we sit down for a few minutes?' She closed her eyes tight in despair as she realised how this might sound to him. Would he think she was about to throw herself at him again, and take to his heels?

To her relief, without any hesitation whatsoever he removed his jacket and spread it on the grass. They sat side by side in companionable silence. It was eerie by the light of the pale moon; all shadows and animal sounds. An owl hooted somewhere close and she shivered at the sound, pulled her cardigan closer around her body and hugged herself. Jim put his arm around her waist and pulled her close. They were sitting thigh-to-thigh and hip-to-hip, but to her surprise she wasn't in the least bit physically aroused. She certainly had no great desire to ravage him. Remembering the agitated state she had been in the last time they were alone like this she felt a little confused, but glad to be in control of the situation. She felt very much at ease with him. Was this how it would be if they were married? Feeling his gaze, she turned her head and met his eyes. His lips hovered close and then claimed hers. He kissed her passionately – on the lips, the throat and cleavage – and she returned his caresses with warmth but no great passion. She was glad he wasn't trying to take advantage of her and she was quite happy to respond to his kisses. At last he pushed her gently away and rising to his feet, pulled her upright.

They stood face-to-face and, cupping her chin in his hands, he kissed her once more. 'We'd better go now. It's getting late.'

At the door he asked, 'Can I see you tomorrow night?'

Regretfully she shook her head. 'I couldn't expect Mam to babysit two nights in a row. She isn't fit enough, and William can be a right handful at times.'

He smiled wryly. 'I keep forgetting that you're a mother. It will take a bit of getting used to. When can I see you?'

'Give me a ring during the week and we'll fix something up.'

'Okay.' A light kiss on the lips and he climbed into the car and was away.

Susan made sure all the doors were locked and barred for the night. Climbing the stairs, she paused outside her parents' door and listened. All she could hear was the regular snoring of her father. Gently turning the doorknob, she quietly opened the door and peeped in. The cot was empty, but William took up most of the wide bed, arms and legs outstretched while her mother and father hung precariously on the edge of their respective sides.

She debated whether or not to lift William and bring him to her bed, but decided it would be a shame to disturb everyone. With a smile she gently closed the door. This was something that mustn't become a regular habit. The young rascal must be taught to sleep in his own cot or he would get used to the company and she would have trouble later on when she returned to work and needed to get a good night's sleep.

As she creamed off her make-up she went over in her mind the events of the evening. She admitted to herself that she had been a right nasty bitch. Still, it would be worth being thought a bitch if Graham really did stop pestering her. She remembered his strained face and her heart went out to him. If only he and Alison were closer. It was her fault that they weren't! How she regretted that night of lust! If she hadn't been so stupid, her sister and Graham would be married by now and she would probably be engaged to Jim. It hadn't been all her fault, she lamented. Graham had wanted it, too.

Was there any truth in the old wives' tale that everything happened for a purpose? Surely not. What advantage could there be in the sin that she and Graham had committed? Not that they had planned it – no, it had been the result of a series of occurrences.

Try though she did to recapture the comfortable feelings she had experienced with Jim, it was Graham's face she carried into her unsettled dreams.

She dreamt he was pursuing her towards the edge of a high cliff. She shook with terror as she peered over the edge at the angry waves crashing against the jagged rocks far below. Seeing no way of escape, she squared her shoulders and bravely turned to face him, but he wasn't there. She awoke lathered in sweat, her heart pounding against her ribs. The feeling of panic stayed with her for a long time, making sleep almost impossible.

For six wonderful weeks Susan was very contented with her lot; life could not be better. William was coming on like a house on fire. Bright as a button, he viewed the world around him with gurgles and smiles. She was due to return to work at the beginning of September and was looking forward to it. The weather continued to be fine and warm with just the odd dull or wet day. Graham had had a relapse after the night out at the dance. He was confined to bed for three weeks and Alison spent a lot of time at his home. Once he was on his feet again, she went about with a smug smile on her face like the cat who had stolen the cream. It appeared to all concerned that her every wish was Graham's command. He certainly appeared to be living up to his promise to make Alison happy and stay out of Susan's hair. What more could she ask?

She saw Jim twice a week; he wanted to see her more often, but tentative efforts to get him to include William in some outings so that they could go out on a Sunday afternoon, for instance, had so far failed. This worried her somewhat, but she convinced herself he needed time to get accustomed to her being a mother. Hadn't he said, 'It will take a bit of getting used to'?

To her joy she received a letter from Donald Murphy. Being a maintenance fitter, he had to work during the annual summer holiday, which in Darlington was the last week in July and the first in August. Now he wrote to inform Susan that, starting the second week in August, he was thinking about visiting Northern Ireland to see for himself some of the places she had told him about. He intended travelling up through Scotland to Stranraer and crossing on the ferry to Larne, and wanted to know if he could possibly call and see her and her wee son while he was over? He also asked if she could recommend a good guest house. He would have a three-week break.

As it turned out, Alison was accompanying Graham and his parents to Killarney the first two weeks that Donald would be in Belfast and she was quick to suggest that he could have her room, as it was much bigger than the spare room. It was with trepidation that Susan approached her father and asked if she could offer Alison's room to Donald for a fortnight.

'And what has Alison got to say about that?'

'It was her suggested it, Dad. And Donald was a true friend to me when I lived in Darlington. I could always rely on him.'

Trevor's eyebrows gathered in a frown. 'Is he . . .'

'No,' she anticipated his question. 'He's not William's father.'

'Then by all means invite him to stay.'

Inwardly she marvelled at how her father had mellowed in his attitude towards Catholics. There had been a time when he would not have allowed one over his doorstep, let alone hold a civil conversation with one. Now he and Jim got on quite well together. She gave into her instinct to hug him. He released himself quickly from her embrace, but, although embarrassed, she could see he was nevertheless pleased.

She replied that day to Donald's letter, assuring him of a good Irish welcome, and informed him that he was to stay at her parents' home. Once he knew dates and times, he was to be sure to let her know immediately what ferry he would be on and when he would arrive, so that she could arrange for someone to meet him at Larne harbour and pilot him to Belfast, him being a stranger to the Emerald Isle.

During her stay in Darlington, Donald had endeavoured to teach her how to drive and had been quite pleased with her efforts. Now she regretted not keeping it up. It would be so handy to be able to drive. Her father's car often sat unused in the garage at weekends because neither she nor Alison had a driving licence. Perhaps Jim would give her some driving lessons if she asked him? Men were not very forthcoming where women learner drivers were concerned, but perhaps if she worked on him, he might just agree to teach her.

Her excitement bubbled over when she told Jim about Donald coming to visit. They had been to the cinema and were sitting in the car outside the house talking when she told him the news. At first she didn't notice his withdrawal as she babbled on about how good Donald had been to her. Eventually she broached the subject of learning to drive.

'Maybe you'll give me some driving lessons, Jim. Donald will be so surprised if I can drive. He warned me to keep it up or I'd just lose all my confidence. I was coming along great, too. Then I got word about Mam and I had to come home. Will you help me, Jim?'

It was some seconds before she realised he was not responding to her. She turned in her seat and eyed him warily. 'Is anything wrong?'

'You seem very excited at the idea of meeting this bloke again.'

'I am.' She warned herself to be careful; not to give Jim cause for jealousy. 'He was a very good friend to me when I was over at Aunt Edith's. I'd have been lost without him.'

He still refused to meet her eye. 'Is he William's father?' he asked flatly.

To her surprise she found that she wanted to lash out at him and tell him to mind his own bloody business. After all, she at last despairingly admitted to herself, he had shown very little interest in William so far, so what did it matter who the father was? Then she remonstrated inwardly. He had the right to know the truth, but it was something she could never tell him. If anything was to come of their relationship, he would have to take her at face value.

'No, he's not!' Her tone of voice brooked no further questions.

He ignored her reticence and suddenly reached out and gripped her hands tightly. 'Susan, it would be easier all round if you would only tell me the father's name. Surely you can trust me not to broadcast it?' His tone deepened. 'Can't you see? I need to know,' he cried in anguish.

If she were to confess to him now, she could imagine how he would react the next time he saw Graham. There was no way he could act normally and all her conniving would be in vain. Leaning towards him, her eyes beseeched him. 'Jim, I can't! I can never tell anyone.'

'Why not?' he cried in bewilderment. 'You make it sound like a virgin birth! Did you not realise what was going on until it was too late, or something? Is that why? Did he take advantage of you?'

She remembered the intensity of her brief union with Graham, the pain and the pleasure, and cried, 'No! No, far from it. I can never accuse him of that. It was by mutual consent.'

He threw her hands from him in disgust. All the doubts and dark thoughts he had harboured for a long time erupted. They came into his mouth and, without thought of the consequences, he spewed them out in despair. 'You must have been seeing this guy while you were dating me all those months ago,' he accused. Ignoring her wild shake of the head and the piteous moans of denial coming from her lips, he continued. 'Were you, Susan? If we had done it that night, would you have palmed William off as mine? Eh, Susan? Is that why you were so keen? Was I intended to be the fall guy? When I didn't play ball, is that why you ran off to England?'

The enormity of this tirade was like an icy wind blowing through her, leaving her numb to the core. She gaped at him in horror, eyes and mouth stretched wide. How could he think that of her? All these weeks while he dated her he had been harbouring these terrible dark thoughts. Distraught, she cried, 'How can you think that?'

'Why not? Can you blame me? You certainly have never shown such passion since,' he muttered bitterly.

Slowly a hot rage consumed her at his audacity. How

dare he! All this time he had been waiting for her to throw herself at him again. Who did he think he was? Well, he would have a long wait! Never again would she risk rejection such as she had been subjected to at his hands. Her tongue was sharp when at last she found her voice and upbraided him, 'Shall I tell you why that is?' she hissed. 'It's because I'm afraid that maybe this time you might think I'm easy prey and that I'll let you have your way with me and then run away again, perhaps leaving me with another child. Besides which, you're not exactly the world's most passionate lover yourself, you know! It's not too hard for me to control my emotions when I'm with you. We may as well be an old married couple for all the passion you show.' Aghast at the effrontery of her remarks, she fumbled for the door handle. The close confinement of the car was becoming unbearable. She must get away before he insulted her further, in retaliation. He would never forgive her for attacking his ego like that. But it was true! There had been no great moments of passion between them, as once there had been. Even at the dances when they had danced close together, there was no great awareness; no longing to be alone. Not on her part, anyhow. He must have noticed it too. She had been foolish enough to think it was out of respect for her.

Before she could open the door, his hands suddenly gripped her shoulders, shook her and roughly pulled her towards him. 'You want a display of passion, do you? Eh? How about this?' His lips were brutal as they crushed against hers, and she tasted blood as she frantically tried to escape his savage kiss. 'And this!' She struggled to be free, but he held her firmly in one arm and his free hand was relentless in his endeavour to hurt. He tore wildly at her blouse. It was of flimsy material and the buttons gave easily under his attack. Pushing her bra roughly to one side, he cupped her breast and kneaded it with sharp, cruel fingers. 'Is this how you like it? Eh, Susan? Is this how it was with him? Do you like it rough?'

With one last desperate push she managed to free herself from his grasp and this time her groping hand found the door handle. Gripping the ends of her blouse together with one hand to hide her nakedness, she grabbed her bag, stumbled from the car, almost falling, and raced blindly up the steps. With hands that shook she had the key out, the door open and was through it before he had time to get out of the car.

He gazed after her in stunned silence. Dear God, what on earth had possessed him to attack her like that? He, who had never once lifted a hand or raised his voice in mock anger at his sisters when they were disobedient? He looked down at his hands; they were trembling, and no wonder! He was shaking all over. He started to get out of the car – he had to beg her forgiveness, explain how her silence had been tormenting him all these weeks. He must somehow get her to understand that he was only human and needed to know the truth. Then he sank back in his seat in defeat, his hands washing over his face in anguish. She could never have a rational conversation with him now. Not the state she was in. And who could blame her! How she must hate him. He might wake the whole household if he went after her. He cringed when he pictured how Trevor would react if he saw her torn blouse. Head in hands, he sat for some time regaining control of his shaking body, then slowly set the car in motion and drove away.

Passionless! Did you ever hear the like of it? She thought him passionless. He wanted to weep at the very idea. If only she knew the times he had wanted to ravage her; arouse her to awareness such as she had known before and, declaring his love, ask her to marry him. Well, why hadn't he, he ranted inwardly? Because he wasn't sure how she felt towards him. What if he was unable to arouse her? The emotions they used to ignite in each other at the slightest provocation were no more. He had hoped to rekindle them. Now it was too late. He had ruined everything by losing his self-control like some wild beast. Besides, now there was the child to consider. He found he couldn't work up any great enthusiasm for this other man's offspring. Perhaps if she had trusted him enough to tell him the father's name he might have felt differently. Then this would never have happened. Surely he had the right to know his identity, if they were to marry.

Susan stood trembling with her back pressed against the door in the dark hall, willing him to go away. What if he came to the door and created a scene and woke her father? There would be hell to pay. At last she heard the engine start up and, with a sigh of relief, pushed herself away from the door. It was too early to lock up for the night. Alison couldn't be home yet. They had made arrangements to leave their door key on the hall-stand so that the last one in would know to lock and bar the door. There was no sign of Alison's key. Wearily, she climbed the stairs. Perversely, now that Jim was gone, she derided him for not following her. He must surely have known how upset she was; why hadn't he tried to put matters right? Offered some kind of apology for his bullish behaviour? But then, could she ever forgive him?

She paused outside her parents' bedroom, but all was silent, except for the usual rhythmic snoring from her father. William must be in his cot. Continuing on up the stairs she entered the nursery. She had managed to get William into a routine whereby he slept in his cot most of the night and had insisted that her parents bear with her and use the intercom when babysitting. He lay in his usual spreadeagled position with the bedclothes kicked off. Bending over the cot, she gently caressed his small head and pulled the blankets back over him before entering her own room and quickly undressing.

She had just pulled on her pyjama coat when she heard light footsteps on the stairs. A tap on the door and her mother entered the room, holding the other half of the intercom.

'I thought you might need this, Susan,' she whispered.

'Thanks, Mam, but really, you shouldn't have got out of bed. You should have just turned it off. After all, he's right next door to me, I would have been sure to hear him.'

'It's still quite early. Your father is snoring away, but I was reading.' She peered intently at her daughter. 'Are you all right, love?'

'Yes! Why wouldn't I be?'

'I have a confession to make. I was on my way to the bathroom and I glanced out of the landing window earlier on and I saw you leave Jim's car. You seemed in

Mary A. Larkin

a big hurry to get away from him. Have you two had a tiff?'

Suddenly it all proved too much for Susan and, covering her face with her hands, she sank down on the bed. 'Oh, Mam. I don't know what to do. Jim doesn't want William.'

Quickly crossing the floor, Rachel sat down beside her and put a comforting arm across her shoulders. 'Perhaps he just needs time?'

'You must surely have noticed, Mam, how we never take William out with us? Even when Jim's in the house he pays little attention to him. He's yet to hold him.'

'You can't very well take him to a dance or the pictures, Susan,' Rachel reasoned gently.

'He wants to see me more often, but I've tried to get him to take me and William out at weekends. You know, to the park or the beach, even over to the zoo. Just to let him get to know what a lovely baby William is, but Jim never takes the hint. He just doesn't want to know.'

'From what I've heard, he seems to be a nice, hard-working, caring lad. Even your dad likes him, and you know how he feels about you girls dating Catholics. Not many men would support their families like Jim has, since his father died. Perhaps that's why he's reluctant to take on someone else's responsibilities. Don't be too rash, Susan. Give him more time.'

'Time won't change anything. You see, he insists on knowing who the father is.'

'Ah, now, Susan. He has the right to know. Surely you can at least confide in *him*?'

'That's just it! I can't, Mam! Once he knows, his

opinion of me would be so low, he'd walk away for ever. So I'd be daft to tell him.'

This revelation left Rachel aghast. 'Ah, love,' she muttered in despair. 'What's going to become of you? No matter who you meet, they will want to know the truth.'

'Yes, I know! And there's those I could tell, and they would respect my wishes and it wouldn't make any difference to them. But not Jim! Mam, I wish I could explain. It's all such a sorry mess. I only wish I could tell the truth. Get it off my chest. Indeed, it would be a relief! But too many people would be hurt.' Tears continued to flow.

Bewildered, Rachel gathered her close, at a loss how to comfort her daughter. Who on earth was this mystery man? 'Don't take it so much to heart, love. If he's the one for you, he will marry you in spite of everything. If not, you'll meet someone else. You're young! You've your whole life ahead of you.' She rocked her daughter gently until at last the sobs petered out and the tears stopped.

Dabbing her eyes with the corner of her pyjama jacket, Susan said, 'You're right, Mam. But if he comes back tomorrow – not that I think he'd have the audacity, but if he does – I don't want to see him. You'll make some excuse for me, won't you? I need time to think.'

'All right. I'll do my best,' Rachel promised sadly.

Next morning Susan was appalled to see bruises on her upper arms and breast. She hadn't realised Jim had been so brutal. But then, she did bruise easily, she reminded herself, only to cry in retaliation that he had no right to abuse her at all! No right whatsoever!

She had to get out of the house in case he returned. There was no way she could face him at the present time. She would phone Ruth and see if she was free, and if so, perhaps they could go to the park for a picnic. This plan, however, was quickly abandoned. Ruth would guess right away that something was wrong and would wheedle the truth out of her, and she didn't want to make any confessions she might later regret.

At breakfast Alison gazed at her in concern. 'You look awful this morning, Susan! Are you ill?'

'No, William was restless during the night. I didn't get much sleep.'

'Was he? I didn't hear him. But of course I was home late and was out like a light as soon as my head hit the pillow.'

Rachel came to Susan's rescue. 'I was thinking that perhaps your father . . .' An eyebrow was raised towards the foot of the table, where Trevor was scanning the morning paper as he ate breakfast.

Aware of the sudden silence, he glanced up. 'Did someone speak to me?'

'I was wondering if you would run us all down to Enniskillen to visit my parents today. They haven't seen William since shortly after he was born. They would be so pleased.'

'I don't see why not. But it will only be a flying visit, mind. I don't fancy driving home late at night. I'd probably fall asleep behind the wheel.'

'That will be fine. Eh, Susan, don't you agree?'

'I'd love that, Mam.' Susan shot her a grateful glance. 'I'll go and prepare all I need to bring with me for William.'

'I'm afraid you'll have to count me out,' Alison said, suppressed excitement in her voice. 'I'm going over to Graham's house today.'

'So what's new?' Rachel said drily. 'You practically live there now. I take it you and Alma have resolved your differences by now?'

'She's not a bad old soul once you get to know her,' Alison assured her mother. 'And, what do you think? We're going to look at some houses today. If we find anything suitable, there might be a Christmas wedding after all.'

'Is Graham well enough?' Rachel asked in concern.

'Not really. It will have to be a very quiet affair in a registry office.'

'Ah, Alison, would it not be better to wait and have a nice big church wedding?'

A very definite shake of the head disputed this idea. 'Graham wants to get away from his mother's fussing as soon as possible.'

'That's no reason to rush into marriage. Don't you rush into anything just to suit everybody else!' Rachel admonished. 'Is this what you want?'

'The sooner we're settled in our own home, the better. Everything will be all right then.'

Then? Did that mean that everything wasn't all right now? Rachel was worried and tried to get her husband's opinion. 'Did you hear that, Trevor? There might be a Christmas wedding after all.'

Coming from the depths of his newspaper, Trevor muttered, 'Eh? What's that? Did anyone speak to me?'

Tut-tutting, Rachel sighed. Trevor could be very irritating at times. If he had been listening, instead of lost in that silly newspaper, he might have come up with something constructive. She repeated, 'Alison and Graham might get married at Christmas after all. What do you think of that?' Silently, she willed him to question the wisdom of it.

But no! A grin split her husband's face in two and, to her disappointment, he cried, 'I think that's a grand idea!'

'And I have another bit of news for you,' Alison announced.

They waited patiently for her to continue. She kept them in suspense for some moments until at last Rachel cried, 'Well? Go on, tell us.'

'I'm learning to drive. I've put in for my test and, if I pass, Graham is going to buy me a car. Isn't that wonderful?'

'I hope you realise how lucky you are, Alison. See and show Graham the respect he deserves,' Trevor warned.

'Oh, I will. Believe me, Dad, I will.'

Susan felt a twinge of jealousy. Not, she assured herself, because her sister was marrying Graham. Or indeed because she was learning to drive – a desire that had brought things to a head between herself and Jim. But because everything seemed to fall into her sister's lap without much effort on her part, whilst nothing seemed to go right for her.

The trip to Enniskillen was most enjoyable. When their eldest daughter Edith had run off with a married man, a Catholic, William and Jane Wilson had managed to weather the furore that followed. The scandal had threatened to ruin their marriage. William had been bitter and unforgiving, but Jane had sided with her daughter, saying that she must follow her heart. Most of their neighbours had been understanding, knowing they had no control over events. Others had condemned them as weaklings for having no control over their daughter. A year later Rachel had somewhat redeemed their standing by marrying Trevor Cummings, a wealthy Protestant businessman.

With Rachel's marriage, William and Jane were free to get on with their lives and had left their Shankill Road enclave and, using most of their savings, had retired to a little village on the outskirts of Enniskillen, a move they never regretted. Their cottage was set well back from the lane in a garden still abundant with late summer flowers, whose perfume permeated the air. The hills in the background were ablaze with pink and purple heathers. They were sitting in the garden await-ing the arrival of their daughter and family, and ushered them inside for a cup of tea before taking advantage of the good weather and retiring to the conservatory at the back of the cottage.

Both grandparents were captivated by baby William and not a word of censure or curiosity was passed on how he had come about. He was their great-grandson and that was all that mattered. To Susan's surprise, her grannie found an opportunity to have a quiet word in her ear.

'I don't want to pry, love, but you seem to be unhappy. Can I help in any way?'

'Ah, Grannie, I didn't mean to be a wet blanket.'

'Don't be silly, girl! It's been a pleasure having you

here. I just sense a deep, hidden unhappiness. Am I right?'

Susan sighed and confided in her. 'It's just . . . well, the man I love doesn't appear to want William.'

'Not want that beautiful wee baby?' A stern expression settled on her grannie's face. 'You're better off without him, love,' she assured her granddaughter. 'Any man who wouldn't want that lovely wee baby must need his head examined. He's not worth his salt!'

Susan laughed outright at her grannie's words. 'Do you know something, Grannie? You're probably right.'

'Remember, Susan, if you need to get away from it all for a while, bring William here. Okay? I know we get harsh winters, but nevertheless this house is warm and comfortable. We'd be delighted to have you.'

Tears brimming on her eyelashes, Susan hugged the slight figure of her grannie close. 'Thanks, Grannie. You're a dear. Actually, everybody has been very supportive, considering how I've fallen from grace. I've a friend coming over from England on a visit in a few weeks' time. Perhaps I could bring him here for a few days and let him sample some of this lovely countryside?'

'Just you do that! That would be wonderful, love. We'll be glad of the company.'

It was quite late when they returned to Belfast. When they turned off North Circular Road and rounded the corner of Old Cavehill Road, the first thing to catch Susan's eye was Jim's car parked on the opposite side of the road near the house. Pretending not to notice it, she turned her head away, and when her father drew to a halt in the driveway she hurried from the car and quickly entered the house. Perhaps if she continued to ignore him, Jim might get the message and stay away. To complicate matters still further, a taxi pulled up behind her father's car and Alison jumped out, followed more cautiously by Graham.

In the hall, under the harsh glare of the electric lights, Susan gasped in concern when she saw how ill Graham looked. Dark rings under baggy eyes and a pallid face that looked as if it had caved in. He noted her reaction and smiled wryly. 'I'm not as bad as I look. I just did too much too soon.' He paused to gaze down at the sleeping child in Susan's arms. When his eyes met hers again the bleakness within their depths caught at her heartstrings.

'You shouldn't have gone to the Orpheus that night, Graham,' she admonished. 'It was an unnecessary risk you took and it's set you back months.'

He shrugged. 'Not quite unnecessary,' he disagreed wryly. 'It cleared the air and showed me where I stood with you.'

'What are you two whispering about?' Alison asked gaily. Putting a possessive hand on his arm, she drew him away. 'Come in and sit down, love.'

A knock on the door sent Susan hurrying to climb the stairs, clutching William in her arms. 'I'll just put him in his cot.' Feeling all the surprised eyes on her, she explained, 'He's out to the world. It's been a long day for the poor wee soul.' She had a good idea it would be Jim at the door.

She was right! Out of sight at the head of the stairs, she paused and strained her ears. Her father's voice reached her. 'Come in, Jim. Susan has just gone up to put William to bed. We've been to Enniskillen and the good fresh air there has knocked him out. She shouldn't be too long. Come in and join the rest of us in the lounge.'

Tears blinded her as she gave her son a quick wash, put on his nightclothes and laid him in his cot. Locked into his night's sleep, he barely stirred during her administrations. Gazing down on his rosy cheeks and parted pink lips, she agreed with her grannie. Any man who turned away from this wee bundle of joy did indeed need his head examined. She delayed as long as she dared and at last reluctantly descended the stairs.

'Ah, there you are, Susan. Jim's been waiting for you,' her father greeted her.

Jim's eyes met hers across the room and she saw the regret and anxiety in them. He rose and crossed the floor to her. 'Can we go for a short walk, Susan?' he said quietly. 'We need to talk.'

'I'm very tired, Jim. And William might wake any minute looking for his bottle. Perhaps we could meet tomorrow night and talk?'

He hesitated, then nodded in agreement. 'Where?'

'Let's meet outside the GPO about seven and take it from there. Eh?'

'Yes, that would be fine.'

Soon after he made his excuses and left the house.

Chapter Eleven

Jim waited twenty anxious minutes outside the GPO gazing blindly at the passing pedestrians. Convinced that Susan wasn't going to show up, he was about to go home in despair. Relief flooded through him when he saw her dodging in and out of the crowds on Royal Avenue towards him, brown hair lifting in the light breeze and cheeks pink with exertion. His heart lightened at the sight of her. Would she ever forgive him? He had said some awful things to her in the heat of the moment. If she did forgive him, would he be able to persuade her to his way of thinking?

She halted in front of him, breathless. 'I'm sorry to be so late, but William was restless and I couldn't very well leave Mother to cope with him. I had to stay until he settled down.'

He forced a smile to his lips. This was something he would have to get used to if he was to further their relationship. The child would always come first now. If only it were his child, it wouldn't be a problem! In fact if the truth be known, he would be delighted. But it wasn't his and, as things stood, he would have to be more resilient if he wanted to win her over. 'You don't have to apologise, Susan. Where would you like to go?'

She had noted the smile and guessed the trend of his thoughts. Her child had to be loved, not tolerated. Why didn't he give himself a chance to get to know William? She shrugged and his spirits dropped at her apparent indifference. 'I've no idea. Somewhere quiet where we can talk.'

'Mooney's lounge bar is quiet on a Monday night, shall we head there?'

'Great! That sounds fine.' In her opinion it was great. She didn't want to be completely alone with him, in case her heart overruled her head.

They walked along Royal Avenue and she was very aware of his height and breadth. Crossing Castle Junction, they headed for Cornmarket where Mooney's pub graced one corner. The public bar was crowded as usual, but as Jim had predicted the lounge was practically empty. A few girls chatting noisily at a table in the middle of the room and a couple gazing dreamily at each other over their glasses at a side table. Once inside, he led her to a corner table.

'What would you like to drink?'

'I'll have a Pernod and lime with ice, please.'

Conversation had been sparse between them so far, and Susan couldn't think of any excuse he might come up with that could possibly put things back on an even keel, in her eyes. Her heart was heavy as she watched him standing at the bar. She admired his long, lean body, broad shoulders and dark good looks. He was so handsome! Her idea of the perfect partner. Had she been describing him in writing, she would have labelled him Adonis. She had thought they were well matched. As if aware of her scrutiny, he turned and met her glance, a slight smile playing at the corners of his mouth. Confused, she looked away, embarrassed colour lighting up her face.

Blinking hard to contain the tears that threatened to fall, she gazed blindly down at her hands clasped on the table in front of her and thought of the high hopes she'd had of a future with Jim. What a fool she'd been! While she had convinced herself that he really cared, he'd been harbouring awful doubts about her. As if she would ever have tried to con him into accepting another man's child as his. He could never undo the harm he had caused to her self-esteem.

Slipping into the seat opposite her, he placed her drink close to hand. She lifted the glass and without looking at him said, 'Thank you. Cheers,' and sipped at the pale-green liquid.

When he had acknowledged her salute with raised glass, he gently removed hers and placed it to one side, then tightly gripped both her hands within his own. In spite of the warm atmosphere, they were icy-cold and trembled in his grasp. Her gaze remained downcast.

'Look at me, Susan,' he whispered.

Reluctantly, great tear-filled eyes were lifted to his and he was full of remorse at how much pain he was causing her. 'What I did was terrible and unforgivable, Susan. I know that! And I'm ashamed of myself.' His head swayed in distress. 'I can't believe I acted like that. It shows the stress I've been under these past weeks. I've tried and tried, until I think I'm going round the bend, to put a face to the father of your child, but it's beyond me. No one I know fits the bill. I can't remember you showing interest in any other man. But I swear I will never act like that again. Do you think you could ever find it in your heart to forgive me?'

'I realise I was partly to blame,' she conceded. 'And I do forgive you. But I honestly think it would be better if we didn't see each other again, Jim. There's no way I can see a future together for us.'

'Listen, Susan.' His voice was urgent. 'I want to explain something to you.'

Wordlessly, she gazed at him. Could he possibly put matters right? She doubted it, but nevertheless a flicker of hope kindled deep within her.

'First, I want you to know that I love you dearly. There has never been anyone else as far as I'm concerned. Since I met you I've never looked at another woman, let alone touched one. Never wanted to. Do you believe me?'

She did not answer; just gazed fixedly at him. Could he really love her, yet treat her like he had? She wasn't sure, so she remained silent.

Desperate to get his point across, he pleaded, 'Susan, please believe me. I really do love you. That's why I was so gobsmacked when I saw you were pregnant. It didn't take much arithmetic to figure out you had been seeing him at the same time you were dating me. And I never guessed! I just couldn't take it in. I wanted to walk away! Put you out of my life for good. What with Mam getting married and all, I'd such great hopes for us. Then you turned up big with another man's child and it was as if you were a different Susan from the one I knew. Still, if I'd been more understanding that night, things might have turned out different. But I didn't understand your desperate need. I could only feel this deep need to possess *you*. And to realise that you were mine for the taking? I couldn't take advantage of you like that. That's why I treated you with scorn and walked away. Fool! I was a fool. I wish now I'd stayed! Just how much I wish I'd stayed you'll never know. Then none of this would have happened. But you see, I thought I was doing you a good turn. I never dreamt that someone else was involved. Someone who wouldn't show you the respect you deserved. And he didn't, you know. No matter what you say. Whoever he is, he took advantage of you.'

Jim fell silent and she thought of her brief time with Graham. He hadn't taken advantage of her. It had been mutual. She opened her mouth to defend him, but Jim was continuing.

'However, I was totally out of order when I accused you of trying to implicate me. You're too decent a person to do anything underhand like that.'

Sifting through his words, she was able to see his point of view, but could not understand why he had never contacted her, later, before she was aware that she was pregnant and had run away in despair.

She voiced her thoughts. 'Why did you never get in touch with me again? I mean, you must have known I was ashamed of my carry-on that night.'

'I couldn't, Susan. Ma's auld fellow hadn't come on the scene then and I was in no position to offer you marriage. In my opinion, nothing else is good enough for you. That's where I'm different from this other bloke. I do love you dearly. Too much to use you for my own needs.'

She desperately wanted to believe his protestations of

love, but found that she couldn't. Had he not been harbouring awful doubts about her for weeks? Had he not mauled her? How could he do that if he loved her? When they were together she had imagined they were happy enough – not as wildly happy as they had formerly been, but a quiet, settled happiness. Had these doubts been festering away in his heart? He had practically confessed that he had been waiting for her to throw herself at him! If she had, would he then have thought her a slag? There was no way she would ever know. She could never comprehend the way his mind worked. And she must never for one minute forget that he *had* cruelly manhandled her. There was no excuse for that.

Sadly she shook her head. 'It wouldn't work, Jim.'

'Could we not give it a try?'

'I can't tell you the name of William's father. And you won't be happy otherwise.'

He sighed. 'I've been thinking about that, and I realise you must have very good reasons. I think perhaps I could learn to live with it.' He gripped her hands tighter still. 'Listen, our firm is sending two workers over to the parent company in California for a year's training in some new design methods. I've been offered the chance to go.'

These words killed off the last shred of hope. She tried to sound pleased for him. 'That's a wonderful opportunity for you.'

'For us, Susan! For *us!* I want you to come with me.'

'Me? I don't understand.'

'I would be going out in about three months' time. We could be married quietly in the registry office before then. Think about it, Susan. A honeymoon in America!'

'You're forgetting about William.'

'No, I'm not! But we would be better on our own. The other fellow who's going is single.'

'Would you not be better going as a single man?'

'I want you to come with me. I told the boss I wanted to get married and he said, "No problem! What better place for a honeymoon than America?" Think of it, Susan . . . A honeymoon in California. Could William not stay with your parents? It's obvious they dote on him.'

'And you didn't think to mention that I had a son?'

'I thought we'd be better on our own, Susan,' he admitted. 'And I don't think a child would be permitted. I mean, I am going out there to work. It's a bonus them letting you go along.'

'Let me get this straight. You want me to marry you and go to America with you . . . but without my son? You must know I could never leave William behind, no matter what the circumstances were.'

Aware that he wasn't convincing her, he nodded slowly, his eyes wary.

'And what about when we come back? What then, Jim?'

'I have to confess I haven't thought that far ahead, Susan.' He felt the colour rise in his face and he hoped she wouldn't notice. Because he *had* given it a lot of thought! He pictured Susan's parents rearing William. After all, they could afford it and he would want for nothing. Susan and he would hopefully have children of their own one day. Susan was far from stupid and he felt she must be aware of his duplicity. He was not surprised when she rose swiftly to her feet, almost upsetting the drinks.

She gazed sadly down on him. 'What kind of person do you think I am, Jim? Do you really think I could turn my back on my beautiful wee son? I thought you knew me better than that.'

Tight-lipped, he replied, 'Why not? His father obviously did!' He regretted the words the instant they left his mouth, but it was too late. Would he never learn?

He didn't see her hand coming and received the full strength of her wrath, as it made contact with his cheek with such force that it drove his head back on his shoulders.

'I can't believe how rotten you are, Jim Brady! You're certainly making a career of insulting me. This much I can tell you! William's father would marry me tomorrow if I gave him the go-ahead. What do you think of that?'

'Then why don't you marry him?'

'Hah! I'll tell you one of the reasons why. Because, poor fool that I am, I actually believed I still loved you. But you certainly hit that on the head once and for all. I don't want to see you ever again. Do you hear me?' Tears blinded her as she hurried from the pub. How could she ever have thought him Mr Wonderful? He was nothing but a selfish, two-faced pig.

Jim sat sipping his pint, aware of the covert glances directed at him. What did he care what anyone thought? He smiled slightly as he gingerly fingered his throbbing cheek. Susan could certainly pack a wallop. It looked as if he would be going to America on his own after all. If he had put in a bigger effort to show willingness where the child was concerned, he might have been able to persuade her that everything would be okay when they returned. No good thinking along those lines now. He loved kids and couldn't understand why he couldn't warm to William. His aversion to the child disturbed him somewhat. How could he be a good, loving father to him, feeling the way he did? The idea that Susan had cared enough to have a relationship with another man hurt him beyond measure. Especially since it must have been while she was professing to love him. Still, surely he could overcome his dislike and learn to love this child. He drained his glass and rose slowly to his feet. He cordially saluted the people who were now smiling openly at him. One young girl even shouted, 'Hey, gorgeous, we'll be here next week if she doesn't come back to you.' Another, 'Good luck, mate.' A cheer went up as he left the bar.

Locked in misery, Susan was unaware of the concerned glances that came her way as she queued for the bus. As she paid her fare the conductor, an elderly man with daughters of his own, asked kindly, 'Are you all right, love?'

She nodded and attempted a smile, but failed miserably. Climbing to the upper deck, she sat with bowed head and tried to get a grip on her emotions.

The journey home seemed endless, but at last she was at her own front door. Her mother was crossing the hall with William in her arms when Susan let herself into the house.

A glance in her daughter's direction brought Rachel to an abrupt halt. 'Susan, what's wrong, love?'

Taking the child from his grandmother's arms, Susan

clasped him close to her breast. 'You should hear the plans Jim Brady has in mind for us,' she wailed and at last the tears fell like rain and she wept bitterly, great drops falling down unchecked on William's head.

Concerned, Rachel patted her shoulder consolingly. 'Look, I was just about to heat William's bottle. Take him into the lounge and, when it's ready, I'll come and you can tell me all about it.'

A few minutes later she found her daughter sitting on the edge of the settee rocking back and forth in a distraught state. William was howling in sympathy with her. Reaching for the child, Rachel spoke soothingly to him and admonished her daughter. 'Stop that racket, for heaven's sake. You're terrifying the poor wee soul.' When William's sobs petered out, she wiped his blotched face and offered him his bottle. He snuffled, still in distress for another few seconds, then with a sigh snuggled close and sucked contentedly.

Only then did Rachel give her full attention to her daughter. 'Now, tell me about these plans Jim Brady has in mind for you.'

Rachel heard her out in silence, her mind digesting her daughter's words of woe. Unable to bear it any longer, Susan gulped back a sob and cried, 'Well, what do you think of that? Isn't he just one cruel, heartless bugger?'

'Hush, we'll have less of that language in this house, if you don't mind.'

'Sorry, Mam. It's just . . .' She shrugged dejectedly. 'I'm so disappointed.'

'Let's get one thing straight. Do you love Jim Brady?'
'Yes! God help me! He'd need to, I can't help myself.'

Rachel looked down at the now sleeping child. She could not comprehend how this child had come about if her daughter loved Jim Brady so much. A sudden thought entered her mind, to be pushed away in horror. If Susan had been raped she would not have covered up for the man. Unless . . . it was someone close. Someone they all knew. Hadn't she said that to tell his name would cause one hell of a scandal? Impossible! No one they knew would do a thing like that.

Susan noticed the worried expression flitting across her mother's face. 'Mam? What are you thinking? Good or bad, I want your opinion. What do you think I should do?'

Rachel tried to free her mind from the dreadful thoughts that swirled around in it. 'I'm thinking,' she said slowly, 'that it might be a good idea if you married Jim. That is, if you're absolutely sure you love him?'

'Mam! Whether I love him or not doesn't enter into it!' Susan was horrified that her mother could even think of her leaving William. 'How can you condone him asking me to leave my son behind?'

'Because obviously it would be the proper thing to do. It would give you a chance to enjoy married life together, without Jim having the constant reminder of your infidelity. Once he was sure of your love he might feel differently towards William. And . . . you know yourself that William would be well looked after by your father and me.'

Susan was looking at her mother, mouth agape. 'I can't believe I'm hearing this. From you of all people, Mam.'

'Well, you did ask my advice. You've got to be realistic,

Susan. You say you love Jim! He wants to marry you! So go for it! I bet when you come back he won't be able to resist William and everything will work out in the long run.'

Scandalised, Susan retorted, 'Don't you realise that babies' memories are short? William will have forgotten me in a year's time.'

'A year's nothing in a baby's life, Susan. As long as he's loved and cared for, I admit he won't necessarily miss you. But he will quickly get to know you again.'

Susan stood rooted to the spot for some moments. She wanted to scream in frustration, grab her son and rush from the house, but common sense prevailed. Where could she go? Instead she gave her mother a baleful glare and, turning on her heel, left the room.

A short while later Rachel heard the front door slam and sat motionless, feeling that she had failed her daughter. But if Jim persuaded Susan to marry him, there was no way Rachel was going to encourage them to take William with them. For a whole year? No way at all. He had become too precious to her.

Some thirty minutes later Trevor found her still clasping the sleeping child and rocking gently to and fro. 'Is he poorly?' he asked in concern.

Great haunted eyes gazed up at him. 'Jim Brady wants Susan to marry him.'

Perplexed, Trevor asked, 'Is that not a good idea? Oh, I know he's a Catholic and normally the idea would upset me no end, as you well know, but all children need a father and Jim seems a reliable kind of bloke.'

'His firm is sending him and another chap to America on a training course and he wants Susan to marry him and go with him. They'd be away for a year. He wants her to leave William with us.'

Still feeling very much in the dark, Trevor asked softly, 'And do you not feel well enough to look after him? Is that why you look so worried? You know I'd do all I can to help, and I'm sure Alison would pull her weight too. We can even employ a nanny if need be.'

'No! Susan won't go unless she can take William with her. What will we do if Jim agrees to take him? They could like America so much that they might even settle over there.'

Slowly Trevor sank down on to the settee beside her. Now he could see only too well why she was so worried. 'We can't let that happen, Rachel.'

'I know. But it's out of our hands. I advised Susan to marry Jim and go, but she acted as if I was a traitor.'

'Is she upstairs?'

'No. She ran out of the house as if the devil himself was after her. Oh, Trevor, I feel I've let her down badly.'

He slipped to his knees beside her, the better to see the sleeping child. In the months since he was born this wee fellow had wormed his way into his grandfather's heart. Their whole life seemed to revolve around him. In the midst of her worries, Rachel felt joy creep into her heart as she gazed at them both, so close together. 'Look, Trevor,' she whispered, 'look at him!'

Bewildered, he examined his grandson's features. 'What am I looking for?'

'Can't you see? He's a smaller version of yourself. You must surely see the resemblance?'

Slowly Trevor examined his grandson feature by feature. He couldn't believe William's nose was like his, but then it would be on a smaller scale. And definitely not the eyes. Although they were closed, he knew they were a different colour entirely from his. However, as the child moved restlessly in his wife's arms he saw what she meant. The shape of the brows, the contours of the face . . . why, it was a miniature of the face that looked out of the mirror at him every morning when he shaved.

'Well?' Rachel's voice throbbed with urgency.

Trevor placed an arm around his wife and pressed his cheek to hers. 'I see what you mean, and I'm sorry I ever doubted you, love.'

Rachel closed her eyes and sent a prayer heavenwards, thanking God for his mercy. Now she could forget that mad fling she had indulged in shortly before her marriage. What had possessed her she would never know. He had been a handsome man, it was true, but she hadn't loved him. Love had never entered into it. Trevor had been away at the time and she had agreed to go to the Plaza with the girls she worked with in Gallaher's tobacco factory.

All the armed service men who came into Belfast harbour frequented the Plaza ballroom, soldiers and sailors alike. Hans had been a Norwegian sailor and she had agreed to go out with him. One date had led to another. She had been vulnerable at the time, missing Trevor, and Hans' compliments and gentle caresses had persuaded her it would do no harm – he would take care, he assured her. One night his attentions and soft words of persuasion had aroused her so much, she had let lust rule her head. Once the deed was done, however, she had been riddled with guilt and had refused to see Hans again.

To her dismay he had actually sought her out, coming to her workplace in York Road and hanging about outside, waiting for her. Trevor was due home soon and, terrified he would find out, she had begged Hans not to mess up her life. At last she had persuaded him that he really would ruin her life if he carried on in the same way. He had given in to her wishes, but, professing to love her, had insisted that she take his address in case she changed her mind.

When Susan had been premature and had resembled none of the family, Rachel had been terrified, especially in the face of Trevor's suspicions. Because of her guilty secret she hadn't blamed him for doubting her. There had been moments in their marriage when she had fought the desire to tell him about Hans and clear the air once and for all. Now she was glad she hadn't. There could be no doubt now that Susan was Trevor's daughter. He need never know her well-kept secret.

Suddenly her heart contracted with fear as shameful thoughts entered her mind. There could be another reason why William resembled him so much; why Trevor gave in so easily and accepted Susan and her child back into the family home.

Cupping her cheek with his hand, Trevor turned her face towards him. 'I really am sorry for doubting you, love.'

Eyes full of dread met his. How could she think these terrible things about her husband, Susan's father? But was he responsible? She was very much aware that these things did happen. Remembered such a case happening in the street where she grew up. There had been a terrible scandal. It had broken up the family! The father had eventually been arrested and imprisoned. But he had been an unsavoury character. Nothing at all like Trevor.

'It doesn't matter, I understood your fears,' she whispered. But when, above the sleeping child's head, he sought her lips, she turned her head aside. She would have to question Susan closely and insist on knowing the man's name. Her daughter was making life impossible for them all by her obstinate silence.

'I'll make it up to you, love. I promise.'

'I know you will. Just give me time.'

Susan's mad rush sent her up the side of the Cave Hill at a gallop. Halfway there she had to pause for breath, sitting on the trunk of a fallen tree and wiping the tears from her face. A man walking his dog passed her and bid her the time of day. She returned his greeting and then let her thoughts hold sway. Imagine her mother, of all people, advising her to leave her son behind. She would never have believed it possible if she hadn't heard it with her own two ears. Her own mother! She couldn't get over it. Had the whole world gone crazy? After she had regained her breath, more slowly now, she continued on up the hill until she was standing on the brow looking out over Belfast Lough.

A heat haze made everything ethereal and she felt ghostly spirits must surely be hovering about observing her. 'Is anyone I know out there,' she whispered softly. 'Any spirits of dead friends or relatives? If so, please help me to do what's right.' Suddenly memories of nights when much younger came to her, when she and her schoolfriends had gathered together on the hill to tell ghost stories and see who could terrify the others the most, as they sat in a ring, clasping hands. Shivers ran down her spine as the memories unfolded. It was alleged that caves hidden below the brow of the hill were used for satanic meetings. What if there was any truth in the rumours and she was calling on the wrong kind of spirits for help? Could you unwittingly make a pact with the Devil? With a last fearful look around she hurriedly retraced her footsteps, glancing apprehensively over her shoulder now and again until she reached the foot of the hill and civilisation.

Feeling more at ease, her thoughts turned to Donald. She was glad he was coming over on a visit. He would be a pleasant change from Jim and Graham. They had been very close friends, so perhaps she would feel able to confide in him and find out what he thought about her marrying Jim Brady and going to America for a year without William. Good God! What was she thinking of? Was there even the slightest of chances that she might marry Jim? Of course not. She could never leave William behind for a whole year. Why, she would miss out on so much: the cutting of his first tooth; his attempts to crawl; maybe even his first unaided steps.

Against her will Jim's words came back to tempt her. A honeymoon in California with the man she loved would be out of this world. It was a wonderful opportunity. Too good to be missed. Was there any way he could be persuaded to bring William with them? No! Not after the way she'd reacted to his proposal, slapping his face in public like that. He would never come anywhere near her again. She had surely burnt her bridges.

All day Sunday she moped about the house, barely speaking to her parents. Rachel tried to work up the courage to confront her daughter, find out the truth once and for all. Seeing his wife's distress, Trevor thought her worry was in case Susan went to America and took William with her. He warned her not to try and soft-soap Susan, but to let things take their own course.

Three days later Susan was proved wrong about Jim's intentions. On Tuesday morning there was a letter in the post for her. The handwriting was only slightly familiar and her thoughts flew to Donald. Was he cancelling his holiday? It was with trepidation that she opened it.

Colour rushed to her face when she saw it was from Jim. It was so unexpected; she had thought she would never hear from him again. All eyes were on her and she pushed it unread into the pocket of her skirt and continued to eat her breakfast.

'Aren't you going to tell us who the letter's from?' teased Alison. 'Have you a secret admirer.'

'It's none of your business, Alison.'

'You're blushing so much I just had to ask.'

'Did no one ever tell you that curiosity killed the cat?'

'Ah well, I suppose all will be revealed soon enough.' A glance at the clock brought Alison quickly to her feet. 'Is that the time it is? I'll have to run or I'll be late. See you all tonight.'

Trevor was as usual lost in the morning paper and hadn't noticed anything untoward. Susan studiously avoided her mother's eye and Rachel knew better than to pursue the matter. The writer of the letter would be revealed when – and only when – her daughter thought fit.

As soon as she was free, Susan locked herself in the bathroom and, sitting on the edge of the bath, pulled the letter from her pocket. It was quite brief. In it Jim expressed his sorrow at the way things had turned out on Saturday night. He took all the blame for failing to impress her, saying he had been insensitive in the extreme and did not blame her for slapping him on the Monday. He asked if they could please be friends and offered to give her some driving lessons before her friend arrived from England. Suggesting Wednesday evening as a starting date, he said he would be outside the gates at seven o'clock. If she failed to show he would understand and wished her all the best for the future.

Susan sat gazing into space for some time debating what she should do. Feeling as she did about him, could they be just good friends? It was worth a try. After all, not all friends became lovers – look at her and Donald, for instance. She might be only too glad of Jim's friendship one day. So what had she to lose?

Hearing William gurgling, she left the bathroom and went to attend to him. He always wakened in a happy mood, but if he was ignored for too long he would soon give off. Her mother cornered her later, whilst she was bathing William.

'Susan, I'm going to ask you a question and I want you to tell me the truth, mind.' Rachel was so agitated that she was wringing her hands in apprehension.

From her position kneeling beside the baby bath, Susan sat back on her heels and gazed at her in amazement. The state her mother was in, if Susan said 'Boo',

Rachel would probably have fainted on the spot. She held her tongue and waited.

'Were you raped?'

Susan couldn't believe her ears. 'Pardon?'

'You heard me.'

Susan's mouth dropped open. 'Catch yourself on, Mam.'

'Well, were you? Are you covering up for some man?'

'Look, Mam, believe me, I'd never be so noble. If I'd been raped, you can bet your sweet life everybody would have known all about it. Do you think I'm daft or something? I'd never let any man get away with the likes of that.'

'Why be so secretive then? Why not speak out and set everybody's mind at rest.'

'Because, as I've said time and time again, it's nobody's business but mine, and too many people would be hurt. Why are you suddenly so hot and bothered?'

'You would tell me if you'd been raped, wouldn't you?' Rachel persisted. 'Even if it is someone we all know?' Her voice was ragged with worry and Susan gazed at her in bewilderment.

'Mam, believe me, I wasn't raped!'

'Convince me, please. Tell me the man's name.'

'Mam, what's got into you? I wasn't raped. You'll just have to take my word for it.'

Hand pressed to her mouth to stifle a sob, Rachel turned and left the room.

Pulling a towel from the hot rail, Susan lifted her wriggling bundle of joy out of the bath and carried him to the nursery. She was confused beyond measure; could not comprehend what her mother was getting at. Did she suspect Graham was the father and thought her sister should be informed? Well, tough! She had no intention of opening that can of worms. Not even to please her mother.

The first meeting with Jim was an awkward affair. On Wednesday evening she watched from the landing window and saw him arrive dead on seven o'clock. Tightly gripping her handbag, she quickly descended the stairs and was out the door without anyone detaining her.

When he spotted her coming down the drive, Jim left the car and came round to open the passenger door for her. 'Thank you for coming. I don't deserve it.'

'After what I did? I'm sorry I slapped your face in public like that,' she said ruefully. 'Were you very embarrassed?'

He shrugged. 'Just a bit, but I got over it. Actually, it got me a lot of sympathy from those girls. They cheered me when I eventually left the bar.' He had opened the car door but was blocking access to it. 'How well do you drive, Susan? I've no idea. Would you like to start now?'

'Oh no,' she cried in alarm. 'Let's go somewhere there isn't a lot of traffic, please. I'm sure to be very rusty.'

He laughed and opened the door wide for her.

He drove up to the zoo car park and stopped the car. 'This should do the trick.' He turned in his seat to look at her. 'Susan, what happened between us lately can't be ignored. I just want to say I'll be going to America in three months' time and so far the firm thinks you are coming with me. If you feel you care enough to marry me, let me know. Meanwhile, I'll be only too happy to teach you to drive.'

'Thank you, but don't count on it, Jim. William must always come first.'

'I realise that now.' He squeezed her arm gently. 'Let's swap seats. I want to see how well you drive.'

Donald left his car in the garage at Cockerton to get it serviced and walked up West Auckland Road to tell Edith he was going over to Ireland for a holiday. 'Why, that's wonderful news!' she cried. 'Will you be anywhere near Belfast?' she asked excitedly.

'Not only will I be near Belfast, but I'll be staying there.' He laughed happily as he informed her, 'Susan has invited me to stay in her home. What do you think of that?'

'That's marvellous!' She nodded wisely. 'They'll see that you have a good time while you're with them, so they will. If I get some wee presents for them all, will you take them over for me? That is, if you're driving over?'

'I am, yes, taking the car, and of course I'll deliver your presents.'

'I wish I was going with you,' she lamented.

'Now that's an idea, Edith. Why don't you come with me? I'd be glad of the company and there's stacks of room in the car. And you know they'd be glad to see you.'

Edith's voice was sad. 'If only I could, but we're too busy at the moment. This good weather is bringing so many visitors to Darlington. Not just on market days, but every day. It wouldn't be fair to leave Billy to cope on his own. Especially at weekends.'

'Would Jack not help out at weekends?'

'Can you see Margaret letting him? She gripes enough as it is because he can't afford a car to squire her about. That wee girl wants to run before she can walk. There's no way she would let him give up his free time to help out. And mind you . . . we wouldn't ask him to do it for nothing.'

'Put it to Billy anyhow,' Donald urged. 'See what he says.'

'No. No, it wouldn't be fair putting the onus on him. He would only insist on me going with you. Perhaps in the autumn when we're not so busy, he and I will get over for a week. That wee baby of Susan's looks lovely in the photographs she sent over. I'd love to see him. But forget about me. Do you need anything, son? How are you off for money?'

'I couldn't take your hard-earned cash, Edith! But it's more than generous of you to offer.'

'It would be a loan, but you could take your time paying it back.'

'Not even for a loan! Cash flow is most important in business. You need a little capital behind you in case of the unexpected. Thanks all the same, but I'll manage.'

'Quite the little businessman,' she laughed. 'But if you should need help, sure you won't be too shy to ask?'

'Thanks, Edith, you're a pal. I'll bear it in mind.'

'Hush, here's Billy now. Don't mention me saying I'd like to go to Belfast.'

'Look who I picked up along the way,' Billy cried as he stood, still hidden from view, behind the open living-room door.

A little head came around the door, face alight with laughter.

'Why, it's a little angel.' Edith swooped on her grand-daughter and, taking her from Billy's arms, hugged her close. 'How's my little darling today?' she crooned.

Margaret followed Billy into the room, her eyes brightening noticeably when she saw Donald. 'She's a bit off-colour. We had taken her out for a breath of fresh air when Billy spotted us, and insisted we come home with him. I didn't notice your car outside, Donald?'

'It's in getting serviced.'

Jack followed her into the room. 'We won't be able to stay too long, mind,' he warned when his eyes fell on Donald.

'Well, I'm sure you can all at least take time to have a cup of tea,' Edith reasoned. 'I've a lovely fresh Madeira cake.'

'You've convinced me, Edith,' Donald chuckled.

'I second that,' Margaret agreed, and planked herself down on the settee beside him. So close it wasn't decent. He squirmed as Jack glared at him. Why was he glaring at him? Why didn't he control his wife, instead of taking it out on him? He wanted to upbraid Jack, but what good would it do? He moved as far away from her as possible, but she edged along after him and patted the space on the other side of her, as if they were making room for her husband. Jack looked at her and wasn't fooled. The venom in his eyes was almost tangible as his eyes raked their faces. For a moment Donald braced himself, convinced that Jack was about to lunge at them in a rage, but with a stifled oath he turned on his heel and left the room. They heard the front door slam and Margaret, with a smug smile, snuggled closer to Donald.

'Isn't this nice,' she whispered.

They were alone, Billy having taken Angela out to see the birds in the back garden, while Edith was in the kitchen making the tea. With a contented sigh, Margaret wiggled her body along the length of his, pressing closer still; rubbing her cheek against his sleeve.

Appalled at her effrontery in her mother-in-law's house, Donald growled, 'You're asking for trouble, girl.'

She smiled sweetly at him. 'No, you're reading the signs all wrong, Donald. It's a bit of lust I'm after. Just good, old-fashioned sex, you know! God knows, my life is so drab I could do with a bit of excitement in it.' Daringly she placed a hand on his thigh and gently caressed it.

He pushed it away. 'You're shameless!'

'No. Wrong again. Just bored. You know, you could put a stop to my boredom, Donald. And then everybody would be happy. And the best of it is, no one need be any the wiser. We could be very discreet about it.'

'You don't know the meaning of the word.'

'Oh, but I do. You'd be surprised.' The hand was back and she laughed softly when she saw the effect it was having. 'It's very obvious to me you still find me attractive, Donald, and it would do no harm to give in to your urges. I promise never to tell anyone.'

He was on his feet and away from her caressing hand and the unwanted effect it was having on him. 'Are you actually looking for a divorce?' he hissed into her face.

'Jack dotes on Angela. He'd never divorce me,' she said confidently. 'Unless of course I forced him to.' A speculative look came into her eye. 'Would you be interested, Donald, if I was free?' Her mouth twisted in a wry grimace as she assured him, 'You needn't worry about Jack. I can manage him. He's putty in my hands.'

'More fool him! Do you know something? You're sick! You don't know when you're well off.' With these words, Donald left her and went off to join Edith in the kitchen.

Edith eyed him covertly as he gazed blindly out of the window. 'Is Margaret up to her old tricks again?'

He turned a look of surprise on her. 'What do you mean?' he asked apprehensively.

She laughed sadly. 'Do you think I'm blind, son? I know what's going on. It will do you good to get away from her for a while, before she wears you down.'

'What I don't understand, Edith,' he cried in frustration, 'is why Jack doesn't put his foot down. Show her who's boss.'

'I think he's afraid! If they have a showdown, he doesn't know whether you'll be waiting to take her on. Will you, Donald?'

He puffed out his cheeks and expelled his breath loudly. 'I've had enough of Margaret to last me a lifetime, thank you.'

'I'm glad to hear that, son. To be truthful, I wasn't sure. She's a very attractive woman – and a very determined one at that. She likes to get her own way.'

'I suppose, if I had any sense, I'd get out of Darlington. Give their marriage a chance.'

'Why? Why should you be the one to move? This is your home town. You've always lived in Darlington, and I for one would be sorry to see you go. As for your mother? Why, she'd be devastated. Here, take this tray in, son. Let Margaret make herself useful for a change, being mother. I'll give Billy a shout when I cut this cake, and follow you in.'

They hadn't heard Jack return, but he sat at the opposite end of the settee from Margaret, looking the picture of misery.

'Edith says will you pour, Margaret?'

'Sure.'

Her pale hair swung down around her face as she bent over the tray, casting mysterious shadows around her eyes and mouth. She really was lovely to look at. A pity her demeanour wasn't as nice. Still, Donald could understand why Jack put up with her tantrums. His eyes ran down her body, lingering on the curve of her hips. Yes, she still had the power to arouse him, in spite of the fact that he didn't like her any more. He could understand why Jack was so besotted with her. Raising his head, he met Jack's baleful glare and blushed with shame at the road his thoughts had taken. He really would be glad to get away from them both for a while.

Edith passed the plate of Madeira cake around and, feeling the tension hanging in the air, sought to break it. 'Has Donald told you he's going over to Ireland in a couple of weeks' time?'

Margaret's head reared back. 'No, he hasn't mentioned it. My, but you're a dark horse. When did you decide on this, Donald?'

'Just lately.'

'Are you going over to Susan?'

'Yes.' He didn't elaborate and she gazed down at her plate. With Jack sitting there she didn't dare show too much concern; he was upset enough already.

Billy broke off putting small morsels of cake into his

granddaughter's mouth. 'Did I hear you right? Is Trevor Cummings actually letting you stay in his house?'

Looking apprehensive, Donald nodded his head. 'Is there any reason why he shouldn't?'

'No, no. But he must have changed his spots. There was a time he would hardly pass the time of day with a Catholic. Or perhaps he doesn't know you're a Catholic. Is that it?'

Seeing a worried frown gather on Donald's brow, Edith admonished her husband. 'Stop teasing, Billy. You're worrying the lad. Don't you listen to him, Donald. If Susan says you can stay in their house it must be all right.'

'Are you going over to make an honest woman of her, Donald?' Margaret asked maliciously.

'Not really, but I'll tell you this much: if I think there's a chance she'll have me, I'll certainly ask her to marry me. You couldn't meet a nicer girl.'

'Huh! That's a matter of opinion.'

'I think most people like her, Margaret.' Donald drained his cup and rose to his feet. 'That was worth waiting for, Edith. The cake was delicious. I'll have to be shoving off now.'

Margaret came to the door of the kitchen as he placed his cup in the sink. 'I would like to send something over for the baby. Will you call in and see us before you go, Donald?'

Not wanting to give her an excuse to follow him over to the sink and make a fool of him again, he joined her at the doorway, where they were in full view of the others. 'I will surely, Margaret. As soon as I know when I'm leaving I'll give you a tinkle and you can leave your gift with Edith. I'll be picking some things up from here before I go.' He had raised his voice just loud enough for everyone to hear.

'I'll buy something tomorrow.' She looked meaningfully at him. 'Perhaps we'll have a drink with you before you go? Wouldn't that be nice, Jack?'

No answer was forthcoming from her husband, but undeterred she continued, 'We'll see you before you go, Donald.'

Not if I can help it, Donald thought and, bidding them all good day, left the house.

On a fine Saturday morning two weeks later Donald left Darlington early in the morning on his journey up to Stranraer and the cross-channel ferry. He was booked on a late afternoon sailing, but never having been to Scotland before wanted to take his time and see all the beautiful scenery Susan had raved about. Billy had also warned him about all the small villages and towns he would pass through, which would slow his journey down somewhat; especially Dumfries, where the traffic was usually bumper-to-bumper on Saturdays.

The further he got away from Darlington, the more relaxed he became. In spite of all his best endeavours to elude her, Margaret had at last caught up with him the night before. He had been collecting the gifts that Edith was sending over to all her family when Margaret arrived with her present for Susan's baby, just as he was about to leave. Edith had apologised for letting her know he was coming, but as she pointed out, Margaret had phoned knowing that Donald was leaving the next morning and had asked if she could come over with a present for Susan's baby, so what could she do but agree?

Jack was on the late shift, Margaret explained when she arrived, and so, wanting to catch Donald, she had left Angela with her neighbour for a while to come over with her present for the baby. 'You're a hard man to catch,' she said and eyed him reproachfully, knowing full well that he had managed to elude all her attempts to waylay him en route from work.

Glad that her gifts were already packed into the boot, Edith asked, 'Have you time for a cup of tea, Margaret? Billy will be out some time yet, but if you can wait he'll give you a lift home as soon as he gets here.'

'I don't want to impose on my neighbour by being away too long. If I do stay for a cuppa, will you give me a lift home, Donald? It would save me waiting for a bus. They're few and far between at this time of evening.'

Reluctantly he agreed, and fifteen minutes later they left Cockerton and headed over to Albert Hill. She was very quiet and this worried him. Just what was going on in that conniving little mind of hers? he wondered.

He drew the car up in front of her house but made no attempt to get out. She turned in her seat and those big, dark eyes of hers mocked him and the full, sensuous lips pouted seductively at him. With a rueful smile she shook her head. 'I do believe you're afraid of me, Donald Murphy. I wonder why? Could it be that you don't trust yourself?'

'Good night, Margaret. I'll see you when I get back.'

'Ah now, Donald. You're not getting off as lightly as that.' A key was thrust at him. 'Here, open the door while I fetch Angela.'

Before he could object she was out of the car and he had no option but to follow her. Planning to leave the minute she came back with the child, he opened the door and entering the small hall waited there. He had to admit that Margaret had hit the nail on the head. He didn't trust himself and had no intention of being manoeuvred any further into the house. To his dismay, in spite of his determination, he had to move into the living room to allow a young man who returned with Margaret, carrying a sleeping Angela in his arms, to enter the house. He looked surprised when he saw Donald and acknowledged him with an abrupt nod.

'In here, Joseph.'

Joseph hesitated. 'Don't you want me to carry her upstairs, Margaret? She's getting quite a weight, you know.'

'No, in here will be fine, Joseph. Lay her on the settee, please. If need be, Donald can carry her upstairs before he goes.' She introduced them. 'Joseph, this is Jack's friend. Donald, this is my next-door neighbour. He lives in the house you used to rent.'

The men exchanged nods and then Joseph, with a quizzical look at Margaret, took his leave.

'Sit down, Donald.'

'I'm afraid I'll have to be going now, Margaret. I've still a lot of packing to do.'

'Why do I not believe you? In my experience, men just throw their belongings together at the last minute, especially when travelling by car. As a rule they don't worry about packing the way women do.'

'I must be the exception to the rule then. Good night, Margaret.'

'You must hold on for a minute or two, Donald. I can't leave Angela on her own in case she rolls off the settee. I need to get her nightclothes down.'

It was on the tip of his tongue to offer to carry the child upstairs, but he caught the words back in time. Look where that could lead.

As if she had read his mind Margaret laughed aloud. 'For heaven's sake sit down, Donald. I'm not going to eat you! I won't be a minute.'

He sat on the edge of the settee and watched the sleeping child. With her golden curls and rosy cheeks, she looked a picture. If things had worked out differently that could be his daughter lying there. If they had married as planned, would Margaret still be discontented with her lot? He imagined so. She would always want what she couldn't have. He'd had a lucky escape.

Was life already laid for you? A matter of whatever will be, will be? Was there someone out there waiting for him? What about Susan Cummings? Who knows? He had questioned Edith about Susan's marriage. Had tried to find out if she was divorced or in the process of being divorced. Edith had been very evasive and had advised him to speak to Susan about it when he was over there. Well, he'd do that! It would be nice to get married and have children of his own. Perhaps one day he and . . .

His thoughts were interrupted by Margaret returning to the living room. She had changed into a loose garment – Donald wasn't sure, but he thought it was called a housecoat. It was of fine material and clung to her full breasts. It was obvious that she had nothing on under it. She had also taken time to brush her hair and, although dusk was falling, it still caught the light that filtered through the window and moved like quicksilver around her face and shoulders.

His breath caught in his throat at the beauty of her and as desire made itself felt. He rose quickly to his feet. 'I'll have to be going now.' His voice was shaky and silently he cursed himself. He knew she was aware of his agitation.

'Bear with me another few minutes, Donald.'

She disappeared into the kitchen and reappeared with a bottle of whiskey and two glasses. 'Remember, I promised to share a drink with you before you left. I wanted Jack to invite you out for a meal with us, but he wouldn't hear tell of it. I can't think why. So . . .' She placed the glasses on a small table and half-filled them with whiskey. 'I believe in keeping my promises.' A glass was thrust at him. 'Safe journey over and back,' she said softly.

Feeling it would be churlish to refuse, he said 'Thanks' and raised the glass to his lips. Darkness was closing in on them and he reached for the light switch.

Quickly setting down her glass, Margaret was there before him, covering the switch with her hand. 'Don't, Donald.' She was so close her breath was fanning his face and her perfume was wafting around him. 'Don't fight it! No one will ever know. You want me. I know you do. So why not? Eh, why not? I made a mistake, but there's no need for us to suffer for ever. We were meant to come together.' She moved closer and raised her face for his kiss.

Feeling his control slipping, he tried to move away but relentlessly she followed, all the while subtly using her body to excite him. Distracted, he thought: why not indeed? He was a mug trying to resist her. After all, you never missed a slice from a cut loaf. As she frequently pointed out, no one need ever know. Susan's face rose before his mind, but he ignored it. No promises had been made there. All she had ever offered him was friendship and for all he knew her marriage may have been reconciled. She had never willingly discussed it with him, but she had said there was a man she was in love with. So why was he letting thoughts of her trespass on this passionate moment?

Margaret was in his arms now; warm and willing. Only a fool would push her away. He crushed her close and his lips trailed her face and neck before savagely covering her mouth. Her lips were soft and moist and worked hungrily under his. He opened her housecoat and caressed her full breasts. The child stirred on the settee and settled down again, but he had been distracted. He raised his head to gaze at her in bewilderment. What was he thinking of? Well, that was obvious enough! But why? Why was he coveting his mate's wife? Jack Devine, God help him, had enough on his plate without him adding to his worries. She pulled his head down towards her and whispered urgently, 'You can't stop now, Donald.'

'I can't do this to Jack.'

'Why not? He did it to you.'

'Two wrongs don't make a right, Margaret. And who knows? I'm beginning to think he did me a good turn. Besides, I don't want to join a queue, and that Joseph guy next door seemed to know his way about here earlier on.'

'Joseph means nothing to me. You must believe that. It's you I want. I've always wanted you.'

Gripping her arms, he put her firmly from him.

'You fool! You stupid fool!' she cried. 'It's only an act after all. A bit of excitement.'

'No, Margaret. In most people's books it's a betrayal.'

In one last desperate attempt to delay him, opening her housecoat and arms wide she cried, 'Look! Look what you're missing.'

A quick glance was all he needed to warn him he must get out of here before it was too late. Roughly pushing past her, he opened the door and hurried to his car. As he eased it away from the kerb, he wasn't surprised to see Joseph, in the rear mirror, leave his house and approach the one next door. Nor was he surprised to see him being admitted. He smiled wryly. Ah, well . . . that's the way the cookie crumbles, he thought. Was he a fool to turn down what was being offered on a plate, so to speak?

Pushing all thoughts of his old flame from his mind, he concentrated on the road ahead. At this hour of the morning it was clear. Dawn was breaking, the sun a fiery ball rising behind him and giving a pink blush to fields and hedges as it rose slowly in the sky, like an artist's brush creating a scene in watercolour. He had never seen anything like it in his life before. He drove through Barnard Castle and over Bowes Moor, before stopping in a lay-by to enjoy all this peaceful beauty. He delayed for twenty minutes looking out over the moors; watching the transformation, with only the wary sheep for company. Then, with a sigh of contentment, he continued over the moors until he reached Penrith, where he left the scenic route for the more mundane motorway towards Carlisle, one of the signs he had been told to watch out for. Half an hour later he passed Carlisle and was crossing the invisible border into Scotland.

Soon he came upon a road sign pointing off the dual carriageway, indicating Dumfries and Stranraer, his ultimate destination. Following these directions, he was surprised to come across another road sign pointing to Gretna Green. Doing a quick calculation of the time it would take to reach Stranraer from here, he decided he was well ahead of schedule, so he made a detour to take a walk round Gretna Green. He was enthralled by the different stories displayed around the blacksmith's shop: some sad, some downright hilarious, but all with the same theme – romance. Stories of lords and ladies eloping to marry their true loves. Stories, too, of girls and boys, considered by law to be too young to marry in their own countries, eloping to Gretna Green to take their wedding vows. As in days of old, some even got married over the blacksmith's anvil. All too soon he had to leave this romantic setting behind and continue on his way.

He was delayed slightly driving through Annan due to the Saturday traffic and shoppers. Feeling a bit peckish as he neared Dumfries, he remembered Billy telling him about one of the fish-and-chip shops where he wouldn't be disappointed with the fare. Finding a car park by a river, he went in search of the shop. Billy was right of course. The fish and chips were delicious and were washed down with a Coke. A glance at his watch warned him that he had better get cracking and go at a steady pace from now on, just in case of any unforeseen hold-ups. He passed through lots of beautiful villages and along the twisting road with the sea shimmering in the bright sunlight below on his left, until he finally arrived at Stranraer harbour with a little time to spare. He booked in at the terminal and was directed into a line of cars.

Locking the car, he went to the terminal café and ordered some sandwiches and a pot of tea. Thus refreshed, he settled down to await the call for all motorists to return to their cars, reflecting on his journey so far. He would certainly give the west coast of Scotland some priority when he next considered taking a holiday.

Chapter Twelve

The short crossing over on the ferry to Larne had been pleasant. So calm and warm Donald had spent all two and a half hours on the upper deck watching Scotland receding in the distance and the shores of Ireland eventually appearing on the horizon. Susan had phoned the night before and explained she would be waiting in the lorry park at Larne harbour and to be sure to watch out for her. As soon as the first vehicle rolled down the ramp she would get out of the car and watch for him.

He pictured her as he had last seen her, anxious and stressed and big with child, and wondered how she would look now. The PA system interrupted his musing, informing drivers to return to their vehicles and foot passengers to gather at some point or other. With a last appraising glance at the fast-approaching Larne harbour, Donald joined the other drivers and passengers and descended the iron companionway down into the bowels of the ship. Waiting for the great iron doors to open and release the cars and vans and wagons, he sat, his thoughts occupied with Susan. Would her husband be with her? Would she be foolish enough to think he would be glad to hear her marriage had been salvaged?

God forgive him, but he hoped a divorce was in the pipeline. There didn't seem much substance to this shadowy husband and Susan deserved a real man. But he could be wrong. Perhaps when he met the guy he would be impressed by him. Only time would tell! Twenty minutes later he was bumping noisily down the ramp on to *terra firma*.

Donald's first sight of Susan brought to the surface all the latent feelings she had once aroused in him. He remembered when he had first become aware of her sensuality on High Row and his pulse quickened. She looked beautiful in a white sleeveless top and brief white shorts, her limbs a golden honey colour. Her figure was neat and trim and the sun caught the chestnut highlights in her hair. Suddenly, to his surprise, he recaptured the feel and smell of her in his arms as if it were yesterday. To his dismay, however, she was accompanied by a tall, dark-haired man. He was deeply tanned and wore a white sports shirt and shorts. Donald smiled as it crossed his mind that the pair of them would make a good advertisement for Persil. Was this the husband?

He steered the car out of the flow of traffic and, leaving it, joined Susan and her companion on the pavement. 'You look wonderful, Susan,' he exclaimed and dared to kiss her on the cheek. To his delight she threw her arms around him and hugged him close.

'It's great to see you again, Donald.' She swung away from him but stayed in the circle of his arm. Indicating her companion, she said, 'This is my friend, Jim Brady. Jim, you must feel you already know Donald, since I've talked of nothing else since I knew he was coming.'

Jim thrust his hand at Donald and wryly agreed. 'I do indeed. Susan thinks the world of you. Apparently you were there for her when no one else was, and for that I am grateful to you.'

Donald gripped the proffered hand and inwardly lamented this man's handsome good looks. Jim's words had a possessive ring to them and this dismayed Donald even more. 'Pleased to meet you, Jim,' he said, his voice pleasant, his demeanour neutral.

'Donald, you'll be glad to hear that Jim has been giving me driving lessons. I drove all the way here,' Susan announced proudly.

A delighted grin split Donald's face. 'I'm glad to hear that! That's very good news. You were doing very well before you left Darlington.'

'She's a natural! She'll have no bother passing her test.' Jim's words of praise warmed her heart. He really had been making an effort these past few weeks. Why couldn't she just forgive and forget?

'Jim will lead the way back to Belfast, Donald, and I'll go in your car. Then you can bring me up to date about everybody across the water.'

'Right!' Jim took control. 'Donald, my car is over in the lorry park. Give me a few minutes and then Susan will direct you to me and we'll get on our way.'

Jim strode off, admiring eyes following his progress. Donald gazed thoughtfully after him, feeling pale and insignificant compared to Jim. And to imagine that he had thought he had a tan! He glanced down at arms that now appeared yellow in the face of the other man's tanned limbs.

Susan tugged at his sleeve to get his attention and

gazed smilingly up into his face. 'I really am so pleased to see you. Mam is looking after William, and Dad is mowing the lawn. All in your honour. They're looking forward to meeting you, and Mam will have a meal ready for us.'

At once all his attention was hers. After all, tanned skin didn't make the man, and she and Jim didn't appear to be all that close. 'Billy Devine had me a bit worried about your dad. Said he wasn't too fond of Catholics. Mind you, Edith didn't contradict him, but she assured me that you would look after me.'

Susan laughed aloud. 'I've discovered lately my dad's bark's worse than his bite. Don't worry about it. Everything's going to be just fine. You're even having our Alison's bedroom while you're here. It's much bigger than the guest room. She left for Galway this morning with Graham and his parents.'

'How is Graham?'

'I don't see very much of him these days. But I hear he's still a bit wobbly on his legs. They say he will eventually get back to his old self. It looks like a Christmas wedding is on the cards.'

Donald eyed her closely, wanting to ask her how she felt about this. He held his tongue. Perhaps he had just imagined that Graham was interested in Susan, after all. If that were the case, he was hardly likely to be planning to marry her sister, and Susan certainly didn't seem in the least perturbed.

'I think we've delayed long enough. Let's go find Jim, eh, Donald? In case he thinks we've got lost already,' she laughed.

When Jim saw Donald's car coming along the lane

between the high container lorries, he eased slowly into his path and Donald fell in behind him. The journey to Belfast had commenced. In his rear-view mirror Jim could see Susan chatting away to Donald and he was worried. Were they closer than Susan had led him to believe? He had thought he was making headway with her these past weeks, and would maybe be able to persuade her to marry him, but seeing how well she and Donald were getting on, he felt uneasy. This guy would be living under the same roof as Susan for the next three weeks; how could he further his own cause while Donald was there?

In the car Susan sat twisted in her seat to gaze at Donald. 'How is Edith and Billy?'

'Doing very well, as far as I can make out. Edith would have liked to come over with me, but they're far too busy. She wants to see your wee son in person.'

'Oh, I wish she had come with you,' she said wistfully.

'She said her and Billy would probably come over in the autumn.'

'Good! Mam will be so pleased.' A smile creased Susan's face as she asked after her cousin and his wife. 'How is Jack and the wonderful Margaret?'

'Jack should put his foot down where that girl's concerned,' he retorted. 'She's far too brazen, that one!' He squirmed in his seat as he remembered how he had almost succumbed to temptation with her the previous night.

'Ah! So she's still making passes at you, mm?' Susan queried knowingly. Watching the red colour rise from his collar to hairline, she felt sad. 'Don't let her ruin your life, Donald. She's not worth it. You deserve better.'

'What about you? Is Jim your estranged husband?'

She laughed ruefully, 'Oh, Donald, there's so much I must explain to you. And I will, I promise. But not now. Later! We have three whole weeks to talk. That is, if you don't mind me trekking about with you?'

'I'll be very glad of your company, Susan. Remember, I've never been to Ireland before, so I'll need a guide to show me around.'

Contented, she relaxed back in her seat with a sigh and started pointing out places she thought might be of interest to him during the rest of the drive.

When they arrived at the house Jim declined her invitation to stay for a meal, saying he needed to have a shower and a change of clothes if they were to go to the Orpheus that night.

Clapping a hand to her mouth in dismay, Susan cried, 'I completely forgot to mention the dance. Perhaps you're too tired to go, Donald, after travelling all day?'

Her eyes questioned him and he was quick to respond. 'Not too tired to see this famous dance hall of yours.' He had a feeling Jim would expect Susan to go, whether he went or not, and he had no intention of losing out.

'That's smashing! Jim and I go every Saturday night.'

'I'll pick you up then, a bit later than usual, eh, Susan? Give you both a chance to get ready. Say about half-eight?'

'That'll be fine, Jim. And thanks for all your help and for letting me drive your car to Larne.'

'No problem.'

Without another glance she climbed the steps, as her mother appeared at the door with William in her arms and her father hovering in the background.

Donald watched her, a slight frown on his brow, feeling that she was being very abrupt with Jim. 'Thanks for all your bother, Jim. See you tonight,' he said before following Susan up the steps.

'Donald, this is my mother and father.' She reached for William as she introduced them.

'Come in, son.' Rachel stepped aside and motioned him inside. 'I'm very pleased to meet you at last.' Seeing Jim turn away, she said in surprise, 'Are you not coming in, Jim?'

'No, I'll see you and Mr Cummings later. Bye for now.'

Trevor gripped Donald's hand. 'Glad to meet you, son.'

'The pleasure's all mine, Mr Cummings. Thanks for putting me up.'

'Uncle Billy had him a bit worried about you, Dad.'

'No doubt! We never did see eye to eye. How is Billy and Edith?'

'Well! Very well. They send their regards. And this must be William.' Tentatively Donald touched a chubby arm and was rewarded with a toothless grin. 'He's beautiful, Susan. The photographs you sent over don't do him justice.'

'Tell me, why do we always stand about in the hall when someone visits?' Trevor complained. 'Come into the lounge, Donald, and sit down. Would you like a lager before your meal?'

'That would be appreciated, Mr Cummings.'

'While you pour the drinks, Trevor, I'll check on the

dinner.' Rachel bustled off in the direction of the kitchen.

'While Mam and Dad are busy, fetch your bags in and I'll show you up to your room,' Susan offered.

Donald disappeared and returned loaded down with parcels. 'These are all presents. Most of them are from Edith and Billy. A small gift from me for the baby and a box of Thornton's continental chocolates for your mother. Edith says you can't get them over here?'

'No. Maybe some day they'll open a shop over here, but not so far. Mam will be delighted.'

'That one in the blue wrapping paper is from Margaret and Jack.' He glanced at Susan and they shared a smile.

'Just leave them all on that coffee table in the corner there, Donald,' she said, suppressed laughter in her voice. She could imagine Margaret making a big thing out of getting the gift to Donald. 'We'll enjoy opening them after dinner. It'll be like Christmas, so it will. Meanwhile, get your bags in and follow me.'

Ascending the stairs behind her, he couldn't keep his eyes of her slim, tanned thighs and well-rounded calves. She turned on the landing to await him and he blushed as she caught his appraising glance.

A smile played about her wide, sensuous mouth. 'In here.' She threw open the bedroom door and stood aside for him to enter.

He gazed around Alison's room in admiration. 'This is lovely. Are you sure your sister won't mind?'

'Not in the slightest. You will be more comfortable here than in the guest room. It's much bigger. As you can see, I've put on plain bedclothes. I trust you won't be too overwhelmed by the flowered curtains and pink carpet, will you?'

He moved closer and whispered, 'It's a secret fetish of mine, to be surrounded by feminine things.'

Eyes wide, she whispered back, 'Don't tell me you wear women's underwear as well?'

'No, I'm fighting that urge. But I think I'm slowly losing the battle.'

They enjoyed a good laugh together and she was struck anew by how easy he was to get on with, and by just how much she liked him. 'We had better go down or your beer will be flat and Mam will be getting worried in case the dinner spoils.'

He held out his arms. 'Let me carry William down for you, he looks a right handful.'

She handed the child over and Donald hugged him against his chest. Her heart was sad as she watched him cuddle her son. This was no act put on for her sake! It was obvious he was genuinely fond of children. If only Jim could be more like Donald it would solve a lot of her problems.

After dinner her parents disappeared into the kitchen and, rising to her feet, Susan said, 'Alas, time marches on. I'm afraid I won't have time to open the presents now. Mam and Dad can go ahead and open theirs if they like. Donald, I'm sorry about this. I should have realised we'd be pushed for time, but I can't let Jim down. Would you prefer to stay here and rest yourself?'

'To be truthful, I'm looking forward to the dance. The presents can keep until tomorrow. Shouldn't I offer to help with the dishes?'

'They just have to be loaded into the dishwasher and Mam will have all that organised by now. Here she is now. Mam, if I leave William's things out, will you get him ready for bed? We're running late.' ·

'You know I will! You two away and get ready.'

'Thanks, Mam. Donald, come on and I'll show where everything is and you can have a shower while I decide what to wear. I think we can just about make it for half-eight. So let's get a move on.'

Jim arrived on the dot and Trevor crossed the hall and admitted him as Susan came down the stairs looking flushed and happy. Donald joined them from the lounge, where he and her parents were getting to know each other.

'I'll just say good night to William and then we'll go.'

'Here he is!' Rachel came from the lounge with William in her arms. 'Donald was nursing him and he's almost asleep.'

They all kissed the sleepy baby, except Jim, who was aware of Donald's appraising look but was unable to do anything about it. Lately he had made tentative attempts to include the child in outings with him and Susan, but she didn't seem to notice. As for suddenly becoming all loving towards him in front of her parents, that was beyond him. They'd only think him a hypocrite.

To his relief they were at last outside and climbing into the car. The Orpheus was packed, but the doorman recognised Jim and Susan as regulars and allowed them through.

Claiming priority over her, Jim asked for the first dance. With a smile of apology at Donald, she followed Jim on to the floor. 'You look lovely tonight, Susan.'

'Thank you.'

'You suit that colour.'

She wore a pale primrose-coloured cotton dress. Short-sleeved and full-skirted, it showed off her tan and called attention to her slim legs. Glancing down at it, she smiled. 'One of last year's, I'm afraid. I have to be careful with my savings now I've William to think about. I can tell you, I'll be glad to get back to work and earn some extra cash. That's another thing, Jim. If I was to consider your proposal, I'd forfeit all right to my job. There's no way they would keep it for another year.'

'But if we were married, you wouldn't need to work.'

'With William not being yours, I'd always feel the need to be independent.'

'You're talking nonsense now, Susan. When we marry I'll be responsible for him.'

'*If* we marry!' she reminded him. 'Please don't be counting on it, Jim,' she warned.

A frown puckered his brow. 'Susan, I'll still see you while Donald is here, won't I?'

'I don't see why not. Donald is unlikely to want me hanging around him every night. I shall show him the sights during the day and we'll be going to Enniskillen to visit Grannie and Grandad for a couple of days. Edith has sent presents over for her parents. But other than that, I'm sure Donald will want to do his own thing.'

Jim wasn't so sure about this. 'Will you make a point of seeing me as usual on Tuesday and Thursday for your driving lessons?' he asked anxiously. 'You won't want to miss out now that you're doing so well.'

'I don't think you need worry about my lessons, Jim. I'm sure Donald will let me have a go behind the wheel when the roads aren't too busy.'

'You know that's not what I'm worried about! I must see you, Susan, on a regular basis, otherwise how can I hope you will change your mind and marry me?'

'I never made any promises, Jim,' she cried in dismay. 'You said we could be friends.'

Before he could reason with her the music ended and she quickly left his arms and headed to where Donald was waiting. The next dance was a foxtrot and Donald, with a flourish, led Susan on to the floor. Jim watched bleakly as they executed the steps together in perfect harmony. So much for hoping that Donald had two left feet. He was as good a dancer, if indeed not better, than himself.

They danced in silence for some minutes, giving themselves up to the joy of the music. Susan found that she wanted to move closer to Donald and this confused her. She was inclined to keep Jim at arm's length now, not wanting to give him any false impressions. But surely, if she loved Jim, she would be unable to resist contact with him?

To resist the urge, she broke the silence. 'Well! What do you think of the Orpheus, then?'

'It's not what I expected. From the way you spoke of it, I thought it would be more like the Pali.'

'No, that's the Plaza ballroom you're thinking of. Here and the Club Orchid are where we usually dance.'

'Ah, I remember now. The Plaza is where all the servicemen go. Isn't it?'

'That's right.'

The music once again drew to a halt and she reluctantly left Donald's arms and crossed the floor towards Jim.

Jim noted her reluctance and greeted them abruptly. 'Would you like a drink?'

'Yes, please. Excuse me while I go and powder my nose.'

The two men headed for the bar. 'What would you like to drink, Donald?'

'Allow me, please. What will you have?'

'Just an orange juice, thank you. Remember I'm driving.'

'What about Susan?'

'She usually has a pineapple juice.'

Donald ordered the drinks, and whilst they waited for them to be poured, he said tentatively, 'Look, Jim, if I'm in the way, tell me. I don't want to trample on anyone's toes.'

'I'll give it to you straight, Donald. I go to America in about nine weeks' time. I've asked Susan to marry me and accompany me to the States. We were once very close, but I'm afraid I made a mess of it. However, I'm still hoping she'll change her mind and come with me.'

'I see.'

'I hope I can depend on your cooperation?'

'Is she divorced, then?'

'Divorced? What are you talking about?'

'I was under the impression she was married and seeking a divorce.'

Susan caught the tail-end of this sentence as she joined them. Red-faced, she said, 'Hi! I'm here. Is that my drink?'

Donald lifted the drink from the bar and handed it to her. His eyes questioned her, but she refused to meet them. Jim watched them both, completely in the dark. What was Donald talking about? Surely Susan couldn't have married over in England? Was her lover English? Impossible! William was conceived while she was dating him. Of that he was certain!

During their next dance together, Jim showed his bewilderment. 'What on earth's Donald talking about? He seems to think you're married.'

'I know. I'll have to explain to him later on. You see, Aunt Edith thought it would look better if I wore a wedding ring while living with her. Just to keep tongues from wagging. It made no difference to me what people thought, but since I was living in her house I wore it to please her. And it had its purposes. It kept Donald from thinking of me in a personal way. If you know what I mean.'

'Was he interested?'

'No. He was suffering from a broken heart. The girl he was to marry ran off with my cousin Jack. Donald was devastated. He was lonely and so was I. We were good company for each other.'

His voice tight, Jim asked, 'Was that as far as it went?'

Taken aback by his forthrightness, she retorted, 'Not that it's any of your business, but there was never anything but friendship between us.'

He nuzzled his face in her hair and his voice was heartfelt. 'Thank God for that! I don't think I could bear for you two to be under the same roof if you had ever been intimate.'

Thinking how close it had been many a time, she allowed Jim to continue to hold her close. She was afraid of him seeing the guilt she knew was written all over her face, even though she and Donald hadn't actually gone the whole way.

The next dance she forestalled Donald when he opened his mouth to question her. 'Donald, I'm well aware I owe you an explanation. But this isn't the time, or the place. I promise I'll tell you all when we get home tonight. All right?'

Noting how close she and Jim had been dancing, he was inclined to think he had unwittingly been the cause of this and was annoyed, and showed it. 'I suppose it will have to be!' he said abruptly.

She didn't blame him for being annoyed and said soothingly, 'I promise to tell you all I can tonight.'

'That sounds as if I'm not going to learn everything?' he grumbled.

'No. Not quite everything. As I say, I'll tell you as much as I can.'

The house was in darkness when they arrived home. Jim had been very quiet since her disclosure about the wedding ring and now Susan asked tentatively, 'Are you coming in for a cup of coffee, Jim?'

Aware that she had no intention of lingering outside with him for a while, like she usually did, he considered her offer. He was cold sober, but Donald, although far from drunk, had sunk a few beers. He didn't particularly want to go in and watch them together. It was obvious that Donald thought a lot of Susan, and if he happened to do or say anything in the least out of place, Jim knew, the mood he was in, that he would be likely to punch him. However, he decided he had better accept Susan's offer of coffee or she might think he was in a huff. And who knows, perhaps after what he had told Donald about hoping to marry Susan, Donald might retire and leave them alone. Jim was doomed for disappointment.

Inside, Donald slumped into a chair and showed no intention of going to bed. He felt quite tipsy. That was because he was tired to start with, after all the travelling. Then the heat of the Orpheus and all that dancing hadn't helped him relax. On top of all that, a few pints were enough to intoxicate him.

Jim followed Susan into the kitchen and watched as she poured milk into a pot to make the coffee. 'I'm afraid it will have to be instant coffee. I like mine made with milk – what about you?'

'That's fine by me.' He stood drumming his fingers on the table. 'Donald's quite drunk. Will it be safe to leave you alone with him?' he asked apprehensively.

Turning from the stove, she gaped at him in amazement. 'He only had three pints.'

Ah, so she'd been counting! 'Sometimes if you're tired, as he obviously must be after all that travelling today, even one pint is enough.'

'I don't understand? Enough for what?'

'I think you know what I mean! What if he tries it on?'

'He won't! But even if he does, it takes two, you know.'

Jim shrugged his shoulders slightly in frustration, but she took offence at what she thought he was implying. Moving closer to him, she hissed into his face, 'You really do have a very low opinion of me, Jim Brady! You must think I have the morals of an alley cat.'

'Susan, I think nothing of the kind! Do you think I'd want to marry you if I thought that?' He wrapped his arms around her and gripped her close. 'I love you,

Susan, and I'm afraid to leave you alone with him. It's obvious he likes you.'

'That shows how much you trust me.' The milk boiled over on the stove and, breaking away from him, she ran to rescue it. 'Now look what you've made me do.'

'Can I be of any assistance?' Donald stood blinking in the doorway. Although unable to hear what was said, he had been aware of the heated whispered conversation in the kitchen and had forced himself alert to deal with anything unexpected.

Jim threw him a look that verged on loathing. 'No, I was just about to leave. See you Tuesday night, Susan.' Without another word to Donald he left the house.

'What's got into *him*?'

'Jealousy.' Susan's voice was grim as she mopped angrily at the overflow of milk.

'I should have gone on up to bed and left you two alone.'

'It wouldn't have made any difference! I never bring him in on a Saturday night. I do love him, you know, and I don't want to be tempted to do something I might later regret. If I ever do marry him, it will be because I'm sure he wants to be a father to William, not because I was frustrated enough to lose my self-control. We say good night in the car and that's as far as it goes.'

'He told me earlier on he wants to marry you, soon.'

'Oh, did he indeed? And what brought that on?'

'I think he realises I care for you and was warning me off.'

'That was stupid of him! I told him you and I are just good friends.'

'He has eyes in his head, Susan, he can see that I care for you a lot.'

'But that's just it. You don't!'

'I do.' The words were said quietly, yet filled with conviction.

'I see.' Her voice was sad as she spooned instant coffee into the cups and poured the milk. Handing a cup to him, she preceded him into the lounge. 'I think I'll soon change your mind about that. Come on, it's time I removed your rose-tinted glasses once and for all and put you in the picture.'

She perched on the edge of the settee and Donald sat down beside her, but sank back into its depths. Choosing her words carefully, Susan began her narrative.

She told him the whole rigmarole of meeting Jim at the Club Orchid ballroom and how, in spite of warnings from her friend Ruth, she had fallen in love with him. For some months everything had been rosy. Then, when Jim had tried to break it off, she had accused him of having met someone else. Of course she knew in her heart this wasn't so, she stressed, for they were so very much in love. He'd convinced her there was no one else, saying that he was thinking only of her and didn't want her to waste any more of her youth on him. There was no way he could ever marry her.

'He's Catholic and I thought it was because I was a Protestant, and I even offered to go and live with him. He explained he had too many commitments to his family.

'I was distraught when I discovered I was pregnant.'

Donald stirred restlessly beside her when he heard these words and she hurried on before he could interrupt. 'Aunt Edith seemed the only solution. I took the easy way out. I left my parents a note and went over to Darlington. Aunt Edith was wonderful. She hated deceiving Mam, but allowed me to stay. Later, when she suggested I should wear Billy's mother's wedding ring, I agreed to please her – and the rest you know.'

Donald heard her out in silence. The silence stretched and she glanced round at him, thinking that perhaps he had fallen asleep. But no, his gaze was bright and alert.

'Did you understand all that, Donald?'

'I'm still digesting it. However, I'm a bit confused. You forgot to say how or when you got pregnant. According to your story, only Jim could be the father, but why then does he resent the child?'

'He isn't the father, and I won't tell him who is. That's why he resents William.'

Donald ran his fingers through his hair in frustration. Was it the drink that was making him feel thick and stupid? 'I can't say I blame him, Susan. You appear to have been pulling the wool over everyone's eyes. Am I right?'

She nodded and bent her head in shame. Put like that, it did sound disgraceful.

'Susan, do you realise if I had known you were free, things would have been very different back in Darlington?'

'No, they wouldn't! Don't forget you were, and probably still are, in love with Margaret.'

'Not any more I'm not. Even then, with a bit of

encouragement, I could have fallen in love with you. But you kept putting up all these obstacles between us.'

'Well, for a start I was pregnant! And I really do love Jim. There has never been anyone else for me but him.'

'I don't believe that! I don't know what it was like before, but now, as far as I can see, there's a great big void between you and him. Whether you're aware of it or not.'

'I'm very well aware of it. Do you think I'm stupid? But that's only because he wouldn't accept William.'

'And now?'

'He says if we get married he'll make William his responsibility.'

'Responsibility? Is that good enough for you, Susan? I've only been here a few short hours, but I noticed that he seemed to steer clear of the boy.'

'If we married, it would be different. He wouldn't be able to help loving William.'

'You really believe that? You don't think he might always resent him?'

'Of course I believe it. Even Mam thinks everything would work out all right.'

'You've asked your mother's advice about something as important as this?'

'Yes,' she whispered, close to tears now. How could she ever have expected Donald to understand and advise her? She had even thought she would have his blessing.

He put his arm around her and pulled her back against the warmth of his body. 'Listen, Susan. It seems to me everybody is looking out for their own selfish ends, here. Your mother, for instance, obviously doesn't want to lose contact with her grandson, so thinking you love Jim Brady, she will encourage you to marry him with an easy conscience. Then she will have William to herself for a whole year. And she can be sure that you won't be tempted to stay in America, while William is over here. She and your father dote on the child. Much as they love you, it's William who will come first. I've seen the same situation over at Edith's. She and Billy will put up with anything – anything at all – in order to keep Margaret sweet so that she won't leave Jack.'

She jerked her head back to look up at him. 'Do you think she might?' she gasped, eyes wide in apprehension.

'How would I know? She's bored and finds anything in trousers attractive.'

'But you wouldn't . . .'

'Let's get something straight, Susan. I'm no saint. I'm flesh and blood, and remember we can all be tempted.'

'We managed to build up a strong friendship between us,' she reminded him.

'Ah, come off it, Susan. We came close to making love a number of times and you know it!'

'And why do you think I put a stop to it, eh? It was because Jim was always there in my mind, and you – huh! – were obviously still besotted with Margaret.'

He frowned. 'Do I detect a note of complaint there? At that time I had reason to think your husband was the obstacle . . . Hah! What a sham that was. Eh, Susan? Was it Margaret all along? Is that what you're saying?'

His hands were gently caressing her shoulders and arms, trying to ease the tense muscles.

She tried to break his hold. 'I don't know what you mean.'

'I think you do. Even though you were pregnant, if you hadn't pretended to have a phantom husband in the background, we might very well have become lovers and eventually married.'

She tried to rise, but his hands tightened on her shoulders. 'I think we've rambled on long enough for one night. Let's go to bed.'

His arms gathered her close and a rueful smile twisted his lips. 'I wish you really meant that, Susan.'

She lifted her head to chastise him and his lips were there, waiting. She willed herself to look away, but was lost and without further ado he kissed her. It went on and on, and all the emotions she had been bottling up since William's birth were there crying for release. Gently his lips left hers and he put her away from him.

'Listen to me, Susan. Don't marry Jim unless you're absolutely sure you do love him. It won't be an easy commitment if he finds he can't love William. The child will always come between you.' She opened her mouth to assure him she did indeed love Jim Brady, but recalling the longing in her just now, in Donald's arms, she closed it again.

He continued, 'I'll be here for the next three weeks and if I can win you over, I think we could make a go of it. I've always thought we'd make a great match. If not, Jim will have a further six weeks to plead his case. So be prepared! All's fair in love and war! Now, let's go to our separate beds before I forget I'm a gentleman.'

'Donald . . .'

'Let's play it by ear. Eh? But I warn you! Be prepared, because I'll be hugging and kissing you every chance I get.'

She pressed her lips firmly closed. Imagine! She had just been about to say that she couldn't think of anything nicer. She really did like playing with fire.

The next few days passed in a happy blur. Sunday started off wet but warm and Susan, much to the displeasure of her father, attended Mass with Donald in St Patrick's Church on Donegall Street. Afterwards she gave him a tour of how Belfast looked on a wet, quiet Sunday morning.

Rachel had an Ulster fry-up ready for them when they returned and Trevor had obviously been warned to hold his tongue where Mass was concerned. Susan hid a smile at his endeavours to be amicable. Then the presents were opened and a few tears were shed by Rachel and Susan at the goodness of the people over in Darlington. Vera Crabtree had also enclosed a gift for William with Edith's lot. In the afternoon they visited Belfast Castle and Bellevue Zoo, Donald insisting on taking William along with them, which pleased Susan no end.

The evening was spent quietly at home and Susan watched as Donald lay on the carpet and amused her son with soft toys and rattles. He also used all his considerable charm on her parents. Becoming aware that this young man just might be interested in his daughter, Trevor started asking questions about his future prospects and was pleased at what he gleaned from Donald. Warning bells, however, rang loud and clear in Rachel's head as she took stock of all this information. She realised that if Donald and Susan were to marry, they might settle down in England. She buried her fears within her, assuring herself it was unlikely to happen.

Didn't her daughter love Jim Brady? And nice as Donald was, he couldn't hold a candle to Jim in the good-looks stakes.

Monday was spent touring the Antrim coast. They had passed through Glenarm, Glenariff, Cushendall and Cushendun and stopped for a cup of tea in Ballycastle before reaching Bushmills, where Donald purchased a bottle of the famous Black Bush whiskey at the distillery to take home to Billy Devine.

On the way back they stopped at Carrickfergus. Susan was amazed at how much Donald knew about the history of Carrickfergus and some of the towns and fishing villages they had passed through.

'You never cease to amaze me! I'm ashamed to say, you know more about the local history than I do. And I live here for heaven's sake.'

He laughed at her awed expression and informed her, 'I was very good at history when at school. It was my favourite subject and I've read a lot of books about Ireland.'

'Are you enjoying yourself then?' she asked diffidently. 'I mean, you would say if you would prefer to be alone, wouldn't you? You aren't bored with me and William trailing along?'

They were sitting in a sheltered spot in the grounds of the castle overlooking Belfast Lough, eating the picnic lunch prepared by Susan. William was asleep in his carrycot, exhausted by all the fresh air according to Susan. There was no one else about and it was as if they were cut off from civilisation. Moving closer, he put his arm around her shoulders.

'I can honestly say I'm far from bored.'

'I'm glad to hear that. Okay then, tomorrow we'll . . .'

He put a finger to her lips. 'Tomorrow, we won't travel far. I think you owe it to Jim to see him and go for your usual driving lesson. I don't want to take unfair advantage of him.'

With laughter in her voice, she said, 'I thought you said all's fair in love and war?'

'I still think that, but I feel sorry for him. I fear he's fighting a losing battle and there's not much he can do about it.' A finger under her chin, he tilted her face towards his. 'For instance, he's not in a position to do this.' His lips were soft and tender on hers. She squirmed, wanting more, but he again put her gently from him. At her frustrated sigh he smiled and said, 'All in good time.'

Tuesday night she was ready when Jim came to collect her. He breathed a sigh of relief.

Opening the driver's door, he said, 'In you go. I think we'll go straight into town tonight. It's time you learnt to drive in the city traffic for a change and it won't be too busy at this time of night. We'll get you used to the traffic lights and do a bit of hand signalling on the way.'

'Oh, no!' she cried aghast as she slid behind the wheel. 'There are plenty of car parks and quiet streets about. I'd be too nervous to go anywhere else.'

'You're a very good driver, Susan. You could do anything you set you mind on. It's all about confidence. Remember that when you take your test.'

'There will be no hurry with that.'

'Not if I have my way and you come to America with me.'

'Jim . . .'

'I know. You don't want to talk about it. But I can hope, can't I?' Her expression was glum and he promised, 'No more talk about America tonight. After you've conquered the town, you can drive me out to the Chimney Corner Inn. I've booked a table for dinner.'

She smiled. 'If I've to conquer the town first we'll never get there. You might very well starve.'

'Look, Susan, think positive. Now prepare to turn right at these traffic lights coming up.'

She immediately tensed. She hated taking right-hand turns.

'You can do it, Susan. You've done it before. Just relax.'

To her relief, she managed the hand signal and manoeuvre without any difficulty and his words of praise warmed her heart. Nevertheless she was glad when at last her lesson in town was over. Ten minutes later they were passing through Glengormley on their way to the Chimney Corner. She was feeling more relaxed now and enjoying the driving. She even managed a perfect reverse into a parking spot in the car park.

After they had perused the menu and ordered, he inquired after Donald. 'Well, have you been squiring Donald around the sights?'

'Not really. We visited the castle and the zoo on Sunday and yesterday we went along the coast road as far as Bushmills. We went into the distillery and Donald bought a bottle of Black Bush to take home to Billy. On the way back we stopped at Carrick castle for a picnic. He thought the scenery was out of this world.'

'That's nice. The weather's holding out rightly for him. Does he intend going down south?'

'Yes. He's taking off tomorrow for Dublin. I left him and Dad poring over road maps. I wouldn't be a bit surprised if Dad takes a couple of days off and goes with him. They get on remarkably well, you know . . .'

'You're not going to accompany him then?'

'No, William has a touch of the sniffles and I want to keep him indoors for a couple of days. It's probably all that sea air that brought it on.'

The relief Jim experienced was profound. At last he had something to be thankful to William for. And better still, Susan didn't appear in the least bit disappointed not to be accompanying Donald. 'Then I'll see you as usual on Thursday night?'

She nodded and he asked tentatively, 'Can we go to the pictures or somewhere after your driving lesson?'

'I would like that, Jim, because I won't be able to see you on Saturday night. As I've already told you, Aunt Edith has sent over some presents for her parents, and when I phoned Grannie she said to come down at the weekend, when there would be a sing-song in one of the local pubs and we would enjoy it.'

He swallowed his disappointment and smiled gamely. 'I must admit that time is dragging for me at the moment. I hate the thought of you two being together so often. But still, he will only be here a few weeks, and he's well aware you're my girl. Isn't he?'

She nodded and agreed with him. 'Yes, he is.' However, she didn't meet Jim's eyes and the arrival of their starters put an end to the topic.

Back home, when he drew the car to a standstill in the driveway, Susan turned to him. 'I enjoyed myself tonight,

Jim. Thank you very much. Would you care to come in for a coffee?' Her eyes teased him. 'After all, you didn't get the last one.'

'I'm sorry about that. It was very childish of me.'

'Never mind.' She made to get out of the car, but a hand on her arm stopped her. For some unknown reason, the last time he had tried to stop her leaving the car entered her mind and she went rigid. He immediately let go his hold. 'Susan? Surely you don't . . .'

'I'm sorry. I don't know what came over me just now. I honestly haven't even thought of that night in a long while.'

'I was just going to say I wouldn't come in for coffee. Stay and talk to me for a while, like you usually do.'

'I can't. Donald will know we're here and he'll wonder why you aren't coming in.'

'If Donald is any kind of a man at all, he will know very well why I want to stay out here with you.'

Sensing that he was feeling hurt, she relaxed and put her hand on his arm. 'I'm sorry. Of course I'll stay . . . for a short while.'

With a sigh of relief he put his arm around her.

For all his warnings, except for that one time at Carrickfergus, Donald hadn't hugged and kissed her. Just the odd peck on the cheek, leaving her wanting more. Now Jim was nuzzling her neck and whispering endearments in her ear and she found it quite pleasant. More than pleasant! She turned in his arms and returned his caresses. Sensual longing was apparent in her hands and mouth. It was a half-hour later when she sighed and said that she must go in.

Delighted at her show of passion, which had been

sorely lacking of late, Jim reluctantly released her from his embrace. 'Good night, my love. See you Thursday night.'

To her dismay, Donald had retired when she at last entered the house. Only her mother was downstairs. 'Would you like a cup of tea or coffee?' she asked.

'No, thank you, Mam. I'm tired, I'll go on up to bed.'

'Your dad and Donald are off early in the morning – that's why they went to bed early.'

'Is Dad going with Donald, then?'

'Yes, I'm glad to say. He deserves a break. Did you enjoy the meal?'

'Oh, it was so-so.'

'But you enjoyed being with Jim.'

Bewildered, Susan nodded.

'You do still intend marrying him, don't you?'

'Now, Mam, I never said I was going to marry him! I said I'd think about it.'

'You love him, so what's there to think about?'

'William! Remember him? Your grandson?'

Hesitantly Rachel said, 'Promise you won't let Donald sway you.'

'If I let Donald influence me, it will be because I'm not sure of my feelings, and it wouldn't be fair to marry Jim unless I'm sure of how I feel.' Seeing a worried frown gather on her mother's brow, Susan said, 'Don't worry your head about me, Mam. I'm a big girl and I'll do what's best for all concerned. Now away you go to bed. I'll lock up.'

'Good night, Susan. I only hope you know what you're doing.'

Donald heard Rachel climb the stairs and debated

whether or not to go down and have a chat with Susan. Unable to bear the long wait while she said good night to Jim, he had made his excuses and retired to his room. What on earth were they doing out there? As if he didn't know! On the landing he paused to look out and, through the partly misted car windows, could just about see them. The figures in the car were in a tight embrace. Appalled at the intense jealousy that engulfed him, he regretted the plans he had made to go south with Trevor the next day. What if he returned to find Susan engaged to Jim?

Donald came back from the south full of the wonderful architecture of Dublin and the fantastic scenery they had encountered on their travels. They had spent the first day visiting the most popular attractions in the capital, going into museums, cathedrals and the like – and of course the pubs, 'for a wee drop of the cratur'. They had a stroll around St Stephen's Green and even managed a quick visit to Trinity College. Darkness was falling when they eventually got to their hotel, exhausted but happy with their day's adventure.

Next morning, after a hearty Irish breakfast, they travelled across country to Galway. Trevor drove while Donald acted as navigator, stopping along the way at Athlone for coffee and to stretch their legs. They arrived in Galway town late morning and parked the car. It was a warm, bright sunny morning as they stood by the bay looking out over the calm, shimmering water. As they stood admiring the view Donald couldn't resist humming 'Galway Bay', bringing a loud guffaw and a friendly punch on the shoulder from Trevor.

'I didn't hear you singing yesterday when we passed through Drogheda,' chided Trevor.

'Should I have?' Donald was somewhat mystified.

'Well, you were humming 'Galway Bay' here.'

'So?'

'*The Boyne* runs through Drogheda.'

'I think you're losing me, Trevor.'

'Oh, never mind. I was only joking anyway. Where's your sense of humour?'

Donald was slightly offended. 'Here, hold on a minute, Trevor. I've a very good sense of humour if you must know. It's just that I don't understand what you're going on about. I do remember passing through Drogheda, and I do know the River Boyne runs through it. So what?'

'Listen, son. Did you ever hear of William III, known over here as King Billy?'

At last the penny dropped. 'Oh! Now I know what you're going on about.' Donald laughed. 'You're talking about the *Battle of the Boyne*, where William defeated King James II. Why didn't you say that in the first place?'

'God, give me strength.' Trevor was looking skywards, shaking his head in mock frustration. He was nevertheless impressed that this young Englishman would have knowledge of this bit of information. But then again, hadn't Susan mentioned this very fact to him and Rachel – just how knowledgeable Donald was of Irish history.

'Let's go for a short drive along the coast, before we look for somewhere to eat,' suggested Trevor.

'I'm all for it,' replied Donald, and they headed back to the car.

* * *

They drove slowly along the coastal road as far as Clifden before returning to Galway for their lunch. They found an upstairs steak house on the main street and had to wait some time before being served. They both agreed the meal, complemented by a fine red wine, was well worth the wait. After lunch they took a stroll around the town, stopping for a short while to listen to the buskers in the square. Later, as they sat on a bench watching the world go by, Trevor had a sudden thought.

'Look, Donald, do you remember that John Wayne film . . . *The Quiet Man?*'

'This isn't another one of your "guess the song" games, is it? Of course I remember it. I don't think there'd be too many people who wouldn't. Why do you ask?'

Trevor was getting a little bit excited now. 'If my memory serves me right, there's a village not a stone's throw from here called Cong. And that was the outside location for the shooting of that very film. Now then, what do you think of that?'

'Well, I have to admit, Trevor, I don't know what to think.' Donald was beginning to get on Trevor's wavelength at last and waited for his reply.

'Do you fancy taking a drive up to have a look? You never know, we might even run into Barry Fitzgerald with a bit of luck.' They both had a good laugh at his wit.

'Not to mention Ward Bond,' suggested Donald.

'Ah yes, Ward Bond.'

'I said not to mention him,' laughed Donald. 'It must have been that wine we drank, giving us a fit of the giggles.'

'Okay, let's get back to business. If we go to Cong we

can always go home that way, instead of going back through Dublin. What do you think?'

'I think that's a brilliant idea, Trevor. That way we'd be able to see more of Ireland, instead of backtracking through places we've already seen,' he said as he eagerly dug out his trusty map of Ireland and proceeded to pore over it, with Trevor looking over his shoulder.

'There's Cong, there, at the top of Lough Corrib,' said Trevor, stabbing at the map with a finger.

Donald traced the road further north. 'We could then go up through Castlebar and further north to Sligo,' he exclaimed running his finger up the map. 'Where do we go from there?'

'We'll cut across to Enniskillen and from there it's plain sailing all the way back to Belfast, so to speak.'

'Enniskillen? That's where we're going on Saturday isn't it?'

'Yes! But we won't call in on Susan's grandparents. It would only spoil the women's pleasure. You know what they're like! So we'll pass on through.'

'You know what's best, Trevor.'

'Right then, we'd better be getting a move on if we want to have a look around John Wayne country before it gets too late,' said Trevor, getting to his feet and giving his back a good old stretch.

An hour later, after a leisurely drive through some lovely scenery, they were standing outside the large gates of Ashford castle.

'It's in there where that big fight between Big John and Victor McLaglen took place,' said Trevor with an all-knowing tone. 'Let's take a walk around the village and see if we can get a cup of tea. Or maybe you'd like a pint of the black stuff, Donald, eh?'

'Thanks, but tea will be fine. I'm already getting too much of a liking for the Guinness over here and I'll probably take over the driving on the way back, now I know in which direction we're heading.'

They hadn't gone far when they found a little corner café and sat down, 'to take the weight off our feet,' said Trevor as they waited for the tea and home-baked cake. The walls were lined with framed photographs of some of the locals posing with the crew and cast of *The Quiet Man*. Donald, seeing them for the first time, got up and walked around the café scrutinising each and every picture, passing comments to Trevor in the process. Feeling more refreshed they went for a stroll through the village, which didn't take very long. They stood on a bridge watching a pair of swans feeding lazily on a pond and then made their way back to the castle gates and into the castle grounds. Feeling a bit tired from the stifling heat of the day and from walking about, they planted themselves down under a large chestnut tree and sat there for some time in companionable silence, each – more than likely – imagining Maureen O'Hara being dragged bodily across this beautiful countryside, or maybe the horserace down on the shore, or the high-light of the film – that big fight. Who in their right mind could ever forget that?

It was Trevor who intruded on their tranquillity. 'Look, Donald, if we sit here any longer daydreaming, I'll fall asleep. We'd better pull ourselves together and get a move on if we want to find somewhere to stay the night, before it gets dark.'

Reluctantly they left the idyllic Cong in their wake as they headed north towards Castlebar, where they booked into a B&B and went out to find somewhere to eat. And perhaps 'a wee dram', suggested Trevor with a smile. He was really enjoying this young man's company.

Next morning they were heading up towards Sligo and then across to Enniskillen, passing alongside the beautiful Lough Erne, on the final stage of their travels. As they travelled along the motorway to Belfast, Donald thanked Trevor for his company and remarked on the places they had passed through and visited. 'We certainly saw a lot of places in such a short time,' he remarked. 'I'd love to take more time out and tour around the south for, say, a couple of weeks. It was a fantastic couple of days. Wasn't it?'

'You can say that again, Donald. On second thoughts, don't bother, son.' Another loud laugh. 'Seriously, though. Do you know something? This is the first break I've had in five years and I really needed it. I've enjoyed it every bit as much as you. And do you know something else? I enjoyed your company tremendously,' he confessed. 'And do you know something else, son? I'm going to make damned sure, pardon my French, that me and Rachel take a holiday every year from now on. What's the use of slogging yourself half to death, six days a week, fifty-two weeks a year, and not getting any enjoyment out of it? You can't take your money with you when the Big Man calls, you know. Oh no, I've had a right eye-opener this last couple of days. From now on I'm going to be a changed man. Take things a lot easier and not drive myself into an early grave.'

Donald had listened in silence to every word as they approached the end of the motorway, before he finally spoke in a very solemn voice. 'Okay, that was a very good confession. Now, for your penance I want you to say three Hail . . .'

They both had a good old laugh at that and were still laughing as they pulled into the driveway of Trevor's home.

Chapter Thirteen

Trevor had assured Donald he would enjoy himself in Enniskillen and it certainly lived up to his expectations. Susan's grandparents welcomed him so warmly that he immediately felt at home. He particularly liked Jane, as she reminded him of his own mother.

It started to rain as they travelled along the motorway on Saturday morning. 'It would have to start raining now,' grumbled Susan.

'I'm not complaining. It's only a shower. I've been very lucky with the weather so far. Two light showers in a week? Your dad couldn't get over us having no rain at all while we were down south.'

She smiled at him. 'You're right, of course, but I did so want you to see Enniskillen at its best.'

'I've a confession to make, Susan. We passed through Enniskillen on the way home yesterday, so I've already seen it bathed in sunshine and it looks a grand town. Don't you worry! With you for company, I'll enjoy myself, rain or shine.'

They shared a smile. They hadn't had a chance to talk since he had returned with Trevor the night before. He was anxious about how things had progressed between her and Jim. Now, diffidently, he ventured to ask, 'How are you and Jim getting along?'

She shrugged nonchalantly. 'Oh, the same as usual.'

'He hasn't yet persuaded you to marry him, then?'

'Not yet, though sometimes I think it would be for the best. Other times I worry about leaving William behind and that puts me off.'

Much relieved to hear this, Donald tried to be fair towards his rival in love. 'At the moment I'm cramping his style. When I go home next week things will be different.'

'Oh? So you've decided *we* wouldn't be suited after all?'

Surprised at this question, he debated whether to admit seeing her and Jim in the car on Tuesday night; it sounded as if he'd been spying on them. And so he had! He shrugged inwardly. May as well come clean and clear the air. 'I saw you and Jim in the car on Tuesday night and you seemed to be getting on all right.'

She turned in her seat and gaped at him. 'Were you spying on us?' she asked, aware that she was blushing, as the memory of Tuesday night's episode crossed her mind.

'No! No, I wasn't! I just happened to glance out the landing window on my way to bed.'

'Huh! Do you expect me to believe that?' Receiving no reply, she dared to ask, 'And just what did you see, eh?'

He smiled wryly as he admitted, 'As a matter of fact, very little. The windows were all steamed up and, since it wasn't a very cold night, my imagination went into overdrive.'

'Did it indeed? Well, I'll have you know that we did have a good old cuddle. Any objections?'

'No, why should I?' His voice was abrupt. So much for being honest. 'You're a free agent after all.'

'Do you know something? I enjoyed it. A girl likes to be kissed now and again, you know. Not being promised hugs and kisses that never materialise. Some people are just all talk! No action. Know what I mean?'

Aghast at this outburst, her face blazed with colour. Now he would think she was throwing herself at him.

Noting her high colour, he said gently, 'Give me a chance, Susan. I didn't want to rush you. But, believe you me, all that's about to change. I'll have you screaming for mercy before we leave Enniskillen. You mark my words,' he promised.

She was saved from replying by sounds from William, whose carrycot was strapped to the back seat. He soon settled down again, but the conversation was not pursued, as Donald was by now commenting on the countryside as they cruised along towards County Fermanagh.

Donald had insisted on buying her grandparents some little token to show his appreciation of their kindness, so after a hearty lunch they spent a few hours in the town centre shopping and looking at buildings of historic interest that Susan thought would be of interest to him. She mentioned there was a pottery up near the border which produced the world-famous Belleek china and Donald jumped at the chance, suggesting they should visit it while they were in the region.

'I might even get a gift there for Edith,' he said.

They travelled up alongside the Lough Erne, a route that was by now becoming quite familiar to Donald.

'This is the road your dad and I came down on our way home from Cong yesterday,' he said nodding towards Upper Lough Erne. 'Isn't that view something else? You could spend your whole holiday on one of those cruisers.'

'Well, that's what a lot of tourists actually do,' Susan replied. 'And it is a lovely view. Mind you, I wouldn't fancy being out on the lough if it were raining.'

'I suppose if you were really into boats, you wouldn't care what the weather was like,' Donald replied.

Before long they were in Belleek and followed directions to the factory. They spent an hour browsing over the magnificent displays of china.

'Look at some of those price tags,' said Susan. 'They'd take your breath away. Wouldn't they, Donald?'

'They sure would, but I'm just admiring the craft.'

'You men! You never see the important things, do you?'

He just smiled at her and shrugged his shoulders. He did, however, manage to afford a pair of delicate china candlesticks for Edith.

'She'll be delighted with them. I noticed some china ornaments in her display cabinet, when I was over there,' Susan enthused.

On their way out of Belleek, Susan noticed that one of the pointers on the road sign indicated Bundoran. 'Do you fancy a visit to the seaside before we return to Grannie's? It's only a short distance over the border.'

'Why not! We've plenty of time.'

A short time later they were sitting by the seaside, each enjoying a bag of fish and chips.

* * *

Donald was suitably impressed with his day's travels and his praise of Enniskillen and the surrounding countryside, when they returned to the cottage, pleased Susan's grandparents.

That night William and Jane shooed them out of the house and down to the pub while they pampered baby William; warning them not to hurry back, as they would give William a bath and put him to sleep in the carrycot.

Susan and Donald sat in the corner of the olde-worlde pub and sang along with the rest of the customers to the traditional music played by the two fiddlers. He kept her in the circle of his arm, hugging her close and kissing her every now and again. It was with reluctance that they rose to go. The bar was still open, though it was after one o'clock in the morning. As for the fiddlers, they looked as if they could go on playing all night.

Nearing the end of August, it was still quite warm outside. The rain had stayed at bay, bright stars studded the clear sky and the air smelt fresh and earthy. Putting an arm around her shoulders, Donald pulled Susan close as they made their way back to the cottage.

She eased away from him. 'You don't have to overdo it, you know, Donald.'

'Overdo what?'

'You know rightly what I'm talking about,' she admonished him. 'All that kissing and hugging. I know it's all a big show after what I said earlier today.'

They were now at the cottage, which was in darkness. He secured the gate and followed her up the path in silence, but when she would have unlocked the front door, he closed his hand over hers and, pulling her against him, kissed her in a long satisfying kiss.

They were both breathless when he eventually released her. 'That's what I call a real kiss, Susan. I've wanted to do that constantly, but felt I was betraying Jim's friendship. See what I mean?'

'Not really.'

'I mean, have I your permission to court you? Is there any chance you might consider marrying me? Otherwise it would be a waste of time continuing like this, and might cause bad feeling all round.'

Her look was appealing. 'How can I know, Donald? Eh, tell me that. How can I know if you don't try?'

'Fair enough. Jim Brady will just have to look out for himself, then.'

Once more he drew her into his arms and she willingly lifted her face for his kisses.

After that it was no holds barred and Susan felt loved and desired. He didn't overstep the mark once, but during their stay at Enniskillen his attention was passionate and loving, and all thoughts of Jim Brady melted into insignificance, at least for the time being.

Her grandmother gave Susan her blessing. When they were making their farewells on Monday morning she whispered in her ear, 'I hope to hear of a wedding in the not too distant future, girl. Donald is a fine young man and it's obvious he cares for William as well as you, and that's most important for your future happiness.'

Whether Susan put Jim wise to the situation, Donald did not know nor did he care. She went for driving lessons with Jim as usual during the week. On Tuesday night Trevor took Donald to Dunmore Park to the grey-hound racing and on Thursday night they visited a few of the city-centre pubs. Thus he was out late both nights and returned when Jim had long departed, so he was not tempted to spy on Susan and Jim in the car again.

Donald was quite confident about his chances with Susan. The only snag, as far as he could see, was that he would be here such a short time, while Jim would have much longer to win her over. How would Susan react if they all went to the Orpheus on Saturday night? Donald smiled at the idea. She would probably flirt with both of them and he would be none the wiser.

Donald was alone with William when a car pulled up to the front of the house on Friday. Trevor was at work and Susan and her mother had gone shopping in preparation for Alison coming home the next day, leaving Donald babysitting. Lifting the child up in his arms, he entered the hall and waited for a knock on the door. To his surprise a key turned in the lock and a young blonde girl with big sparkling blue eyes stepped inside. She set down the suitcase she was carrying and beamed at him.

'Hello. You must be Donald,' she said. 'I'm Alison, Susan's sister.'

Donald was struck dumb, such was the effect this girl was having on him. Shifting William on to his left arm, he clasped the small, firm hand offered to him and, unable to find his voice, nodded in greeting, still holding her hand.

Embarrassed at his reaction, Alison gently withdrew her hand and gave her attention to the child. 'And how's my lovely wee nephew?' she crooned and stretched out her arms for him, hugging him close. 'Oh, how I've missed you.'

To Donald's relief Graham staggered in, weighed down with parcels. 'Hello, Donald. Nice to see you again. I do declare Alison has brought twice as much back with her as she had going.' Dropping the parcels, he approached Donald with hand outstretched.

'You're looking well, Graham,' Donald greeted him.

'You too, Donald. You too.'

'Ah, but I haven't been in a car crash and, may I say, what a car to crash in!'

Graham grinned, displaying a flash of even white teeth set in a tanned face. 'Thank God it was the car that was a write off and not me. It was touch and go for a while, you know, whether or not I'd ever walk again. But I must admit this holiday has done me all the good in the world. The weather down south was marvellous for a change and we spent most of the time lying about in the sun. We did, however, manage a tour of the Ring of Kerry. The scenery was out of this world. Is there no one else at home?'

'Susan and her mother are in town doing a bit of shopping. They weren't expecting you until tomorrow.'

'That's Alison's fault. She wants me to take her to the Orpheus tomorrow night, now that I'm steadier on my feet. If the truth be known, I think it's just so she can show off her tan. Will you be going to the dance?'

'As far as I know, we are going to a dance in somewhere called the Floral Hall.'

'Oh, that's up at Hazelwood, near the zoo. Is it a ticket do?'

'Yes, it was Jim who got the tickets.'

'I'll give him a ring and see if he can get another two. But look, Donald, I'll have to rush on now. I've Mam and Dad waiting in the car. I'll see you when I come back later for Alison.'

'I look forward to it.'

The door closed on Graham, and Donald drew a deep breath before joining Alison in the lounge. She was kneeling on the floor playing with William and his heart lurched in his breast at the beauty of her. He should have been prepared for this, he chastised himself. Hadn't Susan intimated that her sister was beautiful?

'Is anything wrong?' she asked, a puzzled frown ruffling a smooth brow. 'You needn't worry about giving up your room, you know. I'll be staying at Graham's while you're here.'

Glad that she had given him an excuse for his awkwardness, he smiled. 'Are you sure it'll be no bother?'

'No bother at all! There's no shortage of rooms in his house.'

William started to whimper and Alison asked anxiously, 'Is he due a feed?'

A glance at his watch and Donald cried, 'Lord, yes. I'll just heat a bottle for him.'

'You look after him and I'll attend to the bottle.'

As if drawn by a magnet, he followed her into the kitchen, William in his arms.

She glanced over her shoulder at him. 'Are you enjoying yourself here?'

'Yes, I'm having a marvellous time. I've been all over and seen some wonderful places. Of course there's lots I haven't seen, but time goes by so quickly. Last weekend we visited your grandparents in Enniskillen. We had a great time.'

'I enjoy going there too. What did you think of the country pubs? I love them.'

'I enjoyed them immensely. We have working men's clubs over in England and I must say they put on some marvellous acts in their concert rooms. A lot of Irish groups and comedians are very popular. The two fiddlers playing in the pub last Saturday would go down a treat over there. They'd have the women up dancing on the tables. I thoroughly enjoyed the Irish music and the sing-songs. It was smashing.'

'I'm glad you enjoyed yourself.' She tested the bottle on the inside of her wrist. 'There you are. Will you give it to him, while I unpack and sort out some fresh clothes to take to Graham's house tonight?'

He held William out to her. 'First, let me carry those cases upstairs for you.' He was already halfway across the hall, but paused when struck by a thought. 'Where will I put them?'

'Just dump them in the spare room at the end of the landing for the time being.'

Once away from the effect her presence was having on him, Donald sat on the edge of the bed in the spare room and tried to justify his behaviour. What was he playing at? He had practically convinced Susan they were meant for each other and here he was drooling over her sister. And that very same sister was engaged to Graham, and Jim was still clinging to the hope that Susan would marry him. Even if she did decide to marry Jim, that wouldn't clear the way for him and Alison; there was still Graham to consider. Why would she look at him anyway? He was hardly God's gift to women. What a mess! He had better get a grip, before he made a complete idiot of himself. Rising to his feet, he drew a deep breath and exhaled slowly to steady his nerves, before descending the stairs.

Now that he had his emotions under some semblance of control he found Alison easy to get on with. She kept the conversation going, asking after her relatives in England and how her grandparents were faring in Enniskillen, and how he was getting on with her father. Donald was not to know that Alison was usually very quiet and reserved and it was nerves that put her in such a talkative mood. This big fellow made her feel uneasy; albeit in the nicest possible kind of way, she still felt uneasy.

After dinner that evening, Susan sat on the bed and watched her sister pack some things to take to Graham's. 'Did you have a nice time?' she asked.

'Very quiet, but I enjoyed myself. It gave me and Graham a chance to get to know each other.'

'With his parents there?' Susan's voice was sceptical.

'Don't sound so surprised, Susan. They were very understanding and took themselves off for hours at a time. And the hotel was marvellous, great food and plenty of entertainment each evening. I think Graham and I will be very happy together.'

'What about Graham? Is his walking getting any better?'

'He's coming along fine. He even manages to shuffle round the dance floor now. Are you going to the Orpheus tomorrow night?'

Susan shook her head. 'We're going to the Floral Hall. Victor Sylvester and his orchestra are playing there, and Jim and I thought it would . . .'

Alison's eyes widened. 'Oh, is the big romance back on again?'

'I'm not sure yet, but in the meantime he has been giving me driving lessons.'

'I see.' Alison smiled wisely. 'Is this dance a ticket-only do?'

'Victor Sylvester? What do you think? However, Donald says that when Graham heard about it, he said he would ring Jim to see if he could possibly get two extra tickets.'

'You won't mind us tagging along?'

'Not in the slightest. Anything new on your wedding front?'

'No date set yet, if that's what you mean, but it'll be in the not too distant future. Graham wants a place of his own.'

'Will it be before Christmas, do you think?'

'I really don't know. Why all this sudden interest?'

'Well, you see, I've also had a proposal of marriage . . . two, actually.'

'Huh! Two? You're not letting the grass grow under your feet, are you?' Alison sat down on the bed beside Susan and gazed at her wide-eyed.

Susan laughed at her sister's amazement. 'Yes, two. Jim is going to America on contract for his firm and he wants me to marry him and go with him. He would have to leave here in about six or seven weeks, so my wedding would be a hurried affair in the registry office. I don't want to spoil your plans, so what do you think?

Do you think it would interfere with your wedding plans if I were to marry soon?'

'Don't you worry your head about me! There's no chance of us getting married in a couple of months' time. Having said that, I don't want it too near Christmas, either. But I'm sure Graham won't mind waiting until the spring. Easter would be nice, so it would. But I'll say this much: we'll all sure as hell miss William. We kept talking about him the whole time we were away.'

This admission surprised Susan. 'Did you indeed?'

'He's so quiet that you might find this hard to believe, but Graham is very fond of him.'

Hiding her concern, Susan replied, 'That's the snag! Jim wants me to leave William with Mam and Dad. It will only be for a year.'

'Huh! He's a gag! There's no way you'll leave William for a week, let alone a year. Why, as far as a baby is concerned, it's a lifetime. I know I wouldn't chance it! Although, mind you, Graham and I would be delighted to help out.'

Susan's heart dropped. Her sister was just confirming all her own misgivings.

'You said you'd had two proposals?' Alison prompted her.

'Yes, Donald thinks we could make a go of it, and I must say he is more attached to William than Jim is.'

Alison rose to her feet and, crossing the floor, opened a drawer and rummaged unnecessarily about in it. Why did the mention of Donald make her blush? Had Susan noticed? When Susan and her mother had returned from town she had stayed as far away from him as she could, for he made her feel so uncomfortable. During dinner she had been aware of his frequent probing glances and now Susan had intimated that she might marry him. Could she bear to have Donald for a brother-in-law? Turning to face her sister, she said, 'But you love Jim, don't you?'

'I don't really know any more. To tell you the truth, I'm all mixed up.'

'For heaven's sake, Susan, you used to be nuts about him! When you first fell out I thought you'd die of a broken heart. He was all you ever talked about.'

'I know, but he was my first love and I always imagined your first romance is always in Technicolor, as it were. You must know what I mean? Graham's *your* first love. You see, I've grown up now. I'd never let a man get a grip like that on me again. I'm also very attracted to Donald. He's one of the best, and such fun to be with.'

Alison was at a loss to understand her sister's reasoning. She didn't know what she meant about your first love being in Technicolor. All she knew was that she had envied the deep, sensual magnetism between her sister and Jim Brady. It had been there in the air all around them. She wished she could feel that way about Graham, but so far it hadn't happened. As yet the ground hadn't even shivered – let alone moved – when she was in his company.

'Just be careful, Susan,' she warned gently. 'You and Jim were very committed to each other at one time.' The sound of the doorbell brought her to attention. 'That'll be Graham. Will you go down and talk to him till I finish off here?'

It was reluctantly that Susan left the room and descended the stairs. She had seen Graham just once since that awful night at the Orpheus and he'd looked dreadful. How would he look now? More importantly, how would he behave? Would he still live up to his promise? It was her mother who crossed the hall and opened the door.

Giving him a warm hug, she said, 'Graham, it's wonderful to see you. You do look so much better.'

'Thank you, Rachel. I must confess I do feel much better now. Almost back to my old self, as a matter of fact.'

'That's good to hear, son. Come into the lounge, Donald and Trevor are there.'

'Thanks, Rachel. I'll just have a quick word with Susan first.'

He stood at the foot of the wide staircase and watched Susan descend, a sad smile on his face. She looked lovely to him, and putting a hand on each shoulder he kissed her lightly on the cheek. 'You're looking very attractive, if I may say so.'

She smiled into his eyes, seeking reassurance. 'You can pay me compliments like that any time you feel like it.'

His hold on her tightened. 'Ah, Susan, there's so much I would like to say to you. If only . . .'

Dismayed, Susan whispered warningly, 'Graham, remember your promise . . . please.'

Slowly he released his hold on her. 'Forgive me and don't worry. I don't intend breaking my word. It hasn't been easy, you know, staying away. It's so long since I last saw you.' Seeing that she was becoming agitated, he said gently, 'Don't look so worried. I'll behave. Where is that lovely wee son of yours?'

'He's asleep, so he is.'

Unheard by Susan, Alison was descending the stairs. Her voice reached them. 'Are you staying for a while, Graham?'

'I certainly am. I want to renew Donald's acquaintance, and I'm hoping Susan will let me have a look in on her son.'

'Of course she will. I can see a big difference in him in just two weeks and it's much longer since you've set eyes on him. Take him up, Susan, and I'll make some coffee.'

Slowly Susan retraced her steps, followed by Graham. 'You've lost a bit of weight,' he admonished her.

'Just a little. I want to be slim if I decide to get married.' She had reasoned that the sooner he knew her plans, the better. Shock made his step falter and he gripped the banister tightly. Concerned, she swung round to face him. 'Are you all right? Is it your back?'

Pain in his voice, he retorted, 'Do you care?'

'Look, Graham, you know I don't wish you any harm.' She had reached the door of the nursery and gently pushed it open. He preceded her into the room and stood looking down on his son.

He was overcome at the sight of the chubby, pink cheeks and long, curly lashes. 'Alison's right. He has grown. It's not fair, you know, Susan. You're breaking my heart with all this secrecy.'

'Look, for the last time he isn't yours.' Fear of being overheard made her keep her voice low, but it was tight with anger and he hastened to pacify her.

'Don't worry. I'll stick to my word.' With a gentle touch on the baby's head he pushed abruptly past her and descended the stairs.

Susan stood by the cot looking blindly down at her child, her mind in turmoil. How could she ever contemplate leaving William to grow under Graham's suspicious, probing eye for a whole year? She hadn't even considered that angle! All she had worried about was William forgetting her. There was no way she could marry Jim. She had been daft even to consider it. She must tell him at the first possible opportunity; not keep him waiting and hoping in vain. Good! That was one decision taken out of her hands. She would tell him at the dance tomorrow night, in case she was tempted to change her mind if she waited much longer.

Having made up her mind about Jim, Susan felt bereft. She realised now that she had intended marrying him all along. If that was the case, why was she stringing Donald along? As insurance against unforeseen hitches? Besides, she did care a lot for Donald! As he had implied, they would make a good couple. If they did marry, she would make him a good, faithful wife and William would be reared over in Darlington, well out of harm's way. But not too far away for her parents to visit any time they felt like it.

Jim managed to get another two tickets for the dance. It was a special occasion, with Victor Sylvester and his orchestra playing. A big enough occasion for Susan to wear her new ruby dress. She tried it on once again. Tonight, as she examined her reflection in the mirror, she didn't feel in the least bit attractive in it. She had hardly slept a wink the night before, and there were dark shadows under her eyes. She felt depressed and dreaded telling Jim the bad news. Slowly she removed the dress. What a waste! Would she ever wear it? Perhaps at another time in the future she might feel more comfortable in it and wear it for Donald. But not tonight! Not when she was sending her beloved Jim away for good; never again to feel his strong arms around her. Thank God Donald would· be there to console and support her. What would she do without his understanding? He was her mentor indeed.

When Jim arrived Donald offered to drive them to the Floral Hall, insisting that it was Jim's turn to have a few beers. Outside the white, round-shaped building, Susan stopped and waited for Donald's reaction.

'Well? What do you think of it?'

He seemed to come to with a start. 'Well, it certainly looks wonderful from here.'

Taken aback by his lack of interest, she entered the building with the two men and excused herself to go and deposit her wrap in the cloakroom, while they went to the men's room.

They had agreed to meet Graham and Alison inside. The ballroom was packed and the men were delighted to discover that Graham had already secured a table by the windows overlooking the duck pond. As she approached them, Susan noted how well Donald and Jim looked in dark lounge suits with crisp, white shirts and black bow ties, but she had never seen Graham look so handsome. Usually he dressed in pale colours, greys and blues, but she thought with his fair colouring and fine physique he carried off his dark suit and white shirt with such panache!

Alison had bought a new dress whilst in Cork. Of pale blue silky material, it fitted her like a glove, made her eyes glow like sapphires and she exuded sensuality. The dress had narrow shoulder-straps and the men's eyes were drawn like a magnet to her tanned cleavage.

Susan now regretted not wearing the ruby dress; she felt quite frumpy in a white sheath, little knowing that it complemented her dark looks and showed off her long, slim legs. Graham caught her appraising glance and winked, with a hint of a smile playing at the corners of his mouth. Embarrassed, she instinctively moved closer to Donald.

This move upset Jim and when Victor Sylvester announced the first dance of the evening, with a slight bow in her direction he said, 'Would you like to dance, Susan?'

Reluctantly she left Donald's side and followed him on to the dance floor.

As if under compulsion, Donald immediately turned to Graham. 'Is it all right if I ask Alison for this dance?'

Taken aback, Graham stretched out a hand, palm upward. 'If Alison doesn't mind?' He glanced at her. She did mind! The affect Donald was having on her frightened her. But what could she say? A slight nod of the head gave her consent. Graham shrugged. 'Be my guest, Donald.'

He watched them take to the floor, a bewildered look on his face. What was Donald playing at? He had noticed Susan's movement towards Donald and Jim's quick intervention. Was that why he had rushed on to the floor with Alison? Did he want to keep a close eye on Susan?

With a shake of the head Graham·dismissed the idea and turned his thoughts to his own problems. Now that he had seen William again he was regretting his promise to Susan. If only he could talk it over with someone? But who? No matter to whom he confided his doubts, the cat would be out of the bag and Susan would never forgive him. Besides, he had no real proof that William was his. No proof at all! Just a gut feeling! Only Susan knew the truth. The old adage that sprang to mind was really true. You could always be sure of the mother, but the father could be open to speculation.

Embarrassed at his impulsive gesture, Donald was stiff and awkward as he led Alison around the dance floor. Mortified, he glanced down at her only to discover that she was eyeing him covertly from under long, golden lashes, a slight smile on her face at his discomfort. He apologised. 'I'm sorry. I'm not usually so impetuous, but I might not get another chance to dance with you tonight.'

She wanted to ask him if it mattered, but was afraid of what his answer might be. Before they left the house Susan had confided in her that she had made up her mind not to marry Jim after all. Seeing Alison's reaction had only reinforced her own feelings, that it would be wrong to leave William for such a long time. Did that mean Susan was going to accept Donald's proposal?

He grimaced in apology as he trod on her toes. 'Believe it or not, I'm no country yokel, you know. I can dance as well as the next one.'

'Perhaps if you just relaxed a little and led me around, instead of pushing me away from you, we'd manage better,' she teased.

A chuckle started deep within him and erupted. She

joined him in laughter and, before she knew it, he was sweeping her in and out of the dancers, their steps in perfect harmony.

She was light as a feather in his arms and he gave himself up to the exultation of holding her close. He had never experienced emotions like this in his life before. And he had actually thought he loved Margaret McGivern? He shook his head at the very idea. How could he have been so stupid?

Alison's heart was racing so fast she thought he must surely hear it. What on earth was the matter with her? Donald was only a man, after all. All too soon the dance was over. She thanked him and, withdrawing from his arms, headed back to the table. She felt as if there were gentle electric currents pulsating through her.

He danced the next dance with Susan. It was a slow foxtrot and as they swayed to the rhythm of the music she confided in him. 'I've decided that it would be wrong to marry Jim and leave William behind.'

His heart sank. 'Have you told him yet?'

'No, I can't find the right words to let him down as lightly as possible.'

'Don't be too hasty. Be sure it's what you want, Susan.'

A bewildered frown puckered her brow. 'I thought you'd be pleased.'

'I want what's best for you and the child, Susan.'

'Don't you want me any more?'

'Of course I do. I promise I won't let you down.'

She moved closer, her face almost against his chest, hiding her expression. What did he mean, he wouldn't let her down? It sounded as if he was making some kind of sacrifice for her sake.

They finished the dance in silence and over her shoulder Donald's eyes found and followed Alison. As if under some hypnotic charm, her eyes were drawn to his. They gazed at each other and she had difficulty tearing her glance away. His mother had always told him that some day he would meet a girl and he would know right away that she was the one for him. He had laughed at the very idea of it, but she had said, 'You mark my words, son!' Now it had come about, but too late for him. He was practically engaged to her sister.

Later on in the evening Jim waltzed Susan out into the grounds of the dance hall. Leading her away from the building to one of the benches strategically placed for viewing Belfast Lough, he waited until she was seated, then sat close beside her. They gazed down over the lough for some moments in silence.

'It's beautiful, isn't it?' she whispered.

'It is. We'll miss Belfast when we go away. America will be a completely different kettle of fish for us.'

She squirmed restlessly. Now, she must tell him, *now*. Before she could form the words to break it gently, he spoke again.

'What's wrong, Susan? You've been like a cat on a hot griddle all evening.' He put his arm around her and tilted her face towards his. His kiss was hungry, and to her dismay she found herself reciprocating. It would be wonderful to marry him. If only they could take William with them. If only he would accept the child. When his hands started to explore her body, with a strangled groan she found the strength to push him away.

He recoiled, gazing at her in hurt bewilderment.

Reaching for his hand, she clasped it between her own. 'Forgive me, Jim, and please try to understand. I've something to tell you,' she whispered in a shaky voice.

'From your expression I assume it's bad news?'

'I can't come to America with you. Please understand. I can't leave William for a whole year. It wouldn't be fair on the child, especially at such a young age. He needs me now!'

'Your parents would look after him well. You know that. There's no sweat there, and he's young enough not to miss you.'

'That's not what I'm worried about.'

'What then?'

Deciding to be truthful, she said, 'I'm afraid if I decide to go, his father will make himself known. Not deliberately, but it could happen and I'm not willing to risk it.'

'I wish I could understand why you're so loyal to this guy,' he snarled. 'You must love him, Susan, to shield him like this.'

'Don't be silly! It's not him I'm shielding.'

It was on the tip of her tongue to tell him the truth. After all, once he knew it was Graham, he would see her for the slut she was and want nothing more to do with her. He would go away quietly. Who was she kidding? He would go straight back in and give Graham the length of his tongue. He'd make all kinds of accusations. That's what he'd do! There would be no stopping him! And it would snowball out of all proportion. Then what would her sister and her parents think of her and Graham? They'd be scandalised! The shame of it, the humiliation! She couldn't bear ever to let that happen.

Jim was eyeing her intently. 'Whether you believe it or not, Susan, I think you're in love with this guy and you don't even realise it.'

Tears shone in her eyes as she tried to convince him. 'I'm not! I tell you, I'm not.'

'All right. If you say so. Don't get yourself all upset. Now listen to me, Susan. Please don't rush into anything with Donald until you're absolutely certain. Sure you won't? I'll be here for a while yet, so if you change your mind just let me know. All right?'

She nodded and he kissed her briefly on the lips. 'You're getting cold! Let's go back inside.'

Their table was empty. 'Would you like a drink?'

'Yes, please. I'd like a Coke.'

Jim had barely left when Graham appeared. 'Dare I ask you for this dance, Susan?'

With a nod she rose to her feet and followed him on to the dance floor. 'Where's Alison?'

'Dancing with Donald. She seems to have made a big impression on him. I haven't seen much of you tonight – or her, for that matter.'

'I was out in the grounds for a while with Jim. I've told him I can't go to America after all.'

He successfully hid his relief. 'And what did he have to say about that? Has he asked you to wait for him?'

She shook her head despondently. 'No. He thinks I'll change my mind.'

'And what do you think, Susan?'

'I don't know what to think. I'm so confused.'

He saw the tears glistening on her lashes, threatening to fall. 'Let's get out of here.'

She found herself outside again, on a different bench and with a different man holding her. It had become quite cool and she shivered slightly. Removing his jacket, he placed it around her shoulders and gathered her tightly against him.

She tried to oppose him. 'No, Graham. I can't take your coat, you'll be cold.'

He wanted to say 'I've got my love to keep me warm', but she might take umbrage and storm off, so he remained silent. She felt safe and warm in his arms and instinctively snuggled closer. He was so tender that she longed to experience again his sweet lovemaking; that feeling of oneness. If only . . . Aghast at her line of thought, she lifted her head and gazed at him.

Her expression puzzled him and he said, haltingly, 'What is it?'

She shook her head, bewildered at the thoughts flitting across her confused mind. 'Nothing. Just a passing thought.'

'I must confess, Susan, I'm glad you're not going to marry Jim Brady. I think you'd be doing the wrong thing.'

'What difference does it make whom I marry?'

'Because, while we're both single, I can hope for a miracle.'

'Oh, Graham, Graham.' An urge to offer him her lips was so strong it almost overwhelmed her. She struggled from his embrace, leaving him holding the empty coat. 'I'll have to go inside and repair my make-up.' She was off before he could say another word.

He watched her go with bleak eyes. Why did life have to be so complicated?

In the cloakroom Susan powdered her nose and the dark shadows around her eyes. She looked as awful as she felt. Thank goodness the dim lights in the ballroom would help to camouflage her unhappiness. She practised putting a bright smile on her pale face, then decided to go in search of Donald. She was disappointed in him. He had not lived up to her expectations as a comforter and mentor. She had hardly seen him all evening.

Earlier, Donald had casually asked Alison to show him the grounds around the Floral Hall. It was with trepidation that she allowed him to whisk her off the dance floor and through one of the open French windows. Putting an arm around her shoulders, he walked her to the edge of the lawn and stood gazing over the lough in amazement. 'I can't understand Susan not mentioning this view to me.'

'She can't remember everything, and besides she has a lot on her mind tonight and you're not exactly looking after her, if you don't mind my saying so.'

He did mind! He minded very much any criticism from those lovely, sensuous lips. 'I don't know what you mean.'

'Don't you? She told me you had also proposed marriage?'

'Yes, I did. I thought we were well suited,' he admitted. 'But that was before I met you.'

She twisted round to face him and he immediately put his other arm around her, circling her waist. 'What on earth do you mean? What have I got to do with it?'

His heart sank as he gazed down on her lovely

features. His emotions were so strong that he had been certain she must feel the same. Surely these intense feelings that gripped him could not all be one-sided? He gave in to temptation and kissed her. Shock coursed through her and then a wonderful feeling of release as she returned his kiss. Terrified at the wave of emotions that raged through her at his touch, she angrily pushed him away.

'Don't you dare kiss me like that,' she cried, angrily dabbing at her bruised lips with the back of her hand. 'You've no right at all.'

'I thought there were two of us sharing that kiss,' he chided gently.

'You were taking advantage of me! That's what you were doing.'

'Don't you feel anything at all for me, Alison?' he cried.

'No. Why should I? I hardly know you.' She was being far from honest. The affect Donald was having on her frightened the life out of her. She had never experienced anything like it in her life before, but she had no intention of admitting it. She didn't want any disruptions in her life right now. She was happy with it as it was. Graham could give her everything she ever wanted.

'I don't believe you don't have some feelings for me,' he insisted gently and reached for her again.

Fright, and the need to get away from him, made her speech strong. 'You're one arrogant English bastard, so you are! Practically engaged to my sister and now trying it on with me. Are they all like that over there?'

If she had struck him with her clenched fist Donald couldn't have looked more taken aback. 'I'm sorry. You're right of course.' He stepped quickly away from her. 'I had no right to assume you felt the same as me.' With these words he turned on his heel and left her.

Tears blinding her, she sought solace in the cloakroom. She bumped into Susan on her way out. One look at Alison's face and her sister followed her back in.

'What on earth's wrong with you?'

Blowing her nose, Alison replied, 'Nothing! I was outside. The air is very cold. I think it's a touch of hay fever. What would be wrong with me?'

Hay fever at this time of night? Not for one minute taken in by her lame excuses, Susan said bluntly, 'You look awful, so you do.'

Alison was repairing her make-up and was refusing to meet her sister's eyes in the mirror. She spared her a fleeting glance and retorted, 'You don't look so good yourself.'

'I've a good excuse. I've just told Jim I can't marry him.'

'And what about Donald? Do you love him?'

'I care deeply for him, but it's not the same as love.'

'But is it enough for marriage?'

'Well, you see, Donald is also in love with someone else, so I suppose we understand each other.'

Startled, Alison gaped at her in the mirror. Had Donald confessed his feelings for her, to her sister? Surely not. 'Did he say who this someone else was?'

'He didn't have to. You see, I saw for myself. The girl he really loves married our cousin Jack.'

Rage rose in Alison's breast. He really was an arrogant bastard! There now, he had reduced her to swearing again. Who would want to take on a man like that? He must make a pass at all the girls. Thank God she hadn't succumbed to his advances. For a moment it had been touch and go, she admitted, because whether she liked it or not, Donald was capable of awakening unwanted feelings deep within her.

Controlling her temper, she said curtly, 'Then you are well suited.'

'What do you mean?'

'Both nursing broken hearts? That's a great basis for marriage, so it is. Taking each other on the rebound.' Returning her compact to her purse, she turned to face Susan. 'Thank goodness I have Graham. He can be depended upon, so he can.'

'Oh, can he indeed?' Susan's temper flared and she railed at her sister. 'Let me tell you something, Alison Cummings . . .' Horrified at her outburst, she took a deep breath and finished lamely, 'No man can be relied on. They only think of themselves. "What's in it for me" is their motto. You remember that! Even your wonderful Graham is no different.' She turned aside, dismayed to think she had almost blurted out the truth.

'No, not Graham,' Alison stated with confidence and left the cloakroom with an exaggerated flounce.

Susan wanted to call her back and wipe the smug look off her face, but how could she without letting the cat out of the bag? After all the sacrifices she had made to keep her great secret, she had no intention of doing that.

Graham and Alison were taking to the floor when she arrived back at the table. The other two men were sitting with faces as long as wet weekends. Wearily Susan joined them. 'What a miserable night this has turned out to be. Such a waste! Victor Sylvester! One of the best bands around and look at us sitting here, pictures of misery.'

'I don't think any of us has very much to smile about at the moment,' Jim agreed and nodded to a glass of Coke on the table. 'That's your Coke, but I'm sure it's flat by now.'

Belatedly she remembered him going to the bar. It seemed so long ago. By the look of the Coke it *was* a long time ago. 'I'm sorry, Jim. While you were at the bar Graham asked me to dance, and then I was talking to Alison in the cloakroom. She seems upset about something and I didn't want to leave her alone,' she lied. She looked over at Donald and was surprised to see him wince and squirm in his chair.

'Did she say what had upset her?' he asked.

'No, she just implied that all men were useless, except her Graham of course.'

They lapsed into silence for a while, then Jim rose to his feet. 'Susan, there's no point me hanging around here any longer. I'll get a taxi home. Can I have another dance before I go?'

'Sure.' With a quick glance at Donald, Susan excused herself and followed Jim. 'Are you sure you don't want to come back to the house for a while? You could have a few drinks and stay overnight.'

He smiled wryly. 'If you had said you were coming away with me and I was celebrating, I'd be only too glad to go back with you. As it is, at the moment I feel a bit depressed. Mind you, I haven't given up all hope yet. You might still change your mind. Meanwhile, I'll stay out of the way and see how Donald fares. Okay?'

'If that's what you want.'

'It's better this way. I'm not comfortable when he's around.'

'Does that mean I won't see you at all next week?'

'There'd be no point, Susan. Not while he's here.'

'But I will see you before you go?'

He smiled wryly. 'Mm. I'm still hoping you'll change your mind and come with me.'

'Don't count on it, Jim.'

'Fair enough. Now, let me hold you close one last time, for old times' sake . . . just in case.'

It was about an hour after Jim had bid them all good night that the National Anthem was played. As Susan stood to attention she glanced around her at all the happy, smiling faces. Even Alison looked happy as, arm through his, she pressed close to Graham, who looked his usual sombre self. Donald looked withdrawn and grim. She herself felt down in the dumps.

Both men were sober, having arrived in their own cars. They said good night at the entrance to the car park and headed in the direction of their vehicles. Graham's was parked at one end and Donald's at the other.

Once home, Susan quickly left the car. She was in a quandary. The journey had been travelled in silence. Too short a journey for there to be an atmosphere, but still, surely Donald could have said something? Anything!

'Tea? Coffee?'

'I'll have a beer, if there is any, thank you.'

'There's some in the fridge. Help yourself and would you pour me a brandy, please? I want to get into something more comfortable.' Realising how this might sound, she felt annoyed at herself. Well, she would soon put a stop to it if he tried anything on. He'd been anything but good company all evening.

Donald was sitting on the settee, a glass of beer in his hand. Her brandy was sitting on a small occasional table between the settee and an armchair. Her dressing gown covered her from head to toe and, resisting the urge to sit beside him on the settee, she lifted the brandy and sat down on the chair.

She had looked in on William and the sight of this precious baby of hers convinced her that she had done the right thing in sending Jim away. Whilst changing into her nightwear she had relived the evening in her mind and came to the conclusion that it was all her fault it had been such a big flop. After all, she needn't have told Jim of her decision tonight; Tuesday would have been soon enough. Donald was here on holiday! It was up to her to see that he enjoyed himself. Hadn't he looked after her over in Darlington?

'Donald, I'm sorry.'

He seemed in a stupor and it was some moments before her words penetrated his mind. If she hadn't known this was his first drink, she would have thought him intoxicated.

'I'm sorry. What did you say?'

Concerned, she moved over and joined him on the settee. 'I said I'm sorry I spoilt the night out for us. I could have told Jim some other time.'

He reached for her hand and squeezed it. 'It's not your fault, Susan. I should have been more understanding.' Inwardly he ranted, 'Instead of making a fool of myself over your sister.' How would he be able to face Alison again? He couldn't! He'd have to make some excuse and go home early.

'Donald, let's go away for a couple of days next week, eh? We could go to Donegal. It's beautiful up there at this time of year.' Susan was getting carried away and continued excitedly, 'A friend of Dad's has a cottage there. He rents it out now and again to friends. If it's free this coming week, how about us going there? Now that Alison is home and able to lend a hand with William, I could ask Mam to take over for a few days and we could go on our own. What do you think?'

It was like a lifeline being thrown to him. To get away from this house and not have to face Alison? His prayers had been answered. Putting an arm around her shoulders, he agreed with her plans. 'That sounds a great idea, Susan. I'd like that! I've heard a lot about Donegal.'

His hopes of a clear escape were dashed at her next words. 'Alison and Graham are coming to dinner tomorrow, so I'll ask Alison then if she'll help out with William and, if she agrees, I'll phone Dad's friend. Okay?'

He nodded despondently. So he wasn't off the hook after all. How could he sit through dinner, making inane conversation, while Alison was there? He just couldn't do it! Perhaps he could think up some excuse and take off after Mass tomorrow. He turned to her in desperation. 'I was thinking of taking off after Mass in the morning, Susan. I'm not used to sitting around in someone's house and being tended to hand and foot. I need some time to myself. Just for the day. Would you be offended if I did?'

Grey eyes full of hurt met his. 'Why? Have I done something awful, Donald?'

'No! No, of course you haven't . . .'

'Then why are you acting like this?' She paused, struck by a thought. 'You know, just because I've turned down Jim's offer, don't think I'm about to trap you into marriage. As Alison was quick to point out tonight, two broken hearts are no basis for a happy marriage, so we would have to take our time and see how things go. One step at a time, no strings attached.'

'Why would Alison say that?' he asked, completely bewildered.

'Oh, we were just talking earlier on, and she didn't think it would be fair of me to marry you if I loved Jim. I explained to her that it was your idea and that you were also getting over a broken heart, so you knew just how I felt. And I *do* think we could make a go of it, Donald, I really do.'

'I suppose you told her all about Margaret, and how Jack had run off with her?'

At his tone of voice, her eyes narrowed and, drawing back from him, she slowly withdrew her hand from his clasp. 'Did I do wrong? After all, Alison is family. She won't be telling anyone else.'

Dear God, what must Alison be thinking of him? He rose quickly to his feet. 'I'm tired, Susan. If you don't mind, I think I'll go on up to bed. Good night.'

Open-mouthed, she stared after him. What on earth had got into him? She smiled wryly as she looked down at her dressing gown and a bitter laugh escaped her lips. Had she really thought that she might have to beat him off? Good God, he had practically run away from her. The smell of the brandy was suddenly nauseating. Entering the kitchen, she poured it down the sink and turned on the tap to wash it away. It was as well her father was unaware of such waste or there'd be wigs on the green, she thought, as she made her way to bed.

The journey home to Graham's house had also been conducted in silence. Alison did not find this unusual. She was used to Graham's long silences. Sometimes she thought Graham was more like an older brother than a sweetheart, but this suited her fine. She didn't want an intense affair, if it was going to cause such an upheaval. And it did! Tonight she had experienced that for herself. For one wild moment she had wanted to give herself up to Donald Murphy and let him devour her.

She turned to Graham in the hall. 'Do you mind if I go on up to bed? I've a bit of a headache.'

Concerned, he moved towards her. 'Is it very bad? Shall I get you a couple of aspirin?'

'I have some up in my room. I'll be all right after a good night's sleep.'

Silently she willed him to sweep her into his arms and ravish her. Make her aware that he could also invoke those feelings that Donald had aroused. He kissed her chastely on the brow. 'Happy dreams, love.'

She moved feverishly against him. 'Kiss me properly, Graham.' Again she urged him: make me want you. Bewildered, he took her in his arms and put a lot of feeling into the kiss, but although she pretended to reciprocate it, she felt nothing. Not even the slightest tingle in her toes. This hadn't bothered her before, so why now? Because now she knew how different it could be. When they drew apart she gently brushed his face with her fingers. 'Thank you. Good night, love.'

Disappointed, she climbed the stairs despondently. Why did Donald Murphy have to come into her life at this time, when everything was going so smoothly?

Donald left the house for early Mass in St Patrick's and afterwards crossed over the Queen's Bridge towards County Down. Let Susan make his excuses, he thought. He just couldn't face Alison so soon after making such a fool of himself. What must she be thinking of him? Supposedly nursing a broken heart; willing to take Susan on as a wife, and trying to seduce Alison last night! Because that's how it would look to her. She had practically said so, hadn't she?

He passed through a town named Hollywood and couldn't help smiling as he pictured John Wayne and Maureen O'Hara again. He reached Bangor and stopped for a coffee and a stroll along the promenade, looking at yachtsmen carrying out various tasks of maintenance on their boats. After a while he sat on the sea wall and browsed over Trevor's road map before moving on round the coast.

He made short stops at places like Donaghadee, Portavogie and Ardglass, eventually arriving in Newcastle at the foot of the Mourne mountains in the late afternoon.

He mustn't go home too early or all his manoeuvres would have been in vain. It was a wasted day really. He got no pleasure from all this lovely countryside; his mind was lamenting the loss of Alison. The loss? What was he thinking of? He had never had her in the first place, and now through his own stupidity he never would.

He spent some time at the beach and walking around the souvenir shops, examining the usual ware you'd expect to find in any holiday resort, yet buying nothing. He soon tired of this fruitless browsing and went looking for a café for a bite to eat.

A glance at his watch reminded him that it was time to be moving on, so he took the inland route through Ballynahinch on his way back to Belfast.

It was late evening when he returned. There was no sign of Graham's car in the drive and he gave a sigh of relief. He had been reprieved. It was Trevor who answered his knock.

'I don't know what our Susan's thinking of. She should have given you a key so that you could come and go as you please, not have to stand knocking on the door like a stranger.'

'Or the tick man,' joked Donald. 'Anyway, she knew I wouldn't be too late getting back.' Donald made his excuses. 'I hope you didn't mind me taking off like that, Trevor.'

'Not at all, son. We all need a bit of respite now and again, just to get our heads showered, especially when we are surrounded by strangers. I've done the same myself many a time, I can tell you. And not just with strangers.'

Rachel had quietly followed her husband into the hall and stood nearby. 'I'm just about to make a pot of tea. Are you hungry, Donald?'

'Until you mentioned grub, Rachel, I didn't realise how hungry I was.'

'I'll make some sandwiches then. William is a bit restless. Susan's up there with him, she shouldn't be too long.'

'If you'll excuse me, I'll just nip upstairs and freshen up.'

He paused at the second flight of stairs, wondering if he should go up to see William. Then, hearing a thin wail and Susan's words of endearment as she soothed her son, he decided against it. After a quick wash he changed into a sports shirt and slacks and left his room.

Alison was just coming out of the spare room and he stopped in dismay. With an embarrassed nod he was about to pass her, but with a tentative gesture she stopped him. 'I've been waiting for you. Can we talk?'

He nodded and with a motion of her head she invited him into the spare room. Inside the room, she closed the door and stood with her back to it, apparently at a loss for words.

He waited in bewildered silence and at last twigged what must be wrong. 'You want your room back. Is that it? I'll move my stuff over here now. It won't take too long.'

He moved towards the door, but she remained with her back to it, barring his escape. Her big blue eyes swam with tears. 'I want to apologise for my behaviour towards you. You must think me a right prude, getting on like that about a kiss.'

'It's all right,' he said gently. 'If you're a prude, that's how I'd want you to be.' He stopped in confusion. She wouldn't want to hear this kind of talk from him. 'What's up?'

'I wasn't truthful with you.'

He stood looking perplexed and she found that she couldn't find the right words to explain what she meant. How do you tell a man that he got under your skin so much that you couldn't stop thinking about him? She found she couldn't. Reluctantly moving away from the door, and with a limp wag of her hand, she said, 'Anyway, thanks for listening.'

Aware something was amiss, he hesitated. 'Am I missing something here?'

She raised her head and their eyes locked. The look said it all. Warning himself not to take anything for granted, he slowly reached for her. She willingly entered his arms and they stood, savouring the feel of each other.

It was when he tried to claim her lips that she whispered, 'What are we going to do about Susan and Graham?'

He gazed down in wonder at her. 'I can't take it in! Does this mean that you *do* care for me?'

'Do you think I'd be here if I didn't? I didn't want this to happen! I was happy with my lot till you came along, but it wouldn't be fair my marrying Graham feeling like this about you. And if you married Susan, I'd always be looking at you and wondering . . .' she rambled on.

Joy was flooding through him, making him light-headed. 'Don't you worry about Graham and Susan. I'll see to them,' he promised and finally kissed her.

They clung together for a long time until at last he gently eased her away from him. Gazing down at her flushed, happy face, he asked, 'Are you sure about this?'

She nodded and smiled sadly. 'Very sure. The effect

you have on me is indescribable. I've been up all night trying to talk myself out of it, but in vain. I believe in my heart we were fated to meet. I think I love you.'

'Well, I don't *think* I love you. I *know* I do. Mind you, I won't be able to support you the way Graham can, but I'll do everything in my power to make you happy, my love.'

'I know you will. I'm a pretty good judge of character.' She gave him a slight push towards the door. 'You had better go downstairs before they start wondering where you've got to. I'll hang back here for a while and get my breath back.' The smile she gave him was breathtaking in its happiness.

Rachel had laid out a variety of cold meats and salad, crusty bread and soft rolls, tea and coffee. They were all gathered around the dining table when at last Susan was free to leave William. When she joined them, her eyes met Donald's and he gave her a huge grin. Surprised at the change in him, she gave him an abrupt nod and took her place at the table.

During the course of the conversation Susan told him that her father had managed to get his friend's cottage for three days. Adding, 'Mam and Alison are more than willing to look after William, so we have three whole days free to enjoy ourselves.'

'According to the forecast the weather is about to break,' Trevor warned. 'And Donegal can be very bleak when it rains, but no doubt you young ones will be able to find something to amuse yourselves,' he muttered, not altogether happy at the idea of what they might get up to.

Alison sat with bowed head. Surely, after her declaration of love, Donald would refuse to go to Donegal for three whole days alone with her sister? It would be unbearable for her to stay behind, picturing them enjoying themselves.

He nodded in agreement. 'Sounds great. I'll see another bit of Ireland before I go home.'

She lifted her head, mouth open at his words. He caught her eye and gave a slight shake of the head, which she took to mean he wouldn't go. Well then, he should tell them here and now and then they would all know where they stood. To her frustration he remained silent.

After the meal the women retired to the kitchen to tidy up and Donald came to a decision.

He and Trevor were in the lounge when he tentatively ventured, 'Don't think me nosy, but are you happy about your daughters' choice of men?'

Unable to hide his surprise at Donald's audacity, Trevor answered honestly enough, 'Graham is a fine, upstanding gentleman and I think Alison will be happy with him. As for Susan? Well now, I can't figure out just who she intends marrying. For a while there I thought you might even be in the picture.' He smiled wryly. 'It shows how much I've changed, when I don't even object to a Catholic as a son-in-law.'

'Then you wouldn't object to me marrying one of your daughters?'

Eyebrows raised, Trevor asked, 'Are you about to ask for Susan's hand in marriage?'

Donald laughed aloud. 'No. I'm just paving the way.'

'I'd be happy if Susan married you.'

'Do you not think that Graham is a bit too settled for Alison?'

'It has never crossed my mind. Although, mind you, Rachel has her doubts about them.'

'Has she indeed?'

'She has, but she won't interfere.'

'What if she's right and Alison changes her mind?'

'I don't think she will, son. Graham is a good catch and Alison will want for nothing. She knows a good thing when she sees it.'

She would want for nothing except excitement and passion, Donald acknowledged to himself.

The evening passed uneventfully. Donald, not wanting to call attention to them, eluded all Alison's attempts to get him alone. It would cause too much speculation and he must talk to Susan first; square things with her. He owed her that much. He was annoyed when Alison, tired of his antics, took matters into her own hands.

'I don't think I'll stay the night after all. I may as well see Graham tonight and come back in the morning.'

'But I've made up the bed in the spare room for you,' Rachel objected.

'I know, Mam.' She flicked a quick glance in Donald's direction and was pleased to see the perturbed look on his face. 'But I'm sure Graham will be glad of my company for a few hours. I'll come back early in the morning.'

'If you're determined to go, I'll run you over,' Trevor offered.

'Let me, Trevor. It will save you getting your car out

of the garage.' Donald rose to his feet and reached for his car keys.

Pleased that her ploy had paid dividends, Alison headed for the stairs. 'I'll fetch my bag. I won't be a minute.'

However, when she returned to the hall, Susan was also waiting. 'I'm coming along for the ride. I need to get out for a bit,' her sister informed her.

Donald was afraid to meet Alison's eye and they trooped out to the car in silence, Susan taking her usual place in the front beside Donald and leaving a disgruntled Alison to climb into the back.

At Graham's house, with an abrupt 'Good night', she left the car and entered the house without so much as a backward glance.

Susan gazed after her in amazement. 'What on earth's got into her? Is it my imagination, or is everyone acting strange this evening?' Donald had turned the car and was heading back. Now she turned to him. 'Well, say something. Why are you all acting so strange?'

Drawing the car into a lay-by, he reached for her hand. 'Susan, I've some explaining to do.'

'Well, thank God for that! I was beginning to think I was going round the bend or something.'

'Do you love me?'

'Huh?'

'Do you love me enough to marry me right away?'

'Ah now, wait a minute. I thought we had decided to take things easy. One step at a time?'

He was roughly caressing her hand and she pulled it away from him. 'Look, whatever's wrong, spit it out.'

'I don't want to hurt you, but things have changed

for me. And I wouldn't for the world let you down if I thought you loved me.'

'But you were so sure we could make a go of it. Why the change of heart? You mean you no longer care for me?'

'I care very dearly for you. I hope we can always remain close friends. But you see, I've fallen in love with someone else.'

Her mind went blank for some seconds, then ran amok as she tried to make sense of his words; tried to make a connection. 'You met someone at the dance last night! That's why you were acting so strange!' She shook her head as if to clear it. 'Still . . . I never saw you with anyone in particular.' She laughed derisively. 'So, some girl looked at you and you fell in love with her. Just like that. Is that what you're saying? Well, I don't believe you! It can't just happen like that.'

'Not quite like that. But as far as I'm concerned, a look was all it took,' he contradicted her. 'At first she wouldn't admit to feeling the same as me. Now she does.'

'You spent the day with her!' she accused. 'That's why you took off! Huh, so much for looking after me.'

'I'll keep my word, if that's what you want.'

'So second best is good enough for me?'

'Isn't that what you'd be offering me?'

She sat silent for a long time. He spoke the truth. He *was* her second choice. Suddenly the truth dawned on her and she swung round in her seat in amazement. 'My God, it's our Alison, isn't it?'

He nodded, shamefaced. 'I'm sorry it had to happen this way.'

'I think you're in for a big disappointment, Donald.
Our Alison knows which side her bread is buttered.
Graham can give her everything she wants, whereas you
. . .' She spread her hands wide to show what she
thought of his prospects. 'Sorry to be so blunt, but there
it is.'

'She's willing to throw in her lot with me.'

'I don't believe you.'

'It's the truth! She said so.'

She waved her hands about in distress. 'I need to
think. Let's go home.'

As he drew the car to a standstill in the drive, he
said, 'You understand I can't go to Donegal with you
now? It wouldn't be fair on Alison. That's why she was
so upset and stormed off like that.'

'Oh, let's on no account upset our Alison. What about
me? Don't I deserve some consideration, some sympathy?'

He put a hand on her arm. 'Of course . . .'

She threw his hand off. 'Give over! I don't want to
hear any more excuses.'

'What are you going to do?'

'I don't know,' she hissed. 'I need time to think! I'll see
you in the lounge after Mam and Dad have gone to bed.'

Throwing herself on top of the bed, Susan beat on her
pillows with clenched fists. 'Hell roast the two of them!'
she muttered. She didn't deserve to be treated like this.
That Donald, of all people, should let her down devastated her. And what about poor Graham? How would
he take it? Very well, an inner voice assured her. In fact,
she thought he might even be relieved. She felt calmer

thinking of Graham. He alone would be composed in this crazy state of affairs. She lay for a long time thinking and at last reached a decision.

She heard her mother and father retiring for the night. Giving them fifteen minutes to get settled, she looked in on William and then quietly descended the stairs. Donald rose to his feet when she entered the lounge.

'Sit down,' she ordered. 'I've a proposition to make.'

He sank down on to the settee again, while she remained standing. 'This shouldn't take too long. As you know, I intend returning to work in a couple of weeks' time. Tomorrow morning I'll pretend to get a phone call asking me to go and see my boss. I'll insist that Alison accompanies you to Donegal to show you around.'

'Are you sure about this?'

'No! But can you come up with anything better?'

'Can't we just tell the truth?'

'That wouldn't suit me at all. I insist we do it my way.'

Thinking that she wanted to save face, he went on, 'What about Graham? Shouldn't he be told the truth?'

'I'll explain to him. When he comes tomorrow night to see Alison, I'll tell him the truth. All of it. Do you agree?' He nodded and she continued, 'Tell Alison to let Graham come here as planned. As if nothing has changed. Okay?'

'Will you be all right breaking the bad news to him?'

She laughed abruptly. 'Do you know something, Donald? I don't think he'll be exactly heartbroken. Good night.'

Getting quickly to his feet, he crossed to her and made to take her in his arms.

'Don't! There is only one man I'll ever let touch me again. I only hope I haven't left it too late. Me and my worrying about other people. That's why I got into this situation in the first place! What do other people matter when your own future is at stake? No one worried how I might feel!'

He gazed at her, uncomprehending. 'I wish I could be more helpful. I feel such a heel.'

'And well you may! I wouldn't have believed you'd act this way. Some mentor you turned out to be.'

'I couldn't help myself, honestly. I fell in love. It happens,' he said abjectly.

'Tell me, Donald, if Alison hadn't returned your love, would you still have pursued me?'

He shrugged. 'How do I know what I'd have done?'

She cried in frustration, 'Agh, away to bed. I'll see you in the morning.'

The realisation of how stupid she'd been ate away at her mind, keeping sleep at bay. She had kept her true feelings under wraps all these months. Had ignored all the signs that she loved *Graham*. And this was the outcome; everyone suiting themselves. Doing what *they* wanted. What if Graham had changed his mind where she was concerned and really believed now that William was not his son? God knows she had denied it often enough. The very idea sent her into a spasm of tears and she sobbed herself into a fitful sleep.

Heavy-eyed, she was passing through the hall next morning just as the phone rang. It was Alison. Not wanting to ask outright if Donald had put her sister in the picture, she dithered.

'I was wondering what time you're leaving for Donegal?'

Keeping her voice low, Susan said, 'You can stop pretending. Donald told me everything last night.'

'Susan, I'm sorry. I couldn't help myself. It just happened.'

'Huh!' Susan gave a disgusted grunt, then sighed. 'I suppose these things do happen. Listen, here's what you must do. You will take my place and go to Donegal with Donald.'

'I can't do that! What will Mam and Dad think?'

'I'll pretend this call is from my boss asking me to go in and see him today. Since he has held my job open so long, they'll understand that I must go.'

'What do I tell Graham?'

'Nothing!' Her voice was sharp. 'You'll tell him nothing. Is that clear? I'll explain to him when he comes round tonight expecting to see you here.'

'That wouldn't be fair, leaving you to do all the dirty work.'

'I want to. I've a lot of explaining to do and I may as well clear the air once and for all. Look, just in case you're tempted to let the cat out of the bag, I'll send Donald over for you now. Tell Graham you'll see him tonight as usual, all right?'

'Are you sure, Susan? I feel guilty as hell about all this.'

'Just do as I say and everything will work out fine. I hope,' she muttered under her breath.

'I didn't catch that last wee bit, Susan.'

'You weren't meant to. See you soon.'

* * *

Later that morning Susan and her mother waved Donald and Alison off and returned to the house. William was letting them know he was awake and Susan took the stairs in a rush. Deep in thought, Rachel went into the kitchen to prepare the child's bottle. There was something going on here, but she couldn't put her finger on just what.

Climbing the stairs, she stood in silence at the door of the nursery and watched her daughter bath and dress her grandson. 'Susan, is anything wrong?'

'Not really.' Seeing that her mother was about to argue, she looked appealingly at her. 'Mam, bear with me. No more questions now, and soon I'll be able to tell you all my secrets – everything.'

'What time are you going to the office?'

Deciding to be truthful, Susan said, 'I'm not.' Rachel's mouth opened, but her daughter forestalled her. 'Please, Mam? Remember, no questions. I would like to go into town this afternoon and get my hair cut and set. Will that be all right with you?'

Her mother nodded dumbly. She would never understand this oldest daughter of hers. She was an enigma.

The morning dragged, but the afternoon flew in. Trevor was surprised when he returned from work and discovered Susan still in the house.

'What happened?' he asked in bewilderment. 'I thought you were all set to go to Donegal today.'

Avoiding her mother's eye, Susan lied convincingly. 'Mr Kennedy rang this morning, about me coming back to work, so I had to go into the office for a short time today to discuss it with him. Alison went with Donald to show him around. Act as courier, as it were.'

'Oh.' Trevor's eyebrows rose as he turned this news

over in his mind for a few moments. Susan could practically hear his thoughts ticking over. 'Can I assume
they'll be back tonight, then?' he asked.

'No, they'll stay the three days.'

A frown gathered on her father's brow. 'What has
Graham to say about that?'

'He doesn't know yet. He's coming over here after tea
tonight. I'll explain everything to him then.'

'That should be interesting!' Trevor remarked, tight-
lipped.

Trembling like a leaf, for the third time Susan tried on
the ruby dress and fearfully eyed her reflection in the
mirror. She felt every bit as glamorous as she looked.
The dress hugged her slim figure and the warm colour
reflected in her cheeks. Her new hairdo played a big
part in her transformation. Cut short and shaped close
to the head, it emphasised the delicate planes of her
face and her long, slender neck.

She recalled her friend Ruth Vernon's words of praise
in the boutique. 'You look absolutely gorgeous in it.
You'll never look so lovely again.' Susan smiled to herself
in the mirror as she ran her hands over the dress,
smoothing invisible creases, glad that Ruth had
persuaded her – even bullied her – into buying it. She
prayed it would win back Graham's affection.

She stepped into navy court shoes just as the doorbell rang. Quickly leaving the bedroom, she hurried
downstairs. The lounge door opened and, before she
could stop him, her father was opening the front door.

'Hello, Graham. Come into the lounge. I'm afraid
Alison . . .'

'Dad, if I could have a minute alone with Graham, please?' Susan interrupted, her voice slightly louder than usual.

At the sound of her voice both men turned and looked at her. Graham's breath caught in his throat at the sight of her. She was a vision to behold. This beauty should be his wife, he lamented inwardly. He couldn't just stand aside and let her walk off with someone else. What kind of man was he? No! To hell with the promises he had made. He was going to fight tooth and nail to win this beautiful woman over.

Trevor's gaze slowly travelled from head to toe. Why, he thought belatedly, had he always imagined Alison the beauty of the family? Here before his very eyes was a different kind of beauty. 'You're looking well, girl. If I may say so. Is that a new dress?' he blurted out. It was the best he could come up with on the spur of the moment.

'Yes, Dad.' Susan's eyes were fastened on Graham's, 'I bought it for a very special occasion. Now, could I have a quiet word alone with Graham, Dad?'

With a final appraising glance, Trevor nodded at Graham and, entering the lounge, closed the door behind him.

There was still a distance between her and Graham. He was still standing by the front door, she on the bottom stair tread. It felt like a chasm. He stood as if galvanised to the spot. At last she forced her feet into action. Heading for the dining room, she said, 'Can I have a word with you in here, Graham?'

He came to with a start and followed her into the room. Except for the evening light filtering in through the nets on the window, the room was in deep shadow. He reached for the light switch but her voice stopped him.

'Leave it for a moment, Graham. I've a lot of explaining to do and it'll be easier for me in the dark. To be truthful, I'm terribly ashamed of myself.'

Slowly his arm dropped to his side. She was remembering the times she'd had difficulty keeping him at arm's length; practically fighting him off. Now, when she longed for the comfort of his arms, he was standing like a statue. Had she left it too late? Had his love for her finally died after all her rejections of him?

As for Graham, he couldn't make head nor tail of what was going on. Susan had never looked lovelier, but he wasn't daft enough to think she was all dressed up for his benefit. Had she decided to marry Donald and wanted to break the news to him personally? Didn't she realise that, no matter who was the harbinger or what way the news was delivered, it would only break his heart?

'Graham, I don't know where to start. I'm so afraid,' she stuttered.

'If it's bad news, Susan, just get it over with. I'm getting used to hearing bad news from you.'

Big, haunted eyes full of pity gazed at him. Pity was something he didn't want from her. 'Have you decided to marry Donald after all?' he asked abruptly.

'*No!* What made you think that?'

'Well, it looks like Jim's out of the picture now, so I thought marriage to Donald would be the next obvious thing on your agenda. To be truthful, I don't know what to think any more where you're concerned. It's one big hurt after another. I just can't take any more.'

Her heart sank. Had she really been as fickle as that? How could he possibly have any deep feelings left for her, the way she had treated him? 'I've been an awful fool,' she admitted. He remained silent and she continued, 'I worried about what other people would think. Who might get hurt. I was afraid of a scandal and as a result . . .' She paused and licked her lips, suddenly parched '. . . I deprived you of the right to acknowledge William as your own son.'

He abruptly straightened to his full height, his chin jutting out as he absorbed these words. 'Are . . . are you admitting William is *mine*?'

'Yes.'

'Why the sudden change of heart? Are you saying I can have him? Is that it? Does Donald not want to rear him after all? Was it all one big show to let people see what a great fellow he was?'

Exasperated, she cried, 'This has nothing to do with Donald! You're not listening to me.'

'Forgive me, Susan, I'm all at sea here. I don't know what to think. You've lost me completely.'

'Look!' She spoke deliberately. 'Donald and Alison have fallen in love.' Her voice had gone flat. This was not going as she had hoped. And she didn't blame him in the slightest. After the way she had treated him? After all the rejections and denials? She had said some terrible things to him and now she expected him to sweep her into his arms and utter declarations of love, saying that everything would be hunky-dory.

Tears spilled over at the loss of him. She hoped the darkness would hide them, but he saw them glistening in the half-light and was immediately all concern. In three steps he was beside her, dabbing at the tears with his handkerchief.

'Don't cry, Susan. I can't bear it when you cry. What can I do to help?'

She blew her nose loudly and peeped up at him through wet lashes. 'You could try holding me and kissing me,' she whispered.

He needed no further bidding and, once in his arms, all restraint fled. She devoured his lips, his face and his lips again. 'Oh, I've been such a fool.'

'Hush. Forget it.' Tears were now streaming down his own face. 'Just convince me I'm not dreaming and you really do love me.'

For some time she did just that, until they were both brought to their senses by cries from William. They rushed into the hall. Rachel had beaten them to it.

Grinning from ear to ear, Graham looked askance, 'Are we going to let them all know?'

At Susan's nod of assent, he gently put a delaying hand on Rachel's arm. 'Susan wants to have a quiet word with you and Trevor, Rachel.'

'And what about William?' Rachel cried with an anxious glance up the stairs.

'I'll attend to my son.' Graham took the stairs two at a time, singing at the top of his voice.

'*Your* . . . son?' Rachel shrieked and looked to Susan for confirmation.

Placing an arm gently around her mother's shoulders, Susan said, 'Mam, remember I said I'd tell you everything when the time was right? Well, that time has now come. But I think you'd better sit down first. Besides, I have to break the news to Dad as well, so come into the lounge.'